The Complete Strategy & War Collection (Vol. 4)

History of the Peloponnesian War & On the Nature of Things
— Strategy, Power and the Roots of Conflict

A Modern Translation

Adapted for the Contemporary Reader

Lucretius | Thucydides

Translated by Tim Zengerink

Table Of Contents

Preface - Message to the Reader

What If You Could Help Rebuild the Greatest Library in Human History?

Thousands of years ago, the Library of Alexandria stood as the crown jewel of human achievement — a sanctuary where the collected wisdom of every known civilization was gathered, preserved, and shared freely.

And then, it was lost.

Through fire, conquest, and the slow erosion of time, humanity lost not just books — but ideas, dreams, discoveries, and stories that could have changed the world forever.

Today, the Library of Alexandria lives again — and you are invited to be a part of its restoration.

Our mission is simple yet profound:

To rebuild the greatest library the world has ever known, and to translate all timeless works into every language and dialect, so that no seeker of knowledge is ever left behind again.

By joining our movement to rebuild the modern Library of Alexandria, you become part of an unprecedented mission:

- **Unlimited Access to the Greatest Audiobooks & eBooks Ever Written:**

   Instantly explore thousands of legendary works—Plato, Shakespeare, Jane Austen, Leo Tolstoy, and countless more. All instantly available to read or listen, placing a complete literary universe at your fingertips.

- **Beautiful Paperback & Deluxe Editions at Printing Cost**

  Own any title as an elegant paperback, deluxe hardcover, or stunning collectible boxset—offered to you at true printing cost, delivered straight to your door. Build your personal Library of Alexandria, crafted for beauty, built for durability, and worthy of proud display.

- **Fresh Translations for Modern Readers—in Every Language & Dialect**

  Enjoy timeless masterpieces reimagined in clear, contemporary language—no more outdated phrases or obscure references. Alongside the original versions, we're tirelessly translating these classics into every language and dialect imaginable, ensuring accessibility and understanding across cultures and generations.

- **Join a Global Renaissance of Literature & Knowledge**

  You directly support expanding our library, publishing deluxe editions at true cost, translating works into all global languages, and bringing humanity's greatest stories to people everywhere. By joining today, you're not just preserving a legacy of masterpieces; you set in motion a powerful wave of literary accessibility.

Become a Torchbearer of Knowledge.

Join us for free now at **LibraryofAlexandria.com**

Together, we will ensure that the light of human wisdom never fades again.

With gratitude and a shared love of knowledge,
The Modern Library of Alexandria Team

Visit:

www.libraryofalexandria.com

Or scan the code below:

Introduction

Conflict and Cosmos:
War, Nature, and the Logic of Power

At first glance, Thucydides and Lucretius may appear to belong to different universes. One is a historian of war, detailing the brutal intricacies of a civilizational struggle between Athens and Sparta. The other is a poet-philosopher, illuminating the physical and metaphysical structure of reality through atomism and natural philosophy. Yet placed side by side in The Complete Strategy & War Collection (Vol. 4), their writings reveal a startling synergy: both aim to strip away illusion, to uncover the hidden structures that govern human behavior, and to expose the forces—natural and political—that drive conflict, decay, and transformation.

Thucydides' History of the Peloponnesian War is perhaps the most psychologically and politically penetrating work of history ever written. In it, war is not a temporary aberration, but a fundamental consequence of human ambition, fear, and competition. His realism offers no comfort, only insight. He shows how democratic idealism can become tyranny, how power reveals character, and how the struggle for dominance tears at the fabric of civilization.

Lucretius' On the Nature of Things, by contrast, seems to float above the battlefield. But his purpose is no less urgent: to free humanity from fear—especially the fear of gods and death—by explaining that the universe is composed of atoms and void, ruled not by divine punishment but by physical necessity. His Epicurean vision is philosophical warfare: a campaign against superstition and suffering, fought with poetry, logic, and science.

By pairing these two authors, this volume does something rare. It unites the external conflict of empire with the internal conflict of the soul. It offers not just strategies for winning battles, but frameworks for understanding why we fight them, what we fear, and what we might become if we see clearly. This introduction will explore how Thucydides and Lucretius, in radically different voices, converge on the deepest themes of human existence: power, fear, perception, and freedom.

Thucydides:
Power, Fear, and the Anatomy of Political Collapse

Written in the fifth century BCE, Thucydides' History of the Peloponnesian War chronicles the epic struggle between Athens and Sparta—two great powers vying for dominance in the Greek world. But Thucydides was not interested in mere chronology. He sought to uncover the deeper causes of conflict, the psychology of leaders and citizens, and the corrosive effects of power on moral and civic life.

Thucydides begins with a bold claim: the Peloponnesian War was the greatest war in history up to that point, and he intends to write not just for his own time, but for all time. His history is not folklore or mythology—it is an autopsy. He examines not only what happened, but why it happened.

Central to his analysis is the famous triad of motivation: fear, honor, and interest. These are the true causes of war, not the superficial reasons leaders give. For Athens, the rise of power led to fear in Sparta. For Sparta, fear led to preemptive aggression. This interplay of psychological and strategic imperatives sets the stage for a long, brutal, and ultimately ruinous war.

Thucydides provides unmatched portraits of political and moral transformation. In the plague of Athens, we witness societal breakdown. In the Melian Dialogue, we see realpolitik laid bare—Athens tells Melos that "the strong do what they can, and the weak suffer what they must." In the Sicilian Expedition, we see the tragic arc of hubris, miscalculation, and collapse.

What makes Thucydides so enduring is not just his diagnosis of war, but his understanding of human nature. He shows how democratic assemblies become mobs, how leaders are shaped and destroyed by ambition, and how crises reveal the true character of individuals and societies. He offers no utopia, only clear-eyed analysis.

His history is not moralistic, but it is moral. It demands that we confront uncomfortable truths: that ideals can be corrupted, that power often rewards ruthlessness, and that civilization is more fragile than we care to admit. In an age of political volatility and global competition, his voice resonates as powerfully as ever.

Lucretius:
Atoms, Fear, and the Liberation of the Mind

Titus Lucretius Carus, writing in the first century BCE, composed one of the most extraordinary poems in Latin literature: De Rerum Natura (On the Nature of Things). Six books of philosophical verse, it explains the physical, ethical, and metaphysical principles of Epicureanism. Lucretius seeks to free his readers—not through conquest, but through understanding.

His core thesis is that the universe consists of invisible atoms moving through the void. All things—life, death, perception, consciousness—arise from these atoms' interactions. There are no gods controlling the cosmos, no afterlife of torment or reward, no fate imposed by divine will. The soul, too, is material, and dissolves at death. Therefore, fear of punishment after death is irrational—and damaging to human happiness.

Lucretius is not simply teaching physics; he is waging a philosophical war against fear. Fear, especially of death and the gods, is the root of much human suffering. It leads to superstition, tyranny, and violence. By replacing fear with knowledge, he believes, we can attain ataraxia—a serene, undisturbed state of mind.

The poem is rich with scientific insight: the nature of sensation, the patterns of weather, the origins of the universe, and the mechanics of disease. But it is also deeply psychological. Lucretius understands the anxieties that plague the human heart and offers a cure: not faith, but reason; not myth, but nature.

His style is passionate, even ecstatic. He writes not just to instruct, but to move. His verse evokes the vastness of the cosmos, the beauty of natural order, and the freedom that comes from letting go of illusions. Though rooted in ancient atomism, his philosophy anticipates modern scientific naturalism and secular humanism.

Lucretius may not speak of generals or campaigns, but he too addresses conflict—the internal battle between ignorance and knowledge, fear and wisdom. He reminds us that true freedom begins in the mind.

Synthesis:
War Without and Within

In bringing Thucydides and Lucretius together, this volume creates a bridge between the outer and inner theaters of human conflict:

• Thucydides shows how nations fall into war through power dynamics, perception, and ambition. He studies how societies fracture, how leaders rise and fall, and how the quest for dominance devours its architects.

• Lucretius shows how individuals fall into suffering through fear, ignorance, and false belief. He offers a vision of liberation not through conquest, but through comprehension.

Both men are concerned with the hidden structures of reality— whether the political structures of war or the atomic structures of matter. Both believe that by seeing clearly, we can act more wisely. Both reject comforting fictions in favor of difficult truths.

Thucydides does not promise peace; Lucretius does not promise salvation. But together, they offer something more enduring: perspective. They show that human beings, driven by fear and desire, often become the architects of their own destruction—but also that understanding, whether of war or of nature, can give us the power to change.

This volume is not just about strategy in the battlefield sense. It is about strategy in the broadest sense: how to live, how to govern, how to think, and how to be free.

Welcome to The Complete Strategy & War Collection (Vol. 4). May the realism of Thucydides sharpen your perception of power, and may the clarity of Lucretius free your mind from fear—so that you can engage the world not only with strength, but with wisdom.

History of the Peloponnesian War

Thucydides

Book I

Chapter I

The History of Greece from the Earliest Times to the Start of the Peloponnesian War

Thucydides, an Athenian, set out to document the history of the war between the Peloponnesians and the Athenians from its outset, believing it would be a conflict of great magnitude, surpassing any war that had come before. His anticipation was well-founded. Both sides had reached a peak of military and logistical preparedness, and the rest of the Hellenic world was poised to choose sides, with many allies ready to join the fray. This was, in fact, the most extensive movement in history, not only for the Greek people but for a significant portion of the barbarian world—possibly even for all of humanity. Although the events of ancient times and those immediately preceding this war are unclear due to the passage of time, the evidence gathered from as far back as possible suggests that nothing of comparable scale, whether in warfare or in other matters, had occurred before.

For example, the land now called Hellas (Greece) did not have a stable population in ancient times. Migrations were frequent, with tribes readily abandoning their homes under the threat of superior forces. Without trade, secure communication routes, or freedom of movement by land or sea, they cultivated only enough land to meet their basic needs. They lacked capital and did not develop the land extensively, as they could not predict when an invader might come to seize their resources. With no walls to protect them, they had little reason to settle permanently, moving from place to place and building neither large cities nor achieving any lasting form of greatness.

The regions with the richest soil were the most frequently conquered: Thessaly, Boeotia, most of the Peloponnese (except for Arcadia), and other fertile parts of Hellas. The abundance of resources in these areas encouraged individual wealth and power, which in turn fostered internal divisions and conflicts that led to ruin. Fertile lands also attracted invaders. In contrast, Attica, with its relatively poor soil, remained free from internal strife and retained the same population over the centuries. This stability supports the idea that frequent migrations stunted growth in other regions. Attica became a safe haven for powerful individuals from other parts of Hellas who had been displaced by war or internal conflict. These newcomers, becoming part of the Athenian community, contributed to a rapid population increase in Athens. This growth eventually led to overpopulation in Attica, forcing the Athenians to establish colonies in Ionia.

Thucydides thus begins his history by exploring how these early migrations and conflicts shaped the unique character and trajectory of Greece, setting the stage for the immense struggle of the Peloponnesian War.

Another point that strongly reinforces my belief in the fragility of ancient times is the lack of unity among the Greeks before the Trojan War. There is no evidence of any collective action across Hellas, nor was there even a unified name for the region. In fact, before the time of Hellen, son of Deucalion, the term "Hellas" did not exist. Instead, the land was identified by the names of its various tribes, especially the Pelasgian. It wasn't until Hellen and his sons gained power in Phthiotis and were invited as allies into other cities that the name "Hellenes" gradually spread, city by city, through these connections. Yet, even then, it took considerable time for this term to be widely adopted across the region.

The best evidence for this is found in Homer, who lived long after the Trojan War. Nowhere does he call the Greeks "Hellenes." Instead, he uses names like Danaans, Argives, and Achaeans, referring to different groups. He also never uses the word "barbarian," likely because the Greeks had not yet distinguished themselves with a single identity separate from the rest of the world. Thus, before the Trojan War, the Hellenic communities—both those who first adopted the name "Hellenes" and those who later embraced it for the entire people—were too weak and too isolated from each other to coordinate any united action.

In fact, it wasn't until they became more accustomed to seafaring that they could undertake such an expedition. According to tradition, the first known ruler to establish a navy was Minos. He took control of the waters now known as the Hellenic Sea and dominated the Cyclades, where he established the earliest colonies, expelled the Carians, and appointed his sons as governors. To secure revenue for himself, he aimed to suppress piracy in these waters.

At that time, as sea travel became more common, both the Hellenes and coastal barbarians increasingly engaged in piracy, often led by their most powerful men. These raids were driven by greed and a need to support the poor. They would descend upon towns that lacked walls, typically collections of scattered villages, and plunder them. Far from being shameful, such acts of piracy were seen as a source of honor and livelihood. In fact, some people on the mainland still honor successful raiders, and old poets often depict people casually asking travelers, "Are you pirates?"—implying that those questioned felt no need to deny it, and their questioners saw no reason to criticize it.

This tendency toward raiding extended to the land as well, where the same lawlessness prevailed.

Even today, many regions of Hellas continue to live by these ancient customs. For example, the Ozolian Locrians, the Aetolians, and the Acarnanians, along with others from this part of the mainland, still carry arms as a regular part of their daily lives. These people retain this tradition as a remnant of the old piratical practices that once dominated the region. At one time, all of Hellas followed this custom. Carrying weapons was a necessity for survival since settlements were often unfortified, and travel was hazardous due to frequent conflicts. For the Greeks, as for many barbarians, wearing arms was as integral to everyday life as farming or trading.

The persistence of this lifestyle in certain parts of Hellas reflects a time when the same habits were widely practiced across the land. The Athenians were the first to abandon this armed lifestyle, gradually adopting a more refined and luxurious way of living. It was only in recent times that wealthy older Athenians gave up wearing linen undergarments and securing their hair with gold grasshopper clasps— a fashion that had spread to their Ionian relatives and remained popular among older men there for generations. In contrast, the Spartans set a different trend, one that emphasized simplicity. They encouraged a plain manner of dress, which the wealthy embraced to resemble more closely the common people. They also led the way in public athletic practices, stripping naked and oiling themselves for gymnastic exercises. Previously, athletes, even in the Olympic Games, wore belts around their waists. It was only recently that this custom ended. To this day, in some parts of Asia, where boxing and wrestling contests are still held, fighters wear belts. Many similarities can be observed between the ancient Greek way of life and that of the barbarians today, particularly in their customs and daily practices.

As for the placement of their towns, the shift came later, when increased seafaring and greater resources allowed for better fortification and trade. Coastal areas began to feature walled towns and settlements on isthmuses to facilitate commerce and defend against rival neighbors. Yet the original towns, both on the mainland and the islands, had been built inland or far from the shore, as piracy was so prevalent that coastal living was dangerous. Pirates preyed on each other and raided all coastal inhabitants, regardless of their involvement in seafaring.

The islanders were also notorious pirates. Many of these pirates were Carians and Phoenicians, who had colonized most of the islands. Evidence of this was uncovered during the purification of Delos by the Athenians during the war. In excavating all the graves on the island, they found that more than half of those buried there were identified as Carians, recognized by their distinctive weaponry and burial methods, which matched practices still followed by the Carians.

The situation changed with the rise of Minos, who established a powerful navy and brought greater security to the region. He colonized most of the islands and drove out the pirates, making sea travel and trade safer and more frequent. As communication by sea improved, the coastal populations shifted their focus toward accumulating wealth, gradually adopting a more stable lifestyle. Some communities even began to fortify their towns with walls, leveraging their newfound prosperity for defense. The desire for wealth led weaker settlements to accept the dominance of stronger ones, while those with more resources grew powerful enough to subdue smaller towns. This accumulation of wealth and consolidation of power set the stage for greater collective ambitions, culminating in the expedition against Troy—a moment when the Greeks finally united for a large-scale, organized campaign, symbolizing the shift toward a more cohesive and powerful Hellas.

In my view, Agamemnon was able to gather his great army not so much because of the oaths sworn by Tyndareus's suitors to support him, but rather due to his own superior power and influence. According to the most reliable traditions passed down by the Peloponnesians, it all began with Pelops. Pelops arrived in the region from Asia, bringing with him great wealth, which quickly allowed him to gain power among a population that was poor. His influence became so profound that, though he was an outsider, the land eventually came to be named after him. This power grew even more under his descendants.

After Eurystheus was killed in Attica by the Heraclids, his rule in Mycenæ was left to Atreus, who was his maternal uncle. Eurystheus, before setting out on his campaign, had entrusted Mycenæ and its governance to Atreus, as they were family, and Atreus had left his own homeland following the death of Chrysippus. When Eurystheus failed to return, Atreus accepted the Mycenæans' invitation to take over the throne, a decision they made partly out of fear of the Heraclids. Atreus's power appeared substantial, and he had won the support of the people. Thus, he assumed control of Mycenæ and the other lands once ruled by Eurystheus, and with this, the power of Pelops's line surpassed that of Perseus's descendants. This extensive influence eventually passed to Agamemnon.

Agamemnon's strength was further reinforced by his naval superiority, which was unmatched by others of his time. Therefore, it seems that fear played just as large a role as loyalty in securing the cooperation of the various Greek leaders in this expedition. The size and strength of his navy are evident in Homer's accounts: not only did Agamemnon command the largest fleet among the allies, but he also supplied ships for the Arcadians. If Homer's account is considered trustworthy, he also describes Agamemnon as "king of many islands and of all Argos."

Agamemnon's power was primarily land-based, which implies that he could only have held sway over the nearby islands—and even then, not many—through his control of a formidable fleet. His naval capabilities thus allowed him to assert his dominance over both land and sea, creating the kind of influence necessary to lead the combined forces to Troy.

From this expedition to Troy, we can deduce much about earlier ventures. Mycenæ may have been a modest city, and many towns from that period might seem relatively minor by today's standards. However, that should not lead us to dismiss the accounts from poets and tradition regarding the scale of the forces assembled. For example, if Sparta were to fall into ruin, leaving only the temples and the foundations of its public buildings, future generations might underestimate its power based solely on appearances. Sparta occupies two-fifths of the Peloponnese, leading the entire region and maintaining numerous allies beyond its borders. Yet, as the city is not built in a centralized form, nor adorned with grand temples and monuments but instead is arranged in a cluster of villages in the old Hellenic style, it might seem underwhelming to the casual observer.

On the other hand, if the same fate befell Athens, the opposite impression might arise. The striking and consolidated layout of

Athens, with its temples and public structures, would likely suggest to onlookers that its power was double its actual strength. Therefore, we must be cautious not to judge a city's power merely by its physical appearance; a town's true influence is often not fully revealed by what remains of its architecture. The scale of Agamemnon's armament likely surpassed all prior expeditions, though it still fell short of what we would consider substantial by modern standards. Homer's epic references twelve hundred ships; for the Boeotian ships, he mentions a complement of one hundred and twenty men per vessel, while the ships of Philoctetes had fifty. From this, we can assume Homer was suggesting a range of the maximum and minimum crew sizes. He provides no other details on the ships, implying that most carried similar numbers.

Furthermore, Homer's account reveals that these men were both rowers and warriors. For instance, the crew of Philoctetes' ships consisted entirely of archers who also manned the oars. It's unlikely that there were many additional non-combatants aboard, aside from the kings and senior officers. Crossing the open sea, they carried supplies and weaponry in ships without decks, fitted out in the simple piratical style of the time. If we calculate an average crew size based on the largest and smallest ships, the overall number of men would seem relatively modest, given that they represented all of Hellas. This limited force was likely due not to a shortage of men but to a scarcity of funds. Sustaining the army with provisions was difficult, so they reduced their numbers to levels sustainable by local resources.

Even after their initial victory upon arrival—without which they could not have built their fortified naval camp—there is no evidence of them deploying their full strength. Instead, they seem to have relied on farming the Chersonese and conducting piracy to supplement their supplies. This strategy allowed the Trojans to prolong the conflict, as the Greeks' dispersed forces left only a portion of their troops on constant duty, making it easier for the Trojans to resist them. Had the Greeks brought abundant supplies and maintained a continuous siege without scattering their forces for piracy and agriculture, they would have likely conquered the Trojans quickly, as they managed to hold their ground even with a divided force. Essentially, had they maintained focus on the siege itself, the capture of Troy would have demanded far less time and effort.

This shortage of funds reflects the limitations of earlier campaigns as well. Thus, even the famed Trojan expedition, considered grander than its predecessors, can be seen, based on its actual results, as less impressive than its reputation suggests—an impression fostered by the poets but not entirely supported by the practical realities of the campaign.

Even after the Trojan War, Greece remained in a state of instability, continually uprooting and resettling, unable to achieve the peace necessary for true growth and development. The prolonged delay of the Greek heroes returning from Troy led to revolutions and civil strife in nearly every city. Many of those exiled by these conflicts went on to found new cities. Sixty years after the fall of Troy, the Thessalians expelled the Boeotians from their land in Arne, forcing them to settle in present-day Boeotia, formerly known as Cadmeis. Some of the Boeotians had already been present there before, and even took part in the expedition to Troy. Twenty years after this, the Dorians and the descendants of Heracles took control of the Peloponnese. With so many displacements and migrations, a long period had to pass before Greece could reach a state of lasting peace, undisturbed by further upheavals. Only then could the Greeks begin to establish colonies: Athens sent settlers to Ionia and most of the islands, while the Peloponnesians founded cities in parts of Italy, Sicily, and other areas in Hellas. All of these colonies arose after the Trojan War.

As Greece's power grew and wealth became more desirable, states began to amass greater revenues, leading to the establishment of tyrannies in many cities. Previously, governance had taken the form of hereditary monarchies with specific, limited powers. But now, with increasing resources, many Greek states turned to naval pursuits, focusing their efforts on the sea. Corinth is credited as the first Greek city to adopt what would become the modern style of shipbuilding; it was here that the first galleys were built. Ameinocles, a shipwright from Corinth, famously constructed four ships for the Samians, marking a significant advancement in naval technology. This event took place nearly three hundred years after the end of the Trojan War. Additionally, the earliest recorded naval battle in Greek history was fought between the Corinthians and the Corcyraeans, roughly two hundred and sixty years after the Trojan War.

Situated on an isthmus, Corinth had long been a center of trade, as most of the movement of goods between regions within and beyond the Peloponnese passed through Corinthian territory. This position brought significant wealth to Corinth, as reflected in the epithet "wealthy" often used by ancient poets to describe the city. This financial strength enabled Corinth to develop a strong navy, which it used to combat piracy and secure its position as a commercial hub for both land and sea trade, allowing it to reap the benefits of a robust revenue.

Later, the Ionians developed significant naval power during the reigns of Cyrus, the first Persian king, and his son Cambyses. While at war with Cyrus, the Ionians briefly commanded the Ionian Sea. Polycrates, the tyrant of Samos, also amassed a powerful fleet during Cambyses's rule, using it to subdue many islands, including Rhenea, which he dedicated to Apollo of Delos. Around the same period, the Phocaeans, while founding Marseilles, defeated the Carthaginians in a naval battle. These were among the most formidable fleets of the time. However, despite the many generations that had passed since the Trojan War, most of these navies still consisted mainly of the old-style fifty-oared ships and longboats, with few true galleys in their ranks.

It was not until shortly before the Persian Wars and the death of Darius, Cambyses's successor, that the tyrants in Sicily and the Corcyraeans began to amass fleets with a significant number of galleys. Before this period, there were no notable navies in Greece, aside from a few ships possessed by cities like Aegina and Athens, which consisted mostly of the simpler fifty-oared vessels. Only at the close of this era, when the conflict with Aegina and the threat of the Persian invasion loomed, did Themistocles successfully persuade the Athenians to construct the fleet that would later prove decisive at the Battle of Salamis. Even then, these ships were not fully decked, reflecting the early stage of Greek naval development.

Thus, Greece's transition from land-based power to a force focused on the sea was gradual and often hindered by internal strife, resource limitations, and evolving ship technology. The process accelerated in response to external threats, ultimately allowing the Greeks to rise as a significant naval force in the face of the Persian invasion.

Thus, the navies of the Greeks during this period, though modest by later standards, were of critical importance to those who developed them, serving as powerful tools for revenue generation and territorial control. Despite their limitations, these fleets enabled the Greeks to reach and conquer the islands, with smaller territories falling most easily to their advances. On land, however, there were no wars that significantly expanded power. Instead, land conflicts were limited to minor skirmishes between neighboring regions. There were no large-scale campaigns aiming for conquest, nor were there any alliances of subject cities around a central power, or cooperative expeditions among equal states. Greek warfare was primarily local, with rival cities and nearby territories clashing for limited goals. The closest thing to a coalition was the conflict between Chalcis and Eretria, where several Greek states aligned with one side or the other, but this was an exception rather than the rule.

In addition to these limitations, the growth of Greek power was frequently hindered by various local challenges. The Ionian Greeks, for example, experienced rapid advancement until they encountered the expanding Persian Empire under King Cyrus. After defeating Croesus and taking control of the lands from the Halys River to the sea, Cyrus moved to conquer the Greek coastal cities, sparing only the islands, which were later subdued by Darius and the Phoenician navy.

In regions ruled by tyrants, these leaders' focus on personal gain and family power further restricted collective progress. Such rulers prioritized security above all, often isolating themselves from broader Greek affairs and limiting their ambitions to minor disputes with nearby cities. While they had their own local conflicts, they generally avoided anything that might endanger their hold on power. This was true in mainland Greece, though it should be noted that tyrants in Sicily achieved far greater power than their mainland counterparts. In Hellas as a whole, however, we see long-standing conditions that made the Greek states incapable of uniting for substantial, national purposes or of pursuing any robust action independently.

These factors—fragmented warfare, local rivalries, interference from powerful empires like Persia, and the self-serving policies of tyrants—created persistent obstacles to the formation of any unified or ambitious Greek state. For much of this period, the Greek world remained a collection of small, independently focused city-states, unable to organize themselves for significant collective goals or to achieve any lasting cohesion in their actions.

Finally, there came a turning point when the tyrants in Athens, along with the long-standing tyrannies throughout most of Greece, were decisively overthrown by Sparta—except for those in Sicily. Sparta, though originally plagued by long-standing factional conflicts after the arrival of the Dorians, managed at an early stage to establish solid laws and maintain a unique stability, remaining free from tyrants. This political stability allowed Sparta to retain its form of government for over four hundred years, even up to the end of the recent war, and enabled it to play a leading role in regulating the affairs of other Greek states.

Not long after Athens rid itself of its tyrants, the famous Battle of Marathon took place between the Medes and the Athenians. A decade later, the Persian forces returned with a massive fleet intending to subjugate all of Greece. Facing this immense threat, Sparta assumed command of the allied Greek forces due to its superior military power, while Athens, deciding to abandon its city, transformed its citizens into a naval force, retreating to their ships and committing to a new life on the sea. Together, the Greeks repelled the barbarian invasion, but this coalition quickly fractured into two factions, divided between those who had opposed the Persian King and those who had aided him.

Athens soon rose as the leading naval power, while Sparta remained the preeminent military force on land. For a brief period, the alliance between these two powerful city-states held. But the fragile peace eventually shattered when Sparta and Athens clashed directly, dragging their respective allies into a protracted conflict that would involve nearly every Greek city-state, even those that initially tried to stay neutral. Thus, the entire period from the Persian Wars to this current conflict, punctuated by occasional interludes of peace, saw each state frequently embroiled in warfare—either with each other or against their own rebellious allies. These continual hostilities provided both Athens and Sparta with extensive military experience, honed in the crucible of constant danger.

Sparta's policy towards its allies was one of control rather than financial extraction. Rather than demanding tribute, Sparta sought to secure its allies' loyalty by installing oligarchies that would support its interests. Athens, in contrast, gradually deprived its allies of their fleets and instead imposed monetary contributions on all, with the exception of Chios and Lesbos. As a result, when the two states eventually went to war, each found itself possessing greater resources individually than the combined strength they had once shared when the alliance was intact.

In presenting the findings of my inquiries into these early times, I acknowledge that not every detail will be easy to accept. People commonly accept all traditions as they are presented, rarely questioning their accuracy. For example, most Athenians mistakenly believe that Hipparchus was the ruling tyrant when he was assassinated by Harmodius and Aristogiton, unaware that Hippias, the eldest son of Pisistratus, was actually in power, while Hipparchus and Thessalus were his brothers. The events unfolded when Harmodius and Aristogiton, intending to kill Hippias, suspected—at the very moment they were to act—that their accomplices had informed Hippias of the plan. Believing he had been warned, they shifted their attack to Hipparchus, finding him near the temple of the daughters of Leos, where he was preparing the Panathenaic procession, and there killed him rather than abandon their plot entirely and risk their lives in vain.

These instances highlight the importance of critically examining historical traditions, as misunderstandings and distortions often obscure the true course of events.

There are many other misconceptions among the Greeks, even about recent history that hasn't been obscured by time. For example, some believe that the Spartan kings each hold two votes, when in reality, they have only one. Others think there is a company named Pitane among the Spartans, though no such unit exists. This shows how little effort people make to investigate the truth, readily accepting the first story they hear. However, based on the evidence I've presented, I believe the conclusions I've drawn are trustworthy. They won't be shaken by poetic exaggerations or by the chronicles of storytellers who prioritize appeal over accuracy; these accounts often touch on subjects outside the reach of evidence, and over time, they have drifted into legend, losing their historical value. Setting aside these unreliable sources, we can be content with the knowledge that our inquiry has relied on the clearest available evidence, reaching conclusions as precise as one might expect for such ancient matters.

Turning to this war: while it's common for participants in any conflict to overstate its significance and, once it ends, to return to admiring earlier events, an honest examination of the facts reveals that this war surpassed previous ones in scale and impact.

Regarding the speeches in this history, some were delivered before the war began, and others during it. Some I heard firsthand; others I gathered from various sources. It was rarely possible to remember them word for word, so I have crafted the speeches to convey what I believe each speaker would have said in each situation, adhering as closely as possible to the essence of their actual statements. For the narrative itself, I did not rely on the first source available, nor did I even fully trust my own memory. My account is based partly on what I witnessed myself and partly on accounts provided by others, always subjected to the strictest possible checks. My conclusions required considerable effort, as accounts of the same events from different witnesses often conflicted, sometimes due to lapses in memory and other times due to bias. The lack of romantic embellishment in my work may make it less engaging, but if it proves useful to those seeking a precise understanding of the past to interpret the future—since human nature suggests that the future will resemble the past—I will be satisfied. My aim has been to create a work not meant to gain temporary applause but to endure as a lasting resource.

The Persian War, often hailed as the greatest achievement of the past, reached a swift conclusion with just two battles by sea and two by land. In contrast, the Peloponnesian War dragged on for an extraordinary length of time, and though long, it was unmatched for the calamities it brought upon Greece. Never before had so many cities been captured and destroyed, some by foreign invaders, others by Greek factions, often resulting in the displacement of entire populations. Never had there been such widespread exile and bloodshed, whether on the battlefield or through internal factional strife. Ancient tales, which once seemed unbelievable, suddenly appeared credible: there were massive and violent earthquakes, an unprecedented frequency of solar eclipses, severe droughts that led to famines in various places, and the devastating, deadly outbreak of plague.

All these calamities coincided with the recent war, initiated by the Athenians and Peloponnesians with the dissolution of the thirty-year truce made after the conquest of Euboea. As for the reasons they broke the treaty, I will begin by detailing their grievances and points of contention, so that no one may later ask what caused such a vast conflict among the Greeks. The true cause, in my view, was one that was carefully concealed: the rapid rise of Athenian power and the fear this provoked in Sparta made the war unavoidable. Nevertheless, I will present the stated reasons given by both sides that led to the treaty's breakdown and the outbreak of hostilities.

Chapter II

The city of Epidamnus was situated on the right side of the entrance to the Ionic Gulf, in a region inhabited by the Taulantians, an Illyrian tribe. Epidamnus was originally a colony of Corcyra, established by Phalius, son of Eratocleides, of the Heraclid family, who had been summoned from Corinth, the mother city, according to ancient custom. The Corcyraeans were joined in this venture by some Corinthians and other Dorians. Over time, Epidamnus flourished and grew populous. However, internal strife, reportedly arising from a war with neighboring barbarian tribes, weakened the city, and much of its former power was lost. Ultimately, a factional struggle led to the expulsion of the nobles by the people. These exiled nobles allied with the barbarians and launched attacks on Epidamnus by both land and sea.

With pressure mounting, the Epidamnians sent representatives to Corcyra, pleading with their mother city to intervene. They asked the Corcyraeans to mediate between them and the exiled nobles and to assist them in the war against the barbarians. To strengthen their appeal, the ambassadors sat as suppliants in the temple of Hera, hoping to secure a favorable response. Yet, the Corcyraeans refused to grant their request, dismissing them without any offer of aid.

Left without support from Corcyra, the Epidamnians were unsure of their next step. They decided to consult the oracle at Delphi, asking whether they should hand their city over to Corinth and seek assistance from their founders. The god advised them to submit their city to Corinthian protection. Acting on this counsel, the Epidamnians went to Corinth, explaining their ancestral connection to the Corinthians, recounting the oracle's words, and appealing for help to prevent their city's downfall. The Corinthians agreed to assist, viewing the colony as rightfully theirs due to its founding ties to Corinth. Additionally, the Corinthians had long held a grudge against the Corcyraeans, who, unlike other colonies, refused to honor their mother city with customary deference at public gatherings or sacrifices. This resentment was fueled by Corcyra's wealth, considerable military strength, and pride in its naval heritage, which traced back to its legendary inhabitants, the Phaeacians. Corcyra's navy had become a source of great pride and power, and when the war began, they boasted a fleet of one hundred and twenty galleys, a testament to their maritime prowess.

Thus, the appeal of Epidamnus to Corinth and the strained relations between Corinth and Corcyra over matters of honor, heritage, and power became catalysts for conflict, setting the stage for a larger struggle in the Greek world.

All these grievances made Corinth eager to fulfill its promise of aid to Epidamnus. Volunteers were recruited as settlers, and a force made up of Corinthians, as well as allies from Ambracia and Leucas, was organized. They marched overland to Apollonia, another Corinthian colony, to avoid the possibility of interference from Corcyra's navy. When the Corcyraeans learned that Corinthian settlers and troops had arrived in Epidamnus and that the city had been surrendered to Corinthian protection, they were incensed. They quickly launched a fleet of twenty-five ships, soon reinforced by others, and demanded that the Epidamnians restore the exiled nobles and dismiss the Corinthian garrison and new settlers. (The Epidamnian exiles had previously appealed to Corcyra, invoking the graves of their ancestors as they pled to be restored.) However, the Epidamnians refused.

In response, Corcyra assembled a fleet of forty ships, bringing the exiles with the intention of reinstating them and enlisting support from Illyrian forces. They positioned themselves outside Epidamnus, issuing a proclamation that any natives or foreigners who wished to depart unharmed could do so, while those remaining would be treated as enemies. When this ultimatum was ignored, the Corcyraeans laid siege to the city, located on an isthmus. Upon hearing of Epidamnus's siege, Corinth gathered an armament and announced the establishment of a new colony there, promising full political equality to all participants. Those who were unwilling to leave immediately could still share in the colony by paying a fee of fifty Corinthian drachmae. This offer attracted many, with some preparing to sail at once, while others paid the required fee. Expecting resistance from Corcyra, Corinth sought assistance from allied cities to provide an escort for their fleet. Megara prepared eight ships, Pale in Cephallonia four, Epidaurus five, Hermione one, Troezen two, Leucas ten, and Ambracia eight. Meanwhile, Thebes and Phlius were asked for monetary support, and Elis was asked to provide hulls, while Corinth itself contributed thirty ships and three thousand heavy infantry.

Upon learning of these preparations, the Corcyraeans sent representatives to Corinth, accompanied by envoys from Lacedaemon and Sicyon, to negotiate. They demanded that Corinth recall its garrison and settlers, arguing that the city had no rightful claim to intervene in Epidamnus. However, if Corinth believed it had legitimate claims, the Corcyraeans offered to submit the matter to arbitration by mutually agreed-upon Peloponnesian cities, with the colony going to whichever side the arbitrators deemed appropriate. They were also open to consulting the oracle at Delphi for a final verdict. Corcyra warned that if Corinth disregarded these offers and escalated to war, they would be forced to seek allies in places they would rather avoid, even if it meant breaking old ties for new support.

Corinth responded that if Corcyra withdrew its fleet and allied barbarians from Epidamnus, negotiations could proceed; however, arbitration was impossible while the siege continued. The Corcyraeans countered by proposing that Corinth withdraw its own troops from Epidamnus as well, or that both sides agree to maintain the current positions and an armistice until a decision could be reached.

Ignoring all proposals for peace, the Corinthians, once their ships were manned and their allies gathered, sent a herald ahead to formally declare war. They then set out with a fleet of seventy-five ships and two thousand heavy infantry, bound for Epidamnus to confront the Corcyraeans in battle. The fleet was commanded by Aristeus, son of Pellichas, Callicrates, son of Callias, and Timanor, son of Timanthes, while the land troops were led by Archetimus, son of Eurytimus, and Isarchidas, son of Isarchus. Upon reaching Actium, a site in Anactorium at the mouth of the Ambracian Gulf, where a temple to Apollo stood, the Corinthians were met by a Corcyraean herald, who arrived in a small boat, warning them to turn back.

Meanwhile, the Corcyraeans prepared their ships for battle. Many of their vessels had been retrofitted, with old ships reinforced to ensure their seaworthiness. When the herald returned without a peaceful response from the Corinthians, the Corcyraeans launched their fleet of eighty ships (forty of which were still engaged in the siege of Epidamnus) and set out to confront the enemy. In the ensuing naval battle, the Corcyraeans achieved a decisive victory, sinking fifteen Corinthian ships. That same day, the besieged city of Epidamnus surrendered under terms imposed by the Corcyraean forces: the foreign troops would be sold into slavery, while the Corinthian defenders were held as prisoners of war until further decision.

After their victory, the Corcyraeans erected a trophy on Leukimme, a promontory on Corcyra, and executed all captured soldiers except the Corinthians, who were retained as prisoners. Following their defeat, the Corinthians and their allies returned home, leaving the Corcyraeans in control of the seas around the region. The Corcyraean fleet went on to raid the territory of Leucas, a Corinthian colony, and destroyed Cyllene, the harbor of the Eleans, as punishment for their support of Corinth with ships and money. For nearly the entire period following the battle, the Corcyraeans dominated the surrounding seas, harassing Corinth's allies with their cruisers.

Eventually, Corinth, frustrated by the hardships inflicted on its allies, sent out additional ships and troops late in the summer, establishing a defensive encampment at Actium and around Chimerium in Thesprotis to protect Leucas and other friendly cities. In response, the Corcyraeans set up their own camp at Leukimme. Despite their proximity, neither side took further action, and they remained in a standoff until the end of summer, eventually withdrawing as winter approached.

Enraged by the ongoing conflict with Corcyra, Corinth spent the following year and the one after that building up a powerful fleet. Ships were constructed with urgency, and rowers were recruited from across the Peloponnese and the rest of Greece, lured by substantial bounties. Hearing of Corinth's extensive preparations, the Corcyraeans, who lacked any allies in Greece since they had not joined either the Athenian or Spartan alliances, decided to seek help from Athens and form an alliance. Meanwhile, Corinth, learning of Corcyra's plans, sent its own envoys to Athens to prevent an alliance that might strengthen the Corcyraean navy and hinder Corinth's control over the conflict.

An assembly was called in Athens, where representatives from both Corcyra and Corinth presented their cases. The Corcyraean envoys began with the following argument:

"Athenians! When a people, like us, who have not previously provided significant aid or support to their neighbors, approach others to request assistance, they can be justly asked to meet certain initial requirements. They should first demonstrate that granting their request is either beneficial or, at the very least, safe. They must also show that they will remain grateful for the favor. If they cannot satisfy these points, they should not be surprised if their request is denied. The Corcyraeans believe that, alongside our plea for help, we can give you satisfactory reasons on these points, which is why we have sent envoys to you.

Our current situation, however, places us in an unusual and, admittedly, somewhat contradictory position. On one hand, we acknowledge the inconsistency in our approach; we are a state that has never before sought alliances with our neighbors, and yet here we are, asking you to ally with us. On the other hand, our longstanding policy of isolation, which we once considered wise, has left us dangerously exposed, making our request not only inconsistent with our history but also a matter of necessity. Our strategy was based on the belief that by avoiding alliances, we could also avoid being drawn into conflicts of others' making. Yet, as events have shown, this policy now appears shortsighted and has left us vulnerable.

In the recent naval battle, we succeeded in repelling the Corinthians on our own. But they have since mustered an even larger force, drawing support from the Peloponnese and other Greek states. Recognizing our inability to stand against them alone and understanding the grave threat that defeat would pose, we have come to you and to others, asking for help. We hope you will understand that our abandonment of our previous stance on isolation is not rooted in any underhanded motive; rather, it is the outcome of a miscalculation. We misjudged the risks of standing alone, and now we see the need to seek support beyond our shores to preserve our independence."

"There are many reasons why, if you choose to grant our request, you will have good cause to congratulate yourselves. First, because you will be assisting a power that, while itself peaceful, suffers from the injustices of others. Second, because everything we hold dear is at stake in this struggle, and by welcoming us under these conditions, you will demonstrate goodwill that will remain embedded in our hearts with lasting gratitude. Third, aside from yourselves, we are the greatest naval power in Hellas. And consider, what better fortune could come your way, or more effectively dishearten your enemies, than for a power whose alliance you would have valued to approach you of its own accord? We deliver ourselves into your hands, without cost or risk, offering you an opportunity to earn high regard among the Greeks, gratitude from those you aid, and a significant addition to your strength.

"Examples of such opportunities are rare in history—a state not only seeking assistance but able to offer as much security and honor as it receives. It may be argued that we would only prove useful in the event of war. To this, we respond that any who believe such a war is distant are gravely mistaken. They ignore the jealousy Sparta holds toward you and its desire for conflict, or the influence Corinth wields there—a state that is not only your rival but is actively attempting to subdue us as a precursor to turning against you. Corinth aims to prevent our alliance by conquering us first, thus avoiding the challenge of fighting us both. They plan to gain an advantage over you by either crippling our power or turning it to their benefit. Therefore, our best response is to act first—Corcyra offering alliance, and you accepting it. Instead of waiting to thwart Corinth's plans, we should take the initiative and make plans of our own.

"If Corinth claims that accepting an alliance with one of its colonies is improper, let them be reminded that colonies honor their mother cities when treated fairly but grow distant when subjected to injustice. Colonies are not founded to be enslaved by those left behind but to be equal partners. Corinth has wronged us—that much is clear. When invited to submit the Epidamnus dispute to arbitration, they chose to pursue it by war rather than by a fair settlement. Let their treatment of us, their kin, serve as a warning to you: don't be deceived by their arguments or swayed by their demands. Concessions to adversaries lead only to regret, while a firm stance against them greatly increases the likelihood of your security."

"If anyone argues that accepting us as allies would breach the existing treaty between you and Sparta, we respond that we are a neutral state, and the treaty clearly allows any neutral Hellenic state to join whichever side it chooses. It is unreasonable that Corinth can gather men for its navy not only from its allies but from across Hellas—including a significant number from your own subjects—while we are denied both the alliance that the treaty entitles us to and any outside assistance, and that you would be accused of wrongdoing for agreeing to our request. In truth, we would have greater reason to feel wronged if you rejected our appeal. We, who pose no threat to you, are seeking help in a time of need, while Corinth, the aggressor and your enemy, faces no opposition from you and even recruits resources from your own territories. This shouldn't be the case—you should either prevent Corinth from recruiting within your domain or allow us the support you see fit to provide.

"Your best policy is to openly offer us support. The advantages are many, as we stated at the outset, but one stands out: nothing could confirm our good faith more than the fact that we share a common enemy with you—a powerful enemy fully capable of punishing any betrayal. There's a crucial difference between refusing an alliance with a land power and refusing one with a maritime power. Your priority should be to eliminate any significant naval force apart from your own; failing that, to ally with the strongest available. If some of you see the wisdom of our argument but fear it may lead to a breach of the treaty, remember that your strength alone will intimidate opponents regardless of their accusations. On the other hand, refusing our alliance out of caution won't make you any less vulnerable to a strong enemy.

"Keep in mind that this decision impacts Athens just as much as it does Corcyra. If you want to secure Athens' interests as well as your own, you must take this opportunity to gain a crucial ally now, as war is almost upon you. By bringing Corcyra to your side, you acquire control over a position with enormous strategic importance. Located along the route to Italy and Sicily, Corcyra can block naval reinforcements traveling between Peloponnese and those regions, making it an ideal stronghold.

"To put it plainly, this decision has significant consequences. Consider that there are only three major naval powers in Hellas—Athens, Corcyra, and Corinth. If you let two of these unite by allowing Corinth to absorb us, you will face the combined fleets of Corcyra and Peloponnese on the seas. But if you accept us, our fleet will stand with yours in the coming struggle, enhancing your power and securing your interests."

The Corcyraeans, having made their case, painted themselves as the victims of injustice and accused us of waging an unprovoked war. Before addressing their plea for alliance, it is necessary to clarify these allegations so that you may better understand the foundation of our claims and why their request should be denied. They claim their policy of isolation, their historical refusal to join alliances, was driven by moderation. In reality, this policy was a tool for selfish and exploitative ends, not a testament to restraint. Their conduct clearly reveals that they are not interested in having allies, not out of principled moderation, but because they wish to avoid scrutiny. They do not want witnesses to observe their actions or anyone questioning their behavior, let alone allies who might object to their conduct.

Their geographical position has also contributed to this approach, as Corcyra's location makes them largely self-sufficient, meaning they rarely need to engage with others. Instead, they exploit their situation, exercising authority over those who are forced by circumstance to land on their shores. When they injure others, they act as their own judges, arbitrating conflicts on their own terms since they seldom venture out, yet constantly welcome ships from abroad into their ports, where these visitors are at the mercy of Corcyra's power. Their supposed 'neutrality' is not a noble effort to avoid the wrongdoing of others, but a shield to enable them to monopolize wrongdoing for themselves— a convenient cover that permits them to use force where they can, deceive where they must, and enjoy the profits of their actions without consequence or shame. Were they the upstanding and fair-minded people they claim to be, they would engage with other states, not to avoid accountability but to uphold justice in their dealings. Instead, their independence has enabled them to evade these responsibilities.

The truth is, their conduct has been anything but honorable, either toward us or their neighbors. Their relationship with us, their mother city, has long been marked by disrespect and, more recently, open hostility. They argue, 'We were not sent out to be mistreated.' But we reply, 'We did not establish a colony to be insulted by our own settlers. We intended to be their leaders and to be accorded due respect.' Our other colonies honor and respect us, and we enjoy close bonds with our settlers across the Hellenic world. The fact that Corcyra alone shows discontent suggests that their grievances are unjustified and that we have every right to confront them. We are not acting without cause. Their rejection of us is not rooted in any wrong on our part but in arrogance bred from their wealth and sense of independence.

If the Corcyraeans believed we were wrong, they should have yielded to our authority and earned our respect by doing so; their humility would have been a testament to their integrity, and it would have been disgraceful for us to exploit such moderation. Instead, they have acted with increasing insolence, and nothing illustrates this more than their actions at Epidamnus. Despite Epidamnus being our dependency, they showed no interest in it during its hardships, until we intervened to restore order. Only then did they seize it and now occupy it with force. Such disregard for our claim demonstrates their audacity, pushing their defiance to new heights.

Their plea for alliance and their accusation of our alleged wrongdoing ignore these underlying issues. Their supposed moderation is simply a mask for a policy of self-interest, shielding themselves from accountability while benefiting at others' expense. This, in truth, is the source of the conflict between us, and why we believe they are undeserving of your aid and alliance."

"As for their claim that they wished to resolve the matter through arbitration, it's clear that this offer came only after they felt secure in their advantageous position. Such a suggestion, coming from a party who has already seized control and sits safely entrenched, hardly deserves the respect due to those who genuinely seek a peaceful resolution. They only proposed arbitration after besieging Epidamnus and realizing that we would not passively accept their aggression. By then, the offer of arbitration was a convenient pretense, not a sincere attempt to resolve the issue justly. Now, after committing these wrongs, they come here to urge you to join them—not in an alliance grounded in honor, but in one rooted in their offenses—and they ask you to stand with them, even though they are openly hostile to us.

"If they had truly valued justice, they should have reached out for your support while they still held a position of strength, not at this moment when they face the consequences of their actions and find themselves in peril. Instead, they have waited until they are vulnerable, now seeking the support and protection they once had no intention of offering you. They are asking you to open your defenses to those who, when in power, had no desire to share their influence with you and who now bring upon you the same level of reproach that we direct at them, for offenses you had no part in. Fairness would dictate that they share their power with you first before they ask you to share your protection with them.

"Our grievances are real and our opponents have clearly demonstrated their greed and aggression. Now, however, let us explain why, in fairness, you cannot accept them into your alliance. Yes, the treaty allows any state not already aligned to join whichever side it chooses. But that provision wasn't meant to shield states that seek to cause harm to others; it was meant for those in genuine need of support, not for those seeking refuge only because of defection. The clause was not designed for those who would bring, to the power unwise enough to receive them, conflict instead of peace. And that is precisely what you will invite if you take them in and disregard our warning. Accepting them means you cannot remain our friend; by joining their aggression, you would also incur the consequences inflicted upon them by those who defend against it. You are in the best position to remain neutral, and if neutrality is impossible, then you should align with us rather than them. We, at least, have an established treaty with you, while you have no formal bond with Corcyra, not even a truce.

"Do not set a precedent of supporting defectors. When Samos defected, we did not cast our vote against you. The other Peloponnesian powers were divided over whether they should support the Samians, yet we told them outright that each state has the right to discipline its own allies. If you establish a policy of taking in and assisting every offending state, then you risk the loyalty of your own dependencies, who may be tempted to come over to us under similar conditions. Such a precedent would ultimately weigh more heavily on you than on us.

"In sum, these Corcyraeans have acted out of arrogance and self-interest, disregarding us as their parent city, and now they seek to drag you into their conflict under a guise of fairness. We caution you against allowing their provocations to compromise the peace between us. Reflect carefully on the implications of offering them your support, as you risk disrupting the equilibrium and facing potential threats to your own alliances and stability."

"This, then, is the right we assert under Hellenic law. But beyond this, we appeal to your gratitude and offer advice, grounded in a history of support that should not be forgotten. We remind you that, unlike enemies, we pose no threat to you, and though our friendship does not entail frequent contact, it has proven solid in moments of need. Recall, for instance, when you were in desperate need of ships for the war against Aegina before the Persian invasion. Corinth supplied you with twenty vessels. That aid, along with our stance during the Samian rebellion, when we prevented Peloponnesian support for Samos, was crucial for you: it allowed you to conquer Aegina and punish Samos.

"We provided this support at critical times—moments when states often disregard all past relations in pursuit of victory. In such crises, even former enemies who aid a cause are viewed as friends, and former friends who oppose it are seen as adversaries. Nations often disregard their true interests in their singular focus on triumph. Let this reminder weigh on you as you consider your present course. Let your youth hear from their elders of our aid in your time of need, and may they resolve to repay it accordingly. Let them not only see the justice in our appeal but understand the wisdom of honoring it, even with talk of war in the air.

"Not only is the straight path often the wisest, but the very war that the Corcyraeans use to frighten you into a reckless decision remains uncertain. The potential enmity of Corinth should not be risked lightly in the face of mere speculation. Rather, it would be prudent to offset the negative perception your recent actions with Megara have created. Timely acts of friendship have a remarkable ability to dissolve old grievances, even when the facts seem irreconcilable. And while the allure of a powerful naval alliance with Corcyra may tempt you, respect for the sovereignty of other leading powers offers a far more stable foundation than any short-term advantage that would jeopardize long-term peace.

"In our prior support of you, we have already set a precedent—at Lacedaemon we argued that every state has the right to manage its own allies. We now call upon you to extend this same principle to us and not to repay our past loyalty with harm to our interests. Rather, return us like for like, recognizing that in a time of crisis, the one who offers support is the truest friend, while the one who obstructs is the greatest foe. As for the Corcyraeans—do not ally with them against us, nor encourage their wrongful actions.

"In doing so, you will honor our past support and act in your own best interest."

These were the words of the Corinthians.

After the Athenians had listened to both sides, two assemblies were held to discuss the matter. In the first assembly, there was a clear inclination toward Corinth's arguments. However, by the second meeting, the mood had shifted, and Athens resolved to form an alliance with Corcyra, albeit with specific conditions. This would be a defensive alliance, not an offensive one, meaning that Athens would not be required to support Corcyra in any attack on Corinth. The agreement would not violate the existing treaty with the Peloponnese, as the Athenians could join Corcyra only in cases of defensive necessity. Each ally was obligated to support the other in case of invasion, whether of their own territory or that of an ally.

The Athenians recognized that a war with the Peloponnesians seemed increasingly inevitable, and they were unwilling to see a significant naval power like Corcyra fall to Corinth. If Corinth and Corcyra could weaken each other in their struggle, this could serve as useful preparation for a potential confrontation between Athens and the Peloponnesian states. Additionally, Corcyra's strategic location on the route to Italy and Sicily made the alliance particularly attractive. With these considerations in mind, Athens accepted Corcyra as an ally and, shortly after the Corinthians departed, sent ten ships to aid them. These ships were commanded by Lacedaemonius, son of Cimon; Diotimus, son of Strombichus; and Proteas, son of Epicles. The Athenian commanders were instructed to avoid direct conflict with the Corinthian fleet unless absolutely necessary. If the Corinthians sailed to Corcyra and attempted to land on Corcyraean territory or in any of their holdings, the Athenian fleet was to do everything possible to prevent it, with the intention of avoiding any breach of the treaty.

Meanwhile, the Corinthians completed their preparations and set sail for Corcyra with a fleet of one hundred and fifty ships. Of these, Elis contributed ten, Megara twelve, Leucas ten, Ambracia twenty-seven, Anactorium one, and Corinth itself provided ninety ships. Each contingent operated under its own admiral, while the Corinthian fleet was commanded by Xenoclides, son of Euthycles, alongside four colleagues. Departing from Leucas, the Corinthian fleet made landfall on the coast directly opposite Corcyra. They anchored in the harbor of Chimerium, within the territory of Thesprotis, near the city of Ephyre, which lies a short distance inland. By this city, the Acherusian lake empties into the sea, taking its name from the Acheron River, which flows through Thesprotis and into the lake. Nearby, the Thyamis River forms the boundary between Thesprotis and Kestrine, with the point of Chimerium rising between the two rivers. Here, the Corinthians set up camp.

Upon spotting the Corinthian fleet, the Corcyraeans prepared a fleet of one hundred and ten ships, led by Meikiades, Aisimides, and Eurybatus, and stationed themselves near the Sybota isles with the ten Athenian ships in attendance. They positioned their land forces on Point Leukimme and were bolstered by a thousand heavy infantry who had arrived from Zacynthus to support them. Meanwhile, the Corinthians also had land allies on the mainland, as the local barbarians, longstanding allies of Corinth, gathered in large numbers to aid them. The two sides, with their respective allies, prepared for the imminent confrontation, each bolstered by the forces they had managed to gather for this pivotal battle.

When the Corinthians were fully prepared, they gathered three days' provisions and set out from Chimerium under cover of night, ready for combat. At dawn, as they sailed onward, they spotted the Corcyraean fleet approaching them from the open sea. Both sides quickly recognized one another and arranged themselves for battle. The Corcyraeans placed the Athenian ships on their right wing, with the rest of their line organized in three divisions, each commanded by one of their three admirals. The Corinthians, in turn, arranged their forces with the Megarian and Ambraciot ships on their right wing, the remaining allied ships in the center, and on the left the swiftest ships of the Corinthian navy, positioned to confront the Athenians and the Corcyraean right wing.

At the signal, both fleets engaged. The battle was fierce and drawn-out, yet lacking in sophisticated tactics—it more closely resembled a battle on land. Both sides had placed a large number of heavily armed soldiers on their decks, along with archers and javelin throwers, relying on a traditional style of armament. When the ships collided, the sheer number of vessels made it nearly impossible to disengage. Victory depended primarily on the infantry stationed on the decks, who fought in close ranks, while the ships held their positions. There were no advanced naval maneuvers like breaking through enemy lines; instead, brute strength and courage dictated the outcome, with raw force replacing tactical skill.

The battle soon became chaotic, with confusion spreading through every part of the clash. Meanwhile, the Athenian ships kept close to the Corcyraeans, reinforcing their allies whenever they were under heavy attack and intimidating the Corinthian forces, although the Athenian commanders held back from full engagement due to their orders to avoid direct conflict. On the Corinthian right wing, the fighting went poorly. The Corcyraeans managed to overpower the Corinthians in this sector, driving them back to the coast in disorder with twenty ships. The Corcyraean forces then sailed up to the Corinthian camp, found it deserted, burned the empty tents, and plundered what they could. Thus, the Corcyraeans emerged victorious on their right flank, defeating the Corinthian allies there.

However, on the Corinthian left wing, where Corinth's best ships were concentrated, they met with success. The Corcyraean forces were outmatched here, made worse by the absence of the twenty Corcyraean ships pursuing the retreating Corinthians. Observing their Corcyraean allies struggling, the Athenians began to intervene more openly. Initially, they held back from direct charges, but as the Corcyraeans' defeat on this wing became more apparent and the Corinthians pressed harder, the Athenians abandoned restraint. In the thick of the fight, distinctions fell away entirely, and the confrontation escalated to a point where Corinthians and Athenians found themselves openly attacking each other.

In the end, both fleets were locked in a bitter and confused struggle, and the Athenians, despite their earlier orders, found themselves fully drawn into the battle alongside the Corcyraeans.

After the rout, the Corinthians, rather than focusing on securing and towing away the damaged hulls of the Corcyraean vessels they had disabled, concentrated on killing the men aboard, cutting them down as they passed through the shattered ships. They showed little interest in taking prisoners. In the chaos, they even killed some of their own allies by mistake, unaware that their right wing had been defeated. The vast number of ships on both sides and the wide area of the sea they covered made it nearly impossible to distinguish between friend and foe once the fleets had fully engaged. This battle was greater in scale than any previous naval conflict among Hellenes in terms of the number of ships involved.

After chasing the Corcyraeans back to land, the Corinthians turned their attention to collecting the wreckage and the dead. They managed to gather most of them and transported them to Sybota, the gathering point for the allied land forces provided by their barbarian allies. Sybota, a deserted harbor in Thesprotis, served as their rendezvous. Once they had completed this task, the Corinthians regrouped and prepared to sail against the Corcyraeans once more. In response, the Corcyraeans, along with the remaining Athenian ships, readied all their seaworthy vessels, fearing that the Corinthians might attempt a landing on their territory.

As the day wore on and the battle song, or paean, was sung to signal the attack, the Corinthians suddenly began to pull back. They had spotted twenty additional Athenian ships approaching—sent as reinforcements by Athens, which rightly anticipated that the initial ten vessels would be insufficient to protect Corcyra. These new ships, which the Athenians sent out to strengthen their presence, were spotted first by the Corinthians. Fearing that this was just the advance guard of a larger Athenian fleet, they began to retreat, uncertain of how many more ships might follow. The Corcyraeans, who hadn't yet seen the new Athenian ships due to their position, were initially puzzled by the Corinthian withdrawal. But then some of them caught sight of the ships on the horizon and raised the alarm, realizing reinforcements had arrived. With nightfall approaching and the Corinthians in retreat, both sides withdrew, ending the battle as darkness fell.

That night, as the Corcyraeans gathered at their camp on Leukimme, the twenty Athenian ships, under the command of Glaucon, son of Leagrus, and Andocides, son of Leogoras, approached through the sea scattered with corpses and wreckage, and reached the Corcyraean camp not long after they were first sighted. Initially, the Corcyraeans feared these were enemy ships, but they soon recognized the vessels and welcomed their arrival as the Athenian reinforcements dropped anchor.

At dawn, the thirty Athenian ships, now joined by all the seaworthy Corcyraean ships, set out toward Sybota, where the Corinthian fleet was stationed, to test if they would engage again. The Corinthians sailed out from their anchorage and lined up in formation in open waters, but beyond this, they took no further action. They had no intention of initiating another attack, as they now faced fresh Athenian reinforcements and were constrained by several pressing issues: they needed to safeguard the prisoners held on their ships, lacked resources to repair their vessels in this remote area, and were primarily concerned with how they would manage their return voyage. They feared that the Athenians might view the previous engagement as a violation of the treaty, potentially blocking their departure and escalating the situation into open hostilities.

In light of these challenges, the Corinthians focused on finding a way home, wary of the possibility that the Athenians might consider the treaty broken due to the confrontation and prevent their return journey.

The Corinthians, uncertain of how the Athenians might react, decided to send a small group in a boat without the formal herald's staff, testing the waters, so to speak. Upon reaching the Athenians, these envoys addressed them as follows: "Athenians, you are acting unjustly in initiating a war and violating the treaty. We are here to punish our enemies, but we find you actively blocking our path in arms. If it is your purpose to prevent us from sailing to Corcyra or any destination we choose, and if you are indeed set on breaking the treaty, then take us here and treat us as your foes." As they spoke, the Corcyraean forces nearby called out to the Athenians to seize the envoys and kill them. The Athenians, however, replied, "We are not initiating war, Peloponnesians, nor are we violating the treaty. The Corcyraeans are our allies, and we are here to support them. If you wish to sail elsewhere, we will not stand in your way; but if you intend to proceed against Corcyra or any of its territories, we shall oppose you as best we can."

With this reply from the Athenians, the Corinthians began preparations to return home. They erected a victory trophy at Sybota on the mainland, while the Corcyraeans, retrieving wreckage and the bodies scattered by the night's currents and winds, set up their own trophy on Sybota, on the island, also claiming victory. Each side had its own reasons for declaring triumph. The Corinthians argued they had the upper hand during the main part of the battle until nightfall, secured most of the wreckage and dead, and held roughly a thousand prisoners while sinking close to seventy Corcyraean ships. The Corcyraeans, on the other hand, had destroyed about thirty Corinthian vessels and, with the arrival of the Athenians, recovered wrecks and dead on their side of the battlefield. They also saw the Corinthians retreat upon sighting the Athenian reinforcements and noted that the Corinthians declined to engage after the Athenians' arrival. Thus, both sides laid claim to victory.

During their return voyage, the Corinthians captured Anactorium, a strategically located city at the entrance of the Ambracian Gulf. This city had been a shared settlement between Corcyra and Corinth, but was taken through treachery. The Corinthians installed their own settlers there and then headed home. Of the Corcyraean prisoners, 800 were sold as slaves, while 250 were kept and treated well in the hope that, once released, they might sway Corcyra's loyalty toward Corinth. Many of these captives held prominent positions in Corcyra, increasing the likelihood of influence upon their return.

In this manner, Corcyra managed to sustain its political independence despite Corinth's aggression, and the Athenian ships departed. This incident marked the first major cause of Corinth's animosity toward Athens: that they had taken up arms against them in alliance with Corcyra during a time of treaty.

Almost immediately after this, new disputes arose between the Athenians and Peloponnesians, further fueling tensions leading to war. Corinth, nursing a desire for revenge, began to devise plans, while Athens grew increasingly wary of Corinth's intentions. The Potidaeans, who inhabited the isthmus of Pallene, were a Corinthian colony but also tributary allies of Athens. Concerned that they might be swayed by Perdiccas and the Corinthians to revolt, and thereby encourage other allied states near Thrace to join them, Athens ordered the Potidaeans to dismantle their wall facing Pallene, provide hostages, remove their Corinthian magistrates, and discontinue the practice of annually accepting new officials from Corinth.

These measures against the Potidaeans were taken by Athens soon after the battle at Corcyra, as the hostility of Corinth had become openly apparent. Additionally, Perdiccas, son of Alexander and king of the Macedonians, who had once been a friend and ally, had now become an adversary. This enmity developed after Athens allied with Perdiccas's brother, Philip, and Derdas, who were aligned against him. Alarmed by these developments, Perdiccas appealed to Lacedaemon, hoping to draw Athens into a broader conflict with the Peloponnesians. Simultaneously, he sought to align Corinth with his cause, aiming to incite the Potidaeans into rebellion. He also reached out to the Chalcidians and Bottiaeans, urging them to join the revolt. He believed that, with these neighboring states as allies, he would be better equipped to sustain a war against Athens.

Realizing the potential threat and seeking to prevent the spread of revolt among the cities, Athens acted decisively. They were preparing to send thirty ships and a thousand heavy infantry to Macedonia, under the command of Archestratus, son of Lycomedes, along with four others. Athens instructed these commanders to take hostages from the Potidaeans, dismantle the wall facing Pallene, and maintain vigilance over the neighboring cities to prevent any uprisings.

Meanwhile, the Potidaeans sent envoys to Athens, hoping to dissuade the Athenians from taking further action. At the same time, they, along with representatives from Corinth, traveled to Lacedaemon to secure support if the need arose. When extended negotiations with Athens failed to yield favorable results, and realizing that the Macedonian-bound Athenian fleet would likely also target them, the Potidaeans took action. They received a promise from the Lacedaemonian government that, if Athens attacked Potidaea, they would invade Attica in retaliation. Encouraged by this promise, the Potidaeans forged an alliance with the Chalcidians and Bottiaeans and declared their revolt.

Perdiccas also persuaded the Chalcidians to abandon their coastal cities and regroup inland, fortifying themselves at Olynthus as a stronghold. To support those who followed his advice, he provided them with territory in Mygdonia, near Lake Bolbe, as a temporary home during the war against Athens. The Chalcidians thus abandoned their towns, relocated inland, and prepared for the impending conflict.

When the thirty Athenian ships arrived near the Thracian territories, they found Potidaea and its allies already in open revolt. Seeing that their current forces were insufficient to engage in a dual campaign against Perdiccas and the allied cities, the Athenian commanders redirected their efforts to Macedonia, their original objective. There, they established a base and waged war in alliance with Philip and the brothers of Derdas, who were invading from the interior of the country.

With Potidaea now in open revolt and Athenian ships positioned along the Macedonian coast, the Corinthians, alarmed for the security of Potidaea and regarding its fate as closely tied to their own, organized reinforcements. Volunteers from Corinth and mercenaries from across Peloponnese assembled, forming a force of sixteen hundred heavy infantry and four hundred light troops. Command of the expedition was given to Aristeus, son of Adimantus, a longstanding friend of the Potidaeans, whose personal reputation inspired many of the Corinthian volunteers to join. This force reached Thrace about forty days after Potidaea's defection.

Upon learning of the revolt and Aristeus's advance, the Athenians acted swiftly. They dispatched two thousand of their own heavy infantry and forty ships to quell the uprising, under the command of Callias, son of Calliades, along with four other commanders. Arriving in Macedonia, they found that the earlier Athenian force of a thousand men had recently seized Therme and were laying siege to Pydna. The newly arrived Athenians joined the siege for a time, but due to urgent news from Potidaea and the arrival of Aristeus, they hastily reached an alliance with Perdiccas, withdrew from Macedonia, and advanced toward Potidaea by way of Beroea and then Strepsa. Their attempt to capture Strepsa proved unsuccessful, so they continued their march toward Potidaea. Their force consisted of three thousand Athenian heavy infantry, allied soldiers, six hundred Macedonian horsemen led by Philip and Pausanias, and seventy ships that sailed along the coast, advancing gradually. After three days, they reached Gigonus and set up camp.

Meanwhile, the Potidaeans and their Peloponnesian allies, under Aristeus's command, had taken up a defensive position on the isthmus near Olynthus, facing the direction from which the Athenians would approach. They established a marketplace outside the city and prepared for the impending battle. The allies appointed Aristeus as the commander of all infantry forces, while Perdiccas, having defected from his alliance with Athens, took charge of the cavalry, assigning Iolaus as his representative. Aristeus's strategy was to keep his forces on the isthmus and meet the Athenian assault head-on, while positioning the Chalcidians and other allies outside the isthmus, and deploying Perdiccas's two hundred cavalry in Olynthus. This arrangement would allow them to strike at the Athenian rear when the Athenians attacked, effectively surrounding them.

The Athenian general Callias and his colleagues anticipated this strategy and sent their Macedonian cavalry and some allied forces to guard Olynthus, aiming to prevent any interference from that direction. The Athenian forces then broke camp and advanced towards Potidaea. Upon reaching the isthmus, they found the enemy prepared for battle and quickly arranged themselves for combat. Soon after, the two sides engaged. Aristeus's wing, composed of Corinthians and other elite troops, managed to rout the opposing Athenian wing and chased them a fair distance. However, the remaining Potidaean and Peloponnesian forces were overcome by the Athenians and retreated within the city walls.

Returning from the pursuit, Aristeus saw that the rest of his army had been defeated. Facing a difficult decision, he ultimately chose to consolidate his forces and make a direct dash into Potidaea. This maneuver was perilous, as they endured a barrage of projectiles, but he managed to lead most of his men to safety through the sea along the breakwater, although a few were lost in the attempt.

Meanwhile, reinforcements from Olynthus—about seven miles away and visible from Potidaea—had started advancing upon seeing the battle signals, intending to assist. However, the Macedonian cavalry intercepted them, preventing them from joining the fight. When the outcome of the battle became evident and the signals were taken down, the Olynthian forces withdrew back within their walls, and the Macedonian horse returned to the Athenian side. Thus, neither side had effective cavalry support during the battle.

After the victory, the Athenians erected a trophy and agreed to a truce, returning the bodies of the dead to the Potidaeans. The Potidaeans and their allies suffered around three hundred casualties, while the Athenians lost about one hundred and fifty soldiers, including their general Callias.

The Athenians now set up fortifications against the wall on the side of the isthmus and stationed their forces there. However, they did not construct any works on the Pallene side, as they felt they lacked sufficient manpower to maintain a garrison on the isthmus while simultaneously moving to Pallene to establish fortifications there. They feared that dividing their forces would leave them vulnerable to an attack by the Potidaeans and their allies.

Back in Athens, when word arrived that Pallene was undefended, sixteen hundred heavy infantry were dispatched under the command of Phormio, son of Asopius. Upon reaching Pallene, Phormio set up his base at Aphytis and marched towards Potidaea in steady stages, devastating the countryside as he advanced. Since no enemy troops dared to confront him in open battle, he proceeded to build fortifications against the wall on the Pallene side. With these works completed, Potidaea was fully besieged—cut off by land on both the isthmus and Pallene sides, and by sea with Athenian ships enforcing a blockade.

Observing that Potidaea was thoroughly surrounded and with little hope of relief except through an intervention from the Peloponnese or some other unlikely turn of events, Aristeus advised the defenders to allow all but five hundred men to leave the city under cover of favorable winds. He believed this would extend their limited food supplies, and he volunteered to be among those who would stay behind. However, he was unable to convince the defenders to follow this plan. Deciding to pursue other options, he slipped past the Athenian guardships and escaped the city.

Once outside, Aristeus joined forces with the Chalcidians and continued the war effort. He ambushed the citizens of Sermylians, killing many in a surprise attack, and he kept up communication with the Peloponnese, attempting to arrange a way to secure reinforcements. Meanwhile, after securing the siege of Potidaea, Phormio led his sixteen hundred troops on raids through Chalcidice and Bottica, capturing several towns and continuing to harass the region.

Chapter III

Congress of the Peloponnesian Confederacy at Lacedaemon

The Athenians and Peloponnesians had underlying grievances against each other: Corinth's complaint was that her colony of Potidaea, along with Corinthian and Peloponnesian citizens within it, was under siege; Athens' grievance against the Peloponnesians was that they had incited a member of her alliance and a contributor to her revenue to revolt and were now openly fighting against her alongside the Potidaeans. Yet despite these actions, the formal state of peace still held for a time, as this was considered a private venture on Corinth's part rather than a declaration of war.

However, the siege of Potidaea ended any semblance of Corinthian restraint. With her own men trapped inside Potidaea and the security of the town at stake, Corinth decided it was time to act. She called on the allies to gather at Lacedaemon and brought formal charges against Athens, accusing her of violating the treaty and infringing on the rights of Peloponnese. Alongside Corinth, the Aeginetans—though not officially represented for fear of Athens—pressed their case in secret, claiming they were denied the independence guaranteed to them by the treaty. The Lacedaemonians extended their summons to any allies or cities that felt similarly aggrieved by Athenian overreach, and then held an assembly where complaints against Athens could be aired. Many stepped forward with their grievances, including the Megarians, who detailed a lengthy list of offenses, highlighting in particular their exclusion from the ports of the Athenian empire and the market of Athens—clear violations, they argued, of the terms of peace.

Last to speak were the Corinthians. Allowing those before them to fuel the discontent, they finally took the floor and delivered a speech as follows:

"Lacedaemonians! Your confidence in your constitution and social structure often leads you to treat our warnings about other states with a degree of skepticism. This skepticism does reflect a form of moderation, but it also exposes a certain limitation in your knowledge of foreign affairs. Time after time, we have sounded the alarm about Athenian ambitions, and each time, instead of examining our reports, you dismissed them as self-serving. Rather than gathering the allies for discussion before matters worsened, you postponed action until we are now deeply affected—at a point where we, as those who have borne the brunt of Athenian aggression and Lacedaemonian disregard, have the right to speak most directly.

"Now, if these violations of Hellenic rights were conducted covertly, you might not be fully informed, and we would need to bring you up to date. But the reality is visible to all: Athens has imposed servitude on some and intends it for others, especially among your allies. What more evidence do you need? You have seen Athens admit Corcyra into her sphere through deceit and maintain it against our objections with force. You have seen her lay siege to Potidaea, a place that is strategically critical to any action against the Thracian towns, while Potidaea herself could have offered a significant naval contribution to the Peloponnesian cause.

"Isn't it time to ask what Athens really intends? Her actions point toward systematic subjugation, with prolonged preparations and actions that are clearly designed for an impending war. Are we to continue waiting as Athens grows bolder, absorbing one ally after another? How long before these actions, unchecked by us, escalate beyond any response we might later be able to muster? This is no time for inaction, Lacedaemonians; we stand at a critical juncture and urge you to defend the freedom of Hellas."

"For all this, the responsibility falls on you. It was you who allowed Athens to fortify her city after the Median War and later to build her long walls. You—who have repeatedly allowed the freedom of not only those she has already subdued but also those who are still your allies—to be endangered. For when a people is subjugated, the blame lies not only with the oppressor but also with the power that could have prevented it, especially if that power holds itself up as the defender of Hellenic liberty.

"At last, we are gathered here. It was no small feat to convene, and even now, our purpose remains unfocused. This should not be a time to debate the reality of our grievances but to consider how we shall defend ourselves. Athens has already taken up arms, casting aside words for action, fully prepared while we hesitate. We understand all too well the method of Athenian expansion and the subtlety of its advance. She may draw confidence from thinking you simply don't perceive her designs, but what truly drives her is the sense that you do see and yet choose not to intervene. Among all the Hellenes, only you, Lacedaemonians, remain passive, relying on appearances of strength rather than real deeds, letting your adversary grow rather than stopping her early on. You wait until her power is double what it was at the beginning, instead of dealing with it decisively at the outset.

"Once, the world believed it could rely on you. But it seems, Lacedaemonians, that the reputation exceeded the reality. We recall that when the Persian invader approached, he was able to reach the Peloponnese from the farthest ends of the earth without meeting any force of yours substantial enough to halt him. That was a distant enemy, we acknowledge. But Athens is close, and yet you remain indifferent to her actions. Against Athens, you rely on defense rather than offense, putting your fate in the hands of fortune by postponing confrontation until she is much stronger than before. Consider this: it was largely Persia's own miscalculations that brought her downfall, not any effective resistance from you. And if Athens has failed to conquer us outright, it has been due more to her own errors than to your protection.

"Indeed, many who once relied on your support found themselves defeated because their trust in you kept them from making the necessary preparations. We are here today because we refuse to share that fate. We urge you to act—not to watch—but to seize this moment, while action is still possible, to defend the freedom of Hellas and uphold the strength of your own word and reputation."

"We hope that none of you will see these words of warning as words of hostility. Friends remonstrate with those who err; accusations, they reserve for those who have harmed them. Moreover, we believe we have as much right as anyone to point out a neighbor's faults, especially as we reflect on the sharp contrast between our nations, a contrast that you, perhaps, have yet to fully recognize. Have you truly considered the nature of the adversary you would face in Athens? They are entirely unlike you—vastly and utterly different. The Athenians are quick to embrace innovation, launching bold designs with both speed and audacity; you, on the other hand, are conservative, focused on preserving what you have, slow to adapt, and, when compelled to act, prone to caution. They are adventurous, often pushing beyond their limits and daring beyond their judgment, buoyed by optimism even in perilous times. You, however, often attempt less than your power permits, mistrust even your well-reasoned plans, and treat danger as if it were inescapable.

"Promptness and action define the Athenians; for you, it is delay and hesitation. They are rarely at home, constantly pressing outward to expand their holdings, while you rarely leave home, fearing that your advance will jeopardize what you leave behind. They capitalize swiftly on victory and are slow to yield after defeat. They give their bodies unstintingly for their country, reserving their intellect and strategic resources carefully for her service. To them, an unexecuted scheme is a real loss, and even a successful endeavor only modestly satisfying. If a plan fails, they quickly replace it with new ambitions, as if they have the rare power to transform hopes into achievements, driven by the pace at which they bring their plans to life. They labor through trouble and danger daily, with little time to enjoy; they seem born to gain rather than to savor, and their idea of respite is to fulfill whatever the moment demands. For the Athenians, a quiet life is more burdensome than tireless action. To sum up their character, one could say that they were born to take no rest themselves and to give no rest to others.

"This, Lacedaemonians, is Athens—your adversary. And still, you hesitate, failing to understand that true peace endures longest for those who not only use their power justly but also show a resolute unwillingness to tolerate injustice. Your notion of fair play seems based on the belief that, as long as you refrain from harming others, there's no need to risk your own stability by intervening to stop others from causing harm. Perhaps you might manage such a policy if you were surrounded by nations like your own; but as we've shown, your ways are outdated compared to Athens'. Just as in art, so in politics: it is a law of nature that advancements prevail. Established customs may best suit peaceful societies, but constant demands for action require constant progress in method. This is why Athens' long experience has led her further down the path of innovation than you.

"Let this, at least, be where your delay ends. Now is the time to aid your allies—Potidaea in particular—as you promised, by a prompt invasion of Attica. Do not abandon friends and kin to their fiercest enemies, forcing the rest of us, in despair, to seek support elsewhere. Such a move would not violate the oaths sworn before the Gods, nor the pledges witnessed by men. Breaking a treaty is the fault not of those forced by neglect to seek new bonds but of the power that fails to stand by its allies. Act now, and we will remain at your side. It would be unnatural for us to seek new allies, nor would we find one so well-matched. Therefore, make the right choice, and strive to preserve Peloponnesian prestige under your leadership, just as it flourished under that of your forebears."

"Such were the words of the Corinthians. There happened to be Athenian envoys present at Lacedaemon on other business. Upon hearing the accusations brought against them, they felt compelled to address the assembly. Their purpose was not to directly answer the complaints of the various cities but to urge a more measured consideration of the situation, and to caution against a hasty decision.

They also aimed to remind the Lacedaemonians of the might of Athens, hoping to persuade them to favor peace over conflict. So, with permission, the Athenians came forward and spoke:

"We did not come here intending to debate with your allies; our mission was to discuss other matters on behalf of our state. But the intensity of the charges we hear leveled against us compels us to respond. Our intention is not to dispute the cities' grievances—indeed, this is not the setting for formal accusations or defenses—but to prevent you from being misled into decisions of enormous consequence by the words of your allies. We wish to present a broader view, to demonstrate that our claims are justified, and to show that Athens deserves your respect and consideration. We won't go back to ancient times, where tradition rather than experience would be our source. But we will refer to recent history, particularly the Persian Wars, a topic we are weary of revisiting. Nevertheless, if our past actions are raised as a foundation for current disputes, they deserve mention here—not merely to deter hostility but to establish a true record of events, showing you the strength and character of the adversary you would face should you choose to go to war with us.

"We recall that at Marathon, we stood at the front, facing the barbarian alone. When he returned, we realized we couldn't match him on land, so we evacuated our people, took to our ships, and joined the battle at Salamis. This crucial act prevented the Persians from attacking the Peloponnesian cities one by one, shielded by their formidable fleet. Had they been able to do so, no defensive alliance would have held. The proof is seen in Xerxes' own retreat. Once defeated at sea, he recognized that his strength had been broken and, with most of his army, withdrew as swiftly as possible.

"In this struggle, we Athenians were not only fighting for ourselves but for the freedom and security of Hellas. We endured great sacrifices and risked much, but the victory secured was shared by all. You, Lacedaemonians, took part in the peace that followed and reaped the rewards of the safety we fought to secure. We ask only that you acknowledge the role we played, the risks we faced, and the contributions we made. Let that acknowledgment deter you from entering hastily into a needless struggle. Remember that Athens, should she be forced to stand as your adversary, is formidable, tested, and has proven her strength in battle for the good of all Hellas."

"Such, then, was the outcome of that critical time, and it became clear that the fate of Hellas hinged on her fleet. In securing that outcome, we Athenians provided three indispensable contributions: the largest number of ships, the most capable commander, and unwavering patriotism. Our fleet made up nearly two-thirds of the four hundred ships, and Themistocles, our leader, was instrumental in drawing the enemy into the straits, ensuring victory for our collective cause. This leadership earned him honors from you—honors not often granted to a foreign visitor. In our courage, too, we had no rivals. Without reinforcements, knowing that everything behind us had already been subjugated, we held fast. We abandoned our city, sacrificed our possessions, yet instead of breaking ranks or retreating, we stood firm in our ships, prepared to face the enemy without bitterness toward those who failed to assist us. We claim, therefore, that we did as much for you as we did for ourselves. For you, at least, still had homes to defend and the hope of returning to them; fear for your own safety brought you to the fight as much as the duty to protect us. But we left behind a city reduced to ruins, risking our lives for a future based only on hope and shared in your salvation as well as our own. Had we acted differently—choosing submission to the Persians out of concern for our territory—your own naval inferiority would have left the enemy's victory uncontested.

"Surely, Lacedaemonians, for the patriotism we demonstrated at that time, as well as for the soundness of our judgment, we do not deserve the hostility we now face from Hellas, especially regarding our empire. That empire was not seized by force; rather, we were invited to lead, as you declined to continue the fight against the Persians, and the allies turned to us for leadership. Circumstances then compelled us to expand our influence as we did—primarily out of fear, although honor and interest also played a part. In time, as others began to resent our authority and revolt, it no longer seemed safe to relinquish our empire, especially when those who left us would likely fall under your control. And in such grave matters, who can blame a people for securing their own interests in the face of considerable risk?

"Even you, Lacedaemonians, have used your dominance to shape the Peloponnesian states as you see fit. If, at the time in question, you had continued the struggle and faced the resentment that comes with leadership, it is likely that you, too, would have become burdensome to the allies and would have had to choose between maintaining order and safeguarding yourselves. Therefore, it is hardly surprising, or against common practice, that we accepted the leadership entrusted to us and resisted giving it up under the pressure of three compelling motives—fear, honor, and self-interest. We did not create this precedent; it has always been the way of the world for the weaker to yield to the stronger. Moreover, we believed we were deserving of the position, and you, too, shared that view until considerations of self-interest led you to invoke justice—a standard rarely invoked to restrain ambition when opportunity aligns with strength. Praise is due to those who, while not refusing dominion, exercise justice beyond what their power requires."

"We believe that our fairness could be best understood if others found themselves in our position. Yet our own moderation has strangely resulted in criticism rather than approval. Our decision to settle disputes with our allies in Athenian courts under impartial laws, despite our right to decide them as we see fit, has branded us as litigious. No one questions why other empires, with far stricter rule, avoid such complaints; it's simply that where brute force prevails, law becomes unnecessary. Our subjects, however, are so accustomed to being treated as equals that any perceived injustice, whether it arises from a legal ruling or from our imperial authority, makes them forget their fortune in retaining most of their possessions and dwell instead on the few losses they endure. Had we enforced our authority with pure coercion, disregarding law entirely, they likely would have accepted that the weaker must yield to the stronger without question. People, it seems, are more embittered by what they see as a betrayal within legal bounds than by outright force; the former feels like being tricked by an equal, the latter like being commanded by a superior. They somehow endured far worse from the Persian and yet find our rule harsh. This is not surprising, for present hardships weigh heavier on the vanquished than past wrongs.

"One thing is clear: if you were to overthrow us and assume our position, the popularity you currently enjoy due to fear of us would soon fade, especially if your approach mirrors your brief role in leadership against the Persian. Not only is your internal life governed by rules that differ greatly from those of other Hellenes, but when abroad, your citizens follow neither these rules nor the broader customs of Hellas.

"So we urge you to deliberate carefully, for the matter at hand is one of great consequence. Don't let the clamor of others drive you toward actions that may bring misfortune upon yourselves. Consider how unpredictable war can be; once it begins, it often becomes a matter of uncertain outcomes that neither of us can fully foresee. It is easy to make the mistake of rushing into conflict only to pause and discuss after disaster has struck. But neither of us, we believe, is yet so misled. While reason still guides our choices, we ask that you uphold the peace and honor your oaths, resolving any grievances through arbitration as agreed. Otherwise, we call upon the gods who witnessed those oaths, and if you initiate conflict, we will match whatever course of action you pursue to defend ourselves."

"Such were the words of the Athenians. After hearing the grievances of their allies and the response from the Athenians, the Lacedaemonians made all withdraw, and deliberated privately on the matter. The majority opinion leaned toward the same conclusion: the Athenians were indeed acting as aggressors, and the time for declaring war was at hand. Yet before any final decision could be made, Archidamus, the king of Lacedaemon—a man widely respected for his wisdom and moderation—stood before them and offered the following counsel.

"Lacedaemonians, I have lived through many wars and can speak with the voice of experience. Among you are men of my own age who will not succumb to the all-too-common trap of desiring war out of inexperience or misplaced confidence in its supposed advantages and safety. This potential war with Athens, I must stress, would be an undertaking of immense scale and complexity. Consider the difference: when we engage in conflict with Peloponnesians or other neighboring cities, our forces are well-matched in strength and proximity, allowing us to act swiftly and manage different fronts effectively. But here, we face a people living in a distant land, deeply skilled in naval warfare, and prepared in every imaginable way—whether in their substantial public and private wealth, the number and capability of their ships, their cavalry, heavy infantry, or their population, which is unparalleled in all Hellas. Beyond that, they have an alliance of tributary states supporting them. What reason, then, do we have to start such a war rashly? Wherein lies the confidence to drive us to rush into conflict unprepared?

"Do we put our trust in our fleet? In this, we are undeniably weaker, and if we are to train ourselves to match their capabilities, it will take considerable time. Or do we rely on our wealth? Again, we fall short. Our treasury is not sufficient for such a protracted conflict, and we are hardly ready to contribute from our private resources. Perhaps we think our superiority in heavy infantry and land forces gives us an edge—strength that could allow us to invade and devastate Athenian territory. But the Athenians are not solely dependent on their land; they control other territories within their empire, and they can easily import any necessary supplies by sea.

"Consider, too, any thoughts we might have of inciting their allies to rebellion. Most of their allies are on islands or distant lands, and supporting them would require a fleet at least equal to the Athenians'. How then should we approach this war? Unless we can either gain superiority at sea or sever their access to the wealth that fuels their fleet, we are likely to encounter only setbacks. And once we commit ourselves, our honor and reputation will bind us to continue the conflict, especially if it is perceived that we initiated hostilities. Let us beware of the dangerous illusion that this war might end swiftly simply because we ravage their lands. I worry instead that we may leave this war as a legacy for our children to fight, as it is far-fetched to imagine that the Athenians would submit merely because of the loss of their territory, nor will their battle-hardened experience in war easily bend to our efforts.

"Athens is not a city that would ever give up quickly or capitulate because of hardships. They are a people accustomed to fighting for their position and maintaining their dominance, and if pressed by us, they will not hesitate to increase their commitment. They may well counter with fresh resources, and they possess a fleet that is already formidable. And if we, in our eagerness, find ourselves unprepared, what then will we do? Shall we continue indefinitely, or admit our lack of foresight when we can no longer sustain the campaign?

"We must also consider our resources carefully. We are not a people who store vast reserves of wealth nor rely on external resources. We may initially commit enthusiastically, but we are, by nature and custom, a cautious people, reluctant to burden ourselves with sustained effort over the long term, especially when so far from home. So if we go to war without an assured way to strike directly at their power—be it by sea or by breaking their alliances and revenue streams—we might find that we are fighting on their terms, not ours.

"I urge you to consider this fully before making a decision. The cost of war will fall heavily upon us if we underestimate the difficulty of the path ahead. We must not be swept up by the moment or allow ourselves to be driven solely by the grievances and urgencies voiced by our allies. To be cautious is not a sign of weakness but of wisdom. Let us take counsel from past conflicts and approach this situation with the consideration it deserves. The Athenians are ready and eager for war; they are skilled, determined, and well-prepared, and this will not be a conflict that ends in a single season.

"Not that I would advise you to stand by idly while they harm our allies or to ignore their schemes; rather, I suggest that we do not rush headlong into war. Instead, let us first send a delegation to remonstrate with them—firmly, yet not in a tone that suggests we are itching for conflict, nor one that implies we are willing to concede to them either. This will buy us time to strengthen our position. First, let us seek allies—Hellenic or barbarian, it matters not so long as they bring naval strength or financial support to our side. The principle of self-preservation should dispel any criticism of seeking help from foreign powers, especially among those, like us, who are the targets of Athenian expansion.

"Second, we should develop our resources at home to ensure that when we do enter into conflict, we do so from a position of readiness. If our envoys' words do persuade the Athenians to step back, then we benefit without engaging in hostilities. But if they refuse to heed us, then after two or three years of bolstered preparation, we will be much better positioned to confront them if we deem it necessary. By that time, our readiness—combined with carefully chosen words—might even influence them to reconsider their approach, especially if they still enjoy the unspoiled fruits of their land and are not yet facing the desperation of a full-scale war. In this way, their territory becomes, in a sense, a valuable hostage—a bargaining tool that we control without yet damaging. The longer we refrain from laying waste to it, the stronger our leverage remains, and we avoid pushing them into desperation, which would only make them a more formidable adversary.

"However, if we allow ourselves to be swept up by the grievances of our allies and prematurely devastate their lands, we risk inflicting a twofold blow upon Peloponnese: the disgrace of striking before we are fully prepared, and the complications of managing a protracted conflict. Adjustments to address grievances, whether from cities or individuals, are achievable through careful diplomacy. But a war launched impulsively by a coalition of states, each with its own agendas and grievances, quickly grows unwieldy and cannot easily be honorably resolved.

"Do not mistake this deliberation for cowardice. Our confederation of cities must carefully consider any action against Athens, for their allies are as numerous as ours, and they contribute financially to Athens' cause. In this kind of war, money is as crucial as arms, if not more so, especially in a confrontation between a land power like ours and a naval power like theirs. Therefore, our first priority must be to gather funds, and we should not be rushed into action by our allies' voices before we have done so. Given that the greatest responsibility for the outcome, whether successful or disastrous, will fall upon us, it is our prerogative to make a thorough and composed assessment of the situation before taking any decisive step."

"And the caution and deliberation for which our character is often criticized should not cause you to feel ashamed. If we rush into war unprepared, our haste will only prolong the struggle. Remember, we are a free and illustrious city, and always have been. What others call 'slowness' is, in truth, our wise moderation—a quality that has protected us from becoming arrogant in success and yielding to despair in hardship. We are not easily swayed by flattery into taking foolish risks, nor do we allow accusations to goad us into actions that our judgment does not approve. We are both strong in war and prudent in thought, and it is our sense of order that brings us these qualities. Our strength in battle comes from self-discipline, which instills honor and, in turn, courage. Our wisdom arises from an education that balances knowledge with respect for our laws, instilling a level of self-restraint that keeps us from defying them.

"We are not overly inclined to speculate about impractical matters or to indulge in endless analysis of an enemy's plans without the courage to confront them in action. Rather, we assume our enemy's strategies are well-considered and ensure that our own preparations are equally sound. Victory should rest on the strength of our preparations, not on hoping for the enemy's mistakes. And we should not assume vast differences between one man and another, but instead recognize that the true advantage lies with those trained in the strictest discipline.

"These principles, passed down to us by our forebears, have always been to our benefit, and we should not abandon them. We must not let the urgency of a single day force us to decide a matter that will affect many lives, fortunes, and cities—a matter where our honor and reputation are also deeply at stake. Instead, we should proceed thoughtfully and prudently. Our strength gives us the unique ability to do just that.

"As for the Athenians, send envoys to them regarding Potidaea and to address the grievances of our allies. If they offer a legal settlement, we should respect that, for to attack someone who offers arbitration is against our principles of law. Meanwhile, let us continue our preparations for war. This approach will be best for us and most daunting for our enemies."

These were the words of Archidamus. Then Sthenelaidas, one of the ephors for that year, came forward and addressed the Lacedaemonians as follows.

"The Athenians' lengthy speech, I must admit, is beyond my understanding. They spent much time praising themselves but failed to deny that they are indeed harming our allies and all of Peloponnese. If they once acted nobly against the Mede but now behave unjustly towards us, then they deserve to be punished twice over—first, for no longer being the allies they once were, and second, for having become antagonistic toward us. We, meanwhile, have remained the same, consistent in our actions and intentions. And if we have any wisdom, we will not ignore the wrongs suffered by our allies, nor delay until tomorrow the duty of aiding those in need today.

While others may have wealth, fleets, and armies, what we have is invaluable: loyal allies, and we must not abandon them to the Athenians' designs, nor resort to mere legal arguments or deliberations over what is clearly beyond words. We are not harmed in mere speech but in action, and our response must likewise be swift and powerful. It would be wrong to suggest that long deliberation has any place in facing injustice—such delay is more fitting for those who are plotting wrongdoing, not for those defending against it. Therefore, Lacedaemonians, I urge you to vote for war as Sparta's honour demands. Let us neither permit Athens to expand her power further nor forsake our allies to their ruin. With the gods at our side, let us rise against those who aggress against us."

With these words, Sthenelaidas, as ephor, put the matter directly to the Lacedaemonian assembly. He declared that he could not judge which side had the louder acclamation—since decisions were traditionally made by acclamation rather than by vote—but his intent was to prompt an open declaration, increasing their commitment to war. He instructed: "All Lacedaemonians who believe the treaty has been broken and that Athens is guilty, move to this side," indicating a specific spot, "and all who hold the opposite view, to the other." The assembly members stood and divided, with a clear majority siding with the belief that Athens had indeed broken the treaty.

They immediately called upon their allies, informing them that they believed Athens to be guilty of injustice and declaring their intent to convene all the allies for a collective vote. They resolved that if a majority agreed, they would proceed to war as a united decision. After this, the delegates returned to their cities without delay, while the Athenian envoys soon followed, having concluded their diplomatic business.

This decision by the assembly—judging the treaty broken and leaning toward war—was made in the fourteenth year of the thirty-year truce signed after the Euboean affair. The Lacedaemonians ultimately chose to declare war on Athens, less because of their allies' persuasions and more due to their apprehension over the increasing power of Athens, seeing most of Hellas already under her sway.

Chapter IV

From the end of the Persian War to the beginning of the Peloponnesian War, Athens saw a remarkable transformation from a city-state recovering from invasion to a dominant power with a far-reaching empire. The path by which Athens expanded her influence unfolded as follows: After the Persian forces were driven out of Europe, decisively defeated by the combined Hellenic forces both at sea and on land, those Persians who escaped to their ships retreated to Mycale. There, the forces of the Hellenes, led by Leotychides, king of the Lacedaemonians, destroyed the remaining Persian fleet, after which Leotychides and the Peloponnesian allies returned home.

However, the Athenians, alongside their allies from Ionia and the Hellespont—regions that had revolted against the Persian King—chose to remain. They turned their efforts to Sestos, a strategic stronghold still occupied by the Persian forces. Throughout the winter, the Athenians and their allies laid siege to the city. Eventually, the defenders were compelled to evacuate, allowing the Hellenes to seize control. Victorious, they returned to their respective cities from the Hellespont region.

Back in Athens, the Athenian people, having endured the barbarian's invasion, immediately set to work re-establishing their lives. They brought their families and remaining possessions from the places of refuge they had used during the war. With their people back, they set about reconstructing their city and fortifying it with new walls. Only a few fragments of the old defensive perimeter remained intact, as most of the walls and houses had been left in ruins by the Persian occupation. Some buildings stood as they had served as quarters for the Persian officials during the war.

The Lacedaemonians, perceiving the Athenians' intentions to rebuild their city's fortifications, quickly dispatched an embassy to

Athens. In truth, they wished for Athens and other cities outside the Peloponnese to remain without walls, primarily driven by the concerns of their allies, who were alarmed by Athens' rising naval strength and the bravery she had shown in the war against the Medes. They urged the Athenians not only to refrain from constructing defensive walls but also to join them in dismantling whatever fortifications were left intact in cities beyond the Peloponnesian region. The Lacedaemonians framed their request in terms of collective security, arguing that, in the event of another invasion by the barbarian, there should be no fortified stronghold like Thebes available for the enemy's use. They proposed that Peloponnese would serve as the stronghold for all, providing both a retreat and a defensive base.

When the Lacedaemonians finished speaking, Themistocles, who had devised a strategy, advised the Athenians to promptly send him as an envoy to Sparta, but to delay dispatching his fellow envoys until the wall had been raised to a defensible height. He also directed the entire Athenian population, including men, women, and children, to devote themselves to the construction of the wall. No structure, whether private or public, was to be spared if it could contribute materials for the fortifications. With these instructions, Themistocles set off for Sparta, assuring the Athenians that he would manage all matters diplomatically.

Upon reaching Lacedaemon, Themistocles did not immediately request an audience but instead sought to buy time by making various excuses. When questioned by the authorities about his delay in appearing before the assembly, he explained that he was waiting for his colleagues, who were delayed by matters in Athens. He reassured them that his fellow envoys would arrive soon. At first, the Lacedaemonians trusted him, as they respected his previous friendship. But as more reports came in from other sources confirming that construction on the walls was progressing, the Lacedaemonians grew suspicious.

Themistocles, aware of their rising doubts, urged them not to rely on rumors and suggested they send reputable inspectors to verify the situation firsthand. The Lacedaemonians agreed and sent a delegation to Athens. However, Themistocles had secretly sent word to the Athenians, instructing them to delay the Spartan envoys as much as possible, without resorting to overt detention, until he and his fellow envoys were ready to leave. By now, Themistocles' colleagues, Abronichus and Aristides, had joined him, bringing news that the walls had been raised to a defensible height. Themistocles feared that the Lacedaemonians might detain him and his colleagues if they learned of the completed fortifications, so the Athenians, following his instructions, held the Spartan inspectors as long as possible.

With his colleagues now by his side, Themistocles formally addressed the Lacedaemonians. He declared openly that Athens was indeed fortified to a level sufficient to ensure the safety of its people and their independence. He asserted that any future Spartan or allied embassy to Athens should proceed on the understanding that the Athenians were fully capable of determining their own and the common Hellenic interests. He reminded the Lacedaemonians that Athens had acted independently when it decided to evacuate its city and take to its ships in the face of the Persian threat—a decision made without prior consultation with Sparta. Yet, when acting in concert with the Lacedaemonians, Athens had demonstrated sound judgment and had proven to be an equal in deliberation and contribution.

He emphasized that the Athenians believed it was only proper for their city to be fortified, both for their own safety and for the stability of the Hellenic league. He noted that meaningful and balanced counsel in the alliance could only come from those with sufficient military strength. Athens would either require all members of the confederacy to be without walls or consider her decision to fortify as just and beneficial to all.

The Lacedaemonians showed no outward signs of anger towards the Athenians when they learned of the walls being built. Their mission, it seems, had been intended less to obstruct than to influence the direction of Athenian policy, and their relations with Athens were still amicable due to the patriotic role Athens had played in the struggle against the Mede. Nevertheless, their unfulfilled expectations undoubtedly caused them some private irritation. However, the envoys from both sides returned home without voicing any complaints.

In this manner, the Athenians succeeded in constructing the city walls swiftly. Evidence of the hurried construction remains visible to this day: the foundation comprises stones of every shape and size, hastily placed without any careful fitting. Some stones even bear the marks of their original use in tombs, with sculpted surfaces and column fragments mixed in indiscriminately. As the circumference of the city was expanded, every available material was put to use, driven by a pressing need for speed.

At this time, Themistocles also urged the Athenians to complete the fortification of Piraeus, a project that had been initiated during his term as archon. His recommendation was based on the strategic advantage of Piraeus, which boasted three natural harbors, making it ideal for a fortified naval base. Themistocles saw this as an opportunity for Athens to establish itself as a dominant sea power. He envisioned a future where Athenian strength lay not only on land but in the control of the seas, laying the foundation for what would become an empire based on naval supremacy.

He advised that the walls of Piraeus be built to exceptional thickness, and traces of these fortifications remain visible, showing the sturdy construction he proposed. Stones were transported by pairs of wagons that met at the building site, where they were assembled to create a wall with double thickness. The structure contained no rubble or mortar but consisted of massive, square-cut stones tightly fitted together and bound with iron and lead on the outer sides. Although the wall was only completed to about half the height he had envisioned, Themistocles had designed it so that it would be resilient against potential attackers. His goal was to allow a minimal defensive force to protect Piraeus, enabling the majority of the Athenian fighting force to be deployed in the fleet.

It was clear that Themistocles prioritized the fleet, anticipating that an enemy assault would be more likely by sea than by land. He even advised the Athenians to consider the harbor and fleet at Piraeus as their greatest assets, suggesting that, should they ever be forced to retreat, they should rely on the security of Piraeus and their naval strength. Thus, after the Mede's retreat, the Athenians not only completed the city walls but also began construction on other fortifications and buildings, taking the first steps toward a new era of maritime power and influence.

Meanwhile, Pausanias, the son of Cleombrotus, was appointed by the Lacedaemonians as the supreme commander of the Hellenic forces. Leading an initial force of twenty ships from Peloponnese, he was joined by the Athenians with thirty ships and a contingent of allies from across Hellas. Together, they launched a campaign against Cyprus, capturing most of the island, and soon turned their efforts against Byzantium, which was under the control of the Medes, ultimately compelling it to surrender. At this time, Spartan supremacy in military leadership was uncontested. However, Pausanias's harsh and overbearing conduct quickly began to alienate the Hellenic allies, particularly the Ionians and other recently liberated communities. Disturbed by his behavior, they appealed to the Athenians, asking them as kin to take the lead and prevent any further abuse of authority by Pausanias.

Recognizing both an opportunity and a responsibility, the Athenians accepted the request and resolved to curb Pausanias's influence, seeing it as a chance to establish their own leadership and shape the course of events to align with their interests. In response to the complaints from allied states, the Lacedaemonians decided to recall Pausanias for an inquiry. Numerous and severe accusations had reached them, brought forward by various Hellenes who had journeyed to Sparta. It was said that Pausanias had adopted more of a tyrant's demeanor than that of a Hellenic general. This recall arrived just as tensions had led most of the allies, except for the soldiers from Peloponnese, to abandon his command and align with the Athenians instead.

Upon Pausanias's arrival at Sparta, he faced condemnation for his oppressive and arrogant conduct in his interactions with the allies. However, he was cleared of the most serious charges, including allegations of collusion with the Medes, though this accusation remained one of the most prominent and seemingly well-founded against him. Despite this acquittal, the Lacedaemonians decided against reinstating him as commander. Instead, they sent out Dorkis and a few other leaders with a modest force to take his place, but these new commanders quickly realized that the allies were no longer willing to accept Lacedaemonian leadership. Observing the shift in loyalty toward Athens, Dorkis and his colleagues returned to Lacedaemon.

The Lacedaemonians ultimately decided not to send any further commanders to assume the role of supreme leader. They feared that whoever took on the command might fall into the same pitfalls as Pausanias, succumbing to the same hubris and detachment. Additionally, they were eager to bring their role in the Median War to an end and had confidence in Athens's capabilities to lead the Hellenic cause. At this juncture, the Athenians still held friendly relations with Sparta, and so the Lacedaemonians were willing to step back, allowing the Athenians to assume the mantle of leadership in the Hellenic League. This pivotal shift marked the beginning of Athens's growing influence, as they were now recognized not just as allies but as the leading power in the alliance against the Medes and other threats to Hellenic freedom.

With the allies willingly transferring the leadership to Athens due to their aversion to Pausanias, the Athenians assumed command and organized the confederation against Persia. They determined which cities would contribute ships and which would contribute money, intending, as they claimed, to retaliate against the Persian King by attacking his lands in retribution for past invasions. This period saw the Athenians establish the office of "Treasurers for Hellas" to manage the tribute payments, which were initially set at four hundred and sixty talents. Delos was chosen as the location for the common treasury, and meetings of the allies were held in the sanctuary there. Thus, Athens began its period of leadership with a coalition of independent allies who worked collectively through resolutions passed at a shared congress.

From this foundation, Athens led a series of campaigns and administrative undertakings during the years between the Median War and the outbreak of the current conflict. These campaigns were waged against Persia, their own rebellious allies, and occasionally against Peloponnesian powers that crossed paths with Athenian interests. I recount these events here to fill a gap left by earlier historians, who either focused solely on Greek affairs before the Median War or limited themselves to that war alone. Hellanicus did briefly address these events in his Athenian history, yet he lacked precision in dates and detail. Furthermore, the history of these developments provides critical insight into the ascent of Athenian imperial power.

The first significant action was the capture of Eion on the Strymon River from the Medes, under the command of Cimon, son of Miltiades, during which the inhabitants were enslaved. Following this, the Athenians seized Scyros, an island in the Aegean inhabited by the Dolopians, and settled it themselves. Next, they engaged in a conflict with Carystus, a city on Euboea. The rest of Euboea remained neutral, and Carystus ultimately surrendered on agreed terms.

Soon after, Naxos attempted to break away from the confederation, which led to a conflict, ending with the city's forced return after a siege. This marked the first instance of an allied city being subdued for attempting to leave the league—a precedent Athens would follow with other cities as conditions necessitated. A common reason for these defections was related to unpaid tribute, unfulfilled commitments to supply ships, and reluctance to participate in military service. The Athenians enforced strict adherence to these obligations and earned resentment from allies as they imposed these demands upon those not accustomed to nor inclined toward continuous military exertion.

Moreover, the Athenians gradually moved away from their initial stance as egalitarian leaders, exerting stricter control over the confederation. Many allies, seeking to avoid the burdens of service, opted to provide money instead of ships, hoping to remain in their homes rather than commit to active duty. Athens used these monetary contributions to build up her naval strength, while the allies—lacking military resources and experience—were left vulnerable and without recourse if they attempted to revolt.

The next significant events occurred on land and sea at the river Eurymedon, where the Athenians, joined by their allies, engaged the Medes. Under the leadership of Cimon, son of Miltiades, the Athenians triumphed in both a land battle and a sea engagement on the same day, ultimately capturing and destroying the entire Phoenician fleet of two hundred ships. This victory secured substantial control over the region.

Not long afterward, conflict arose with the Thasians, who revolted due to disputes over trading centers along the Thracian coast and a valuable gold mine they held. In response, the Athenians sent a fleet to Thasos, defeated the Thasians at sea, and landed forces on the island. Concurrently, Athens dispatched ten thousand settlers, both from their own citizenry and from allied states, to establish a colony at Ennea Hodoi, later known as Amphipolis. After taking Ennea Hodoi from the Edonians, the settlers attempted to advance further inland but met fierce resistance. Near Drabescus, a town of the Edonians, they were defeated and wiped out by the united Thracian tribes, who viewed the settlement as an aggressive encroachment on their territory.

Meanwhile, as the Thasians continued to suffer under Athenian pressure and siege, they appealed to the Lacedaemonians for help, requesting an invasion of Attica to divert the Athenians. The Lacedaemonians secretly agreed, intending to act on this request, but their plans were disrupted by a powerful earthquake that struck Sparta. This disaster led to a massive uprising, with the Helots, along with the Thuriats and Aethaeans of the Perioeci, seceding to Ithome. Many of these Helots were descended from the old Messenians enslaved after a previous war, which is why they were all commonly referred to as Messenians.

Engaged in a long struggle with the rebels at Ithome, the Lacedaemonians called upon their allies, especially the Athenians, to assist. The Athenians responded with a force led by Cimon, owing to their skill in siege warfare, which the Lacedaemonians had come to value after recognizing their own limitations. This marked the first significant fracture between Athens and Sparta. Despite the Athenians' assistance, the Lacedaemonians grew wary of their allies' presence, particularly distrusting the Athenians' ambitious nature and differing cultural origins. Concerned that the Athenians might be swayed by the besieged in Ithome to incite political changes within Spartan territory, they discreetly dismissed the Athenians, claiming they no longer required their aid.

The Athenians, however, perceived this as an insult, understanding that their dismissal was rooted in suspicion rather than genuine necessity. Deeply offended by what they viewed as unwarranted distrust, the Athenians returned home and, without delay, severed their alliance with the Lacedaemonians formed during the Medean War. They then entered into an alliance with Argos, a long-standing enemy of Sparta, and simultaneously forged a pact with the Thessalians, solidifying mutual oaths of allegiance with both. This marked a significant shift in Greek politics and alliances, as Athens moved away from Sparta and began to align with those who opposed her.

Meanwhile the rebels in Ithome, unable to pAfter a prolonged ten-year resistance, the defenders at Ithome finally surrendered to the Lacedaemonians, agreeing to terms that required their complete departure from Peloponnese under a safe escort, with the stipulation that they would never return. Any of them found in Peloponnese in the future would become the property of whoever captured them. This decision was influenced by an ancient Delphic oracle instructing the Lacedaemonians to release the suppliant of Zeus at Ithome. So, the defeated left, taking with them their children and wives. They were welcomed by Athens, who harbored resentment toward Lacedaemon at that time, and were given land at Naupactus, which Athens had recently captured from the Ozolian Locrians.

Shortly thereafter, Athens gained a valuable new ally, the Megarians, who left the Lacedaemonian alliance due to conflicts over border disputes initiated by Corinth. The Athenians took control of Megara and Pegae, constructing long walls from the city to the port of Nisaea, where they stationed an Athenian garrison. This strategic move by Athens stoked intense resentment from the Corinthians, as it established Athenian influence right next to Corinth.

During this period, Inaros, the son of Psammetichus, a Libyan king near Egypt, led almost the entire region of Egypt in revolt against the Persian King Artaxerxes. From his base at Marea, above Pharos, Inaros assumed leadership of the rebellion and called upon Athens for assistance. Responding to his call, Athens withdrew two hundred ships, their own and those of their allies, from an expedition to Cyprus. The Athenian fleet arrived in Egypt, took control of the Nile, and captured two-thirds of Memphis. They then turned their attention to the last stronghold, the White Castle, where Persians, Medes, and Egyptians loyal to Artaxerxes had taken refuge, holding out against the rebellion.

In this way, Athens continued to extend its influence, seizing opportunities to weaken both the Persian Empire and its opponents in Hellas, and expanding its presence across the region.

The Athenians, having launched a campaign from their fleet at Haliae, encountered forces from Corinth and Epidaurus. In this engagement, the Corinthians claimed victory. However, shortly after, the Athenians clashed with the Peloponnesian fleet near Cecruphalia, where the Athenians emerged triumphant. This was soon followed by a significant escalation when war broke out between Aegina and Athens, leading to a fierce naval battle off Aegina, with both sides supported by their respective allies. The Athenians ultimately won, capturing seventy enemy ships and landing forces on Aegina, where they began a siege led by Leocrates, son of Stroebus. In response, the Peloponnesians, eager to aid Aegina, dispatched a contingent of three hundred heavy infantry to reinforce the Aeginetans. This force had previously been stationed with the Corinthians and Epidaurians.

Meanwhile, the Corinthians and their allies took strategic positions on the heights of Geraneia, proceeding to invade the Megarid, calculating that Athens, with a substantial number of forces deployed in Aegina and Egypt, would struggle to assist the Megarians without abandoning the siege of Aegina. However, Athens, rather than pulling troops from Aegina, mustered an army from the older and younger men left in the city and sent them under the command of Myronides to meet the Corinthians in Megarid. After an intense, evenly matched battle, both sides believed they had achieved victory. Nevertheless, the Athenians set up a trophy, subtly claiming an edge in the confrontation. Prompted by the criticism of their elders, the Corinthians returned about twelve days later to set up their own victory trophy. The Athenians, seizing the opportunity, launched a sortie from Megara, ambushing and defeating the Corinthians' party as they erected their trophy. During the ensuing retreat, a sizable contingent of Corinthian forces mistakenly veered into a walled field with a deep trench around it and no exit. Familiar with the terrain, the Athenians surrounded them with heavy infantry and encircled them with light troops, stoning the trapped Corinthians and inflicting heavy losses. The remaining Corinthian forces retreated to Corinth, significantly weakened by this costly engagement.

Around this period, Athens commenced the construction of the Long Walls leading to the sea, one toward Phalerum and the other toward Piraeus, solidifying their city's defenses and strategic coastal access. At the same time, the Phocians launched an attack on Doris, the ancestral land of the Lacedaemonians, seizing one of its three towns, Boeum, Kitinium, and Erineum. In response, Lacedaemon dispatched a force led by Nicomedes, son of Cleombrotus, to aid the Dorians, as he commanded on behalf of King Pleistoanax, who was still a minor. This Spartan force consisted of fifteen hundred heavy infantry and an additional ten thousand allied troops. After compelling the Phocians to restore the captured town under negotiated terms, the Spartans began their return journey. They considered crossing the Crissaean Gulf by sea but feared interception by the Athenian fleet. Alternatively, a return via Geraneia posed risks, as the Athenians controlled Megara and Pegae and habitually guarded the difficult pass, making it treacherous. Additionally, the Lacedaemonians had received reports that the Athenians intended to block their way.

Consequently, the Spartans decided to remain in Boeotia temporarily to strategize a safer route. Another motive for delaying their departure was covert encouragement from certain Athenian factions who opposed democracy and sought to halt the construction of the Long Walls. With suspicions aroused, the Athenians mobilized their full forces, joined by a thousand Argives and various allied contingents, amassing a total of fourteen thousand troops. This move was partly due to concerns that the Lacedaemonians were plotting against Athenian democracy. Cavalry from Thessaly, one of Athens' allies, initially joined the Athenian forces but defected to the Lacedaemonians during the battle.

The battle that decided much of the future course of events took place at Tanagra in Boeotia. After intense fighting and significant casualties on both sides, the Lacedaemonians and their allies emerged victorious. Following their success, they advanced into the Megarid, where they ravaged the land, cutting down fruit trees before making their way back across Geraneia and the isthmus to return home.

However, the Athenians did not leave these actions unanswered; sixty-two days after the battle, they marched into Boeotia under the command of Myronides, engaged the Boeotians at Oenophyta, and decisively defeated them. This victory allowed the Athenians to take control of Boeotia and Phocis, consolidating their power in the region. They proceeded to dismantle the walls of the Tanagraeans, took a hundred of the wealthiest men from the Opuntian Locrians as hostages, and completed the construction of their own long walls.

Following these successes, Athens compelled the Aeginetans to surrender, with terms that included the destruction of their walls, the surrender of their fleet, and an agreement to pay tribute to Athens moving forward. Continuing their aggressive momentum, the Athenians launched a naval expedition around the Peloponnese under Tolmides, son of Tolmaeus. This campaign saw them burn the Spartan arsenal, capture the Corinthian town of Chalcis, and conduct a landing at Sicyon, where they defeated the Sicyonians in a pitched battle.

Meanwhile, the Athenians and their allies who had embarked on the Egyptian campaign were still actively engaged in that theatre and faced the fluctuating fortunes of prolonged warfare. Initially, the Athenians held the upper hand in Egypt, leading the Persian King to dispatch Megabazus, a Persian official, to Lacedaemon with a significant sum of money intended to bribe the Peloponnesians to invade Attica and force the Athenians to abandon their Egyptian operations. However, when this strategy failed to yield results, and the funds were largely spent without success, the king recalled Megabazus. In his place, he sent Megabuzus, son of Zopyrus, with a powerful Persian force to Egypt.

Upon his arrival, Megabuzus swiftly turned the tide, defeating the Egyptians and their Athenian allies in battle and eventually driving them out of Memphis. He then besieged them on the island of Prosopitis, where the Hellenic forces held out for a year and a half. In the end, Megabuzus implemented a decisive tactic: by redirecting the waters of the canal into a new channel, he left their ships stranded on dry land and effectively joined most of the island to the mainland. This maneuver allowed him to cross over on foot and capture the island, bringing a ruinous end to the Greek campaign in Egypt after six years of conflict. Out of the massive Athenian force, only a few managed to escape through Libya, eventually reaching safety in Cyrene, while the majority perished in Egypt. With this, Egypt reverted to Persian control, although Amyrtaeus, the king of the marshlands, continued to resist. Due to the marsh's difficult terrain and the military skill of its inhabitants, he managed to evade capture. However, Inaros, the Libyan leader who had instigated the revolt, was ultimately betrayed, captured, and crucified.

In the meantime, Athens had dispatched a reinforcement squadron of fifty ships from the Athenian fleet and its allies to aid the forces in Egypt. Unaware of the collapse of the Athenian position, these ships arrived at the Mendesian mouth of the Nile. They were quickly attacked both from land by the Persian forces and from the sea by the Phoenician navy. Most of the Athenian ships were destroyed in the ensuing fight, with only a handful managing to escape. Thus concluded the ambitious and ultimately disastrous Egyptian expedition of the Athenians and their allies.

During this time, Orestes, son of Echecratidas, the exiled Thessalian king, persuaded the Athenians to assist in restoring him to power. The Athenians, together with their Boeotian and Phocian allies, set out for Thessaly and arrived at Pharsalus. While they managed to secure the area immediately surrounding their camp, they dared not venture further due to the presence of the formidable Thessalian cavalry. Consequently, they were unable to capture the city or accomplish any of their objectives, and eventually returned home, bringing Orestes back with them without having achieved anything significant.

Soon after, the Athenians dispatched a thousand troops aboard ships stationed at Pegae, a city that was under their control. Led by

Pericles, son of Xanthippus, they sailed along the coast to Sicyon. Upon landing, they successfully engaged and defeated the Sicyonians who opposed them. They then joined forces with the Achaeans and crossed over to Acarnania, where they laid siege to the city of Oeniadae. However, despite their efforts, they were unsuccessful in capturing the city and thus returned to Athens without further gains.

Three years after these events, a truce was established between the Athenians and the Peloponnesians, lasting for five years. Freed from immediate Hellenic conflicts, the Athenians turned their attention to Cyprus, launching an expedition with two hundred ships drawn from their own forces and those of their allies under the command of Cimon. Of these, sixty ships were dispatched to Egypt at the request of Amyrtaeus, the rebel leader in the marshes of Egypt. The remaining fleet began a siege of the city of Kitium in Cyprus, but due to Cimon's death and shortages of provisions, they were forced to abandon the siege. Later, they encountered and defeated a combined force of Phoenicians, Cyprians, and Cilicians near Salamis in Cyprus, securing victory in both the land and sea battles. Following these successes, they returned to Athens, along with the squadron previously sent to Egypt.

Meanwhile, the Lacedaemonians undertook a sacred war, seizing control of the temple at Delphi and placing it under Delphian control. Shortly after their withdrawal, the Athenians countered by occupying the temple themselves and returning it to the Phocians, further stirring tensions.

Some time later, the towns of Orchomenus, Chaeronea, and other areas in Boeotia came under the control of Boeotian exiles who had gathered forces hostile to Athens. In response, the Athenians dispatched a force of a thousand heavy infantry, accompanied by allied contingents, under the leadership of Tolmides, son of Tolmaeus, to reassert control. They captured Chaeronea and enslaved its inhabitants, leaving a garrison before beginning their journey home. However, as they were returning, they were ambushed at Coronea by

Boeotian exiles from Orchomenus, supported by Locrians, Euboean exiles, and others with shared grievances against Athens. In the ensuing battle, the Athenians were defeated; some of their men were killed, while others were captured. To secure the release of their captives, the Athenians agreed to a treaty that required them to withdraw from Boeotia, allowing the Boeotian exiles to return to their homeland and regain their independence.

Not long after, Euboea revolted from Athens. Pericles quickly led an Athenian army across to the island to respond to the unrest. However, while he was in Euboea, he received urgent news: Megara had also revolted, the Peloponnesians were poised to invade Attica, and most of the Athenian garrison in Megara had been overrun, with only a few soldiers managing to escape to the fortress at Nisaea. The Megarians had even allowed Corinthian, Sicyonian, and Epidaurian forces into their city before they declared their revolt. Faced with this alarming development, Pericles rapidly withdrew his army from Euboea to attend to the crisis closer to home.

Shortly afterward, the Peloponnesians invaded Attica, advancing as far as Eleusis and Thrius. Under the command of King Pleistoanax, son of Pausanias, they ravaged the region but did not push further and eventually retreated. The Athenians then returned to Euboea, this time more determined, with Pericles leading the campaign. They subdued the entire island. While most of Euboea was pacified through negotiated agreements, the people of Histiaea were treated more harshly; they were expelled from their homes, and the Athenians took over their lands.

Following their campaign in Euboea, the Athenians concluded a truce with the Lacedaemonians and their allies for thirty years, relinquishing their holdings in the Peloponnese, specifically Nisaea, Pegae, Troezen, and Achaia, as part of the terms.

Six years into this truce, a conflict arose between the cities of Samos and Miletus over the control of Priene. The Milesians, having been bested in the conflict, sought help from Athens, bringing their grievances against Samos to the Athenians. They were joined by certain Samians who were intent on overturning the existing government in their city. The Athenians, seeing an opportunity, sailed to Samos with forty ships, imposed a democratic government, took hostages—fifty boys and fifty men from prominent families—and stationed them in Lemnos. After leaving a garrison in Samos to secure the new order, the Athenians returned home.

However, some Samians who had escaped to the mainland orchestrated a counter-move. They reached an agreement with influential figures in the city and formed an alliance with Pissuthnes, the Persian satrap of Sardis. With his support, they mustered a force of seven hundred mercenaries and crossed over to Samos under the cover of night. Once back on the island, they quickly subdued the democratic faction and retrieved their hostages from Lemnos. Declaring open rebellion, they handed over the Athenian garrison to Pissuthnes and immediately prepared an offensive against Miletus, with Byzantium also joining their revolt.

Upon hearing of the Samian uprising, the Athenians swiftly mobilized sixty ships and sailed to Samos. Sixteen of these vessels were dispatched to Caria to intercept the Phoenician fleet and to recruit reinforcements from Chios and Lesbos, leaving forty-four under Pericles to confront the Samian navy. Off the island of Tragia, they encountered a Samian fleet of seventy ships, twenty of which were transport vessels, as they were returning from Miletus. The Athenians emerged victorious in the ensuing battle.

Soon, Athens reinforced its fleet with an additional forty ships from home, along with twenty-five ships from Chios and Lesbos. They landed on Samos, established control on land, and laid siege to the city with three walls, securing both land and sea approaches. With intelligence of an impending Phoenician fleet sent to aid Samos, Pericles took sixty ships and sailed urgently towards Caunus and Caria to intercept it. During his absence, the Samians launched a surprise attack, catching the Athenian camp unprepared. They destroyed lookout ships and defeated the hastily launched Athenian vessels, seizing control of the surrounding waters for two weeks, during which they freely moved supplies and reinforcements.

However, Pericles soon returned, reinstating the siege and cutting off Samian resistance. Reinforcements continued to bolster the Athenian forces, with forty more ships from Athens under Thucydides, Hagnon, and Phormio; twenty ships under Tlepolemus and Anticles; and an additional thirty ships from Chios and Lesbos. Realizing their situation was hopeless, the Samians capitulated after a grueling nine-month siege. The terms of surrender required them to dismantle their city walls, provide hostages, surrender their navy, and cover the expenses of the war through installment payments. The Byzantines, who had also revolted, agreed to return to Athenian control under previous terms.

Chapter V

After this period, and not long thereafter, events led us to the familiar conflicts at Corcyra and Potidaea and the disputes that ultimately became the grounds for the present war. All the conflicts among the Hellenes, as well as with the barbarian, took place within the fifty years following Xerxes' retreat from Greece and before the onset of this war. During these years, the Athenians steadily strengthened their empire and built their power at home to an extraordinary level. While the Lacedaemonians were well aware of this growing dominance, they opposed it only briefly and largely remained inactive for much of this period, typically reluctant to go to war unless it was absolutely necessary. This hesitation stemmed partly from their own internal conflicts, but eventually, they could no longer ignore the expansion of Athenian influence, which started to encroach upon their own allies within the Peloponnesian League.

The Lacedaemonians reached a point where they felt that tolerating Athens' dominance any further was impossible. Believing that the time had arrived to confront this growing threat directly, they resolved to make a full effort to weaken Athens by initiating a war.

Although the Lacedaemonians had already concluded that Athens was responsible for breaking the treaty, they still sent a delegation to Delphi to consult the oracle. The response, according to reports, promised that if they committed all their strength to the war, victory would be theirs, and assured them that the god Apollo would be with them, whether called upon or not.

Despite having the oracle's favorable reply, the Lacedaemonians wanted to gather the support of their allies once more and secure a collective vote in favor of war. After the allies' ambassadors assembled and a congress was held, each of the confederates voiced their opinions, with the majority condemning Athens and urging immediate war. The Corinthians, who had already been lobbying the other cities individually to ensure their votes for war (out of fear that delays would endanger Potidaea), also attended this gathering. On this occasion, they spoke last, presenting their perspective in the following speech:

"Fellow allies, we can no longer accuse the Lacedaemonians of negligence in their duties as leaders. They have voted for war themselves and called us here for this purpose. Their responsibility as our leaders includes not only handling internal matters fairly but also ensuring the well-being of all states, particularly when these states have entrusted them with their leadership in exchange for special honors. As for us, those who have had prior dealings with Athens are already well aware of the need to guard against their overreach. To those states more inland, removed from the main routes of commerce, we stress that if they fail to support the coastal powers, they risk weakening the very channels through which their goods are exported and imports received. They must not view this as an irrelevant matter, for, without doubt, allowing the coast to fall will one day extend the danger to the interior. Therefore, they should recognize that their own welfare is closely tied to what we now discuss.

"For these reasons, we urge you not to hesitate to exchange peace for war. The wise may remain passive when uninjured, but the brave abandon peace for war when wronged, while still ready to embrace peace again should an opportunity arise. They are neither drunk on the glory of battle nor passive when it comes to their defense. Indeed, it would be a mistake to cling to the illusion of peace at the expense of one's safety, for inactivity is the swiftest way to lose that very tranquility. On the other hand, pursuing war recklessly, trusting blindly in success, is equally dangerous. Countless poorly conceived plans have succeeded merely by the ineptitude of an opponent, while many carefully crafted ones have failed due to unforeseen challenges. Confidence is easy when merely theorizing; but in action, fear can unravel the best of plans.

"As for our current decision, if we now take up arms, it is because we are driven by clear grievances and a legitimate cause. Once Athens is chastised, we can choose to cease hostilities. Our strengths—superiority in numbers, military experience, and steady obedience to orders—suggest we are well-positioned for success. We will raise a capable navy, leveraging resources from places like Olympia and Delphi, and use these funds to lure Athens's foreign sailors with higher pay. Athens's power relies heavily on mercenaries, while ours rests on our citizens, who are more committed to the cause. A single naval defeat could severely undermine Athens. And should this conflict continue, it will give us more time to strengthen our naval skills; when we are equal in skill, our courage will surpass theirs. While our natural advantages cannot be taught, we can match their technical knowledge through diligent practice.

"The money required for these efforts will come from our own contributions. After all, nothing could be more disgraceful than allowing Athens's allies to finance their own servitude while we, the free, refuse to invest in our own vengeance and survival. Should we hold back now, the wealth we save will only be claimed by Athenian greed and used to support our undoing.

"We also have numerous ways to carry on this war, including the incitement of revolts among Athens's allies—a method which will cut off their revenue and, by extension, weaken their strength. Further, we can establish fortified posts within their territory and devise various unforeseen strategies to press our advantage. For war is, more than anything else, unpredictable and adaptable, relying not on rigid plans but on resourceful, timely responses to emerging situations. In these moments of unpredictability, the side that faces the turmoil with patience and calm will gain the most security; while the side that lets anger drive its actions will only meet with disaster. Let us also remember that if this were merely a series of small disputes over territory between neighboring cities, the issue might be easier to tolerate. But in Athens, we face an opponent who rivals our entire coalition in power and exceeds the capacity of any one of us alone. Without a unified stance, both as a league and as individual states, Athens will have no difficulty in conquering each of us in turn, with disastrous consequences.

"Consider what such conquest would mean: the total loss of our freedom and the imposition of pure and unalterable servitude. This is no mild threat—it is an outcome that should provoke alarm across the Peloponnese, for it would mean that countless states would be subjugated by a single power. If this happens, it will be either because we lacked the resolve to resist or because we were too fearful, and such an outcome would mark us as unworthy descendants of those who once secured freedom for Hellas. We would be allowing a tyrannical state to rise within Hellas, undermining the very principle we uphold within our cities—the rejection of sole rulers. If we fail to prevent this, we are guilty of three failings of the gravest kind: a lack of foresight, courage, and vigilance. Surely, none among you believe that we can afford to dismiss Athens lightly—a fatal underestimation that has led to ruin for so many in the past. Indeed, the term 'contemptible' now describes those who fall into this trap of arrogance and neglect, having been the undoing of countless states.

"However, reflecting on the past holds no value unless it serves the present. For the future, we must focus on preserving what we currently have and redoubling our efforts to keep it. Hard work has always been the foundation of our virtue and strength, passed down through generations, and now is not the time to abandon this heritage simply because our resources have increased. Indeed, it would be shameful to squander in times of plenty what was achieved in times of hardship. We must advance into this conflict with boldness, not only because of the many compelling reasons at hand but also because the gods themselves command it, promising to stand with us. The rest of Hellas will join this struggle, some out of fear of Athens's power, and others out of common interest.

"We will not be the ones breaking the treaty by going to war, for it is Athens that has violated the peace through its actions. The gods themselves, in urging us to this fight, affirm that the treaty has already been broken. We will not be dismantling the peace; rather, we will be supporting a treaty that Athens has already violated. Let it be clear: treaties are not undone by those who resist oppression, but by those who commit aggression."

"Your present position, viewed from any angle, clearly justifies you in choosing to go to war; we urge this step in the interests of all, reminding you that a common cause is the strongest bond, whether between cities or individuals. Act now, therefore, to aid Potidæa—a Dorian city suffering siege by Ionians, a reversal that defies the natural order—and to stand up for the freedom of the rest. We cannot afford further delay, as delay only leads to immediate disaster for some of us and, should it be known that we have gathered in council yet fear to protect ourselves, it would spell eventual ruin for the rest. Do not hesitate, allies; rather, see the necessity of this crisis and the wisdom of the counsel offered. Vote for war—not out of disregard for its immediate dangers, but with an eye to the lasting peace it will bring once we have acted. For only through conflict can we secure a peace that will endure. To cling to safety in hopes of avoiding danger is far from the best path to lasting security.

"We must recognize that the tyrant city, Athens, which has established itself in Hellas, stands as a threat to us all, harboring ambitions of universal empire—some already fulfilled, others openly pursued. Let us then rise together, confront it, reduce its strength, and secure the safety of our future as well as the freedom of the Hellenes who remain under its control."

These were the words of the Corinthians. After hearing the arguments from all, the Lacedaemonians presented their own perspective and called for a vote from each allied state, treating great and small alike. The majority cast their votes in favor of war. Yet, though the decision was made, immediate action was impossible due to a lack of preparation. It was resolved that each state would promptly procure the necessary means for the campaign, ensuring no undue delay. And indeed, despite the time needed for organization and preparation, less than a year passed before Attica was invaded, marking the open beginning of the war.

This interval was spent in sending embassies to Athens with specific grievances, intended to establish a more solid pretext for war should Athens ignore these demands. The first Lacedaemonian embassy to Athens ordered the Athenians to expel "the curse of the goddess," referring to an ancient and ominous tale known well among the Athenians. This curse stemmed from events involving Cylon, an Athenian of high birth and an Olympic victor, who had married into the powerful family of Theagenes, the tyrant of Megara. Seeking power in Athens, Cylon consulted the oracle at Delphi, which told him to seize the Acropolis during the grand festival of Zeus. Confident in this guidance, Cylon gathered forces from his father-in-law and enlisted his supporters to help in his attempt. When the Olympic festival in the Peloponnese arrived, he seized the Acropolis, hoping to establish himself as a tyrant. He took the oracle's reference to the grand festival of Zeus to mean this event, as it seemed natural for an Olympic victor to strike during the games. However, he overlooked the possibility that the festival mentioned might be held in Attica, and that it might be the Diasia, the Attic festival for Zeus Meilichios, held just outside Athens, where the people sacrificed bloodless offerings in a unique local tradition.

Despite this possible misinterpretation, Cylon attempted his coup. The Athenians, alerted to his plot, quickly rallied and laid siege to the Acropolis. As the days passed and fatigue set in, most of the Athenian citizens withdrew, leaving the nine archons in charge with full authority to resolve the matter. These nine archons, it should be noted, held significant sway in political and military affairs at that time. Inside the Acropolis, Cylon's forces began to suffer from severe hunger and thirst. Seeing their dire straits, Cylon and his brother managed to escape, abandoning the rest of their men, who were forced to take sanctuary at the Acropolis altar in desperation. Some of the Athenians, tasked with maintaining the siege, were moved by the men's plight and promised them protection if they would leave the temple. But as soon as the besieged exited the sacred area, they were slaughtered by the Athenians. A few who had sought refuge at the altars of the "awful goddesses" were cut down even as they clung to these holy sites. This sacrilege led to the entire event being viewed as cursed, with those who committed the murders, along with their descendants, marked as accursed. These cursed individuals were expelled multiple times—first by the Athenians themselves, later by Cleomenes of Lacedaemon in collaboration with a faction of Athenians who opposed them. The exiles were hunted, and even the bones of those long dead were dug up and cast out. However, despite all efforts to banish them, these families returned, and their descendants continued to live in Athens.

This ancient curse was now the very one the Lacedaemonians demanded the Athenians remove. Their motives, as they professed, were rooted in reverence for the gods, but the Lacedaemonians had another, more strategic reason: Pericles, the influential Athenian statesman, was a descendant of one of these cursed families through his mother. They believed that if Pericles were somehow disgraced or exiled, it would significantly weaken Athenian resistance and advance their own interests. They knew this demand was unlikely to succeed, but they aimed to turn Pericles' heritage against him, hoping to sway the Athenians into seeing him as an unwelcome force, thus planting the notion that he bore responsibility for any conflict that might arise.

For his part, Pericles, the most powerful figure in Athens, opposed any accommodation with Lacedaemon and continually encouraged his fellow citizens to prepare for the inevitability of war.

The Athenians responded by demanding that the Lacedaemonians purge themselves of the "curse of Taenarus." This curse originated when the Lacedaemonians violated the sanctity of the temple of Poseidon at Taenarus. There, they had forcibly removed Helot suppliants who had sought sanctuary, only to lead them away and execute them. It was widely believed that this sacrilegious act led to the devastating earthquake that later struck Sparta, a punishment from the gods. In addition, the Athenians called upon the Lacedaemonians to cleanse themselves of the "curse of the goddess of the Brazen House." This curse had its roots in the actions of Pausanias, a Lacedaemonian commander whose misconduct and treasonous plots had cast a lasting shadow over Sparta.

After his initial recall from the Hellespont, where he had been commanding Spartan forces, Pausanias was tried by the Spartans and, though acquitted, was no longer granted a public command. Undeterred, he covertly took a galley from Hermione and sailed back to the Hellespont as a private citizen. While he claimed his return was to aid in the Hellenic war, his true purpose was to pursue secret dealings with King Xerxes, whom he aimed to serve in his quest for power over Hellas. Pausanias's ambitions had taken root earlier, during his time in Byzantium. There, after capturing the city from the Medes, he had detained several high-ranking relatives and allies of the Persian king. He covertly sent them back to Xerxes, orchestrating their release as an apparent escape, thereby ingratiating himself with the king. This act was carried out with the assistance of Gongylus, an Eretrian whom Pausanias had entrusted with command over Byzantium and with responsibility for the prisoners.

Alongside the prisoners, Pausanias sent a letter to Xerxes, containing his bold propositions. The letter, later uncovered, read: "Pausanias, the general of Sparta, eager to serve you, returns these prisoners to you as an act of goodwill. I propose, with your approval, to marry your daughter and make Sparta, along with the rest of Hellas, subject to you. I am confident that, with your cooperation, I can achieve this." Pausanias concluded by requesting that Xerxes send a reliable emissary to facilitate further correspondence. This communication delighted Xerxes, who saw in Pausanias a willing collaborator. Without delay, he dispatched Artabazus, son of Pharnaces, to implement his commands and to deliver a letter back to Pausanias. Artabazus was ordered to replace Megabates as the governor of Daskylion and to bring Xerxes' letter and seal to Pausanias in Byzantium, enabling Pausanias to act on behalf of the king.

In his response, Xerxes' letter read: "King Xerxes greets Pausanias. For saving the lives of those you returned to me from Byzantium, you have my everlasting gratitude, marked within our royal house. Your proposals please me greatly. Spare no effort in fulfilling your promises to me. Neither the cost of gold and silver nor the number of troops required shall hinder you. Work boldly with Artabazus, a trusted man whom I send to aid you. Pursue our shared aims with courage, for both our honor and mutual interest."

This exchange laid bare Pausanias's treachery. His ambition to rule Hellas as a Persian-backed despot, revealed in these correspondences, had embroiled Sparta in dishonor and in the curse of the goddess of the Brazen House, thus tainting the entire city.

Once celebrated by the Hellenes as the hero of Plataea, Pausanias, after receiving the letter from the Persian king, grew more arrogant and distanced himself from his former life. He adopted the customs of the Persians, wearing Median attire, moving through Thrace under guard by Medes and Egyptians, and maintaining a lavish Persian-style household. His actions and demeanor—impossible to hide even in small gestures—betrayed the lofty ambitions he harbored, causing him to alienate others and gain a reputation for being difficult to approach and quick-tempered. His overbearing behavior drove away many allies, pushing them towards the Athenians and weakening his influence.

This conduct soon reached Lacedaemon and led to Pausanias's first recall. Nevertheless, he returned to the Hellespont in a vessel from Hermione, again without Spartan orders. Soon, news arrived that he had been expelled from Byzantium by the Athenians and had taken refuge in Colonae in the Troad, where he was said to be scheming with the Persians. No longer willing to tolerate his actions, the Spartan ephors sent him a herald along with a scytale—a message engraved on a wooden staff—ordering him to return or be branded as a public enemy. Pausanias, anxious to avoid suspicion and confident in his ability to bribe his way out of trouble, returned to Sparta once more. Initially imprisoned by the ephors, who possessed the rare power to detain even a regent, he managed to negotiate his release and offered himself for trial.

The Spartans, however, lacked definitive evidence against Pausanias that would justify severe punishment, particularly given his royal family status and his current position as regent for his young cousin, King Pleistarchus, the son of Leonidas. Although proof of overt treason was missing, his disregard for traditional Spartan ways, along with his admiration for foreign customs, made him a subject of intense suspicion. His actions, such as inscribing his name alone on the Delphic tripod dedicated by all the Hellenic cities after the victory over the Persians, had already been perceived as a serious breach. The inscription, which originally read:

"The Mede defeated, great Pausanias raised

This monument, that Phœbus might be praised."

was erased by the Spartans, who replaced it with an inscription honoring the combined efforts of all the cities in the campaign. This early display of vanity was now interpreted as an omen of Pausanias's current aspirations.

The ephors also learned that Pausanias was secretly communicating with the Helots, the oppressed class of Spartan society, encouraging them to rebel and promising them freedom and citizenship if they would join his cause. Despite this alarming intelligence, the ephors hesitated to act, adhering to their policy of restraint and caution when dealing with a Spartan citizen of high rank.

The breakthrough came when a man named Argilus, a former favorite and trusted aide of Pausanias, grew suspicious after noticing that previous messengers sent by Pausanias to Artabazus had never returned. Fearful for his life, Argilus carefully broke the seal on the letter he was supposed to deliver, disguising his actions by forging the seal so that it could be resealed if needed. Inside, he found his suspicions confirmed: there was a postscript ordering his own execution after delivering the letter.

This revelation shattered the last doubts of the ephors and provided the proof they needed to confront Pausanias's disloyalty.

After seeing the incriminating letter, the ephors were now convinced of Pausanias's betrayal, yet they wanted to secure an undeniable confession from him. They arranged for the man who had exposed the plot to meet Pausanias at the sanctuary of Taenarus. The man constructed a divided hut, allowing some of the ephors to hide and listen in secret. When Pausanias arrived, he inquired why the man had taken refuge as a suppliant. In response, the man accused Pausanias of plotting his death and recounted all his prior loyal services as a messenger between Pausanias and the Persian king. Pausanias admitted everything, urged the man not to be upset, and pledged to support him. He then asked him to continue with their mission without delay.

The ephors, having overheard this conversation, now possessed irrefutable proof. They initially refrained from taking action but began preparing to arrest Pausanias once he returned to the city. It is said that, as Pausanias was walking down a street, he noticed the expression on one of the ephors' faces and sensed what was about to happen.

Another ephor, moved by compassion, discreetly signaled a warning to him. Realizing the danger, Pausanias dashed towards the temple of the goddess of the Brazen House, seeking refuge there just as the ephors closed in on him. Entering a small chamber within the temple to shield himself from exposure to the elements, he remained there, hoping to avoid immediate capture.

Although he had initially eluded them, the ephors took decisive action. They removed the roof from the chamber to confirm his presence, then sealed him inside by blocking the doors and posted guards outside to ensure he could not escape. Determined to bring his life to an end without violating the sanctuary, they left him there to starve. Eventually, Pausanias weakened and was on the verge of death. The ephors pulled him out of the temple just before he died, sparing the temple itself from becoming the place of his death. Shortly after being brought outside, he passed away.

Initially, the Lacedaemonians intended to dispose of his body in the Kaiadas, the chasm where they cast criminals. However, they eventually chose to bury him nearby. Later, the oracle at Delphi declared that the Lacedaemonians must transfer Pausanias's remains to the site of his death within the temple grounds, as his actions had brought a curse upon them. They were also commanded to give two bodies in place of Pausanias's as an offering to the goddess of the Brazen House. To fulfill this mandate, they dedicated two bronze statues in his stead. The Athenians, upon learning of these events, countered by advising the Lacedaemonians to drive out what the oracle itself had branded as a curse.

Returning to the matter of Pausanias's involvement with the Persians, evidence emerged during the investigation that implicated Themistocles. Consequently, the Lacedaemonians dispatched envoys to Athens, requesting that Themistocles be punished just as Pausanias had been. The Athenians agreed to this course of action. However, Themistocles had already been ostracized and was residing in Argos, often traveling to various parts of the Peloponnese. Therefore, the

Athenians joined forces with the Lacedaemonians to pursue him wherever they could find him. But Themistocles, catching wind of their intentions, fled from the Peloponnese to Corcyra, where he had supporters.

The Corcyraeans, however, were unwilling to offer him refuge, fearing it would harm their relations with both Athens and Lacedaemon. They helped him cross to the mainland instead. Pursued closely by his enemies, Themistocles found himself with few options. Desperate, he sought refuge at the court of Admetus, the king of the Molossians, despite their prior enmity. Admetus happened to be away, but his wife advised Themistocles to make a powerful appeal by sitting with their child on the hearth, the most sacred spot for supplicants. Upon his return, Admetus found Themistocles thus positioned and heard him out. Themistocles explained that he was no longer a threat, imploring Admetus not to take revenge on an exile over past grievances. He argued that to surrender him would be equivalent to condemning him to death.

Moved by his words, Admetus raised Themistocles and his son from the hearth in a gesture of protection. When the Lacedaemonian envoys arrived shortly thereafter, Admetus steadfastly refused to hand him over. Instead, he secretly arranged for Themistocles to travel overland to Pydna, a city within Alexander's Macedonian domain, to begin his journey toward the Persian court. From Pydna, he boarded a merchant ship bound for Ionia, but a fierce storm pushed them into the vicinity of an Athenian fleet blockading Naxos. Fearing capture, Themistocles revealed his identity to the ship's master, promising a reward if he was kept hidden. The shipmaster, accepting the offer, ensured no one left the vessel and waited out the storm until they could sail to safety. Eventually, they reached Ephesus, where Themistocles rewarded the shipmaster generously, drawing upon resources he had hidden in Argos and received from friends in Athens.

Now able to proceed, Themistocles traveled further inland, guided by a local Persian escort. He sent a letter to the new Persian king,

Artaxerxes, son of Xerxes, who had recently ascended the throne. In his letter, Themistocles introduced himself as the one who had once inflicted significant harm on the Persian empire in his defense of Greece. Yet he claimed he had later done more to assist than harm Xerxes by facilitating his retreat from Greece, including allowing the bridges at the Hellespont to remain intact, a false claim that he cleverly presented as an unreturned favor. Now, he explained, he had come to offer his services to Persia, being pursued by the Greeks because of his allegiance to the Persian king. He requested one year to prepare before presenting himself in person to explain his intentions.

In this manner, Themistocles, once a hero of Greece, sought refuge in the very empire he had once opposed, navigating complex allegiances and the dangers of his political exile.

It is said that the King approved of Themistocles' intentions and encouraged him to proceed as planned. During the year he had requested, Themistocles dedicated himself to learning the Persian language and studying the customs of the empire. When he finally presented himself at court, he quickly gained a high level of respect and influence, which no Greek had ever achieved before or since. His reputation was bolstered by his remarkable past achievements, the ambitious promises he made of aiding in the conquest of Greece, and, most importantly, by the clear proof of his capabilities in everyday matters.

Themistocles possessed an extraordinary natural intelligence that allowed him to navigate situations of great urgency and complexity with remarkable insight. His intuitive grasp of crisis management was unmatched—he had a rare ability to make sound decisions quickly, even when there was no time for extensive deliberation. He was also a gifted predictor of future developments, envisioning both near and distant outcomes with impressive accuracy. Although he had not studied formally, he could analyze situations and apply theoretical knowledge to his actions. In areas where he lacked firsthand experience, his judgments were nonetheless sound.

His foresight into hidden dangers and opportunities in the future was unparalleled, enabling him to navigate uncharted territory with confidence. When considering his natural abilities alongside the minimal formal training he had, it is hard to deny that Themistocles excelled over others in responding to urgent situations with an almost instinctive precision. His death, it is believed, was ultimately caused by illness, though there is a legend suggesting that he took his own life by poison after realizing he could not fulfill his promises to the King. A monument was later erected to him in the marketplace of Asiatic Magnesia, where he had been appointed governor. The King had rewarded him with the revenues of Magnesia, which provided fifty talents a year, for bread; Lampsacus, known for its fine wine, for wine; and Myos for other provisions. According to tradition, his remains were secretly brought back to Attica by his family and buried there, honoring his wishes, as the Athenians themselves could not bury a convicted traitor on Athenian soil without breaching their own laws.

Thus concludes the story of Pausanias and Themistocles, the Spartan and the Athenian, two of the most celebrated figures in Greece during their time.

Returning to the Lacedaemonians: after the first embassy and its demands—which concerned expelling the cursed individuals and which has been discussed earlier—they soon sent a second embassy with new instructions. This mission called on the Athenians to lift the siege of Potidaea and respect the independence of Aegina. Most significantly, it demanded that Athens revoke the decree against Megara, which excluded the Megarians from Athenian markets and harbors. The Lacedaemonians hinted that war could be avoided if Athens would agree to this single condition. However, the Athenians were unwilling to concede, citing grievances against the Megarians, who they accused of encroaching on sacred lands and harboring runaway Athenian slaves.

Finally, a third delegation arrived, bearing what was essentially the Lacedaemonian ultimatum. The ambassadors—Ramphias,

Melesippus, and Agesander—made no reference to prior disputes but delivered a simple message: "Lacedaemon wishes the peace to continue, and there is no reason why it should not, if you would leave the Hellenes independent." In response, the Athenians convened an assembly to discuss the proposal. Various speakers rose, advocating either for war or for peace through a compromise involving the Megarian decree. Ultimately, Pericles, son of Xanthippus, stood up to speak. Known as the most influential statesman of his time, renowned for both his strategic insight and his effectiveness in action, Pericles offered his counsel on how Athens should respond.

"There is one principle, Athenians, which I hold firmly through all situations, and that is to make no concessions to the Peloponnesians. I am aware that the bold spirit that often inspires people to prepare for war does not always endure through the trials of actual combat; that as circumstances evolve, so too do resolutions. Yet, I find that once again, almost word for word, you ask me for the same counsel as before, and so I urge those of you who have chosen to be persuaded to go to war, to maintain the resolve you now express, even in the face of setbacks, or else, if success should come, to abandon all claim to credit for your wisdom in that success. Often, outcomes are as much a product of fortune as they are of human plans; it's common to blame chance for whatever defies our expectations.

"It has long been evident that Lacedaemon harbored designs against us, and their intentions are even clearer now. The treaty stipulates that both sides must submit disputes to arbitration and, in the meantime, keep possession of their holdings. But the Lacedaemonians have never proposed any such arrangement to us, nor have they accepted our proposals for peaceful settlement. Instead, they choose to seek resolution through war, preferring conflict over negotiation. And now they come before us not with pleas, but with orders. They demand that we lift the siege of Potidaea, grant independence to Aegina, revoke the Megara decree, and finally, issue us an ultimatum that we 'leave the Hellenes independent.'

"I ask you not to believe that we would be entering a war over a mere trifle by refusing to revoke the Megara decree, which stands foremost among their complaints, as though yielding on this point would ensure peace. Nor should you indulge any pang of guilt as if we would be fighting for an insignificant cause. This 'trifle' is a test of our resolve and autonomy. Should we yield here, it will only signal to them that we are vulnerable to intimidation and open the way for greater demands. A steadfast refusal, on the other hand, will make it unmistakably clear that they must deal with us as equals. So make your decision now: either submit to them before harm befalls us, or, as I firmly believe we must, prepare for war without concern for the perceived gravity of the issue, resolved not to yield or to endanger the security of our holdings.

"For demands made by an equal, delivered as orders rather than proposed as negotiations, whether trivial or monumental, can have only one purpose—to impose submission. To give ground now will be to court slavery by degrees."

"As for the war and the comparative resources of each side, a careful evaluation will not reveal any weakness in Athens. The Peloponnesians, preoccupied with their farms, are without substantial private or public wealth and lack experience in prolonged overseas warfare. Their limited funds restrict their ability to sustain extensive campaigns, even within their own borders. Unlike us, they do not command the sea, and their resources are ill-suited for the continuous costs of a long war. The maintenance of a war relies more on capital than on sporadic contributions. Farmers are generally more inclined to offer themselves in person than to part with their wealth; they may be confident that they'll survive the dangers of combat, but they worry that their finances could be drained far too quickly, especially if the conflict drags on longer than anticipated, which seems likely.

"In a single battle, the Peloponnesians and their allies might have the strength to challenge the entirety of Hellas, but their capacity to sustain a drawn-out war against an opponent of a different character is hindered by their lack of unified direction. Their confederacy operates through a council where every state has equal voting power and prioritizes its own interests, which results in delays and inaction. Some allies prioritize personal vendettas, while others seek only to protect their resources. Slow to convene, they spend very little time on the collective goals, devoting the bulk of their attention to local concerns. Each state believes that its own neglect will not affect the overall outcome, assuming that others will handle what is required. Consequently, through this shared complacency, the strength of their alliance gradually fades.

"The primary limitation they will face is a shortage of funds. The slow pace at which contributions are collected will result in frequent delays, yet the critical moments in war do not wait. We should not be overly concerned about the possibility of their constructing fortifications in Attica or their navy's potential. Creating a rival city, even in times of peace, is no small feat, and establishing one in enemy territory with Athens fortified against it would be even more difficult. A mere outpost may harass our land with minor raids and entice some deserters, but it cannot prevent us from sailing into their lands, fortifying positions of our own, and retaliating through our naval superiority. Indeed, our mastery at sea is more advantageous for ground campaigns than their military skills would be if brought to bear on naval operations.

"Familiarity with the sea is not something they can acquire easily. We have been perfecting our skills since the Persian invasion, and if even we have not yet achieved mastery, what can be expected from an agrarian, land-focused population that will be constantly thwarted by our patrolling squadrons? They might risk an engagement with a small force, buoyed by their numbers and confidence in their inexperience, but the sight of our large, seasoned squadrons will keep them at bay. Without consistent practice, their inexperience will lead to blunders, which will, in turn, erode their morale. Seamanship, like any craft, requires focused dedication; it cannot simply be taken up as a part-time endeavor. It demands full commitment, leaving little room for other pursuits.

"Thus, when all these factors are considered—our resources, our naval expertise, and the Peloponnesians' many disadvantages—Athens stands in a strong position to withstand this conflict and ultimately prevail."

"Even if the Peloponnesians were to attempt tapping into the treasuries at Olympia or Delphi to secure funds, or even to try tempting our foreign sailors with higher pay, we would still have ample means to counter them. The reason for this confidence lies in our capacity to man our fleet with our own citizens and resident aliens who are loyal to Athens. We possess a larger and more skilled class of sailors, especially among our native coxswains, than the rest of Hellas combined. Further, the foreign sailors under our command have every reason to stay loyal. The temporary lure of higher pay is hardly sufficient to tempt them into the peril of outlawry, severing ties to their homeland and choosing a precarious allegiance with the Peloponnesians. A few days' high pay would not compensate for such risks, and thus, they are unlikely to defect.

"This assessment of our situation should give a clear picture of the relative weaknesses of the Peloponnesians. Athens is free from such shortcomings and boasts advantages unmatched by them. If they attempt to invade our territory, we shall retaliate by launching naval expeditions against theirs. In such a contest, they will quickly discover that ravaging all of Attica would not equate to losing even a small portion of Peloponnesian land, as they would have no alternative supply lines to compensate for their losses without facing us directly in battle. Meanwhile, we have access to vast territories on both the continent and islands, thanks to our naval supremacy. Think of the power of controlling the sea! Imagine us as islanders—could there be a more impregnable position? This is the perspective we should adopt, maintaining an islander's mindset by prioritizing our navy and city over our lands and rural properties. We must avoid the pitfall of risking direct combat with the Peloponnesians simply to protect our land and homes. Any defeat would mean not only the loss of our defenses but also of our allies, who provide the core of our strength. Once we lose the ability to respond to their calls for help, they will desert us immediately. We must therefore value our people over our land and homes, for only men, not houses or fields, can defend a city. If I thought I could convince you, I would suggest we burn our own lands and homes to show the Peloponnesians that nothing can force us into submission.

"There are ample reasons to hope for a successful outcome, provided we avoid engaging in reckless expansion while prosecuting the war. In fact, I am more wary of the harm we could bring upon ourselves than of any strategy the enemy might employ. Further details and strategic recommendations can be discussed as necessary, but for now, let us respond to these envoys. Let us tell them that we are willing to allow Megara access to our markets and ports when the Lacedaemonians are prepared to lift their own prohibitions against us and our allies—since nothing in the treaty compels us to make this concession otherwise. On the matter of leaving cities independent, we will do so only if the cities were indeed independent when we originally signed the treaty. Furthermore, any 'independence' must be one not subservient to Spartan interests but genuinely reflective of each city's will. We are also open to any legal procedures specified by our agreements and are resolved not to initiate hostilities ourselves, although we will respond to any aggressions directed toward us. Such a response, in my view, aligns with both the dignity and rights of Athens. The certainty of war may be inescapable, but the more firmly we prepare for it, the less eager our adversaries will be. Great threats often lead to even greater glory, both for communities and individuals.

"Our fathers resisted the Medes with far fewer resources than we possess now. They even chose to abandon their city yet maintained a strength in strategy and boldness that allowed them to fend off the enemy and elevate our standing to its current heights. We must honor their legacy by confronting our enemies through every available means, with the resolve to pass on an undiminished empire to future generations."

These were the words of Pericles. His wisdom won over the Athenians, who voted to respond to the Lacedaemonians as he recommended. They stood firm in their resolve not to yield to dictation but were open to addressing the complaints in a fair and legal manner, as outlined in the truce. The envoys departed without obtaining concessions and did not return.

Thus, these were the grievances and points of conflict between the two major powers that led up to the war, stemming initially from the events at Epidamnus and Corcyra. Communication and contact persisted despite these disputes, although it was strained and laden with suspicion. Even in the absence of formal declarations, actions unfolded on both sides that were tantamount to breaches of the treaty and moved them closer to open hostilities.

Book II

Chapter VI

The Peloponnesian War had officially begun, with the Athenians and Peloponnesians, along with their respective allies, fully committing to open hostilities. Communication was restricted solely to formal emissaries, and conflict proceeded without pause. The history unfolds sequentially, following events season by season, summer to winter.

The thirty-year truce established after the Athenian conquest of Euboea held for fourteen years but faltered in the fifteenth year. This year marked the forty-eighth year of Chrysis as priestess in Argos, the ephorate of Aenesias in Sparta, the penultimate month of Pythodorus's archonship in Athens, and half a year after the battle of Potidaea. At the very start of spring, a contingent of over three hundred Theban soldiers led by their Boeotarchs, Pythangelus and Diemporus, infiltrated Plataea, a Boeotian town aligned with Athens, under cover of night. The city's gates were opened by a Plataean named Naucleides, who, along with his supporters, sought to seize power by killing the leaders of the opposing faction and bringing the city under Theban control. This plot was coordinated with Eurymachus, a prominent Theban who wielded significant influence. The town of Plataea had long-standing enmity with Thebes, and with war on the horizon, the Thebans aimed to catch their adversary off-guard during peacetime before outright war erupted. Their entry was facilitated by the absence of posted guards, allowing them to slip into the town unchallenged.

Upon reaching the marketplace, the Theban soldiers set down their arms, intending to secure the town. While Naucleides and his faction urged immediate action against their enemies, the Thebans chose a different approach. They preferred to make a conciliatory offer, aiming to win over the townsfolk rather than resorting immediately to violence. A herald announced a message to the citizens, inviting them to rejoin their Boeotian compatriots under Theban leadership, believing that a peaceful appeal might encourage the city's surrender.

The Plataeans, shocked by the unexpected occupation, initially overestimated the size of the Theban force, misled by the obscurity of night. Taken by surprise, they temporarily accepted the terms and remained still, assured by the Thebans' peaceful demeanor. However, during the discussions, some Plataeans realized that the Thebans were fewer in number than they had initially thought. Emboldened by this discovery, the majority of the Plataeans, loyal to Athens, decided to counterattack, confident they could overwhelm the invaders.

Acting swiftly, they moved from house to house by breaking through the walls, allowing them to gather discreetly without exposing themselves in the streets. They positioned wagons as barriers, creating a makeshift defense to block the roads. Taking advantage of the early morning darkness, they set their plan into action, hoping that the element of surprise, combined with their knowledge of the town, would enable them to prevail over the disoriented Thebans. They attacked swiftly and aimed to close in on the Thebans before dawn broke. In daylight, they feared the Thebans would rally and resist effectively; in the darkness, however, they anticipated that the Thebans would be thrown into disarray and struggle to defend themselves in unfamiliar territory. Seizing the moment, the Plataeans launched their assault and swiftly engaged the Thebans at close range.

The Thebans, realizing they had been outmaneuvered by the Plataeans, tried to form a defensive stance and repel the attacks from every direction. Despite their best efforts, they managed to fend off their attackers two or three times. However, the noise and chaos increased as the Plataean men attacked with renewed vigor, and the women and slaves joined in, yelling from windows and rooftops and hurling stones and roof tiles at the Thebans. Heavy rain had also fallen throughout the night, adding to the confusion. At last, overwhelmed by the relentless assault, the Theban morale broke, and they scattered in retreat through the town, desperately seeking an escape route.

Many Thebans, unfamiliar with the town's layout, struggled to find their way out. Their predicament was worsened by the muddy streets, the darkness of the last quarter moon, and the keen knowledge of the terrain by the Plataean defenders, who used these advantages to intercept and cut off many of the fleeing Thebans. Only the gate by which they had entered remained accessible, but a Plataean defender had jammed it shut by driving a javelin spike into the bar, effectively sealing it. This final obstacle forced the Thebans into a chaotic flight, dispersing them across the town.

Some of the Thebans, in desperation, attempted to escape by climbing onto the city walls and jumping off, though many fell to their deaths. A few managed to discover an abandoned gate, and, acquiring an axe from a woman, broke through the bar; however, the noise of their escape attempt soon alerted the Plataeans, allowing only a handful to get out alive. Others met their end in various isolated parts of the city, where they were trapped and killed by the pursuing

Plataeans. A large group, misled by the appearance of a nearby building close to the city wall with open doors facing the street, rushed inside, believing it was an exit gate leading outside the city. The Plataeans quickly saw that they had unintentionally trapped themselves and debated whether to set the building on fire to kill them all at once or to consider other ways of handling the situation. Eventually, the Thebans still scattered around town surrendered themselves and their weapons, placing themselves at the mercy of the Plataeans.

Meanwhile, the rest of the Theban force that had been scheduled to join the initial infiltration party before dawn was delayed on the way due to the heavy rain and the consequent swelling of the Asopus River, which made crossing difficult. Their march was further hindered by the rain-soaked ground. By the time they reached Plataea, they found that their comrades had either been killed or captured. Realizing they were too late to assist those inside the city, they turned their attention to those Plataeans still outside the walls. Since the surprise attack had occurred in a time of peace, many Plataean men, along with their livestock, were still in the fields. The Thebans hoped to capture some of these as hostages, who could then be exchanged for any of their own men taken alive by the Plataeans. But the Plataeans, suspecting their intentions, swiftly sent a herald to warn the Thebans against any action that might provoke a reprisal against their captured comrades. They informed the Thebans that if they withdrew without harm, they would consider surrendering the prisoners.

The Theban version of events claims they were promised the release of their men through an oath. However, the Plataeans dispute this, insisting they only agreed to future negotiations rather than any immediate release, and they deny any oath was taken. In any case, after the Thebans withdrew from Plataean territory without causing harm, the Plataeans brought all their people and livestock safely within the city walls and promptly executed the prisoners. Among the 180 Thebans killed was Eurymachus, the influential figure with whom the Plataean traitors had colluded.

After securing their city, the Plataeans sent word to Athens about the incident, returned the bodies of the dead Thebans under a truce, and organized their defenses in anticipation of further conflict. In Athens, news of the attack reached the city immediately after it happened, prompting the Athenians to arrest all Boeotians present in Attica. They also sent a herald to Plataea with strict orders to spare the lives of the Theban prisoners until they received instructions from Athens. However, as the initial messenger had departed Plataea at the time of the Theban entry, and a second had left just after the Thebans' defeat and capture, news of the executions had not yet reached Athens, and the directive was given in ignorance of the men's fate. Upon arrival, the Athenian herald learned that the prisoners had already been executed.

Following this, the Athenians marched to Plataea to fortify its defenses, supplying provisions and stationing a garrison in the city. They also evacuated the non-combatants, including women, children, and older men, to Athens.

"Men of Peloponnese and allies, we have come together for a great and just cause. As you know, Athens has long oppressed our fellow Hellenes, abusing her power and disregarding the sacred bonds between allies and states. We cannot sit by and allow this unchecked ambition to continue. This war is not a pursuit of conquest, but of liberation—our aim is to restore to each city its own laws and its freedom, to ensure that no single power may dominate Hellas in the way Athens has. Remember that our unity here today is a testament to our shared purpose. Each of you has come from a different state, yet all have felt Athens' injustice, either directly or through your kin and allies.

"Many of you may already know the nature of our Athenian adversaries, yet it is worth reminding ourselves of the resolve we must bring to this undertaking. The Athenians are bold and tireless; they are skilled in adapting quickly to new circumstances and possess a fleet that has long kept them in dominance over the sea. But they have grown overconfident, and in that arrogance lies their vulnerability. They believe they can fight us on our terms, but we will show them the error in this. This war will not be swift or simple; we face an enemy who has grown powerful from tribute and allies, but they are not invincible, especially when they are attacked from within as well as from without.

"Know, too, that we shall not be fighting alone. Many cities look to us as liberators, and many, weary of Athenian dominion, will rally to our side as this war unfolds. They need only to see that we, as the united Peloponnesian League, are resolved and prepared to go the distance in this fight. They will join us if we prove to them our commitment, if we show them we are willing to face the hardships and sacrifices necessary to bring down the Athenian power.

"Your courage and discipline will be tested, as will your endurance, but this struggle demands nothing less from each of us. We must be steadfast, knowing that we fight for a freedom worth any hardship, a freedom for which our ancestors also fought. We enter this conflict as defenders, not aggressors; as men protecting our homes and our allies from a force that has long grown careless in its rule. Athens will discover that her sea power cannot defend her land, nor her wealth buy her freedom from the consequences of tyranny.

"So let each man remember the honor of his home, the duty he owes his fellow citizens, and the justice of our cause. We will fight as one, united by our shared purpose and undivided in our resolve to see this through. Let every man who holds his city and his family dear prepare himself, and together we shall bring Athens to understand the true strength of a free Hellas. Stand firm, and be resolved; our strength lies in our unity and in the justice of our purpose. We fight not only for ourselves, but for all those who wish to be free."

With this, Archidamus urged the Peloponnesian and allied forces onward, ensuring they understood the weight of their cause and the importance of their unity. His words were met with enthusiasm and resolve, for the men recognized that the freedom of Hellas, not mere revenge, was at stake. Inspired, they prepared to march upon Attica, knowing that they would soon meet the Athenians in a conflict that would test the mettle and resolve of both sides.

"Peloponnesians and allies, we stand on the threshold of a monumental campaign, one our fathers would regard with pride and all of Hellas watches with hope. Our ancestors often ventured into battles both within and beyond Peloponnesian borders, and the elder men among us have known the trials of war. Yet, even they did not embark with a force as powerful as the one we now assemble. We carry with us not only a formidable army but also the reputation and expectations of Hellas, a reputation that calls us to prove ourselves worthy of our history and of the respect of those who look to us for relief from Athens' rule. The eyes of all Hellas are upon us, cheering for the downfall of the oppressive power of Athens.

"Some among us may assume, due to our numbers and strength, that the Athenians will avoid meeting us in open battle. But such assumptions should not lead us to any complacency. We must remain vigilant and disciplined. Officers and men from every city must prepare as if the enemy could appear before them at any moment. The course of war is unpredictable, and even the strongest force can be weakened by overconfidence. A cautious readiness has, in many instances, triumphed over sheer numbers. Confidence is a valuable asset, but in an enemy's land, caution and readiness are equally essential. Our troops, ready to strike but also guarded against surprise, will be best equipped to gain victory and secure their own safety.

"Our adversary, Athens, is far from defenseless. She is a city well-equipped for war, fortified at every turn. They may even take the field against us, and if not yet prepared to meet us outside their walls, they may soon rally to defend their land as they see us pressing forward, laying waste to their fields, and consuming what they hold dear. For any city, witnessing the ruin of its homeland stirs the fiercest resolve, and men who might otherwise hesitate are often driven to action when they see their own possessions in flames. This is especially true of the

Athenians, who are more accustomed to bringing destruction upon others than to seeing it at their own doors.

"Knowing the power of the enemy we face, and the impact our actions will have on our legacy, I urge you to approach this campaign with the discipline and unity that define great armies. Be swift to obey orders, for in the field, the safety and success of a force as vast as ours depend on unity of command and disciplined cohesion.

"With these words, Archidamus dismissed the assembly and, as a last attempt to avoid bloodshed, sent Melesippus, son of Diacritus, as a herald to Athens, hoping the Athenians might reconsider their stance now that they saw our forces assembled and on the march. However, under the leadership of Pericles, Athens had already resolved not to allow any envoy from Lacedaemon to enter their city once the Spartan army had set forth. Melesippus was denied an audience, instructed to leave Athens' borders the same day, and told that future embassies would only be received if sent from Lacedaemonian territory.

"Before departing, Melesippus, understanding the gravity of the situation, offered these parting words: 'This day will be the beginning of great misfortunes for the Hellenes.' Once he returned to our camp and delivered the Athenians' final response, Archidamus, now certain that Athens would not yield, began his advance with the assembled forces, crossing into Athenian lands.

"Meanwhile, the Boeotians, sending a contingent of cavalry to support the Peloponnesian advance, turned their forces toward Plataea and began laying waste to the surrounding lands. With the march into Attica now underway, the war that had been long anticipated had finally begun, setting the stage for a struggle that would shape the destiny of all Hellas."

While the Peloponnesians were still gathering at the Isthmus or on the march before their invasion of Attica, Pericles, son of Xanthippus, one of Athens' ten generals, anticipated that Archidamus, the Spartan king and his friend, might spare his estate during the invasion. This consideration troubled Pericles, as he feared that such an act might seem suspicious or imply that he was secretly cooperating with the enemy. Such a scenario could either stem from Archidamus' personal inclination or perhaps even a ploy by Lacedaemon, aiming to discredit him, especially given their earlier efforts to stir mistrust by demanding the expulsion of his family for the alleged curse. To prevent any potential doubts among the Athenians, Pericles publicly addressed the assembly. He declared that, although he and Archidamus were friends, he would not allow any personal relationship to harm the state. If the enemy indeed left his property untouched, he vowed to donate it entirely to the public, ensuring it could not be used against him as a mark of suspicion.

Pericles then reiterated his advice to the Athenians, urging them to prepare fully for the impending war. He stressed that they should move their property from rural areas into the safety of the city and avoid open battle with the invading Peloponnesian forces. Instead, he advised, they should stay within the city walls, fortify their defenses, and focus on readying their formidable fleet, as Athens' real strength lay in her naval power. He also highlighted the importance of maintaining strict oversight of their allies, emphasizing that the tribute from these states, which formed the financial backbone of Athens, was essential to sustaining the war effort. He reminded them that success in this conflict would depend not only on their military might but also on their financial stability and strategic conduct.

He then outlined the state's financial position, underscoring Athens' impressive resources. The annual tribute from allies alone generated about six hundred talents of silver. In addition to this revenue, the Acropolis held approximately six thousand talents of coined silver, remaining from an initial treasury of nine thousand seven hundred talents, which had partly been used for various public works, including fortifications and expenses related to Potidæa. Moreover, the city's wealth extended beyond coined silver. Pericles cited the vast quantities of uncoined gold and silver housed in both public and private offerings, religious vessels, and spoils from the

Persian wars—valued collectively at about five hundred talents. Furthermore, he mentioned the other treasures located in different temples throughout the city, arguing that in an extreme crisis, even these could be drawn upon. If Athens were ever in desperate need, they could even resort to using the golden ornaments from the statue of Athena herself. He assured the citizens that the statue contained around forty talents of pure gold, which was crafted to be removable and could therefore be borrowed and restored in times of peace. Such assurances of financial strength were meant to reinforce confidence, proving that Athens was far from defenseless on the economic front.

He proceeded to detail the military resources of Athens, beginning with the city's land forces, which included an impressive thirteen thousand heavy infantry soldiers. Additionally, there were another sixteen thousand troops stationed in garrisons and on home defense duty within the city limits. This defensive force consisted of both the oldest and youngest among the city's citizens, along with resident aliens equipped with heavy armor. Pericles outlined the city's strategic defenses, mentioning the Phaleric wall, which stretched four miles before it joined the main wall encircling Athens. Of the city wall's nearly five miles, a significant portion was manned, although certain sections, such as the area between the Long Wall and the Phaleric wall, were left unmanned. He described the Long Walls leading to Piraeus, extending about four and a half miles, of which the outer wall was fully garrisoned. Lastly, he mentioned the perimeter of Piraeus, including Munychia, which spanned nearly seven and a half miles, with roughly half of it under guard. This extensive fortification network underscored Athens' readiness to withstand a prolonged siege.

In addition to the land forces, Pericles pointed to Athens' cavalry, which consisted of twelve hundred mounted soldiers, including archers on horseback, as well as sixteen hundred foot archers. The city's naval strength was equally formidable, with three hundred war-ready galleys, which formed the core of Athens' offensive and defensive power. Pericles argued that, with these resources, Athens held a favorable position to face the war. Their preparedness on land

and sea, combined with a strategic reliance on the navy, gave Athens a significant advantage over the Peloponnesians, who lacked comparable maritime strength. Pericles reassured the citizens that Athens was more than capable of sustaining itself against any initial hardships of the war, and with proper conduct and caution, they could expect a favorable outcome.

By underscoring Athens' extensive financial and military resources, Pericles aimed to instill a sense of confidence and resilience in the citizens, reminding them that they possessed the means to endure the hardships ahead and to stand firm against the Peloponnesian threat. The Athenians, recognizing the wisdom in his counsel, prepared themselves as he advised, rallying under his leadership to face the trials of war.

The Athenians took Pericles' advice to heart and began to move their families, belongings, and even the woodwork of their homes into the city. They dismantled their houses in the countryside and transported the materials to Athens. Their livestock, including sheep and cattle, was sent across the sea to Euboea and other nearby islands for safekeeping. This relocation was not easy, as most Athenians were deeply connected to the rural life, having always lived and worked in the countryside.

Athenians had long been a people rooted in rural lifestyles, perhaps more than most other Greeks. In the earliest times of Attica, under the rule of Cecrops and the first kings up until Theseus, the region was divided into independent townships, each with its own administration and local magistrates. In those days, each township managed its own affairs independently, without consulting the king of Athens except during times of conflict or crisis. The various townships even had the authority to make war on the central government in Athens if they saw fit, as evidenced by the Eleusinians, who waged war against King Erechtheus with Eumolpus as their leader.

However, the rule of Theseus brought change. Known for his intelligence and strength, Theseus united the region by abolishing the independent councils and magistrates of these smaller cities and merging them into a single council in Athens. Although each family retained ownership of its private lands and homes, politically, all of Attica now had one center—Athens. The unification created a stronger state, and upon Theseus's death, he left behind a powerful and cohesive nation. To commemorate this unity, he established the Synoecia, or Feast of Union, which remains a state-funded festival honoring the goddess Athene. Athenians still celebrate it, recognizing the strength that this unification brought.

At that time, Athens was smaller, comprising mainly the citadel and the southern area below it. This southern orientation is evident from the location of temples to various gods, which are clustered within or near the citadel. Besides the temple of Athene, temples to Olympian Zeus, Pythian Apollo, Earth, and Dionysus "in the Marshes" were situated in this southern part of the city. This latter temple, dedicated to Dionysus, is also significant for hosting the ancient Dionysia festival, still celebrated by the Athenians and their Ionian descendants in the month of Anthesterion. Many other older temples also remain in this area, a testament to the long-standing religious and cultural heart of Athens.

Additionally, a natural spring, later modified and named Enneacrounos, or Nine Pipes, by the ruling tyrants, was an essential water source and was originally known as Callirhoe, or Fairwater. Located close to the citadel, this spring was used for ceremonial purposes, including weddings and religious rites. Despite renovations, the Athenians maintained some of the ancient traditions surrounding its use.

The deep historical significance of the citadel as Athens' original center has left a lasting impression. Even now, Athenians refer to the citadel as "the city," a term that reflects its enduring role as the heart of Athens.

The Athenians, having long lived in scattered communities across Attica, retained a deep attachment to their rural way of life. Even after Theseus centralized governance in Athens, many Athenians continued to reside in the countryside with their families, carrying on the old traditions. This attachment persisted into the current conflict, making it especially difficult for them to uproot now. The recent restoration of their homes and sacred sites after the Median invasion deepened their reluctance to leave. The need to abandon their ancestral temples and familiar lands filled them with grief, as each person saw the countryside as an integral part of their heritage and identity.

When they arrived in Athens, only a few found accommodations in their own homes or with relatives and friends. The vast majority, however, had to seek shelter wherever they could—in unbuilt areas of the city, in temples and shrines dedicated to heroes, with the notable exception of the Acropolis, the temple of Eleusinian Demeter, and other sacred places traditionally kept closed to the public. Even the area known as the Pelasgian ground, which lay below the citadel and was forbidden for habitation due to an ancient curse, was now occupied out of necessity. This plot of land had been the subject of a prophetic warning from Delphi, which ominously cautioned, "Leave the Pelasgian parcel desolate; woe worth the day that men inhabit it!" This oracle was interpreted by many to mean that grave misfortunes would come from inhabiting the land. Yet, as I see it, if the prophecy came true, it was because the war's hardships forced them to build on the plot, not that the occupation itself was the cause of the troubles. The god had foreseen that a dire time would force the Athenians to settle there, marking a bleak period for Athens.

Amid the shortage of space, many Athenians sought shelter in the towers along the walls or in any other place they could find. Despite their efforts to find housing, the city was overwhelmed by the influx of rural citizens. Later, they divided sections of the Long Walls and parts of Piraeus into lots, where some were eventually able to settle. Throughout this challenging time, the Athenians remained focused on preparations for war. They rallied their allies, organized an impressive fleet of a hundred ships for an expedition to the Peloponnese, and meticulously prepared for the long struggle ahead.

Meanwhile, the Peloponnesian army, advancing into Attica, reached the border town of Oenoe. Positioned strategically between Attica and Boeotia, Oenoe was fortified and served as a stronghold for Athens during times of war. The Peloponnesians set up camp and prepared for a siege, using various war engines in their attempt to breach the town's defenses. However, this prolonged siege delayed their advance and caused considerable frustration. Archidamus, the Spartan king leading the invasion, was already under suspicion for being too moderate and possibly sympathetic toward Athens, due to the cautious measures he had taken in planning the campaign. This latest delay at Oenoe intensified the soldiers' dissatisfaction, who believed that an immediate advance would have caught the Athenians unprepared, with much of their property still in the open. They felt the delay had given the Athenians precious time to secure their belongings, which might have been left exposed if the invasion had moved forward more swiftly.

However, Archidamus's motives were different. He anticipated that the Athenians, unwilling to see their lands ravaged, might surrender before their property suffered any harm. Confident that such a strategy would lead to a more favorable outcome, he chose to wait, believing that this approach would avoid unnecessary destruction while still achieving their objectives.

After Archidamus made repeated assaults on Oenoe to no avail, and with no envoy from Athens appearing to negotiate, he finally abandoned the siege and moved deeper into Attica. The attack began about eighty days after the Thebans' initial attempt on Plataea, right in the peak of summer when the grain was ready for harvest. Archidamus, son of Zeuxis and king of Lacedaemon, led the Peloponnesian army, and they advanced as far as Eleusis and the Thriasian plain. There, they established a camp, ravaged the surrounding lands, and even routed some Athenian cavalry near Rheiti, or "the Brooks." Keeping

Mount Aegaleus to their right, they pressed on through Cropia, eventually reaching Acharnae—the largest of the Athenian townships—where they settled in for a prolonged raid on the land.

Archidamus chose to halt and establish a base at Acharnae, rather than pushing immediately into the heart of the Athenian plain, for a calculated reason. He speculated that the Athenians, driven by the enthusiasm of their youth and their recent military successes, might be provoked into defending their land. This encampment at Acharnae was meant as a deliberate incitement, hoping to spur them to action. Archidamus believed that the Acharnians, with their formidable corps of three thousand heavy infantry and their lands at risk, might be unwilling to stand by while their territory was destroyed. He hoped they would demand a sally from Athens to engage the invading force, forcing the entire Athenian army into battle.

However, if the Athenians held back and did not rise to his bait, Archidamus saw this restraint as a strategic advantage. By devastating the lands of the Acharnians, he expected that the rest of the city would be less motivated to risk lives defending other parts of the territory in future invasions. Once the Acharnians had accepted the loss of their own land, he reasoned, they would be less inclined to push for resistance to protect lands further afield, potentially creating divisions within the Athenian ranks. This strategy would allow him to devastate the Athenian plains and even approach the city walls with minimal resistance in the future.

Meanwhile, as long as the Peloponnesian forces remained at Eleusis and in the Thriasian plain, there was hope among the Athenians that they might not press any closer. Memories resurfaced of the previous Peloponnesian invasion fourteen years earlier, led by Pleistoanax, son of Pausanias, which had halted at Eleusis and Thria without advancing further. Pleistoanax's retreat had led to his exile under suspicion of bribery, with many Athenians now hoping for a similar outcome. However, when the Peloponnesians established their position at Acharnae, barely seven miles from Athens, the mood in the city became one of frustration and urgency. With the ravaging of their lands occurring right before their eyes, younger Athenians—who had never before witnessed such a direct threat, unlike the older citizens who remembered the Median wars—felt humiliated by the enemy's encroachment. As passions ran high, many young Athenians urgently called for an immediate sortie to confront the Peloponnesians.

Throughout the city, people formed small groups, debating hotly whether to sally forth. While some fervently pushed for an attack, others advised caution, fearing a rash decision might endanger Athens. Oracles of varying interpretations circulated, each taken up by different factions in the debate. The Acharnians, whose lands were being devastated, were particularly vocal, pressuring the rest of the population to defend their interests.

Pericles, however, remained steadfast. Despite becoming the target of criticism for not leading out the army, he chose to maintain a firm stance against any hasty military action. Knowing the dangers of allowing an emotionally charged assembly to dictate policy, he refrained from calling a public meeting or encouraging debate on the matter. Instead, he focused on maintaining order within the city and preparing defensive measures, while deploying small contingents of cavalry to deter the enemy's raiding parties near the city.

A minor skirmish occurred at Phrygia, where Athenian horsemen, alongside their Thessalian allies, engaged the Boeotian cavalry. Though the Athenians initially gained the upper hand, they were ultimately driven back when Boeotian infantry joined the fight. A few Athenian casualties resulted, but their bodies were recovered the same day without a truce. The next day, the Peloponnesians raised a victory trophy, marking their success. The Thessalian forces who had come to Athens's aid included contingents from several cities: the Larisaeans, Pharsalians, Cranonians, Pyrasians, Gyrtonians, and Pheraeans. The commanders included Polymedes and Aristonus from Larisa, who led opposing factions, and Menon from Pharsalus, along with other generals from the different Thessalian cities.

Since the Athenians continued to refuse battle, the Peloponnesians moved on from Acharnae, shifting their focus to other demes located between Mount Parnes and Brilessus, which they plundered thoroughly. During the occupation of Attica, the Athenians dispatched their prepared fleet of a hundred ships, carrying a thousand heavy infantry and four hundred archers. Commanded by Carcinus, son of Xenotimus; Proteas, son of Epicles; and Socrates, son of Antigenes, this fleet set sail to cruise around Peloponnese. The Peloponnesians, after exhausting their supplies, finally left Attica, retreating through Boeotia by a different route than they had used on entry. While passing Oropus, they ravaged the territory of Graea, held by the Oropians under Athenian rule, and then dispersed back to their home cities in the Peloponnese.

Following their departure, the Athenians took preventive measures for the future. They established permanent land and sea posts at strategic locations for regular defense throughout the war. Additionally, they set aside a special fund of a thousand talents from the moneys stored in the Acropolis, strictly reserved for use only in the event of an emergency sea attack by the enemy. Any proposal to access these funds for other purposes would be treated as a capital offense. They also dedicated a fleet of a hundred of their best galleys, complete with captains, specifically reserved for this emergency.

Meanwhile, the Athenian fleet, supplemented by fifty ships from Corcyra and other allied vessels in the region, continued cruising along the coast of Peloponnese, raiding coastal territories. One of their stops was Laconia, where they attempted an assault on Methone, a town left nearly defenseless due to its weak walls and lack of a stationed garrison. However, Brasidas, son of Tellis, a Spartan commander in the area, quickly intervened. Learning of the Athenian attack, he rallied a hundred heavy infantry and charged through the dispersed Athenian forces, who were occupied with the town's wall, successfully making his way into Methone. Although he lost a few men in the process, Brasidas managed to secure the town, earning recognition from Sparta as the first officer to distinguish himself in the war. Following this setback, the Athenians resumed their voyage.

Continuing along the coast, they reached Pheia in Elis, where they ravaged the countryside over two days and defeated a selected force of three hundred soldiers who had come from the nearby Vale of Elis to defend the area. However, as a sudden squall approached, the Athenians, lacking a safe harbor nearby, decided to re-embark on their ships and sailed into the port of Pheia by rounding Point Ichthys. Meanwhile, some Messenians and other allies who were unable to board the ships traveled by land, capturing Pheia. The fleet soon sailed back to pick up the land troops, but they evacuated Pheia once the main Elean army approached.

After regrouping, the Athenians continued their coastal campaign, raiding various other locations as they cruised along the Around this same period, the Athenians dispatched a fleet of thirty ships to patrol the coast of Locris and to guard Euboea, with Cleopompus, son of Clinias, appointed as commander. During the campaign, Cleopompus led raids along the coastal settlements, capturing Thronium and seizing hostages from the city. He also defeated the Locrians at Alope, who had gathered to defend their territory from Athenian incursions.

That summer, the Athenians undertook another significant measure by expelling the Aeginetans, including their families, from the island of Aegina. This decision was justified on the grounds that the Aeginetans had played a central role in inciting the war. Additionally, the close proximity of Aegina to the Peloponnesian coast made it strategically desirable for Athens to secure the island with their own colonists. Not long afterward, the Athenian settlers were established there. The exiled Aeginetans found refuge in Thyrea, a territory granted to them by Lacedaemon. This grant was not only a gesture of Spartan hostility toward Athens but also a reward to the Aeginetans, who had rendered services to Sparta during the Helot revolt following the earthquake. Thyrea, situated on the border of Argolis and Laconia and extending to the sea, became the new home for many Aeginetans, while others dispersed across Hellas.

This summer also saw an unusual natural phenomenon: a solar eclipse at midday, early in the lunar month, casting the sun into the shape of a crescent and revealing some stars before it returned to normal.

During this period, the Athenians changed their stance toward Nymphodorus, son of Pythes, an influential Abderite and brother-in-law to Sitalces, King of the Thracians. Previously seen as an adversary, Nymphodorus was now made the Athenian proxenus (public host) and was invited to Athens. The Athenians sought his influence to secure Sitalces as an ally. Sitalces, son of Teres, ruled the Odrysian kingdom, which his father had established as the dominant power in Thrace, a region largely divided among independent tribes. Notably, this Teres bore no relation to Tereus of Daulis, the mythical figure linked to the story of Procne, Pandion's daughter from Athens, and the famous tale involving the nightingale, often called the Daulian bird in poetry. The two figures not only lived in different parts of Thrace but also belonged to different lineages.

With Nymphodorus's mediation, the Athenians succeeded in forming an alliance with Sitalces, who promised military support in the form of Thracian cavalry and light-armed troops to assist Athens in its conflicts with the Thracian cities and with Perdiccas of Macedon. Nymphodorus further facilitated a reconciliation between the Athenians and Perdiccas, prompting Athens to restore the town of Therme to Macedon. In turn, Perdiccas joined forces with the Athenians and their general Phormio in a joint campaign against the Chalcidians. Consequently, Athens gained powerful allies in Sitalces, son of Teres, King of the Thracians, and Perdiccas, son of Alexander, King of the Macedonians, strengthening their position in the region.

Meanwhile, the Athenian fleet of one hundred ships continued its operations around the Peloponnesian coast. They succeeded in capturing Sollium, a town that belonged to Corinth, and subsequently handed over its city and lands to the Acarnanians of Palaira, further cementing their alliance. Moving next to Astacus, the Athenians seized the town, expelling its ruler, Evarchus, and thus securing another ally within their confederacy. Following this, they directed their attention to the island of Cephallenia, which they brought under Athenian influence without resorting to violence. Cephallenia, located off the coasts of Acarnania and Leucas, consists of four regions: the Paleans, Cranians, Samaeans, and Pronaeans, all of whom now fell into the Athenian sphere of influence. After this string of successes, the fleet returned to Athens.

Towards the autumn of this same year, the Athenians undertook a massive military campaign into the Megarid. Under the command of Pericles, son of Xanthippus, they gathered a force that included not only Athenian citizens but also resident aliens, marking one of the largest Athenian armies ever assembled. This enormous force was possible because Athens had not yet been struck by the devastating plague that would soon ravage the city. The army included around ten thousand heavy infantry, all Athenian citizens, along with an additional three thousand stationed at Potidaea. Furthermore, the incursion was supported by at least three thousand resident aliens and a large contingent of light-armed troops. They ravaged most of the Megarid territory, dealing a significant blow to the region before withdrawing.

Shortly after, the fleet that had been patrolling Peloponnese, upon returning to Aegina, received word of the full Athenian force gathered in Megara and joined the land forces. With both land and sea power concentrated, it was likely the largest Athenian army in history. This operation became a yearly tradition; annually, the Athenians would invade the Megarid, sometimes with their cavalry alone and sometimes deploying their full forces. This practice continued throughout the war, until Athens eventually captured Nisaea.

Towards the close of summer, the Athenians fortified the deserted island of Atalanta, located off the Opuntian coast, to prevent privateers from Opus and other parts of Locris from raiding Euboea.

This fortification represented a strategic defense against the incursions threatening their territory and resources. Thus, the summer concluded with Athens strengthening its military hold across the region.

In the following winter, Evarchus, the ousted ruler of Astacus, sought to regain his position. He convinced the Corinthians to assist him, prompting them to dispatch a force of forty ships and fifteen hundred heavy infantry. Evarchus also recruited mercenaries to bolster his efforts. Corinthian commanders Euphamidas, son of Aristonymus; Timoxenus, son of Timocrates; and Eumachus, son of Chrysis led the operation. They succeeded in reinstating Evarchus at Astacus but failed in their subsequent attempts to capture additional positions along the Acarnanian coast. Forced to abandon their plans, they began their journey home.

While returning, the Corinthians made a stop in Cephallenia, where they launched a raid on the territory of the Cranians. However, a planned negotiation with the Cranians ended in betrayal; the Cranians suddenly attacked, resulting in the loss of several Corinthian troops. The Corinthians, taken by surprise and suffering casualties, hastily withdrew and resumed their journey home.

In that same winter, the Athenians observed their ancestral custom of honoring those who had fallen in the war by holding a public funeral at the state's expense. The ceremony, observed with solemnity and respect, followed a well-established tradition. Three days prior to the burial, the bones of the deceased were displayed in a tent set up for this purpose, and friends and relatives came to pay tribute, bringing offerings according to their own wishes. On the day of the funeral, a solemn procession was held. Coffins made of cypress wood were carried on wagons, each coffin designated for a particular tribe and containing the bones of that tribe's fallen warriors. Additionally, there was one empty bier decorated and carried in honor of the missing—those whose bodies had not been recovered.

The procession, open to all citizens and foreigners who wished to join, moved slowly through the city, accompanied by the wailing of female relatives as they expressed their grief. The dead were then laid to rest in a public cemetery in the most beautiful suburb of Athens, a site reserved for the warriors who died in battle. Only those who fell at Marathon were buried on the battlefield itself, a tribute to the exceptional valor they had shown. After the burial, a man chosen by the state for his wisdom and reputable character was invited to deliver an oration honoring the fallen. This tradition, held with reverence throughout the war whenever needed, was now observed for the first time in this conflict, and Pericles, son of Xanthippus, was selected to deliver the eulogy.

When the time came, Pericles stepped onto a high platform near the graves to address the assembled crowd, ensuring he could be heard by all. He began his speech with solemnity, honoring the tradition of commemorating the dead, and acknowledging the responsibility of such an address:

"Many before me have praised the wisdom of those who established this custom of delivering a speech at the burial of those who fell in battle. They say it is fitting to honor the fallen with words. For my part, however, I would consider their deeds themselves to be the most eloquent of all tributes, shown here in this state-funded funeral. The valor displayed in their actions speaks louder than any words could; and I almost wish that so many worthy reputations did not rest on the words of one speaker, whose success or failure could color their memory. To do justice to the deeds of so many brave men is difficult; to speak with accuracy of all that they have done risks alienating listeners. Close friends and relatives, who know every detail of their loved one's achievements, may feel that justice has not been done to their memory, while those less acquainted with the facts may hear of great acts and, measuring them against their own limitations, doubt their truth. People are often comfortable with praise only so long as they believe they could achieve the same; when they cannot, envy and disbelief arise. Yet, as our ancestors have made this tradition a law, I must do my best to honor it, aiming to meet your varied expectations and respect the law."

Pericles then began with Athens' past, acknowledging the founders of the city. "It is right and just that we begin by honoring our forefathers, for they lived in this land from generation to generation, preserving it for us, their descendants, through their courage and determination. If we owe gratitude to those more distant ancestors, even more so do we owe it to our fathers, who increased our inheritance by building the empire we now hold, sparing no effort to pass on their achievements to our generation. Furthermore, we who are gathered here today have in our time contributed to this empire, expanding its reach and strengthening our home city, which has become self-sufficient in both peace and war.

"The accomplishments by which we obtained these dominions, and the courage displayed by us and by our ancestors in resisting both Hellenic and foreign aggressors, are tales familiar to all, too well-known to require my repetition here. Instead, I wish to speak of the path we took to reach our current power, of the political institutions and customs that enabled our rise, and of the character that grew from these. This, I believe, is a fitting subject to address before I honor these men; it is a matter from which all of us, whether Athenian or visiting foreigner, may take instruction.

"Our system of government does not copy the institutions of our neighbors; rather, we serve as an example to others. It is called a democracy because power rests not in the hands of the few but of the many. Our laws afford equal justice to all in their private disputes, and our social status is not determined by class, but by merit. Public offices are not restricted to those with privilege or wealth, but are open to all citizens of merit, regardless of social standing. Poverty does not bar one from service to the state if he has something to contribute to the welfare of the city.

"In our private lives, we are free and tolerant, but in public affairs, we uphold the law. We respect the magistrates and laws, particularly those laws that protect the oppressed and those unwritten rules whose violation brings disgrace. Furthermore, we are lovers of beauty without extravagance and lovers of wisdom without softness. Wealth, to us, is not merely an opportunity for ostentation but a resource to be wisely and practically used; and poverty is no disgrace as long as one seeks to better one's condition.

"We enjoy our lives in a spirit of celebration, and we find happiness in our homes without letting pleasure detract from our discipline. The very source of our courage in battle is our ease of living; we are fearless not because we are hardened by deprivation but because we are prepared for whatever may come. We fight not out of compulsion but by choice, trained both by mind and spirit, so that our strength lies in our freedom and our commitment to defend what we hold dear. Thus, we are not ashamed to acknowledge that we love our city and that our unique way of life binds us to defend it."

Pericles' speech not only honored the dead but also underscored the ideals of Athens. His words inspired those gathered, reminding them of the courage required to defend their city, their way of life, and the memory of those they had lost. The Athenians, moved by his words, found renewed purpose, recognizing that their city was not just a place but an ideal worth every sacrifice.

"Our constitution does not imitate the laws of neighboring states but rather serves as a model for others. We govern ourselves by favoring the many rather than the few, which is why our system is called a democracy. Our laws provide equal justice for all in their private disputes, without regard for social class. Advancement in public life is determined by a person's merit and ability, not by their wealth or social status. Nor does poverty prevent anyone from serving the state; if a person can contribute to the public good, their lack of rank is no obstacle.

"The liberty we enjoy in our government also extends to our everyday lives. We are not overly vigilant of each other's personal choices, nor do we resent our neighbor for living as he pleases. We refrain from imposing judgmental looks that, although harmless in practice, only serve to offend. Yet, while we value ease in our private lives, we are not without discipline in public life. Our freedom does not lead to lawlessness; rather, respect for our laws is our greatest safeguard, teaching us to obey our magistrates and the laws that protect the injured—whether written down or simply understood as common codes of decency.

"Moreover, we provide ample means for relaxation and recreation to refresh the mind after business. Our city is alive with festivals, games, and sacrifices throughout the year. The beauty of our private dwellings adds daily pleasure, helping to chase away gloom, while the greatness of our city brings the products of the world into our harbor. For Athenians, the luxuries and goods of foreign lands are as accessible as those of our own, an advantage that enriches our lives.

"In our military conduct, too, we stand apart from our rivals. We keep our city open to the world, never forbidding foreigners from learning or observing, even if our enemies sometimes benefit from this openness. Rather than rely solely on strict training or rigid policies, we trust in the innate courage of our citizens. Our rivals, in contrast, train their youth with rigorous discipline from a young age in the hopes of cultivating bravery. But here in Athens, we live freely, with leisure, and still prove ourselves just as ready to face danger whenever it arises. Evidence of this can be seen in the fact that the Lacedaemonians do not invade our territory without the help of all their allies, while we Athenians enter a neighbor's territory without such support, and even when fighting on foreign soil, often overcome those defending their own land.

"Our combined forces have never faced an enemy all at once, for we are required to maintain both our naval strength and our presence on land across countless expeditions. Thus, when others encounter only part of our strength, a victory over a small force is hailed as a triumph over Athens itself, while a defeat is exaggerated as a setback for our entire people. Yet if we, accustomed to lives of ease rather than grueling labor, and fortified by courage drawn not from constant training but from our very nature, are still willing to face risks when needed, we possess a double advantage: we are free from the strain of constant hardship in preparation, and we confront danger in the moment with the same bravery as those who live in unceasing discipline.

"In this way, we experience the best of both worlds: we are neither burdened by the constant pressure of military training nor unprepared for the demands of battle. Our unique blend of freedom, culture, and courage allows us to enjoy life while still being formidable on the battlefield, meeting challenges not out of compulsion but by deliberate choice."

"Nor are these the only qualities in which our city merits admiration. We cultivate a sense of refinement without lapsing into extravagance and embrace knowledge without allowing it to soften us. We see wealth as a means to practical ends rather than as something to flaunt, and we place the true shame of poverty not in acknowledging it but in resigning oneself to it without striving to overcome it. In Athens, our public leaders do not ignore their private concerns, nor do our ordinary citizens, engaged in daily work, relinquish their interest in public matters. Uniquely, we view those who neglect public affairs not as harmlessly unambitious but as wholly unproductive. Here, each citizen, if not always an originator, can at least be a discerning judge. We do not see open debate as an obstacle to action; rather, we regard it as a necessary foundation for all wise decisions.

"In our endeavors, we exhibit a rare combination: the highest courage coupled with prudent deliberation, united in the same people. Generally, bold decisions spring from ignorance, while caution arises from reflection, yet we manage to merge daring with thoughtfulness. Surely, the truest courage belongs to those who understand fully both hardship and ease yet never shy from the call of duty. In our generosity, too, we are unparalleled, winning friends by giving rather than by receiving favors. Naturally, it is the one who gives a favor who becomes the truest friend, driven by an enduring desire to foster goodwill, while the recipient feels a quieter bond, knowing any return will be less a gift than a repayment. Only Athens confers its benefits unreservedly, acting not out of cold calculation but with an unhesitating confidence in our own generosity.

"To put it simply, Athens is indeed the school of Hellas, and I doubt if any city or people in the world can produce an individual, self-reliant yet versatile, as adaptable and resourceful in varied circumstances as the Athenian. This is not an empty boast, spoken to suit the occasion, but a truth demonstrated by the greatness of our state, which we have built by adhering to these principles. Athens, among all cities, is found to be as grand in reality as she is in reputation, providing no cause for her enemies to regret their choice of rival, and no grounds for her subjects to question the justice of her rule. In fact, Athens will command the respect and admiration of both her contemporaries and those yet to come, as we have made our power known not through words alone but through mighty acts. Unlike others, we do not rely on a Homer or another poet to lend our fame a passing charm through song; instead, we have compelled every sea and every land to become a witness to our boldness, leaving behind enduring monuments wherever we ventured, whether for noble or harsh purposes.

"This is the Athens for which these men, in defense of her sovereignty and dignity, fought and died with unwavering valor. They faced death so that their city might live in freedom and greatness. And so, it is only fitting that each of us who remains be ready to endure any hardship in her cause, following the example of those who have gone before."

"Indeed, if I have lingered at length upon the virtues of our city, it is to illustrate that our stake in this struggle is unlike that of those who, lacking such blessings, have little to lose. Moreover, I wished to ground the praise of the men over whom I now speak in concrete proofs, rather than mere sentiment. Much of that praise is already complete; for Athens, as I have celebrated her, is precisely what the courage and dedication of these men and others like them have made her. Their fame, unlike that of most men in Hellas, stands in full measure to their worth. And if any test of worth is sought, it lies in their final act, which not only marked the fulfillment of their merit but, in many cases, even revealed it for the first time. There is a fairness in holding that a man's steadfastness in the service of his city should shield him from the memory of lesser faults; for a single virtuous act can outweigh a lifetime of smaller failings, and his value as a citizen should balance any shortcomings he may have had as an individual.

"Not one of these men allowed wealth, with its promise of future comforts, to weaken their resolve, nor did poverty, with its distant hope of prosperity, tempt them to shrink from danger. No, they held vengeance upon the enemy dearer than any personal comfort or security, seeing in it the most glorious of risks. Resolute, they embraced the danger, made certain of their revenge, and deferred their personal hopes. Entrusting the uncertainty of success to fortune, they chose instead to act with boldness, relying on their own courage. They decided to die resisting rather than to live submitting. They fled only from dishonor and faced danger with unwavering courage, ultimately escaping not from their fears but from the zenith of their glory.

"These men, thus, died as Athenians should. You, their survivors, must resolve to meet the enemy with equally steadfast courage, even as you may pray for a more fortunate outcome. But let not your patriotism rest on mere words or ideals; instead, see with your own eyes the greatness of Athens, and let this vision fill your hearts with love and devotion for her. Then, as the magnitude of our city dawns upon you, consider that it was by courage, duty, and an unyielding honor in action that men achieved all this. They did not allow any personal setback to deprive their city of their strength; they offered it to her, laying down their lives as the highest tribute they could give. For this common sacrifice, each one has won a fame that time cannot diminish. And though they are interred in a single tomb, it is not the physical grave that truly honors them, but the grander and more eternal shrine in which their glory is preserved—the memory that will live on through stories and deeds long after their bones have turned to dust.

"Heroes have the whole earth as their tomb; in distant lands, where monuments bear witness to their sacrifice, they live on in every heart, in a memory etched not in stone but in the spirit of those who cherish their courage. Let these men be your model, and understand that happiness is born of freedom, and freedom of valor. Shrink not from the dangers of war, for it is not the destitute who should cling tightly to life—they have little to lose—but rather those to whom life still holds unknown possibilities, whose fall, should it come, would be felt most keenly. To a man of spirit, the disgrace of cowardice would weigh infinitely more than the unperceived death that meets him in the midst of his vitality and patriotism.

"In this spirit, may you go forward, inspired by the example of those who have fallen, and take comfort in the knowledge that, should the same fate befall you, you will join their company in a glory that transcends death. For as long as Athens endures, so too shall the memory of those who defended her, imperishable, and honored in the hearts of her people."

"Comfort, not condolence, is what I offer to the parents of the fallen here today. Life is uncertain, and our destinies are woven by countless, unseen threads. Yet blessed are those who, like your sons, have drawn such a noble end—a death that brings renown and preserves the joy in which they lived. Still, I recognize the difficulty in these words, especially for those who will be reminded daily, by the sights and sounds of other families, of the treasures they once cherished. For grief is not felt as sharply for that which was never known, but for the loss of what has become familiar, beloved, a part of life itself.

But those of you who are young enough to have more children should find strength in that hope; new sons may both ease the weight of your grief and contribute to the strength of the state. For when a man brings to his city the shared burdens and hopes of a father, he brings greater wisdom to his judgments and a juster perspective. To those among you who are past your prime, reflect upon the fortune you have known in your life so far, and be consoled by the fame that will keep the memory of the departed alive. The desire for honor, unlike so many earthly pursuits, does not wither with age; rather, it sustains us in life's final years, bringing a joy that mere wealth can never match.

"To the sons and brothers of these heroes, I must say, I foresee a challenging path for you. For when a man has passed on, he is naturally praised, and even the most exceptional among the living find it difficult to rival, let alone surpass, his memory. The living contend with envy and rivalry, while those who have fallen are honored with a pure respect unmarred by competition. Still, you should strive to embody the virtues of your fathers and brothers, so that you may stand worthily beside their memory.

"And to the widows who will now live on in their absence, I say only this: your strength lies in embodying the finest qualities of our people. The greatest honor for a woman lies in being spoken of as little as possible—whether for good or ill. Quiet strength, dignity, and virtue: these are your finest traits.

"Thus I complete my duty, speaking as best I can according to our law. In words, I have done what I am bound to do; in deeds, these men already have received the public honor due them, and their children will be reared to manhood at the state's expense. This provision stands as a public reward, a prize of valor bestowed upon both the fallen and their families, and it is through such rewards that the state nurtures its finest citizens.

"And now, having paid your respects and heard the final words of tribute, you may depart in peace."

Chapter VII

This plague thus began to devastate Athens soon after the Lacedaemonians arrived in Attica, marking the onset of the second year of the war with unrelenting suffering. Rumors spread that it had originated in Ethiopia, then traveled through Egypt and Libya before descending upon the crowded and vulnerable city. As it struck Piraeus first, some whispered that the Peloponnesians had poisoned the water reservoirs, though there was no proof. From Piraeus, the disease spread quickly through Athens, claiming a staggering number of lives and overwhelming every attempt to contain it.

The Athenians, despite their best efforts, found themselves helpless against this unknown affliction. Physicians, as they attempted to aid the sick, succumbed more rapidly than anyone due to their constant exposure. The temples and altars, once places of hopeful supplication, became crowded with the sick, their prayers met only with silence. Soon, even the rites of supplication and divination were abandoned as the city plunged into despair, its people left to confront the unyielding catastrophe alone.

As the disease advanced, its symptoms appeared with chilling suddenness. Individuals in good health were abruptly overtaken by extreme heat in their heads, their eyes inflamed and bloodshot. The infection gripped the throat and tongue, coloring them with blood and causing breath that reeked with a foul odor. Sneezing and hoarseness followed swiftly, leading to sharp pain in the chest and a relentless, hacking cough. In many cases, the illness would reach the stomach, which resulted in agonizing distress and the expulsion of bile of various colors. This phase often led to dry, spasmodic retching, accompanied by violent cramps that either receded quickly or lingered unbearably.

Externally, the body displayed a strange mix of heat and rashes. Though not extremely feverish to the touch, the skin turned a deep reddish or livid shade and was covered with pustules and small ulcers. Internally, however, the afflicted burned with such intensity that they could hardly endure the lightest clothing, preferring to remain unclothed or, if possible, plunge into cold water to soothe their agony. In desperation, some of the neglected patients threw themselves into the public water tanks, maddened by an insatiable thirst that tormented them day and night. Yet, whether they drank or refrained, their suffering remained the same. The inability to rest or find sleep added to their despair, each day blurring into the next with no relief in sight.

Remarkably, although the body did not initially waste away, most succumbed on the seventh or eighth day to the relentless fever and internal inflammation. For those who endured past this critical period, the disease would descend into the bowels, causing severe ulceration and a virulent diarrhea that sapped the last of their strength, typically leading to death. The infection traced a devastating path through the entire body, beginning in the head and then ravaging each internal system it touched. For those who survived, the disease left cruel reminders in the form of lingering afflictions: many lost their extremities, such as fingers and toes, and some became blind. Even among those who recovered, some experienced a complete loss of memory, unable to recall their own identity or recognize their family and friends.

This unprecedented disaster left the Athenians in a state of hopeless confusion, and it altered the fabric of daily life in the city. The fear of contagion separated families and friends, and the usual bonds of trust and support were weakened. The character of the people, shaped by the city's shared hardship and grandeur, began to change under the strain, as Athens grappled with a crisis that tested not only its resilience but also its very identity.

The suffering caused by this plague was beyond words, and its effects almost too severe for human strength to bear. Yet, the most extraordinary sign of its nature, distinguishing it from any ordinary illness, was how even scavenging animals—both birds and beasts that normally fed on human remains—avoided these bodies. Although many lay unburied, these animals either stayed away or died shortly after touching the corpses. People noticed that certain birds vanished entirely, and no scavengers were seen near the bodies. The disease's effects were perhaps most easily observed in animals like domestic dogs, whose suffering mirrored the deadly toll it took on people.

This was a plague like no other. Despite the variety of symptoms that appeared from person to person, the illness shared a chilling consistency: Athens was free of all other typical ailments; those that did arise inevitably concluded with this same plague. Some died without receiving any care, while others perished despite having every available comfort. No treatment could be deemed reliable; what helped one person seemed to worsen another. Strong constitutions offered no protection, as the disease struck the healthy and the weak without discrimination, leaving them all to perish even under the strictest regimen of diet and care.

The most devastating aspect of the illness, however, was the despair that gripped anyone who began to show symptoms. Those stricken would fall into deep hopelessness almost immediately, which weakened their ability to fight back, making them easier victims to the disease. It was horrifying to see individuals die like animals, having contracted the illness while nursing others. This alone drove the death toll higher than ever. For fear of contagion, many people avoided visiting their sick friends and neighbors, leaving the ailing to die alone. Whole households were sometimes emptied because no one remained to care for them. Conversely, those who did tend to the sick often caught the illness and died themselves. This was especially true of those with a sense of duty or honor, who felt morally compelled to care for their friends and family. As they stayed by the bedsides of the dying, they eventually became overwhelmed by the disease and perished alongside them.

Survivors of the illness, however, became figures of hope and comfort for those still sick. Having endured the ordeal, they showed compassion without fear, knowing firsthand what it was like. For them, the worst seemed over; they rarely, if ever, contracted the illness a second time. Their survival brought admiration from others, and they themselves felt an elated, almost vain belief that they were now immune not only to this plague but to all illnesses.

The calamity worsened as refugees from the countryside, fleeing the Peloponnesian invasion, poured into the city. Athens was unequipped to shelter this influx; people crowded into makeshift huts and cramped living spaces during the height of summer's heat. Disease spread unchecked among these close quarters. Dead and dying individuals lay piled atop each other, while others, half-dead, stumbled through the streets and clustered around any available water source, desperate for relief. Temples, once revered as holy places, were soon filled with the dead and dying, lying unburied and abandoned where they fell. As the crisis spiraled out of control, people lost all sense of order, disregarding sacred spaces and any former customs.

The usual rites and customs for burial became meaningless, as the city's resources and families were exhausted by the sheer scale of death. Those without the proper means to bury their loved ones often resorted to shocking practices. Overwhelmed by grief and necessity, some would throw their deceased onto any nearby funeral pyre, even one prepared for strangers, igniting it if it was not yet burning. Others, carrying their dead, would approach a stranger's burning pyre and toss their loved one's body onto it before hurrying away.

The plague was a relentless ordeal for Athens, sparing no one and stripping away any semblance of normal life. With no end in sight, this once-great city found itself reduced to desperation, its people grasping at whatever means they could to survive, mourn, and cope in a world that had descended into chaos.

The plague not only devastated lives but also unleashed a wave of reckless indulgence and disregard for morals or restraint. People now openly pursued what they might have hidden before, no longer feeling the need to be discreet. The plague's unpredictability brought about rapid changes in fortune; those who once had nothing suddenly inherited wealth, while the prosperous could die overnight. Consequently, a new outlook took hold: spend what you have while you still live, since both life and wealth seemed so fleeting. Concepts like perseverance or traditional ideas of honor no longer appealed to people, who now doubted whether they'd even live to see such ambitions fulfilled. Instead, immediate pleasure became the most desirable and logical goal, with indulgences seen as both honorable and practical in a world where tomorrow wasn't guaranteed.

Neither divine reverence nor the rule of law was a deterrent. The gods, they reasoned, offered no solace or protection, as the devout and the impious seemed equally doomed; and laws held little power when death was already a constant threat, sparing no one. Rather than fearing the judgment of courts, people felt a harsher fate hovered permanently over them. Under this grim shadow, the immediate impulse was to seize whatever joy they could.

This dire state of affairs pressed heavily upon the Athenians. Within the city, death was rampant; outside, their land lay ravaged. In their distress, people clung to an ancient verse, remembered by the elders and repeated in their grief:

"A Dorian war shall come and with it death."

A debate quickly arose over whether the verse originally said "death" or "dearth" (famine). However, given the current devastation, it seemed only natural to believe "death" was the word, a belief strengthened by their suffering. Still, it's easy to imagine that if, in the future, a Dorian war should arrive accompanied by famine, people would likely recall the verse to fit that tragedy instead.

There was also the memory of an oracle given to the Lacedaemonians, known to some Athenians, foretelling that if they fought with all their might, victory would be theirs, and the god himself would support them. The plague seemed to lend credence to this prophecy. As soon as the Peloponnesians set foot in Attica, the plague struck, wreaking havoc on Athens but sparing Peloponnese almost entirely, afflicting only Athens and the most densely populated towns.

With the pestilence devastating the population, the Peloponnesian forces pressed forward, ravaging the lands of the Athenian plain and advancing as far as the region of Paralia, up to Laurium, the site of the Athenian silver mines. They destroyed first the areas facing Peloponnese, then those facing Euboea and Andros. Pericles, though still general, remained resolute in his strategy. Just as he had done during the prior invasion, he resisted the calls to send the Athenians out to confront the Peloponnesians directly, holding firm to his conviction to keep the citizens within the walls.

While the Peloponnesians still occupied the Athenian plain but had yet to reach the Paralian region, Pericles prepared a substantial naval expedition to target the Peloponnesian coast. Commanding a fleet of a hundred ships, he mobilized four thousand Athenian heavy infantry and three hundred cavalry, the latter transported for the first time in improvised horse carriers made from old ships. The fleet also included fifty vessels provided by allies from Chios and Lesbos. Setting out, they left the Peloponnesians behind in Attica as they sailed to Epidaurus in the Peloponnese. Here, they ravaged the surrounding territory and even attempted an assault on the city, though they ultimately failed to capture it. Moving on from Epidaurus, they laid waste to the lands of Troezen, Halieis, and Hermione, all coastal towns in the Peloponnese. They then sailed to Prasiai, a coastal town in Laconia, sacked part of its territory, and plundered the town itself before returning home. By then, the Peloponnesians had withdrawn from Attica, leaving it in ruins.

During the entire period of the Peloponnesian occupation of Attica and the Athenian naval expedition, the plague continued to claim lives, both among those on the ships and within Athens. It was even rumored that the Peloponnesians were quickened in their retreat from Attica out of fear of the plague, as deserters informed them of its spread within the city and the burials they observed from afar. Nevertheless, this invasion was the longest of its kind, lasting around forty days, during which they ravaged the entire region.

In that same summer, Hagnon, son of Nicias, and Cleopompus, son of Clinias—who served as Pericles' colleagues in command—took the same Athenian armament Pericles had recently used and embarked on an expedition against the Chalcidians near Thrace and the still-besieged Potidaea. Upon their arrival, they brought siege engines against Potidaea and used all possible means to breach the city. But despite their efforts, they were unsuccessful, achieving neither the capture of Potidaea nor any other significant objective. The plague struck them here as well, inflicting severe losses, even infecting previously healthy soldiers who had avoided the disease during the prior campaign. Phormio and his sixteen hundred troops only escaped because they were stationed farther from the Chalcidians. Ultimately, Hagnon returned to Athens, having lost over a thousand men out of the original four thousand heavy infantry within about forty days, though those remaining at Potidaea continued the siege.

Following the Peloponnesians' second invasion, a noticeable shift occurred in the Athenians' morale. Their lands had been devastated twice, and the dual burden of war and pestilence weighed heavily on them. Frustration and resentment grew against Pericles, whom they now blamed as the instigator of the war and the source of all their suffering. Many Athenians, desperate to end their afflictions, favored negotiating peace with Lacedaemon and even sent a delegation to pursue this end. However, the ambassadors returned empty-handed, and the Athenians' despair deepened, with all of their frustrations directed at Pericles. Perceiving the mounting anger and hopelessness and anticipating such a reaction, Pericles, who remained general, convened an assembly. His purpose was twofold: to restore the shaken confidence of the people and to guide them from their resentful state toward a more steadfast and hopeful outlook. With these aims in mind, he addressed the assembly, speaking to the Athenians as follows:

"I anticipated the anger that has been directed at me, understanding well the reasons for it. That is why I have called this assembly: to remind you of certain truths and to urge you not to let your suffering lead you into unreasonable blame against me or despair over our circumstances. I believe firmly that the strength of our state provides greater security to each of us individually than any temporary personal comfort could bring if the state itself were diminished. Even the wealthiest and most secure individual cannot escape ruin if his country falls, while a strong and thriving state always offers refuge and support to its citizens in times of personal misfortune. Therefore, if the commonwealth can bear the individual's losses but the individual cannot bear the loss of the commonwealth, then each of us must surely prioritize its defense. This is not the time to let private distress cloud your concern for our public safety or lead you to reproach me for advocating for war, nor to regret your own decision to vote for it.

"Some may feel anger toward me now, but I stand here as someone who, I believe, has not only knowledge of what policy is right but also the skill to communicate it, and who, moreover, is driven by genuine patriotism and integrity. Without the knowledge, a leader's advice would be pointless; without the ability to communicate it, it would lack influence; without a love for the state, he would lack the drive to defend it, and without integrity, he would be tempted by self-interest. If you believed I had some measure of these qualities when you first accepted my counsel and supported going to war, there is little reason now to accuse me of having misled you.

"War may indeed seem foolish to those who can avoid it and who face no immediate danger. But if we faced only two choices: submission that sacrificed our independence or the risk of hardship with a hope to preserve it, then I say it is the refusal to take on that risk that is truly blameworthy. I am still the same man with the same principles; it is you who have changed. You accepted my advice when you were secure but now, in hardship, you regret it, not due to any inherent flaw in the strategy itself but because of your own wavering resolve. Every one of you now feels the personal hardship, yet the benefits of this struggle are still distant and unclear, making it hard to endure when our endurance is most needed. The rapidity and unexpected severity of our setbacks, compounded by this sudden plague, have understandably shaken you. However, being

Athenians—citizens of a great and historic state, raised with the values of courage and resilience—you should be prepared to face even the harshest trials without faltering in your commitment to the city's glory.

"Grieve, if you must, for the losses you bear personally. But do not let these private sorrows cloud your focus on the safety of the commonwealth. Instead, draw from our shared legacy of strength and press forward with determination, knowing that our city's reputation requires us not only to live up to but to surpass the expectations placed upon us. Remember, the eyes of all Hellas are upon us, and neither history nor posterity will forgive us if we let our courage falter when our city needs it most. Let us, therefore, cease to dwell on our individual troubles and instead unite in our efforts to secure the common safety and preserve the dignity of Athens."

"If you feel daunted by the demands that this war imposes and are fearful that these efforts may end in failure, remember the many reasons I have shared with you, proving that such fears are misplaced. But if those reasons seem insufficient, I will now point out another advantage from the sheer scale of your empire, one I suspect you may not fully appreciate and that I have not raised before. Although it may sound bold, I would not mention it now were it not for the undue discouragement I see among you. Many of you may think our power extends solely over our allies, but let me tell you the truth. The world of action comprises two arenas: land and sea. In one of these, the sea, you are entirely dominant—not only in terms of your current reach but also in terms of how far you choose to extend it. Simply put, your naval strength allows your ships to travel wherever they will, without any power on earth, not even the King himself, being able to oppose them. So, while you might see the loss of your lands and homes as a great deprivation, you should recognize that our naval supremacy gives us a form of power that is far more substantial. Rather than lamenting the temporary loss of your physical estates, you should view them as minor sacrifices, like the gardens or luxuries that merely adorn a substantial fortune. Understand this: the freedom preserved through your efforts will enable us to restore all that we've lost. But should you submit, even what remains to you will surely be taken. Our fathers did not receive these possessions from others; they won them through their own labor and defended them steadfastly. They passed them on to you, and now it falls to you to prove yourselves their equals. To lose what has been secured is far more shameful than to fail in striving for something new. Thus, face your enemies not just with resolve but with disdain, for contempt of one's foes is born of genuine strength.

"Moreover, blind confidence can inspire courage, even in the faint-hearted. But contempt—true disdain—is reserved for those of us who, through thoughtful reflection, are assured of our superiority. When both sides have the same odds, knowledge fuels bravery, as it replaces vague hope with a firm expectation grounded in real resources and capabilities, lending a strength far more reliable than mere desperation.

"Your country, therefore, rightfully demands your service to sustain her in the glory she has achieved. These honors are a source of pride for you all, and you cannot reject the responsibilities of empire yet still lay claim to its rewards. Remember, too, that you are fighting not only to preserve your freedom but also to protect your empire and secure yourselves against the dangers bred by the enmities that come with it. It is too late to retreat, even if any among you now feel a sudden preference for a simpler, 'honorable' existence free from ambition. For what you hold, if I may speak frankly, is akin to a tyranny; perhaps it was bold to seize it, but relinquishing it now would be reckless. And if any who are inclined toward this unambitious perspective persuade others, they could swiftly undo the state. In truth, they would meet the same fate even if they could remain entirely isolated, for the unambitious can never be safe without vigilant protectors. In short, these gentle qualities may suit a subject city, content in quiet servitude, but they do not befit a ruling power like ours.

"But do not be swayed by such citizens or allow your anger to turn upon me—who, if I advised war, only cast the same vote you yourselves gave. The enemy has invaded your land and acted as anyone would expect if his demands were denied. We anticipated this, and while the plague has come upon us as an unforeseen blow—one point on which our plans were mistaken—this alone should not be a reason for blame, unless you are also prepared to credit me with any unexpected success that chance may bring. Remember, too, that calamities beyond human control must be met with resignation, while human adversaries must be confronted with determination; this was always the Athenian way, and I urge you to uphold it now.

"Recall that Athens stands as the most renowned city in the world because she has never bowed before adversity; she has invested more lives and energy in her pursuits than any other city, and has won an empire greater than any known. Even if, in line with nature's course, we are someday compelled to yield, it will still be remembered that we held sway over more Hellenes than any other state, faced the greatest wars, and inhabited a city unmatched in wealth and strength. These accomplishments may draw criticism from those with lesser ambition, but they will stir emulation among the energetic and envy among those who lack them. Indeed, history shows that to rule often brings unpopularity and resentment, but true wisdom willingly accepts this burden for a noble cause. Hatred is fleeting, yet the glory of the present and the legacy we build endures forever, unforgotten.

"Therefore, let your choice be made for glory to come and honor today; pursue both with immediate and dedicated action. Do not send envoys to Sparta; do not betray any sign of faltering under the weight of your present hardships. For it is those who are least shaken by adversity and who respond most readily to it with strong hands and clear minds who are the greatest men and build the greatest communities."

These were the arguments by which Pericles aimed to relieve the Athenians of their anger and refocus their minds away from their immediate troubles. As a city, they accepted his words; abandoning all thought of negotiation with Sparta, they directed renewed vigor toward the war effort. Yet, as individuals, they continued to feel the sting of their losses—ordinary citizens deprived of their modest means, and the wealthier classes grieving over estates and properties reduced to ruin. Above all, they faced the bitterness of war instead of the peace they had once enjoyed. Public sentiment against Pericles persisted until he was fined. Not long after, however, the fickle crowd restored him to the office of general and entrusted their affairs to him once again, their private grievances now dulled by time and their acknowledgment of his value in public service renewed. They recognized that he was the best leader they had in times of national crisis.

During the peace, under Pericles' leadership, Athens flourished under a steady and measured policy, reaching its peak of greatness. With the onset of the war, he demonstrated a clear understanding of his city's strengths and limitations. Pericles lived two years and six months into the conflict, and his predictions grew all the more evident after his death. He had advised a cautious approach, emphasizing a focus on the navy, avoiding unnecessary expansions, and refraining from risking the city's security unnecessarily during wartime. He promised that this strategy would bring about a favorable outcome. However, the Athenians did the opposite. Private ambitions and personal interests led them into actions unrelated to the war, actions that were unfair to both themselves and their allies. These pursuits brought honor and gain only to individuals, while their failures brought great losses upon the state in its struggle.

The reasons for this deviation are not hard to understand. Pericles' rank, ability, and integrity allowed him a unique authority over the populace; he led them, rather than being led by them. Seeking no power through improper means, he had no need to flatter the public and could even risk displeasing them by opposing their moods. When he saw them unduly confident, he would curb their arrogance; if they succumbed to panic, he would restore their confidence. Thus, under Pericles, what was nominally a democracy became, in essence, rule by the foremost citizen. With his successors, it was different. Being on more equal footing with one another and all vying for dominance, they surrendered state policy to the will of the masses. As was inevitable in a powerful and sovereign city, this led to a multitude of misjudgments, including the disastrous Sicilian expedition. This venture failed less due to a miscalculation of the enemy's strength than from the failure of those who sent it to provide adequate support, being more engaged in internal rivalries for control over the people. These rivalries not only weakened military operations abroad but also sowed the seeds of civil discord at home.

Despite suffering significant losses in Sicily and experiencing increasing internal strife, the Athenians managed to hold out for three more years against their original foes, who were joined by revolting allies and the King's son, Cyrus, who financed the Peloponnesian fleet. Ultimately, it was their internal conflicts that led to their defeat. This overwhelming wealth of resources was precisely what Pericles had anticipated would enable Athens to triumph over the unassisted forces of the Peloponnesians.

In the same summer, the Lacedaemonians and their allies launched an expedition with a hundred ships against Zacynthus, an island off the coast of Elis inhabited by Achaean colonists from the Peloponnese and allied with Athens. They landed a thousand Lacedaemonian heavy infantry under the command of the Spartan admiral Cnemus. After raiding most of the territory, they withdrew when the inhabitants refused to surrender and sailed back home.

As summer drew to a close, a group of envoys from Corinth and Lacedaemon, including Aristeus, Aneristus, Nicolaus, Stratodemus, and Timagoras of Tegea, along with a private citizen named Pollis from Argos, set out on a mission to Asia to persuade the Persian King to join the war effort and provide financial support. On their way, they stopped in Thrace to seek the favor of Sitalces, son of Teres, hoping he might abandon Athens as an ally, support the beleaguered Potidaeans who were under siege by Athenian forces, and offer them a safe passage across the Hellespont to Pharnabazus, who could escort them to the King.

At the same time, Athenian ambassadors, Learchus, son of Callimachus, and Ameiniades, son of Philemon, happened to be with Sitalces. They appealed to Sadocus, Sitalces' son and an Athenian citizen, persuading him to prevent the envoys from reaching the King and thus thwart their plans to harm Athens. Sadocus acted promptly: he arranged for the envoys to be seized as they journeyed through Thrace to their ship and handed them over to the Athenian ambassadors, who took them to Athens. There, the Athenians, fearing the potential harm Aristeus could still bring due to his role in stirring trouble in Potidaea and their territories in Thrace, ordered their execution on the same day without trial. They threw their bodies into a pit as an act of retaliation, recalling how the Lacedaemonians, at the onset of the war, had mercilessly executed and discarded the bodies of Athenian and allied traders seized around Peloponnese, even those of neutral states.

Around this time, late in summer, Ambraciot forces, together with a large number of local barbarian allies, launched an attack on Amphilochian Argos and the surrounding region. Their enmity with Argos had deep roots. The city had been established by Amphilochus, son of Amphiaraus, who, upon returning from the Trojan War and finding matters unsatisfactory at home, founded this city by the Ambracian Gulf, naming it after his homeland. Argos grew to be the most important city in Amphilochia. Much later, facing hard times, the people of Argos invited the Ambraciots, their neighbors, to join their colony, which led the Argives to adopt Greek speech. Eventually, however, the Ambraciots turned against them, seizing control of the city and driving the Argives out. The displaced Argives allied with the Acarnanians, and together they sought help from Athens. Athens responded by sending the general Phormio with thirty ships. Upon arrival, the Athenians took the city by storm, enslaving the Ambraciots, and the Acarnanians and Amphilochians took up shared residence in Argos. This event sparked the alliance between Athens and Acarnania and marked the beginning of Ambraciot hostility toward Argos. During the war, the Ambraciots amassed forces, including Chaonian and neighboring barbarian troops, and mounted an offensive against Argos. They managed to devastate the surrounding lands but were ultimately unable to breach the city itself. Defeated, they returned home, and their allied forces dispersed.

These events brought summer to an end. As winter set in, Athens dispatched twenty ships under the command of Phormio to patrol the Peloponnesian coast from Naupactus, monitoring all naval movement in and out of Corinth and the Gulf of Crisa. Six additional ships were sent under Melesander to Caria and Lycia to collect tribute and prevent Peloponnesian privateers from establishing a base in those waters, which would threaten the merchant routes from Phaselis, Phoenicia, and the nearby regions. However, Melesander's campaign in Lycia met disaster; he was killed in battle, along with a portion of his forces.

That winter, the Potidaeans, now suffering unbearable famine, could no longer hold out against the Athenian siege. Despite repeated invasions by the Peloponnesians into Attica, the Athenians had remained committed to the siege, spending vast resources, nearly two thousand talents. Provisions were utterly exhausted in Potidaea, and desperate acts, including cannibalism, were reported among its citizens. In their dire straits, they approached the Athenian generals Xenophon, Hestiodorus, and Phanomachus with terms for surrender. Observing the toll on their forces in such a vulnerable position and the enormous costs already incurred, the generals agreed to the surrender terms: the Potidaeans, their families, and allies could leave with a few possessions and a small allowance for their journey. They scattered across Chalcidice and other regions as their circumstances allowed.

Upon learning the terms, the Athenians criticized their generals for making concessions without direct instructions, believing Potidaea would have ultimately surrendered unconditionally. Eventually,

Athens sent its own settlers to Potidaea, establishing a new colony there.

Thus concluded the second year of the war, chronicled by Thucydides.

Chapter VIII

The Plataeans listened to Archidamus's offer and withdrew to consult amongst themselves. After deliberating, they returned with the answer that they could not accept his terms. They explained that their loyalty to Athens, which had protected them and held their families, made it impossible to comply without putting themselves in grave danger once the Spartan forces left, as neither the Athenians nor the Thebans could be trusted to respect the neutrality Archidamus proposed. Despite the assurances offered, they could not risk the chance of being overtaken by either side once they were unprotected. In response, Archidamus, seeing no change in their stance, prepared to invest the city.

After a brief period of negotiation, the Spartans proceeded to lay siege to Plataea. They began by constructing a mound against the walls, intending to use it as a platform from which to launch attacks. The Plataeans, however, worked tirelessly to counteract these efforts, building up their own walls and creating obstacles to slow the advance of the mound. Night and day, the Plataean defenders added to their fortifications and prepared to resist, while the Spartans, undeterred, continued the siege. As the mound rose, the Plataeans devised additional tactics to render it useless, digging tunnels beneath it to destabilize the structure and cause it to collapse. The struggle over the mound was prolonged and marked by intense effort on both sides, with the defenders displaying resourcefulness in countering each Spartan move.

Elsewhere that summer, the war continued. In the waters near the Peloponnesian coast, the Athenian commander Phormio led a fleet of twenty ships and managed to secure a significant victory. His naval skills and the discipline of his crews allowed him to outmaneuver a much larger Peloponnesian fleet, resulting in a victory that added to his renown. Phormio's success at sea provided a boost to Athenian morale, as his tactics and boldness inspired confidence in their naval power, offsetting the bitter news of the ongoing siege at Plataea. With his fleet stationed near Naupactus, Phormio maintained control of the area and continued to harass Peloponnesian shipping routes, demonstrating Athens's dominance on the sea despite the challenges they faced on land.

In the north, meanwhile, a separate front of the war unfolded. Sitalces, the Thracian king and Athenian ally, launched a substantial campaign against Macedonia. He sought to enforce his claims over certain territories and exert influence in the region. The Athenians had previously formed an alliance with Sitalces, and his move against Macedonia represented an extension of their strategy to destabilize hostile territories. Sitalces's invasion, though vast and encompassing large numbers of Thracian tribes, ultimately faced difficulties in sustaining momentum, as the Macedonian forces retreated and evaded open confrontation. Although the campaign did not yield a decisive outcome, it served as a reminder of the complexities and geographical reach of the Peloponnesian War, extending beyond the primary Athenian and Peloponnesian rivalry into wider Greek territories.

Thus, the third year of the war saw Athens striving to maintain its influence through sea power and distant alliances, while on the ground, the siege of Plataea reflected the harsh realities and determination of both sides. The Athenians, emboldened by Phormio's successes, looked to their navy as their most formidable asset, while the Plataeans fought for survival against overwhelming odds. The conflict between Sparta and Athens continued to intensify, expanding its reach and impacting regions far beyond their immediate territories.

When they had given Archidamus this message, the Plataeans returned to their city and, after consulting with their people, informed him that they wished to communicate his proposal to the Athenians.

If the Athenians agreed, they would be prepared to accept his terms; meanwhile, they requested a truce, during which he would refrain from ravaging their lands. Archidamus, respecting this appeal, agreed to pause his operations for the time necessary for the Plataean envoys to travel to Athens and return. While awaiting the response, he ordered his troops to cease all ravaging of Plataean territory.

The envoys made their way to Athens, conferred with the Athenian leaders, and returned with the following response for the Plataeans: "The Athenians declare, Plataeans, that they have never in the past, since we became their allies, abandoned us to any enemy. Now, as then, they pledge to stand by us, helping us to the extent of their resources, and they urge us, by the oaths our forefathers swore, to honor the alliance and remain unwavering in loyalty."

With this message delivered, the Plataeans made their decision. They resolved to stand firm beside Athens, despite the likely destruction of their lands and the hardships ahead. Thus, instead of accepting further negotiations, they responded from the walls to Archidamus, stating that it was impossible for them to agree to the Lacedaemonian terms. When he received this answer, Archidamus, seeing no alternative, performed a solemn appeal to the gods and heroes of Plataea: "You gods and heroes of this land, be witnesses that we did not come here as the original aggressors, nor are we acting out of violation of our common oath. We entered this territory only after the Plataeans abandoned their duty to our shared pledge, which was once offered to you before the battle with the Medes and blessed by you. Now, we act not out of malice, but out of rightful vengeance against those who have broken faith. Grant that the Plataeans be justly punished for their transgressions and that those who seek redress be favored in their cause."

With this invocation to divine justice, Archidamus ordered his forces to prepare for a full siege. They began by erecting a palisade around the town, crafted from the fruit trees they had felled, encircling Plataea to block any escape or resupply. Next, they undertook the construction of a massive mound against the city walls, hoping that, with the vast numbers involved, they could complete the work quickly and breach the fortifications. To construct this mound, they harvested timber from Mount Cithaeron, layering the wood in a lattice structure to create a stable framework, and then packed it with earth, stones, and whatever materials could aid in its stability and height.

For seventy continuous days and nights, the Peloponnesians worked in shifts, some resting and eating while others toiled. The Lacedaemonian commanders supervised each contingent to ensure that progress continued without pause. Meanwhile, the Plataeans, watching the mound grow higher day by day, developed their own countermeasures. They erected a wooden wall atop their existing fortifications, packing the interior with bricks gathered from nearby buildings. Timbers reinforced this structure, binding it to prevent collapse as it rose. Additionally, they draped the wall in hides and skins to shield the woodwork from fire and to allow the workers to defend the fortification safely. Thus, as the Peloponnesian mound grew, so too did the Plataean defenses.

Recognizing, however, that a direct assault from the mound could still threaten them, the Plataeans devised a further tactic. They secretly dismantled part of the wall where the mound leaned against it, hauling away the earth that had accumulated. By bringing the mound's materials into the city, they intended to slow its advance, ensuring that each step the enemy gained was met with an equal measure of rSeeing their efforts stymied, the Peloponnesians filled the gap in the mound by packing it with clay wrapped in reed matting, creating a dense, stable barrier that could not easily be removed like loose soil. The Plataeans, undeterred, adapted their strategy again. They began to dig a tunnel from inside the city, calculating the direction to burrow beneath the mound. Once they had reached under it, they began surreptitiously removing its material from below. For a time, the Peloponnesians had no idea their mound was slowly being undermined. Although they continued to add material from above, they found it mysteriously failing to grow as expected, as the removed soil caused it to settle and collapse from beneath.

But fearing that even these efforts might eventually prove insufficient against the overwhelming enemy numbers, the Plataeans conceived yet another defensive measure. They halted the construction of their original wall facing the mound and instead built a crescent-shaped wall, extending from each end of the original wall back into the city, forming a secondary line of defense. This inner crescent was designed to create a fallback position if the main wall was breached. It would force the enemy to restart their efforts, building a new mound if they wished to breach this inner fortification, all while exposing themselves to missile fire from both flanks as they advanced inward.

As the mound continued to rise, the Peloponnesians brought forward siege engines, some aimed specifically at the great building the Plataeans had erected to counter the mound. One such engine, deployed atop the mound, struck the wall with great force, breaking down a substantial section and alarming the Plataeans. In response, they deployed a new defense: they suspended large wooden beams by long iron chains from poles extended over the wall. Whenever a battering ram threatened a particular spot, they would hoist the beam high and, timing it just right, release it so it would swing down with tremendous momentum, crashing into the nose of the battering ram and rendering it useless.

Thus, the Plataeans continued to fend off the enemy's advances, using both ingenuity and determination to hold their city against the odds.

Following the failure of their engines and the setbacks from the Plataeans' countermeasures, the Peloponnesians recognized that their existing tactics were insufficient to capture the city. Seeking an alternative approach, they decided to try setting the city ablaze. They thought that with the help of a favorable wind, they might destroy the town by fire, sparing themselves the cost and time required for a prolonged siege. The Peloponnesians gathered massive amounts of brushwood and piled it against the walls, filling the area between the mound and the city wall. They then heaped the faggots as far into the city as possible from their elevated position on the mound. When the wood was in place, they ignited it with sulfur and pitch, unleashing a fierce blaze that grew into one of the most intense fires ever witnessed from human action, far exceeding anything the Plataeans could have anticipated.

This fire presented a severe threat to the Plataeans, blocking much of the city and posing an almost inescapable danger. The Peloponnesians hoped that a strong wind would fan the flames further into the town, making escape impossible. Yet, as the flames roared, a fortunate turn of weather—a sudden downpour accompanied by thunder—doused the fire, saving the city from imminent destruction. Thus, the Plataeans narrowly escaped the catastrophe, which could have decimated the town had the weather favored the enemy's hopes.

After the failure of their fiery assault, the Peloponnesians resigned themselves to the prospect of a blockade. They left a portion of their forces on-site while dismissing the remainder, and they set to work constructing a wall of circumvallation around Plataea. To accomplish this, they divided sections of the construction among the contingents from different allied cities, digging a ditch on both the inner and outer sides of the wall, and using the excavated soil and materials to form bricks. By the time of the rising of the star Arcturus, the wall was complete. They then stationed sufficient forces to man half of the wall, while the Boeotians took responsibility for the other half, and the rest of the Peloponnesian forces returned to their cities.

Earlier, anticipating the prolonged siege, the Plataeans had sent their non-combatants—women, children, the elderly, and those not fit for fighting—to Athens. Left within the city were four hundred Plataean citizens, eighty Athenians, and a hundred and ten women who were tasked with baking bread for the defenders. This was the entirety of the besieged, as no other individuals, whether free or enslaved, were present within the walls. Thus, the arrangements for the blockade of Plataea were set, initiating a long and grueling siege that would test the endurance and resolve of those trapped inside.

That summer, in coordination with their campaign against Plataea, the Athenians launched a parallel offensive against the Chalcidians in the Thracian region and the Bottiaeans. Commanded by Xenophon, son of Euripides, along with two fellow generals, they marched with two thousand heavy infantry and two hundred cavalry. Timing their arrival to coincide with the ripening of the corn, they hoped not only to destroy crops but also to persuade Spartolus, a city in Bottiaea, to surrender through internal support from sympathetic factions. However, opposing factions in the city had secretly requested aid from nearby Olynthus, which quickly responded by sending a garrison of heavy infantry and other troops.

These reinforcements soon confronted the Athenians outside Spartolus. In the initial engagement, the Athenian heavy infantry managed to push back the Chalcidian heavy infantry and their allies, who then retreated into the city. However, the Chalcidian cavalry and light troops successfully countered the Athenian horse and light infantry. Boosted shortly afterward by the arrival of additional targeteers from Crusis and further reinforcements from Olynthus, the Chalcidian forces, emboldened by their initial success, launched a renewed assault. They pressed the Athenians, who were retreating to their baggage divisions. The Chalcidians employed hit-and-run tactics, advancing whenever the Athenians showed signs of weakness, but retreating under cover of missile fire whenever the Athenians pressed forward. The Chalcidian cavalry, riding at will, eventually broke the Athenian lines, causing a rout and pursuing them over a considerable distance. The survivors sought refuge in Potidaea, later recovering their dead under a truce, and returned to Athens with the remnants of their force, having lost four hundred and thirty men, including all their generals. Meanwhile, the victorious Chalcidians and Bottiaeans erected a trophy, collected their own dead, and dispersed to their respective cities.

Later that summer, the Ambraciots and Chaonians, intent on subjugating all of Acarnania and detaching it from Athenian influence, convinced the Lacedaemonians to dispatch a fleet and a thousand heavy infantry. They argued that a combined assault by land and sea would make it impossible for the Acarnanians to mobilize effectively. They envisioned capturing Zacynthus and Cephallenia in quick succession, thereby obstructing the Athenian cruises around the Peloponnesian coast. This campaign even held the potential for capturing Naupactus, a strategic point for Athenian control. In response, the Lacedaemonians sent a small fleet under Cnemus, the high admiral, with the heavy infantry and ordered the fleet to assemble promptly at Leucas.

The Corinthians, driven by their close ties with the Ambraciots (a Corinthian colony), showed particular enthusiasm, while ships from Corinth, Sicyon, Leucas, Anactorium, and Ambracia gathered at Leucas. Cnemus, taking advantage of Phormio, the Athenian commander stationed off Naupactus, successfully maneuvered his thousand heavy infantry past Athenian blockades into the Gulf, immediately preparing for the land campaign. His Hellenic forces comprised Ambraciots, Leucadians, Anactorians, and the thousand Peloponnesians, with additional barbarian forces, including a thousand Chaonians led by Photys and Nicanor. Joining them were Thesprotians, Molossians, Atintanians led by Sabylinthus, the guardian of their young king Tharyps, and Paravaeans led by King Oroedus, along with a thousand Orestians under Oroedus' command on behalf of King Antichus.

Additionally, a thousand Macedonians, sent by Perdiccas in secret from the Athenians, arrived late and did not participate in the initial expedition. Without waiting for the Corinthian fleet, Cnemus pressed on through Amphilochian Argos, sacking the unfortified village of Limnaea before advancing towards Stratus, the Acarnanian capital. They were confident that if Stratus fell, the rest of Acarnania would quickly follow.

The Acarnanians, faced with a dual threat—an invasion by land and an approaching fleet from the sea—chose not to organize a centralized defense. Instead, each town's residents remained to defend their own homes, while they sent an urgent appeal for aid to Phormio. However, Phormio explained that, with a Corinthian fleet on the brink of departure, he could not leave Naupactus vulnerable. Meanwhile, the Peloponnesian and allied forces advanced on Stratus in three distinct divisions. They planned to set up camp near the city and attempt an assault on its walls if negotiations failed.

Their march formation was strategic: the Chaonians and other barbarian troops held the center, flanked on the right by the Leucadians, Anactorians, and their followers, and on the left by Cnemus leading the Peloponnesians and Ambraciots. However, each division kept a significant distance from the others, sometimes even losing visual contact. The Hellenic divisions proceeded cautiously, aiming to set up a secure camp. In contrast, the Chaonians, known for their reputation as fierce warriors among the continental tribes, grew overconfident. Without pausing to establish a camp, they surged forward with the rest of the barbarian troops, hoping to capture Stratus by assault and claim the victory as their own.

The Stratians, observing this overextension of the Chaonians and realizing the impact their defeat would have on the morale of the Hellenic divisions behind, prepared an ambush. They stationed troops around the town's outskirts and, as the Chaonians advanced, attacked them up close from both the city and the ambuscades. Panic quickly swept through the Chaonians, leading to heavy casualties. Seeing their comrades retreat, the other barbarian forces also turned and fled. Due to the separation between divisions, neither the Peloponnesian nor the Leucadian contingents were initially aware of the battle; they assumed they were still marching toward the encampment.

When the fleeing barbarians suddenly broke through their lines, the Hellenic divisions opened ranks to let them pass, then consolidated their forces and held their ground, staying put for the remainder of the day. The Stratians, lacking the full support of the other Acarnanians, refrained from engaging in a direct assault. Instead, they relied on their skill with slings, harassing the Peloponnesians from a distance. This form of long-range assault severely troubled the Peloponnesians, who found it difficult to move without their armor, while the Acarnanians excelled in this type of combat.

When night fell, Cnemus quickly withdrew his forces, retreating to the river Anapus, about nine miles from Stratus. The following day, he arranged a truce to recover his dead. Then, with reinforcements from the friendly city of Oeniadae, he moved his forces back there, ensuring safety before the Acarnian reinforcements could arrive. Each contingent soon dispersed, returning home, while the Stratians set up a victory trophy to commemorate their battle with the barbarian forces.

Meanwhile, the fleet from Corinth and other allies in the Crissaean Gulf, intended to support Cnemus and prevent the coastal Acarnanians from aiding their inland counterparts, found itself unable to carry out this mission. Around the same time as the engagement at Stratus, they were intercepted by Phormio and his squadron of twenty Athenian ships stationed at Naupactus. Phormio kept a close watch on the Corinthian fleet as it hugged the coast, waiting for an opportunity to confront them in open waters. However, the Corinthians and their allies had not expected naval combat, having come prepared only to transport troops to Acarnania. Their ships, more suited for carrying soldiers than for battle, were far from ideal for facing the Athenian fleet. Moreover, they did not anticipate that Phormio's twenty ships would dare to engage their forty-seven.

As the Corinthian fleet coasted along the shore, they spotted the Athenian vessels mirroring their movements. When they attempted to cross from Patrae in Achaea to the opposite mainland en route to Acarnania, they again saw the Athenians, this time advancing from Chalcis and the river Evenus to intercept them. The Corinthians attempted a covert night departure, slipping their moorings to avoid detection, but were soon spotted by Phormio's vigilant fleet. Finally, they were forced to face the Athenians in open waters.

The Peloponnesian commanders, each from the contributing states, prepared for the confrontation. The Corinthian leaders, Machaon, Isocrates, and Agatharchidas, organized their fleet into a broad, defensive circle with prows facing outward and sterns inward, encircling their smaller support vessels in the center. They positioned their five fastest ships ready to respond to any point where the Athenians might press an attack.

The Athenians, formed in a tight line, sailed around the Peloponnesian fleet repeatedly, forcing them to shrink their defensive circle with each pass. Phormio had previously instructed his men to feign attacks without fully engaging, waiting for his signal. His strategy relied on unsettling the Peloponnesians, expecting that, unlike troops on land, their ships would eventually lose order, especially if a wind rose from the gulf—a typical occurrence in the early hours. Phormio guessed that the chaotic effect of such a wind, combined with the close maneuvering, would cause the Peloponnesian vessels to collide with each other and disrupt their formation.

When the wind finally came, Phormio's expectations were realized. Hemmed into a narrow area, the Peloponnesian ships faltered, unable to maintain formation as the gusts and waves tossed them against one another and their smaller support craft. This chaos was only worsened by the clashing oars and shouting from crews trying to right their ships, while officers' orders and signals were drowned out by the disorder. Taking advantage of the moment, Phormio gave the signal to attack. The Athenians charged, quickly sinking the ship of one of the enemy's admirals and disabling any vessels they encountered, plunging the Peloponnesian ranks further into confusion. With no hope of rallying, the Peloponnesian fleet retreated to Patrae and Dyme in Achaea.

The Athenians pursued, capturing twelve enemy ships and taking many prisoners. They then sailed to Molycrium, where they erected a trophy on the promontory of Rhium and dedicated one of the captured ships to Poseidon before returning to Naupactus. Meanwhile, the remaining Peloponnesian vessels regrouped and made their way along the coast from Dyme and Patrae to Cyllene, the Eleian dockyard, where Cnemus and the fleet from Leucas, who had been unable to reach Stratus in time, joined them.

The Lacedaemonians, baffled by the defeat, sent commissioners—Timocrates, Bradidas, and Lycophron—to the fleet with orders to regroup and achieve a more favorable outcome in the next engagement, determined not to be chased from the seas by a smaller Athenian force. The commissioners, finding it difficult to accept defeat, were convinced the loss was due to mismanagement rather than any inherent disadvantage in their fleet. They quickly began gathering reinforcements and refitting their ships for another confrontation.

Meanwhile, Phormio sent a message to Athens detailing his victory and warning of the Peloponnesians' renewed preparations, urging them to send reinforcements swiftly as he anticipated another battle soon. Athens responded by dispatching twenty more ships, though these were first diverted to Crete. This detour was at the request of Nicias, a Cretan from Gortys and Athenian ally, who suggested attacking the hostile town of Cydonia, partly to benefit his own allies, the Polichnitans, who were neighbors to the Cydonians. The Athenian fleet sailed to Crete, where they, along with the Polichnitans, laid waste to the lands of Cydonia, but adverse winds and poor weather caused significant delays in reaching Phormio.

While the Athenians were delayed in Crete, the Peloponnesians at Cyllene prepared for battle and moved along the coast to Panormus in Achaea, where their land forces awaited them. Phormio, with his original fleet of twenty ships, followed suit and anchored at Molycrian Rhium, on the Athenian-friendly side of the strait. Across from him, the Peloponnesian fleet of seventy-seven ships anchored near the Achaean Rhium, not far from Panormus. For about a week, the two fleets remained stationed opposite one another, each practicing and readying for battle. Phormio held back from entering the straits, knowing it favored the enemy, while the Peloponnesians hesitated to venture out into open waters after their previous defeat.

However, Cnemus, Brasidas, and the other Peloponnesian commanders were eager to fight before Athenian reinforcements could arrive. Recognizing that the recent loss had shaken their men's confidence, they gathered the troops together to encourage them, saying:

"Peloponnesians, although the recent defeat may cause some to fear this coming battle, there is truly no reason for apprehension. In the last engagement, we were hardly prepared, as our primary goal had been a land expedition rather than naval combat. Moreover, the fates of war worked against us that day, and perhaps a lack of experience contributed to our initial setback. But remember, it was not cowardice that led to our defeat, nor should the spirit of determination, which remains alive within us, be diminished by one unfortunate outcome. It is a mark of true bravery to remain resolute, despite the chance of an unexpected loss.

"Consider that, although we may not yet match the enemy in naval experience, our courage far exceeds theirs. Their expertise might aid them if they had the valor to apply it effectively under pressure. However, a faint heart makes any skill useless in the heat of danger. In the face of fear, presence of mind vanishes, rendering knowledge and skill ineffective. Let us counter their skill with our bravery and turn their complacency from victory into a reason for our triumph. We have the advantage of greater numbers, home waters, and the support of our heavy infantry, while they are far from their allies and accustomed to fighting without such backup. Typically, strength in numbers and better positioning are key to victory.

"Let us also treat our previous mistakes as lessons for the future. Steersmen and sailors, stay focused on your specific duties, without breaking formation or leaving your assigned positions. We, your commanders, will make all preparations necessary and will leave no room for excuses in the case of poor conduct. Those who show bravery will be duly honored, while any who shirk their duty will face the punishment they deserve."

The Peloponnesian commanders rallied their forces in this way. Meanwhile, Phormio, seeing his own men gathering in worried groups and visibly discouraged by the enemy's numbers, felt it was crucial to restore their confidence. He had long instilled in them the idea that no numerical advantage could truly threaten them, and they had come to believe that Athenians need never retreat from any number of Peloponnesian ships. But sensing their spirits faltering now, he gathered them to bolster their resolve and offered the following words:

"I see, men, that the enemy's numbers have made you uneasy, so I have called you together to prevent you from fearing something that is not truly formidable. Remember, the Peloponnesians have already been defeated by us once, and even they don't believe they can match us on equal terms—hence, they've brought so many ships. They rely on their usual confidence in land combat, presuming that it will serve them just as well at sea. But here, on our element, we hold that same advantage; they have no more courage than we do, and each of us excels in the domain where we are experienced. Furthermore, the Lacedaemonians, who impose their rule on their allies for their own prestige, have pushed many of these men into danger unwillingly. Without such compulsion, they would hardly dare a second encounter after their defeat. So don't overestimate their spirit.

"You, by contrast, have the advantage in morale. Your recent victory alone is cause enough for them to fear you, as they likely believe that we would not face them again unless we intended to accomplish something equally remarkable. An opponent relying on sheer numbers often trusts in strength rather than will, while the one who voluntarily faces such odds must draw on deep internal reserves. Thus, the Peloponnesians are more intimidated by our 'recklessness' than they would be by a more 'calculated' force. Many large armaments have been bested by smaller ones due to a lack of skill or courage—both of which we possess in abundance.

"As for the battle itself, I will avoid fighting within the narrow straits and will not sail in there at all. Against a larger, poorly maneuvered force, our smaller, swifter ships need open water, where we can spot the enemy from afar, charge effectively, or retreat if pressed. Cramped spaces make it impossible to flank, break through, or execute the agile tactics that give us the advantage. In such narrow confines, combat turns into a clash of numbers rather than skill. I will make sure we avoid these pitfalls.

"Stay at your posts, alert and attentive to commands, especially given the short distance at which we are eyeing each other. In battle, remember that discipline and silence are vital—qualities that prove valuable in war generally, and especially in naval engagements. Act with the same courage that has carried you before. This fight is critical: to crush the Peloponnesians' hopes at sea and to ease Athens' worries. And remember, you've beaten most of them already, and a defeated force rarely returns with the same conviction."

Phormio's words resonated deeply among his men, rallying their courage and reinforcing their trust in his leadership. Inspired by his confidence and seasoned guidance, they prepared for the encounter with fresh resolve. Meanwhile, the Peloponnesians, observing that the Athenians refused to sail into the gulf and the narrow straits where the larger Peloponnesian fleet held the advantage, devised a strategy to compel Phormio to follow them. At dawn, the Peloponnesians arranged their ships in a tight formation, sailing four abreast. Their aim was to provoke Phormio into a position disadvantageous to his smaller and more agile fleet.

Organizing their ships with careful intent, they moved in the direction of their own coast within the gulf. Their right wing, leading the formation, was reinforced by twenty of their fastest and best-equipped ships. They positioned these in anticipation that, should Phormio interpret their move as an approach toward Naupactus and move to intercept, the Athenians would be forced into a narrow, vulnerable formation along the shoreline. In this position, Phormio's ships would not have the space to maneuver as they usually did in open water. Moreover, the Peloponnesian ships on the right wing could swiftly close in and cut off the Athenian escape, thus isolating and surrounding them with the intent to strike decisively.

As the Peloponnesians had anticipated, Phormio, alarmed at the possibility of an attack on Naupactus—which, at that moment, was practically defenseless—quickly embarked his fleet and sailed along the coast toward the town, his ships strung out in a single file formation along the shore. His ships, closely hugging the coastline, were now exactly where the Peloponnesians had hoped: inside the gulf and within the narrow waters near the shore. Seeing this, the Peloponnesian fleet, already prepared and waiting for such a chance, received the signal to turn in unison. Without hesitation, they tacked sharply and bore down on the Athenians, advancing at full speed to close off the escape routes and to engage their prey in close quarters.

In the ensuing moments of high tension, the eleven leading Athenian vessels managed to break free of the Peloponnesian wing, swiftly moving into open water before the opposing line could fully encircle them. However, the remaining ships in Phormio's formation found themselves caught in the Peloponnesian trap. Hemmed in by the advancing Peloponnesians, they struggled to break free, but with the shore to one side and the Peloponnesians bearing down on them from the other, their situation grew increasingly dire. Several Athenian ships were overtaken and driven ashore, where they became immobilized and vulnerable. The Peloponnesians captured these ships, some by towing them away empty, while others were seized with their crews still aboard, who were either slain or forced to abandon ship by swimming for their lives. In one instance, the Messenians leapt into the sea armed and waded into the fight, boarding the Peloponnesian ships to rescue some of the captured Athenian vessels. These efforts proved successful in saving a few ships, but overall, the Peloponnesians held the upper hand.

So far, the Peloponnesians had the advantage; their strategy had outmaneuvered the Athenians, leaving Phormio's fleet partially disabled. Meanwhile, the Peloponnesian right wing pursued the eleven Athenian ships that had narrowly escaped the ambush and reached open water. These eleven managed to outpace their pursuers, save for one vessel, and reached the safety of Naupactus, where they anchored just off the shore near the temple of Apollo. There, they formed a defensive line, their prows facing outward toward the enemy, ready to repel any further approach. The Peloponnesians, triumphant and emboldened by their success, slowly approached, chanting their victory paean as they closed in on the remaining Athenian ships, anticipating an easy capture.

One Athenian ship, however, lagged behind, pursued by a Leucadian vessel that was out in front of the other Peloponnesian ships. In the harbor, there was a large merchant ship anchored nearby, and the lone Athenian ship deftly maneuvered around it, using it as cover. Seizing an opportune moment, the Athenian ship then swung around sharply, and, catching the pursuing Leucadian off guard, rammed her amidships. The impact dealt a critical blow, sinking the Leucadian vessel swiftly.

The sudden reversal sent a shock through the Peloponnesian ranks. The unexpected sinking of the Leucadian ship sowed confusion and panic among them. Some ships halted abruptly, their crews unsure of how to proceed in the midst of the disruption. Others inadvertently clashed with one another or found themselves dangerously close to the Athenians, whom they had assumed would remain on the defensive. The disorder among the Peloponnesians left them vulnerable to the Athenians' counter-maneuvers. Adding to the chaos, some Peloponnesian ships, unfamiliar with the local waters, ran aground in the shallow areas, further compounding the confusion and breaking the cohesion of their line.

Seizing the moment, the Athenians, reinvigorated by the turn of events, launched a bold counterattack from their defensive positions near the shore. The sudden shift in momentum allowed Phormio's remaining ships to charge the disarrayed Peloponnesian fleet, exploiting the confusion that had taken hold. The Peloponnesians, caught off-guard by the Athenian resurgence, now faced a counteroffensive they had not anticipated, transforming what had seemed a sure victory into a hasty struggle to regain control and escape the reach of the Athenian counterattack.

Thus, the engagement shifted, with the Athenians, once on the defensive, now pressing their advantage, and the Peloponnesians scrambling to extricate themselves from the chaos that Phormio's fleet had unleashed.

With morale boosted by the sudden victory, the Athenians let out a triumphant cheer, and without hesitation, they launched a spirited attack on the disordered Peloponnesians. Already thrown into confusion by their failed assault and clumsy maneuvers, the Peloponnesian fleet hesitated only briefly before breaking formation and fleeing back toward Panormus, the port from which they had originally set out. The Athenians gave swift chase, taking advantage of their enemy's disarray. In the pursuit, they captured six of the Peloponnesian vessels that lagged behind, retaking the Athenian ships that had been initially disabled and towed by the enemy. Some of the fleeing Peloponnesian crews were killed in the pursuit, while others were captured and taken as prisoners.

One of the ships that went down was the Leucadian vessel that had collided with the merchantman. Aboard was the Spartan Timocrates, who, unable to bear the shame of defeat, took his own life just before the vessel sank. His body was later found washed ashore in Naupactus' harbor, a tragic emblem of the day's ferocity.

On their return, the Athenians set up a trophy to commemorate their unexpected victory. They gathered the wreckage of the battle along with the bodies that had drifted to their shore, and then, under a truce, returned the Peloponnesian dead to their commanders. The Peloponnesians, despite their losses, also set up their own trophy, celebrating the initial victory they had achieved in disabling the Athenian ships close to shore. They dedicated a captured Athenian ship at the Achaean Rhium as a symbol of their partial success in the early stages of the encounter.

However, fearing the approach of reinforcements from Athens, the Peloponnesians decided to retreat. All but the Leucadian vessels withdrew, sailing back through the Crissaean Gulf toward Corinth to regroup and avoid further losses. Not long after their retreat, the twenty Athenian ships sent to support Phormio finally arrived at Naupactus, having missed the decisive battle.

With the summer ending and winter approaching, the Peloponnesians docked their fleet in Corinth and the Crissaean Gulf to await the next season. However, Cnemus, Brasidas, and the other Peloponnesian commanders found themselves persuaded by the Megarians to take advantage of Athens' overconfidence in her naval supremacy. The Peloponnesians hatched an audacious plan to raid Piraeus, Athens' vital port, which, due to the Athenians' dominance at sea, had been left unguarded and completely exposed.

The plan called for speed and stealth. Each Peloponnesian rower was instructed to carry only his oar, cushion, and rowlock thong, and to march overland from Corinth to the Athenian side of the sea. Their destination was Megara, where forty ships lay idle in the docks of Nisaea. Once there, they would quickly launch these vessels and make a surprise dash to Piraeus, catching Athens completely off guard. With no Athenian fleet on watch and no signs of an imminent attack, the Peloponnesians believed they could exploit Athens' sense of security. They reasoned that a direct assault would likely go undetected in the port city, which had grown complacent in its supremacy at sea.

As night fell, they moved swiftly to put their daring plan into action. Reaching Nisaea, they launched the ships under cover of darkness and sailed toward the Athenian coast. Yet, despite their initial plan to strike Piraeus itself, they hesitated, likely daunted by the potential risks and the uncertainty of success. Reports suggest that a sudden shift in the wind might also have deterred them. Rather than pressing on to Piraeus, they instead redirected their course toward the part of Salamis facing Megara, where a small Athenian fort guarded the island's waters along with a squadron of three ships stationed to block any vessels attempting to sail in or out of Megara.

In a rapid and unexpected assault, they attacked the fort, catching the garrison off guard. The Peloponnesians seized the three ships, towing them away empty. With Salamis now partially undefended, they spread out, raiding the island and wreaking havoc on its settlements. This surprise strike on Salamis sent shockwaves through the region, serving as a stark reminder to the Athenians of their vulnerability despite their stronghold at sea. The Peloponnesians' daring raid, while falling short of their initial plan to seize Piraeus, marked the close of a dramatic and turbulent campaign season.

Meanwhile, a series of fire signals flashed across the region, spreading alarm to Athens. The city descended into one of the worst panics of the entire war, each quarter of Athens struck by the same terror. In the city itself, people believed that the Peloponnesian fleet had already breached Piraeus, while in Piraeus, residents feared that Salamis had fallen and that the enemy might appear in their harbor at any moment. In truth, had the Peloponnesian forces shown a bit more courage and commitment to their plan, this outcome was indeed possible. Nothing—neither the wind nor the proximity of Athens—would have stood in their way had they pressed on to seize Piraeus.

At the break of dawn, as the scope of the situation became clearer, the Athenians rallied in full force. Ships were hastily launched, and in the midst of a chaotic scramble, soldiers and citizens boarded the fleet to sail to Salamis, determined to defend their territory. Meanwhile, the Athenian forces on land assembled in Piraeus, establishing a vigilant guard against any potential surprise attack.

As the Peloponnesians spotted the Athenian fleet approaching in the distance, they realized that their window for action was rapidly closing. Though they had already pillaged much of Salamis and seized both plunder and captives, they hastily set sail, retreating back to Nisaea. Additionally, their ships, which had long sat idle before being launched for this sudden expedition, were causing them some concern. Many had taken on water, and they feared these aging vessels might not survive another prolonged stint at sea. With these anxieties mounting, they opted for a swift return, carrying off their spoils and the three Athenian ships captured at the Fort of Budorum.

Upon their return to Nisaea, the Peloponnesians docked their vessels and continued the remainder of their journey on foot to Corinth. Meanwhile, when the Athenians arrived at Salamis, they found the enemy already gone. With a mix of relief and frustration, they turned back toward their own shores, realizing how narrowly they had avoided a direct assault on Piraeus. This close call drove home the necessity of greater vigilance in the future. From that point forward, the Athenians fortified their defenses at Piraeus, closing off their harbors and implementing additional security measures, aiming to prevent any further episodes of such vulnerability.

Around the same time, as winter began, Sitalces, son of Teres and king of the Odrysians in Thrace, launched an expedition against Perdiccas, son of Alexander, king of Macedonia, as well as the Chalcidians in Thrace's neighboring regions. His motives were twofold: to enforce an unfulfilled promise from Perdiccas and to keep a commitment he himself had made. Previously, when Perdiccas faced pressure early in the war, he had promised Sitalces that, in exchange for the king's intervention with Athens on his behalf and the prevention of his rival brother Philip's return, he would meet certain terms. However, he had failed to follow through on these promises. Additionally, Sitalces had entered into an alliance with Athens, pledging to put an end to the Chalcidian resistance in Thrace. It was these dual aims that Sitalces sought to achieve in his campaign.

Along with him, Sitalces brought Amyntas, the son of Philip, whom he planned to install on the Macedonian throne, as well as some Athenian envoys who were at his court to discuss these matters, accompanied by Hagnon as their general. The Athenians had agreed to assist him in the campaign against the Chalcidians with a fleet and as many troops as they could assemble.

Sitalces began by rallying his own people, the Odrysians, and then proceeded to call upon the Thracian tribes within his dominion, which spanned the lands between the Haemus and Rhodope mountain ranges, extending as far as the Euxine Sea (Black Sea) and the Hellespont. He then summoned the Getae, who lived beyond the Haemus Mountains, along with other tribes settled to the south of the Danube near the Euxine, all of whom shared similarities with the Scythians and were mounted archers like the Getae.

In addition to these forces, he called upon the fierce hill-dwelling Thracian warriors, known as the Dii, who mostly inhabited the mountainous region of Rhodope. Some of these hillmen came as mercenaries, while others volunteered. Sitalces also drew support from the Agrianes, Laeaeans, and the Paeonian tribes under his rule. These territories stretched to the Paeonian Laeaeans and the river Strymon, which originated in Mount Scombrus and flowed through the lands of the Agrianes and Laeaeans; here, Sitalces' realm ended, and the lands of the independent Paeonian tribes began.

Additionally, bordering the Paeonians were the Triballi—another independent group—and the tribes known as the Treres and Tilataeans. These tribes lived to the north of Mount Scombrus, stretching westward as far as the river Oskius, which shared a source with the rivers Nestus and Hebrus in a vast, rugged mountain range connected to Rhodope. This grand mobilization of forces from varied regions and tribes showcased the extensive reach of Sitalces' influence and highlighted the diverse mix of warriors he brought together for his ambitious campaign against Macedonia and the Chalcidians.

The Odrysian kingdom under Sitalces extended along the coastline from Abdera on the Aegean Sea to the mouth of the Danube on the Black Sea (the Euxine). The seaboard of this empire was so vast that, following the shortest route, a merchant vessel with favorable winds would require four days and four nights to complete the journey. Traveling by land along the shortest path, a fit man could cover the distance from Abdera to the Danube in about eleven days. Such was the kingdom's expanse along the coast.

Inland, the reach of Sitalces' empire extended from Byzantium up to the lands of the Laeaeans and the river Strymon, a journey of thirteen days on foot for a robust traveler. During the reign of Sitalces' successor, Seuthes, the wealth of this empire reached its peak. The annual tribute collected from the various barbarian regions and Hellenic cities under Odrysian control amounted to roughly four hundred talents in gold and silver. Along with this tribute, additional gifts were given in great quantities, including not only gold and silver but also textiles, both plain and embroidered, as well as various goods presented not only to the king but also to Odrysian nobles and high-ranking officials. Unlike the Persian kingdom, where it was customary to bestow gifts upon others, the Odrysians practiced the opposite tradition, where it was expected to request and receive. Not giving when asked was considered more disgraceful than asking and being refused. Though this practice existed elsewhere in Thrace, it was most prevalent and pronounced among the powerful Odrysians, to the extent that little could be achieved without a bribe or present.

This considerable wealth and custom of gift-taking made the Odrysian kingdom a formidable power, one that surpassed all others in Europe between the Ionian Gulf and the Black Sea in terms of revenue and general prosperity. In numbers and military capability, the Odrysians ranked second only to the Scythians, a people known for their overwhelming numbers and martial prowess. The Scythians had such vast manpower that even a united Asian power would struggle to defeat them, though they lagged behind other nations in intelligence and the sophistication of civilized life.

It was this powerful Odrysian empire that Sitalces now prepared to lead into battle. Once all his preparations were in place, he set out with his army for Macedonia, advancing first through his own lands and then over the desolate mountain range of Cercine. This range divided the territories of the Sintians and the Paeonians. Sitalces crossed by a route he had previously carved by clearing timber during an earlier campaign against the Paeonians. Moving through these mountains, with the Paeonian lands to his right and those of the Sintians and Maedians to his left, Sitalces and his forces eventually reached Doberus in Paeonia. Throughout the march, he suffered no notable losses except for a few to illness; on the contrary, he saw his forces grow as many independent Thracians joined him, lured by the prospect of plunder. The army that he brought together for this campaign was said to be an impressive force of about 150,000 troops. Most of these were infantry, though roughly a third were cavalry, primarily contributed by the Odrysians and, to a lesser extent, by the Getae. The fiercest among his infantry were the independent swordsmen from the Rhodope Mountains, while the remainder of the troops, though less skilled, presented a formidable strength due to their sheer numbers.

Gathering in Doberus, Sitalces and his army prepared to descend from the highlands upon Lower Macedonia, where Perdiccas ruled. Although the Lyncestae, Elimiots, and other inland tribes were of Macedonian descent and politically aligned with the Macedonians, they still maintained their own separate governments. The territory now recognized as coastal Macedonia had been acquired by Alexander, father of Perdiccas, and his ancestors, who were originally Temenids from Argos. These Temenids had gradually expanded their territory, driving out other groups: they expelled the Pierians from Pieria, who subsequently settled at Phagres and other locations under Mount Pangaeus, beyond the river Strymon, with the region between Mount Pangaeus and the sea still known as the Pierian Gulf. The Bottiaeans were similarly driven from their homeland of Bottia and later settled near the Chalcidians. Additionally, Alexander's lineage managed to secure a narrow strip of land in Paeonia along the river Axius, extending to Pella and the coast, as well as the Mygdonia region lying between the Axius and the Strymon rivers by ousting the Edonians.

The Eordians were largely eradicated from Eordia, although a small number survived around the area of Physca, and the Almopians were expelled from Almopia. The Macedonians, through these conquests, took possession of regions belonging to neighboring tribes, adding areas like Anthemus, Crestonia, Bisaltia, and parts of central Macedonia, collectively now known as Macedonia. At the time of Sitalces' invasion, Perdiccas, son of Alexander, ruled this entire expanse.

Overwhelmed by the sheer scale of the Thracian invasion, the Macedonians refrained from facing Sitalces' army in open combat and instead retreated into the fortified locations that dotted the region. At this period, Macedonia had relatively few fortifications compared to later times, as most of these defensive structures were constructed under the rule of Archelaus, Perdiccas' son. Archelaus, upon ascending to the throne, not only improved the kingdom's fortifications but also implemented straight roads and significantly developed the kingdom's military capabilities in cavalry, heavy infantry, and other resources, achievements surpassing those of the previous eight kings combined.

With their initial position established in Doberus, the Thracian forces proceeded first to attack areas that had formerly been governed by Philip. They successfully took Idomene by force, while towns like Gortynia, Atalanta, and several others surrendered willingly, likely out of loyalty to Philip's son, Amyntas, who accompanied Sitalces. The Thracian army then besieged Europus but, failing to capture it, moved on to devastate other regions of Macedonia, specifically those lying westward from Pella and Cyrrhus. They did not venture farther south into Bottiaea and Pieria, instead focusing their efforts on ravaging Mygdonia, Crestonia, and Anthemus.

The Macedonian forces, unable to match the Thracian army's numbers, did not even contemplate engaging them with infantry forces. Instead, they harassed the Thracians in small skirmishes using their cavalry, bolstered by allied reinforcements from the interior regions. These Macedonian horsemen, heavily armored with cuirasses and highly skilled in combat, managed to disrupt the Thracian forces wherever they struck, causing significant damage in localized charges. However, the Macedonian cavalry soon recognized the peril of becoming entangled within the dense ranks of the Thracian masses. This risk led them to cease their assaults, as they judged their strength insufficient to make a decisive impact against the overwhelming numbers of the Thracian army.

While Sitalces was still in the field, he opened negotiations with Perdiccas, focusing on the issues that had initially prompted his campaign. However, it soon became clear that the Athenians, having doubted his commitment to the venture, had not sent the fleet they had promised. Although they did dispatch gifts and representatives, they failed to provide substantial reinforcements. Frustrated but determined, Sitalces redirected a large portion of his forces toward the Chalcidians and Bottiaeans, besieging them within their walls and systematically ravaging their lands. As his army swept across these regions, the communities to the south, including the Thessalians, Magnetes, and other Thessalian-controlled tribes, along with the Hellenes extending as far south as Thermopylae, grew increasingly apprehensive. They feared the massive Thracian army might press further and prepared accordingly. Similar concerns spread among the independent Thracian tribes beyond the Strymon River to the north, such as the Panaeans, Odomanti, Droi, and Dersaeans. Even among the Hellenes who were hostile to Athens, there was talk that Sitalces, as Athens' ally, might extend his campaign southward against them.

Despite holding a formidable position in Chalcidice, Bottice, and parts of Macedonia and inflicting substantial damage upon these regions, Sitalces gradually realized that his primary objectives remained unmet. Moreover, his army, now stretched thin across a foreign land, faced growing shortages in provisions and struggled with the increasingly harsh winter conditions. These difficulties prompted Sitalces to reconsider his course. At the urging of his nephew and highest-ranking officer, Seuthes, son of Spardacus, Sitalces decided to retreat. Unbeknownst to him, Seuthes had been covertly swayed by Perdiccas, who had promised him his sister Stratonice's hand in marriage along with a generous dowry if he persuaded Sitalces to withdraw. Thus, after a campaign lasting thirty days—eight of which were spent in Chalcidice—Sitalces led his army back to Thrace. True to his word, Perdiccas later fulfilled his promise, giving Stratonice to Seuthes. This concluded the ambitious but ultimately inconclusive expedition of Sitalces.

During the same winter, following the dispersal of the Peloponnesian fleet, Phormio and the Athenian forces stationed in Naupactus undertook an expedition along the Acarnanian coast. They sailed to Astacus, disembarked, and marched inland with four hundred Athenian heavy infantry and four hundred Messenians. Their mission was to secure strategic loyalty, which they achieved by expelling suspected traitors from towns such as Stratus and Coronta and reinstating Cynes, son of Theolytus, as the ruler of Coronta. However, facing unfavorable conditions, they decided against advancing on Oeniadae, the only town in Acarnania still hostile to them. Winter's wet weather, combined with the unique geography of the region, made a campaign against Oeniadae nearly impossible. The Achelous River, originating from Mount Pindus and flowing through Dolopia, the Agraean and Amphilochian territories, and finally the Acarnanian plains, converges with the sea near Oeniadae. Here it forms marshy lakes, rendering the terrain impassable for an army in winter.

Opposite Oeniadae lay a cluster of small, uninhabited islands known as the Echinades. Positioned close to the river's mouth, these islands were steadily being connected to the mainland by the Achelous' silt deposits, a process that had already linked some islands to the coast and seemed likely to continue. The powerful current of the Achelous, with its deep and turbulent waters, carried sediment that accumulated around the islands. Due to their irregular positioning, which prevented a direct flow into the sea, the islands acted as natural barriers, trapping the sediment. This formation story lent itself to an ancient legend concerning Alcmaeon, son of Amphiaraus. According to the tale,

Alcmaeon, haunted by the guilt of his mother's murder, was instructed by Apollo to seek refuge in a land that had not been exposed to the sun or existed at the time of his crime. Eventually, he noticed the newly formed land around the Achelous, deemed it untainted by his past, and chose to settle there. In time, he established a settlement that his son Acarnan would eventually rule, thereby giving the region its name.

After securing what they could in Acarnania, Phormio and the Athenian force returned to Naupactus. With the coming of spring, they set sail for Athens, bringing back the captured ships and exchanging prisoners taken in the previous battles on a man-for-man basis. Thus, the winter ended, and with it, the third year of the war, as chronicled by Thucydides.

Book III

Chapter IX

The next summer, as the grain was nearing harvest, the Peloponnesian forces and their allies once more invaded Attica, under the leadership of Archidamus, son of Zeuxidamus, king of the Lacedaemonians. They set up camp and began ravaging the lands, but as in previous years, the Athenian cavalry took every opportunity to harass them. The Athenians, where terrain allowed, kept the Peloponnesian light-armed troops from advancing close to the city and restricted their movement, thereby limiting the damage they could inflict on the immediate surroundings of Athens. After exhausting their provisions, the invaders dispersed, each contingent returning to its respective city.

No sooner had the Peloponnesians withdrawn than news reached Athens of a rebellion brewing on Lesbos. All of Lesbos, save for the city of Methymna, had risen against Athenian control. The Lesbians had actually intended to revolt even before the war began, but the Lacedaemonians, wary of entanglements at the time, had declined their request. Now, however, facing increased pressure, the Lesbians were forced to revolt sooner than they had originally planned. While still finalizing their harbor fortifications, preparing ships, and completing walls, they were also engaged in gathering archers, grain, and other supplies from the Pontus region. It was then that the city's rivals—the Tenedians, who harbored long-standing enmity, the Methymnians, and some dissidents within Mytilene itself loyal to Athens—tipped off the Athenians. They informed Athens that the Mytilenians were aiming to bring the whole island under their control and that their military preparations were in collaboration with the Boeotians, their ethnic kin, and the Lacedaemonians, as part of a plan for an imminent revolt. They warned Athens that unless immediate action was taken, the city could lose control over the strategically valuable island of Lesbos.

Athens, however, was under immense strain, burdened by the devastating plague and by the ongoing war, which had only intensified. Reluctant to believe that a core ally like Lesbos could so openly betray them, the Athenians at first dismissed the reports, partly influenced by their own hope that it was simply a rumor. However, they decided to send an embassy to Mytilene to investigate and persuade the city to abandon the unification of Lesbos and halt its military buildup. The embassy returned unsuccessful, finding the Mytilenians unmoved by their arguments. Alarmed by this confirmation, the Athenians realized they needed to act decisively. Hastily, they dispatched a fleet of forty ships that had been originally prepared for a circumnavigation of Peloponnese. This force was placed under the command of Cleippides, son of Deinias, and two other commanders. The Athenians had received intelligence that a grand festival honoring Apollo at Malea, outside Mytilene, was soon to be held, drawing large gatherings of people from the city. They calculated that, by making swift progress, they might catch the Mytilenians off guard while the population was occupied with the festival. The orders were clear: if their surprise attack succeeded, all would be well; but if the Mytilenians had been forewarned and thwarted the attempt, the fleet was to demand that they surrender their ships and dismantle their walls. Should the Mytilenians refuse, Athens would declare open war.

The fleet promptly set sail, while the Athenians detained ten Mytilenian triremes that had been serving in the Athenian fleet under the terms of their alliance, placing the crews under arrest. Despite Athens' precautions, a Mytilenian managed to slip out of the city, crossing over to Euboea and then making his way to Geraestus, where he found a merchant vessel on the verge of departure. He boarded the ship and, sailing with great speed, arrived in Mytilene three days after setting out from Athens. Receiving his warning in time, the Mytilenians canceled the festival at Malea and took urgent steps to bolster their defenses. They placed barricades around the unfinished portions of their walls and reinforced the defenses around the harbor to guard against an imminent Athenian assault.

With this rapid mobilization, the Mytilenians were able to prepare for the arrival of the Athenian fleet, setting the stage for the beginning of a new and turbulent chapter in the war, as Lesbos attempted to break free from the Athenian sphere of influence.

When the Athenians arrived and saw that the Mytilenians had indeed been alerted to their plans, the generals issued their demands. The Mytilenians, however, refused to comply, and hostilities soon broke out. Caught off guard and forced into war without the time or resources to prepare, the Mytilenians initially attempted a defense by sailing out with their fleet to confront the Athenians just outside the harbor. They managed a brief show of resistance, but were ultimately driven back by the superior Athenian fleet. Realizing that they could not sustain a confrontation, the Mytilenians immediately sought to negotiate, hoping to reach an agreement that might at least cause the Athenians to withdraw their forces temporarily. The Athenian generals, uncertain if they could successfully subdue the entire island of Lesbos, accepted the offer to negotiate, and an armistice was arranged.

Under the terms of the temporary truce, the Mytilenians sent a delegation to Athens, including one of the informants who now regretted his role in exposing Mytilene's plans to revolt. The envoys aimed to plead the innocence of the Mytilenians' intentions and persuade the Athenians to recall their fleet. Yet the Mytilenians, fearing a harsh response from Athens, did not rely solely on diplomatic appeals; they discreetly sent another galley to Lacedaemon, hoping to secure military aid from Sparta. The Athenian fleet, stationed at Malea to the north of Mytilene, did not detect this clandestine mission.

The Mytilenian envoys endured a challenging voyage across open waters to reach Lacedaemon, where they began negotiating for Spartan support. Meanwhile, the Mytilenian envoys to Athens returned without achieving any favorable outcome, and it became clear that Athens had no intention of recalling its fleet or forgiving the island's rebellion. Faced with the failure of their diplomatic mission, Mytilene and the rest of Lesbos, save for the loyal Methymnians, formally entered into open hostilities. Mytilene now gathered forces from the island and prepared to mount a serious defense. The Methymnians, along with a small group of allies from Imbros, Lemnos, and other cities still aligned with Athens, joined the Athenians against Mytilene.

In an initial engagement, the Mytilenians launched a full-scale sortie against the Athenian encampment, resulting in a fierce battle. Though the Mytilenians managed to gain a slight upper hand, they did not have the confidence to hold their ground overnight and withdrew back within their walls. After this clash, the Mytilenians became more cautious, preferring to bide their time in hopes that reinforcements from the Peloponnesian League might soon arrive to support their cause. Their morale was bolstered when two envoys, Meleas, a Lacedaemonian, and Hermaeondas, a Theban, arrived at last. Though they had set out before the insurrection began, they had been delayed and only now managed to slip into Mytilene by sea after the recent battle. Upon arrival, they advised the Mytilenians to send another delegation to Sparta to reinforce their plea for aid, a suggestion the Mytilenians promptly acted upon.

Meanwhile, the Athenians, observing the lack of action from the Mytilenians after their initial sortie, felt emboldened. They called upon their allied forces, who responded swiftly, encouraged by the Mytilenians' evident hesitation and lack of vigor. The Athenians then moved their fleet to a new position south of the city, establishing fortified camps on both sides of Mytilene, effectively initiating a siege. With both harbors blockaded, the Mytilenians found themselves cut off from the sea. However, the Mytilenians, along with the rest of Lesbos now united with them in revolt, maintained control over the countryside, while the Athenians held a limited area around their camps and used Malea as their naval station and market.

While this conflict persisted in Mytilene, Athens also launched a separate campaign during the same summer. They sent thirty ships to raid the Peloponnesian coast under Asopius, son of the esteemed general Phormio. The Acarnanians, who had previously allied with Phormio, specifically requested a commander from his family. Asopius' fleet raided the shores of Laconia, but he soon dispatched the majority of his ships back to Athens, choosing to continue with only twelve vessels to Naupactus. There, he assembled a land force with the Acarnanians and launched an expedition against Oeniadae, his fleet moving along the river Achelous while his army devastated the surrounding lands. When the defenders showed no signs of yielding, Asopius released the land forces and sailed on to Leucas. However, while making an assault on Nericus, he was ambushed by local defenders with support from coastal guards, resulting in his death and the loss of most of his forces. The Athenians recovered the bodies under truce and withdrew to their ships.

Thus, the war in Mytilene continued through the winter, with Athens tightening its siege and the Mytilenians anxiously awaiting aid from Sparta.

The Mytilenian envoys, instructed by the Lacedaemonians to come to Olympia so the rest of the allies could hear their case, awaited the opportunity to present their speech following the festival, during the Olympiad in which the Rhodian Dorieus achieved his second victory. Addressing the Lacedaemonians and their allies, the envoys began:

"Lacedaemonians and allies, we are well aware of the established opinion among the Hellenes: those who revolt in times of war and abandon their previous allies are often welcomed by new allies only for their potential utility, while generally being regarded as traitors to their former friends. This judgment may indeed be just when the revolt is unfounded—where there is harmony in policy, mutual interests, and balanced strength. Yet our case with the Athenians is far different. We seek not only alliance with you but also understanding of our motives for taking this step in a time of conflict, despite the seeming honors Athens bestowed on us during peace.

"In requesting your alliance, we are compelled to speak with honesty, for we know that no lasting friendship or stable alliance is possible between parties unless they share a foundation of mutual trust and understanding. Without this harmony of purpose, misunderstandings will breed conflicting conduct, leading only to discord. Our alliance with Athens began at a time when you Lacedaemonians withdrew from the Persian War, while the Athenians remained to continue the struggle. Back then, we joined them not for any conquest of the Hellenes, but to liberate Greece from the threat of Persia. For as long as Athens led us honorably, we were willing allies. But when we saw them shift their ambitions from resistance against the Mede to a desire for domination over their allies, our confidence was shaken, and our suspicions aroused.

"We were not alone in this. Yet, lacking the unity or organization to effectively defend ourselves due to the influence and votes of many of the confederates who were subjugated, only we and the Chians were able to maintain a semblance of independence, contributing contingents while still technically free. Yet trust in Athens as a leader became difficult; for it was clear they would not hesitate to reduce all who once stood beside them to subjects, should they acquire the power. We had reason to believe we might one day face this same fate.

"Had each state maintained its independence, perhaps we would have been assured they'd refrain from such acts. But when they began enslaving the majority, leaving only us as equals, we became an anomaly—a reminder of the freedom that once existed. As Athens grew in strength, our position of solitary independence became an irritation to them, while our resources became increasingly inadequate to defend ourselves against their rising power.

"This disparity introduced an inherent risk. The only secure foundation for any alliance is a balance of power, where neither side can easily impose its will without consequence. With the Athenians treating us equally for now, they did so only because they had calculated that political maneuvering and persuasive rhetoric would serve their ambitions more effectively than brute force. As long as we remained nominally independent, they could lead the larger powers against the smaller states, gradually stripping them of allies. By the time they would eventually confront us, their empire would be firmly established.

"Moreover, our navy has long been a point of unease for them; they feared that our fleet might one day join with yours or another power, challenging their supremacy. Only the careful relations we maintained with the commons of Athens and their shifting leadership preserved our freedom. Yet we recognized that, if not for the outbreak of this war, we could not have held our independence for much longer, considering what we saw happening to others around us.

"We appeal to you now, not because we seek revenge or wish to trade one alliance for another lightly, but because we believe this is the only way we can preserve our city and our freedom. Our motives are rooted in self-preservation and a desire for a fair and balanced alliance, one that respects our sovereignty rather than seeks to suppress it. We ask you to consider our plight and grant us a place among your allies, for we believe we have as much at stake in this war as you do, and that our cause aligns with the greater good of all Hellenes who value their freedom over submission."

This speech laid out the Mytilenians' reasoning for their defection, hoping to secure the trust and support of the Lacedaemonians and their allies. Their appeal focused on Athens' shift from liberator to oppressor, a transformation that left them little choice but to seek new allies who would respect their independence and share their values.

The Mytilenian envoy continued, addressing the Lacedaemonians and their allies with earnest appeal:

"Consider this, Lacedaemonians and allies: how could we genuinely place our trust in such a forced alliance? We joined them against our natural instincts; for fear in war made them court us, while in peace it was fear that held us in submission. Any true friendship was replaced by mutual apprehension; we remained in their alliance not out of mutual respect but out of necessity, bound more by fear than by loyalty. In such a precarious arrangement, the party that first found a glimmer of hope or the possibility of escape would inevitably break faith. To reproach us for taking the initiative to free ourselves, rather than waiting to see if they would act against us, is to misunderstand our plight. If we were in a position to counter their ambitions and withstand their tactics, we wouldn't need to be under their rule at all. They always had the liberty of offense; we must now claim the liberty of defense.

"These, Lacedaemonians, are the reasons for our decision to revolt—sufficient, we believe, to explain our actions and to alert us to our own immediate danger. We sought refuge long ago, even while peace lasted, but were rejected. Now, upon the invitation from Boeotia, we have seized the chance and revolted—against Athens, yes, but also for the greater Hellenic cause. We could not stand by and assist Athens in the oppression of our fellow Hellenes, nor wait until they finally subjugated us. Though our uprising has come about hastily and without thorough preparation, this very urgency calls for your support; it is vital for you to accept us as allies and to send swift assistance. By doing so, you not only demonstrate loyalty to your friends but also gain a tactical advantage over your enemies. Never has there been a moment as opportune as this.

"The Athenians are weakened by disease and drained by the war. Their ships are either patrolling your coastlines or engaged here in the blockade against us. Should you press forward with a combined assault on both land and sea this summer, they will find it nearly impossible to muster a sufficient defense. Either they will abandon their blockade or be forced to divide their fleet to defend their territory, weakening themselves further.

"Do not regard this as a distant problem that need not concern you. Lesbos may seem far, yet we are a strategically essential ally in this war. Contrary to popular belief, the conflict will not be won within the walls of Attica but in the lands that sustain it. Athens draws her strength from her allied cities; without their contributions, her power crumbles. If we are reduced, the Athenian alliance will be stronger than ever; no other state would dare to rebel, and our own considerable resources would bolster their ranks. Worse yet, we would suffer a fate even harsher than those already enslaved. But if you offer us timely support, you gain not only an ally with a formidable navy, addressing your current lack, but also a foothold to encourage others to break free from Athenian rule.

"Show yourselves, then, as the liberators of Hellas, and you will find the tide turning in your favor. By stepping forward, you dispel any notion that Lacedaemon fails to support those willing to defy Athens. In essence, you will rally the allies to your side and gain the advantage in this struggle. Let this moment not be wasted; seize the opportunity, and together we shall make a stand for true freedom."

Thus, with impassioned words, the Mytilenians appealed to the Lacedaemonians, urging them to grasp the moment and solidify their role as liberators in the eyes of all Hellas. Their plea emphasized the strategic significance of Lesbos and promised to sway the course of the war if they were aided in their revolt against Athenian oppression.

The Mytilenian envoy, with earnest words, concluded his appeal to the Lacedaemonians and their allies:

"Show the Hellenes that their faith in you is not misplaced, and honor the protection of Olympian Zeus under whose temple we now stand as suppliants. Grant us your alliance and defend us, the Mytilenians, who are willing to risk everything for a cause that benefits not only ourselves but all who would be freed from Athenian oppression. Do not abandon us to our fates, where our loss would signify a greater harm to all Hellas if you refuse us aid. Be the steadfast allies we and the other Hellenes believe you to be."

The fervent appeal struck a chord with the Lacedaemonians and their confederates. After listening to the Mytilenians, they decided to take action in their favor. The Lesbians were accepted into the Lacedaemonian alliance, and it was agreed that an invasion of Attica would be organized. The Lacedaemonians issued orders for all their allies to gather at the Isthmus as quickly as possible, with two-thirds of their forces prepared to join the march. The Lacedaemonians arrived first at the Isthmus and began constructing devices to transport their ships across the narrow land bridge from Corinth to the Athenian side, aiming for a coordinated assault by both sea and land.

However, the enthusiasm of the Lacedaemonians was not matched by that of their confederates. Many of the allies were slow to respond, preoccupied with the harvest season and wearied by the frequent calls for expeditions. This delay in assembling forces slowed their preparations considerably.

Meanwhile, the Athenians had learned of these developments and recognized that the enemy's plans were fueled by a belief that Athens had been significantly weakened. Determined to counter this perception and display their strength, the Athenians decided to take action without drawing on the forces already engaged in the blockade of Lesbos. They manned a hundred ships, crewed by Athenians except for the knights, the Pentacosiomedimni, and the resident aliens. This fleet then sailed to the Isthmus, where they demonstrated their naval power by launching raids along the coast of the Peloponnese at will, proving their continued capability to project force.

This bold maneuver took the Lacedaemonians by surprise. Seeing the Athenian fleet so active and undeterred, they began to doubt the Mytilenians' claims and the extent of Athens' supposed vulnerability. The absence of their allies, compounded by reports that the Athenian fleet had been raiding Spartan lands, further frustrated the Lacedaemonians, who decided to abandon their plans and return home.

Following this, they resolved to send a separate fleet to Lesbos to aid the Mytilenians. They ordered a total of forty ships to be assembled from their allied cities, appointing Alcidas, their high admiral, to lead this expedition. Meanwhile, the Athenian fleet of a hundred ships, seeing the Lacedaemonians withdraw, also returned to Athens.

This period saw Athens at the peak of her naval strength. When the war had begun, she had perhaps an even greater number of first-rate ships in commission at one time. A hundred ships were then designated to guard Attica, Euboea, and Salamis; another hundred circled Peloponnese, while others were stationed at Potidaea and various other posts, totaling around two hundred and fifty ships engaged in active service in a single summer. This substantial mobilization, alongside the campaign at Potidaea, exerted a considerable strain on Athenian finances. The siege of Potidaea alone required significant resources, with a force of three thousand heavy infantry stationed there, each soldier drawing a daily allowance of two drachmae—one for himself and another for his servant. This expense was maintained until the siege's conclusion, despite sixteen hundred men under Phormio having departed earlier. Furthermore, the ships involved in these efforts were also compensated at the same rate, leading to a heavy initial drain on Athens' financial reserves. This marked the largest and most resource-intensive fleet the city had ever deployed.

Around the time the Lacedaemonians gathered at the Isthmus, the Mytilenians, joined by their mercenaries, attempted a land assault on Methymna, hoping to capture it through inside assistance. However, their assault failed, and they withdrew, moving on to the towns of Antissa, Pyrrha, and Eresus. At these locations, they focused on securing and reinforcing defenses, building up the walls before hurrying back to Mytilene. Meanwhile, the Methymnians, seeing an opportunity after the Mytilenians left, launched an attack on Antissa. They met fierce resistance; the Antissians, supported by their own mercenaries, made a successful sortie, defeating the Methymnians, who fled with significant casualties.

When this reached Athens, the Athenians, aware that the Mytilenians now had dominance in the surrounding countryside and that their own forces were struggling to contain them, sent reinforcements. At the beginning of autumn, Paches, son of Epicurus, was dispatched with a thousand Athenian heavy infantry. The soldiers rowed themselves to Mytilene, where they constructed a continuous wall encircling the city, with strongpoints fortified along strategic sections. With this construction, Mytilene was effectively blockaded by both land and sea as winter drew close.

However, the Athenians still needed funds for the ongoing siege. Having already raised two hundred talents from their citizens—an unprecedented levy—they sent a fleet of twelve ships under Lysicles and four commanders to collect further contributions from their allies. This fleet cruised to various locations, gathering resources along the way. Lysicles himself ventured inland from Myus, in Caria, crossing the broad plain of the Meander River toward the hill of Sandius. There, he encountered resistance from the Carians and people of Anaia, who launched a fierce assault in which Lysicles and many of his soldiers were killed.

At the same time, the besieged Plataeans were facing their own desperate situation. Hemmed in by the Peloponnesians and Boeotians, they found themselves running out of provisions and losing hope of rescue from Athens. With few options left, they decided to attempt a daring escape by breaching the enemy's walls. This plan was devised by Theaenetus, a soothsayer, and Eupompides, a general. Initially, all the besieged agreed to participate; however, as the danger became more apparent, about half of them withdrew, leaving around two hundred and twenty determined to press forward.

Their escape was meticulously planned. They constructed ladders to match the exact height of the enemy wall by counting the layers of bricks visible from their side. Since this side of the wall was not entirely whitewashed, they were able to see and count the bricks clearly. By having multiple people count simultaneously and repeatedly, they minimized the risk of error, ultimately calculating the height needed for their ladders from the measurements of the bricks.

The Peloponnesian wall surrounding Plataea was built in a complex dual-layer structure: two parallel lines encircled the city, with one side facing Plataea and the other facing outward to guard against any Athenian assault. The space between these two walls—about sixteen feet wide—was filled with soldiers' huts, designed as one long defensive block. This double wall was fortified with battlements along both sides, making it appear as one thick defensive barrier. Every ten battlements was interrupted by a large tower, which spanned the entire width of the wall, linking the inner and outer sides without a passageway around it. On stormy or rainy nights, the guards would abandon the exposed battlements to shelter inside the covered towers, positioned closely together for efficient defense.

With their plan in place, the Plataeans waited for a stormy night, hoping that poor weather would drive the enemy off the battlements and into the towers, allowing them to make their escape under the cover of darkness.

With the Peloponnesian wall structured as described, the Plataeans, having finalized their preparations, waited for a night when stormy weather with high winds and heavy rain would conceal their escape. Choosing such a night with no moon, they set out, led by those who had devised the plan. Crossing the ditch surrounding their city, they reached the Peloponnesian wall undetected. The storm drowned out any sounds of their approach, and they moved spaced apart to avoid being heard if their weapons clashed. For added stealth, they wore only minimal armor and had the left foot shod for better grip on the muddy ground.

Arriving at a section between the guard towers where they knew the battlements to be unguarded, those carrying the ladders moved first, setting them against the wall. Next came twelve lightly armed Plataean soldiers, equipped with just a dagger and a breastplate, led by Ammias, son of Coroebus, who climbed first, followed by his men— six scaling each tower. After them, more light troops followed, armed with spears. For easier movement, their shields were carried by others who would pass them over once they reached the top and were ready to engage with the enemy.

While many had already mounted, one Plataean accidentally dislodged a tile as he climbed, alerting the guards in the towers, who raised the alarm. The noise stirred the Peloponnesian troops, who rushed to their posts in confusion, unable to discern the nature of the attack due to the dark, stormy conditions. At the same time, the Plataeans within the city launched a diversionary attack on the opposite side of the wall to draw the defenders' attention away from the escape point.

This diversion caused the Peloponnesian soldiers to become further disoriented, each staying at his own station, unsure of where the actual attack was coming from. The three hundred soldiers assigned for emergencies hurried outside the wall toward the area of the alarm. To signal an attack, fire signals were lit, aimed toward Thebes for support. But the Plataeans inside the city anticipated this and had prepared a set of false signals to confuse the enemy. These decoy signals were displayed immediately, rendering the Peloponnesian signals unintelligible to their allies, thus preventing the Thebans from accurately interpreting the situation or sending timely assistance.

This meticulous and well-coordinated escape plan allowed the Plataeans to stay concealed from the Peloponnesians for as long as possible, enhancing their chances of evading immediate capture and making a successful getaway under cover of night and storm.

Once the first members of the scaling party had reached the top of the wall, they quickly secured both towers by overpowering and killing the sentinels. They stationed themselves within the towers to block any enemies attempting to come through, and set up ladders from the wall to allow more men to climb up. From the tops and bases of the towers, they used their arrows and missiles to fend off approaching Peloponnesians, enabling the main body of Plataeans to plant more ladders against the wall. Knocking down sections of the battlements, the escapees crossed over between the towers. As each soldier made it across, he moved to the edge of the ditch, using his bow and spear to cover his comrades, dissuading any pursuers attempting to stop them on the wall.

When most of the group had made it across, the soldiers stationed on the towers descended, though the last of them had some difficulty. They headed towards the ditch just as the Peloponnesian three hundred—a rapid-response force—arrived, carrying torches that illuminated their approach. Positioned on the edge of the ditch and hidden by the dark, the Plataeans shot arrows and threw javelins at the exposed parts of their enemies' bodies. The torchlight cast on the Peloponnesians made them visible targets, while the obscurity kept the Plataeans hidden, allowing even the last of their group to cross the ditch. They faced a challenging crossing: the ditch had a thin sheet of ice—not solid enough to walk on—that made it difficult to wade through. Additionally, an eastern wind had blown in snow, raising the water level, so they had to fight against the water's strong current. Nevertheless, the fury of the storm helped cover their movements and enabled them to complete their escape.

Once across the ditch, the Plataeans set out together, initially taking the road toward Thebes and passing the shrine of the hero Androcrates on their right. They reasoned that the Peloponnesians would be least likely to suspect them of fleeing toward enemy territory. Their plan worked: the Peloponnesians pursued them in the opposite direction, with torchlight illuminating the path to Athens and Cithaeron, where they expected the escapees would be headed.

After traveling about half a mile toward Thebes, the Plataeans altered course, taking a mountain path leading toward Erythrae and Hysiae. Reaching the safety of the hills, they continued on to Athens, where they finally found refuge. In all, two hundred and twelve men completed the daring escape, although a few had returned to the city before scaling the wall, and one archer was captured at the outer ditch.

Meanwhile, the Peloponnesians, realizing the pursuit was futile, abandoned their chase and returned to their positions. Back in Plataea, those inside the town remained in the dark about the success of the escape. Hearing from those who had returned that no one had made it across, they sent out a herald at dawn to arrange a truce for the recovery of the bodies, only to learn the truth shortly afterward.

In this way, the daring escape of the Plataean contingent was accomplished, and the survivors made it safely to Athens.

Towards the end of that same winter, Salaethus, a Lacedaemonian, was sent from Lacedaemon on a galley to Mitylene. Upon arriving, he secretly made his way to Pyrrha by sea and then traveled overland, following the course of a riverbed, where he found a breach in the Athenian circumvallation. Using this hidden route, he successfully slipped into Mitylene undetected. Once inside, he informed the magistrates that an invasion of Attica by the Peloponnesians was imminent, that a fleet of forty ships would soon arrive to relieve Mitylene, and that he had been dispatched to oversee these efforts and manage the situation. His news gave the Mitylenians renewed hope, and they promptly abandoned any plans to negotiate with the Athenians. Thus, the winter came to an end, concluding the fourth year of the war as chronicled by Thucydides.

In the following summer, the Peloponnesians dispatched a fleet of forty-two ships to Mitylene, under the command of Alcidas, their high admiral. Simultaneously, they and their allies launched an invasion of Attica, aiming to divide the attention of the Athenians with simultaneous threats and make it harder for them to respond to the fleet heading toward Mitylene. The invasion of Attica was led by Cleomenes, who acted on behalf of King Pausanias, son of Pleistoanax, who was still a minor. This time, instead of only ravaging lands that had previously been untouched, they extended their pillaging to areas overlooked in prior invasions, making this assault particularly harsh on the Athenians. The enemy lingered longer than in previous campaigns, systematically laying waste to the land as they awaited news of success from the fleet in Lesbos, expecting that it would by now have reached Mitylene. However, when none of the anticipated outcomes materialized and their provisions ran low, they withdrew and dispersed to their various cities.

Meanwhile, the Mitylenians, seeing their supplies dwindling and the Peloponnesian fleet slow to arrive, found themselves cornered into seeking peace with the Athenians. Salaethus, who had ceased to expect the fleet's arrival, made a desperate attempt by arming the common people with heavy armor—something they had not previously possessed—in the hopes of making a direct attack against the Athenians. But as soon as the commons found themselves armed, they refused to obey their leaders and, gathering in groups, demanded that all remaining provisions be shared equally among them. They also threatened to negotiate with the Athenians themselves and surrender the city if their demands were not met.

Realizing that they could not control the situation and fearing for their safety if they were excluded from any peace terms, the authorities conceded and negotiated directly with Paches, the Athenian general, agreeing to surrender Mitylene unconditionally. They allowed the Athenian forces to enter the city under the agreement that they would be permitted to send an embassy to Athens to present their case. Paches, in turn, promised that no harm would come to any of the citizens until the embassy returned. Although these were the official terms of the surrender, the leaders who had originally sought an alliance with Lacedaemon were so paralyzed with fear upon the Athenians' entrance that they took refuge at the city's altars. Paches, seeing this, assured them of their safety, removed them from the altars, and sent them to Tenedos, where they would remain until Athens made a final decision on their fate.

In addition to securing Mitylene, Paches also sent a few ships to seize Antissa and implemented other military measures he deemed necessary to fortify the area and maintain control over the region.

Meanwhile, the Peloponnesians in the fleet of forty ships, who were supposed to rush to Mitylene's aid, instead delayed by moving slowly around Peloponnese and then proceeding leisurely through the remaining distance. They reached Delos undetected by the Athenians stationed in Athens, then moved on to Icarus and Myconus, where they first heard of Mitylene's fall. To verify this news, they sailed to Embatum in the region of Erythrae about seven days after Mitylene's capture. Here, learning that the news was true, they debated their next course of action. Teutiaplus, an Elean officer, addressed the commanders with the following proposal:

"Alcidas and my fellow Peloponnesian commanders, my counsel is to sail directly to Mitylene without delay, striking before our presence here is known. Likely, the Athenians will be off guard, as it's common for an army that has just captured a city to be lax. Their naval defenses, especially, will be at ease, not expecting an enemy attack. Even their land forces, after their victory, are likely scattered across the town, inattentive. If we act quickly and launch a sudden nighttime attack, we may well succeed with the help of any supporters still loyal to us within the city. We must not fear the risk; these are the moments when the unexpected can lead to victories, and when an opportunity like this presents itself, the truly skilled general knows it is time to strike."

Teutiaplus's advice, however, did not convince Alcidas. After his proposal was dismissed, several Ionian exiles and the Lesbians in the fleet suggested a new plan, proposing they capture a nearby Ionian city or the Aeolic town of Cyme to establish a base from which they could stir up a revolt in Ionia. This idea, they argued, held promise; they were likely to be welcomed by the people and could simultaneously deprive Athens of a major source of income while burdening her with the costs of any blockade attempts. The hope was also to attract Pissuthnes to their side, adding further strength to their campaign. Yet Alcidas was equally unreceptive to this idea, anxious instead to return to Peloponnese as swiftly as possible now that he had arrived too late to save Mitylene.

Consequently, he departed Embatum and moved along the coast, anchoring briefly at Myonnesus, a Teian town, where he ruthlessly executed many of the prisoners he had taken en route. Arriving at Ephesus, envoys from the Samians of Anaia visited him with a warning. They argued that by slaughtering men who had never opposed him—people who were unwilling allies of Athens, not his enemies—he was undermining his own purpose. They told him he was more likely to create foes than to gain allies by such actions. Heeding their advice, Alcidas freed all the Chians still in his custody, as well as some of the other prisoners he had taken. Many of the people along the coast, seeing the Peloponnesian ships, had not fled as they might have from an enemy; instead, they had approached, assuming they were Athenian vessels, as it was almost unthinkable that Peloponnesian ships would be bold enough to cross into Ionia while the Athenian navy held dominion over the seas.

From Ephesus, Alcidas swiftly set sail and fled, having been sighted by two Athenian galleys, the Salaminian and Paralian, while still anchored near Clarus. Now fearful of being pursued, he aimed to cross the open sea and avoid making landfall anywhere until he reached Peloponnese. Meanwhile, word of his presence spread quickly, reaching Paches and causing widespread alarm. Ionia, being unfortified, was especially vulnerable; people feared that even a brief passage of the Peloponnesians along the coast could lead to raids and pillaging. The Salaminian and Paralian ships, after spotting Alcidas at Clarus, confirmed his location to Paches, who then immediately set off in pursuit.

Paches chased him as far as the isle of Patmos, but seeing that Alcidas had gained too much distance, he abandoned the chase. It was perhaps fortunate, he thought, that he had not encountered Alcidas somewhere that would have required blockading and drawn out the pursuit. On his return journey, Paches stopped at several locations along the coast, including Notium, the port of Colophon. This town had become the refuge of Colophonians after their main city was captured by Itamenes and the barbarian forces brought in by a factional conflict. This takeover had occurred around the same time as the second Peloponnesian invasion of Attica.

The Colophonians at Notium had fallen into factional strife once more. One faction had aligned with Median supporters from the upper town and enlisted Arcadian and barbarian mercenaries from Pissuthnes, establishing a separate fortified quarter for themselves. The opposing Colophonian faction, exiled by these actions, called on Paches for help. Paches arranged a parley with Hippias, the commander of the Arcadians in the fortified quarter, with an agreement that if they failed to reach an understanding, Hippias would be safely returned. However, upon meeting, Paches took him into custody and, launching a sudden assault, captured the fortified area by surprise. He executed the Arcadians and the barbarians there, then brought Hippias into the fort as promised, only to seize and kill him once inside.

Having subdued the fortress, Paches handed over Notium to the Colophonian faction opposed to the Medians. Later, Athens sent settlers to formally colonize the place under Athenian law, consolidating all Colophonians found in surrounding cities into this new settlement.

Afterward, Paches proceeded to Mitylene, where he reduced the towns of Pyrrha and Eresus. He captured Salaethus, the Lacedaemonian commander, who had been hiding in the city, and sent him along with the detained Mitylenians at Tenedos and any others suspected of involvement in the revolt, back to Athens. Paches then dispatched the bulk of his forces home, remaining behind with a portion of the troops to restore order in Mitylene and the rest of Lesbos as he deemed necessary.

From Ephesus, Alcidas swiftly set sail and fled, having been sighted by two Athenian galleys, the Salaminian and Paralian, while still anchored near Clarus. Now fearful of being pursued, he aimed to cross the open sea and avoid making landfall anywhere until he reached Peloponnese. Meanwhile, word of his presence spread quickly, reaching Paches and causing widespread alarm. Ionia, being unfortified, was especially vulnerable; people feared that even a brief passage of the Peloponnesians along the coast could lead to raids and pillaging. The Salaminian and Paralian ships, after spotting Alcidas at Clarus, confirmed his location to Paches, who then immediately set off in pursuit.

Paches chased him as far as the isle of Patmos, but seeing that Alcidas had gained too much distance, he abandoned the chase. It was perhaps fortunate, he thought, that he had not encountered Alcidas somewhere that would have required blockading and drawn out the pursuit. On his return journey, Paches stopped at several locations along the coast, including Notium, the port of Colophon. This town had become the refuge of Colophonians after their main city was captured by Itamenes and the barbarian forces brought in by a factional conflict. This takeover had occurred around the same time as the second Peloponnesian invasion of Attica.

The Colophonians at Notium had fallen into factional strife once more. One faction had aligned with Median supporters from the upper town and enlisted Arcadian and barbarian mercenaries from Pissuthnes, establishing a separate fortified quarter for themselves. The opposing Colophonian faction, exiled by these actions, called on Paches for help. Paches arranged a parley with Hippias, the commander of the Arcadians in the fortified quarter, with an agreement that if they failed to reach an understanding, Hippias would be safely returned. However, upon meeting, Paches took him into custody and, launching a sudden assault, captured the fortified area by surprise. He executed the Arcadians and the barbarians there, then brought Hippias into the fort as promised, only to seize and kill him once inside.

Having subdued the fortress, Paches handed over Notium to the Colophonian faction opposed to the Medians. Later, Athens sent settlers to formally colonize the place under Athenian law, consolidating all Colophonians found in surrounding cities into this new settlement.

Afterward, Paches proceeded to Mitylene, where he reduced the towns of Pyrrha and Eresus. He captured Salaethus, the Lacedaemonian commander, who had been hiding in the city, and sent him along with the detained Mitylenians at Tenedos and any others suspected of involvement in the revolt, back to Athens. Paches then dispatched the bulk of his forces home, remaining behind with a portion of the troops to restore order in Mitylene and the rest of Lesbos as he deemed necessary.

"I have long believed that a democracy is poorly suited to wield empire, and never more so than in this moment, as I see you reconsidering the fate of Mitylene. Because you live among yourselves without fear or suspicion of hidden plots, you project the same trust onto your allies. Yet, you fail to recognize that indulging their pleas or succumbing to your own feelings of pity exposes you to grave risks and earns you no gratitude for your leniency; you forget that your empire is maintained by force, not mutual goodwill, and your subjects are subdued not by their loyalty but by the clear superiority of your strength. What disturbs me most is the constant shift in policy we seem to embrace, and our apparent unawareness that poor but stable laws are better for a city than good laws weakened by frequent change. Stability, even without brilliance, serves the public more reliably than cleverness that bends with every new argument. History shows that practical men manage affairs better than the overly ambitious. The latter, always eager to outwit the laws and override proposals, often ruin their own cities; while the cautious, who respect both the laws and each other's ideas, and who focus on judging fairly rather than debating endlessly, succeed more often. Such men should guide our deliberations, rather than those swayed by cleverness and competition.

"I stand by my original stance and am amazed by those who have reopened Mitylene's case, thus giving the guilty a reprieve and tempering the victim's rightful anger with delay. Justice is most effective when it follows quickly on the heels of wrongdoing. I am equally astonished that anyone would argue that Mitylene's betrayal somehow benefits us, while our loss harms our allies. Such a person must either be astonishingly confident in his rhetoric, hoping to sway us by sophistry, or else has motives other than the public good. When we indulge in such debates, we hand others the reward and bear the risk ourselves. The fault lies with those of you who treat these debates like spectacles, taking opinions at face value and judging ideas based more on their delivery than their merit. You have become easy prey to new ideas, always skeptical of established judgments, quick to applaud innovations, and dismissive of familiar conclusions. Each of you, it seems, longs to be a speaker, or at least to match wits with those who are, rushing to praise clever arguments without reflecting on their true implications.

"In essence, you pursue ideals that are detached from the realities of our city, failing to truly understand the conditions you actually live in. You are more captivated by the pleasure of eloquence than committed to the demands of governance, resembling an audience at a rhetorician's performance more than a council deciding the fate of a city."

"To keep you from falling into this error, I will explain why no state has ever harmed you as grievously as Mitylene. I can sympathize with those who revolt out of genuine oppression or who are forced to do so by the enemy. But here we are dealing with a state that enjoyed its independence, security, and high standing among us, that had its own fortified island and navy, fearing no enemy except by sea—and even there they were fully capable of defense. For such a state to act as Mitylene has done is not mere revolt, which implies some measure of oppression; it is outright betrayal and an unprovoked attempt to ruin us by siding with our most bitter enemies. Their crime is graver than any mere war to expand their own power; it is a deliberate and unwarranted act of hostility against their benefactors.

"Mitylene's actions were not due to hardship; they rebelled despite their prosperity, ignoring the fate of their neighbors who had rebelled before them and suffered for it. They acted out of sheer arrogance, driven by ambition beyond their means. They made their choice not out of necessity, nor because they had been provoked, but because they believed the timing favorable and sought might over right. This kind of reckless ambition often arises when success comes unexpectedly. People tend to manage adversity more capably than prosperity, for great fortune tends to breed insolence, while restraint keeps men grounded. Indeed, our fault was in treating Mitylene with special regard; had we treated them as we did others from the beginning, they would not have grown so presumptuous. Human nature responds as much to kindness by becoming arrogant as it does to firmness by respecting limits.

"Let us now punish them as their crime deserves, and do not make the mistake of condemning the aristocrats alone while absolving the people. The fact is that all the citizens took up arms against us; they could have sided with us, choosing their city's safety, but instead they chose rebellion. Reflect on this: if we punish the ally who is compelled to rebel as lightly as we do one who revolts of their own free will, then what is to stop any other ally from rebelling? With no distinction between forced defection and deliberate betrayal, we are telling our allies that the reward for a successful revolt is freedom, and the penalty for failure is not severe enough to deter them.

"Thus, we are left to expend both lives and resources in quelling one rebellion after another, exhausting ourselves on states that should be our allies. If we succeed, we gain only a broken city, no longer a productive ally; if we fail, we gain yet another enemy, while our time and resources are drained battling those who should be helping us fend off our real foes."

"No hopes, whether offered by eloquence or purchased by wealth, nor any appeals to human frailty, should soften your resolve against the Mitylenians. Their offense was committed not under compulsion, but with malice and forethought; mercy is rightly reserved for those who transgress unwillingly. Therefore, as I advised before, I urge you not to reverse your original decision nor yield to three weaknesses that most threaten an empire—pity, sentimentality, and indulgence. Compassion is owed only to those who might return it, not to those who are our perpetual foes and will never have mercy for us in turn. Orators who wrap these issues in sentiment can find more suitable platforms for their talents than this one, where our city pays dearly for brief rhetorical delight, while they themselves reap applause for elegant phrases. Indulgence, too, should be reserved for those with whom future friendship is possible, not for men who will remain as hostile as they were before.

"To put it simply, if you take my advice, you will treat the Mitylenians with the justice they deserve and uphold what is most beneficial to us. A different decision would do little to endear them to us, but would, in effect, be a self-condemnation. If the Mitylenians had been justified in rebelling, it would mean that we are unjust in ruling them. But if, whether right or wrong, you intend to maintain this empire, then you must uphold the principles upon which it rests. Punish the Mitylenians as your interests demand, or else abandon your empire and embrace virtue without its attendant risks.

"Think carefully, then, about giving them the same treatment they intended for you. Don't let those who narrowly escaped their schemes be softer than the very conspirators who plotted against them. Consider what they would have done if they had won: they initiated this aggression and, had they succeeded, would have pursued you to the utmost, knowing that a victim of betrayal left alive is far more dangerous than one with no such grievance. So let us not betray ourselves; remember the urgency you felt when the threat was near, and now, with the advantage of safety, don't let weakness sway you or let the memory of the danger fade. Repay them justly, showing our other allies that the price of rebellion is death. Once this is understood, you will not so frequently have to leave your true enemies unattended while you handle rebellions among your own allies."

These were the words of Cleon. Then Diodotus, son of Eucrates, who had also spoken strongly in the previous assembly against the death penalty for the Mitylenians, rose to speak in reply.

"Therefore, I do not blame those who have reopened the Mitylenian case, nor do I support the idea that critical matters should not be repeatedly examined. The two greatest enemies of wise decisions are haste and passion; haste accompanies thoughtlessness, and passion narrows our perspective. Some argue that actions should not depend on debate, but anyone who says this is either ignorant or self-serving: ignorant if they believe that the uncertain future can be grasped in any other way, self-serving if they hope to silence opposition by slander when they know their own case lacks merit. Worse yet is the accusation that speakers give counsel only to profit from it. If only lack of wisdom were the charge, an unsuccessful speaker might at least retain a reputation for honesty; but to imply dishonesty is to mark the speaker as both foolish and corrupt, whether he fails or succeeds. This system robs the city of sound advice by silencing its advisors with fear. Indeed, if our speakers are so accused, it would almost be better if none could speak at all, for then fewer missteps might be made. A good citizen wins support by out-arguing his opponents, not by intimidating them; and a wise city, while not granting undue honors, will not turn away genuine advice. A failed proposal should not disgrace its originator; instead, they should be free from suspicion and able to offer counsel honestly.

"Our city does not follow this approach. Here, the moment someone is thought to be advising for personal gain, we harbor such resentment—even for possible gains that may not materialize—that we overlook the value of his advice to the city. This suspicion extends equally to sound counsel and bad, making plain and honest advice as mistrusted as the most dubious suggestions. Consequently, those who propose extreme measures feel they must rely on deceit, and those who speak plainly also feel compelled to shade their words to gain trust. The result is that only the city suffers, for it rarely benefits from forthright, honest guidance, and even well-meaning advice is suspected of hidden motives.

"Given the stakes involved, we orators must look further ahead than the audience judging us in the moment. As your advisors, we bear a burden that you do not share, for if both you who decide and we who propose paid equally for mistakes, your judgment would surely be more measured. Instead, you place the blame for any error or misfortune on the advisor alone, while you, the audience, bear none of the responsibility.

"I have not come forward to defend or accuse Mitylene; our question as sensible men is not about their guilt but about what best serves our interests. Even if I could prove their guilt without question, I would not advocate for their death unless it served us well; nor would I urge mercy if it did not clearly benefit the city. Our deliberation here should be for the future, not merely for the present moment. Cleon argues that capital punishment for rebellion would serve as a deterrent;

however, I see the opposite as more effective and ask you not to be swayed by his arguments that, though they may seem justified given your anger at Mitylene, do not serve our broader goals. This is not a trial seeking retribution but a political council to consider how Mitylene may serve Athens best.

"Yes, many societies impose death for even minor crimes, yet hope still leads people to take risks. No one ever undertakes a perilous venture without a belief in success, however improbable. Has any city ever rebelled without thinking it could find resources, either from itself or its allies, to support the undertaking? Both cities and individuals make mistakes, and no penalty has ever completely prevented wrongdoing. Were it otherwise, laws would not have evolved, growing increasingly severe as people repeatedly disregarded earlier punishments. The death penalty has been enacted in many cases, yet it is still often disregarded. Either a punishment more severe than death must be devised, or we must admit that these harsh penalties alone fail to restrain people.

"The truth is that as long as poverty gives men the courage of desperation or wealth fills them with pride and ambition, the urge to take risks will remain. Driven by ambition and the desire for gain, hope and greed push individuals and cities alike into danger. Hope, often the seed of daring plans, convinces people of the ease of success, while greed follows behind, spurring on the action. These forces, though unseen, are more powerful than any visible threat. Fortune often emboldens the reckless by lending unexpected aid, tempting people to challenge even greater forces, particularly in cities where the stakes are immense—freedom or dominion. In such cases, each individual overestimates his strength, emboldened by the collective will.

"In the end, it is naïve to believe that human nature can be restrained by law or any other deterrent. Once people have set their minds upon a course, they will pursue it regardless of penalties. We are dealing with forces beyond control through law alone; the only course, therefore, is to consider what is expedient, not what seems just in a moment of passion.

"We must avoid a misguided policy that relies on the death penalty as a deterrent and leaves rebels with no hope for reconciliation or early atonement. Imagine the effect: as it stands now, a city that sees its revolt failing can negotiate while it still has resources, repay expenses, and resume paying tribute. But if rebels expect the same punishment regardless of when they surrender, which city wouldn't prepare more thoroughly and resist to the last? Under such conditions, surrender becomes futile, forcing us to incur the expense of long sieges and, if successful, only gaining a destroyed city that can no longer contribute the revenue upon which we rely. Instead of playing strict judges to our own detriment, we should act with moderation, aiming to restore our subjects' productivity and ensure their future allegiance through careful administration rather than terrifying punishments. Presently, we reverse this logic: when a subject state, held down by force, inevitably rises for independence, we consider ourselves bound to punish it severely, rather than prudently preventing such insurrections in the first place and making the fewest possible responsible once subdued.

"Consider, then, the error in Cleon's proposal. As things stand, in all the cities, the common people are your allies, seldom revolting alongside the oligarchs. If forced into rebellion, they quickly turn against the insurgents, leaving you with the majority on your side. But if you execute the people of Mitylene—who took no part in the revolt and who, once armed, surrendered the town—you would be killing those who acted as your benefactors. Worse, this action would hand an advantage to the ruling classes, who, knowing you'll punish everyone indiscriminately, will draw the common people to their side the next time they rise. Instead, even if the people were guilty, it would be wiser to overlook it to preserve the goodwill of the one group still friendly to us. In short, maintaining our empire requires us to tolerate some injustice willingly rather than to kill—however justified—those we need to keep alive. Cleon's notion that justice and expediency can align in punishment is contradicted by experience: justice often demands a different course than expediency.

"Therefore, acknowledge this to be the most sensible approach—not motivated by excessive pity or leniency, which, like Cleon, I do not advocate—but based on the solid facts before us. I urge you to take a balanced course: try those whom Paches sent to Athens as the main culprits in the rebellion, but let the others remain untroubled. This course is best for our future security and delivers a strong message to our adversaries by showing that wise strategy is more potent than impulsive aggression."

These were Diodotus's arguments. The two speeches presented sharply opposing viewpoints, and the Athenians, despite their shifting sentiments, proceeded to vote. The result was almost evenly split, but Diodotus's proposal narrowly won. Immediately, a second galley was dispatched in haste to Lesbos, as there was a real fear the first ship might already have arrived and the city could be destroyed before a reprieve was issued; the first galley had a lead of only about a day and a night. To ensure a swift journey, the Mitylenian envoys provided the crew with wine and barley cakes and made generous promises for timely arrival. Driven by the urgency, the crew worked tirelessly, eating on the go with meals made from barley cakes kneaded with oil and wine, sleeping only in shifts to keep the oars in motion.

Fortunately, the winds were favorable. The first galley, bound by its grim orders, proceeded at a steady pace, while the second vessel pushed ahead at full speed. They arrived almost simultaneously—just as Paches had finished reading the original decree and was on the brink of carrying it out, the second ship entered the harbor and averted the slaughter. Mitylene's narrow escape from devastation was nothing short of miraculous.

However, the prominent rebels whom Paches had sent to Athens as instigators were, on Cleon's motion, executed, numbering more than a thousand. The Athenians also demolished Mitylene's walls and seized their fleet. Although they imposed no tribute, they divided nearly all Lesbos's land, except for that of the Methymnians, into three thousand lots. Of these, three hundred were set aside as sacred for the gods, while the remainder were assigned by lot to Athenian proprietors, who settled on the island. The Lesbians agreed to pay two minae per year in rent for each allotment, cultivating the land themselves. Athens also took control of Mitylene's territories on the mainland, making them fully subject to Athenian rule. Thus ended the events in Lesbos.

Chapter X

Fifth Year of the War—Trial and Execution of the Plataeans—Corcyraean Revolution

During the summer following the reduction of Lesbos, the Athenians, under the command of Nicias, son of Niceratus, launched an expedition against the island of Minoa, located near Megara. Minoa had served as a fortified outpost for the Megarians, who had constructed a tower there to monitor the surrounding waters. Nicias sought to secure this position to enable the Athenians to maintain a closer blockade over Megara, eliminating the need to operate from more distant points like Budorum and Salamis. This move aimed to prevent Peloponnesian ships and privateers from sailing out of Minoa undetected, as had often happened, and to restrict any potential supply routes to Megara.

The initial objective involved taking control of two towers situated along the Nisaea side of Minoa, which provided the Megarians with a defensive vantage point. Nicias's forces, using siege engines brought by sea, succeeded in capturing these towers and gaining access to the channel between the island and the mainland. Once these defenses were secured, Nicias moved to sever all remaining connections between Minoa and Megara by constructing a wall on the mainland at a location where a bridge across a marsh allowed the Megarians to send reinforcements to Minoa. In a few days, the wall was completed, effectively isolating Minoa. Nicias then constructed additional fortifications on the island itself, left a garrison in place to maintain control, and withdrew with his forces.

Around the same time in the summer, the Plataeans, having exhausted their supplies and unable to sustain the ongoing siege, surrendered to the Peloponnesians. Weakened by hunger and lacking any means of effective resistance, they had little choice. An attack had recently been made on their walls, which they were unable to repel, signaling their vulnerability. Observing their desperate state, the Lacedaemonian commander chose not to storm the town. Instead, he followed his orders from Lacedaemon, which advised restraint to ensure that Plataea would appear to have voluntarily come over to the Lacedaemonian side. This approach was meant to leave Plataea out of any future agreements that might require returning conquered towns to their original allies.

A herald was sent to the Plataeans, proposing that they surrender voluntarily, accept the Lacedaemonians as their judges, and agree to submit to punishment only after due process. Given their weakened position, the Plataeans accepted these terms and surrendered their town. The Peloponnesians provided them with provisions for several days while awaiting the arrival of five Lacedaemonian judges from Sparta. When these judges arrived, the Plataeans were presented with a single question, without any formal charges being laid: had they, the Plataeans, done any service to the Lacedaemonians or their allies in the current war?

Faced with this unexpected question, the Plataeans requested permission to present a fuller defense. Two of their representatives were chosen to speak on behalf of the town: Astymachus, son of Asopolaus, and Lacon, son of Aeimnestus, the proxenus of the Lacedaemonians. These two came forward and began to address the judges.

"Lacedaemonians, when we surrendered our city, we did so with the understanding that we would be granted a fair trial, one that would respect the due process of law. We believed that the judgment would come from you alone, Lacedaemonians, whom we considered most likely to dispense justice fairly. We never anticipated being subjected to this form of trial or that anyone other than yourselves would hold judgment over us, as is now happening. Under these circumstances, we fear we have been deceived twice over: first, in the nature of the trial, which seems to pose a question that is the most dire of all; and second, by the possibility that impartiality might not be observed here. We are especially troubled by the fact that no accusation was presented for us to respond to, forcing us to ask for permission to speak, and by the phrasing of the question—so brief that if we were to answer truthfully, it might condemn us, and if falsely, we could easily be contradicted.

"Nevertheless, here we stand, left with no choice but to speak openly, taking any risk, for we could hardly remain silent without being haunted by the thought that speaking might offer us a chance at survival. Yet, even as we speak, we encounter another challenge: the difficulty of convincing you. If we were strangers, we could perhaps present new evidence that would shed light on our position. But as you know us well, there is little we can say that would be new or surprising to you. We worry, not that you believe we have wronged you directly, but rather that, to satisfy others, we are forced into a trial with a verdict that may already be determined.

"Nevertheless, we will speak to what we believe is right, addressing not only our conflict with the Thebans but also your honor as Lacedaemonians and our record of loyalty to Hellas. We trust that, by reminding you of our past actions, we may appeal to your sense of fairness and justice.

"To the question of whether we have done any service to the Lacedaemonians or their allies during this war, our answer depends on whether you regard us as friends or foes. If you consider us as enemies, then surely we have done no more harm than abstaining from helping you; if as friends, then it is you who have wronged us by coming to attack. We have always acted honorably in times of peace and in the face of the Mede. We were the only Boeotians who stood alongside you in defense of Hellenic freedom against the Persians, refusing to join our kinsmen who collaborated with the enemy. Although we are an inland people, we supported the fleet at Artemisium and took our place by your side at the battle that unfolded upon our own soil, where we fought with you and Pausanias. Moreover, we participated in other struggles for Hellas, contributing far beyond our capacity as a small state.

"Do not forget, Lacedaemonians, that we came to your aid when Sparta faced a crisis. During the great panic that gripped you after the earthquake, when the Helots revolted and took refuge in Ithome, we did not hesitate. We sent a third of our citizens to assist you. This was no small commitment; it was an act of loyalty and sacrifice at a time when you needed it most. We did so because we believed in the unity of Hellas and trusted in the common cause we shared with you.

"On those great and historic occasions, this was the course we chose, though now we find ourselves in conflict with you. But it was not by our choice that we became your enemies. The blame lies with you. When we sought your aid against the Thebans who oppressed us, you turned us away and advised us to approach the Athenians, our neighbors, because you found our plea inconvenient due to your distance. Since then, we have never acted unreasonably toward you, nor would we have done so. When you asked us to abandon the Athenians, we refused, but not out of ill will toward you. They came to our aid against Theban aggression when you declined to intervene, and, having received benefits from them, we could not abandon them without dishonor, especially after we had gained their citizenship by our own choice and with their goodwill. It would have been shameful to turn our backs on them then. It is only fair, therefore, that the responsibility for any errors committed by Athens or Sparta in their positions of power should fall upon the leaders who dictated those actions, not the followers who, out of necessity or duty, obeyed them.

"As for the Thebans, their wrongs against us have been numerous, culminating in the aggression that led to our present plight. You know well how, during a time of peace, and even at a sacred time, they violated our city, seizing it without warning. We were forced to defend ourselves, as is universally acknowledged as just, according to the natural law permitting resistance to an unjust invasion. Thus, it is wrong that we should now suffer for defending our own city. If you weigh their hatred and your own present interests as the measure of justice, then you would be valuing convenience over righteousness, rather than serving as impartial judges. While they may appear useful to you in this moment, do not forget that in times of dire need, when all Hellas was under threat, we stood by your side in ways more valuable than any present utility they offer. Now you are the ones causing fear, while back then we all faced terror together under the threat of the barbarian's yoke, and Thebes chose to stand with him.

"Therefore, it is just to consider our loyalty and sacrifice at that time as outweighing any supposed error now. We acted then with great patriotism, at a time when few Hellenes dared stand against Xerxes' might. There were many safer paths than resistance, yet we were among those who chose the difficult road, preferring honor over easy safety, and we were celebrated for it. And here we stand again, having chosen the honorable path, aligning with Athens not just for gain but for what seemed right. And yet, we now fear death for following those same principles. If there is to be true justice, let it mean consistent treatment in similar cases. Policy, then, should not be a tool of convenience, but rather a demonstration of lasting gratitude for loyal allies, along with a practical regard for one's own interests.

"Let the memory of our deeds for Hellas not be forgotten. We are the same people who once joined you in defending all that we hold dear, and now we ask only that our past sacrifices and alliances be considered fairly alongside whatever accusations may have been brought against us. Let the justice we once helped uphold stand firm for us now."

"Think about this too: at this moment, the Greeks see you as an example of worth and honor. If you pass an unjust judgment on us in this case—which is not some minor issue, but one where both you as judges and we as prisoners have a reputation to uphold—take care that people do not feel anger over an unfair decision by those more honorable than the ones being judged, and over the placing in your temples of spoils taken from us, the Plataeans, who have served all of Greece. It will indeed be shocking for Spartans to destroy Plataea and for you to erase from the map of Greece a city whose name your fathers honored on the tripod at Delphi for its service, just to please the Thebans. We have reached such a depth of misfortune that while the success of the Persians would have ruined us, it is now the Thebans who have replaced us in your favor; and we have been faced with two of the worst dangers possible—first, the threat of starving to death if we had not surrendered our city, and now, the threat of being tried for our lives. So, we Plataeans, who have struggled beyond our strength in the cause of the Greeks, are now rejected, abandoned, and left without help, with none of our allies standing by us, and left wondering if we can even rely on you as our one remaining hope.

Yet, in the name of the gods who once watched over our alliance, and because of the good we have done for Greece, we beg you to change your minds; to reconsider the decision that we fear the Thebans may have convinced you to make; to reclaim the gift you have given them so that they do not bring you shame by killing us; to gain a pure rather than a tainted gratitude, and to avoid rewarding others at the cost of your own honor. Though our lives may be taken quickly, it will not be easy to erase the shame of the deed, as we are not enemies who deserve punishment but friends who were forced to take up arms against you. Sparing our lives would thus be a fair judgment; remember also that we are prisoners who surrendered of our own will, holding out our hands for mercy, and whose killing Greek law forbids, as we have always been your friends. Look at the graves of your fathers, those who were killed by the Persians and buried on our land, whom year after year we have honored with garments and offerings, and the first-fruits of all that our land produced in each season, as friends from a friendly land, and allies to our former comrades in battle. If you do not judge rightly, your actions would be the complete opposite of ours. Think of this: Pausanias buried them here, believing he was laying them to rest in friendly soil and among friendly people; but if you kill us and give the Plataean land to the Thebans, you will leave your fathers and relatives in hostile land, among those who killed them, denied the honors they now enjoy. Furthermore, you will enslave the land where Greece's freedom was secured, ruin the temples where they prayed before defeating the Persians, and take away the ancestral sacrifices from those who founded and established them."

"It would not bring you honor, Spartans, to go against the common law of the Greeks or the traditions of your own ancestors, nor to kill us, who have been your allies, simply to satisfy someone else's hatred, especially when we have done you no harm. It would be far more honorable to spare us, moved by reasonable compassion; not only thinking of the terrible fate awaiting us but also considering who we are as people and the fact that no one can know when misfortune might strike, even those who don't deserve it. We, as we have the right and the need to do, beg you, calling upon the gods at the altar where all Greeks worship, to listen to our plea, to remember the oaths your fathers swore, which we now invoke—we beg you by the graves of your fathers and appeal to those who have passed on to save us from falling into the hands of the Thebans, to prevent their closest friends from being handed over to their most hated enemies. We remind you also of that day when we performed the most honorable deeds by your fathers' sides, and we who are now likely to suffer the most dreadful fate. Finally, we do what is required but most difficult for those in our situation—to stop speaking, as the end of our words draws us closer to the danger to our lives—in conclusion, we declare that we did not surrender our city to the Thebans (we would have chosen a dishonorable death by starvation over that), but instead trusted you and surrendered to you; it would be only fair, if we fail to convince you, to put us back where we were and let us face whatever comes. And at the same time, we plead with you not to hand us over—we, your supplicants, Spartans, who trusted in your honor, we Plataeans, the first among the Greek patriots—not to deliver us to the Thebans, our most hated foes, but to be our protectors, and not, while you are freeing other Greeks, to condemn us to destruction."

These were the words of the Plataeans. The Thebans, fearing that the Spartans might be swayed by what they had heard, came forward and asked to speak as well, arguing that the Plataeans had been allowed to speak at length against their wishes, rather than being confined to a simple answer to the question. With permission granted, the Thebans began their speech as follows:

"We would not have asked to speak if the Plataeans had simply answered the question briefly, rather than turning around and accusing us, adding a long defense on matters irrelevant to the current issue and not even the subject of accusation, as well as praise for things that no one disputes. However, since they have done so, we feel it is necessary to respond to their accusations and counter their self-praise, so that neither our bad reputation nor their good reputation influences you, but that you can hear the real truth from both sides and make your decision accordingly."

"The origin of our dispute was this: We settled in Plataea sometime after the rest of Boeotia, along with other areas where we had driven out mixed populations. The Plataeans refused to acknowledge our authority, as was initially agreed, separating themselves from the other Boeotians and betraying their own people. We then used force, and in response, they went over to the Athenians and, with them, caused as much harm as they could, for which we retaliated.

"Later, when the barbarian invaded Greece, they say they were the only Boeotians who did not side with the Persians, which is where they boast most and criticize us. We claim that if they didn't side with the Persians, it was because the Athenians didn't either; just as later, when the Athenians attacked the rest of the Greeks, the Plataeans were again the only Boeotians who sided with Athens. And consider what kind of governments we had during these times. Our city then didn't have an oligarchy where all the nobles had equal rights, nor a democracy, but rather the form of government closest to tyranny—the rule of a narrow group. These rulers, hoping to strengthen their own power through the success of the Persians, kept the people down by force and brought the Persian into the city. The city, as a whole, was not in control of itself when it acted this way, and it should not be blamed for mistakes made while deprived of its proper government. Look only at how we acted after the Persians left and we regained our constitution; when the Athenians attacked the rest of Greece and tried to take over our land, much of which they had already gained through political factions. Did we not fight and win at Coronea to free Boeotia, and aren't we now contributing actively to the freedom of the rest, supplying horses and a force greater than any other state in the alliance?"

"This should be enough to explain our association with the Persians and defend us from blame for it. Now we will try to demonstrate that it is actually you who have harmed the Greeks far more than we ever did, and that you deserve far harsher punishment. You claim that it was because of our threats that you became allies and citizens of Athens. If that were truly the case, then your actions should have been limited to calling in the Athenians for protection specifically against us, without joining them in attacks against others. If, at any point, you felt they were pushing you into conflicts that went beyond your intent or duty, you had options. Sparta was already an ally against the Persians, as you have repeatedly insisted; this alone should have been enough to deter us and allow you to deliberate with safety and independence. However, despite these possibilities, you chose—entirely by your own decision and without any force applied—to align yourselves completely with Athens, thereby supporting its broader agenda.

"You argue that it would have been shameful for you to betray those who had once helped you. But isn't it far more shameful and even unjust to abandon all the Greeks—your fellow allies who were fighting to liberate Greece—just to stay loyal to Athens, who was actively trying to subjugate it? Thus, your response to Athens was neither fair nor honorable, since you called them to your aid, as you claim, only because of our supposed aggression, but then became their partners in oppressing others, going beyond simple gratitude into complicity. True disgrace lies in failing to respond with equal support to those who supported you, rather than merely failing to repay an unjust demand.

"Furthermore, while you now insist that you were the only Boeotians not to side with the Persians out of loyalty to Greece, it's quite clear that your choice was made only because Athens had made that choice first, and you wanted to follow them in opposition to the rest of us. And now you expect credit for actions that were done more to please your Athenian neighbors than to uphold any true loyalty to Greece. This is simply unreasonable. You made your choice to stand with Athens, and now you must bear the consequences alongside them, whether good or bad.

"Also, you cannot claim that the old alliance should protect you now. You abandoned that alliance yourselves by supporting, rather than resisting, Athens' subjugation of other allies like the people of Aegina. And you did this not because anyone forced you to, as was the case in our own past conflicts, but freely, while still under the same institutions you live by to this day. You chose to support Athens willingly, with no one compelling you.

"Finally, even before you were besieged, an offer was made to you to remain neutral, to align with neither side in this war. You chose not to accept it. So, who is more deserving of the Greeks' disdain than you, who sought to harm them under the guise of honor? The past virtues you claim are now proven to be false reflections of your character. The true nature of your motives has been revealed beyond question: when Athens chose the path of injustice, you eagerly followed them."

"Here, then, is our account of why we unwillingly associated with the Persians, while you willingly aligned yourselves with Athens. The last offense that you bring against us, as you claim, is our so-called unlawful invasion of your city during a time of peace and festival. On this point, too, we cannot see that we were more at fault than you were. If we had, on our own initiative, attacked your city with an armed force and ravaged your lands, then indeed, we would be guilty; but if it was your own leading citizens—those with wealth and status—who, wanting to end your foreign alliances and bring you back into the common Boeotian fold, invited us in of their own free will, where, then, is our crime? In situations of wrongdoing, those who initiate an action bear more responsibility than those who respond. That said, in our view, neither they nor we acted wrongly. These were your own fellow citizens, men with even more at stake than you, who opened their gates to us and let us into their city—not as enemies but as allies—to prevent the worst among you from becoming more harmful; to restore justice to the honorable; to correct principles without targeting individuals, as you were not being banished from your city, but rather being brought back to your true community, not made enemies of anyone, but made friends to all.

"Our actions make it clear that we did not come with hostile intent. We did no harm to anyone but publicly invited all who wished to live under a united Boeotian government to join us. You, at first, accepted willingly, reached an agreement with us, and remained calm until you saw that our numbers were few. Now, it may be true that our entry was less than fully fair since we came without the direct consent of your broader population. But in return, you did not act with fairness yourselves. Instead of, as we had done, refraining from violence and persuading us to leave through peaceful means, you turned on us, breaking your own agreement, and killed some of us in battle. This much we do not resent, as there is a degree of justice in open combat; but others among us who held up their hands in surrender, and to whom you had promised safety, you mercilessly slaughtered. If this is not abhorrent, what is? After committing these three offenses in succession—the breach of your agreement, the murder of our men afterward, and the outright lie that you would spare them if we refrained from damaging your lands—you still maintain that we are the guilty ones and hope to avoid the punishment you deserve. But if these judges rule justly, you will face justice for all your actions together.

"Such, Spartans, are the facts. We have explained them at length, both for your benefit and our own, so that you may feel assured that a fair sentence on these prisoners is deserved, and so that we may confirm the justice of our cause for vengeance. We also wish to prevent you from being swayed by hearing of any past virtues they may claim, if indeed they had any at all: such appeals belong to those who have suffered injustice, but for offenders, they only add to the weight of their guilt, as they act in defiance of their own better character. Nor should they gain any sympathy through tears and lamentations, by invoking the tombs of your ancestors or speaking of their own pitiful state. In response to this, we point to the far worse fate of our young men, slaughtered at their hands; their fathers either died at Coronea while bringing Boeotia to your side or sit as sorrowful old men by empty hearths, having every reason to call for justice upon these prisoners. Pity belongs to those who suffer undeservedly, while those who suffer justly, as they do, should only be met with scorn. As for their present miserable condition, they have only themselves to blame, as they knowingly rejected a better alliance. Their reckless actions were not provoked by anything we did; it was their hatred, not justice, that drove their choices. Even now, the punishment they face does not truly satisfy what we have lost; they are sentenced by law, not, as they claim, as suppliants seeking mercy in battle, but as prisoners who surrendered under an agreement to stand trial.

"Therefore, Spartans, uphold the Greek law that they have violated; grant us, who have been wronged by them, the justice that we have rightfully earned through our efforts. Do not let their speeches take priority over our rights, but instead, set an example for all of Greece that the competitions you hold are not just for words, but for meaningful actions. Good deeds can be easily stated, but those who commit wrongdoing must cover it with lengthy speeches to hide its shame. If those in power judged all cases as you are doing now, asking one straightforward question of all parties and judging accordingly, people would be less tempted to dress up their bad actions with fine words."

"Such were the words spoken by the Thebans. The Lacedaemonian judges, after hearing both sides, decided that it was fair to ask the Plataeans if they had provided any assistance to the Lacedaemonians during the war. This question seemed justified because the Spartans had previously invited the Plataeans to remain neutral, in keeping with the original covenant made by Pausanias after the defeat of the Persian forces. Additionally, before the siege began, the Spartans had again extended an offer of neutrality to the Plataeans under those same terms. Since the Plataeans had rejected this offer, the Lacedaemonians believed that they were now freed from their obligations under the covenant due to their consistent loyalty and goodwill. Feeling that they had been wronged by the Plataeans, they brought each prisoner forward individually and asked each one a single question: whether they had performed any service for the Lacedaemonians and their allies during the war. When each answered that they had not, they were led away and executed, without exception.

In total, no fewer than two hundred Plataeans were put to death, along with twenty-five Athenians who had joined them during the siege. The women captured were taken and sold into slavery. The city itself was then given to some political exiles from Megara and to the remaining Plataeans who had supported the Thebans, allowing them to inhabit it for roughly a year. Later, however, the city was razed to the ground, with every structure demolished to its very foundations. In the ruins, the Thebans constructed a large inn, measuring two hundred feet square, with rooms on both the upper and lower levels, using the roofs and doors from Plataean houses to complete the building. Additionally, from the iron and bronze found in the Plataean walls, they crafted couches, which they dedicated to Hera, for whom they also built a stone chapel measuring one hundred feet square. The Plataean land was confiscated and leased to Theban tenants on ten-year terms.

The Lacedaemonians' harsh treatment of Plataea throughout this affair was primarily intended to please the Thebans, who were seen as valuable allies in the ongoing war. Thus ended the city of Plataea, ninety-three years after it had first allied itself with Athens.

Meanwhile, the forty Peloponnesian ships that had been dispatched to support the Lesbians and that we last saw fleeing in open water with the Athenians in pursuit, were caught in a storm off the coast of Crete. The storm scattered the fleet, but they eventually regrouped and returned to the Peloponnese. There, at Cyllene, they joined thirteen more galleys from Leucas and Ambracia, and met with Brasidas, the son of Tellis, who had recently arrived to assist Alcidas as an advisor. After the failed expedition to aid the Lesbians, the Lacedaemonians decided to strengthen their naval forces and make their way to Corcyra, where a revolution had broken out. Their goal was to reach Corcyra before the twelve Athenian ships stationed at Naupactus could be reinforced from Athens. Brasidas and Alcidas, in response, began their preparations accordingly."

"Such were the words delivered by the Thebans. After careful consideration, the Lacedaemonian judges concluded that it was reasonable to question the Plataeans on whether they had contributed any assistance to the Lacedaemonians or their allies during the war. This line of questioning seemed fair and justified, given that the Spartans had previously offered the Plataeans the opportunity to remain neutral. This offer of neutrality was in line with the original covenant established by Pausanias after the Persian defeat, which encouraged non-aligned Greek states to abstain from involvement in conflicts. Even more recently, the Spartans had extended a similar offer to the Plataeans before the siege, presenting the same conditions for neutrality. However, as the Plataeans chose to reject this proposal, the Lacedaemonians felt that they had acted in good faith and that their obligations under the original agreement had now been voided. Furthermore, they believed they had legitimate grievances against the Plataeans, who, they felt, had acted in opposition to Spartan interests. With this in mind, the Lacedaemonians proceeded to bring the Plataeans forward one by one, asking each individual the same question—whether they had performed any service for the Lacedaemonians and their allies during the war. When each prisoner answered that they had not, they were promptly led away and put to death, without exception or reprieve.

In total, not fewer than two hundred Plataeans were executed in this manner, alongside twenty-five Athenians who had been present with them during the siege. The women of Plataea were taken as slaves, further symbolizing the Lacedaemonians' complete control over the city's fate. Following these executions, the Lacedaemonians granted the city to political exiles from Megara and to the remaining Plataeans who had supported the Theban cause, allowing them to inhabit the city for approximately a year. Subsequently, however, they made the decision to destroy Plataea entirely, demolishing every structure down to its very foundations. In the area where the city once stood, the Thebans constructed a large inn, measuring two hundred feet square, with rooms surrounding a central courtyard, both on the upper and lower levels. To complete this structure, they repurposed the roofs and doors from Plataean homes, which had been dismantled during the city's destruction. Additionally, the remaining iron and bronze from the Plataean walls were used to craft couches, which they dedicated to the goddess Hera, in whose honor they also built a stone temple measuring one hundred feet square. The land of Plataea was seized and leased to Theban citizens on ten-year terms, further cementing the city's absorption into Theban control.

The Lacedaemonians' decision to act so decisively against Plataea was largely motivated by a desire to maintain good relations with the Thebans, who were considered valuable allies in the ongoing war effort. Thus, the city of Plataea came to its tragic end, precisely ninety-three years after first becoming an ally of Athens.

Meanwhile, the forty Peloponnesian ships that had been dispatched to assist the Lesbians, and which were last seen fleeing across the open sea with the Athenians in pursuit, encountered a powerful storm off the coast of Crete. The violent weather scattered the fleet, forcing each vessel to make its way back to the Peloponnese on its own. Eventually, they regrouped at Cyllene, where they found thirteen additional galleys from Leucas and Ambracia. Here, Brasidas, the son of Tellis, had also recently arrived, sent as an advisor to Alcidas. The Lacedaemonians, recognizing the failure of the attempt to assist the Lesbians, had resolved to fortify their naval presence and redirect their focus toward Corcyra, where a political revolution was underway. Their objective was to reach Corcyra before reinforcements could be sent to the twelve Athenian ships stationed at Naupactus. In response to this urgent need, Brasidas and Alcidas promptly began preparations for the upcoming mission."

"After a day of ceasefire, hostilities resumed. Victory went to the commoners, who held the advantage due to their greater numbers and stronger positions. The women also fought bravely alongside them, throwing roof tiles from the tops of buildings and supporting the fighting with remarkable courage, showing strength beyond what was typically expected of them. As dusk fell, the oligarchs, now in full retreat, feared that the triumphant commoners would storm the arsenal and kill them all. In desperation, they set fire to the houses around the marketplace and the lodging-houses to block the commoners' advance, sparing neither their own property nor that of their neighbors. This resulted in a great loss of goods belonging to merchants, and it almost caused the city's total destruction. If the wind had picked up and fed the flames, the entire city might have been lost.

With the fighting paused, both sides kept their positions and remained alert throughout the night, each guarding against a possible attack. During this time, a Corinthian ship managed to slip away, taking advantage of the commons' victory, while most of the mercenaries also left the city under the cover of darkness, escaping to the mainland.

The next day, the Athenian general Nicostratus, son of Diitrephes, arrived from Naupactus with a fleet of twelve ships and five hundred Messenian heavy infantry. He immediately tried to mediate and worked to negotiate a resolution. Through his efforts, he persuaded both sides to reach an agreement: ten of the primary leaders of the recent violence would stand trial, though they soon fled, while the rest would commit to live together peacefully, cooperating and making terms with each other. Furthermore, both factions agreed to form a defensive and offensive alliance with Athens. With this agreement settled, Nicostratus prepared to depart. However, the leaders of the commons requested that he leave five of his ships with them to deter any further hostile moves from their adversaries. In return, they offered to provide five of their own ships to accompany him back. Nicostratus agreed, and no sooner had he given his consent than the commons began enlisting their enemies to crew the ships. Fearing they would be sent away to Athens against their will, many of these individuals sought sanctuary in the temple of the Dioscuri as suppliants.

Nicostratus attempted to calm them, reassuring them that they had nothing to fear and urging them to rise from their place of refuge, but his efforts proved unsuccessful. The commons then seized upon this as an opportunity, claiming that their opponents' refusal to join the fleet was proof of their untrustworthy intentions. They began to arm themselves, entering their opponents' houses to confiscate weapons, and would likely have killed some of them if Nicostratus had not intervened. Seeing these actions unfold, the rest of the opposing faction, numbering no less than four hundred, took sanctuary in the temple of Hera as suppliants. The commons, concerned that these men might resort to some desperate measure, eventually persuaded them to leave the temple peacefully and escorted them across to an island opposite the temple, where they provided them with supplies.

At this critical point in the revolution, on the fourth or fifth day after the men had been moved to the island, a fleet of Peloponnesian ships arrived. These fifty-three ships had been stationed at Cyllene since their return from Ionia and were still under the command of Alcidas, though Brasidas was also on board, serving as an advisor. The fleet anchored at Sybota, a harbor on the mainland, and at daybreak, they set sail for Corcyra."

"The Corcyraeans, thrown into great confusion and panic due to both the chaos within their city and the advancing enemy fleet, immediately began outfitting sixty ships. Despite the Athenians advising them to let the Athenian vessels sail out first and then follow in formation with all their ships together, the Corcyraeans sent out each ship as soon as it was manned. When these vessels, launching in such a disorganized manner, approached the enemy fleet, two ships immediately deserted. In other ships, the crews fell into fights among themselves, and there was a complete lack of coordination in everything they attempted to do. Observing the disorder among the Corcyraeans, the Peloponnesians took advantage of the situation, placing twenty of their ships in position to directly oppose the Corcyraean forces, while aligning the rest of their fleet against the twelve Athenian ships, which included the notable vessels Salaminia and Paralus.

The Corcyraeans, attacking recklessly and in scattered groups, found themselves weakened by their own lack of discipline. Meanwhile, the Athenians, wary of the large number of enemy ships and the risk of being surrounded, did not dare to directly engage the main body or even the center of the division facing them. Instead, they chose to focus on the enemy's flank, successfully sinking one vessel in the process. In response, the Peloponnesians quickly formed a defensive circle, prompting the Athenians to row around them in an attempt to break their formation and cause confusion. Recognizing the Athenians' strategy, the division facing the Corcyraeans, fearing a repeat of the disastrous defeat at Naupactus, moved to support the rest of their fleet. With this maneuver, the entire Peloponnesian fleet now closed ranks and advanced together against the Athenians, who began to retreat slowly, rowing backward to maintain distance, while buying time for the Corcyraeans to withdraw safely. This allowed the

Athenians to keep the enemy fleet occupied. The sea battle continued in this manner until sunset.

As night approached, the Corcyraeans feared that the Peloponnesians would pursue their victory by launching a direct assault on their town, rescuing the Corcyraean men who had taken refuge on the island, or carrying out another decisive attack. In response to this fear, they transferred the men back to the temple of Hera and posted guards throughout the city to prepare for any sudden attack. However, despite their victory in the naval battle, the Peloponnesians did not attempt to attack the town directly. Instead, they took possession of the thirteen Corcyraean ships they had captured and sailed back to the mainland from which they had initially set out.

The following day, even with the Corcyraeans still in a state of disorder and alarm, the Peloponnesians once again refrained from launching an assault on the city. Although Brasidas, who was acting as an advisor, reportedly urged Alcidas, the Peloponnesian commander, to strike while the Corcyraeans were vulnerable, Alcidas chose not to take such direct action. Instead, they disembarked on the promontory of Leukimme and laid waste to the surrounding countryside, causing further harm without directly challenging the city itself."

"Meanwhile, the commoners in Corcyra, still deeply fearful that the Peloponnesian fleet might launch an attack on the town, decided to negotiate with the suppliants and their allies as a means to protect the city. They managed to persuade some of them to board the ships, of which they had equipped and manned thirty in anticipation of the expected assault. However, the Peloponnesians, after ravaging the countryside until midday, chose to sail away. Toward evening, they received word via beacon signals that sixty Athenian ships under the command of Eurymedon, the son of Thucles, were approaching from Leucas. The Athenians had dispatched these ships as soon as they received news of the revolution in Corcyra and of the Peloponnesian fleet, under Alcidas, preparing to sail there.

In response to this new threat, the Peloponnesians quickly set off for home, sailing by night along the coast. They even went so far as to haul their ships across the Isthmus of Leucas to avoid being spotted rounding the cape, and from there continued on their way. Once the Corcyraeans became aware of the arrival of the Athenian fleet and the departure of the enemy forces, they brought the Messenian forces stationed outside the city walls into the town for additional security. They then ordered the fleet they had manned to sail around to the Hyllaic harbor. While this maneuver was underway, they began systematically killing their enemies—those they could lay hands on were immediately put to death, and those they had earlier persuaded to board the ships were executed as soon as they came ashore.

Following this, they turned their attention to the sanctuary of Hera, where they convinced about fifty men to stand trial. However, upon judgment, all fifty were condemned and executed. Observing these executions, the remaining suppliants who had refused to stand trial understood the fate awaiting them. In despair, they turned upon each other within the sacred grounds, taking their own lives in any way they could. Some hanged themselves on trees, while others used whatever means they could find to end their lives.

During the seven days that Eurymedon remained in Corcyra with his sixty ships, the Corcyraeans were consumed with slaughtering those citizens whom they considered enemies. Although the main accusation was that these individuals were attempting to overthrow the democracy, many others were killed out of private grudges. Some were slain by debtors who saw an opportunity to erase their obligations by eliminating those they owed money to. Thus, death took on every conceivable form, and, as is often the case in such times of civil turmoil, there were no limits to the atrocities committed. Fathers killed their own sons, and even suppliants were dragged from the altars or killed upon them. In one particularly horrific act, some were even walled up inside the temple of Dionysus, left to die within its sacred enclosure."

"The course of the revolution was marked by extreme bloodshed, and its impact was even greater because it was one of the first such uprisings to take place. As time went on, it could be said that nearly all of the Greek world was thrown into turmoil. Popular leaders in different cities sought to bring in the Athenians as allies, while oligarchs invited the Lacedaemonians to support their causes. In times of peace, there would have been neither the opportunity nor the desire to seek such foreign alliances; but in the midst of war, with factions eager to gain any advantage over their opponents and harm them, the availability of an alliance was a tempting and ever-present option for revolutionary leaders looking to introduce foreign powers into their cities. The suffering and devastation brought upon these cities by revolution were immense and horrific, with events that had occurred and always will occur as long as human nature remains unchanged—though they may vary in intensity and expression depending on the specifics of each case.

In times of peace and prosperity, both states and individuals are generally more inclined toward positive behavior, as they are not abruptly confronted by urgent and desperate needs. However, war disrupts the easy supply of everyday necessities, proving to be a harsh teacher that often levels men's character to match the hardships of their situation. Thus, the revolution spread from city to city, and those places that experienced it later, having learned of previous incidents, often carried the extremity of their actions to even greater heights. This resulted in ever more cunning schemes and more brutal acts of revenge. Words themselves took on new meanings to reflect the altered values of the time. Reckless daring was now viewed as the courage of a loyal ally; cautious deliberation was seen as cowardice disguised by reason. Moderation was interpreted as a cover for weakness, and the ability to consider all sides of an issue was seen as an inability to act on any. Extreme and frenzied aggression came to be associated with manliness, while careful planning was justified as necessary self-defense. Those who advocated extreme actions were trusted implicitly, while anyone who opposed them was regarded with suspicion.

To succeed in a scheme became a mark of cleverness, while detecting another's scheme was seen as even shrewder; but attempting to avoid scheming altogether was viewed as weakening one's party and showing fear of one's opponents. In short, taking preemptive action against an enemy or even suggesting a crime where none had been planned was equally praised, until eventually even family bonds became weaker than party loyalty. Party alliances were bound by an eagerness to pursue any course of action without hesitation. These groups did not aim for the benefits of stable institutions; instead, their ambition was focused on overthrowing them. Their loyalty to each other relied not on shared religious principles but on shared involvement in criminal acts.

When one side offered fair terms, the other, if stronger, would meet them with suspicion rather than trust. Revenge came to be valued above even self-preservation. Oaths of reconciliation were exchanged only as temporary solutions to immediate problems, and they lasted only as long as no better option presented itself. As soon as an opportunity arose, the first person to seize it, catching his enemy unprepared, found this treacherous vengeance even sweeter than an open one. Success through deception not only satisfied personal safety concerns but also brought the reputation of cunning intelligence, which was highly prized. People were more inclined to label a dishonest person as clever than to call an honest one simple, and they felt more pride in being seen as cunning than in being known as trustworthy.

The root of these evils lay in the desire for power, driven by greed and ambition; these passions fueled the relentless violence between opposing factions. Leaders in each city, under the guise of noble causes, rallied support—one side advocating for political equality of the people, the other for a balanced aristocracy—yet each side was ultimately pursuing its own interests, showing little regard for the welfare of the community they claimed to serve. In their struggles for dominance, they committed severe excesses, seeking to outdo one another in acts of vengeance that far exceeded what justice or the state's well-being required. Their only measure was the immediate whims of the moment, invoking either an unjust verdict or brute force to satisfy the hatred of the hour.

Thus, respect for religion held no place with either faction; instead, the art of using fair words to achieve dishonorable ends was highly valued. Meanwhile, the moderate citizens were caught in the middle, suffering at the hands of both sides. They were often destroyed either for refusing to join in the conflict or because their existence provoked envy, which would not allow them to remain unscathed."

"Thus, in the turmoil of the time, every kind of wrongdoing and moral corruption took root in the Greek world. The old values, characterized by a straightforwardness and honor that had once held society together, were openly ridiculed and eventually disappeared. People became divided into opposing factions, where no one could trust another. In such an environment, neither promises nor oaths could be relied upon, as people no longer respected these traditional forms of commitment. Instead, each side, seeing the instability of their world, focused more on self-preservation than on fostering trust. This atmosphere of distrust meant that the simpler minds among them often fared best. Aware of their own limitations and fearful of the cleverness of their opponents, these people were quick to resort to action, as they worried that they might lose out in discussions or be outmaneuvered by the strategies of their more sophisticated adversaries. Meanwhile, their opponents, overconfident in their ability to manage the situation and convinced that they would always have time to respond, often became victims of their own lack of vigilance.

Corcyra provided the first example of most of these crimes. The oppressed, having never experienced fair or just treatment from those in power—only arrogance and contempt—seized their chance for revenge. Meanwhile, those who wanted to escape their usual poverty and desired the wealth of their neighbors saw this as an opportunity to satisfy their greed. And finally, those who had begun the conflict driven not by social class but by party loyalty were soon swept up by their own uncontrollable emotions, resulting in acts of extreme cruelty and brutality. In the chaotic conditions now gripping the cities, human nature—always inclined to rebel against the constraints of law—became completely unrestrained, showing itself openly as a force of unbridled passion, dismissive of justice, and hostile to all forms of superiority. Revenge took precedence over religious respect, and personal gain outweighed any sense of fairness, driven by the destructive power of envy. People often took it upon themselves to dismantle the shared laws that offered a foundation for everyone's safety, particularly in times of hardship, instead of preserving these laws as a safeguard against future dangers.

As the revolutionary passions unfolded in Corcyra's factional conflicts for the first time, Eurymedon and the Athenian fleet departed from the city. Soon after, around five hundred Corcyraean exiles who had managed to escape captured several forts on the mainland. Using these as bases, they established control over the Corcyraean territory on the opposite shore and began launching raids on their fellow citizens still on the island. These attacks were so disruptive that they caused a severe food shortage in the town. The exiles also sent representatives to Lacedaemon and Corinth, seeking support for their return, but having failed in this, they resorted to gathering boats and hiring mercenaries. Approximately six hundred of them then crossed over to the island and, in a symbolic act of final commitment, burned their boats, leaving themselves no option but to conquer or perish. They then ascended Mount Istone, where they fortified their position and began a campaign of harassment against those in the city, gradually gaining control over the surrounding countryside."

"Towards the end of the same summer, the Athenians dispatched a fleet of twenty ships under the command of Laches, the son of Melanopus, and Charoeades, the son of Euphiletus, to Sicily, where a war was ongoing between the Syracusans and the Leontines. The Syracusans had formed alliances with all the Dorian cities in the region, with the exception of Camarina. These Dorian cities had been allied with the Lacedaemonian (Spartan) confederacy from the very beginning of the larger war, though they had not yet actively participated in it. On the opposing side, the Leontines had the support of Camarina and the Chalcidian cities.

In nearby Italy, the conflict also drew in regional allies. The Locrians sided with the Syracusans, while the Rhegians supported their kin, the Leontines. At this point, the allies of the Leontines sent envoys to Athens, appealing to the longstanding alliance between their cities and the Athenians. They emphasized their shared Ionian heritage, hoping to persuade the Athenians to send a fleet to aid them, as they were under siege by the Syracusans, who had blockaded them by both land and sea. Although the Athenians officially sent the fleet in response to this appeal of common ancestry, their true intention was twofold: to prevent Sicilian grain from being shipped to the Peloponnese, thereby depriving their enemies of resources, and to assess the possibility of eventually bringing Sicily under Athenian control.

Upon arriving, the Athenian fleet established a base at Rhegium in Italy. From this strategic location, they coordinated their military actions alongside their allies, carrying on the campaign against the Syracusans and their supporters."

Chapter XI

"Year of the War—Campaigns of Demosthenes in Western Greece—Destruction of Ambracia

Summer had come to an end, and with the onset of winter, the Athenians were once again struck by the plague. Although it had never entirely disappeared, the disease had significantly diminished in its intensity before this resurgence. This second outbreak lasted for a full year, while the first wave had endured for two years. Nothing proved to be more devastating to the Athenians or more damaging to their strength and morale than this return of the plague. During this time, no fewer than four thousand four hundred heavy infantry soldiers and three hundred cavalrymen lost their lives, in addition to an unknown number of common citizens who were never counted. At the same time, Athens and surrounding regions experienced a series of severe earthquakes, notably affecting Athens itself, as well as Euboea and Boeotia, especially the town of Orchomenus in Boeotia.

That same winter, the Athenian forces stationed in Sicily, along with their Rhegian allies, set out with a fleet of thirty ships to attack the Aeolian Islands. These islands, due to their lack of freshwater, could not be easily invaded during the summer. The Aeolian Islands were inhabited by the Liparaeans, a colony from Cnidus, who primarily lived on the island of Lipara, which, though small, served as their main settlement and base of operations for cultivating the other islands—Didyme, Strongyle, and Hiera. In Hiera, the people of the area believed that Hephaestus, the god of fire, maintained his forge, as the island frequently emitted flames at night and smoke during the day. These islands, located off the coast of the Sicels and Messinians, were allies of the Syracusans. The Athenians ravaged the land, but as the inhabitants refused to surrender, they eventually sailed back to Rhegium. This marked the end of winter and the conclusion of the fifth year of this ongoing war, recorded by the historian Thucydides.

The following summer, the Peloponnesians and their allies prepared for another invasion of Attica. Under the command of Agis, son of Archidamus, they marched as far as the Isthmus. However, a series of powerful earthquakes struck the region, and they ultimately decided to abandon the invasion and return home. During this period, earthquakes were occurring frequently in several areas. At Orobiae in Euboea, the sea suddenly receded from the shoreline and then returned as a massive wave, flooding a large portion of the town and leaving some of it permanently underwater. Land that was once dry had now become part of the sea. Many inhabitants perished, unable to escape to higher ground in time. A similar event happened on the island of Atalanta, located off the coast of Opuntian Locris. There, the wave destroyed part of an Athenian fort and wrecked one of two ships that were drawn up on the beach. At Peparethus, the sea also withdrew briefly, though no flooding followed; however, the earthquake there caused part of the town wall, the town hall, and several other buildings to collapse.

In my view, the cause of this phenomenon lies in the earthquake itself. When the shock of the earthquake is especially strong, it forces the sea back; as the water then returns with doubled strength, it creates an overwhelming wave that causes the inundation. Without the occurrence of an earthquake, I do not see how such an event could have taken place."

"During the same summer, various operations were carried out by the different factions involved in the conflict in Sicily. The Sicilian Greek states, or Siceliots, continued their struggles against one another, while the Athenians and their allies engaged in their own campaigns. I will focus, however, on the actions that involved the Athenians, selecting the most significant events.

The death of the Athenian general Charoeades, who was killed in battle by the Syracusans, left Laches as the sole commander of the fleet. Laches, along with the allies, then directed the fleet against Mylae, a town held by the Messinians. At Mylae, two battalions of Messinian troops stationed in the garrison attempted to ambush the Athenians as they landed from their ships. However, the Athenians and their allies successfully countered the ambush, inflicting heavy casualties on the Messinians. Following this victory, they launched an assault on the town's fortifications, compelling the defenders to surrender the Acropolis and accompany them in a march on Messina. Upon the approach of the Athenian forces, Messina also surrendered, providing hostages and other assurances as demanded.

That same summer, the Athenians dispatched two separate fleets. One consisted of thirty ships sent around the Peloponnesian coast under the command of Demosthenes, son of Alcisthenes, and Procles, son of Theodorus. The other, a larger force of sixty ships carrying two thousand heavy infantry, was sent against the island of Melos under the leadership of Nicias, son of Niceratus. The Athenians aimed to subjugate the Melians, who, though islanders, had resisted becoming subjects of Athens and refused to join their alliance. When the devastation of Melos's territory failed to bring about their surrender, the fleet departed Melos and sailed to Oropus, a town in Graea. Arriving at night, the Athenian infantry disembarked and began a march toward Tanagra in Boeotia. There, they were joined by the full Athenian levy, who had arrived according to pre-arranged signals, under the command of Hipponicus, son of Callias, and Eurymedon, son of Thucles. The combined force spent the day ravaging the Tanagraean territory and then set up camp to rest overnight. The following day, after repelling a counterattack by Tanagraean forces and a group of Thebans who had come to aid them, the Athenians captured some arms, erected a victory trophy, and then withdrew—the ground forces returning to Athens, while the naval contingent went back to their ships. Nicias, with his fleet of sixty ships, proceeded along the coast, raiding the Locrian seaboard before returning to Athens.

Around this time, the Lacedaemonians established a new colony at Heraclea in the region of Trachis. They had several motivations for this endeavor. The Malians, who inhabited the area, were divided into three tribes: the Paralians, the Hiereans, and the Trachinians. The Trachinians, suffering heavy losses in a war with their neighbors, the Oetaeans, initially considered seeking protection from Athens. However, fearing that Athens might not provide the security they desired, they instead sent an envoy, Tisamenus, to Lacedaemon. The Dorians, the original kin of the Lacedaemonians, joined the Trachinians in this appeal, as they too were under threat from the same enemy. After hearing their plea, the Lacedaemonians decided to send out a colony. They aimed to assist both the Trachinians and the Dorians and saw the new settlement as strategically advantageous for the ongoing war against Athens. A fleet could be stationed there to threaten Euboea, with a short crossing to the island, and the town would serve as a key waypoint on the route to Thrace. These strategic benefits heightened the Lacedaemonians' eagerness to establish the colony.

First consulting the oracle at Delphi and receiving a favorable response, they sent out settlers, consisting of Spartans and Perioeci, and invited other Greeks who wished to join, excluding Ionians, Achaeans, and certain other groups. Three Lacedaemonians—Leon, Alcidas, and Damagon—were appointed as the colony's founding leaders. Upon arrival, they fortified the newly established city, now named Heraclea, located approximately four and a half miles from the pass at Thermopylae and two and a quarter miles from the sea. They also began constructing docks and fortifications, closing off the side of the settlement facing Thermopylae, near the pass itself, to ensure the defenses could be easily maintained."

"The founding of this new town, intended as a threat to Euboea (with only a short crossing to Cenaeum on the island), initially caused considerable alarm in Athens. However, the anticipated trouble never materialized, as the town did not ultimately pose any significant challenge. The reason for this lay largely with the Thessalians, who controlled the surrounding region and viewed the new settlement as a direct threat to their territory. Concerned that it might become a powerful neighboring force, the Thessalians constantly harassed and waged war on the settlers. Despite the initially high number of inhabitants, drawn from various places to this Spartan-founded town which they assumed would guarantee prosperity, the continual attacks from the Thessalians eventually wore them down.

At the same time, the Lacedaemonians themselves, through their appointed governors, contributed significantly to the town's decline. By governing in a harsh and, in some cases, unjust manner, they drove away many of the original settlers, undermining the town's prosperity and reducing its population. This harsh governance made it even easier for the neighboring Thessalians to weaken the settlement.

During the same summer, around the time the Athenians were held up at Melos, their fellow citizens stationed on thirty ships off the Peloponnesian coast undertook a series of operations. First, they ambushed and killed a group of guards at Ellomenus in Leucadia. They then launched an attack on Leucas itself, assembling a large force with reinforcements that included the entire Acarnanian levy (except for Oeniadae), as well as troops from Zacynthus, Cephalonia, and an additional fifteen ships from Corcyra. Although the Leucadians witnessed the devastation of their land on both sides of the isthmus— where their town of Leucas and the temple of Apollo were located— they refrained from responding, as the enemy's numbers were overwhelming.

The Acarnanians urged Demosthenes, the Athenian general, to construct a wall that would cut off Leucas from the mainland. They believed that such a blockade would ensure the town's capture, ridding them of a persistent and troublesome adversary. However, in the meantime, the Messenians had persuaded Demosthenes that this was an opportune moment to attack the Aetolians, given the large force he now had at his command. The Aetolians were not only long-standing enemies of Naupactus but, if defeated, would open up the rest of the region to Athenian influence.

The Aetolians were known to be numerous and skilled in warfare, yet they lived scattered in unwalled villages and had only light armor, making them, in the Messenians' opinion, vulnerable to a swift attack before they could receive reinforcements. They advised Demosthenes to attack the tribes in a specific order: beginning with the Apodotians, then moving to the Ophionians, and finally targeting the Eurytanians, the largest Aetolian tribe, known for speaking a language reportedly very hard to understand and for eating their meat raw. Once these key tribes were subdued, the Messenians argued, the rest of Aetolia would easily fall into line."

Demosthenes agreed to this plan, not only to satisfy the Messenians but also because he believed that by bringing the Aetolians into alliance with his other continental supporters, he could potentially march against the Boeotians without needing additional forces from Athens. His strategy involved advancing through Ozolian Locris to Kytinium in Doris, keeping Mount Parnassus to his right until he reached the Phocians. He anticipated that the Phocians, either due to their long-standing friendship with Athens or through persuasion, would join his cause. Once he reached Phocis, he would already be on the border of Boeotia.

Thus, Demosthenes set sail from Leucas, even though the Acarnanians were opposed to abandoning the siege of Leucas. When he arrived at Sollium, he informed them of his intentions. However, when the Acarnanians refused to support his plan due to his failure to invest Leucas, Demosthenes proceeded alone. He took with him the Cephallenians, the Messenians, the Zacynthians, and three hundred Athenian marines from his own ships, as the fifteen Corcyraean vessels had already departed. His chosen base was Oeneon in Locris, as the Ozolian Locrians were Athenian allies and were expected to join him with their forces once he moved inland. The Locrians, being neighbors of the Aetolians and familiar with both the terrain and the style of warfare in the region, were believed to be invaluable allies in the campaign.

After spending the night with his army at the sacred precinct of Nemean Zeus—where, according to local lore, the poet Hesiod had been killed by the inhabitants in fulfillment of an oracle foretelling his death in Nemea—Demosthenes set out at dawn to invade Aetolia. On the first day, he captured Potidania; on the second, Krokyle; and on the third, he took Tichium. Here, he paused to send the gathered spoils back to Eupalium in Locris, with plans to advance as far as the territory of the Ophionians. If the Ophionians refused to submit, he intended to return to Naupactus and plan a renewed assault.

Meanwhile, the Aetolians had been aware of Demosthenes' plans from the outset. As soon as his army began the invasion, they rallied in great numbers, with all the Aetolian tribes mobilizing, including even the most remote Ophionians, as well as the Bomiensians and Calliensians, who lived near the Malian Gulf.

The Messenians, sticking to their original advice, continued to assure Demosthenes that the Aetolians would be easily defeated. They encouraged him to move swiftly, urging him to capture each village immediately upon arrival without giving the entire Aetolian nation time to gather against him. Motivated by his advisors and confident in his recent successes, Demosthenes pressed forward without waiting for the Locrian reinforcements, who were meant to supply the much-needed light-armed troops for throwing javelins. He advanced and captured Aegitium, a town located on elevated ground about nine miles from the sea. However, the town's inhabitants fled to the hills overlooking the settlement.

At this point, the Aetolian forces, now assembled, launched their counterattack. They charged down from the hills on all sides, throwing javelins at the Athenians and their allies, then retreating whenever the Athenian forces advanced. As soon as the Athenians pulled back, the Aetolians would renew their attack. For an extended period, the battle continued in this pattern of alternating advance and retreat, in which the Athenians found themselves increasingly at a disadvantage.

The Athenians managed to hold their ground as long as their archers had arrows to shoot, which kept the light-armed Aetolians at a distance. However, once the captain of the archers was killed and his forces scattered, the soldiers found themselves exhausted from repeatedly engaging in the same actions. Pressed hard by the Aetolians' relentless javelin attacks, they eventually broke ranks and fled. Their retreat quickly became chaotic, with soldiers falling into deep ravines and rugged terrain that they did not know, which led many to their deaths. This situation was made worse by the loss of their Messenian guide, Chromon, who had also been killed.

A large number of Athenians were overtaken during the pursuit by the swift, light-armed Aetolians, who cut them down with their javelins. Many others lost their way and ended up in a dense forest with no clear escape route, which was soon set ablaze by the enemy, trapping and killing those within. The Athenian army suffered every form of hardship and horror associated with a disorderly retreat. Those who survived managed to escape with difficulty back to the sea and eventually reached Oeneon in Locris, the point from which they had initially set out.

The losses were heavy among the allies, and around one hundred and twenty Athenian heavy infantrymen perished—all in their prime and among the best soldiers in the city of Athens to fall during the war. Among the slain was also Procles, Demosthenes' colleague in command. The Athenians arranged a truce with the Aetolians to recover their dead and then retreated to Naupactus. From there, they returned to Athens by ship, while Demosthenes remained behind in Naupactus and its surroundings, too fearful to face the Athenians after such a severe loss.

Around the same time, the Athenians stationed along the coast of Sicily conducted a raid on Locris. During a landing from their ships, they defeated the Locrian forces that opposed them and captured a fort on the river Halex.

Later in the summer, the Aetolians, who had already sent envoys to Corinth and Lacedaemon before the Athenian expedition, succeeded in securing support for an assault on Naupactus, which they viewed as responsible for inviting the Athenian invasion. The Lacedaemonians agreed to send a force in early autumn, comprising three thousand allied heavy infantry, including five hundred from Heraclea, the newly established city in Trachis. The expedition was led by Eurylochus, a Spartan commander, along with his fellow Spartans, Macarius and Menedaius.

Once the army had assembled at Delphi, Eurylochus sent a herald to the Ozolian Locrians, as the route to Naupactus passed through their territory. Additionally, he saw an opportunity to sway them away from their alliance with Athens. His principal allies among the Locrians were the Amphissians, who were anxious due to their hostilities with the Phocians. The Amphissians were the first to give hostages to Eurylochus, and they encouraged the other Locrian tribes to do the same, fearful of the invading force.

The neighboring Myonians, who controlled the most challenging mountain passes, were the next to provide hostages, followed by the Ipnians, Messapians, Tritaeans, Chalaeans, Tolophonians, Hessians, and Oeanthians—all of whom ultimately joined the expedition. The Olpaeans agreed to provide hostages but refrained from actively participating in the invasion. However, the Hyaeans initially refused to either join the invasion or give hostages, until one of their villages, Polis, was captured by the Lacedaemonian forces.

Once his preparations were complete, Eurylochus placed the hostages in the town of Kytinium in Doris for safekeeping. He then began his advance toward Naupactus, passing through the territory of the Locrians. Along the way, he seized control of Oeneon and Eupalium, two Locrian towns that had refused to join his campaign. When he reached the territory of Naupactus, he was joined by the Aetolian forces. Together, the combined army laid waste to the surrounding lands and captured the unfortified suburbs of the town. They also seized Molycrium, a Corinthian colony that had been under Athenian control.

Meanwhile, Demosthenes, the Athenian general who had stayed near Naupactus after his defeat in Aetolia, learned of Eurylochus's approach and became concerned for the safety of the town. He appealed to the Acarnanians for assistance, though convincing them was not easy due to their resentment over his earlier departure from Leucas. Despite their initial reluctance, they agreed and sent a thousand heavy infantry to accompany him on his ships. These troops managed to enter Naupactus and reinforce its defenses, saving the town, which had been vulnerable due to its extensive walls and a shortage of defenders.

Seeing that Naupactus had been reinforced and realizing that an assault on the town was now unlikely to succeed, Eurylochus and his forces decided not to return to the Peloponnese. Instead, they withdrew to the region formerly known as Aeolis, now called Calydon and Pleuron, as well as nearby locations including Proschium in Aetolia. While there, they were approached by envoys from Ambracia who proposed a combined attack on Amphilochian Argos, along with the rest of Amphilochia and Acarnania. The Ambraciots argued that conquering these territories would bring all of the mainland under the influence of Lacedaemon. Eurylochus agreed to their proposal, dismissed the Aetolian forces, and settled his troops in the area, waiting for the Ambraciots to mobilize so that he could join them for an assault on Argos.

As summer came to an end and winter set in, the Athenians stationed in Sicily, alongside their Greek allies and some Sicel allies who had defected from Syracuse, launched a campaign against the Sicel town of Inessa. Inessa's acropolis was held by a Syracusan garrison, and despite their efforts, the Athenians were unable to capture the stronghold. During their retreat, the allied forces following behind the Athenians were ambushed by the Syracusans from the fort, resulting in a heavy loss of life among the allied troops.

Following this, Laches and the Athenian forces aboard their ships conducted a series of raids along the coast of Locris. In one engagement near the river Caicinus, they confronted the Locrian forces led by Proxenus, the son of Capaton, defeated them, captured some arms, and then withdrew.

In the same winter, the Athenians undertook the purification of Delos, following what seems to have been an instruction from an oracle. Although Pisistratus, the former tyrant of Athens, had previously purified the island, he had only cleansed the part visible from the temple. This time, however, the Athenians purified the entire island in a more thorough manner. They exhumed and relocated all the graves of those who had died on Delos, and they issued a decree forbidding any future deaths or births to take place on the island. Instead, anyone about to give birth or pass away was to be transported to Rhenea, a neighboring island so close to Delos that Polycrates, the tyrant of Samos, had once tied Rhenea to Delos with a chain and dedicated it to the Delian Apollo during his period of naval dominance.

Following the purification, the Athenians held the Delian games as a quinquennial festival for the first time. In ancient times, Delos had hosted a major festival attended by Ionians and other nearby islanders, who gathered to celebrate with athletic and poetic contests. Cities would send choirs of dancers to participate, much as the Ionians now do for the festival at Ephesus. Evidence of these ancient festivities is found in verses by Homer in a hymn to Apollo: 'Phœbus, wherever thou strayest, far or near,

Delos was still of all thy haunts most dear.

Thither the robed Ionians take their way

With wife and child to keep thy holiday,

Invoke thy favour on each manly game,

And dance and sing in honour of thy name.'

This passage shows that there was once a strong tradition of athletic contests in Delos. Homer also implies a poetic competition in which the Ionians came to compete, as indicated in another part of the same hymn. After describing the dance performed by the Delian women, he closes his praise with the following lines, in which he references himself: 'Well, may Apollo keep you all! and so,

Sweethearts, good-bye—yet tell me not I go

Out from your hearts; and if in after hours

Some other wanderer in this world of ours

Touch at your shores, and ask your maidens here

Who sings the songs the sweetest to your ear,

Think of me then, and answer with a smile,

"A blind old man of Scio's rocky isle."'

Through these verses, Homer attests to the longstanding tradition of a grand festival and assembly at Delos. In later periods, although the islanders and Athenians continued to send choirs and sacrifices to Delos, the contests and most ceremonies faded, likely due to hardships over time. On this occasion, however, the Athenians revived the games, adding horse races as a new feature.

In the same winter, the Ambraciots, fulfilling their promise to Eurylochus when they had retained his army, set out with three thousand heavy infantry to attack Amphilochian Argos. Upon entering Argive territory, they seized Olpae, a fortified hill near the sea that the Acarnanians had previously used as their main judicial center. This stronghold stood approximately two and three-quarters miles from the city of Argos along the coast.

In response, the Acarnanians mobilized part of their forces to defend Argos, while positioning the rest at Crenae, or 'The Wells,' in Amphilochia. There, they established a camp to intercept Eurylochus and his Peloponnesian forces, aiming to prevent their junction with the Ambraciots. Additionally, the Acarnanians sent word to Demosthenes, the Athenian commander from the recent Aetolian campaign, requesting him to lead them in battle. They also summoned the twenty Athenian ships stationed off the Peloponnesian coast under the command of Aristotle, son of Timocrates, and Hierophon, son of Antimnestus.

Meanwhile, the Ambraciots at Olpae, concerned that Eurylochus's forces might not succeed in joining them due to the Acarnanian resistance, sent an urgent message back to their city. They asked for reinforcements, requesting that the entire Ambraciot levy come to their aid, fearing that without additional support, they might either have to fight alone or face significant danger if they attempted to withdraw.

Meanwhile, Eurylochus and his Peloponnesian forces, upon hearing that the Ambraciots had reached Olpae, quickly set out from Proschium to join them. Moving with all possible speed, they crossed the Achelous River and advanced through Acarnania, which they found largely deserted, as most of the population had gone to support Argos. Keeping the city of Stratus and its garrison to their right and the remainder of Acarnania to their left, they traversed the territory around Stratus, proceeding through Phytia, then skirting Medeon, and finally passing through Limnaea. Once they passed Limnaea, they left Acarnania and entered friendly territory belonging to the Agraeans. From there, they crossed Mount Thymaus, part of the Agraean lands, and descended into the territory of Argos under the cover of night. Moving carefully, they passed between the city of Argos and the Acarnanian forces positioned at Crenae, successfully joining the Ambraciots at Olpae.

At dawn, the united forces set up camp at a location called Metropolis. Not long afterward, the Athenian fleet of twenty ships arrived in the Ambracian Gulf to reinforce the Argives. With them came Demosthenes, accompanied by two hundred Messenian heavy infantry and sixty Athenian archers. The Athenian fleet positioned itself off Olpae, blockading the hill from the sea, while the Acarnanians, along with a few Amphilochians (most of whom were forcibly restrained by the Ambraciots), had already assembled at Argos and were preparing for battle. They had appointed Demosthenes as commander of the entire allied army, to lead alongside their own generals.

Demosthenes moved the forces close to Olpae, establishing a camp with a deep ravine separating the two armies. For five days, both sides remained inactive. On the sixth day, they finally arranged their forces for battle. The Peloponnesian army was larger and extended beyond the length of their opponents' line, and Demosthenes, concerned that his right flank might be surrounded, strategically placed an ambush. He hid around four hundred heavy infantry and light troops in a hollow overgrown with bushes. These troops were instructed to rise up and attack the left wing of the enemy from behind at the moment of engagement.

Once both sides were ready, they engaged in battle. Demosthenes took position on the right wing alongside the Messenians and a small contingent of Athenians, while the remaining line consisted of the various Acarnanian divisions and the Amphilochian javelin throwers. The Peloponnesians and Ambraciots formed their ranks in a less organized manner, with soldiers from different regions mixed together, except for the Mantineans, who were massed on the left flank. However, they did not reach the far end of the left wing, where Eurylochus and his troops faced the Messenians and Demosthenes directly.

The Peloponnesians were now fully engaged in battle, and their outflanking wing was on the verge of turning the right flank of their opponents. However, at that moment, the Acarnanians, who had been lying in ambush, attacked from behind. Their sudden assault caught the Peloponnesians completely off guard, breaking their formation almost instantly, as they didn't even attempt to resist. The sudden panic that spread through their ranks led to the rapid collapse of most of their army. The sight of Eurylochus's division, along with their strongest soldiers, being cut down caused even greater terror. Demosthenes and his Messenian troops, positioned in this part of the field, were responsible for much of the success in this area.

Meanwhile, the Ambraciots, known as the best soldiers in the region, along with the troops on the Peloponnesian right wing, successfully defeated the division they faced and pursued them all the way to Argos. However, when they returned from the pursuit, they found that their main body had been defeated. Pressed hard by the Acarnanians, they struggled to make their way back to Olpae. Their retreat was chaotic, with heavy casualties along the way, as soldiers dashed back without any semblance of discipline or order. The Mantineans were the only ones who managed to keep their ranks relatively intact during the retreat.

The battle continued until evening. On the following day, Menedaius, who had taken sole command after the deaths of

Eurylochus and Macarius, was at a loss about how to proceed. Having suffered such a severe defeat, he faced the prospect of a siege, with his forces trapped by land and the Athenian fleet blocking any retreat by sea. Equally unsure of how to retreat safely, he opened negotiations with Demosthenes and the Acarnanian generals, seeking a truce that would allow them to withdraw and also recover their dead.

The Acarnanians agreed to return the bodies, allowing them to set up a trophy and retrieve their own dead, numbering around three hundred. However, they publicly refused to grant a truce for the entire army to retreat. In a covert arrangement, however, Demosthenes and his Acarnanian allies secretly allowed the Mantineans, Menedaius, and other key Peloponnesian commanders and notable figures to leave. This strategy aimed to isolate the Ambraciots and foreign mercenaries, leaving them unsupported, and to damage the reputation of the Lacedaemonians and Peloponnesians among the Greeks in the region by portraying them as self-serving and untrustworthy.

While the Peloponnesians retrieved and hastily buried their dead, those granted permission to leave discreetly prepared for their retreat. During this time, news reached Demosthenes and the Acarnanians that the Ambraciots from the city, responding to the initial message from Olpae, were on their way with their entire force through Amphilochia to join their compatriots, unaware of the defeat that had occurred. Demosthenes immediately prepared to intercept them, sending a strong detachment ahead to secure the roads and occupy strategic positions.

Meanwhile, the Mantineans and others included in the secret truce began leaving Olpae under the pretense of gathering herbs and firewood. They quietly moved out in pairs and small groups, picking up plants and sticks as they went to maintain their cover, until they had put some distance between themselves and Olpae, at which point they quickened their pace to escape. Seeing this, the Ambraciots and others who were left in larger groups started moving as well, thinking it was their turn to depart, and soon began running to catch up.

Initially, the Acarnanians believed that all of them were attempting to leave without permission, and they began to pursue the Peloponnesians. They suspected betrayal and even threw a few javelins at some of their own generals who tried to calm them, explaining that a truce had indeed been granted to certain groups. Eventually, the Acarnanians allowed the Mantineans and Peloponnesians to pass but turned their attack on the Ambraciots, leading to confusion as they tried to distinguish between Ambraciots and Peloponnesians. In the resulting chaos, approximately two hundred Ambraciots were killed. The remaining survivors managed to escape into the neighboring territory of Agraea, where they found refuge with Salynthius, the Agraean king and ally.

Meanwhile, the Ambraciot reinforcements from the city reached Idomene, a location defined by two high hills. The troops that Demosthenes had sent ahead managed to occupy the higher of the two hills after nightfall, completely unnoticed by the Ambraciots, who had climbed up the smaller hill and set up camp there. After their evening meal, Demosthenes and the rest of his army set out; he led half of his forces toward the pass, while the other half took a route through the Amphilochian hills. At dawn, he launched a surprise attack on the Ambraciots, who were still asleep and entirely unaware of the events that had unfolded. They assumed it was their own allies approaching, as Demosthenes had strategically placed the Messenians at the front and instructed them to speak in the Doric dialect, a familiar sound to the sentinels. Given the early hour and limited visibility, the Ambraciot guards were easily deceived.

Demosthenes's forces overpowered the Ambraciot troops almost immediately, killing most of them where they lay and sending the rest into a desperate flight over the hills. However, the surrounding roads had already been secured by Demosthenes's forces, and while the Amphilochians were familiar with the local terrain, the Ambraciots were not. Heavily armored and facing a light-armed enemy, they were at a severe disadvantage, unable to navigate effectively and often stumbling into ravines or ambushes set for them, where many met their end. In their frantic attempts to escape, some even ran toward the sea, not far off, and upon spotting Athenian ships patrolling the coastline, chose to swim out to them. Their fear of falling into the hands of the barbarous Amphilochians was so intense that, in their panic, they preferred to die at the hands of the Athenians if it came to that.

The Ambraciot force suffered devastating losses, with only a few surviving to reach the city. The Acarnanians, after stripping the bodies of their fallen enemies and setting up a victory trophy, returned to Argos.

The next day, a herald arrived from the Ambraciots who had fled from Olpae to the territory of the Agraeans. His mission was to request permission to retrieve the bodies of those who had died in the initial battle, during which they had attempted to leave camp alongside the Mantineans and their allies but without official permission. When he saw the vast array of arms belonging to the Ambraciot troops who had come from the city, he was stunned, unaware of the recent disaster and assuming these arms belonged to his own party.

Someone nearby, noticing his reaction, asked why he seemed so surprised and inquired about the number of Ambraciots killed in the earlier engagement, assuming that the herald was from the troops at Idomene. The herald responded, "About two hundred." His questioner replied, "But the arms you see here are from more than a thousand men." The herald, taken aback, asked, "Then these are not the arms of those who fought with us?" The other person responded, "Yes, if you fought with those at Idomene yesterday." The herald, now bewildered, replied, "But we fought no one yesterday; it was the day before, during our retreat." The other explained, "Regardless, we fought yesterday with the reinforcements that came from Ambracia to join you."

Upon hearing this and realizing that the entire reinforcement from the city had been annihilated, the herald was overwhelmed with grief. Distraught by the scale of the catastrophe that had struck his people, he left immediately without completing his mission or asking again for the dead. This disaster was one of the greatest suffered by any single Greek city within such a short span of time during the war. The precise number of casualties is not recorded here, as the count reported seemed almost too vast to be credible given the size of the city.

Had the Acarnanians and Amphilochians taken Demosthenes's and the Athenians' advice to seize Ambracia, they could have captured it without resistance. However, they feared that having Athens as a neighbor would be even worse than dealing with the current Ambraciots.

Following the battle, the Acarnanians allocated one-third of the spoils to the Athenians, with the remaining portion distributed among the various Acarnanian towns. However, the share designated for the Athenians was intercepted and captured during its voyage back to Athens. The three hundred full sets of armor, or panoplies, currently housed in the temples of Athens were those set aside by the Acarnanians specifically for Demosthenes. He personally transported these to Athens, and this successful campaign significantly eased his return, reducing the risks he faced after the earlier defeat in Aetolia. Meanwhile, the Athenians with the fleet of twenty ships returned to Naupactus.

After Demosthenes and the Athenians departed, the Acarnanians and Amphilochians granted a free retreat to the Ambraciots and Peloponnesians who had sought refuge with Salynthius and the Agraeans. These forces had relocated to Oeniadac from Salynthius's territory. They also established a treaty and alliance with the Ambraciots that would last for one hundred years. This agreement was defensive rather than offensive: the Ambraciots would not be required to support the Acarnanians against the Peloponnesians, nor would the Acarnanians have to aid the Ambraciots against the Athenians. Additionally, the Ambraciots agreed to relinquish any strongholds and hostages they held from the Amphilochians and to refrain from supporting Anactorium, a city hostile to the Acarnanians. With these terms in place, the conflict came to an end.

Shortly afterward, the Corinthians sent a reinforcement of three hundred of their own heavy infantry to Ambracia, under the command of Xenocleides, son of Euthycles. This contingent successfully reached Ambracia after navigating a challenging journey across the mainland. Thus concluded the history of the events in Ambracia.

In the same winter, the Athenians in Sicily, together with their Sicel allies, conducted a raid on the lands of Himera, with the Sicels invading from the interior. The Athenians also sailed to the Aeolian Islands. Upon their return to Rhegium, they found that Pythodorus, son of Isolochus, had arrived to take over command of the fleet from Laches. Representatives from the allies in Sicily had gone to Athens to request additional support, explaining that the Syracusans, who already controlled the land, were now working to assemble a navy to break the blockade that restricted them from the sea. In response, the Athenians decided to outfit forty ships to send to Sicily, hoping that a stronger naval presence would hasten the end of the conflict and also provide an opportunity to train their fleet. Pythodorus was dispatched with a small force, while Sophocles, son of Sostratides, and Eurymedon, son of Thucles, were selected to follow with the main contingent of the fleet.

In the meantime, Pythodorus assumed command of Laches's ships and, near the end of winter, launched an attack on the Locrian fort that Laches had previously captured. However, he was defeated by the Locrians and returned unsuccessful.

At the very start of spring, Mount Etna erupted, as it had on previous occasions, sending out streams of fire that destroyed land owned by the Catanians who live around the mountain. Mount Etna, the largest volcano in Sicily, had not erupted for fifty years; this was the third eruption recorded since the Greeks began settling in Sicily.

These were the main events of the winter, marking the end of the sixth year of this ongoing war, as recorded by Thucydides.

Book IV

Chapter XII

Seventh Year of the War—Occupation of Pylos—Surrender of the Spartan Army in Sphacteria

The next summer, just as the grain began to ripen, ten ships from Syracuse and the same number from Locri sailed to Messina in Sicily. They entered the town with the support of the locals, and Messina broke away from the Athenians. The Syracusans organized this action mainly because they saw Messina as a strategic entry into Sicily and feared that the Athenians might later use it to launch a larger attack. The Locrians joined because they wanted to fight on both sides of the strait and weaken their rivals, the people of Rhegium. Meanwhile, the Locrians invaded the Rhegian land with all their troops to keep them from helping Messina. This move was also encouraged by some exiled Rhegians who were with them, as long-standing internal conflicts had left Rhegium too divided to put up a defense, making it an easier target for invasion. After ravaging the area, the Locrian forces withdrew, leaving their ships to guard Messina while other ships were being prepared to continue the war from that base.

Around the same time, in early spring before the grain had fully ripened, the Peloponnesians and their allies marched into Attica under Agis, the son of Archidamus and king of the Lacedaemonians, and began to devastate the land. Meanwhile, the Athenians sent forty ships they had readied for Sicily, led by the generals Eurymedon and Sophocles, with their colleague Pythodorus already ahead of them. The generals were also instructed to check on the Corcyraeans in the town, who were being harassed by exiles in the mountains. To support these exiles, sixty Peloponnesian ships had recently set sail, thinking they could easily capture the city because of the severe food shortage.

Demosthenes, who had not been engaged in any task since returning from Acarnania, sought and obtained permission to use the fleet along the coast of Peloponnese if he wished.

As they neared Laconia, they learned that the Peloponnesian ships had already reached Corcyra. Eurymedon and Sophocles wanted to proceed directly to the island, but Demosthenes insisted they first stop at Pylos to do what needed to be done before continuing. While they argued, a sudden storm blew the fleet to Pylos. Demosthenes immediately urged them to fortify the location, pointing out that this was his reason for joining the voyage. He showed them there was plenty of stone and timber on site, the location was naturally strong, and much of the surrounding land was uninhabited. Pylos, also known as Coryphasium by the Lacedaemonians, was about seventy-two kilometers from Sparta and located in the ancient territory of the Messenians. The commanders objected, saying there were plenty of deserted headlands in Peloponnese if he wanted to waste the city's resources. However, Demosthenes argued that this site was unique because it had a harbor nearby, and the Messenians, who originally came from this land and spoke the same dialect as the Lacedaemonians, could cause significant trouble for them with raids from here while also serving as a reliable garrison.

After discussing the idea with the company captains and failing to convince either the generals or the soldiers, Demosthenes waited with the others, hindered by the bad weather. Eventually, the soldiers, growing restless and eager for something to do, suddenly decided to go ahead and fortify the area on their own. They began working with determination; lacking proper iron tools, they collected stones and arranged them however they could. When they needed mortar, they carried it on their backs, as they had no proper containers, bending over to keep it balanced and clasping their hands behind them to keep it from falling. They worked tirelessly, aiming to reinforce the weaker spots before the Lacedaemonians arrived, though most of the site was naturally secure and didn't need much extra defense.

During this time, the Lacedaemonians were engaged in a festival and initially dismissed the news, assuming that they could drive out the enemy or easily capture the site whenever they decided to move. They also delayed partly because their main army was still away in Athens. The Athenians fortified the essential areas on the land side within six days, leaving Demosthenes with five ships to hold the position, while the rest of the fleet continued on to Corcyra and Sicily.

When the Peloponnesians in Attica heard of the occupation of Pylos, they quickly returned home, as the Lacedaemonians and their king Agis felt this situation was urgent. Since their invasion had begun early in the season, when the crops were still green, most of their troops had limited supplies. The weather was also unusually harsh for that time of year, making conditions difficult for their army. Several factors led them to end the invasion sooner than expected, and they only stayed in Attica for fifteen days.

Around this time, the Athenian general Simonides gathered a few Athenians from nearby garrisons along with some allies in the region and managed to seize Eion in Thrace, a colony of the Mendaeans and hostile toward Athens, through treachery. However, soon after he took control, the Chalcidians and Bottiaeans arrived and drove him out, causing heavy losses among his soldiers.

Upon the return of the Peloponnesians from Attica, the Spartans, along with the closest Perioeci, immediately marched toward Pylos, while the other Lacedaemonians followed more slowly, as they had just come back from another campaign. Messages were sent throughout Peloponnese, urging forces to come to Pylos as quickly as possible. Meanwhile, the sixty Peloponnesian ships stationed at Corcyra were summoned. The crews dragged the ships across the isthmus of Leucas, managing to avoid detection by the Athenian fleet stationed at Zacynthus, and successfully reached Pylos, where the land forces had already gathered.

Before the Peloponnesian fleet arrived, Demosthenes managed to send two ships without being noticed to alert Eurymedon and the

Athenian fleet at Zacynthus of the threat to Pylos and to call for immediate support. While the ships raced to deliver Demosthenes' message, the Lacedaemonians prepared to attack the fort by both land and sea, assuming it would be easy to capture given its hurried construction and the small garrison defending it. Expecting the arrival of Athenian reinforcements, they planned to block the harbor entrances to prevent the Athenians from anchoring inside.

The island of Sphacteria stretched in a line close to the harbor, serving as a natural shield and narrowing the harbor's entrances. On the side nearest Pylos and the Athenian defenses, there was space for only two ships to pass, while the entrance on the side closer to the mainland could accommodate eight or nine ships. Sphacteria was densely wooded, uninhabited, and around one and a half miles long, with no paths through it. The Lacedaemonians intended to close these narrow inlets by lining up their ships closely, their prows facing outward to the sea. Worried that the Athenians might use the island as a base for operations, they stationed some heavy infantry there and positioned more troops along the coast. This strategy would prevent the Athenians from landing on either the island or the mainland, making both locations hostile to them. Pylos itself, facing the open sea, lacked a harbor and provided no secure point for Athenian ships to support their forces, so the Lacedaemonians anticipated capturing the fort without a naval battle or much risk, as it had been hastily occupied and had limited supplies.

After this plan was settled, they moved the heavy infantry onto the island, selecting them by lot from different companies. Some troops had already crossed in shifts, but the final detachment consisted of four hundred and twenty soldiers, accompanied by their Helot servants, all under the command of Epitadas, son of Molobrus.

Meanwhile, seeing that the Lacedaemonians were preparing a simultaneous attack by land and sea, Demosthenes did not remain idle. He positioned himself along the fortifications and enclosed the remaining ships with a stockade, using the sailors from these vessels as additional defenders. Since they lacked proper shields, most of them made do with makeshift ones woven from willow branches, as weapons were scarce in such a desolate place. The limited equipment they had was gathered from a Messenian privateer and a boat from some visiting Messenians, including forty heavy infantry who joined his defense.

Demosthenes positioned most of his men, both those armed and unarmed, at the strongest points facing inward to defend against a land assault. He selected sixty heavy infantry and a few archers and led them down to the shore, where he anticipated the enemy would likely try to land. Although this area was rocky and faced the open sea, it was the weakest part of the fortifications, as the Athenians, confident in their naval strength, had neglected its defenses. Demosthenes believed that if the enemy managed to land here, they might think they had a good chance of capturing the position. Therefore, he stationed his heavy infantry at the water's edge to block any possible landing and addressed them with the following encouragement.

"Soldiers and comrades in this mission, I trust none of you will waste time thinking too carefully about all the dangers surrounding us. Instead, let us quickly confront the enemy without trying to calculate every risk; this approach gives us the best chance of survival. In critical situations like ours, overthinking is a mistake—facing the danger head-on is our best option. Personally, I believe that most factors work in our favor if we stay strong and don't lose our advantage by fearing the enemy's numbers. One of our strengths is the difficulty of their landing, but this will only work if we hold our ground. If we give way, then despite its natural challenges, the landing will be manageable enough without defenders, and the enemy will become far more dangerous if he manages to retreat after we push him back. It will be much easier for us to repel him while he is still on his ships than once he's landed and meets us on equal terms.

As for his numbers, don't be overly intimidated. Large as their forces may be, they can only approach in small groups due to the limited space for docking. Moreover, the numerical advantage we face isn't that of a land army where conditions are even, but rather of troops confined to ships, relying on many factors to even act effectively. Therefore, I believe their challenges balance out our lack of numbers. Also, I remind you, as Athenians who know what it's like to face landings on hostile shores, how difficult it is to repel a determined enemy who holds his ground, even when faced with crashing waves and the looming ships. Stand firm in this moment, push the enemy back at the shoreline, and save both yourselves and this stronghold."

Encouraged by Demosthenes' words, the Athenians grew more confident and moved down to the water's edge, ready to face the enemy. The Lacedaemonians then launched their assault, attacking both by land and sea, with forty-three ships led by their admiral Thrasymelidas, son of Cratesicles, a Spartan, aiming exactly where Demosthenes had anticipated. The Athenians now found themselves defending from both fronts, as the enemy's ships approached in small groups, each group replacing the last, as not many could dock at once. The Lacedaemonians showed great determination, cheering each other on as they tried to break through and capture the fortifications.

Among them, Brasidas stood out. As captain of a galley, he saw that some captains and helmsmen were hesitant due to the challenging position, fearing they might wreck their ships even where landing seemed possible. Brasidas urged them to put the defense of their land above their concerns for their vessels, declaring that they shouldn't let the enemy establish a foothold in their territory just to save some wood. He encouraged the allies to sacrifice their ships if needed, in gratitude to Lacedaemon for its many benefits, and to drive their vessels onto the shore, land however they could, and take control of the place and its defenders.

Unsatisfied with mere words, Brasidas forced his helmsman to run his ship ashore, and, stepping onto the gangway, attempted to land. However, the Athenians struck him down, inflicting numerous wounds until he collapsed. As he fell into the bow of the ship, his shield slipped off and fell into the sea, later washing ashore, where the Athenians retrieved it and used it as part of the trophy they erected to commemorate this battle. Despite the efforts of the other Lacedaemonians, they struggled to land due to the difficult terrain and the Athenians' unyielding defense. It was an unusual reversal, with the Athenians fighting on land—and on Laconian soil—against Lacedaemonians approaching from the sea. The Lacedaemonians, renowned for their land-based military prowess, were now attempting a seaborne assault on their own territory, while the Athenians, celebrated for their dominance at sea, held firm onshore.

After attacking all that day and most of the next, the Peloponnesians finally halted and, on the following day, sent some of their ships to Asine for timber to construct siege engines, hoping to use them against the high wall near the harbor where landing was most feasible. At this point, the Athenian fleet from Zacynthus, now reinforced to fifty ships with additional vessels from Naupactus and four from Chios, arrived. Seeing both the shore and the island filled with Spartan troops and the enemy's fleet lying idle in the harbor, the Athenians found no suitable place to anchor. They withdrew to the nearby deserted island of Prote, where they spent the night. The next day, prepared to fight in open waters if the enemy chose to confront them, the Athenians resolved that, if the Lacedaemonians stayed put, they would enter the harbor and launch an attack.

The Lacedaemonians did not venture out to meet them and, having failed to block the harbor entrances, remained onshore, busy manning their ships and readying themselves to engage any Athenians who sailed in. Seeing this, the Athenians advanced toward each entrance and attacked the Lacedaemonian fleet, which was now mostly afloat and in line. The Athenians immediately drove them into retreat, pursuing as far as the limited space allowed, damaging many vessels and capturing five, one with its crew aboard. Charging at the rest of the ships that had fled to the shore, they rammed some that were still being manned, seized others that were abandoned, and towed away the empty ones whose crews had fled. Witnessing this, the Lacedaemonians, enraged by the misfortune that had cut off their men on the island, rushed to rescue their ships, even wading into the sea in their armor, grabbing the ships, and attempting to pull them back, each man feeling personally responsible for saving the vessels. The resulting conflict was chaotic and defied the usual naval tactics of both sides, with the Lacedaemonians engaged in a sea battle on land out of desperation, while the Athenians pressed their advantage, effectively fighting a land battle from their ships.

After considerable effort and numerous injuries on both sides, they finally broke off, with the Lacedaemonians salvaging most of their empty ships except those initially captured. Both sides retreated to their camps; the Athenians set up a trophy, returned the dead, secured the wrecks, and began patrolling closely around the island to monitor the trapped garrison, while the Peloponnesians on the mainland, now fully assembled, remained stationed near Pylos.

When word of the events at Pylos reached Sparta, the Lacedaemonians recognized the severity of their loss and resolved to send high-ranking officials to the camp to assess the situation and decide on the best course of action. Observing that aiding their men was impossible and not wanting them to succumb to starvation or be overpowered by numbers, they decided, with the agreement of the Athenian generals, to negotiate a truce at Pylos and send envoys to Athens to arrange a settlement, hoping to secure their men's release as swiftly as possible.

The Athenian generals accepted, and the terms of the truce were as follows: the Lacedaemonians would deliver to the Athenians all the ships that had participated in the recent battle, as well as all warships in Laconia, and would refrain from any assault on the fortification by land or sea.

The terms of the armistice also stated that the Athenians would allow the Lacedaemonians on the mainland to send a set amount of provisions to the men on the island: specifically, each man would receive two quarts of barley meal, one pint of wine, and a portion of meat, while each servant would receive half of this amount. This supply was to be delivered openly and under Athenian observation, with no boats permitted to reach the island except in full view. The Athenians were to maintain their blockade around the island as before, without, however, landing on it or attacking the Peloponnesian troops on land or by sea.

Additionally, if either side violated any part of these terms, the armistice would immediately be rendered void. The truce would remain in effect until the Lacedaemonian envoys returned from Athens. The Athenians would transport the envoys to Athens on a galley and return them, at which point the truce would end, and the ships would be restored to the Lacedaemonians in the condition in which they had been received.

Thus, the armistice was agreed upon, and the sixty ships were handed over. The envoys then proceeded to Athens, where they addressed the Athenian assembly as follows:

"Athenians, we Lacedaemonians have come to you to seek a resolution regarding our men on the island that will serve our interests and uphold our dignity, despite our current misfortune. We hope to speak openly and at length, which is unusual for us. Known for being brief where fewer words suffice, we find it necessary now to be more detailed, as the gravity of the situation calls for clarity and a measured approach. We ask that you listen to us in a spirit of goodwill, not as if we presume to teach or to question your intelligence, but rather as we offer advice to discerning judges on the wisest course of action.

"Your recent success provides you with a valuable opportunity: you can retain what you have gained, while adding honor and renown, and avoid the error of others who, unexpectedly fortunate, fall into the habit of overreaching, grasping continually for more because past gains came with ease. It is often those who have faced both fortune and adversity who are least likely to trust solely in their current strength. Experience has taught this to both our cities.

"If you need proof of this, consider our own misfortune. No power in Hellas stood higher than ours, yet here we are before you, though once we felt in a better position to grant the very requests we now make. This change is not due to a decline in our power or an overreach on our part; our resources remain steady, and our misjudgment was one any might make. Your recent success and the strength your city has gained should not lead you to believe that fortune will always favor you. Sensible people view their gains as precarious and stay level-headed, even in adversity. They understand that war seldom stops where one would like, but follows its own course. Thus, the wise do not become overconfident in success but remain open to peace while fortune remains favorable.

"This, Athenians, is the moment for you to act prudently with us. By choosing peace now, you avoid potential future misfortunes and spare yourselves the reputation of having achieved your present gains by mere chance. Instead, you could leave behind a legacy of strength and wisdom beyond question."

"The Lacedaemonians therefore appeal to you now, calling on you to establish a treaty and bring an end to this costly war. We propose not merely peace, but an alliance—one built on mutual respect and friendship. In every matter and at every opportunity, we hope to establish a lasting partnership between our peoples. In return, we ask for the lives of our men on the island, considering it wiser for both sides to avoid a prolonged conflict that may ultimately rest on mere chance—whether through a fortunate escape or a forced surrender from hunger and isolation. If there is to be a genuine resolution to our long-standing enmity, we believe it will not be through revenge, overwhelming military victories, or by imposing an unfair peace upon a defeated opponent. Rather, real peace is found when the more fortunate party voluntarily sets aside their advantage, guided by compassion, showing a generosity that surpasses expectation and winning over their opponent by offering peace on reasonable terms. In such a case, rather than leaving behind a debt of resentment and a burden of humiliation, one creates a lasting obligation of gratitude, which the recipient feels honor-bound to repay, preserving the agreement out of respect rather than resentment.

"Indeed, it is often observed that people act more generously toward their greatest adversaries than they do in smaller quarrels. By nature, they are inclined to yield to those who first show them respect, just as they are often provoked by arrogance into taking risks they might otherwise avoid. In the present moment, Athenians, we ask you to consider this carefully. If ever there was a time when peace served the interests of both sides, it is surely now. If we do not act, and the situation leads to further irreparable losses, both our peoples will face a deep and lasting hatred that could poison us against each other indefinitely, on a personal as well as political level. You would miss the unique advantages that we now extend to you, while we would lose the chance to resolve our current misfortune through compromise. While the outcome of this situation remains uncertain, and while you still have the chance to gain our friendship and a reputation for wisdom and moderation, let us seize this opportunity to reconcile. Let us choose peace over war and grant the rest of the Hellenic world some relief from the hardships they now endure, hardships for which they will primarily thank you.

"The origins of this war may be unknown to many, yet if peace is achieved, the credit for it will undoubtedly be yours. By deciding on peace, you can establish a genuine and respected friendship with the Lacedaemonians, not through force or demand, but through a noble acceptance of our offer. Consider, too, the many benefits that could arise from such a friendship. With the unity of Athens and Sparta, all of Hellas will look to both of you with respect, recognizing the strength that comes from such a partnership."

These were the words of the Lacedaemonians, believing that the Athenians, already inclined toward a truce yet restrained by certain hesitations, would gladly accept an offer of peace made openly and on such honorable terms, returning the men on the island in exchange. However, the Athenians, confident with the hostages in their possession, felt that the chance for peace would remain available as long as they wished, and instead saw an opportunity to demand more. Cleon, son of Cleaenetus, a popular and influential leader of the time, was at the forefront of this stance, encouraging them to respond with firmness.

The Athenians replied by insisting first that the men on the island must surrender their arms and be brought to Athens. Additionally, the Lacedaemonians were to return Nisaea, Pegae, Troezen, and Achaia— territories previously ceded to Athens under a prior agreement made when Athens, facing a moment of crisis, found a truce necessary. Only once these conditions were met would the Lacedaemonians be permitted to retrieve their men and negotiate a truce for as long as both parties agreed.

The Lacedaemonian envoys, however, made no immediate response to this demand, instead requesting that a select group of commissioners be appointed to discuss each matter more thoroughly and attempt to reach a mutual agreement without the pressures of a public assembly. At this, Cleon launched a fierce attack, accusing the envoys of dishonest intentions, claiming that their refusal to speak openly before the people demonstrated their lack of integrity. He argued that their desire to negotiate privately with a small group was simply a tactic to avoid full transparency. If they had honest intentions, he insisted, they should be willing to present their case publicly.

The Lacedaemonians, recognizing that any concessions made in their current difficult position might later cost them credibility among their allies, could not bring themselves to negotiate openly before the assembly, knowing well that such discussions could ultimately fail. They also understood that the Athenians were unlikely to agree to their requests on moderate terms, given the current balance of power. With no acceptable path forward, the envoys returned to Sparta without achieving any resolution.

With the return of the Lacedaemonian envoys, the armistice at Pylos came to an immediate end. The Lacedaemonians formally requested the return of their ships as per the terms of the truce. However, the Athenians refused, citing alleged breaches of the armistice by the Lacedaemonians, including minor but strategic attacks on the fort, which, though seemingly insignificant, were sufficient grounds to void the truce. They argued that even a slight violation could nullify the agreement, as stipulated by the terms. The Lacedaemonians denied any violation and protested the Athenians' refusal to return their ships, accusing them of dishonorable conduct. Frustrated by this turn of events, the Lacedaemonians departed, now fully committed to intensifying the war.

Both sides prepared for renewed conflict at Pylos with increased energy. The Athenians implemented a strict blockade around the island, patrolling it continuously with two ships circling in opposite directions by day. By night, the fleet, now bolstered by an additional twenty ships sent from Athens, bringing their total to seventy, surrounded the island on all sides except the seaward approach in stormy weather. Meanwhile, the Peloponnesians maintained their camp on the mainland, persistently attacking the Athenian fortifications and vigilantly watching for any opportunity to rescue their stranded men.

Meanwhile, in Sicily, the Syracusans and their allies had gathered the reinforcements they had been preparing and joined the fleet guarding Messina. They intensified their operations, encouraged particularly by the Locrians, who were driven by deep-seated animosity against the Rhegians and had invaded Rhegian territory with all their forces. The Syracusans also saw a chance to test their naval strength. Learning that only a small contingent of Athenian ships remained at Rhegium and that the main Athenian fleet was preoccupied with the blockade at Pylos, they aimed to seize a decisive victory at sea. They hoped that a victory would allow them to besiege Rhegium by both land and sea, leading to its swift capture. This success would give them control over the critical strait between Rhegium in Italy and Messina in Sicily, a narrow waterway too close for Athenian ships to freely command.

This narrow strait, where Sicily is closest to the Italian mainland, is the fabled Charybdis that the poet Homer described as the perilous passage of Ulysses. Known for its treacherous currents formed by the convergence of the vast Tyrrhenian and Sicilian seas, the strait had a notorious reputation for being hazardous to sailors. Here, late in the day, the Syracusan forces, alongside their allies, were drawn into a naval skirmish with a combined fleet of thirty ships against sixteen Athenian and eight Rhegian vessels, triggered by a dispute over a passing boat. The Athenians gained the upper hand in the battle, forcing the Syracusans and their allies into a hasty retreat. Each ship fled independently back to their respective stations at Messina and Rhegium, having lost one vessel as night fell before the engagement was fully resolved.

Following this encounter, the Locrians withdrew from Rhegian territory, while the Syracusan fleet, joined by their allies, regrouped and anchored at Cape Pelorus, in Messinian territory, where their ground forces soon joined them. Observing this, the Athenian and Rhegian fleets advanced toward the shore, where they spotted the Syracusan ships uncrewed and vulnerable. Taking advantage of this, they launched an assault, but during the skirmish, the Athenians lost a ship when it was ensnared by a grappling hook, though the crew managed to swim to safety.

After this initial clash, the Syracusans quickly re-boarded their ships, and while they were being towed along the shoreline back toward Messina, they were again ambushed by the Athenians. However, this time the Syracusans unexpectedly broke out to open water and assumed the offensive, catching the Athenians off guard and causing them to lose another ship. Successfully defending themselves both during the shore-bound journey and in open confrontation, the Syracusans continued on and ultimately sailed safely into the harbor at Messina.

Meanwhile, the Athenians received intelligence that Camarina was on the brink of being handed over to the Syracusans by Archias and his faction. In response, they immediately set sail for Camarina to intervene. Seizing the opportunity while the Athenians were occupied, the Messinese launched a large-scale assault, by both land and sea, on their Chalcidian neighbors in Naxos. On the first day, the Messinese managed to keep the Naxians confined within their city walls and laid waste to the surrounding lands. The following day, their fleet circled around to the Akesines River, ravaging the countryside from the water, while their land forces continued to threaten the city itself.

At this critical juncture, large numbers of Sicels descended from the highlands to support Naxos against the Messinese. Buoyed by the arrival of these reinforcements and expecting further aid from their Greek allies, including the Leontines, the Naxians rallied and launched an unexpected sally from their city. This counterattack was devastatingly effective; they routed the Messinese, killing over a thousand of them. As the remnants of the Messinese forces retreated, they suffered additional losses, harried by the barbarian forces along the route back home. Those who survived eventually regrouped at Messina, while the remaining ships dispersed back to their home ports. With the Messinese now significantly weakened, the Leontines, their allies, and the Athenians took advantage of their vulnerable state. The Athenians attacked by sea near the harbor, while the allied land forces struck from the town's opposite side.

However, the Messinese, along with Demoteles and a contingent of Locrians left to defend the city, launched a surprise sortie. They decisively defeated much of the Leontine army, killing numerous soldiers. Observing this turn of events, the Athenians disembarked from their ships and attacked the Messinese in their disorganized state, driving them back into the town. After setting up a trophy to commemorate their victory, the Athenians withdrew to Rhegium. Following these engagements, the various Greek factions in Sicily resumed their hostilities independently, without further Athenian involvement.

Meanwhile, at Pylos, the Athenians continued their siege of the Lacedaemonians on the island, while the main Peloponnesian forces remained stationed on the mainland. The blockade took a heavy toll on the Athenians, who faced a severe shortage of food and fresh water. The only available spring was a small one within the Pylos citadel, forcing many soldiers to dig into the pebbled shoreline to access whatever brackish water they could find. The cramped conditions of their encampment also added to their discomfort, as there was limited space onshore. Lacking sufficient anchorage for their ships, the Athenians had to rotate their crews, with some taking their meals onshore while others remained stationed at sea.

Their morale waned most, however, due to the unexpectedly prolonged duration of the siege, which they had initially assumed would only take a few days to achieve. To sustain the besieged Lacedaemonians on the island, the Spartans issued a call for volunteers to deliver provisions such as ground grain, wine, cheese, and other essential supplies, promising high rewards and freedom to any Helots who succeeded in the dangerous task. The Helots, eager to seize this opportunity, took to the sea from various points along the Peloponnesian coast, often attempting to approach the island at night. They preferred windy nights, as adverse weather made it harder for the Athenian ships to maintain a close blockade around the island, leaving gaps for the Helots to slip through. Using small boats, they steered toward the island with little regard for their own vessels, trusting they would find Lacedaemonian soldiers waiting at the designated landing sites.

Some of the more daring Helots resorted to swimming supplies underwater into the harbor. Tying bags filled with poppy seeds mixed with honey and crushed linseed to their bodies, they swam covertly to deliver provisions, initially going unnoticed. However, as the Athenians became aware of this tactic, they increased their vigilance and stationed guards to intercept such attempts. Thus, the siege turned into a contest of ingenuity, with both sides employing every possible method to either bring in or block supplies, as the Athenians sought to isolate the Lacedaemonians and starve them into surrender.

At Athens, reports that the army at Pylos was struggling and that supplies were still reaching the Lacedaemonians trapped on the island caused significant worry. The Athenians began to fear the possibility of winter arriving while they were still bogged down in a prolonged blockade. They realized that once winter set in, it would be nearly impossible to transport provisions around the Peloponnesian coast. The terrain around Pylos offered no natural resources to sustain a lengthy siege, and even during the summer months, they had struggled to keep enough supplies coming. Without accessible harbors to facilitate resupply, the blockade would become untenable, leaving the trapped men either able to escape as the siege collapsed or simply waiting for rough weather to create an opening for escape in the boats that brought them provisions.

The Athenians were also increasingly anxious about the Lacedaemonians' silence; they had sent no further envoys to discuss peace. This silence made the Athenians suspect that the Lacedaemonians might feel confident in their position, perhaps indicating that they had found ways to sustain the siege. This growing unease led some to regret rejecting the previous peace proposal. Cleon, recognizing that he was beginning to lose favor for having obstructed the treaty, dismissed the reports as exaggerated, claiming that the informants had misrepresented the situation. When the messengers suggested that, if he doubted them, he could send commissioners to assess the situation directly, the Athenians selected Cleon himself along with Theagenes to investigate.

Aware that this commission would force him either to confirm the reports he had dismissed or be caught in a lie if he claimed otherwise, Cleon took a different approach. Sensing that the Athenians were inclined to take decisive action, he argued that instead of wasting time on fact-finding missions, they should act directly if they believed the reports. He even went so far as to mock Nicias, the son of Niceratus and a general he disliked, by suggesting that any capable leader could resolve the situation swiftly. He boasted that if he were in command, he would already have captured or killed the Lacedaemonians on the island.

Nicias, noting that the crowd was beginning to grumble against Cleon for not acting on his own words, saw an opportunity to turn Cleon's challenge against him. He publicly offered to relinquish his command and allow Cleon to take whatever forces he deemed necessary to resolve the situation. Cleon initially believed Nicias was merely bluffing and was prepared to accept the offer as rhetoric. However, realizing that Nicias was entirely serious and truly willing to step down, Cleon hesitated, suddenly alarmed at the unexpected turn of events. He attempted to retreat, asserting that Nicias, not himself, was the actual general. Nicias, undeterred, reiterated his readiness to step aside and formally relinquished his command over the Pylos campaign, calling on the assembly to witness his decision.

The Athenian assembly, as assemblies often do, eagerly seized on this reversal. The more Cleon tried to withdraw, the more they urged Nicias to resign and insisted that Cleon should lead the expedition. Caught by his own bold words and seeing no escape, Cleon finally agreed to undertake the campaign. He brazenly declared that he was not afraid of the Lacedaemonians and announced his intention to set out without any reinforcements from Athens. He would rely only on the Lemnian and Imbrian troops present in Athens, some targeteers recently arrived from Aenus, and a group of four hundred archers from other regions. With this force, along with the soldiers already stationed at Pylos, he vowed to either capture the Lacedaemonians alive or kill them within twenty days.

The Athenians, amused by Cleon's overconfidence, found his bravado entertaining. Sensible observers, however, reasoned that either outcome would be to their advantage—if Cleon failed, they would be rid of him, and if he succeeded, they would have defeated the Lacedaemonians. After the assembly ratified his command, Cleon promptly chose Demosthenes, one of the generals already at Pylos, as his colleague and accelerated preparations for the expedition. He selected Demosthenes because he had learned that Demosthenes was already considering a direct assault on the island; the troops, worn down by the difficulties of maintaining the blockade, were eager to bring the campaign to a decisive end. Demosthenes himself had gained confidence, as recent fires on the island had cleared much of the dense forest.

Initially, Demosthenes had been hesitant due to the island's natural cover. It was densely wooded and without clear paths, creating an advantage for the Lacedaemonians, who could launch hidden attacks on any approaching force. The thick cover would conceal enemy movements while exposing his own troops, making it easier for the Lacedaemonians to stage surprise attacks. Moreover, if he managed to engage the Lacedaemonians in such dense terrain, he feared that the smaller, more knowledgeable force would hold an advantage over his larger but less familiar troops, who might find themselves unable to support one another effectively.

The recent disaster in Aetolia, where dense woods had greatly contributed to the Athenian losses, lingered in Demosthenes' mind and influenced his planning. Meanwhile, due to limited space, some soldiers were forced to land on the island's outskirts to eat their meals, with guards posted nearby to prevent a surprise attack. During this time, one of the soldiers inadvertently set a small part of the forest ablaze. A strong wind soon spread the flames, and before anyone could control it, almost the entire wooded area was consumed. This unexpected event allowed Demosthenes, for the first time, to clearly see the true number of Lacedaemonians on the island, which he had previously assumed to be smaller due to their modest supply intake. Observing the enemy numbers and realizing the Athenians' growing eagerness for victory, Demosthenes now saw a more favorable opportunity to launch an assault. He began rallying additional troops from nearby allies and advancing other preparations for the attack.

It was at this point that Cleon arrived at Pylos with the forces he had gathered, having previously sent word of his approach. Upon meeting, the first action taken by Cleon and Demosthenes was to dispatch a herald to the Lacedaemonian camp on the mainland, proposing that the men on the island surrender themselves and their weapons to avoid unnecessary risks. They offered to hold the prisoners under lenient terms until a broader peace agreement could be reached.

When the Lacedaemonians rejected this offer, the generals waited a day before implementing their plan. Under the cover of darkness, they embarked all their heavy infantry onto a few ships. Just before dawn, they landed on opposite sides of the island, arriving both from the open sea and from the harbor, with a combined force of around eight hundred men. They quickly advanced toward the first Lacedaemonian outpost on the island.

The Lacedaemonians had organized their defenses in three positions. The first outpost, situated at the point where the Athenians landed, held around thirty heavy infantry. The central, flat area of the island, where the water source was located, was occupied by the main force under the command of Epitadas. At the far end of the island, closest to Pylos, a smaller contingent guarded the precipitous terrain. This area was difficult to access by land, with steep cliffs on the sea side, and contained an old stone fort hastily assembled, which they hoped might serve as a last line of defense in case they were forced to retreat.

The Athenian landing caught the men in the first outpost completely off guard. Still groggy and in the process of arming themselves, they were swiftly overwhelmed and cut down by the Athenian attackers, who had managed to approach without alerting them. The defenders had assumed that the Athenian ships were simply maneuvering into their usual nighttime positions and were not prepared for an assault.

As daylight broke, the rest of the Athenian force disembarked, including the crews of over seventy ships (except for the lowest ranks of oarsmen), as well as eight hundred archers, an equal number of targeteers, Messenian reinforcements, and other soldiers stationed around Pylos, excluding the fort garrison. Demosthenes had organized the troops into units of roughly two hundred, strategically positioning them on high ground to encircle the Lacedaemonians, effectively trapping them and leaving them without a direct opponent to engage.

This tactic left the Lacedaemonians surrounded on all sides, vulnerable to attacks from multiple directions. If they moved to engage an enemy in front, they would be struck from the rear; if they attempted to flank one side, another group would attack from the opposite direction. Demosthenes' plan created a scenario in which the Lacedaemonians would be perpetually outmaneuvered, with Athenian forces always at their back.

Moreover, the light-armed Athenian forces, skilled in ranged attacks, presented a uniquely challenging opponent. Equipped with bows, slings, and throwing weapons, they could strike effectively from a distance, making it nearly impossible for the Lacedaemonians to close in for hand-to-hand combat. The Athenians could retreat quickly, remaining just out of reach, only to regroup and attack again the moment the Lacedaemonians turned away. Demosthenes' strategic vision was evident in every element of the assault, with his primary aim being to keep the enemy off-balance and continuously exposed to attacks from multiple directions, ultimately wearing them down without allowing a close-quarters confrontation.

Meanwhile, the main Lacedaemonian force, led by Epitadas, saw that their forward outpost had been overrun and that the Athenians were advancing in force. Determined to hold their ground, they tightened their ranks and prepared to meet the Athenian heavy infantry face-to-face, with Athenian light troops positioned around them on both flanks and to the rear. However, they struggled to engage effectively. The Athenian heavy infantry remained stationary, refusing to advance, while the light-armed troops on either side bombarded the Lacedaemonians with missiles, preventing them from gaining any ground or capitalizing on their superior close-combat skills. Although the Lacedaemonians managed to push back the light troops whenever they got too close, the Athenian skirmishers, lightly equipped, could quickly retreat to safety, taking advantage of the rugged and uneven terrain. This challenging landscape, coupled with the heavy armor of the Lacedaemonians, made it difficult for them to give chase or maintain a cohesive formation.

As the skirmishing continued, the Lacedaemonians began to show signs of fatigue. Their initial bursts of energy became less frequent, and they struggled to rush forward with the same intensity as before. Observing this, the Athenian light troops grew bolder. They realized that their numbers were vastly greater than the enemy's, and the prolonged engagement had made them more accustomed to facing the Lacedaemonians, whom they now saw as less formidable. The initial terror they had felt at the idea of fighting such renowned warriors dissipated, replaced by a sense of disdain. Emboldened, they attacked en masse, shouting loudly and hurling stones, darts, and arrows with renewed intensity.

The Lacedaemonians, unaccustomed to this chaotic style of combat, were further disoriented by the loud war cries echoing around them. Dust from the recently burned forest rose in thick clouds, obscuring visibility, while missiles rained down from all directions, hurled by the multitude of Athenian assailants. The Lacedaemonians faced a brutal struggle. Their caps and armor offered limited protection, with arrows and broken darts lodged painfully within their gear. The constant noise prevented them from hearing orders, and the dust clouds made it nearly impossible to see their attackers clearly. Surrounded by danger on all sides, they found themselves unable to mount any organized defense or find any means of safety.

After many of their men had been wounded in the cramped battlefield, the Lacedaemonians decided to retreat. They formed a tight formation and withdrew toward the old fort at the end of the island, where their remaining forces were stationed. The Athenians' light troops, seeing them give way, intensified their assault, shouting even louder and pursuing them relentlessly. They struck down any who lagged behind, though most of the Lacedaemonians managed to reach the fort, where they joined the garrison already in place. Together, they lined the fortifications along its full length, ready to defend every vulnerable point against the Athenian assault.

The Athenians pursued the retreating Lacedaemonians but found it difficult to surround them fully due to the strong natural defenses of the terrain. Instead, they launched a frontal attack, attempting to storm the fortified position. The battle continued for hours, with both sides enduring not only the relentless conflict but also the intense heat and thirst of the day. The Athenians pressed forward, determined to drive the Lacedaemonians from the high ground, while the Lacedaemonians, now more securely positioned, fought desperately to hold their ground. Unlike before, the narrow position allowed them to focus on defending against attacks from the front, making it easier to maintain their lines without the fear of being flanked.

For most of the day, the struggle dragged on, with both sides pushing to their limits, neither able to secure a decisive advantage. The Athenians fought to dislodge the Lacedaemonians from their final stronghold, while the Lacedaemonians held firm, knowing that any failure to defend this position would mean certain defeat. The standoff wore down both forces, each contending not only with the physical strain of the battle but also with the oppressive conditions, as they fought on in the relentless heat, through clouds of dust, and without respite.

As the struggle continued with no end in sight, the commander of the Messenians approached Cleon and Demosthenes, suggesting that their efforts were in vain with a direct assault. He proposed that if they gave him some archers and light troops, he would attempt a maneuver to circle around and strike the enemy from behind, finding a way through the terrain that he believed the Lacedaemonians had left undefended. Receiving the troops he requested, he set off from a concealed point, ensuring he would remain unseen by the enemy. With painstaking care, he advanced through narrow, rugged paths, exploiting areas where the natural defenses of the terrain had led the Lacedaemonians to place no guards, trusting that these spots were impassable. After a difficult and careful approach, he managed to flank the Lacedaemonians without being detected, suddenly emerging on high ground at their rear. His unexpected arrival caused dismay among the Lacedaemonians, who now found themselves surrounded, while the Athenians, seeing their advantage, were filled with renewed energy and anticipation.

The Lacedaemonians were now caught between two forces, facing an attack from both front and rear. Their situation echoed the infamous defeat at Thermopylae, where the Persian forces had outflanked the defenders by using a hidden path. Now facing this double threat and weakened by exhaustion and lack of food, the Lacedaemonians began to give ground, unable to sustain their position against the overwhelming odds.

With control of the approaches firmly in Athenian hands, Cleon and Demosthenes, recognizing that any further retreat by the enemy would lead to their complete annihilation at the hands of their soldiers, decided to halt the battle. They restrained their men, hoping to take the Lacedaemonians alive as prisoners to Athens. Thinking that the desperate situation might prompt them to surrender, Cleon and Demosthenes issued a proclamation, offering the Lacedaemonians the chance to lay down their arms and submit to the Athenians, to be treated at their discretion.

Upon hearing the offer, many of the Lacedaemonians lowered their shields and raised their hands in a gesture of surrender. Hostilities ceased, and Cleon and Demosthenes entered into negotiations with

Styphon, son of Pharax, who now led the Lacedaemonian forces. Epitadas, the original commander, had fallen in battle, and Hippagretas, the next in line, lay gravely wounded among the dead. By Lacedaemonian law, command passed to Styphon in the event of the death or incapacitation of his superiors.

Styphon and his officers expressed a desire to send a herald to the mainland to consult with the Lacedaemonian leaders on what action to take. However, the Athenians denied this request, insisting instead that they would summon heralds from the mainland themselves. Messages were exchanged back and forth several times. Eventually, the final messenger from the Lacedaemonians on the mainland delivered the decisive response: "The Lacedaemonians bid you decide for yourselves, provided you do nothing dishonorable."

With this authorization, Styphon and his men conferred and chose to surrender. They laid down their arms and formally handed themselves over to the Athenians. The Athenians guarded the prisoners through the night and prepared to depart the following morning. To mark their victory, they erected a trophy on the island and arranged for the prisoners to be guarded in groups under the supervision of the captains of the galleys. Meanwhile, the Lacedaemonians on the mainland sent a herald to collect their dead.

The final toll of the engagement revealed that four hundred and twenty heavy infantry had originally crossed to the island. Of these, three hundred and twelve survived and were taken alive to Athens, with the remainder having fallen in battle. Among the prisoners, around one hundred and twenty were Spartans, a significant capture. The Athenians suffered only minimal casualties, as the nature of the battle had prevented close combat, sparing them heavy losses.

The entire blockade, from the initial naval engagement to the final battle on the island, lasted seventy-two days. For the first twenty days, while the envoys were away negotiating a peace, the Lacedaemonians on the island received provisions through official channels. During the remainder of the blockade, however, their food was smuggled in by volunteers. Supplies, including grain and other necessities, were found on the island; Commander Epitadas had imposed half rations on his men to conserve their provisions. Following the surrender, both the Athenian and Peloponnesian forces withdrew from Pylos and returned home. Remarkably, Cleon fulfilled his audacious promise, bringing the captured Lacedaemonians to Athens within the twenty days he had confidently pledged.

This event shocked the entire Greek world more than any other incident in the war. The belief had been that no force, nor even the threat of starvation, could compel the Lacedaemonians to lay down their arms; it was expected that they would fight to the last, preferring to die weapon in hand rather than surrender. Many could hardly believe that these prisoners were of the same character as the men who had fought and fallen. When an ally of the Athenians later taunted one of the captured Lacedaemonians, asking if those who had died were truly men of honor, the prisoner replied that "the arrow"—or atraktos—"would be worth a great deal if it could distinguish the honorable from the rest." He referred to the randomness of death in battle, suggesting that the arrows and stones had struck indiscriminately, killing whomever they hit without regard for honor.

Once the prisoners arrived in Athens, the Athenians decided to keep them in custody until peace was achieved. They also decreed that if the Peloponnesians attempted another invasion of Athenian territory, the captives would be executed as a deterrent. Meanwhile, the Athenians maintained their defense of Pylos, and the Messenians from Naupactus took advantage of the situation by sending some of their best men to Pylos. As Pylos was part of their ancestral homeland, they launched a series of raids into Laconia, devastating the region with the added advantage of sharing a common dialect with the locals, which allowed them to blend in more easily and cause greater havoc.

The Lacedaemonians, unaccustomed to this kind of warfare and sudden incursions, soon faced an alarming crisis. Many Helots, the enslaved population of Sparta, began deserting, and the

Lacedaemonians grew increasingly fearful that these attacks could spark a larger rebellion within their territory. Concerned about the potential for unrest, they reluctantly began sending envoys to Athens, despite their pride, to negotiate the return of Pylos and the prisoners. The Athenians, however, sensing their leverage, demanded increasingly advantageous terms, dismissing each envoy without reaching any agreement.

Such were the consequences of the events at Pylos, marking a significant and unforeseen turn in the war.

Chapter XIII

Seventh and Eighth Years of the War—End of Corcyraean Revolution—Peace of Gela—Capture of Nisaea

In the summer following these events, the Athenians launched an expedition against Corinthian territory. The force comprised eighty ships, two thousand Athenian heavy infantry, and two hundred cavalry, transported on specially adapted horse transports. These Athenians were joined by allied troops from Miletus, Andros, and Carystus, all under the command of Nicias, son of Niceratus, along with two other generals. Setting sail under cover of darkness, the Athenian fleet reached land at dawn, arriving at the coast between Chersonese and Rheitus, near the base of Solygian Hill. This site had historical significance, as it was where the Dorians had settled during their ancient conflicts with the Aeolian inhabitants of Corinth. A small village now stood there, called Solygia. The fleet landed on a beach approximately two and a quarter miles from the Isthmus, about seven miles from Corinth, and one and a half miles from the village.

The Corinthians, warned by Argos of the Athenian force's approach, had already moved their troops to the Isthmus to guard against a landing, except for those Corinthians who lived on the far side of the Isthmus and five hundred soldiers on garrison duty in Ambracia and Leucadia. They remained stationed in full force, vigilant for any sign of the Athenians. However, the Athenians managed to slip past under cover of night, landing unnoticed. Once alerted by signals of the landing, the Corinthians left half their forces at Cenchreae to counter any movement toward Crommyon and hurried the rest of their army toward the Athenian position.

Two Corinthian generals led the defense. Battus took a detachment to protect the unfortified village of Solygia, while Lycophron remained with the main force to engage the Athenians. The Corinthians attacked the Athenian right wing, which had landed near Chersonese, before advancing against the remainder of the Athenian forces. A fierce, close-combat battle ensued, with both sides fighting stubbornly. The Athenian right wing and Carystian allies, stationed at the line's edge, initially struggled but ultimately managed to repel the Corinthians, who fell back to a stone wall on higher ground. Regrouping, they renewed the attack, chanting their battle hymn as they charged. They again engaged the Athenians at close quarters. During this encounter, a Corinthian contingent reinforced the left wing, driving the Athenian right wing back toward the sea, where the Athenians and Carystians rallied and forced them to retreat once more.

Elsewhere on the battlefield, the main forces of both armies clashed with equal intensity. The Corinthians' right wing, under Lycophron, held firmly against the Athenian left, fearing that the Athenians might attack Solygia. The prolonged struggle finally tipped in the Athenians' favor, aided by their cavalry, a significant advantage since the Corinthians had none. Gradually, the Athenians forced the Corinthians to retreat up a hill, where they halted and no longer attempted to descend. The heaviest Corinthian casualties occurred during this retreat of the right wing, with Lycophron himself among those killed. Although the rest of the Corinthian forces withdrew in a relatively orderly fashion, they retreated to higher ground to avoid pursuit and regroup.

The Athenians, observing that the Corinthians no longer attempted to re-engage, gathered their own fallen and stripped the dead of the enemy. They then erected a victory trophy. Meanwhile, the Corinthians left to guard Cenchreae, though unable to see the battle because of Mount Oneion, spotted the dust and deduced that a clash was underway. They, along with older Corinthian soldiers from the town, hurried toward the battlefield. Noticing these reinforcements approaching, the Athenians mistakenly believed that additional troops from the Peloponnesus were arriving to reinforce the Corinthians. Deciding to avoid a renewed conflict, they quickly returned to their ships, carrying both the spoils of battle and their own fallen, with the exception of two bodies they couldn't locate. After re-boarding, they crossed over to the nearby islands, from which they later sent a herald to retrieve the two remaining bodies under a truce.

The battle had cost the Corinthians two hundred and twelve men, while Athenian losses were fewer, with just under fifty casualties.

After departing from the islands, the Athenians sailed the same day to Crommyon, located in Corinthian territory roughly thirteen miles from Corinth. There, they anchored and proceeded to ravage the surrounding countryside, spending the night in the area. The next day, they continued along the coast, landing briefly in Epidaurian territory, and then arrived at Methana, situated between Epidaurus and Troezen. Here, they undertook a strategic project, constructing a wall across the isthmus of the peninsula to fortify the location. This stronghold would allow them to launch future raids into the lands of Troezen, Haliae, and Epidaurus. With the fortifications complete, the Athenian fleet then set sail back home.

Meanwhile, as these operations were unfolding, Eurymedon and Sophocles had taken the Athenian fleet from Pylos and sailed toward Sicily. Upon reaching Corcyra, they joined forces with the townsmen to confront the opposing faction that had fortified themselves on Mount Istone. This group, formed after the revolution, had gained control over much of the countryside, severely troubling the local populace. After a successful assault on their stronghold, the garrison retreated to a nearby high ground where they surrendered. They agreed to disband their mercenary forces, lay down their weapons, and submit themselves to the authority of the Athenian people. The Athenian generals transferred the surrendered garrison to the island of Ptychia under a truce, where they would be held until arrangements could be made to send them to Athens. The terms specified that if any prisoner attempted to escape, it would void the treaty for the entire group.

However, the leaders of the Corcyraean commons, fearing that the Athenians might spare the lives of the prisoners, devised a plan to force a different outcome. They secretly contacted a few of the prisoners, sending messengers who, under the guise of friendly advice, suggested to them that it would be wise to escape, claiming that the Athenians intended to hand them over to the hostile Corcyraean people. Persuaded by this, the prisoners attempted to flee, using a boat arranged by their so-called friends. They were promptly apprehended during their escape, which allowed the Corcyraean leaders to declare the treaty void. As a result, the entire group was handed over to the Corcyraeans.

The Athenian generals bore considerable responsibility for this turn of events. Their reluctance to proceed to Sicily, perhaps motivated by the desire to receive credit for escorting the prisoners to Athens, lent credence to the rumors spread by the Corcyraean plotters. With the treaty nullified, the prisoners were confined in a large building by the Corcyraeans, who soon subjected them to a brutal punishment. They were led out in groups of twenty, forced to walk between two lines of heavy infantry, who lined each side. As the prisoners passed through, they were bound together and beaten or stabbed by those along the lines, especially when recognized by a personal enemy. Men carrying whips accompanied them, quickening the pace of any who hesitated or lagged behind.

Around sixty men were led out one by one and executed in this manner, while those remaining inside the building were unaware of what was happening, believing their comrades were merely being transferred to another location. Eventually, however, someone realized the truth and alerted the others. In response, the prisoners cried out, asking the Athenians to end their lives themselves if that was their intent, and refused to leave the building voluntarily. They barricaded themselves inside, determined to prevent anyone from entering.

Unwilling to force entry through the doors, the Corcyraeans climbed onto the roof. Breaking through the roof tiles, they began to rain down arrows and stones upon the prisoners, who tried to shield themselves as best they could. In desperation, many of the captives turned to suicide, using the arrows shot at them to stab themselves in the throat, tearing bedding cords to hang themselves, or ripping their clothing to make makeshift nooses. Others fell to the arrows and stones from above. The horrific scene continued until nightfall, and only as dawn approached did the ordeal end.

At daybreak, the Corcyraeans loaded the bodies in layers onto wagons and transported them out of the city. All the women captured in the stronghold were sold into slavery. In this brutal way, the Corcyraean faction on the mountain was eradicated by the commons. Thus, the intense civil conflict on Corcyra finally ended, at least for the duration of the war, as one faction was effectively wiped out. Following these events, the Athenian fleet resumed its voyage to Sicily, where they continued the campaign with their allies.

Toward the end of the summer, the Athenians at Naupactus, together with the Acarnanians, launched an expedition against Anactorium, a Corinthian city situated at the entrance of the Ambracian Gulf. They captured it through betrayal, and the Acarnanians then took control, settling the town with people from all parts of Acarnania.

With summer over, winter approached. During this season, Aristides, son of Archippus and one of the Athenian commanders assigned to collect funds from the allies, intercepted a Persian named Artaphernes at Eion on the Strymon River. Artaphernes was on a diplomatic mission from the Persian King to Lacedaemon. Taken to Athens, he carried dispatches that the Athenians translated from the Assyrian script. The letters revealed that the Persian King was confused by the Lacedaemonians' requests, as each of their envoys presented conflicting messages. The King suggested they send representatives with a single, clear agenda if they wished to negotiate. The Athenians then sent Artaphernes back to Ephesus in a galley, along with Athenian envoys. However, upon their arrival, they learned that King Artaxerxes, son of Xerxes, had recently died. With this news, the Athenians returned home.

In the same winter, the Athenians ordered the Chians to dismantle their newly constructed wall, suspecting them of planning a revolt. The Chians complied but first secured assurances from Athens that their treatment would remain unchanged, as far as such guarantees were possible. With these events, winter drew to a close, marking the end of the seventh year of the war that Thucydides chronicled.

In the early days of the following summer, a solar eclipse occurred at the time of the new moon, followed by an earthquake in the same month. During this period, Mitylenian and other exiled Lesbians, mostly stationed on the mainland, gathered mercenaries from Peloponnese and recruited additional forces locally. They launched a campaign, first seizing Rhoeteum. However, they soon restored it unharmed upon receiving two thousand Phocaean staters. Following this, they moved against Antandrus, capturing the town through treachery. Their aim was to liberate Antandrus and the other Actaean towns, which had previously been under Mitylene's control but were now held by the Athenians. Fortifying themselves at Antandrus would provide access to plentiful shipbuilding timber from the nearby Mount Ida and other supplies, enabling them to easily raid Lesbos and target Aeolian towns on the mainland.

While the exiles plotted, the Athenians launched their own campaign that summer with a fleet of sixty ships, two thousand heavy infantry, a small cavalry unit, and allied forces from Miletus and other regions, all under the command of Nicias, son of Niceratus, along with Nicostratus, son of Diotrephes, and Autocles, son of Tolmaeus. Their target was Cythera, an island off the Laconian coast opposite Cape Malea, inhabited by Lacedaemonian Perioeci. Annually, Sparta dispatched an official known as the "judge of Cythera" to the island, and a garrison of heavy infantry was stationed there regularly. Cythera was of strategic importance to Sparta, serving as a landing point for trade ships from Egypt and Libya and protecting Laconia's coastline, which faced the threat of privateers from the Sicilian and Cretan seas.

Upon landing with their forces, the Athenians detached ten ships and two thousand Milesian heavy infantry to capture Scandea, a town situated on the coast. Meanwhile, the rest of the force disembarked on the side of the island facing Malea and advanced on the lower town of Cythera, where the Cytherians had assembled. The Cytherians held their ground briefly before retreating to the upper town, where they soon capitulated to Nicias and his fellow commanders, surrendering with the agreement that their lives would be spared. The surrender was expedited by prior negotiations between Nicias and certain Cytherian leaders, allowing the Cytherians to secure terms more favorable than they might have otherwise, given their close ties to the Lacedaemonians and the island's proximity to Laconia.

Following the surrender, the Athenians established a garrison at Cythera, taking control of Scandea near the harbor. They then sailed to Asine, Helus, and several other coastal settlements, making landings and setting up temporary encampments where it suited them. Over approximately seven days, they continued these operations, systematically raiding and devastating the surrounding countryside.

The Lacedaemonians, realizing the Athenians now controlled Cythera and anticipating further raids along their coasts, adopted a cautious defensive strategy. Rather than confronting the Athenians in a unified force, they stationed small garrisons throughout the country, assigning as many heavy infantry to each post as seemed necessary for local defense. Their approach reflected a deepening sense of unease.

The recent blows—the occupation of Pylos and Cythera, compounded by the speed and unpredictability of Athenian attacks—left them in a state of constant alert, fearing internal revolt as much as external aggression. In response, they made the unusual move of establishing a cavalry force of four hundred and adding archers to their ranks, even as they grew increasingly hesitant to engage in battle. Sparta, traditionally structured for land warfare, found itself struggling to adapt to this maritime conflict against the Athenians, who viewed untested opportunities as wasted ones. The series of unexpected losses had demoralized the Lacedaemonians, who now worried about repeating the disaster on the island. Unaccustomed to adversity, they lost confidence in their military capabilities and feared that any attempt at engagement might result in further missteps.

As a result, they allowed the Athenians to raid their coastal regions unchallenged, with local garrisons near the landing points often feeling inadequate and sharing the general apprehension. Only one garrison, near Cotyrta and Aphrodisia, mounted a counterattack. Although their initial charge sent the lightly armed Athenian raiders into disarray, the garrison was forced to retreat upon encountering Athenian heavy infantry, sustaining minor casualties and losing some weapons. The Athenians then set up a trophy to mark their victory before departing for Cythera.

From Cythera, the Athenian fleet continued along the coast, stopping briefly to ravage parts of the countryside at Epidaurus Limera before advancing to Thyrea, in Cynuria, a border region between Argos and Laconia. This area had been granted by the Lacedaemonians to the exiled Aeginetans, in gratitude for their loyalty during the earthquake and Helot uprising, and as a reward for their consistent support of Sparta despite being subjects of Athens.

When the Athenians arrived offshore, the Aeginetans, who had been constructing a coastal fort, abandoned their project and retreated to the main settlement further inland, about a mile from the sea. Although they urged the Lacedaemonian garrison assisting them to take refuge within the town walls, the Lacedaemonians refused, deeming it too risky to confine themselves in the fortifications. They withdrew to higher ground, judging it unwise to confront the Athenian forces directly.

Once ashore, the Athenians swiftly advanced, taking Thyrea by force. They set the town ablaze and plundered its resources. The Aeginetans who survived the initial skirmish were taken prisoner and transported back to Athens, along with Tantalus, son of Patrocles, the Lacedaemonian commander, who was wounded and captured. The Athenians also decided to take a few men from Cythera as hostages, considering it safer to relocate them. They determined that these individuals would be housed on nearby islands, while the rest of the Cytherians would remain on their lands but would be required to pay an annual tribute of four talents. The Aeginetan captives, due to their long-standing enmity with Athens, were condemned to death, and Tantalus was imprisoned along with the Lacedaemonian prisoners previously captured on the island.

In the same summer, the people of Camarina and Gela in Sicily initially reached an armistice. Soon after, representatives from all the Sicilian cities gathered at Gela to discuss a more comprehensive peace. After various speakers presented their grievances and aspirations, Hermocrates, son of Hermon and a prominent Syracusan, rose to address the assembly, giving the following speech:

"If I speak now, fellow Sicilians, it is not because my city is the smallest in Sicily or has suffered the most from this war, but rather to present what I believe to be the wisest course for the entire island. We all know that war is a serious misfortune; explaining this is hardly necessary. No one enters a conflict out of sheer ignorance or avoids it out of simple fear—everyone is driven by the belief that something worthwhile may be gained. For some, the potential reward outweighs the risk, while others prefer to endure hardship rather than make any immediate sacrifice. However, if both sides have misjudged the timing, advice urging peace is precisely what is needed—and that is the situation we find ourselves in now.

"I think we can all agree that we originally went to war to protect our individual interests, and we are here today with the same aim in mind, exploring how to achieve peace. However, if we part from this congress without an agreement that each of us considers fair, it is certain that war will erupt again. Yet as rational people, we must understand that more than our individual concerns are at stake in this assembly. The survival of Sicily as a whole is in jeopardy. I am convinced that Athenian ambition poses a threat to the entire island, and this alone should be reason enough for us to seek peace.

"The name of Athens should compel us more urgently than any words I can offer. Look at the most powerful city in Hellas, carefully observing our conflicts with only a small fleet presently stationed nearby, ostensibly as our ally. Under the guise of supporting us, they are strategically exploiting the natural rivalries between us. If we allow ourselves to be drawn into war, calling on this power for help, we invite a people all too willing to fight on foreign soil, even when uninvited. By wounding each other, we pave the way for them to extend their influence at our expense. We may count on them to return in full strength once they see us weakened, with the intent to bring us all under their control.

"Let us consider this: if we divide ourselves and fight, we risk becoming enfeebled, scattered, and vulnerable. When the Athenians see Sicily divided, they will come not to aid but to conquer, and we will have unwittingly laid the foundations of their dominance. They will then take advantage of our exhaustion and discord, arriving with a much larger force to subjugate the entire island.

Hermocrates paused, allowing his words to sink in, emphasizing the gravity of the situation, before urging the assembly to set aside local grievances for the broader good of Sicily, warning of the looming Athenian threat.

"And yet, as rational men, if we seek allies and risk danger, it should be to expand and enrich our territories, not to destroy what we already have. We must recognize that internal divisions, which are ruinous to any community, will prove equally catastrophic for Sicily if we remain consumed by our local disputes and overlook the common enemy. These considerations should compel each individual and each city to reconcile their differences, uniting in a shared effort to preserve the entirety of Sicily. Nor should anyone believe that only the Dorians are at risk from Athens, while the Chalcidians, by virtue of their Ionian heritage, are safe. The Athenian interest here is not driven by animosity toward any one of our ethnic groups; it is driven by a desire for the wealth of Sicily—a wealth that belongs to all of us collectively.

"We have proof enough in the Athenians' enthusiastic response to the Chalcidians' invitation. The Athenians have lavished their attention on an ally who, despite never truly aiding them, is rewarded almost beyond the formal terms of the alliance. It is not surprising that the Athenians pursue this ambition; I do not criticize those who seek power, but rather those who too readily submit to it. It is natural for people to dominate those who surrender to them, just as it is natural to resist those who try to oppress us. Both impulses are fundamental to human nature. But those who recognize these dangers and still refuse to address them, or those who have come to this assembly without understanding that our foremost obligation is to unite against our common threat, are gravely mistaken. The surest way to eliminate this threat is to make peace among ourselves, for the Athenians threaten us not from their own lands but from those of our own people who have welcomed them here.

"Thus, rather than war leading only to more war, peace can serve to quietly settle our conflicts. Those who come here as allies but with harmful intentions will find themselves without reason to stay if we refuse to give them that opening. As for the Athenians, there are significant benefits to pursuing a wise and prudent policy toward them. Beyond this, given that nearly everyone agrees that peace is our greatest good, how can we reject the opportunity to establish it among ourselves? Do we not see that the benefits we now enjoy and the grievances we wish to redress would be more securely preserved and more readily healed by peace than by war? Peace has its own forms of honor and glory, far less perilous than war, not to mention its many other blessings and the endless miseries that accompany conflict.

"These considerations should lead you to take my words seriously, recognizing that they speak to each of our own interests. And if there are any here who feel confident in their ability to achieve their aims by either strength or right, let them temper their expectations. Many before us have sought to punish wrongdoers, only to fail to bring justice to their enemies and even to lose themselves in the attempt. Likewise, many who have relied on sheer force to secure a gain have, instead of gaining more, ended up forfeiting what they already had. Success in vengeance is not guaranteed simply because a wrong has been committed, nor does confidence ensure victory. The future holds many unknowns; its unpredictability is both the most deceitful and the most instructive of all factors. It teaches us caution, and that caution should lead us to carefully weigh our actions before we turn against one another."

"Let us therefore yield to the natural effect of this undefined fear of the future and the immediate threat posed by the Athenians in our midst. Let us recognize that the challenges of this moment may well explain any setbacks we face in realizing the ambitions we may have each privately entertained. Our first task should be to drive this intruder from our lands. And if a lasting peace among ourselves proves impossible, let us at least establish a truce for as long as possible, postponing our internal disputes to another time. By following this course, we preserve our status as citizens of free states, masters of our own fate, able to choose how we respond to both favor and hostility. But if we reject this opportunity, we risk becoming dependent on others, incapable of defending ourselves from offense, and, at best, aligned with those who might be our worst enemies while estranged from our natural allies.

"As for myself, though I represent a powerful city that could just as easily strike rather than defend, I am ready to make concessions to avoid the dangers before us. I do not wish to see my own interests sacrificed merely to harm my enemies, nor am I so consumed by hostility as to imagine that I control both my plans and the unpredictable forces of fortune. Instead, I am willing to compromise within reason. I call upon the rest of you to act with the same readiness, not because of the force of our enemies, but of our own free will. There is no dishonor in one kin yielding to another—a Dorian to a Dorian, a Chalcidian to his fellow Chalcidian. Beyond our kinship, we are neighbors, sharing this same land, surrounded by the same sea, and known collectively as Sicilians.

"If we are destined to wage war among ourselves, then let us leave that for another day. We may, in the future, gather for new peace treaties after new conflicts, but, if we are wise, we will always stand united against foreign powers, recognizing that a threat to one is a threat to all. Let us ensure that we never again welcome outsiders as allies or mediators within our borders. In so doing, we accomplish two things for Sicily today: we free her from the Athenians, and from civil war. For the future, we secure our freedom at home and lessen any threat from abroad."

Such were Hermocrates' words. The Sicilians heeded his counsel, reaching an agreement to end hostilities, with each city retaining its current holdings. The Camarinaeans, for example, were allowed to keep Morgantina, provided they paid an agreed sum to the Syracusans. The allies of the Athenians informed the Athenian commanders that they would be included in the peace and no longer require their assistance. The generals agreed, and soon after, the Athenian fleet withdrew from Sicily.

Upon their return to Athens, however, the Athenian commanders faced sharp criticism. Pythodorus and Sophocles were banished, and Eurymedon was fined, as they were accused of accepting bribes to leave Sicily when the Athenians might have conquered it. At the height of their success, the Athenian people had grown so confident that they believed nothing was beyond their reach. They were convinced that they could accomplish both the feasible and the impossible, with resources either vast or limited. This overwhelming confidence stemmed from the remarkable successes they had experienced, which had led them to mistake ambition for actual power.

In the same summer, the Megarians within the city, wearied by the constant threat of the Athenians—who invaded their lands twice a year with full force—and troubled by the raids from their own exiled citizens at Pegae, who had been expelled during an uprising led by the popular party, began to wonder if it might be wiser to allow the exiles to return, hoping this would rid the city of at least one of its two sources of suffering. Sensing this unrest, the supporters of the exiles became more vocal in advocating for their return. Meanwhile, the leaders of the popular faction, recognizing that the hardships had weakened the resolve of their own supporters, grew anxious and initiated secret talks with the Athenian generals, Hippocrates, son of Ariphron, and Demosthenes, son of Alcisthenes. They concluded that surrendering the city to the Athenians was safer for them than allowing the return of the banished faction.

It was decided that the Athenians would first seize the long walls extending from the city to the port of Nisaea, nearly a mile away. This move would prevent the Peloponnesian garrison stationed in Nisaea—whose presence ensured Megara's loyalty—from intervening. Afterward, they would attempt to capture the upper town, which they anticipated would surrender more easily once the long walls were secured.

The Athenians, coordinating closely with their allies inside the city, set their plan in motion. They sailed under cover of night to Minoa, the island just off Megara, bringing six hundred heavy infantry under Hippocrates' command. These soldiers concealed themselves in a nearby quarry where bricks for the city walls were once made. Demosthenes, the other Athenian commander, positioned himself even closer, hiding with a contingent of Plataean light troops and Peripoli in the sacred precinct of Enyalius. Only a select few knew of the plan, as secrecy was essential.

Shortly before dawn, the traitors inside Megara began their part of the operation. For some time, they had been smuggling a small boat, mounted on a cart, out through the city gates each night. Claiming it was to raid Athenian positions, they had used this ruse to create a routine. The boat was carried along the ditch to the sea, allowing them to slip past the Athenian blockade stationed at Minoa. Before daybreak, they would retrieve the boat on the cart and re-enter the city, fooling the Megarian authorities into believing they were safeguarding the harbor by keeping the boat concealed.

This night, the cart reached the gates as usual, and the gates were opened to let the boat through. At that moment, the Athenians lying in ambush sprang into action. Spotting the open gates, they raced toward them, aiming to reach the entry before it could be shut. Their Megarian accomplices helped by killing the guards stationed at the gate. Demosthenes led the charge with his Plataeans and Peripoli, and entered through the gates near where the trophy now stands. Once inside, the Plataeans engaged a nearby Peloponnesian contingent who had quickly mobilized, defeating them and securing the gates for the advancing Athenian heavy infantry.

Once inside, the Athenians, as each entered, immediately charged toward the wall. Initially, a few members of the Peloponnesian garrison attempted to hold their position, resisting the Athenians, and some of them were killed in the skirmish. However, the majority were quickly overtaken by fear, panicked by the suddenness of the night attack and the sight of Megarian collaborators fighting alongside the Athenians. Believing that all of Megara had defected, they abandoned their posts and fled. Adding to their confusion, an Athenian herald, acting on his own initiative, called out, inviting any Megarians who wished to join the Athenian side. Hearing this, the Peloponnesians became convinced they were caught in a coordinated assault and retreated to Nisaea for refuge.

By dawn, the Athenians had secured the walls, and unrest spread throughout Megara. Those who had conspired with the Athenians, joined by other members of the popular faction who knew of the plan, advocated opening the city gates to join the battle. According to their arrangement with the Athenians, the gates were to be opened to allow Athenian forces inside, and the collaborators would identify themselves by being anointed with oil to avoid being attacked in the ensuing confusion. The conspirators could proceed with greater confidence, knowing that an additional force of four thousand Athenian heavy infantry and six hundred cavalry, who had marched overnight from Eleusis, were now just outside Megara, ready to intervene.

The plot, however, was suddenly exposed by one of the conspirators, who revealed it to the opposition. Alarmed, the anti-Athenian faction gathered, stating firmly that they should not march out—a course they had never dared attempt even when better prepared—and that it would endanger the city. They warned that, if their counsel was ignored, any fighting would have to take place within Megara itself. Without explicitly disclosing their knowledge of the conspiracy, they held their ground, insisting their advice was best. They stationed themselves by the gates, effectively thwarting the conspirators' plan.

Realizing that their entry into the city was blocked and that a direct capture of Megara was no longer feasible, the Athenian generals turned their attention to Nisaea. They resolved to besiege it, believing that Nisaea's capture would eventually force Megara to capitulate as well. Supplies swiftly arrived from Athens, including iron, stonemasons, and other materials needed to construct a siege wall. Starting from the section of the wall they controlled, the Athenians began building a cross-wall directed toward Megara, extending down to the sea on either side of Nisaea. The army divided the work among themselves, utilizing stones and bricks taken from the surrounding suburb, and cutting down fruit trees and timber to create a palisade where needed. Houses in the suburb were incorporated into the fortifications, and battlements were added where suitable.

Construction continued throughout the day and was nearly complete by the following afternoon. Facing an absolute shortage of food—since their daily provisions had been brought down from the upper city—the garrison in Nisaea grew desperate. With little hope of timely assistance from the Peloponnesians and uncertain about Megara's loyalty, they surrendered to the Athenians. The terms of the capitulation allowed the garrison members to ransom themselves for a specified amount in exchange for their lives. The Lacedaemonian commander and any other Spartans present were left to the Athenians' discretion.

Upon these terms, the garrison surrendered and exited the fort. The Athenians proceeded to dismantle the long walls where they joined Megara, securing Nisaea and advancing their preparations for any future actions.

At this moment, the Lacedaemonian commander Brasidas, son of Tellis, happened to be near Sicyon and Corinth, gathering forces for an expedition to Thrace. Upon hearing that the long walls had fallen, he feared for the Peloponnesians stationed in Nisaea and the security of Megara. He quickly sent word to the Boeotians, requesting that they rendezvous with him as soon as possible at Tripodiscus, a village under Mount Geraneia in the Megarid. Meanwhile, Brasidas himself set out with a force of two thousand seven hundred Corinthian heavy infantry, four hundred Phliasians, six hundred Sicyonians, and the troops he had already gathered, aiming to reach Nisaea before it was fully captured.

However, as he reached Tripodiscus after a nighttime march, Brasidas learned that Nisaea had already fallen. Not deterred, he took three hundred elite troops from his army and approached Megara without alerting the Athenians, who were stationed down by the coast.

His aim was to surprise Nisaea and, if possible, gain entry to Megara to secure the city itself. He urged the Megarians to let his forces inside, asserting that he had a real chance of recapturing Nisaea.

Despite this appeal, neither faction within Megara trusted him enough to open the gates. One faction feared Brasidas might reinstate the exiled Megarian nobles, which could threaten their own influence, while the other worried that the commons, alarmed by this possibility, might turn against them, sparking an internal conflict in plain view of the Athenian forces stationed nearby. Preferring to avoid this risk, both factions decided to wait and see what would transpire, hoping to back whichever side emerged victorious in the inevitable clash between the Athenians and the relieving army.

Brasidas, realizing that he could not force his way into Megara, returned to his main force. At dawn, the Boeotians joined him, having independently resolved to aid Megara, which they viewed as vital to their own defense. Already assembled in full strength at Plataea, the Boeotians immediately sent a force of two thousand two hundred heavy infantry and six hundred cavalry to join Brasidas, while the remainder of their army returned home. This alliance swelled the Peloponnesian ranks to nearly six thousand heavy infantry.

Meanwhile, the Athenian heavy infantry was positioned near Nisaea and the coast, with their light troops dispersed across the plains. The Boeotian cavalry took advantage of this, launching a surprise attack that drove the Athenian light forces toward the sea. This attack caught the Athenians off guard, as they had not anticipated any reinforcements for the Megarians. However, the Athenian cavalry responded by charging the Boeotians, resulting in an extended cavalry skirmish with both sides claiming victory.

The Athenians managed to kill the Boeotian cavalry leader and a few of his comrades who had advanced close to Nisaea. They stripped the bodies, held the field briefly, and erected a trophy to commemorate their tactical success. Later, they returned the fallen under a truce. Yet despite these actions, the outcome of the battle was inconclusive. Both armies withdrew to their respective positions, the Boeotians rejoining their main force while the Athenians regrouped at Nisaea, neither side securing a decisive victory.

Following this, Brasidas moved his forces closer to the coast and to Megara itself, positioning his troops in a strategic location where they remained in battle formation, calmly awaiting an Athenian attack. The Megarians, observing from within the city, waited to see which side would emerge victorious. This approach served Brasidas well for two reasons: by maintaining a defensive stance without directly initiating combat, he was able to demonstrate readiness and resolve. Thus, without the risk of engaging in open battle, he could still claim the day's honor simply by showing force and readiness. Additionally, his visible presence was vital to the situation in Megara. Had he not appeared with his forces, the Megarians would likely have deemed his side defeated and handed the city over to the Athenians.

As anticipated, the Athenians gathered outside the long walls, but, seeing no move from the Peloponnesians, they hesitated. Their generals assessed the situation and deemed the risk too great. They had already achieved most of their objectives without battle, and engaging an enemy with superior numbers offered little gain. Even if victorious, they would only secure Megara, but a defeat would mean the loss of their best heavy infantry. For Brasidas and his allies, the stakes were different; each state represented in his forces risked only a fraction of its total strength, allowing them to be more daring. Consequently, after both sides held their positions without initiating combat, the Athenians ultimately withdrew to Nisaea, while the Peloponnesians returned to their original positions.

With the Athenian withdrawal, the faction supporting the exiled Megarians took the opportunity to act. Viewing Brasidas as the victor and the Athenians as reluctant to engage, they opened the gates to Brasidas and his allied commanders, welcoming them into the city. This entry emboldened their faction, leaving those previously in league with the Athenians paralyzed by the sudden turn of events.

Afterward, Brasidas allowed the allied contingents to return home and himself departed for Corinth, preparing to continue his campaign to Thrace. The Athenians likewise returned home. Meanwhile, the Megarians who had been deeply involved in plotting with the Athenians realized that they were exposed and swiftly disappeared. The remaining Megarians then met with the supporters of the exiles, and together they decided to restore the exiled party from Pegae, binding them by solemn oaths not to seek revenge and to prioritize the city's well-being.

However, once back in power, the returned exiles soon acted against their former enemies. Organizing a review of the heavy infantry, they separated the battalions and selected about one hundred individuals suspected of collaboration with the Athenians. These men were brought before the public assembly, and with an open vote, they were condemned and executed. Following these executions, the restored exiles established a strict oligarchy in Megara. This political order, born from the coup, remained in place for a considerable period, even though it had been instigated by only a small faction within the city.

Chapter XIV

Eighth and Ninth Years of the War—Invasion of Boeotia—Fall of Amphipolis—Brilliant Successes of Brasidas

In the same summer, the Mitylenians were preparing to fortify Antandrus as they had originally planned. Demodocus and Aristides, the Athenian commanders tasked with raising subsidies, learned of these developments on the Hellespont. Their colleague Lamachus had sailed into the Pontus with ten ships, leaving them to deal with the growing threat at Antandrus. The Athenians feared that Antandrus could become a new stronghold like Anaia, a place where Samian exiles had established a base to trouble Samos. At Anaia, these exiles actively aided the Peloponnesians, sending experienced pilots to their fleets, creating unrest in the surrounding region, and providing refuge to exiled enemies of Samos.

Seeing similar risks with Antandrus, the Athenians recognized the strategic importance of acting quickly to prevent it from becoming a fortified haven for their adversaries. Demodocus and Aristides assembled a force from the allied contingents in the area and sailed to Antandrus. They encountered resistance from local troops, but after a hard-fought battle, they defeated these forces and reclaimed the town for Athens, preventing it from falling under hostile control.

Soon afterward, Lamachus, who had been navigating the Pontus, encountered a disaster. While anchored in the river Calex, within the territory of Heraclea, his ships were struck by a sudden flood. Heavy rains had fallen inland, causing the river to swell unexpectedly and wash away his fleet. Lamachus and his forces were forced to abandon their ships and traverse the rugged terrain on foot through Bithynian Thrace on the Asiatic side, eventually reaching Chalcedon, a Megarian colony at the mouth of the Pontus.

In the same summer, the Athenian general Demosthenes arrived at Naupactus with forty ships shortly after returning from operations in the Megarid. Both he and his colleague, Hippocrates, had been approached by certain individuals in Boeotia who wanted to overthrow the existing government and establish a democracy similar to that of Athens. At the center of this plot was Ptoeodorus, a Theban exile. The conspirators planned a coordinated effort to seize strategic locations across Boeotia. One faction had promised to surrender Siphae, a port on the Crisaean Gulf in Thespian territory, to the Athenians. Meanwhile, another group was working to hand over Chaeronea, a town on the border with Phocia and a dependency of Orchomenus, formerly called Minyan Orchomenus and now under Boeotian control. These exiles, well-versed in local dynamics, had even managed to hire troops in the Peloponnese to support their cause.

The plan also involved some Phocians, with Chaeronea bordering the Phocian town of Phanotis. Simultaneously, the Athenians intended to seize the sacred site of Delium, Apollo's sanctuary in Tanagra, positioned opposite Euboea. The goal was for all these maneuvers to occur on a single, prearranged day, preventing the Boeotians from uniting against the Athenians at Delium by preoccupying them with internal unrest.

If successful, the conspirators believed the seizure of Delium and the fortification of other key locations would put them in a position to destabilize Boeotia from within. Even if an immediate revolution did not follow, the presence of Athenian-occupied fortresses would serve as refuges and rallying points for those sympathetic to democracy. The continual harassment of the countryside would further undermine the Boeotian oligarchs, making it easier to effect change over time with the support of the Athenian forces.

To bring this plan to fruition, Hippocrates gathered forces in Athens, preparing to march on Boeotia at the appointed time. Meanwhile, he sent Demosthenes with the forty ships to Naupactus to muster an army of Acarnanians and other allies in the region, with the intention of reaching Siphae to receive the town from the conspirators.

Upon his arrival, Demosthenes discovered that the Acarnanians had already persuaded Oeniadae to join the Athenian alliance, adding strength to the Athenian cause. Demosthenes then continued to rally local allies and advanced to subdue Salynthius and the Agraeans. With these preliminary tasks complete, he concentrated on gathering the resources and forces needed to be ready at Siphae on the agreed-upon day, coordinating efforts to execute this multifaceted plan with precision.

Around the same time that summer, Brasidas began his campaign toward the Thracian cities with a force of seventeen hundred heavy infantry. Arriving first at Heraclea in Trachis, he sent a messenger ahead to his allies in Pharsalus, requesting safe passage for himself and his army across Thessalian territory. In response, several influential Thessalians, including Panaerus, Dorus, Hippolochidas, Torylaus, and Strophacus—the proxenus of the Chalcidians—came to meet him at Melitia in Achaea. They served as his escorts along the journey, joined by other local supporters such as Niconidas from Larissa, who was also a close friend of Perdiccas, the Macedonian king. Crossing Thessaly without an escort was difficult under any circumstances, and it was particularly sensitive for an armed force to pass through another state's territory unbidden. In addition, Thessaly tended to favor the Athenians, so Brasidas knew his progress would require careful diplomacy.

Under different political conditions, particularly if Thessaly had been under a constitutional government rather than its usual close oligarchy, Brasidas likely wouldn't have been permitted to proceed. Even with his escort, he encountered opposition: at the river Enipeus, a group from Thessaly's opposing faction confronted him. They questioned his intentions and opposed his passage, arguing that he had not sought permission from the larger Thessalian community. Brasidas' supporters in the escort explained that they weren't trying to force his way through but were simply accompanying him as a group of friends guiding an unexpected visitor. Brasidas himself responded diplomatically, explaining that he came to Thessaly as an ally, not as an enemy. His arms, he assured them, were directed only against the Athenians, with whom he was at war. He reminded them that there had been no hostility between Thessaly and Lacedaemon, which should allow the two peoples to travel through each other's lands. Nonetheless, he made it clear he would not proceed against their wishes and respectfully requested they let him pass.

This response seemed to satisfy his opposition, and they withdrew. Taking advantage of the lull, Brasidas, urged on by his escort, pressed forward without delay, knowing that a larger force might assemble to block his path if he hesitated. On the same day he left Melitia, he covered the entire distance to Pharsalus, where he set up camp by the river Apidanus. From there, he continued his march, passing through Phacium and eventually reaching Perrhaebia. At this point, his Thessalian escort turned back, leaving the remainder of his journey to the Perrhaebians—subjects of Thessaly—who guided him to Dium, a town within Perdiccas' domain in Macedonia. Dium lay at the base of

Mount Olympus, looking out toward Thessaly, marking his arrival in Macedonian territory and the end of his journey through Thessaly.

Brasidas moved swiftly through Thessaly, avoiding any opposition that might have delayed him, and soon joined up with Perdiccas and the Chalcidian towns in revolt. The Thracian cities that had broken away from Athens, along with Perdiccas, were responsible for his departure from the Peloponnese. These cities, anxious over Athens' recent military successes, saw the need for support. The Chalcidians, in particular, feared that they would be the first target of an Athenian counter-expedition. While other neighboring towns that had not yet openly revolted also encouraged Brasidas' arrival, they did so discreetly. Perdiccas, too, was uneasy due to his past conflicts with Athens, though he was not formally at war with them; his primary goal, however, was to subdue Arrhabaeus, king of the Lyncestians.

The Lacedaemonians, facing ongoing Athenian assaults on their own lands, especially in Laconia, saw this expedition as an opportunity to divert Athenian focus. By sending troops to assist their allies in revolt, they hoped to keep Athens occupied elsewhere. Furthermore, the Thracian towns were prepared to fund the army themselves, making the decision easier for the Lacedaemonians. Another incentive for sending troops, including Helots, was the Lacedaemonians' long-standing fear of rebellion among the Helot population. With the loss of Pylos, the Helots had become more restless, and the Spartans were particularly concerned about potential uprisings. This concern led them to employ a subtle strategy: they announced that any Helot who felt he had distinguished himself in service against the enemy would be granted his freedom. This was intended to single out the most spirited Helots, those most likely to seek freedom, thereby revealing potential rebels. Around two thousand Helots responded, crowning themselves and celebrating their supposed liberation by visiting temples. However, soon afterward, the Spartans secretly executed them, ensuring that no one knew the fate of each individual.

Given this situation, the Spartans readily agreed to send seven hundred Helot heavy infantry with Brasidas, who supplemented his force by recruiting additional soldiers with funds raised in the Peloponnese. Brasidas had pushed for this mission largely on his own initiative, though the Chalcidians were also eager for his leadership. He had proven his capability in every task he undertook at Sparta, and his service abroad would bring significant benefits to his homeland. His fair and moderate behavior in Thrace helped secure the allegiance of many cities, which often preferred voluntary revolt rather than conquest. For the Lacedaemonians, his actions provided valuable bargaining power when negotiating for peace, as they eventually did, since they now held key territories to offer in exchange. Brasidas' campaigns also shifted the burden of war away from the Peloponnese and onto Athenian territories.

Later, after the campaigns in Sicily, Brasidas' reputation for bravery and integrity became widely known, influencing many of Athens' allies to consider switching sides. His conduct set a standard among the Lacedaemonian allies; he was the first Spartan commander they encountered who demonstrated such an impressive character that he left a lasting impression, leading many to assume that others from Sparta would be equally honorable and capable.

Meanwhile, news of Brasidas' arrival in the Thracian region alarmed the Athenians, who quickly declared war on Perdiccas, whom they saw as the instigator of this expedition. Athens also tightened its surveillance over its allies in the area, recognizing that Brasidas' presence posed a serious threat to their influence in the north.

Upon Brasidas' arrival with his forces, Perdiccas immediately prepared to march alongside him with his own troops against Arrhabaeus, son of Bromerus, the king of the Lyncestian Macedonians. Arrhabaeus, Perdiccas' neighboring rival, was a target of longstanding animosity, and Perdiccas sought to conquer him. However, as they approached the pass leading into Lyncus, Brasidas informed Perdiccas that he wished to attempt a diplomatic approach before launching any attacks. Arrhabaeus had already expressed an interest in aligning with the Lacedaemonians and had indicated a willingness to accept Brasidas as an intermediary in his disputes with Perdiccas. The Chalcidian envoys accompanying Brasidas also advised him to handle the situation with caution, suggesting that keeping Perdiccas uncertain might ensure his continued dedication to their alliance.

In addition, when Perdiccas had initially sent envoys to Sparta, they had spoken of his plans to secure several territories around him as allies of Lacedaemon. Brasidas, mindful of this broader strategic opportunity, saw potential in treating the question of Arrhabaeus' allegiance with a larger view in mind. Perdiccas, however, was displeased with this approach. He reminded Brasidas that he had requested his assistance not for mediation but for the suppression of those adversaries he deemed a threat. Further, since he was paying for half of the army's expenses, Perdiccas argued it would be unfaithful to their arrangement if Brasidas engaged in negotiations with Arrhabaeus.

Ignoring Perdiccas' objections, Brasidas held a diplomatic discussion with Arrhabaeus and ultimately agreed to withdraw without invading his territory. Feeling betrayed by this decision, Perdiccas reduced his financial support for the army from half to only a third of its costs, considering that Brasidas had not honored their initial agreement.

Not long afterward, Brasidas turned his attention to Acanthus, a colony of the Andrians, and set out with his Chalcidian allies just before the grape harvest season. The Acanthians were divided over whether to allow him into the city: while one faction, consisting of those who had allied with the Chalcidians to invite Brasidas, supported his entry, the popular party was more cautious. The timing, however, played into Brasidas' favor, as many Acanthians feared for the fate of their unharvested crops if they resisted him. As a result, Brasidas was able to persuade them to let him in alone to present his case before the citizens. Once admitted, he stood before the assembly and, showing a surprising command of rhetoric for a Spartan, prepared to address them directly.

"Acanthians, the Lacedaemonians have sent me and my army to fulfill the very purpose we declared when we first engaged in this war: to liberate Hellas from Athenian control. Our delay in coming sooner was due to our hope that we could bring down Athens through our own efforts, without requiring any risks or burdens from you. But now that we see the need for direct support, we have come ready to stand by you to the fullest extent in this endeavor. I am surprised, therefore, to find your gates closed and our arrival met with hesitation. We had believed that you would welcome us eagerly as allies who had longed for our presence even before we physically arrived. So great was our commitment that we took upon ourselves the hardship of a long and unfamiliar journey to reach you, driven by our shared goal of freedom.

"However, if you now intend to turn us away, it would not only harm your own interests but also cast doubt on the collective freedom of Hellas. By refusing our offer, you not only deny us entry but set a discouraging precedent for others we may approach. If the Acanthians—a respected and significant city—refuse to align with us, then other towns may also hesitate, assuming our mission lacks the promise we profess. People will begin to question the legitimacy of the freedom I offer or, worse, think my force insufficient to shield them from Athenian retaliation. But remember, when I led this very army to relieve Nisaea, the Athenians, despite their greater numbers, declined to face me in open combat. It is unlikely they will muster a fleet to send an equally large force across the sea to confront you here, particularly given the defensive advantages of your position.

"My purpose here is not to harm but to liberate, a commitment I have secured through solemn oaths, ensuring that any allies who join us will retain their full independence. I come neither with deceit nor force, but instead extend my hand to offer support against the Athenians. I urge you to set aside any suspicions about my intentions;

my commitment is genuine, and my ability to protect you is real. Join me confidently and without reservation.

"Some among you may feel reluctance due to private rivalries and fear that my presence might shift power toward one faction. Let me assure you, I have not come to champion any party within your city. I am here to establish freedom in the truest sense, one that does not disturb your existing political structure or subject the many to the few, or vice versa. Such an imposition would be far worse than remaining under Athenian rule. If I were to impose any factional rule, it would bring neither gratitude nor honor to the Lacedaemonians; rather, we would face blame and disrepute. The very reasons that justify our struggle against Athens would apply to us if we acted in this way, and we would be seen as more hypocritical than those who make no claims to justice. For it is more reprehensible for those who claim virtue to use deceptive means than to seize power openly by force, since the former represents mere trickery while the latter, at least, holds the straightforward authority of power.

"It is in our own interest, then, to approach this mission with integrity, and we guard that principle as carefully as you might expect. Beyond the solemn oaths I have sworn, consider how closely our words align with the reality we offer; this alignment alone should convince you that it is in our best interest to uphold the values we proclaim. We seek your friendship on terms that respect your autonomy and restore the collective freedom of Hellas."

"If, despite my arguments, you plead inability to accept our aid and believe that your goodwill alone should protect you from any harm, or if you claim that freedom comes with too many risks for you, and that it should only be extended to those who willingly embrace it rather than forced upon any who resist, then I must take the gods and heroes of your city as witnesses. They will know that I have come with intentions for your benefit, only to be turned away. Should you reject our offer, I will be left with no choice but to compel you by ravaging your land. I shall do this without hesitation, as I am driven by a necessity beyond mere choice. First, I must protect the Lacedaemonians from the harm that would come from you aiding the Athenians with the funds you send them, which would continue if you do not join our cause. Second, I am bound to ensure that no Hellenic city hinders our mission to free Greece from Athenian control. Were it not for this higher purpose, we Lacedaemonians would have no right to compel you to accept freedom, as we do not seek an empire. Our goal is to dismantle imperial power, not establish it, and to ensure that cities like yours do not obstruct the independence we offer to all.

"Therefore, I urge you to consider wisely. Think of the opportunity before you—not only to avoid personal loss but to be part of a historic liberation for all Hellenes. Such an alliance will bring lasting honor to your city and glory to your commonwealth."

These were Brasidas' words. After much discussion on both sides, the Acanthians voted in secret, ultimately swayed by Brasidas' persuasive reasoning and by concerns for their unharvested crops. The majority chose to break away from Athens, though they insisted on additional assurances. They would not allow his army entry until Brasidas personally guaranteed, through oaths sworn by the Lacedaemonian government, the independence of any allies joining their cause. Shortly after this decision, Stagirus, another colony of the Andrians, also joined the revolt against Athens.

These events marked the summer. As winter began, the Athenian generals Hippocrates and Demosthenes prepared for operations in Boeotia. Demosthenes was to take his fleet to Siphae, while Hippocrates would move on Delium. However, a miscalculation disrupted their coordinated timing. Demosthenes sailed to Siphae with a coalition of Acarnanians and other regional allies, only to find his plans betrayed. A Phocian named Nicomachus, from Phanotis, had informed the Lacedaemonians, who then alerted the Boeotians. Boeotian reinforcements arrived swiftly at Siphae and Chaeronea, securing both towns. With their plot revealed, the conspirators within these cities abandoned any attempt to rise up.

Meanwhile, Hippocrates mustered a large force from Athens, including citizens, resident foreigners, and allies, and arrived at Delium after the Boeotian forces had already returned from Siphae. Once there, he began fortifying the sanctuary of Apollo at Delium. The Athenians dug a trench around the temple and sacred grounds, using the earth to build a makeshift wall reinforced with stakes, vines, stones, and bricks from nearby structures. Wooden towers were erected at vulnerable points, and parts of the temple's fallen gallery served as additional barriers.

The fortification effort began on the third day after their departure from Athens and continued on the fourth day and until midday on the fifth. By then, the majority of the defensive works were complete. The Athenian army moved about two kilometers from Delium to begin their journey home. The lighter troops continued onward, while the heavy infantry remained behind, holding their position. Hippocrates stayed at Delium to oversee the final placements of the defensive posts and to ensure that any remaining parts of the fortifications were completed.

During the days of these preparations, the Boeotian forces gathered at Tanagra, rallying soldiers from all their cities. By the time they had assembled in full, they learned that the Athenians had already begun their retreat toward home. The Athenians, however, had only just crossed the border of Boeotia into the territory of Oropos when they halted. Of the eleven Boeotian generals, or Boeotarchs, the majority were against pursuing the Athenians, reasoning that they were no longer technically in Boeotian land and thus no longer a direct threat. But Pagondas, son of Aeolidas, a leading Boeotarch of Thebes, along with his colleague Arianthides, son of Lysimachidas, argued for immediate action, believing that a battle was imperative regardless of the Athenians' current position.

Pagondas took deliberate measures to ready his forces, addressing them in small groups, company by company, so that their defensive lines would remain guarded and their readiness unbroken. When he had gathered each contingent, Pagondas addressed them with urgency and fervor, seeking to rally their spirits and convince them of the necessity of confronting the Athenians in battle. His speech was as follows:

"Boeotians, it is a grave error to think we should only engage the Athenians if we find them firmly within Boeotia. They crossed into our land to erect a fort in hostile defiance, fully intending to harm our homeland. Wherever we find them, they remain our enemies, regardless of whether they are now technically over the border. Our duty is to act decisively, not let them go unchallenged. If anyone among us hesitates under the guise of prudence, let him reconsider. We who defend our own land have a different responsibility than those who merely seek to expand their territories for gain. While they scheme for conquest from positions of ease, our task is to secure what is rightfully ours, to safeguard what we have already, and to prevent any loss.

"Moreover, it is part of our Boeotian heritage to stand against invaders, regardless of where we meet them. But when that aggressor is Athens—a state not only ambitious but also neighboring us—it is all the more crucial that we show strength. Freedom, between neighboring peoples, depends upon the unyielding resolve to defend what is one's own. And with neighbors such as these, who seek not just to conquer nearby lands but to enslave both near and distant peoples alike, there is no choice but to engage them fully and decisively. Look to the plight of the Euboeans and so many others across Hellas—this is what awaits us if we do not act. Most cities fight over contested borders, but we face a foe who, if victorious, will treat all our land as theirs, taking it by force and leaving nothing for negotiation.

"This makes the Athenian threat graver than any other. Powerful states, like Athens, are quick to move against those who merely defend within their own borders. They assume the stillness of such people as weakness. But they hesitate to engage those who actively meet them outside their borders, who dare to strike first when the opportunity arises. We have seen this ourselves: our victory over Athens at Coronea, when past strife allowed them briefly into our land, brought Boeotia the security it enjoys to this day. Let the older among you remember this, and let the younger, heirs to that noble legacy, prove themselves worthy of their forefathers. Trust in the god whose sanctuary has been dishonored by this Athenian fortification, and in the favorable signs we have received from our sacrifices.

"Now is the time to march forward and demonstrate to the Athenians that they cannot simply take what they want by targeting those who won't resist. Let them learn that we are men whose legacy is to fight for the freedom of our homeland, who never unjustly seize the land of others but will never yield our own without a struggle."

Pagondas' stirring words resonated deeply. After weighing his arguments and reflecting on both the immediate danger and the long-term implications, the Boeotians chose to follow his call to arms, preparing to meet the Athenians and defend their land's independence with determination and valor.

With these words, Pagondas successfully persuaded the Boeotians to prepare for an immediate attack on the Athenians. He quickly ordered the camp to be broken, and the army advanced, even though the day was now drawing to a close. As they approached the Athenian forces, he halted his troops on the far side of a hill, which blocked each army from seeing the other. There, out of sight, the Boeotians organized and readied themselves for battle.

Meanwhile, Hippocrates, stationed at Delium, received news of the advancing Boeotians and immediately issued orders for his own troops to assemble into formation. Shortly thereafter, he joined his men, leaving behind a reserve of about three hundred horsemen at Delium to defend the site from a possible attack and to stand ready to seize any opportunity to strike the Boeotian army during the battle. Anticipating this, the Boeotians stationed a detachment specifically to counter these Athenians, ensuring they could not disrupt the main engagement.

When all Boeotian forces were arranged, they advanced over the hill and took their designated positions with great precision. Their numbers included seven thousand heavy infantry, more than ten thousand lightly armed troops, one thousand cavalry, and five hundred targeteers. The formation was structured with the Thebans and their allies holding the right flank, a central position filled by the Haliartians, Coronaeans, Copaeans, and the communities from around the lake, and the left flank manned by the Thespians, Tanagraeans, and Orchomenians. At the extreme ends of both wings stood the cavalry and light troops. The Theban line was drawn up twenty-five shields deep, while the remaining troops arranged themselves in the depth they deemed effective for combat.

On the Athenian side, the heavy infantry formed a consistent depth of eight shields throughout their ranks, matching the Boeotian army in number. Cavalry was stationed on both wings to counterbalance the Boeotian cavalry. Unlike their foes, the Athenians did not possess specialized light-armed troops, as Athens had never integrated a dedicated light-armed force into its military. The majority of light infantry who had joined the campaign were unarmed citizens and foreigners summoned en masse from Athens, and many of them, having left early to head back home, were now absent from the battlefield.

As the armies stood ready, aligned in formation, and prepared to engage, Hippocrates, the Athenian general, moved along the lines, addressing his troops with concise words meant to inspire focus and resilience. His speech, though brief, was designed to reach their minds as much as their hearts:

"Athenians, I will speak but briefly, as true courage needs few words, and you, above all, understand well the cause for which we fight. Do not let yourselves think that we are taking an unnecessary risk in a foreign land. Although we stand in Boeotian territory, this battle is for the security of our own. A victory here means that the Peloponnesians will not again invade Attica without the support of Boeotian cavalry. In a single battle, we can secure both Boeotia and protect Attica from future incursions. So advance with the spirit befitting citizens of the most illustrious city in Hellas, and with the strength of sons whose fathers triumphed under Myronides at Oenophyta, gaining Boeotia itself."

With this speech, Hippocrates aimed to remind his troops of their heritage, invoking both pride in their Athenian identity and the memory of past victories, stirring them to fight with confidence and honor.

Pagondas' address ultimately convinced the Boeotians to confront the Athenians, leading them to break camp swiftly and advance into battle formation, even though the day was nearing its end. As they neared the Athenian forces, they halted just behind a hill that separated the two armies, allowing them to ready themselves out of sight. Meanwhile, Hippocrates, stationed at Delium, received word of the Boeotian approach. He immediately sent orders for the Athenian troops to form lines and, shortly afterward, joined them, leaving behind a small cavalry unit to guard Delium and keep watch for any chance to strike the Boeotians from behind during the clash. The Boeotians, anticipating this, also assigned a contingent to counter this threat.

When all preparations were complete, the Boeotians advanced over the hill and arranged themselves in formation with seven thousand heavy infantry, over ten thousand lightly armed troops, one thousand cavalry, and five hundred targeteers. On the right flank were the Thebans and their allies, the center comprised soldiers from Haliartus, Coronea, Copae, and other nearby towns, while the left included warriors from Thespiae, Tanagra, and Orchomenus. The Theban line was an impressive twenty-five shields deep, with the rest forming ranks at shallower depths according to their preference.

On the Athenian side, the heavy infantry, roughly equal in number to the Boeotians, formed eight shields deep, with cavalry on each wing. Lacking organized light-armed troops, the Athenians found themselves at a disadvantage. Those lightly armed who had joined the campaign were unprepared, mostly gathered as a mass levy from the Athenian citizenry and foreign residents, many of whom had already departed. With both armies ready, Hippocrates moved down the Athenian ranks, giving a brief but pointed speech meant to stir their resolve.

As he made his way through half the army, the Boeotians, having received final instructions from Pagondas, struck up the traditional paean and began advancing from the hill. The Athenians, responding immediately, surged forward to meet them at a run. The two armies clashed with intense vigor, shield against shield. On the Boeotian left, as far as the center, the Athenians gained the upper hand, causing severe losses among the Thespians caught in close quarters, resulting in confusion among the Athenians who, in the frenzy, mistakenly attacked some of their own men. In this section, the Boeotians were ultimately forced to fall back, joining the units still engaged. However, on the Boeotian right, led by the Thebans, the Boeotians managed to push back the Athenians, although the retreat was gradual at first.

At a critical moment, Pagondas, observing the distress on his left, secretly sent two cavalry squadrons around the hill. Their sudden appearance created panic among the Athenians, who mistook them for a larger force. This disruption, combined with the Theban pressure, broke the Athenian lines, and soon their entire army began to flee. Some sought safety at Delium and the coast, others fled toward Oropus and Mount Parnes, pursued relentlessly by the Boeotian cavalry, reinforced by recently arrived Locrian allies. Fortunately for the Athenians, nightfall interrupted the chase, enabling many to escape who otherwise might not have survived. The next day, troops stationed at Delium and Oropus returned to Athens by sea, leaving a small garrison to hold Delium despite the defeat.

In victory, the Boeotians set up a trophy, retrieved their own fallen, and stripped the enemy dead, leaving a guard over the bodies as they returned to Tanagra to strategize an assault on Delium. An Athenian herald arrived to request the return of the bodies, but a Boeotian herald intercepted him, instructing him to wait until his own mission to the Athenians was complete. Upon reaching Athens, the Boeotian herald accused the Athenians of violating Hellenic religious customs, arguing that their seizure and fortification of Delium had desecrated the sacred site by occupying it as though it were ordinary land and by using its water, which the Boeotians touched only for ritual purposes. He conveyed that if the Athenians wished to retrieve their dead, they must first abandon the sanctuary.

In response, the Athenians sent their own herald to clarify their position. They insisted that they had committed no wrongdoing at the temple and would avoid any further harm, emphasizing that they had taken the site only as a defensive measure, not with the intention of desecration. According to Hellenic customs, they argued, conquering a portion of enemy territory granted rights over its temples with the responsibility of maintaining sacred rites, as the Boeotians themselves held temples within lands they had once seized from others by force. If the Athenians had conquered a larger share of Boeotia, they would rightfully have considered it their own. As it stood, they had a legitimate claim to Delium and would not withdraw unless forced. The water, they asserted, had been utilized solely out of military necessity due to Boeotian aggression, not out of a desire to desecrate the sanctuary.

The Athenian herald then posed a challenge: was it not the Boeotians who were impious in prioritizing a demand for religious retreat over the burial rites of the fallen? The Athenians argued that it was contrary to custom for the Boeotians to hold the bodies hostage to compel a withdrawal, claiming that they themselves had occupied Delium by the accepted right of conquest and saw no grounds to relinquish their position. In the Athenians' view, the Boeotians needed only to grant the customary truce for the recovery of the dead, adhering to the long-established practices of Hellenic warfare.

The Boeotians replied to the Athenian demands with a firm stance: if the Athenians truly believed they were in Boeotian territory, they must vacate it before attempting to retrieve their dead. Conversely, if they maintained that they were on their own land, they could do as they pleased—but with the understanding that the Boeotians would not allow the bodies to be reclaimed without their permission. They pointed out that, although the bodies lay on the border in Oropid territory (technically Athenian land), the Athenians could not access them without Boeotian consent. The Boeotians questioned why they should grant a truce over land they did not consider their own, insisting instead that the Athenians vacate Boeotia if they wished to retrieve the remains of their fallen. Receiving this response, the Athenian herald returned, unable to achieve his goal.

Meanwhile, the Boeotians, prepared to capitalize on their victory, summoned darters and slingers from the Malian Gulf, bolstered by two thousand Corinthian heavy infantry who had joined them post-battle, as well as the Peloponnesian garrison recently departed from Nisaea and a contingent of Megarians. This assembled force then advanced on Delium, launching multiple attempts to take the Athenian fortification. Their breakthrough came through an ingenious siege device: they constructed an enormous hollow beam, split and hollowed to act like a pipe, and skillfully reassembled it with iron plating along much of its length. At one end, they suspended a cauldron filled with combustible materials, while an iron pipe connected it to the beam. Mounted on carts, this apparatus was rolled toward the section of the wall predominantly made of vines and timber. Once in position, they attached large bellows to their end of the beam and began pumping air through the pipe into the cauldron filled with burning coals, sulfur, and pitch. This directed blast fanned the flames within, creating a fire so intense that it soon ignited the wooden sections of the wall, forcing the defenders to abandon their posts. With the wall weakened, the Boeotians stormed Delium, overpowering the garrison. Some defenders were killed, about two hundred were captured, and the majority managed to escape by sea, retreating to Athens.

Seventeen days after the initial battle, Delium fell to the Boeotians. Unaware of this defeat, the Athenian herald arrived once more to request the return of their dead. This time, with Delium under their control, the Boeotians granted his request without the stipulations of their previous demands. Nearly five hundred Boeotians had fallen, while close to one thousand Athenians perished, including their general Hippocrates, in addition to numerous lightly armed troops and camp followers.

Following the events at Delium, Demosthenes, after the failure of his operation at Siphae, used the forces he had, including Acarnanian and Agraean contingents and four hundred Athenian heavy infantry, to make a landing on the Sicyonian coast. However, before his entire force had disembarked, the Sicyonians launched a swift counterattack, routing those who had landed and forcing them back to their ships, killing some and capturing others. The Sicyonians then erected a trophy to mark their victory and returned the Athenian dead under a truce.

Around the same time as the events at Delium, Sitalces, the king of the Odrysians, was defeated in battle by the Triballi and killed. His nephew Seuthes, son of Sparadocus, succeeded him, inheriting both the Odrysian throne and the territories in Thrace under Sitalces' rule.

Meanwhile, Brasidas continued his campaign, marching with allied forces from the Thracian region toward Amphipolis, an Athenian colony located on the Strymon River. Amphipolis had a storied history, as the site where Aristagoras of Miletus had once attempted to establish a settlement during his flight from King Darius, only to be driven out by the Edonians. Thirty-two years later, the Athenians tried to colonize it with ten thousand settlers, only for these to be defeated by the Thracians at Drabescus. Nearly three decades later, under Hagnon son of Nicias, the Athenians succeeded in establishing a settlement at what was then called Ennea Hodoi, or Nine Ways. Starting from their nearby port of Eion, just under five kilometers from the new colony, Hagnon constructed Amphipolis, so named because it was nearly encircled by the Strymon River on two sides. A long wall stretched from one bank of the river to the other, creating an impressive and defensible city, visible from both land and sea.

Brasidas advanced swiftly toward Amphipolis, beginning his march from Arne in Chalcidice. He reached Aulon and Bromiscus by dusk, where Lake Bolbe flows into the sea, and, after a brief stop for supper, continued his march through the night. The conditions were challenging due to the stormy weather and light snowfall, which he took advantage of, hoping to catch the inhabitants of Amphipolis by complete surprise, apart from those plotting from within.

The plot to hand over Amphipolis was led by citizens of Argilus, an Andrian colony, who lived both in Argilus and Amphipolis and had been covertly working with Brasidas. The Argilians had long harbored ambitions for the city, resentful of Athenian influence and viewing Brasidas' arrival as the perfect opportunity to act. These conspirators, who had been collaborating with certain discontented Amphipolitans, welcomed Brasidas to Argilus, where they formally revolted against Athens. That night, they escorted Brasidas directly to the bridge over the Strymon River, a critical point near the town with only a light guard, especially since the town's walls did not extend to cover this strategic bridge as they would in later times. Brasidas' forces quickly overwhelmed the guards, some of whom were sympathetic to the conspiracy, while others were taken by surprise due to the storm and the suddenness of the attack. In this way, Brasidas secured control of the bridge and all the possessions outside the town, where the Amphipolitans had established homes.

The speed and efficiency of Brasidas' movement caused shock and disorder among the Amphipolitans. The surprise capture of those outside the walls, coupled with the rapid flight of others back within, created an atmosphere of panic and distrust, especially as factions loyal to Athens and the conspirators vied for control. It is believed that had Brasidas pushed directly into the town without pausing to loot, he might have seized it immediately. Instead, he set up his position outside, effectively controlling the surrounding area and waiting for his allies within to open the gates. However, the faction opposed to the conspirators was strong enough to prevent this from happening, and with the support of Eucles, the Athenian commander assigned to Amphipolis, they were able to send for reinforcements from Thucydides, son of Olorus, the historian and the second Athenian commander stationed in Thrace. Thucydides, stationed on the nearby island of Thasos, only half a day's sail away, quickly mobilized seven ships to rush to Amphipolis, hoping to prevent a surrender or, if that proved impossible, to secure the nearby stronghold of Eion.

Meanwhile, Brasidas, aware that Thucydides might bring reinforcements by sea and bolster the morale of Amphipolis with Athenian support, acted swiftly. He understood Thucydides' considerable local influence due to his rights to the nearby gold mines, which gave him significant connections and resources. Determined to secure Amphipolis before Thucydides' arrival could alter the situation, Brasidas extended an offer of lenient terms to win over the inhabitants. His terms were appealing: he proclaimed that any Amphipolitans or Athenians who wished to remain could retain their property and citizenship, while those preferring to leave would have a five-day window to do so, taking their belongings with them.

These conciliatory terms aimed to reduce resistance and encourage the city's inhabitants to accept Brasidas' presence, hoping they would see him as a protector rather than an oppressor.

The majority of the people within Amphipolis, hearing Brasidas' terms, began to reconsider their options, as they found his proclamation surprisingly reasonable compared to what they had feared. The Athenian residents, though few, were eager to leave, aware that they might face harsher consequences if they stayed, and doubtful about receiving timely reinforcement. Many of the townspeople were not native Athenians but had come from various places and, seeing that the terms allowed them to retain their property and rights, felt a sense of relief. Additionally, some within the walls had relatives or friends who had been captured outside, further inclining them to accept Brasidas' offer. The pro-Spartan faction in Amphipolis, seizing on the change in sentiment, advocated openly for the surrender, further isolating the Athenian general Eucles, who was now ignored by the citizens. In this atmosphere of shifting allegiance, the city formally capitulated to Brasidas on the terms he had set.

By the end of the same day, as Brasidas consolidated his hold on Amphipolis, Thucydides and his ships reached the harbor of Eion, having sailed with urgency to secure it. Thucydides' arrival prevented Eion from falling as Amphipolis had, narrowly missing Brasidas, who would have likely captured it by morning had the relief been delayed. Thucydides immediately took measures to fortify Eion, preparing it against any imminent or future attacks by Brasidas. Those inhabitants of Amphipolis who opted for exile rather than Spartan rule sought refuge in Eion, as permitted by the terms of surrender.

Brasidas, meanwhile, moved quickly to assess the strength of Eion and, hopeful of capturing it, led a fleet of boats down the Strymon River toward the town. Attempting a simultaneous assault by land and river, he aimed to seize the strategic point that extended from the fortifications and thus control the entrance. However, his efforts were thwarted on both fronts as Thucydides' preparations proved effective, and Brasidas withdrew, content for the time being to secure his hold over Amphipolis and the surrounding region.

Brasidas' success in Amphipolis soon inspired neighboring areas to align with him. The Edonian town of Myrcinus, where local king Pittacus had been assassinated by his wife Brauro and the sons of Goaxis, joined the Spartan side. Shortly thereafter, the Thasian colonies of Galepsus and Oesime also shifted their allegiance to Brasidas. Perdiccas, the Macedonian king who had long supported Brasidas' campaign in the region, arrived shortly afterward, contributing to the growing strength of Brasidas' influence and consolidating these new alliances.

The news of Amphipolis falling to Brasidas sent shockwaves through Athens, as the city held significant strategic and economic value for the Athenians. Its access to timber resources crucial for building ships and the steady revenue it generated were of paramount importance. Moreover, the location of Amphipolis acted as a natural barrier to prevent Spartan advances. Previously, even though the Lacedaemonians had gained the cooperation of the Thessalians for travel as far as the Strymon River, they were effectively contained: Athenian ships stationed at Eion monitored the river passage, while on land a large lake adjacent to the river acted as a natural defense against enemy forces trying to penetrate deeper. With the bridge now under Spartan control, however, this crucial defense was compromised, opening up the potential for further Spartan incursions.

This situation stirred fear among the allies of Athens, who were increasingly drawn to the prospect of revolting. Brasidas' moderate and fair treatment of those he conquered, coupled with his declarations that he was waging war to "liberate Hellas" from Athenian dominance, made him a figure of great appeal. As towns subject to Athens heard of the lenient terms granted to Amphipolis and the promises of autonomy, many began reaching out to him covertly, each desiring to be the first to sever ties with Athens. This willingness to revolt, however, rested largely on a miscalculated view of Athenian power—one that was overly optimistic and driven more by wishful thinking than by strategic foresight. Many relied on hopeful assumptions, dismissing the reality of Athenian strength and falling into the common human tendency to envision favorable outcomes without sufficient basis.

This renewed confidence was further fueled by Athens' recent military setback in Boeotia, which had dented their aura of invincibility. Brasidas himself contributed to this confidence, making persuasive but exaggerated claims that Athens had dared not confront his forces directly at Nisaea. Consequently, many allies believed that the Athenians, weakened and wary, would not retaliate if they chose to revolt. Adding to their motivation was the impression that the Lacedaemonians, eager and emboldened by Brasidas' initial successes, would offer unwavering support in the face of Athenian reprisals.

Noting these trends, Athens took preemptive measures by dispatching garrisons to as many towns as possible despite the constraints of winter. Meanwhile, Brasidas also acted swiftly. He dispatched urgent messages to Lacedaemon requesting reinforcements and commenced preparations to construct additional galleys on the Strymon River, likely aiming to bolster his naval presence in the area. However, the Lacedaemonians hesitated to send the requested reinforcements. The leadership was torn between supporting Brasidas' campaign and their desire to prioritize the recovery of Spartan prisoners and negotiate a swift end to the conflict. Additionally, envy and internal competition among Spartan leaders dampened the enthusiasm for fully supporting Brasidas' ambitions.

That winter, the Megarians took advantage of the situation by seizing and demolishing the long walls, which had previously been fortified by the Athenians. Seizing the momentum, Brasidas advanced with his allies to Acte, a narrow promontory that jutted out from the region of the King's Canal, curving towards the sea and culminating in Mount Athos. Acte was a diverse territory, home to a mix of Hellenic and non-Hellenic communities. The towns included Sane, an Andrian colony near the canal facing Euboea, and other settlements like Thyssus, Cleone, Acrothoi, Olophyxus, and Dium. These towns were inhabited by a variety of groups, including Tyrrheno-Pelasgians, who traced their origins back to Lemnos and Athens, as well as Bisaltians, Crestonians, and Edonians. Many of these towns, lured by Brasidas' promises of liberation and autonomy, came over to his side without resistance. However, Sane and Dium chose to resist his advances, compelling Brasidas to ravage their lands in retaliation.

Brasidas' successful campaign in this region further consolidated his control over Thrace and underscored the growing appeal of Lacedaemonian promises of freedom. The movement against Athenian influence was gaining momentum, with Brasidas at the forefront, establishing alliances and winning over city-states through a blend of strategic diplomacy and calculated military pressure. His presence now represented a genuine threat to Athens' hold over its northern territories.

In response to the resistance from Torone, Brasidas promptly organized a campaign to seize the town. Torone, situated in Chalcidice, held an Athenian garrison, but a faction within the city was covertly prepared to facilitate Brasidas's entry. Arriving near the city in the pre-dawn hours, Brasidas stationed his troops close to the temple of the Dioscuri, just outside the city walls. His approach went unnoticed by the majority of Torone's inhabitants and the Athenian garrison, but his allies within the city—prepared and vigilant for his arrival—had been watching for his signal. Upon confirming Brasidas's presence, these partisans brought seven lightly armed men with daggers into the city. Led by Lysistratus of Olynthus, they crept through a lesser-known entrance in the sea wall, quickly overtaking and killing the small guard at the upper fort on the hill, and opened a postern gate to allow Brasidas's forces inside.

Brasidas advanced his main force closer to the city, halting nearby while dispatching a hundred targeteers to be ready to rush in once the city's gates were open and the prearranged signal beacon was lit. As the minutes passed and no signal appeared, the targeteers began to move closer, expecting that the delay might indicate trouble within the city. Meanwhile, the conspirators had finally managed to break through the postern gate and open the main marketplace gates by cutting through the bar. Bringing in some men through the postern, they launched a surprise attack from behind on the city's sleeping residents, igniting the beacon and letting in the remaining targeteers through the market gates.

Upon seeing the signal, Brasidas commanded his troops to advance, leading a powerful charge through the gate amid his men's victorious shouts. This sudden onslaught created chaos among the residents, who were stunned by the attack. Brasidas and the main contingent took the steepest path directly up to the highest part of the town, aiming to capture the entire city at once, while others scaled the wall at a weaker point where timber placed for repairs provided a makeshift ladder. The townspeople, waking to confusion, found themselves overwhelmed as the Lacedaemonians spread through the town. Some residents, loyal to the conspiracy, joined Brasidas and his forces, helping them gain control of key positions.

Caught unprepared, the Athenian heavy infantry—roughly fifty soldiers stationed in the market square—attempted a defense but quickly succumbed. Some fell in combat, while others escaped, either fleeing by land or taking refuge in Lecythus, a fortified corner of the town separated by an isthmus. There, they joined the Toronaeans who had sought Athenian protection.

With dawn breaking and the town secured, Brasidas issued a proclamation to reassure the Toronaeans who had taken refuge with the Athenians. He encouraged them to return to their homes, assuring that they would not face reprisals for their affiliations with Athens. Brasidas also extended an offer of truce to the Athenians in Lecythus, proposing that they evacuate with their belongings, claiming that the fort rightly belonged to the Chalcidians. The Athenians rejected the surrender, though they requested a temporary truce to retrieve their dead. Brasidas agreed to a two-day ceasefire, which allowed both sides to fortify their respective positions.

During this time, Brasidas addressed the Toronaean citizens, delivering a speech similar to the one he had given previously at Acanthus. He cautioned them against viewing those who had orchestrated the town's surrender as traitors, explaining that their intentions were not driven by corruption or self-interest but by a genuine desire for the freedom and well-being of Torone. He urged them to understand that these actions were intended to benefit the city and to provide it with a new opportunity for liberation. Additionally, he assured those who had previously aligned with the Athenians that they had no reason to fear; the Lacedaemonians held no resentment toward them and had come not to harm, but to protect and respect their rights. He suggested that, given time, they would come to trust the Lacedaemonians more than the Athenians, as the Spartans were more just and equitable in their dealings.

Brasidas also called on the Toronaeans to prepare for their role as Lacedaemonian allies, explaining that while past opposition could be forgiven due to Athenian dominance, they would now be held accountable for any future breaches. He urged them to stand resolutely by their new allies, assuring them that the Lacedaemonians would safeguard their freedom and urging them to embrace this new alliance as a path to enduring security and autonomy.

After delivering his encouraging address, Brasidas prepared to launch his assault on Lecythus once the truce expired. The Athenians fortified their position as best they could, using a weak wall and houses outfitted with parapets. On the first day, they managed to repel the initial attack. However, the next day, the Lacedaemonians escalated their efforts, bringing forth a siege engine with the intent of setting fire to the Athenians' wooden defenses. Observing this, the Athenians erected a wooden tower on a nearby house, stocking it with jars and barrels of water, large stones, and numerous defenders to resist the assault.

However, the weight proved too much for the structure, which collapsed with a loud crash. Those nearby, though startled, remained resolute; but soldiers positioned further away mistook the noise for a breach in the defenses. Panic spread among the ranks, and many Athenians, believing the fort was compromised, fled in haste to their ships.

Brasidas saw the disarray among the Athenians and seized the opportunity. He led his forces forward in a swift attack, quickly capturing the fort and killing those left behind. The remaining Athenians evacuated the area, escaping across the water to Pallene. Lecythus contained a temple of Athena, and Brasidas had promised a reward of thirty silver minae to the first man over the wall during the attack. Yet, viewing the victory as one inspired by divine favor, he dedicated the thirty minae to Athena's temple, rather than awarding it to an individual. He then ordered the clearing and razing of Lecythus, consecrating the entire area to Athena.

Brasidas spent the remainder of the winter consolidating control over the towns that had come under his authority, strengthening defenses, and strategizing for future expansions. With the onset of spring, marking the eighth year of the war, both the Lacedaemonians and Athenians agreed to a truce lasting one year. The Athenians anticipated that this would provide time to secure their holdings and prevent further revolts incited by Brasidas, while possibly leading to a broader peace agreement. For their part, the Lacedaemonians calculated that a temporary respite might make the Athenians more amenable to a lasting peace and the return of Lacedaemonian prisoners, hoping that even if Brasidas's momentum continued, they could still recover their men and bring stability to Chalcidice.

The terms of the armistice included the following conditions:

1. Regarding the temple and oracle of the Pythian Apollo, all parties agree that any individual, regardless of origin, may approach and seek guidance at the sanctuary without fear of harm or deceit. This access shall be conducted in the same spirit of reverence and openness practiced by their ancestors. The Lacedaemonians, along with the allies present, pledge to ensure this custom is upheld and will dispatch heralds to the Boeotians and Phocians, requesting that they honor the same terms.

2. Concerning the temple's sacred treasure, it is agreed to pursue and expose any cases of misappropriation. All involved, whether the Lacedaemonians, Athenians, or any other willing parties, are to conduct investigations into potential wrongdoers with integrity and a

strict adherence to ancestral customs. The goal is to preserve the sanctity of the temple's wealth, with all participants agreeing to this shared responsibility.

3. Further stipulations set boundaries to prevent interference and maintain peace. The Lacedaemonians and their allies agree that, should the Athenians sign the treaty, all parties will remain within their respective territories, retaining current holdings. The garrison stationed at Coryphasium will remain within the markers of Buphras and Tomeus, with the outpost at Cythera restricted from interacting with any members of the Peloponnesian League; this prohibition extends equally to Peloponnesian forces, ensuring no communication or collaboration occurs between these garrisons and allied forces. Similarly, the garrisons in Nisaea and Minoa will not cross the route that begins at the gate of the temple of Nisus and stretches to Poseidon's gate and onward to the bridge at Minoa. The Megarians and their allies are equally bound by this restriction, and both sides agree to refrain from engaging in contact. The Athenians may retain control over the captured islands and maintain the terms arranged for Troezen, with each side keeping its current position.

4. As for the right to navigate coastal waters, it is established that Lacedaemonians and their allies may conduct voyages along their shores and the coastlines of their allies. However, such vessels must be limited to oared ships not exceeding a carrying capacity of five hundred talents; warships and larger vessels are strictly prohibited to prevent the escalation of hostilities during the truce.

5. All diplomatic efforts, including the travel of heralds and ambassadors with an unrestricted number of attendants, shall be unhindered. These envoys, tasked with negotiating an end to hostilities and resolving outstanding claims, are granted safe passage through both Athenian and Peloponnesian territories, whether by land or sea, without restriction.

6. Throughout the duration of the truce, neither side is permitted to shelter or accept deserters, whether enslaved or free, from the

opposing forces. Any individual seeking refuge from one side must be denied sanctuary to maintain a stable peace.

7. Finally, all grievances are to be resolved through a system of public law, ensuring that both Athenians and Lacedaemonians settle disputes peacefully. Each side agrees to redress any wrongs through formal legal procedures native to each country, refraining entirely from forceful or hostile methods.

The Lacedaemonians and their allies unanimously approved these articles. However, they extended an invitation to the Athenians: if they had any suggestions for fairer or more just terms, they were welcome to present them at Lacedaemon. The Lacedaemonians assured that any reasonable proposal would not face opposition from them or their allies, but insisted that any representatives sent should possess full authority to negotiate, as the Lacedaemonians themselves would bring delegates with complete powers. The truce was declared for a duration of one year.

The people of Athens formally accepted the terms in the popular assembly. Under the prytany of the Acamantis tribe, with Phoenippus as secretary and Niciades as chairman, a motion was put forth by Laches, invoking the good fortune of the Athenians, to finalize the armistice on the proposed terms. The assembly confirmed this arrangement, stipulating that the truce would take effect immediately, beginning on the fourteenth of the month of Elaphebolion. During this period, ambassadors and heralds would travel freely between the two regions to negotiate a long-term peace. The generals and prytanes were tasked with convening an assembly for the Athenians to discuss the broader peace effort, establishing the process for admitting the representatives from each side to formalize the end of hostilities. The Lacedaemonian ambassadors present took an oath in front of the assembly to uphold the truce faithfully for its entire duration.

On the Spartan side, the armistice was ratified on the twelfth day of the month of Gerastius, with all allies sworn to uphold it. The Libations, symbolizing the oath of peace, were poured by prominent representatives: Taurus, son of Echetimides; Athenaeus, son of Pericleidas; and Philocharidas, son of Eryxidaidas, representing the Lacedaemonians. The Corinthians sent Aeneas, son of Ocytus, and Euphamidas, son of Aristonymus, while Damotimus, son of Naucrates, and Onasimus, son of Megacles, represented the Sicyonians. From Megara, Nicasus, son of Cecalus, and Menecrates, son of Amphidorus were present, as well as Amphias, son of Eupaidas, from Epidaurus. The Athenian generals overseeing the truce included Nicostratus, son of Diitrephes; Nicias, son of Niceratus; and Autocles, son of Tolmaeus. Thus, the truce was formalized, with discussions on a full peace taking place continually throughout the year.

However, as these discussions proceeded, Scione, a town on the Pallene peninsula, unexpectedly revolted from Athens and aligned with Brasidas. The Scionaeans asserted their heritage as Pallenians originally from Peloponnese, descended from Achaean founders who, on their return from Troy, were diverted by a storm to this location, where they eventually settled. Brasidas, eager to support them, crossed to Scione by night. He employed a clever tactic: sending a friendly galley ahead while he followed some distance behind in a small boat. This setup provided him with protection, ensuring that a large ship would target the galley and not his small vessel, while a ship of equal size to the galley would likely engage it directly, giving Brasidas a chance to escape.

Upon arriving safely, Brasidas called a public assembly in Scione, delivering a speech similar to those he had given in Acanthus and Torone. He praised the Scionaeans for their courage and foresight. Though isolated due to the Athenian occupation of Potidaea, which effectively severed Pallene from mainland Greece, they had embraced liberty willingly rather than passively waiting for external liberation. This bold decision demonstrated their willingness to withstand any future challenges. Brasidas assured them that, if his plans succeeded, he would regard them as among the Lacedaemonians' most steadfast allies, and he pledged to honor them accordingly.

In these words, Brasidas sought to solidify their loyalty and prepare them for the trials that lay ahead, confirming Scione's place in the Lacedaemonian alliance and in the larger Greek struggle for independence.

The people of Scione, inspired and uplifted by Brasidas's words, found a new unity of purpose. Even those who initially hesitated or disapproved of the revolt were swayed by the contagious spirit of confidence and determination. Embracing the call to resist Athenian domination, they decided to approach the war with boldness. They welcomed Brasidas with high honors, presenting him as the great liberator of Hellas. The Scionaeans celebrated him publicly, crowning him with a golden wreath as a symbol of his role in freeing them from oppression. Individual citizens, moved by his charisma and leadership, surrounded him, adorning him with garlands as though he were an Olympic athlete who had brought them glory and pride.

In the midst of this celebration, Brasidas took practical steps to secure Scione's position. He left a modest garrison in the town to safeguard its defenses temporarily. Soon after, he crossed back and began organizing a larger force, planning to use Scione as a base to attempt to capture the nearby towns of Mende and Potidaea. He anticipated that the Athenians would attempt to relieve Scione due to its exposed location and its strategic value as a near-island territory. Brasidas also had insider contacts in Mende and Potidaea who were working to betray these towns into his hands, and he sought to capitalize on these connections before Athenian forces could arrive.

While Brasidas was preparing to move against these towns, an Athenian galley arrived, carrying commissioners who bore news of an armistice that had just been declared. Aristonymus represented Athens, and Athenaeus represented the Lacedaemonians. They promptly notified Brasidas of the terms of the ceasefire. While the Lacedaemonian allies in Thrace accepted the armistice, Aristonymus, upon reviewing the timeline of events, noted that Scione had officially revolted after the armistice took effect and thus refused to include it in the terms. Brasidas, however, protested strongly, maintaining that the revolt had occurred beforehand. He steadfastly refused to surrender Scione, arguing that it had joined the Lacedaemonians legitimately, before the armistice was in place.

When Aristonymus returned to Athens with the situation report, the Athenian assembly was incensed at the news of Scione's defiance. Without delay, they resolved to dispatch an expedition to suppress the city. Soon after, Lacedaemonian envoys arrived, arguing that any attack on Scione would constitute a breach of the truce. They claimed that Brasidas's account of the timing was accurate, and they offered to submit the dispute to arbitration to prevent further hostilities. However, Athens, unwilling to risk a decision that might support Scione's revolt, rejected the suggestion. They were enraged by what they saw as an affront—the willingness of even island cities to revolt, emboldened by a belief in Lacedaemonian support on land. The facts, as Athens saw them, indicated that Scione's revolt had occurred two days after the truce, and this detail added weight to their decision. Cleon, an influential leader, succeeded in pushing through a decree that called for the reduction and execution of the Scionaeans. Taking advantage of the temporary lull in fighting, the Athenians began to prepare an assault force to carry out the decree.

Before Athens could mobilize, the city of Mende in Pallene, a colony of the Eretrians, declared its defection from Athens and aligned itself with Brasidas. Although Mende's defection was clearly a violation of the armistice, Brasidas welcomed the town's support, asserting that Athens had itself violated the truce. The boldness of Mende in joining Brasidas stemmed partly from his refusal to hand over Scione to the Athenians, which inspired confidence that he would be loyal to his allies. Furthermore, Mende's conspirators, though small in number, were now desperate to act, as they had engaged in anti-Athenian activities for too long to avoid detection and feared the repercussions if they hesitated further.

The news of Mende's defection infuriated the Athenians even more, who now intensified their preparations for military action against both towns. Brasidas, anticipating their arrival and determined to defend his allies, took proactive measures to protect Scione and Mende from the inevitable Athenian assault. He organized the evacuation of the women and children from both cities, sending them to the relative safety of Olynthus in Chalcidice. Additionally, he dispatched a reinforcement force composed of five hundred Peloponnesian heavy infantry and three hundred Chalcidian targeteers, commanded by Polydamidas, to bolster the defense of Scione and Mende.

With these actions, Brasidas sought to fortify the towns' defenses, rallying their people around the idea of resistance and ensuring that they were prepared to withstand the Athenian offensive. Both Scione and Mende were now heavily involved in the conflict, becoming symbols of defiance against Athenian power, while Brasidas remained steadfast in his commitment to liberating Hellas.

Brasidas quickly gathered his troops, realizing that their position had become highly precarious with the unexpected departure of Perdiccas's forces. Forming his Hellenic heavy infantry into a square formation, Brasidas placed the light-armed troops and non-combatants in the center for protection. The young, agile soldiers were stationed around the square, ready to counter any assault from the advancing enemy. At the rear, he himself stood with three hundred elite soldiers, intending to hold off any immediate attacks and keep their line secure during the retreat.

As his troops anxiously prepared to face the formidable and unpredictable Illyrians, who had now allied with Arrhabaeus, Brasidas delivered an urgent speech to boost their morale. He understood that, given the confusion and fear spurred by the Illyrians' sudden alliance and the disorderly flight of their Macedonian allies, his soldiers were under extreme psychological strain. Standing before his men, Brasidas addressed their apprehensions with resolute words designed to fortify their spirits.

He reminded them that they were experienced warriors, accustomed to facing difficult circumstances, and that they should not be daunted by the formidable reputation of the Illyrians or the betrayal of Perdiccas's forces. "We are not outnumbered as we appear to be," he argued, "nor should we fear an army whose strength lies primarily in intimidation rather than discipline. Stand firm, for those who retreat without reason only increase the boldness of their enemies. Let us show that we are determined and courageous, and they will think twice before rushing upon a force that stands unyielding."

Brasidas encouraged his soldiers to recognize that the Illyrians, although numerous, were less organized and disciplined than the Hellenic hoplites. "They are barbarians," he continued, "and prone to chaos, while you are skilled soldiers who know the value of order and unity. In a tight formation, disciplined and resolved, you are more than their equal." His address reminded them of past triumphs where discipline and cohesion had triumphed over numerical superiority, and he called upon them to rely on their training and to trust one another in the face of adversity.

He emphasized that their retreat was not an abandonment of courage but a tactical maneuver, one which they could execute with dignity and determination. "We do not turn our backs on this foe out of fear but out of necessity," he clarified, "and we shall move with our heads held high. Any who advance upon us will meet with fierce resistance; those who hesitate will fall back, realizing that we are no easy target." Brasidas' confidence and calm in the face of potential disaster reinvigorated his men, filling them with a renewed sense of resilience and solidarity.

With his speech complete and their spirits bolstered, Brasidas prepared his troops to march, fully aware that the discipline and unity he had instilled would be their best defense against the impending assault. His forces, bolstered by his leadership, advanced in square formation, methodically repelling attacks and securing their retreat inch by inch.

In response to the daunting circumstances, Brasidas, showing keen insight and leadership, addressed his Peloponnesian troops with words designed to dispel their fears and strengthen their resolve. Aware that some among them were unnerved by the sheer number and unfamiliar appearance of the barbarian forces, he reassured them, explaining that their courage was innate, not dependent on the presence of allies or an enemy's numbers. He reminded them that the strength of cities like theirs did not stem from overwhelming numbers but from the discipline and experience of a few who naturally lead and dominate through skill in battle.

He highlighted that while the barbarian forces might seem intimidating due to their loud cries, chaotic movements, and the dramatic flourish with which they brandished their weapons, these features were more bluster than true menace. In fact, he argued, their lack of discipline and structured order meant that they were likely to break and flee at the first sign of resistance. This lack of cohesion among the enemy, he observed, meant that any individual within their ranks could easily retreat without consequence, as their style of fighting did not shame those who abandoned their positions. Unlike the organized hoplite ranks of the Hellenes, where each man's bravery and duty to hold his position mattered, the enemy's honor did not rest on steadfastness.

Brasidas emphasized that these barbarians excelled only at intimidation from afar, using loud cries and gestures to unsettle opponents. But, he assured his troops, if they held their ground, these intimidating tactics would quickly falter when faced with a solid line of resistance. The illusion of their power would collapse as soon as the Peloponnesians met them with firm resolve, and those who withstood the initial chaotic rush would find that the barbarian bravado vanished as easily as it had appeared. Indeed, Brasidas portrayed the enemy as relying more on the effect of distant threats than on close combat, where they would reveal their true weakness.

Urging his soldiers to stand firm, he explained that order and discipline would allow them to retire safely when necessary and to withstand the enemy's assaults with fewer losses. Once they reached safer ground, they would know that the barbarian terror was mostly an illusion, effective only against those who showed weakness. By holding firm initially, his troops could avoid the unnecessary panic and casualties that often befell those who fled too soon.

Encouraged by Brasidas's speech, the Peloponnesians began their orderly retreat. Observing this, the barbarians assumed that Brasidas's men were in flight and eagerly charged forward, their shouts and disorganized attacks aimed at overwhelming the retreating force. But Brasidas's tactics caught them off guard: his young soldiers boldly darted out to confront the attackers, and his elite troops maintained a steady defense, resisting each advance and then calmly retreating as the enemy fell back in confusion.

The initial surprise of the Peloponnesians' firm response caused the barbarians to pause, their assumption of an easy victory thwarted by Brasidas's well-executed tactics. Realizing they could not easily overcome the Greeks in open ground, most of the barbarian force redirected their efforts towards the Macedonians, who were scattered and in disarray. The barbarians slaughtered many of the fleeing Macedonians, while a smaller contingent stayed back to continue harassing Brasidas's retreating forces.

Understanding that Brasidas's route led through a narrow pass flanked by hills, the main force of the barbarians hurried to reach and occupy this choke point, intending to trap Brasidas's forces in the most difficult terrain possible. As Brasidas and his men approached this precarious section of the road, they found themselves faced with a potentially deadly ambush, surrounded on all sides by enemies intent on cutting off their escape.

Brasidas, perceiving the barbarians' plan to trap his forces in the narrow pass, quickly ordered his elite three hundred troops to dash forward independently, each man racing to reach the most accessible hill and drive off the small band of enemies already stationed there. This strategic move was designed to secure the high ground before the main body of the barbarian forces could close in and fortify the position. The three hundred attacked fiercely, successfully overpowering the defenders on the hill. Their swift victory struck fear into the larger body of the barbarians, who saw their advanced position lost and their men retreating.

Witnessing their comrades on the heights defeated and the Greeks now controlling the advantageous ground, the main body of the barbarians hesitated. Mistakenly concluding that Brasidas's forces had secured a clear escape route, they pulled back, no longer pursuing the main Greek force as aggressively as before. With the path now less obstructed and the heights secured, Brasidas led his troops forward with greater confidence, navigating towards safety. By the end of the same day, he successfully brought his men to Arnisa, the first town within Perdiccas's territory, where they found refuge.

As they retreated, however, the soldiers vented their anger over the Macedonians' abandonment during the night escape. Spotting any oxen on the road or stray baggage that had been abandoned in the chaotic retreat, the frustrated troops unyoked the animals, slaughtered them, and claimed any provisions left behind. This act of retribution underscored the soldiers' deep resentment toward Perdiccas, who had failed to support them at a critical moment. The betrayal sowed seeds of lasting animosity between Perdiccas and Brasidas, marking a turning point in their alliance. From that point forward, Perdiccas saw Brasidas not as an ally but as an adversary, and he began to shift his allegiance, considering rapprochement with the Athenians and viewing his alliance with the Peloponnesians with distaste.

Following his return from Macedonia, Brasidas arrived at Torone only to discover that Mende had already fallen into Athenian hands.

Realizing that it was too late to intervene directly in Pallene and aid the Mendaeans, he chose instead to fortify his position and keep a vigilant watch over Torone, preparing for any further Athenian aggression. Meanwhile, events were unfolding in Mende and Scione that would demand the Athenians' full attention.

In a campaign carefully organized against these towns, the Athenians deployed a formidable force: fifty ships, including ten contributed by Chios, along with a thousand Athenian heavy infantry, six hundred archers, one hundred Thracian mercenaries, and additional targeteers drawn from allied regions. The Athenian commanders, Nicias, son of Niceratus, and Nicostratus, son of Diitrephes, led this well-equipped force. Sailing from Potidaea, they landed opposite the temple of Poseidon and prepared to attack Mende.

In Mende, the Athenian forces encountered stiff resistance. Three hundred Scionaean reinforcements had bolstered the Mendaean defenders, along with seven hundred heavy infantry led by the Peloponnesian officer Polydamidas. The Mendaeans and their allies occupied a strong hill outside the city, which provided a natural defensive position. Nicias, accompanied by one hundred and twenty light-armed Methonaeans, sixty elite Athenian heavy infantry, and all available archers, attempted to approach the hill via a narrow path. However, he sustained a wound and was forced to halt his advance, unable to dislodge the defenders.

Simultaneously, Nicostratus, leading the rest of the Athenian army, attempted to flank the hill from a different route further away. The steep and rugged terrain, however, threw his troops into disarray, and the entire Athenian force came perilously close to a complete defeat. The defenders from Mende and their allies held firm, showing no signs of surrender. For the remainder of the day, the Athenians found themselves unable to make progress and withdrew to establish a camp, while the Mendaean forces retreated into the city as night fell.

Thus, the initial confrontation ended in a frustrating stalemate for the Athenians, who realized that overcoming the Mendaean defenses would require a more concerted effort.

The following day, the Athenian forces sailed to the side of Mende that faced Scione and took control of the suburb, raiding it throughout the day and looting the surrounding countryside. No one from Mende came out to confront them, partly because the city was in turmoil due to internal conflicts. That night, the three hundred Scionaean soldiers who had previously been supporting the Mendaeans returned to their home city.

The next morning, Nicias advanced with half of the Athenian army towards the border of Scione, continuing to devastate the land along the way, while Nicostratus stationed the other half of the force near the city's main gate on the Potidaean road, close to where the Mendaean and Peloponnesian troops had gathered their arms. Polydamidas, a Peloponnesian officer, began organizing the Mendaeans for a potential sally, trying to rally them to defend the city. However, his attempts were disrupted when a member of the popular faction, voicing opposition to the war, openly defied him by refusing to participate in the battle. This dissenting citizen was seized and roughly handled by Polydamidas, escalating tensions to a breaking point.

The situation quickly spiraled into chaos. The agitated commoners, angered by Polydamidas's violent response, seized their weapons and turned against the Peloponnesians and the aristocratic faction that supported them. This sudden uprising caught Polydamidas and his troops off guard, driving them back in confusion. Fearing that the gates might be opened to the Athenians, whom they suspected of coordinating this revolt, the Peloponnesian forces and their allies fled to the citadel, abandoning the lower part of the city.

With Nicias's detachment already positioned near the city walls, the Athenian army capitalized on the disorder and poured into Mende through its gates, which had been left unbarred. The Athenians proceeded to sack the city with an intensity and ruthlessness as though they had taken it by force, pillaging and wreaking havoc throughout. Even the Athenian generals struggled to rein in their troops, who were close to killing the city's inhabitants in the confusion and fury of the assault.

After taking control of Mende, the Athenian commanders sought to restore some semblance of order. They reassured the citizens that they would retain their civil rights and be permitted to try those among them who were suspected of instigating the revolt. Meanwhile, the Athenians isolated the remaining Peloponnesians and loyalists by constructing a wall around the citadel, sealing off access to the sea on both sides and establishing a garrison to ensure the siege was maintained. With Mende secured, they then turned their attention toward Scione.

In Scione, the Scionaean defenders, joined by Peloponnesian allies, prepared to resist the Athenians by occupying a strategic hill in front of the town. This position provided a natural defensive advantage, as the Athenians would need to capture it before they could fully invest the city. The Athenians launched an assault on the hill, successfully dislodging and defeating the defenders in a fierce battle. Having seized the high ground, they set up camp and raised a victory trophy to mark their success, before beginning preparations to surround Scione with fortifications.

As the Athenians proceeded with their siege works, the Peloponnesian and allied soldiers besieged in the citadel of Mende saw an opportunity to escape. Under the cover of darkness, they managed to bypass the Athenian guards stationed along the seashore and, in a daring maneuver, slipped through the siege lines around Scione. The majority of the besieged soldiers succeeded in entering Scione, reinforcing the defenders within and bolstering their resolve in the face of the Athenian assault.

Thus, with both cities now heavily involved in the conflict, the Athenians faced a renewed challenge, having to maintain pressure on Scione while dealing with the unexpected bolstering of its defenses.

While the siege operations against Scione continued, Perdiccas sent a herald to the Athenian generals, signaling his decision to make peace with Athens, largely due to his resentment toward Brasidas over the retreat from Lyncus. Perdiccas had, in fact, begun discussions with Athens as soon as the retreat took place. At this time, the Lacedaemonian Ischagoras was preparing an overland journey to reinforce Brasidas with an army. However, Nicias, the Athenian general, requested Perdiccas to demonstrate his loyalty to Athens in a tangible way. Perdiccas, now eager to avoid the influx of Peloponnesian troops into his territory, took steps to block their advance. Using his connections among the leading figures of Thessaly, he successfully impeded the progress of the army to such an extent that they did not even attempt to negotiate with the Thessalians for passage.

Despite these obstacles, Ischagoras, along with Ameinias and Aristeus, managed to reach Brasidas. These men had been sent by the Lacedaemonian government to review the situation and to oversee the assignment of Spartan officials to key positions within the cities under Brasidas's control. This was an unusual step, as it involved appointing younger men from Sparta itself to positions of command, thereby bypassing the local population and ensuring greater Spartan control. Brasidas consequently appointed Clearidas, son of Cleonymus, to govern Amphipolis, and Pasitelidas, son of Hegesander, to take charge of Torone.

During that same summer, the Thebans dismantled the fortifications of Thespiae, alleging that the Thespians were inclined toward Athens. This decision was not unexpected, as the Thebans had long sought an excuse to weaken Thespiae and now found an opportune moment to act. The Thespians, who had suffered heavy losses against the Athenians, had lost many of their strongest young men, which rendered resistance unlikely.

The summer also witnessed an incident in Argos where the temple of Hera caught fire. The blaze started when Chrysis, the temple priestess, inadvertently left a lit torch near a cluster of garlands. She fell asleep, and before long, the flames spread throughout the temple. Realizing her error too late, Chrysis fled that same night to the nearby city of Phlius, fearing retribution from the people of Argos, who by law appointed a replacement priestess, Phaeinis. At the time of her flight, Chrysis had served as priestess for eight years and part of the ninth since the outbreak of the war.

By the end of summer, the Athenians had completed their blockade of Scione. After leaving a contingent to maintain the siege, the remainder of the Athenian forces returned home, satisfied with the progress of their efforts.

In the winter that followed, Athens and Sparta remained largely inactive due to the ongoing armistice. However, the Mantineans and Tegeans, along with their respective allies, engaged in a fierce battle at Laodicium in Oresthid. The conflict ended inconclusively; each side had routed one wing of the opposing army, leading both to erect trophies and offer spoils to Delphi as signs of victory. Heavy losses were sustained on both sides, but the outcome was ultimately indecisive. The Tegeans maintained control of the battlefield overnight and promptly set up their trophy, while the Mantineans, who had retreated to Bucolion, only set theirs up later.

As winter neared its end, Brasidas made a bold attempt to capture Potidaea. Arriving under cover of darkness, he managed to place a ladder against the city wall just after the bell-ringing patrol had passed, leaving a narrow window before the guard returned. However, the garrison quickly raised the alarm before Brasidas's forces could mount a significant attack. Realizing that his element of surprise had been compromised, Brasidas led his troops away under the cover of darkness, retreating before dawn.

With this, the winter came to a close, marking the end of the ninth year of the war, as recorded by Thucydides.

Book V

Chapter XV

Tenth Year of the War—Death of Cleon and Brasidas—Peace of Nicias

As the next summer arrived, the truce of one year between the Athenians and Lacedaemonians concluded, having lasted up until the Pythian games. During this period of armistice, the Athenians, acting on a belief that the island of Delos had been marred by a past transgression that tainted its sanctity, expelled the Delians from their homeland. They reasoned that some ancient offense or defilement had persisted since the island's original consecration, and that this oversight had not been fully corrected in the previous purification, when they had removed graves to cleanse the island. With their expulsion from Delos, the displaced Delians were granted the town of Atramyttium in Asia by the local Persian official Pharnaces and migrated there to establish a new settlement.

In the meantime, the Athenian general Cleon persuaded his city to authorize an expedition aimed at subduing the rebellious cities in Thrace as soon as the truce ended. He assembled a considerable force comprising twelve hundred Athenian heavy infantry, three hundred cavalry, a strong contingent from their allied states, and thirty ships. Setting out at the expiration of the armistice, he first stopped at Scione, which was still under siege, to bolster his forces by taking additional heavy infantry from the army stationed there. From Scione, he sailed on to Cophos, a port in the territory of Torone, and prepared for an attack on the city after receiving intelligence from deserters that Brasidas was absent and that the city's defenses were inadequate to resist him effectively.

Cleon's approach was strategic. He dispatched ten ships to sail around and enter Torone's harbor while he advanced with his main force toward the fortifications that Brasidas had recently constructed outside the town to protect its suburb. Brasidas had originally fortified this area by incorporating part of the suburb within the city's defense, even dismantling a portion of the old city wall to unify the fortifications.

At this critical moment, Pasitelidas, the Lacedaemonian commander of Torone, led his limited garrison to confront Cleon's land forces. However, as the Athenian ships rounded into the harbor and began to disembark soldiers, Pasitelidas grew alarmed, fearing that the Athenians might reach the city itself before he could mobilize a defense. Facing pressure both from Cleon's direct assault and the Athenians' rapid approach by sea, Pasitelidas abandoned the outer defenses and fell back into the city to defend it more directly.

Yet, Cleon's strategy proved effective. The Athenians disembarked swiftly, taking the city and overpowering its defenders. They breached the broken-down segment of the old wall and pressed into Torone, capturing the town in a rapid, chaotic engagement. Some of the Peloponnesian and Toronaean forces fell in the skirmish, while others, including Pasitelidas himself, were taken prisoner.

Brasidas, meanwhile, had been hastily advancing to relieve Torone and was only a few kilometers away when he received word of the city's capture. Learning of the defeat, he halted his march and returned, recognizing that it was now futile to attempt a rescue. Cleon and the Athenians celebrated their swift victory by erecting two trophies—one near the harbor and the other by the captured fortification. They enslaved the women and children of the Toronaeans, while the captured men, including the Peloponnesians, Chalcidians, and Toronaeans who had fought against them, were sent to Athens as prisoners, totaling around seven hundred individuals. However, these prisoners were later released and returned to their homes: the

Peloponnesians as part of a subsequent peace agreement and the Chalcidians through an exchange of prisoners with the Olynthians.

In a parallel development, the Boeotians seized Panactum, a fortress located along the Athenian border, through an act of treachery, further escalating tensions. With Torone secured and a garrison left in place, Cleon resumed his campaign. His next objective was Amphipolis, and he set sail along the coastline of Mount Athos, advancing toward his goal of capturing the strategic town.

At approximately the same time, Athens dispatched Phaeax, son of Erasistratus, as an ambassador to Italy and Sicily, accompanied by two colleagues. The purpose of this mission was to assess the political landscape and potentially strengthen alliances. This diplomatic effort was partly spurred by a crisis in Leontini, where, following the withdrawal of Athenian forces from Sicily after a previous peace agreement, significant social discord had erupted. The commoners of Leontini sought to redistribute the land, a move opposed by the upper class, who, aware of this plan, sought assistance from Syracuse to oust the commons. As a result, many commoners were forced to flee, scattering to various locations, while the upper-class citizens of Leontini struck an agreement with Syracuse, choosing to abandon their city and join Syracuse, where they were granted citizenship.

However, not all were content with this arrangement. A faction broke away from Syracuse, occupying areas such as Phocaeae, a district in Leontini, and Bricinniae, a stronghold in the Leontine region. Here, they were soon joined by the exiled commoners and began conducting a form of guerrilla warfare from their fortified positions. When the Athenians learned of these developments, they sent Phaeax with the objective of rallying their allies and convincing the broader Sicilian cities of Syracuse's expansionist intentions, hoping to foster a united opposition and secure protection for the Leontine commoners.

Upon reaching Sicily, Phaeax managed to secure support in Camarina and Agrigentum. However, he faced resistance in Gela, which led him to abandon attempts to persuade the remaining Sicilian cities. Instead, he traveled overland through Sicel territory, stopping at Catana, where he provided assurances to the residents of Bricinniae before ultimately returning to Athens. On his way to and from Sicily, Phaeax also sought to establish friendly ties with certain Italian cities and encountered a group of exiled Locrians returning to Messina. The Locrians, who had been called to Messina during internal conflicts after the peace agreement in Sicily, controlled the city for a period. However, now returning to their own land, they were spared any harm from Phaeax as the Locrians had recently negotiated a peace with Athens due to ongoing conflicts with the Hipponians and Medmaeans on their borders.

Meanwhile, Cleon, who had set out from Torone toward Amphipolis, established a base in Eion. His initial move was an unsuccessful attempt to take Stagirus, a colony of Andros, but he then managed to capture Galepsus, a colony of Thasos, by storm. To strengthen his position, Cleon sent messengers to Perdiccas, requesting that he fulfill his obligations under their alliance and join him with an army. He also sent envoys to Thrace, specifically to Polles, the king of the Odomantians, requesting a contingent of Thracian mercenaries. With these reinforcements on the way, Cleon awaited their arrival while staying in Eion.

Brasidas, aware of Cleon's movements and anticipating an attack on Amphipolis, took up a strategic position on Cerdylium, a hill in the Argilian territory across the river from Amphipolis. From this vantage point, Brasidas could observe any movement by Cleon's forces, giving him an advantage in preparation. He anticipated that Cleon, underestimating the size of his own army, would advance with confidence toward Amphipolis. In the meantime, Brasidas bolstered his defenses, assembling fifteen hundred Thracian mercenaries, a contingent of Edonian cavalry and light troops, and one thousand Myrcinian and Chalcidian targeteers. Altogether, his forces comprised about two thousand heavy infantry, supported by three hundred Hellenic cavalry. He stationed fifteen hundred of these troops with him at Cerdylium, while the remaining forces were under the command of Clearidas within Amphipolis, ready to respond to any Athenian assault.

Encouraged by Brasidas's speech, the men prepared themselves mentally and physically for the impending engagement. Cleon, meanwhile, remained on the hill with his troops, unaware of the advancing danger, still under the impression that his forces held the advantage in their elevated position and, as he perceived it, superior numbers. His soldiers, however, grew increasingly wary, feeling vulnerable due to Cleon's complacency and failure to anticipate any counterattack. They quietly voiced their unease, having observed that Brasidas's forces were nowhere in sight—a fact that could imply either an imminent ambush or a strategic advantage they were not prepared to counter.

Brasidas, understanding that Cleon's men were growing increasingly restless, seized the moment to execute his well-planned assault. He had divided his forces, putting his most dependable soldiers in the charge of Clearidas, ready to deploy from within Amphipolis as soon as Brasidas himself began the attack. Brasidas intended to exploit the element of surprise fully; he knew that a sudden and well-coordinated charge would likely unnerve the Athenians, creating chaos and diminishing their capacity to respond effectively. He hoped that by the time the Athenians perceived the full scale of the assault, it would be too late for them to retreat or organize a proper defense.

As planned, Brasidas led his selected troops swiftly and silently down from the heights of Cerdylium, catching the Athenians by surprise. He moved with a speed and intensity that gave the appearance of a much larger force, aiming directly at the center of Cleon's ranks, where he believed he could cause maximum disruption. As Brasidas's forces bore down on them, Cleon's army struggled to mount a response; the rapid advance threw the Athenians into disarray, with men at the center collapsing under the pressure of the surprise assault. Cleon himself was caught off guard, having anticipated little resistance and expecting to retire leisurely after assessing the town's defenses.

At the same time, Clearidas and his contingent of Amphipolitan and allied soldiers burst out of the gates of Amphipolis as per Brasidas's instructions, charging with fresh force at the Athenians who were already staggered by Brasidas's initial strike. The timing of Clearidas's attack amplified the confusion among the Athenian ranks, as soldiers on Cleon's side now faced enemies on multiple fronts. Those who had managed to keep some semblance of formation against Brasidas's forces now found themselves surrounded and began to panic.

Cleon, now realizing the full extent of Brasidas's strategy and the precarious position of his forces, attempted to rally his troops, urging them to fall back in a more organized manner. However, with panic rapidly spreading through the ranks and the Athenians becoming increasingly demoralized by the sudden attack, any attempt to withdraw coherently devolved into a rout. Cleon himself, ill-equipped for rapid decision-making in the face of battle, turned and attempted to retreat, but in the chaos, he was cut down by pursuing troops, ending his life on the field.

The Athenians, now leaderless and without a clear course of action, broke ranks completely, with men scattering in every direction. The more disciplined Spartan and allied forces under Brasidas and Clearidas systematically pursued the fleeing Athenians, striking down many and capturing others. Some Athenians managed to escape by fleeing toward the river Strymon, attempting to cross or swim to safety, though many were overtaken and lost their lives in the waters.

Brasidas's plan had achieved a decisive victory; his stratagem of using misdirection, speed, and shock had worked perfectly. Despite being outnumbered and facing a well-trained enemy, his tactical brilliance and leadership transformed the encounter into a significant and unexpected Lacedaemonian triumph. With the defeat of Cleon and the scattering of the Athenian forces, Brasidas solidified his reputation and ensured that Amphipolis would remain firmly in Lacedaemonian hands, an outcome that would bolster Spartan influence across the region and strike a severe blow to Athenian confidence.

The battle at Amphipolis thus became a stark reminder to the Athenians of the potential pitfalls of overconfidence and poor leadership. The outcome further shifted the balance of power, providing Sparta with a renewed strategic advantage while marking one of the final engagements in Brasidas's successful campaign against Athenian influence in the north.

After giving his brief but motivating address, Brasidas prepared for the sally and stationed Clearidas with the rest of his forces at the Thracian gates to act as support. His preparations were deliberate, and every move of his force had been closely watched by the Athenians, who could see Brasidas's descent from Cerdylium and his sacrifices near the temple of Athena from their vantage points. Reports soon reached Cleon that a significant enemy force was gathering within the city, and that both cavalry and infantry could be seen massing under the gates, giving the impression that a sally was imminent.

Cleon himself went to observe, but being unprepared for a full-scale engagement without the arrival of reinforcements, he quickly ordered a retreat. He commanded his troops to withdraw along the only practical route—by the left wing in the direction of Eion. However, Cleon, anxious about the speed of the retreat, joined his men in person and made the fateful decision to wheel the right wing, exposing its unshielded side to the enemy.

Seizing this moment, Brasidas, observing the disorganized movements of the Athenian forces, confidently addressed his men. Noting the signs of wavering and confusion among the Athenians— their erratic movements and the way their spears pointed—he declared that such troops were unlikely to withstand a charge. He urged his forces into action, calling for the gates to be thrown open and shouting for an immediate assault without hesitation.

Brasidas then led his men through the palisade gate and one of the primary exits in the long wall, charging at full speed down the road toward the Athenian center, where a trophy would later commemorate this bold attack. With the Athenians already in retreat, his assault was both sudden and intense, targeting the heart of the Athenian formation, which was already disordered and taken aback by his audacious advance. Simultaneously, Clearidas led his detachment out through the Thracian gates, attacking the Athenians from another angle and completing the encirclement.

Caught between Brasidas and Clearidas, the Athenian forces were thrown into disarray. The Athenian left wing, which had begun retreating towards Eion, collapsed first, breaking into a full retreat. At this point, Brasidas advanced toward the right flank. However, in the midst of the attack, he received a severe wound and was carried off the battlefield by his soldiers. Although the Athenians were unaware of his injury, the event momentarily shifted the dynamic. Cleon, seeing the battle take a disastrous turn, attempted to flee but was pursued and killed by a Myrcinian targeteer.

Despite Cleon's flight, the Athenian right flank resisted valiantly, rallying on a nearby hill and fending off Clearidas's advances multiple times. They formed a tight formation, repulsing two or three direct assaults. However, once surrounded and continuously harried by the Chalcidian and Myrcinian cavalry and the targeteers' missile attacks, they eventually broke, descending into chaos and retreating toward the hills. Those who survived the initial clash managed to escape to Eion, but many were cut down by pursuing forces.

Brasidas, meanwhile, was brought into Amphipolis by his men, barely alive but still conscious. He lived long enough to hear of the successful outcome of the battle and the victory of his forces, passing away shortly afterward, proud of the triumph he had achieved. His army, under the command of Clearidas, completed the rout, stripping the bodies of the dead and erecting a trophy to commemorate their victory over the Athenians.

Thus, the battle marked not only a significant Spartan victory but also a turning point in the Peloponnesian War. Brasidas's bold tactics and leadership would leave a lasting legacy, further inspiring Lacedaemonian and allied morale, while the Athenians were left to contend with the loss of both their army and their general.

Following Brasidas's death, all the allied forces gathered, each represented in arms, to honor him with a public burial in Amphipolis. His grave was situated in what would later become the marketplace, underscoring his symbolic importance to the city. Brasidas's tomb was surrounded by an enclosure, marking it as a sacred site. Ever afterward, the Amphipolitans celebrated his memory with sacrifices and rituals, treating him as a hero and bestowing upon him the honor of annual games and offerings. In a dramatic shift of allegiance, they designated him the founder of their city, erasing all physical and symbolic remnants of Hagnon, the original Athenian founder, including any structures he had commissioned. This reflected their gratitude for Brasidas as their protector and their desire to forge a lasting alliance with Sparta, distancing themselves from Athens, now an adversary.

The Amphipolitans returned the bodies of the six hundred Athenians who had fallen in the recent conflict. In stark contrast, only seven of Brasidas's troops had perished, underscoring the chaos and panic rather than a full-scale, organized battle. After reclaiming their fallen, the Athenians retreated by sea, while Clearidas stayed behind to stabilize and govern Amphipolis.

Meanwhile, in another show of Spartan military support, three Lacedaemonian leaders—Ramphias, Autocharidas, and Epicydidas— arrived with a reinforcement of nine hundred heavy infantry for the regions near Thrace. On reaching Heraclea in Trachis, they assessed the conditions and restructured local defenses as they saw fit. Their advance coincided with the summer's end and the significant battle at Amphipolis, affecting their subsequent plans.

At the start of the following winter, Ramphias and his companions moved as far as Pierium in Thessaly. However, facing opposition from the Thessalians, and with news of Brasidas's death, they ultimately turned back to Sparta. They judged that their mission had lost its original purpose without Brasidas's command, especially as the Athenians were no longer actively pursuing hostilities. More pressing, they sensed a shift in the political winds back in Lacedaemon, where sentiment was leaning toward peace.

Directly after the battle of Amphipolis and Ramphias's retreat, both Athens and Sparta began serious considerations for peace. The Athenians, reeling from two recent defeats—first at Delium, and then at Amphipolis—had lost the confidence that had previously driven their resistance to peace talks. They were now worried that their allies, witnessing these setbacks, might seize the opportunity to revolt. Regretting the missed chance for peace after the Pylos affair, Athens recognized the urgency of recalibrating its strategy.

On the Spartan side, expectations that the war would swiftly dismantle Athens's power had faded. Despite devastating the Athenian countryside repeatedly, the Spartans found that Athens remained resilient. The disaster at Pylos, with its uncharacteristic blow to Spartan military pride, and the relentless raids from Pylos and Cythera, had deeply unsettled Sparta. Helot defections added to their fears, stoking the ever-present concern of a Helot revolt, as many Helots were inspired by those who had successfully fled to join the enemy.

Adding to their difficulties, Sparta's thirty-year truce with Argos was nearing expiration. Argos demanded the restoration of Cynuria as a condition for renewal, a demand Sparta was reluctant to meet. Confronted with the prospect of hostilities on multiple fronts—both with Athens and potentially Argos—Sparta was also aware that certain Peloponnesian cities were considering switching sides, a dangerous prospect that could destabilize their coalition.

Thus, both powers, recognizing the war's toll and the mounting risks on their horizons, began to contemplate peace more earnestly than ever before.

These circumstances inclined both Athens and Sparta toward peace, with the Lacedaemonians particularly motivated by their desire to recover the Spartans captured on the island. Many of these captives belonged to leading families, directly connected to the Spartan governing class, which added significant urgency to their release. Although Sparta had sought negotiations soon after the initial capture of their men, Athens, buoyed by victory, had previously dismissed any reasonable offers. However, after their defeat at Delium, and anticipating Athenian receptivity to peace following the loss, Sparta quickly established a one-year armistice, hoping that this temporary truce might pave the way to a more lasting settlement.

With the subsequent defeat at Amphipolis and the deaths of Cleon and Brasidas, who had been the strongest voices for continued hostilities, the political landscape shifted further toward peace. Brasidas, whose military successes and reputation had aligned him with the cause of war, was now absent. Likewise, Cleon, who had previously resisted peace to shield his own questionable actions from scrutiny, was also removed from the scene. This left Nicias in Athens and Pleistoanax in Sparta—leaders in both cities known for their preference for peace—as the primary influencers in favor of reconciliation.

Nicias, esteemed for his consistent good fortune and military achievements, wished to secure his own reputation as a prudent and successful leader. His inclination toward peace stemmed from a desire to avoid unnecessary risks, ensuring a period of stability both for himself and his city. Nicias saw that, by supporting peace, he could protect his legacy as an unblemished statesman who avoided the capricious turns of fortune associated with continued warfare.

Pleistoanax, meanwhile, faced constant political criticism at home. Ever since his return from exile, his opponents had used every setback in the war as an excuse to undermine him, insinuating that his restoration was unpatriotic and even orchestrated through manipulation of the oracle at Delphi. Allegedly, he and his brother

Aristocles had bribed the Delphic priestess to compel successive Lacedaemonian delegations to "bring back the seed of Zeus from abroad" or face misfortune—a strategy that supposedly influenced the city to restore Pleistoanax after his exile of nineteen years. As a result, he had been welcomed back to Sparta with the full honors traditionally given to kings. Yet these accusations lingered, and Pleistoanax recognized that a lasting peace would put an end to the damaging rumors, ensuring his position by depriving his critics of grounds for further attacks tied to wartime misfortunes.

Thus, during the winter, both cities engaged in serious discussions, with negotiations intensifying as spring approached. The Lacedaemonians pressured Athens by issuing orders to their allies to prepare for a fortified occupation of Attica, using this threat to nudge the Athenians toward a resolution. After extended negotiations and mutual demands, a peace agreement was finally reached on the basis of mutual restitution of conquered territories. However, Athens was permitted to retain Nisaea, with each side providing justifications for their acquisitions: the Thebans claimed Plataea had joined them voluntarily, while the Athenians maintained that Nisaea's annexation was achieved through similarly non-coercive means.

With the terms settled, Sparta convened its allies, and the peace treaty was approved by all except the Boeotians, Corinthians, Eleans, and Megarians, who expressed dissatisfaction with the terms. Nevertheless, the majority was sufficient to formalize the treaty, and the parties each swore to uphold the following articles of the peace.

The Athenians and Lacedaemonians, along with their respective allies, established and formally swore to a treaty, city by city, on the following terms:

1. Access to national temples shall be open by land and sea to anyone wishing to sacrifice, travel, consult oracles, or attend games, as customary in each country.

2. Delphi and its sanctuary of Apollo shall be autonomous, governed by Delphian laws, taxed solely by the Delphian state, and

subject to Delphian judiciary, maintaining its own land and people according to traditional practices.

3. This treaty shall be in force for fifty years, binding the Athenians and their allies alongside the Lacedaemonians and their allies, ensuring peace on land and sea, without deception or harm from either side

4. Neither the Lacedaemonians and their allies nor the Athenians and theirs may take up arms with harmful intent against the other party. Should disputes arise, they must be resolved through legal processes and sworn oaths, in accordance with mutual agreement.

5. Amphipolis shall be returned to the Athenians by the Lacedaemonians and their allies. The inhabitants of the cities returned to Athens by Lacedaemon may freely relocate with their possessions, and these cities shall remain autonomous, subject only to the tribute arranged by Aristides. It shall be unlawful for Athens or its allies to wage war against these cities as long as they comply with tribute obligations. The cities involved are Argilus, Stagirus, Acanthus, Scolus, Olynthus, and Spartolus. These cities will be neutral, allied with neither Athens nor Lacedaemon, but may join Athens as allies if they willingly consent.

6. The Athenians will return Coryphasium, Cythera, Methana, and any Lacedaemonians held in Athenian custody, including those in prison and the Peloponnesian forces besieged in Scione. Additionally, Athens will release all individuals in Scione affiliated with the Lacedaemonians, those sent there by Brasidas, and any other Lacedaemonian allies held within Athenian territories.

7. Similarly, the Lacedaemonians and their allies will return any Athenians or their allies that they have in custody.

8. Athens retains the right to take any action it deems appropriate regarding Scione, Torone, Sermylium, and any other cities under its control.

9. Each city shall pledge its commitment to this agreement by swearing an oath. Seventeen representatives from each city shall swear

by their most binding local oaths: "I will abide by this agreement and treaty honestly and without deceit." This oath will also be taken by the Lacedaemonians and their allies, renewed annually, and recorded on stone pillars erected at Olympia, Delphi (Pythia), the Isthmus, and at prominent sites in Athens and Lacedaemon.

10. If any aspect of the agreement is overlooked, both Athenians and Lacedaemonians have the right, in line with their oath, to make amendments as necessary according to their mutual discretion.

The treaty officially commenced with the ephoralty of Pleistolas in Lacedaemon on the 27th day of Artemisium, and in Athens under the archonship of Alcaeus on the 25th of Elaphebolion. Those who swore the oath and performed the ceremonial libations on behalf of the Lacedaemonians included Pleistoanax, Agis, Pleistolas, Damagetis, Chionis, Metagenes, Acanthus, Daithus, Ischagoras, Philocharidas, Zeuxidas, Antippus, Tellis, Alcinadas, Empedias, Menas, and Laphilus. The Athenian representatives included Lampon, Isthmonicus, Nicias, Laches, Euthydemus, Procles, Pythodorus, Hagnon, Myrtilus, Thrasycles, Theagenes, Aristocrates, Iolcius, Timocrates, Leon, Lamachus, and Demosthenes.

This treaty was formally established in spring, just following the end of winter and the city festival of Dionysus, marking exactly ten years, give or take a few days, from the initial invasion of Attica and the onset of this protracted war. Rather than depending on the uncertain timelines marked by magistracies or other offices, this agreement focused on exact seasons—summers and winters— comprising this history, totaling ten full summers and winters in the first phase of the conflict.

Following the conclusion, the Lacedaemonians, who were tasked with initiating the terms of restitution, promptly freed all war prisoners in their custody. They dispatched envoys—Ischagoras, Menas, and Philocharidas—to the Thracian territories to instruct Clearidas to surrender Amphipolis to the Athenians and to ensure their allies adhered to the terms. However, these allies opposed the treaty's stipulations and resisted compliance, while Clearidas himself, aligned with the Chalcidian interests, refused to hand over the town, citing the local populace's opposition. He hastened to Lacedaemon in person, accompanied by envoys from Amphipolis, both to justify his stance against accusations from Ischagoras and others and to see if the Lacedaemonians would reconsider the agreement. Upon realizing that the Lacedaemonians were committed to the treaty, he swiftly returned with new instructions to hand over the city if possible or, at the very least, to withdraw the Peloponnesian forces stationed there.

The Lacedaemonians called on their allies—those present in Lacedaemon and those yet undecided—to ratify the treaty. Yet these allies, still unsatisfied with the terms and demanding a more favorable arrangement, remained steadfast in their refusal. Following their firm response, the Lacedaemonians chose to dismiss them and began negotiating an alliance with the Athenians instead. Believing that without Athens, Argos, which had declined to renew a previous alliance when approached by Ampelidas and Lichas, would be less formidable, the Lacedaemonians anticipated that a pact with Athens would discourage other Peloponnesian states from pursuing hostilities.

After productive discussions with the Athenian delegates, a formal alliance was established between Athens and Lacedaemon, sealed with oaths and with detailed terms laid out for a new era of cooperation and stability.

1. The Lacedaemonians formally agreed to be allies of the Athenians for a period of fifty years, establishing a long-term alliance intended to maintain peace and stability in the region.

2. In the event that an enemy should invade Lacedaemonian territory and cause harm to the Lacedaemonians, the Athenians were bound to provide assistance in the most effective manner possible within their means. Should the enemy withdraw after inflicting damage, that city would be deemed an adversary of both Lacedaemon and Athens and would face retribution from both. Neither party

would conclude a separate peace with this city, ensuring that all actions would be carried out with integrity, loyalty, and without deceit.

3. Conversely, if an enemy should invade Athenian territory and harm the Athenians, the Lacedaemonians were to aid Athens in the most effective way according to their abilities. If the invader subsequently departed after looting, that city would likewise be considered an enemy of both Lacedaemon and Athens, facing punishment from both states. As before, neither Athens nor Lacedaemon would pursue peace independently with the enemy, ensuring an unwavering and faithful response.

4. In the event of a slave uprising against the Lacedaemonians, Athens would commit to assisting with their full strength according to their capability, demonstrating an additional commitment to internal security within Lacedaemon.

5. This treaty would be sworn to by the same representatives from each side who had sworn the prior treaty. Annually, the terms of this alliance would be renewed, with Lacedaemonian envoys visiting Athens for the Dionysian festival and Athenian envoys visiting Lacedaemon for the Hyacinthian festival. Each state would erect a commemorative pillar: in Lacedaemon, near the statue of Apollo at Amyclae, and in Athens on the Acropolis near the statue of Athene. Should either Athens or Lacedaemon wish to amend the alliance by adding or removing provisions, they would be permitted to do so in good faith, allowing flexibility within the framework of the alliance.

The individuals who took the oath on behalf of the Lacedaemonians included Pleistoanax, Agis, Pleistolas, Damagetus, Chionis, Metagenes, Acanthus, Daithus, Ischagoras, Philocharidas, Zeuxidas, Antippus, Alcinadas, Tellis, Empedias, Menas, and Laphilus. The Athenian representatives included Lampon, Isthmionicus, Laches, Nicias, Euthydemus, Procles, Pythodorus, Hagnon, Myrtilus, Thrasycles, Theagenes, Aristocrates, Iolcius, Timocrates, Leon, Lamachus, and Demosthenes.

This alliance was established shortly after the previous treaty was concluded, marking a significant diplomatic milestone. In accordance with these terms, the Athenians released the prisoners taken from the island to the Lacedaemonians, symbolizing a gesture of good faith. Thus, the summer of the eleventh year of hostilities began, and with it, the first ten-year phase of the war drew to a close, covering a decade filled with conflicts, negotiations, and significant developments that shaped the course of both Athenian and Lacedaemonian histories.

Chapter XVI

Feeling against Sparta in Peloponnese—League of the Mantineans, Eleans, Argives, and Athenians—Battle of Mantinea and breaking up of the League

Following the treaty and alliance established between the Lacedaemonians and Athenians, concluding what is often termed the ten years' war, during the ephorate of Pleistolas in Lacedaemon and the archonship of Alcaeus in Athens, the cities that had adhered to the agreements experienced a temporary peace. However, the Corinthians, along with certain cities within the Peloponnesian League, actively sought to undermine this settlement, thereby sparking renewed unrest among the allies and directing fresh hostility toward Lacedaemon itself. Over time, the Athenians also grew increasingly suspicious of Lacedaemon, observing the Spartans' failure to fulfill specific terms of the treaty. Although both parties refrained from direct invasion of each other's lands for six years and ten months, hostilities gradually resumed through indirect confrontations and violations abroad, where an unreliable truce allowed each side to inflict harm upon the other in substantial ways. Ultimately, this erosion of peace led to a breakdown of the treaty and a renewal of open warfare.

Thucydides, the Athenian historian, meticulously documented the events during this period, adhering to a strict chronological sequence of summers and winters. His account extended up to the moment when the Lacedaemonians and their allies succeeded in dismantling the Athenian empire, capturing the Long Walls and the Piraeus. This conflict, inclusive of all intermittent truces and resumed hostilities, spanned a total of twenty-seven years.

Thucydides cautions against any simplistic view that the period of the treaty constituted a genuine peace. From a factual standpoint, the treaty's terms were never fully honored by either side, and frequent violations occurred. In addition to unfulfilled agreements, acts of aggression continued, notably in the Mantinean and Epidaurian conflicts, and other breaches were commonplace. Hostilities persisted unabated in Thrace, and the Boeotians, for instance, maintained only a tenuous truce that was renewed every ten days. Consequently, the entire stretch—comprising the initial decade of war, the unstable armistice, and the subsequent full-scale conflict—together amounted to the twenty-seven years that Thucydides specified. Remarkably, this span of years aligns with predictions based on oracular prophecies, affirming the widespread belief that the conflict would endure for "thrice nine years."

Thucydides notes his direct experience and close observation throughout the duration of the war. As an adult fully aware of the political and military realities of the time, he dedicated himself to discerning the truth of these events. His unique perspective was further shaped by his forced exile after his command at Amphipolis, which granted him the opportunity to observe both Athenian and Peloponnesian actions with an unusual degree of impartiality and proximity. In particular, his exile positioned him among the Peloponnesians, enabling him to witness their strategies and circumstances intimately.

In the following sections, he recounts in detail the chain of events that led to the breakdown of the ten-year truce, the revival of hostilities, and the eventual escalation into renewed warfare, providing an account that is not merely a narrative of battle but an in-depth analysis of the dynamics that perpetuated this protracted struggle.

Following the establishment of the fifty-year truce and subsequent alliance between the Athenians and Lacedaemonians, the

Peloponnesian embassies, having concluded their discussions in Lacedaemon, began their journey back. While most delegations proceeded directly to their respective cities, the Corinthians took a detour to Argos. There, they initiated talks with Argive officials, expressing strong concerns about Lacedaemon's intentions. They argued that Lacedaemon's recent alliance with the Athenians—historically viewed as their sworn enemies—signaled an underlying strategy aimed at dominating Peloponnese rather than preserving its independence. The Corinthians emphasized that the responsibility for defending the region's liberty now rested with Argos. To this end, they recommended that Argos issue a decree inviting any independent Hellenic state to form a defensive alliance with them on the grounds of equality and mutual respect. Moreover, they suggested that a select group of individuals with plenipotentiary authority handle negotiations to maintain confidentiality, thereby avoiding unnecessary exposure if an application was declined. Concluding these discussions, the Corinthians returned home.

The Argive officials who had received the proposal relayed it to their government and citizens, who responded positively. Argos passed a decree, electing twelve representatives authorized to negotiate alliances with any interested Hellenic state—excepting Athens and Lacedaemon, which would require a direct appeal to the Argive assembly. The Argives quickly embraced this initiative, recognizing that conflict with Lacedaemon was increasingly likely as their current truce neared expiration. Additionally, they saw an opportunity to assert leadership over Peloponnese, as Lacedaemon's reputation had suffered from recent setbacks, while Argos enjoyed prosperity and prestige, having maintained neutrality and reaped the benefits of staying out of the Attic war. Consequently, Argos began to position itself as an attractive ally for any Greek city-state that shared its concerns over Lacedaemonian ambitions.

The Mantineans and their allies were the first to join Argos, motivated by apprehension toward Lacedaemon. They had capitalized on the Athenian war to bring substantial portions of Arcadia under their control, fearing that Lacedaemon, once no longer preoccupied with Athens, would move to reassert dominance in the region. Thus, Mantinea eagerly aligned itself with Argos, a city historically opposed to Lacedaemon and governed by a similar democratic system. The defection of Mantinea reverberated through Peloponnese, prompting many other states to contemplate a similar shift. The Mantinean decision to defect suggested, to others, a credible justification for joining Argos.

Additional unease stemmed from a specific clause in the Lacedaemonian-Athenian treaty, which permitted both parties to unilaterally amend the terms of the treaty at their discretion. Many Peloponnesian states viewed this clause as a clear threat to their autonomy, fearing a potential conspiracy between Lacedaemon and Athens to restrict their liberties. Traditionally, any treaty modifications would require the consensus of all allied states. This deviation from convention intensified suspicions, leading various cities to conclude that aligning with Argos was a necessary safeguard. Thus, under a general climate of distrust and fear of hegemony, Argos emerged as a natural counterbalance, offering protection and partnership to those apprehensive of Lacedaemonian intentions.

During this time, the Lacedaemonians, seeing the growing unrest within Peloponnese and realizing that Corinth was behind it, and even considering an alliance with Argos, quickly sent envoys to Corinth in an attempt to prevent this alliance. They accused Corinth of instigating the agitation and reminded her that abandoning Lacedaemon for Argos would be a betrayal of her oaths, especially since she had already failed to comply with the treaty with Athens, which had been accepted on the understanding that the decision of the majority of the allies would be binding unless divine opposition existed. Corinth, however, responded carefully in front of allies who, like her, had also rejected the treaty and whom she had called together for support. Rather than openly listing her grievances—such as Lacedaemon's failure to secure the return of Sollium or Anactorium from the Athenians—Corinth claimed that her refusal to enter the treaty was rooted in her duty to honor the promises she had made to her Thracian allies. Having initially sworn loyalty to them when they rebelled alongside Potidaea, Corinth argued that she could not abandon these allies in good faith. Furthermore, she contended that the phrase "unless the gods or heroes stand in the way" provided her with legitimate grounds for refusing the treaty, as she believed the gods were indeed opposed.

Regarding the proposed alliance with Argos, Corinth stated that she would discuss the matter with her allies and take the course she deemed right. After the Lacedaemonian envoys left, some Argive ambassadors present in Corinth urged the Corinthians to formalize the alliance without delay, but were advised to attend the next Corinthian congress, where such matters would be further considered.

Shortly after this, an embassy from Elis arrived in Corinth. Following instructions from home, they first formed an alliance with Corinth and then proceeded to Argos, where they also allied with the Argives. The Eleans had recently entered a period of enmity with both Lacedaemon and the town of Lepreum. Previously, when the Lepreans were at war with some Arcadians, they had sought help from the Eleans, offering them half their lands in return. The Eleans ended the conflict, but instead of claiming the land, they imposed a tribute of one talent annually to the Olympian Zeus, which the Lepreans paid until the Attic war. Using the war as an excuse, the Lepreans ceased payment, prompting the Eleans to attempt enforcement by force. The Lepreans then appealed to Lacedaemon, submitting the matter for Lacedaemon's judgment. However, the Eleans, doubting Lacedaemon's impartiality, abandoned the arbitration and retaliated by ravaging Leprean lands. Lacedaemon, nevertheless, ruled in favor of the Lepreans, declaring them independent and labeling the Eleans as aggressors. In response, the Eleans invoked the convention, which stipulated that each member should retain what they held at the outset of the Attic war. Disillusioned with Lacedaemon's actions, the Eleans now aligned themselves with Argos, cementing the alliance through their envoys.

Following the Eleans, both the Corinthians and the Chalcidians of Thrace joined the Argive alliance. Meanwhile, the Boeotians and Megarians, aligned with each other, opted to remain neutral. Lacedaemon allowed them this discretion, as they were wary of the democratic Argive model and felt it less compatible with their own aristocratic governments than with Lacedaemon's established political structure.

Around this time in the summer, Athens finally succeeded in capturing Scione. They executed the adult men, enslaved the women and children, and gave the land to the Plataeans to settle in. They also brought the Delians back to Delos, feeling the impact of recent military setbacks and influenced by the commands of the god at Delphi. Meanwhile, the Phocians and Locrians began fighting.

The Corinthians and Argives, now allies, went to Tegea to persuade the Tegeans to leave the Lacedaemonian alliance. They believed that if Tegea, an influential state, could be convinced to switch sides, it would encourage the rest of the Peloponnese to join them. However, the Tegeans refused, saying they would not take any action against Lacedaemon. Disheartened by this, the Corinthians began to doubt that any of the other cities would join their cause. Still, they approached the Boeotians and tried to convince them to form an alliance with Argos and Corinth and join them in taking action. The Corinthians also asked the Boeotians to accompany them to Athens and seek a ten-day truce, like the one the Athenians had made with the Boeotians after the fifty-year treaty. They added that if the Athenians refused, the Boeotians should break their armistice and avoid making any future truces without involving Corinth.

In response, the Boeotians rejected the idea of an alliance with Argos but agreed to go with the Corinthians to Athens. However, they could not secure the ten-day truce they sought; the Athenians replied that the Corinthians, as allies of Lacedaemon, already had a truce. Despite the Corinthians' frustration and accusations of broken promises, the Boeotians kept their ten-day truce with Athens, leaving the Corinthians to accept an informal armistice with Athens.

That same summer, the Lacedaemonians, led by Pleistoanax, the son of Pausanias and king of Lacedaemon, gathered their entire force and marched into Arcadia. Their goal was to support a group within the Parrhasians, who were subjects of Mantinea, that had asked for Lacedaemonian help. They also aimed to destroy the fortress of Cypsela, which the Mantineans had built and garrisoned in Parrhasian territory to threaten Sciritis, a region in Laconia. The Lacedaemonians proceeded to devastate the Parrhasian lands. The Mantineans, who had entrusted their city's defense to an Argive garrison, tried to protect their alliance but couldn't prevent the fall of Cypsela or save the Parrhasian towns. They were forced to retreat to Mantinea. In the end, the Lacedaemonians freed the Parrhasians, destroyed the fortress, and returned home.

In the same summer, the soldiers from Thrace who had accompanied Brasidas were brought back by Clearidas after the treaty was made. The Lacedaemonians decreed that the Helots who had fought alongside Brasidas should be freed and allowed to live wherever they chose. Not long afterward, they were resettled with the Neodamodes at Lepreum, a location on the border between Laconia and Elis, as Lacedaemon was currently in conflict with Elis. However, some Spartans who had surrendered their arms after being taken prisoner on the island raised concerns among the leaders. There was a fear that they might consider their captivity a form of dishonor that could lead them to consider rebellion. To prevent this, these individuals were promptly stripped of their political rights. Although some of them held official positions at that time, they were barred from holding office or conducting any trade. After a period, their political rights were eventually restored.

Also, in this summer, the Dians captured Thyssus, a town allied with Athens, located on the Acte Peninsula near Mount Athos. Throughout the season, relations between Athens and the

Peloponnesians continued, though mutual suspicion arose soon after the treaty. One reason for this distrust was that neither side had returned all the territories listed in the agreement. Lacedaemon, who was supposed to start by returning Amphipolis and other towns, had not fulfilled this obligation. Additionally, she had not persuaded her Thracian allies, the Boeotians, or the Corinthians to accept the treaty, although she repeatedly assured Athens that they would work together to enforce it if necessary. Lacedaemon even set deadlines, suggesting that those who continued to resist would eventually be treated as enemies to both sides, but avoided committing to anything formally.

The Athenians, observing that Lacedaemon was not acting on these promises, started doubting her intentions. Consequently, Athens refused to return Pylos to Lacedaemon, regretted having released the prisoners from the island, and held onto other key positions until Lacedaemon fulfilled her obligations in the treaty. Lacedaemon, in turn, insisted that she had done everything within her power. She had returned the Athenian prisoners of war she held, withdrawn from Thrace, and performed all other duties that were feasible. While she admitted that restoring Amphipolis was beyond her control, she promised to continue pressuring the Boeotians and Corinthians to accept the treaty, recover Panactum, and ensure the return of Athenian prisoners held in Boeotia. Meanwhile, she requested that Athens give back Pylos or, at the very least, withdraw the Messenians and Helots who were stationed there. Lacedaemon proposed that, if necessary, Pylos could be garrisoned by Athenian forces alone.

After a series of discussions throughout the summer, Lacedaemon managed to convince Athens to remove the Messenians, Helots, and deserters from Laconia stationed at Pylos, resettling them in Cranii on Cephallenia. Thus, during this summer, a state of peace and interaction continued between Athens and Lacedaemon.

The following winter, the ephors who had established the treaty left office, and some of their successors opposed the treaty directly. During this time, embassies from the Lacedaemonian alliance and envoys from Athens, Boeotia, and Corinth arrived in Lacedaemon. After extended discussions without any agreement reached between them, the groups dispersed to return to their respective cities. Cleobulus and Xenares, the two ephors most eager to break off the treaty, took advantage of this moment to meet with the Boeotians and Corinthians privately. In this meeting, they advised both groups to act in as unified a manner as possible, suggesting that the Boeotians first form an alliance with Argos. They further advised that after the Boeotians secured an alliance with Argos, they should aim to bring both themselves and the Argives into an alliance with Lacedaemon. This, they said, would make it less likely for the Boeotians to be forced to agree to the Attic treaty. They also argued that Lacedaemon would likely prioritize forming a bond with Argos, even if it meant risking Athenian hostility and the breakdown of the treaty.

The Boeotians knew that Lacedaemon had long hoped for an honorable alliance with Argos, as this would considerably facilitate conducting the war beyond Peloponnese. In the meantime, Cleobulus and Xenares requested the Boeotians hand over Panactum to Lacedaemon, which might be exchanged with Athens for Pylos, thus putting them in a better position if they decided to resume hostilities with Athens.

After receiving these instructions from Xenares, Cleobulus, and their allies in Lacedaemon, the Boeotians and Corinthians departed. While on their way home, they met two high-ranking Argive officials who had been waiting for them on the road. These officials sounded them out on the possibility of the Boeotians joining the Corinthians, Eleans, and Mantineans in becoming Argive allies. They reasoned that, if such an alliance could be formed, the newly united group would have the freedom to make peace or declare war as they wished, whether against Lacedaemon or another power. The Boeotian envoys were pleased to hear such a proposal, which coincidentally aligned with what their friends in Lacedaemon had suggested.

Realizing their interest, the two Argive officials left with a promise to send formal ambassadors to the Boeotians. Upon their arrival home, the Boeotian envoys reported to the Boeotarchs all that had been discussed in Lacedaemon and what the Argives had said during their encounter. The Boeotarchs welcomed the proposal eagerly, as it harmonized with the very suggestions from Lacedaemon. Shortly afterward, Argive ambassadors arrived with the proposed terms, which the Boeotarchs approved, promising to send envoys to Argos to formalize the alliance.

During this time, the Boeotarchs, along with the Corinthians, Megarians, and the envoys from Thrace, agreed first to exchange oaths to support one another whenever needed and to neither wage war nor make peace separately, but only together. Afterward, it was planned that the Boeotians and Megarians, acting in unity, would form an alliance with Argos. However, before the oaths were exchanged, the Boeotarchs presented these proposals to the four councils of the Boeotians, who held the ultimate authority, recommending that they exchange oaths with any cities willing to join a defensive pact with the Boeotians.

Yet, the members of the Boeotian councils did not approve this proposal, fearing that an alliance with the Corinthian defectors would anger Lacedaemon. The Boeotarchs had withheld from them the discussions that had taken place in Lacedaemon and the advice of Cleobulus, Xenares, and other Boeotian allies there, which suggested they ally with Corinth and Argos as a step toward rejoining Lacedaemon. The Boeotarchs believed that, even without sharing these details, the councils would agree to their recommendations. However, faced with this unexpected opposition, the Corinthians and Thracian envoys departed without any agreement having been reached. The Boeotarchs, who had initially planned to secure this pact before pursuing the alliance with Argos, then chose not to bring the Argive matter before the councils or send the promised envoys to Argos. Thus, the plan stalled, and overall, the matter was met with indifference and delay.

During this same winter, Mecyberna, a town garrisoned by Athenians, was attacked and captured by the Olynthians.

During this period, ongoing negotiations took place between the Athenians and Lacedaemonians regarding the remaining territories each still held. Lacedaemon, hoping that Athens would return Pylos if she could regain Panactum from the Boeotians, sent an embassy to Boeotia, requesting that they transfer Panactum and any Athenian prisoners to her, so these might be exchanged for Pylos. The Boeotians, however, refused to comply unless Lacedaemon entered into a separate alliance with them, just as she had with Athens. Lacedaemon understood that this would violate her agreement with Athens, as both had promised not to make peace or engage in war independently. Nevertheless, eager to secure Panactum as an exchange for Pylos, and influenced by factions within her government pushing to dissolve the treaty and favor ties with Boeotia, Lacedaemon eventually signed the alliance. This occurred just as winter transitioned into spring, and shortly after, Panactum was demolished. Thus, the eleventh year of the war concluded.

At the beginning of the following summer, the Argives noticed that the anticipated ambassadors from Boeotia had not arrived, that Panactum was being dismantled, and that a separate alliance had been forged between Boeotia and Lacedaemon. They began to fear that Argos might end up isolated, with the rest of the confederacy shifting towards Lacedaemon. Argos suspected that Lacedaemon had persuaded the Boeotians to destroy Panactum and enter into a treaty with Athens and that Athens might even be aware of this arrangement, leaving no open path for Argos to seek an alliance with her. This had been Argos' fallback option, due to the internal divisions that could emerge if her treaty with Lacedaemon were not continued.

Faced with this difficult situation, Argos feared that her refusal to renew the treaty with Lacedaemon, coupled with her aspirations for supremacy in Peloponnese, would result in having to confront the Lacedaemonians, Tegeans, Boeotians, and Athenians simultaneously.

Consequently, she quickly dispatched Eustrophus and Aeson, two envoys who seemed likely to be well-received, to Lacedaemon. Their mission was to negotiate the most favorable treaty possible with Lacedaemon to secure peace for Argos.

Upon arriving in Lacedaemon, the Argive ambassadors began discussions around the proposed treaty's terms. Their primary request was to resolve through arbitration the question of the Cynurian territory, a long-contested border region containing the towns of Thyrea and Anthene, which the Lacedaemonians currently occupied. Argos suggested that a neutral state or private party might mediate the matter, which had been a source of ongoing conflict between the two sides. Initially, the Lacedaemonians dismissed the idea, indicating they could not permit this land issue to be debated and were only willing to proceed with an agreement based on existing terms. However, after extended deliberation, the Argive ambassadors managed to secure a significant concession from Lacedaemon: a temporary truce of fifty years, with an option to revisit the territorial question under specific conditions.

According to this arrangement, should neither Lacedaemon nor Argos be suffering from war or plague, either side could issue a formal challenge to settle the dispute over Cynuria in a single battle, as they had done in the past when both parties claimed victory. Under these terms, pursuit of the defeated forces would not extend beyond the borders of Argos or Lacedaemon, ensuring the engagement remained a limited affair. While the Lacedaemonians initially regarded this suggestion as absurd, their strong desire to secure Argos's friendship ultimately led them to accept and formally record these terms. However, it was agreed that none of these provisions would become binding until the Argive ambassadors returned to consult with their government, with final oaths to be exchanged at the festival of the Hyacinthia if Argos approved.

The Argive ambassadors subsequently returned home to report on the terms of the treaty. Meanwhile, while Argos was involved in these negotiations, Lacedaemonian envoys—Andromedes, Phaedimus, and Antimenidas—were dispatched to retrieve Athenian prisoners and return them, along with the city of Panactum, to Athens. However, upon arriving, they discovered that the Boeotians had independently demolished Panactum, citing an ancient agreement made with the Athenians following a territorial dispute. According to this pact, neither side would occupy Panactum; instead, both would use the surrounding land for communal grazing.

The Boeotians complied with the Lacedaemonian request regarding the prisoners, handing them over to Andromedes and his colleagues, who transported them back to Athens. Upon delivering the prisoners, the Lacedaemonian envoys also conveyed the news of Panactum's demolition, presenting it as effectively equivalent to a return, reasoning that the city would no longer serve as a base for Athenian enemies.

This announcement infuriated the Athenians, who perceived Lacedaemon's actions as a betrayal. They argued that Panactum should have been restored intact, not razed. Moreover, they had just learned that Lacedaemon had formed a separate alliance with the Boeotians, violating a prior commitment to join Athens in pressuring those reluctant to join the peace treaty. Reflecting on Lacedaemon's various failures to uphold her promises, the Athenians felt deceived, delivered a harsh response to the envoys, and promptly sent them away in anger.

As the division between the Lacedaemonians and Athenians deepened, the faction in Athens pushing to end the treaty quickly mobilized. Leading this faction was Alcibiades, son of Clinias, a young man known for his noble lineage and remarkable ambition. Alcibiades genuinely favored an alliance with Argos but was also driven by a strong sense of personal grievance. He resented the Lacedaemonians for arranging the treaty through Nicias and Laches, neglecting him due to his youth and disregarding the historic relationship between his family and their city. Although this connection as proxeni (host and liaison) had been broken by his grandfather, Alcibiades had recently attempted to renew it by showing favor to the Spartan prisoners taken on the island. Feeling dismissed and disrespected, he initially spoke out against the treaty, arguing that the Lacedaemonians were untrustworthy and had only sought peace to neutralize Argos, after which they would isolate and attack Athens. Now, with this latest incident, he secretly sent a message to the Argives, urging them to come to Athens immediately, bringing proposals of alliance and accompanied by their Mantinean and Elean allies. He assured them the timing was favorable and promised his support in advancing their cause.

Receiving this message, and realizing that the Athenians had not only been excluded from the Boeotian-Lacedaemonian alliance but were also in serious conflict with the Lacedaemonians, the Argives disregarded their recent diplomatic efforts with Lacedaemon. They began to lean towards Athens, considering that in the event of renewed hostilities, it would be beneficial to ally with a city that shared democratic values, had historically been friendly to Argos, and commanded considerable naval power. Seizing the opportunity, the Argives promptly sent ambassadors to Athens to negotiate an alliance, bringing representatives from Elis and Mantinea along to strengthen their case.

Meanwhile, a Lacedaemonian delegation—comprised of Philocharidas, Leon, and Endius, known for their favorable stance towards Athens—arrived in haste, fearing the Athenians might, in their irritation, align themselves with the Argives. They sought to request the return of Pylos in exchange for Panactum and to defend their recent alliance with the Boeotians, emphasizing that it had not been made to threaten Athens. When these envoys addressed the Athenian senate, explaining their purpose and declaring they had full authority to negotiate all outstanding issues, Alcibiades grew concerned that, if the envoys repeated this in the popular assembly, the public might be swayed, resulting in the Argive alliance being dismissed. To prevent this, he devised a cunning plan.

Alcibiades approached the Lacedaemonians and convinced them, under solemn assurances, not to mention their full authority when speaking to the assembly. He promised that, if they followed this advice, he would help them secure the return of Pylos, despite his current opposition to such a concession, and would also resolve other outstanding matters. His true intent was to create a rift between the Lacedaemonian envoys and Nicias, making the former appear inconsistent or insincere before the people, thereby fostering distrust and resentment towards them. This would increase public support for an alliance with Argos, Elis, and Mantinea.

Alcibiades' strategy worked as planned. When the Lacedaemonian envoys addressed the assembly and failed to assert, as they had in the senate, that they possessed full authority to negotiate, the Athenians became frustrated. Spurred on by Alcibiades, who launched into even harsher criticism of the Lacedaemonians, the assembly was on the verge of immediately accepting the Argive, Elean, and Mantinean envoys into an alliance. However, just as matters seemed certain to progress, an earthquake struck, interrupting the proceedings, and the assembly was adjourned without any final decisions being made.

In the assembly held the following day, Nicias argued that, despite the Lacedaemonians' failure to admit that they did not come with full authority and had, in doing so, allowed both themselves and Athens to be misled, it was still in Athens's best interest to pursue peace with them. He advised that they should postpone the proposals made by the Argives and send another delegation to Lacedaemon to ascertain their intentions. Nicias reasoned that prolonging the truce would strengthen Athens's position and weaken that of her rivals. Athens, with her affairs in excellent order, had much to gain by maintaining this period of prosperity, while Lacedaemon, in a much worse state, would only benefit from an earlier chance to test her luck again in war.

Nicias successfully persuaded the assembly to send ambassadors, including himself, to Lacedaemon. Their mission was to invite the Lacedaemonians—if they were truly committed to peace—to restore

Panactum and Amphipolis intact, and to sever their alliance with the Boeotians unless the Boeotians agreed to join the treaty, in line with the stipulation that prohibited either Athens or Lacedaemon from negotiating separately with other parties. The ambassadors were also instructed to emphasize that, had the Athenians wished to be deceitful, they could have already allied with the Argives, who had come to Athens for that very purpose. They set off for Lacedaemon with these instructions and any other grievances that Athens wished to raise.

Upon their arrival, the ambassadors conveyed their demands, ultimately warning the Lacedaemonians that unless they ended their alliance with the Boeotians—should the Boeotians choose not to join the treaty—Athens would instead form an alliance with the Argives and their allies. However, the Lacedaemonians refused to abandon their alliance with the Boeotians, as Xenares, the ephor, and his supporters prevailed in this decision. Still, at Nicias's request, they renewed their oaths, as Nicias feared returning to Athens with nothing to show for his efforts, which could harm his reputation as the architect of the peace treaty with Lacedaemon.

Upon Nicias's return, the Athenians were infuriated when they learned that no progress had been made in Lacedaemon. Feeling that the Lacedaemonians had not honored their promises, they took advantage of the presence of the Argives and their allies—who had been introduced by Alcibiades—and promptly made a treaty and alliance with them, establishing the following terms:

The Athenians, Argives, Mantineans, and Eleans, acting on behalf of themselves and their respective allies, entered into a one-hundred-year treaty. This treaty was to be upheld without deceit or harm by land or by sea.

1. It shall not be permitted for the Argives, Eleans, Mantineans, or their allies to make war against the Athenians or any allies within the Athenian empire; nor shall the Athenians or their allies make war against the Argives, Eleans, Mantineans, or their allies in any way or by any means whatsoever. The Athenians, Argives, Eleans, and

Mantineans shall be allies for one hundred years, under the following terms:

2. If an enemy invades Athenian territory, the Argives, Eleans, and Mantineans shall come to Athens's aid at the Athenians' request. They will assist as effectively as they can and to the best of their ability. If the invader withdraws after looting the land, that state shall be considered the enemy of Argos, Mantinea, Elis, and Athens, and all these cities shall go to war against it. None of the cities may make peace with the offender without the agreement of all the cities involved.

3. Likewise, if an enemy invades the territory of Argos, Mantinea, or Elis, the Athenians shall come to the aid of Argos, Mantinea, or Elis upon request, providing assistance as effectively as possible to the best of their ability. Should the invader withdraw after pillaging, the offending state shall be deemed the enemy of the Athenians, Argives, Mantineans, and Eleans. All these cities shall wage war against it, and no city may establish peace with the offender without the unanimous consent of all.

4. No armed force shall be permitted to pass through the territories of the contracting powers or through the lands of their allies for hostile purposes, nor to sail by sea, unless all cities—namely, Athens, Argos, Mantinea, and Elis—agree to such a passage.

5. Troops sent to provide assistance shall be maintained by their home city for the first thirty days after their arrival in the city that requested aid and likewise upon their return. If their services are needed for a longer duration, the city that requested them shall maintain them at the following daily rates: three Aeginetan obols per day for each heavy-armed soldier, archer, or light-armed soldier, and an Aeginetan drachma per day for each cavalryman.

6. The city requesting aid shall have command over the forces when the war is within its own territory. However, if all cities decide to embark on a joint campaign, the command shall be equally divided among all the cities.

7. This treaty shall be sworn to by the Athenians on behalf of themselves and their allies, and by the Argives, Mantineans, Eleans, and their allies, each city pledging individually. The oath will be sworn over full-grown sacrificial victims in the manner considered most binding in each respective country. The oath shall be as follows:

"I STAND BY THE ALLIANCE AND ITS ARTICLES, JUSTLY, INNOCENTLY, AND SINCERELY, AND I WILL NOT VIOLATE THEM IN ANY WAY OR BY ANY MEANS WHATSOEVER."

The oath was to be administered in Athens by the Senate and the city magistrates, with the Prytanes overseeing it. At Argos, it would be taken by the Senate, the Eighty, and the Artynae, with the Eighty administering it. In Mantinea, the Demiurgi, the Senate, and other magistrates would take the oath, with the Theori and Polemarchs administering it. In Elis, the Demiurgi, the magistrates, and the Six Hundred would swear it, with the Demiurgi and Thesmophylaces overseeing it. The oaths would be renewed regularly: Athenians traveling to Elis, Mantinea, and Argos would renew the oath thirty days before the Olympic Games, while Argives, Mantineans, and Eleans would go to Athens to renew it ten days before the Panathenaea festival. The treaty articles, oaths, and alliance terms would be inscribed on a stone pillar in each city: in Athens at the citadel; in Argos in the marketplace at Apollo's temple; in Mantinea at Zeus's temple in the marketplace. A joint bronze pillar would also be erected at the upcoming Olympic Games. If any additions to the treaty were deemed necessary, any amendments agreed upon by all the cities after consultation would become binding.

Though this treaty and alliance were now formalized, the peace treaty between the Lacedaemonians and Athenians remained intact, with neither side officially renouncing it. Meanwhile, Corinth, although an ally of Argos, did not join this new treaty or the earlier defensive and offensive alliance formed between the Eleans, Argives, and Mantineans. Instead, Corinth expressed satisfaction with the original defensive alliance, which required mutual support without obligating allies to offensive campaigns. Consequently, Corinth stayed apart from her allies and began to reconsider her relationship with Lacedaemon.

At the Olympic Games held that summer—where Androsthenes of Arcadia won victories in both wrestling and boxing—the Eleans barred the Lacedaemonians from entering the temple, preventing them from making sacrifices or competing. The exclusion was due to the Lacedaemonians' refusal to pay a fine imposed on them under Olympic law, which the Eleans had levied because the Lacedaemonians had allegedly attacked Fort Phyrcus and stationed heavy infantry in Lepreum during the Olympic truce. The fine was substantial: two thousand minae, calculated at two minae per soldier in accordance with the law.

The Lacedaemonians sent envoys to protest the fine as unjust, arguing that the truce had not yet been proclaimed in Lacedaemon when the infantry set out. However, the Eleans countered, saying that the armistice had already begun in Elis, where they proclaimed it first, and that the Lacedaemonians' aggression had caught them off guard while they were living peacefully and expecting no hostilities. In response, the Lacedaemonians suggested that if the Eleans truly believed an act of aggression had occurred, it would have been pointless to proclaim the truce in Lacedaemon after the fact. Nevertheless, they had gone ahead and announced the truce, believing no aggression had been committed, and had refrained from further hostilities against Elis from that moment onward.

Despite this reasoning, the Eleans remained firm, insisting that they were convinced an act of aggression had taken place. However, they offered a compromise: if the Lacedaemonians would return Lepreum, the Eleans would forgo their portion of the fine and pay the part owed to the gods on behalf of the Lacedaemonians.

When the Lacedaemonians rejected the first proposal, the Eleans made a second offer: instead of restoring Lepreum, if this was unacceptable, the Lacedaemonians could approach the altar of Olympian Zeus—since they were so eager to gain access to the temple—and swear before all the Greeks that they would pay the fine at a later date. However, this proposal was also refused. Consequently, the Lacedaemonians were banned from entering the temple, performing sacrifices, and participating in the games. They held sacrifices at home instead. The Lepreans were the only other Greeks who did not attend the festival. Concerned that the Lacedaemonians might attempt to sacrifice by force, the Eleans stationed a heavily-armed guard of young men at the temple, joined by one thousand Argives, another thousand Mantineans, and some Athenian cavalry who remained at Harpina during the festival.

There was significant fear in the assembly that the Lacedaemonians might enter with arms, especially after an incident involving Lichas, the son of Arcesilaus, a Lacedaemonian. Lichas was scourged on the course by the umpires because, after his horses won the race, he stepped forward to crown the charioteer, thus claiming ownership of the chariot. Officially, the Boeotian people had been declared the winners, as Lichas was not entitled to enter. This incident heightened tensions, and many feared that a disturbance was imminent. However, the Lacedaemonians kept calm, and the festival passed without further incident.

After the Olympic Games, the Argives and their allies traveled to Corinth to encourage her to join their alliance. There, they encountered some Lacedaemonian envoys, and a lengthy discussion ensued. Ultimately, however, the talks were cut short when an earthquake struck, prompting everyone to return to their respective cities.

As summer ended, a battle occurred the following winter between the people of Heraclea in Trachinia and a coalition of neighboring tribes—Aenianians, Dolopians, Malians, and certain Thessalians—who viewed Heraclea as a direct threat to their lands. Having opposed and harassed Heraclea since its founding, they now succeeded in battle, defeating the Heracleans. Among the fallen was Xenares, son of Cnidis, the Lacedaemonian commander. Thus ended the winter and the twelfth year of the war.

In the first days of the summer that followed, Heraclea had become so weakened that the Boeotians occupied the town, sending away the Lacedaemonian commander Agesippidas for poor governance. They were concerned that Athens might capture the town while the Lacedaemonians were preoccupied with events in the Peloponnese. The Lacedaemonians were nonetheless offended by the Boeotians' actions.

In this same summer, Alcibiades, son of Clinias and now one of the Athenian generals, entered the Peloponnese with a small force of Athenian heavy infantry and archers. In concert with the Argives and their allies, he picked up additional forces from allied cities along his route and led this army through various regions of the Peloponnese, strengthening the alliance and addressing related matters. Among other things, he persuaded the people of Patrae to extend their walls down to the sea. He also intended to build a fort near the Achaean Rhium, but the Corinthians, Sicyonians, and others who would have been affected by the fortification arrived and prevented him from doing so.

Later that summer, hostilities broke out between the Epidaurians and the Argives. The stated reason was that the Epidaurians had failed to send an offering for their pastureland to Apollo Pythaeus, as was required, with the Argives overseeing the temple. However, beyond this pretext, Alcibiades and the Argives were determined to take control of Epidaurus. Securing Epidaurus would help ensure Corinth's neutrality and provide the Athenians with a shorter route to send reinforcements from Aegina, avoiding a longer journey around Scyllaeum. In pursuit of this goal, the Argives prepared to invade Epidaurus on their own, intending to collect the offering.

Around this time, the Lacedaemonians marched out with their entire force to Leuctra, a location on their border facing Mount

Lycaeum, under the command of Agis, son of Archidamus. None of the cities providing contingents were informed of their final destination. However, the sacrifices performed to seek approval for crossing the frontier did not yield favorable results, and the Lacedaemonians decided to return home. They then sent a message to their allies, instructing them to prepare to march after the upcoming month, which happened to be Carneus—a sacred month for the Dorians.

When the Lacedaemonians retreated, the Argives took action. They marched out on the third-to-last day of the month preceding Carneus, designating this day as the same for the entire period they would be out. They then invaded and plundered Epidaurus. The Epidaurians called upon their allies for assistance; however, some used the sacred month as an excuse, while others advanced to Epidaurus's border and remained there, refraining from taking any active part.

While the Argives were in Epidaurus, ambassadors from various cities gathered at Mantinea at the invitation of the Athenians. During the conference, the Corinthian delegate Euphamidas pointed out the inconsistency in their actions. He argued that it made little sense to discuss peace while the Argives, Epidaurians, and their respective allies were facing off in battle. He suggested that representatives from each faction should first separate the armies before resuming peace talks. Following this advice, the ambassadors succeeded in persuading the Argives to withdraw from Epidaurus, and they reconvened afterward. However, the talks once again failed to yield any agreements, and the Argives soon launched another invasion of Epidaurus, looting the countryside.

The Lacedaemonians, in response, advanced to Caryae, but once again, their frontier sacrifices were unfavorable, and they returned home. The Argives, after devastating about one-third of Epidaurian territory, finally withdrew as well. Meanwhile, a thousand Athenian heavy infantry under Alcibiades arrived to assist the Argives, but upon learning that the Lacedaemonian expedition had ended and their presence was no longer needed, they also returned to Athens.

Thus, the summer came to a close. In the following winter, the Lacedaemonians managed to evade the Athenians' watchful eye and sent a garrison of three hundred men to Epidaurus, led by Agesippidas. The Argives, upon discovering this, went to Athens to protest, arguing that the Athenians had allowed an enemy force to pass by sea, violating the treaty clause that forbade allies from permitting enemy movement through their territory. They urged the Athenians to send the Messenians and Helots stationed in Pylos to harass the Lacedaemonians; otherwise, the Argives would consider the Athenians to have broken faith with them.

Influenced by Alcibiades, the Athenians agreed to inscribe at the base of the Laconian pillar that the Lacedaemonians had violated their oaths. They then moved the Helots stationed at Cranii to Pylos to raid the countryside. Otherwise, they remained inactive, as before.

During this winter, hostilities between the Argives and Epidaurians continued, though there were no full-scale battles. Instead, the conflict was marked by raids and ambushes, with minor losses occurring on both sides. Towards the end of winter, as spring approached, the Argives made an attempt to take Epidaurus by surprise. Armed with scaling ladders, they expected to find the city poorly guarded due to the ongoing war and hoped to capture it in an assault. However, they were unsuccessful and returned empty-handed.

Thus, the winter came to an end, and with it, the thirteenth year of the war also concluded.

In the middle of the following summer, the Lacedaemonians, recognizing that their allies the Epidaurians were in dire straits and that much of the Peloponnese was either in rebellion or discontented, decided it was time to intervene if they hoped to halt the spread of instability. As a result, they mobilized their full military force, including the Helots, and set out on a campaign against Argos under the command of Agis, son of Archidamus, the king of the

Lacedaemonians. The Tegeans and other Arcadian allies joined the expedition. Additional allies from across the Peloponnese and beyond gathered at Phlius. The Boeotians arrived with five thousand heavy infantry, an equal number of light troops, five hundred cavalry, and five hundred dismounted horsemen. The Corinthians contributed two thousand heavy infantry, while other allies contributed forces in varying numbers. The Phliasians joined with all available troops, as the army was encamped in their territory.

The Argives had known about the Lacedaemonians' preparations from the outset, yet they delayed taking the field until the Lacedaemonian army was already en route to join the main force at Phlius. Once reinforced by the Mantineans and their allies, along with three thousand heavy infantry from Elis, the Argives set out and encountered the Lacedaemonians at Methydrium in Arcadia. Each army took a position on a hill, and the Argives prepared to engage the Lacedaemonians before they could be reinforced by other allies. However, Agis evaded them by breaking camp during the night and moving to join the rest of the allies at Phlius.

At dawn, the Argives realized Agis's maneuver and, in response, marched first back to Argos and then to the Nemean road, anticipating that the Lacedaemonians and their allies would travel this route. Yet, Agis outwitted them again by taking an unexpected, challenging route. He ordered the Lacedaemonians, along with the Arcadians and Epidaurians, to follow him along this difficult path, allowing them to descend directly into the plains of Argos. Meanwhile, the Corinthians, Pellenians, and Phliasians were instructed to take another steep route, while the Boeotians, Megarians, and Sicyonians received orders to descend via the Nemean road, where the Argives were positioned. This arrangement meant that if the Argives moved into the plain to confront Agis's forces, the Boeotians and their allies could strike them from behind, using their cavalry to press the attack on the Argives' rear.

With these plans in place, Agis led his forces into the plains and began ravaging the territory, including the area around Saminthus and other locations.

In the middle of the following summer, the Lacedaemonians, recognizing that their allies the Epidaurians were in dire straits and that much of the Peloponnese was either in rebellion or discontented, decided it was time to intervene if they hoped to halt the spread of instability. As a result, they mobilized their full military force, including the Helots, and set out on a campaign against Argos under the command of Agis, son of Archidamus, the king of the Lacedaemonians. The Tegeans and other Arcadian allies joined the expedition. Additional allies from across the Peloponnese and beyond gathered at Phlius. The Boeotians arrived with five thousand heavy infantry, an equal number of light troops, five hundred cavalry, and five hundred dismounted horsemen. The Corinthians contributed two thousand heavy infantry, while other allies contributed forces in varying numbers. The Phliasians joined with all available troops, as the army was encamped in their territory.

The Argives had known about the Lacedaemonians' preparations from the outset, yet they delayed taking the field until the Lacedaemonian army was already en route to join the main force at Phlius. Once reinforced by the Mantineans and their allies, along with three thousand heavy infantry from Elis, the Argives set out and encountered the Lacedaemonians at Methydrium in Arcadia. Each army took a position on a hill, and the Argives prepared to engage the Lacedaemonians before they could be reinforced by other allies. However, Agis evaded them by breaking camp during the night and moving to join the rest of the allies at Phlius.

At dawn, the Argives realized Agis's maneuver and, in response, marched first back to Argos and then to the Nemean road, anticipating that the Lacedaemonians and their allies would travel this route. Yet, Agis outwitted them again by taking an unexpected, challenging route. He ordered the Lacedaemonians, along with the

Arcadians and Epidaurians, to follow him along this difficult path, allowing them to descend directly into the plains of Argos. Meanwhile, the Corinthians, Pellenians, and Phliasians were instructed to take another steep route, while the Boeotians, Megarians, and Sicyonians received orders to descend via the Nemean road, where the Argives were positioned. This arrangement meant that if the Argives moved into the plain to confront Agis's forces, the Boeotians and their allies could strike them from behind, using their cavalry to press the attack on the Argives' rear.

With these plans in place, Agis led his forces into the plains and began ravaging the territory, including the area around Saminthus and other locations.

Under the command of Laches and Nicostratus, a thousand Athenian soldiers and three hundred cavalry arrived. Even though the Argives were hesitant to break their truce with the Lacedaemonians, they asked the Athenians to leave and initially refused to present them before the people. It wasn't until the Mantineans and Eleans, who were still in Argos, pleaded that the Argives allowed them to speak. Alcibiades, the Athenian ambassador, told the Argives and their allies that they shouldn't have made a truce without consulting the rest of their allies, and now that the Athenians had arrived, they should resume the war. This argument convinced the allies, who then moved to attack Orchomenos, though the Argives initially held back before eventually joining the others. They all laid siege to Orchomenos, attacking it. They wanted to take this place because the Lacedaemonians had held Arcadian hostages there. Fearing their weak defenses, the Orchomenians, realizing they were outmatched, surrendered on the condition they would join the league, provide their own hostages to the Mantineans, and hand over those the Lacedaemonians had left with them. With Orchomenos secured, the allies debated their next target. The Eleans pushed for Lepreum, while the Mantineans wanted to go after Tegea. When the Argives and Athenians sided with the Mantineans, the Eleans left in anger, and the remaining allies prepared at Mantinea to advance on Tegea, where a faction within had agreed to hand over the city.

Meanwhile, after returning from Argos and securing a four-month truce, the Lacedaemonians criticized Agis for not conquering Argos when they had such a strong alliance ready. When they heard Orchomenos had been taken, they were angrier than ever and nearly decided to destroy Agis's house and fine him ten thousand drachmas. Agis, however, asked for a chance to make up for his failure in the field, promising that if he didn't succeed, they could punish him however they wanted. The Lacedaemonians refrained from fining him or destroying his house. Instead, they established a new rule requiring Agis to have ten Spartan advisors who had to approve any decision to lead an army out of the city.

Around this time, word came from friends in Tegea that unless the Lacedaemonians quickly intervened, Tegea would switch allegiance to the Argives and their allies, if it hadn't already. On hearing this, the Lacedaemonians quickly gathered a large force, including Spartans, Helots, and all their people, and set out for Tegea with more men than ever before. They reached Orestheum in Maenalia, ordering the Arcadians in their league to follow closely, while they advanced to Tegea. When they reached Orestheum, they sent back the oldest and youngest sixth of the Spartans to guard their homes, and the rest continued on to Tegea, where their Arcadian allies soon joined them. They also sent word to Corinth, Boeotia, Phocia, and Locris, urging them to come to Mantinea as quickly as possible. Although they had little time to prepare, they hurried, despite the challenge of passing through enemy lands that blocked their path. Meanwhile, the Lacedaemonians, along with their Arcadian allies, entered Mantinea's territory, set up camp near the temple of Heracles, and began raiding the countryside.

Here, the Argives and their allies spotted the Lacedaemonians approaching and quickly positioned themselves on higher, rugged ground. They organized into a battle formation, ready to meet their opponents. The Lacedaemonians, seeing their foes on this fortified hill, advanced immediately, drawing close enough that they were within range of stones or javelins. At this moment, one of the older Spartan warriors, noticing the enemy's strong position, shouted to Agis, suggesting that Agis seemed eager to "cure one wrong with another." By this, he meant Agis was too eager to make up for his criticized retreat from Argos by risking an overly hasty attack here.

For reasons unknown—perhaps due to the elder's shout, or perhaps following a sudden thought of his own—Agis unexpectedly ordered his troops to pull back without engaging in battle. He led them away into Tegean territory and started redirecting the water flow into Mantinea's lands. This water was a point of constant dispute between the Mantineans and Tegeans, as it caused severe damage to the land it flooded. Agis aimed to provoke the Argives and their allies into coming down from the hill to protect their water supply, thus forcing them to battle on the plains below.

The Lacedaemonians spent the rest of that day focused on redirecting the water. The Argives and their allies were at first baffled by the sudden retreat, confused as to why the Lacedaemonians had approached so close only to turn back without a fight. When it became clear that the enemy was moving away without any intention to engage or to pursue, the Argive soldiers began to criticize their own generals. They remembered how the generals had let the Lacedaemonians escape before, when they had successfully trapped them near Argos, only for the enemy to slip away. Now, yet again, their generals had allowed the Lacedaemonians to withdraw without opposition, as if handing them an easy escape. The Argive soldiers felt frustrated, grumbling that their leaders were betraying their chance to strike while the enemy was vulnerable.

The generals, taken aback by the complaints, eventually gave in and led the Argives and their allies down from the hill to the plain. They set up camp with the intent to confront the Lacedaemonians directly. The next day, the Argives and their allies arranged themselves in their chosen battle formation, prepared to fight if they happened to meet the Lacedaemonians in the field.

Meanwhile, the Lacedaemonians, after finishing their task of redirecting the water, returned to their previous camp by the temple of Heracles. To their surprise, they saw the Argive army positioned just in front of them, fully organized and advancing from the hill. This unexpected sight shook the Lacedaemonians, who couldn't recall ever experiencing such a shock in battle. There was hardly any time to prepare; the troops had to fall into formation quickly, each man rushing to his place, as Agis, their king, took charge of every movement according to Spartan law.

In times of battle, Spartan law dictated that the king gave all commands. Agis relayed his orders to the Polemarchs, who then passed them down to the Lochages. The Lochages communicated them to the Pentecostyes, who then informed the Enomotarchs, who finally gave the commands to the smaller units, the Enomoties. This chain of command allowed orders to be swiftly transmitted throughout the ranks, as nearly every Lacedaemonian unit, save for a few, was structured with officers overseeing officers. In this way, responsibility was distributed among many leaders, ensuring that the army could act as one, even under sudden pressure.

In this battle, the Sciritae formed the left wing; in a Lacedaemonian army, they traditionally held this position alone. Next to them stood the troops of Brasidas from Thrace, accompanied by the Neodamodes. Following these were the Lacedaemonians themselves, organized in company after company, with the Arcadians from Heraea aligned alongside them. Further down the line came the Maenalians, and the Tegeans held the right wing, with a small group of Lacedaemonians stationed at the far end. Their cavalry units were positioned on both wings. This was the battle arrangement of the Lacedaemonians.

On the opposing side, the Mantineans were positioned on the right, as the battle was taking place on their land. Beside them stood the allied troops from Arcadia. Next in line were the thousand elite

Argive soldiers, who had received extensive military training provided by the state. Following them were the other Argive forces, then the allies from Cleonae and Orneae, and finally, the Athenians held the far left, with their cavalry positioned with them.

These were the formations and forces of the two armies. At first glance, the Lacedaemonian army appeared larger, but determining the exact number of either side or their specific units was difficult. Due to the secretive nature of the Lacedaemonian government, their exact numbers remained unknown, and it was common for people to exaggerate the size of their country's forces, making the estimates for their opponents unreliable. However, it was possible to roughly calculate the Lacedaemonian numbers based on the following: there were seven companies in the field, excluding the Sciritae, who numbered six hundred men. Each company consisted of four Pentecostyes, and each Pentecosty had four Enomoties. The first line of each Enomoty included four soldiers, and while the depth of each line wasn't consistent and was left to each captain's choice, they generally stood eight deep. This gave a first-line count, excluding the Sciritae, of four hundred and forty-eight men.

As the armies prepared to engage, each contingent received motivational words from its commander. The Mantineans were reminded that they were fighting to protect their homeland and avoid the return to servitude after having experienced power. The Argives were encouraged to battle for their ancient dominance, to reclaim their former equal standing in the Peloponnese, which they had long lost, and to avenge their grievances against a neighboring enemy. The Athenians were inspired by the promise of winning honor among such brave allies and the glory of defeating the Lacedaemonians in their own region. Victory here would strengthen their influence and ensure the safety of Attica from future invasions.

Meanwhile, the Lacedaemonians, with a different approach, encouraged each soldier quietly, man to man, as they stood in ranks singing their traditional war-songs. They believed that their rigorous training in discipline and action was far more effective in preparing them for battle than any speeches could be. They trusted in the strength that came from their long, intensive training rather than in momentary words of encouragement.

Then, the battle began. The Argives and their allies advanced rapidly, filled with haste and anger, while the Lacedaemonians moved forward slowly, accompanied by the sounds of many flute-players. This was a customary practice in the Lacedaemonian army, not for religious purposes, but to help them advance steadily and keep their formation intact. The music ensured that they marched in rhythm, preventing the disorder that large armies often experience at the onset of battle.

Just before the battle began, King Agis decided on a strategic maneuver. It's common in battles for armies to shift toward their right wing as they advance, which often leads one army's right wing to overlap the enemy's left wing. This happens because each soldier instinctively tries to shield his unarmed side by staying close to the shield of the man on his right. The soldier on the far right sets this movement in motion by pulling away from the enemy, aiming to protect his vulnerable side. This same instinct causes the rest of the soldiers to follow his lead. In this particular instance, the Mantineans extended their right wing well beyond the position of the Sciritae on the Lacedaemonian left, and the Lacedaemonians and Tegeans extended their right wing even farther beyond the Athenians, due to the larger size of their army.

Seeing that his left flank was at risk of being outflanked by the Mantineans, Agis ordered the Sciritae and Brasideans to move out and align themselves with the Mantinean position, leveling the line. He instructed Polemarchs Hipponoidas and Aristocles to fill the resulting gap with two companies drawn from the right wing, thinking that the right side was strong enough to spare some troops, while this shift would reinforce the line facing the Mantineans.

However, because Agis gave these orders as the battle was about to begin and with very little time, Aristocles and Hipponoidas hesitated and did not follow through. This refusal led to their later exile from Sparta on charges of cowardice. Meanwhile, the enemy advanced before the Sciritae (whom Agis had just ordered back into their original position upon seeing the two companies had not moved) could close the gap. In this moment, the Lacedaemonians—though outmatched in tactical skill—demonstrated their courage.

As the two sides clashed, the Mantinean right wing broke through the Sciritae and Brasideans, bursting through the unfilled gap with the support of their allies and the thousand elite Argives. They drove back the Lacedaemonians in a full retreat toward their wagons, cutting down several of the older guards stationed there. Despite this setback on one part of the field, the rest of the Lacedaemonian army, particularly the center where King Agis and the three hundred knights fought, counterattacked against the Argive elders, the five named Argive companies, and the Cleonaeans, Orneans, and Athenians stationed nearby. They routed them almost instantly, with most of the Argive forces fleeing without a fight, some even trampled in their haste to escape.

The Argive army and its allies, having lost ground in this area, found themselves split in two. The Lacedaemonian and Tegean right wing then began to encircle the Athenians and their nearby troops, leaving them trapped between two fronts, already defeated on one side and surrounded on the other. The Athenians might have suffered heavy losses had it not been for the timely support of their cavalry. Observing the distress of his left wing, which was under pressure from the Mantineans and the thousand elite Argives, Agis ordered his entire army to advance to support the weakened section. This move allowed the Athenians and the battered Argive forces to withdraw at a steady pace, as the enemy troops shifted and moved away from them.

Meanwhile, seeing their own allies defeated and the Lacedaemonians advancing with renewed force, the Mantineans, their allies, and the elite Argives broke off from their attack and began to flee. Many Mantineans were killed during this retreat, though most of the elite Argive soldiers managed to escape. However, the retreat was neither rushed nor prolonged. The Lacedaemonians fought stubbornly, holding their ground until the enemy was completely routed. Once they had secured victory, they only pursued the fleeing forces for a short distance, stopping before they had gone far.

This battle was, as closely as I can describe, the greatest in a long time among the Greek states, involving several of the most powerful allies. After securing their victory, the Lacedaemonians stationed themselves in front of the enemy's dead, erected a trophy, and stripped the fallen of their armor. They then gathered their own dead, carried them to Tegea for burial, and returned the enemy's dead to their respective states under a truce. The Argives, Orneans, and Cleonaeans suffered a loss of seven hundred men; the Mantineans lost two hundred, as did the Athenians and Aeginetans, including both their generals. On the Lacedaemonian side, their allies reported minimal losses. Although it was difficult to get an exact figure for the Lacedaemonians themselves, it's said that they lost around three hundred men.

During the battle preparations, the other Lacedaemonian king, Pleistoanax, set out with reinforcements, made up of the oldest and youngest troops, but upon reaching Tegea and learning of the victory, he turned back. The Lacedaemonians then recalled their allies from Corinth and beyond the Isthmus and dismissed them, as they returned home to observe the Carnean festival, which coincidentally fell at that time. This battle erased the accusations of cowardice that had been circulating among the Greeks regarding the Lacedaemonians— criticisms that stemmed from their previous losses on the island and other complaints of slowness or poor management. This victory reminded everyone that, although they had faced setbacks, the Lacedaemonians remained as formidable as ever.

The day before this battle, the Epidaurians took advantage of the absence of the Argive army to launch an attack on the Argive territory. They invaded with all their forces and managed to cut down many of the guards left behind. After the battle, a reinforcement of three thousand Elean heavy infantry and a thousand Athenians arrived to support the Mantineans. Together, these allies set out for Epidaurus while the Lacedaemonians continued celebrating the Carnea. Once there, the allies divided the work among themselves and began constructing a wall around Epidaurus to fortify it. Though most of the forces ceased their work partway, the Athenians completed their assigned section around Cape Heraeum. Once they finished, they collectively left a garrison in the fortification and returned to their respective cities.

With this, summer came to an end. In the first days of the following winter, once the Carnean festival was over, the Lacedaemonians prepared for action again and sent a delegation to Argos with proposals for peace. In Argos, there was already a faction opposed to the democratic government, and following the recent battle, this group was in an even stronger position to sway public opinion toward a truce. Their plan was to first establish peace and then secure an alliance with the Lacedaemonians, after which they intended to overthrow the democratic party. Lichas, son of Arcesilaus and an Argive representative for the Lacedaemonians, arrived in Argos with two proposals from Lacedaemon, offering terms for either continuing the war or agreeing to peace, depending on what the Argives preferred.

After considerable debate, Alcibiades, who happened to be in Argos at the time, persuaded the pro-Lacedaemonian faction to openly advocate for peace. This led the Argives to agree to the proposed truce, which was stated as follows:

The assembly of the Lacedaemonians agrees to treat with the Argives on the following terms:

1. The Argives must return the children they hold from the Orchomenians, as well as the captured men from the Maenalians, and

they must also release the prisoners they hold in Mantinea to the Lacedaemonians.

2. The Argives are required to withdraw from Epidaurus and demolish the fortifications they've established there. If the Athenians refuse to remove themselves from Epidaurus, they will be considered enemies of both the Argives and the Lacedaemonians, as well as enemies of their respective allies.

3. If the Lacedaemonians hold any children from other cities, they are to return each one to his respective city.

4. Regarding the offerings to the god, the Argives may impose an oath on the Epidaurians if they wish, but if they choose not to, they will take the oath themselves.

5. All cities within the Peloponnese, whether large or small, shall be allowed to remain autonomous, respecting the traditions and customs of their individual states.

6. In the event that any forces from outside the Peloponnese invade Peloponnesian land, all parties in this agreement will unite in defense, under terms agreed upon as fair and beneficial for all Peloponnesians.

7. All allies of the Lacedaemonians outside the Peloponnese shall hold the same status as the Lacedaemonians themselves, while the allies of the Argives shall be treated equally with the Argives, maintaining their own lands and possessions.

This treaty shall be presented to all allies, who may approve it or, if they prefer, send the treaty back to their home cities for further consideration before making a final decision.

The Argives initially accepted these terms, and the Lacedaemonian army returned home from Tegea. Soon after, the relations between the Argives and Lacedaemonians grew stronger, and not long afterward, the same faction persuaded the Argives to dissolve their league with the Mantineans, Eleans, and Athenians. Instead, they encouraged the Argives to establish a formal treaty and alliance with the Lacedaemonians, which they did under the following terms:

The Lacedaemonians and Argives agree to a fifty-year treaty and alliance with the following conditions:

1. All conflicts between the two parties will be resolved through fair and unbiased arbitration, in line with the customs of both nations.

2. Other cities within the Peloponnese are invited to join this treaty and alliance as independent and sovereign entities, retaining their current possessions. All disputes among these cities will be settled through fair and unbiased arbitration, respecting the customs of each city.

3. The allies of the Lacedaemonians outside the Peloponnese shall enjoy the same status as the Lacedaemonians themselves, while the allies of the Argives shall enjoy the same status as the Argives, with each group retaining their own lands and properties.

4. For any joint military expeditions that may be necessary, the Lacedaemonians and Argives will consult together and decide upon the course of action most just for their allies.

Any disputes involving city boundaries or other matters, whether within or beyond the Peloponnese, will be resolved through mutual agreement. If one allied city has a dispute with another allied city, the issue shall be referred to a neutral third city chosen by both parties. Disputes between private citizens will be resolved according to the laws of their respective cities.

With the treaty and alliance established, both sides promptly returned anything gained through war or other means. Acting together, they resolved to neither receive any heralds nor envoys from the Athenians unless the Athenians removed their forts and withdrew from the Peloponnese. They also agreed to make no peace or war independently but to act only in unison. Showing their commitment, both the Lacedaemonians and Argives sent envoys to Thrace and to Perdiccas, persuading him to join their alliance. Although inclined to break ties with Athens, Perdiccas did not immediately sever his connection, yet he felt encouraged by the Argives, his ancestral homeland, to take steps in that direction. They also renewed their former oaths with the Chalcidians, taking additional oaths, while the Argives sent envoys to the Athenians, demanding the evacuation of the fort at Epidaurus. The Athenians, realizing their forces there were outnumbered, sent Demosthenes to retrieve their troops. Upon arrival, Demosthenes arranged a gymnastic event to get the rest of the garrison out and then locked the gates behind them. The Athenians later renewed their treaty with the Epidaurians and relinquished control of the fortress.

Following Argos's departure from the alliance, the Mantineans initially resisted but eventually realized they lacked the strength to oppose the Lacedaemonians without Argos's support. They too came to terms with the Lacedaemonians, surrendering control over the towns they had held. Now, the Lacedaemonians and Argives, each fielding a thousand troops, joined forces. The Lacedaemonians first went alone to Sicyon, strengthening its oligarchy, and then united with the Argives to overthrow the democracy in Argos, replacing it with an oligarchy aligned with Lacedaemonian interests. These events unfolded at the close of winter, just before spring, marking the end of the fourteenth year of the war.

The following summer, the people of Dium in Athos revolted against Athenian rule, joining the Chalcidians, while the Lacedaemonians made adjustments in Achaea to further benefit their position. Meanwhile, the democratic faction in Argos, regaining strength and confidence, waited for the Gymnopaedic festival in Sparta to mount an attack on the oligarchs. In a fierce battle within the city, the commoners ultimately prevailed, killing some of their opponents and exiling others. Although the Lacedaemonians received pleas for help from their Argive allies, they initially ignored the messages. Eventually, they postponed the Gymnopaedia and set out to provide assistance. However, upon reaching Tegea and learning of the oligarchs' defeat, they refused to proceed further despite pleas from the survivors, opting instead to return home and resume the festival.

Shortly afterward, envoys from both the victorious Argive democrats and the exiled oligarchs presented their cases in Sparta, where many Lacedaemonian allies were gathered. After extensive debate, the Lacedaemonians declared that the democratic faction had acted unjustly and resolved to march against Argos, though they repeatedly postponed action. In the meantime, the Argive commoners, fearing a Lacedaemonian retaliation, turned once more to Athens, seeking an alliance that they believed would offer significant protection. They began constructing long walls stretching to the sea, hoping that, in the event of a land blockade, they could still receive supplies by sea with Athenian support. Some other Peloponnesian cities supported this construction, and all the people of Argos—men, women, and even slaves—worked on the walls, while carpenters and masons arrived from Athens to assist.

With summer ended, the Lacedaemonians, upon learning about the construction of these walls, marched against Argos along with their allies, excluding the Corinthians. They received intelligence from contacts within the city and were led by King Agis, son of Archidamus. However, the expected support from within Argos did not materialize. The Lacedaemonians did succeed in capturing and dismantling the newly constructed walls. They then attacked the Argive town of Hysiae, killing all the free men captured there, and afterward dispersed to their respective cities.

In retaliation, the Argives launched an expedition into Phlius, plundering it for harboring their exiled opponents, many of whom had taken refuge there, before returning home. During the same winter, Athens took action against Macedonia in response to Perdiccas's alliance with the Argives and Lacedaemonians and his betrayal during an Athenian campaign. This campaign, intended to target the Chalcidians and Amphipolis, was disrupted largely because of Perdiccas's defection, and thus, Athens declared him an enemy. With this, winter came to a close, marking the end of the fifteenth year of the war.

Chapter XVII

Sixteenth Year of the War—The Melian Conference—Fate of Melos

The following summer, Alcibiades sailed to Argos with a fleet of twenty ships and arrested around three hundred individuals suspected of supporting the Lacedaemonian faction. The Athenians promptly detained these individuals on nearby islands within their empire. Soon afterward, the Athenians launched an expedition against the island of Melos, deploying thirty of their own ships, alongside six Chian and two Lesbian vessels. This force included sixteen hundred Athenian heavy infantry, three hundred archers, twenty mounted archers, and about fifteen hundred additional heavy infantry from their allies and the islanders. Melos, a colony of Lacedaemon, had refused to submit to Athenian control as other islands had. Initially, the Melians remained neutral, avoiding involvement in the conflict, but they adopted a hostile stance when the Athenians began to raid and plunder their territory.

Athenian generals Cleomedes, son of Lycomedes, and Tisias, son of Tisimachus, encamped with their forces in Melian territory. Before engaging in any significant damage to the land, they sent envoys to open negotiations. The Melians, however, did not bring the envoys before the people but directed them to speak to the magistrates and a select few. The Athenian representatives addressed the Melian leaders as follows:

Athenians: Since these discussions will not be held openly before the people, and we cannot make our points directly without interruption, perhaps we can speak more frankly. We understand that bringing us before a smaller council means you intend to avoid persuasive arguments that might sway the public unchallenged. To proceed cautiously, we suggest you don't make long speeches yourselves but instead respond directly to anything you find unacceptable in our statements. Let's start with this: do you find our proposal suitable?

The Melian Commissioners responded:

Melians: We agree that a fair, candid discussion is acceptable; however, your military preparations seem at odds with your words. It appears you've come here to impose your will, where any resistance on our part would mean war, and submission would mean servitude.

Athenians: If you're here to discuss mere guesses about the future rather than make decisions for the safety of your state based on present facts, we'll stop now. Otherwise, we're willing to proceed.

Melians: It's only natural for us to be cautious, given our position, and we understand the importance of this discussion for our state's survival. So, as you suggest, let's continue.

Athenians: We won't waste time on long arguments claiming a right to our empire because we defeated the Mede, nor will we suggest we are attacking you because of some wrong you did to us—that would be hard to believe. Instead, we hope that you won't attempt to persuade us by saying you didn't side with the Lacedaemonians, despite being their colony, or by arguing that you've done us no harm. Let's both focus on what's achievable, keeping in mind the reality of our respective positions. As we all know, justice is only relevant when both sides hold equal power, while, in practice, the strong do what they can, and the weak endure what they must.

Melians: We believe it is necessary—even if we must set aside notions of right as you demand and speak only of interest—that you should avoid destroying a shared safeguard, namely, the privilege to appeal to principles of fairness and justice in times of peril, even if the arguments we use may not strictly hold up but still pass for valid. You have a stake in this too, as your fall, should it ever come, would likely invite severe retaliation and serve as a sobering lesson for others to reflect on.

Athenians: The thought of our empire ending, if it should ever happen, doesn't frighten us. A rival like Lacedaemon, even if they were directly against us, isn't nearly as dangerous to the defeated as subjects who might rebel and defeat their own rulers. That is the risk we are prepared to face. Now, we'll explain that we've come here in the interest of preserving our empire, and that what we're saying now is intended for the preservation of your city. We'd rather maintain our rule over you with ease, seeing you preserved for the benefit of both of us.

Melians: And how could it ever be to our advantage to serve while you rule?

Athenians: Because you would gain the benefit of submitting now and avoiding the worst consequences, while we would gain by not having to destroy you.

Melians: So you won't allow us to remain neutral, neither friends nor enemies, and uninvolved on either side?

Athenians: No, because your hostility can't harm us as much as your friendship would undermine us. Your neutrality would serve as evidence to our subjects that we lack strength, while your enmity would affirm our power.

Melians: Is that what your subjects see as justice? To treat those who have nothing to do with your affairs the same as those who are your own colonists or conquered rebels?

Athenians: In terms of fairness, they see both as being alike. If any people remain independent, it's because they have the strength to do so, and if we leave them alone, it's only because we respect their power. By bringing you under our control, we would increase our security, since your position as islanders makes it even more essential that you do not resist the rulers of the sea.

Melians: But have you considered that there might be security in the approach we're suggesting? Since you're dismissing arguments of justice and urging us to follow your interests, we must also explain our interests, if there happens to be common ground. Do you not risk making enemies of all remaining neutrals who will see from our situation that you may one day turn on them too? Isn't this approach likely to increase the number of your enemies, even among those who might otherwise have remained neutral?

Athenians: The truth is, we're not particularly worried about those on the mainland; the freedom they enjoy will keep them from taking preventative measures against us for quite some time. It's the islanders like yourselves, who are outside our empire, and our subjects who resent our control, who are the ones most likely to act recklessly and plunge themselves and us into clear danger.

Melians: If that's the case, then isn't it even more disgraceful and cowardly for us, who are still free, not to attempt every possible option before submitting to your rule—especially when you take such risks to maintain your empire and your subjects are willing to risk everything to escape it?

Athenians: Not if you're being realistic. This isn't a contest between equals where honor is at stake and shame is the penalty; it's a matter of survival and of not opposing those who are far stronger than you.

Melians: Yet we also know that the outcomes of war aren't always determined by numbers alone; fortune sometimes favors the side that seems weaker. Surrendering now would be to give in to despair, but fighting still gives us hope that we can remain free.

Athenians: Hope, that comforting companion of danger, is a reasonable gamble for those with abundant resources, who can afford losses without ruin. But hope tends to be deceptive, and those who gamble everything on it usually see it for what it is only after they're ruined. Unfortunately, when it could still serve as a warning, it's often too tempting to resist. Don't let this happen to you, who are fragile and dependent on a single turn of fate. Don't act like the masses, who, abandoning any security within their reach, turn to invisible hopes, like prophecies and oracles, when tangible hopes run out. These illusions often lead men to ruin.

Melians: We understand the difficulty of facing a power as strong as yours, and we know the struggle will be almost impossible if we don't have equal footing. But we also believe that the gods may favor us, since we are just in this fight while you are unjust. And what we lack in power may be balanced by support from the Lacedaemonians, who, even for the sake of honor alone, are bound to come to the aid of their kin. So, our confidence, in the end, isn't as irrational as it might seem.

Athenians: When you speak of the gods' favor, we believe we have as much reason to hope for it as you do. Our claims and actions are in no way against what people believe of the gods or how they themselves act. We think the gods, like men, naturally rule wherever they have the power. We didn't invent this law; it has existed long before us and will continue long after. We simply apply it, knowing that if you or anyone else held our power, you would act just as we do. So, when it comes to the gods, we feel no fear and see no reason to think we are at a disadvantage.

As for your faith in the Lacedaemonians, which leads you to expect help out of their sense of honor, we can only admire your naivety but don't share in your confidence. The Lacedaemonians are certainly honorable when it comes to their own interests or the laws of their state, but their dealings with others are different. To put it briefly, they're the most consistent we know in seeing what is pleasing to them as honorable, and what is useful to them as just. Such a mindset does not bode well for the safety you are relying on so unreasonably.

Melians: But it's for this very reason that we trust the Lacedaemonians to act in their own interest. We believe they won't betray the Melians, their own colony, as doing so would erode the trust of their friends in Hellas and only aid their enemies.

Athenians: So, you're saying that you don't agree that expediency aligns with security, while justice and honor often come with risk? The Lacedaemonians tend to avoid danger whenever they can.

Melians: We believe they might be more inclined to face danger on our behalf, with more confidence than for others. Our proximity to the Peloponnese makes it easier for them to act, and our shared heritage strengthens our loyalty.

Athenians: Yet an ally doesn't act based on the goodwill of those requesting help but on clear superiority in their own power to act. The Lacedaemonians, more than others, are especially cautious about their resources and rarely take on a neighbor without a large number of allies. Do you really think they would cross the sea to an island when we control it?

Melians: But they have other means. The Cretan Sea is wide, and it's harder for those who control it to intercept ships than it is for those determined to evade capture to get through safely. And even if the Lacedaemonians were unsuccessful, they could still attack your own territory, or strike at the allies you have left, those Brasidas didn't reach. Instead of fighting over lands that aren't yours, you'd then have to defend your own country and your own alliance.

Athenians: You may indeed one day experience the kind of diversion you're hoping for, but you'll discover, as many others have, that the Athenians have never abandoned a siege out of fear of anyone. What surprises us is that, despite saying you would consider the best course for your country's safety, you've mentioned nothing concrete or reliable that could reasonably lead to a secure outcome. Your strongest points lean on hope and the uncertain future, yet your actual resources seem woefully insufficient against the forces we've brought here, making your chances of victory slim indeed. You risk serious error in judgment if, after we depart, you fail to devise a more prudent plan than what you've proposed.

Don't fall prey to the notion of disgrace, which, in situations where defeat is almost certain and unavoidable, has led many to ruin. It's a common tragedy: people often have full awareness of the peril they're facing, yet they let the concept of "disgrace" sway them, misled by the allure of the word itself. They become so fixated on avoiding shame that they willingly walk into disaster, ending up disgraced in a more profound way—through their own miscalculation rather than an unlucky outcome. If you consider this carefully, you'll avoid that pitfall. You'll recognize that it's hardly shameful to submit to the foremost city in Hellas, especially when we offer you moderate terms—becoming a tributary ally while still enjoying your land. With the choice clear between war and security, don't be blinded enough to pick the worst option. Those who avoid challenging their equals, respect their superiors, and show fairness to those below them are generally the most successful. So, think over this carefully when we leave, remembering that it's your homeland you're deciding for. You only have one country, and this decision will determine whether it prospers or falls into ruin.

The Athenians then left the meeting, and the Melians, left alone, decided in line with the stance they had maintained. They replied, "Our decision, Athenians, remains unchanged. We will not, in a moment, strip of its freedom a city that has stood independent for seven hundred years. Instead, we place our trust in the fortune that has preserved us under the gods' favor until now, and in the assistance of men, namely the Lacedaemonians. We will make every effort to defend ourselves. We also invite you to allow us to remain your friends, without hostility toward either side, and to depart from our land under a treaty that we both find acceptable."

This was the Melians' reply. As they withdrew, the Athenians responded, "It appears you are the only ones we've encountered who, judging by these words, place more confidence in the future than in the reality before you, and see distant hopes as certain events. But since you've chosen to rely heavily on the Lacedaemonians, your fortune, and your expectations, it is in these very things that you will ultimately be most deceived."

With that, the Athenian envoys returned to their army. When the Melians showed no signs of surrender, the Athenian generals immediately began their siege, constructing a surrounding wall around the city, with each ally assigned a portion of the work. Once the fortifications were complete, the Athenians withdrew the majority of their army, leaving behind a contingent of their citizens and allies to maintain the blockade by land and sea. This force remained, continuing the siege and cutting off Melos from all outside aid.

Around this time, the Argives launched an attack on the territory of Phlius. However, they suffered a significant loss when eighty of their men were ambushed and killed by the Phliasians, along with Argive exiles who had joined them. Meanwhile, at Pylos, the Athenians were plundering Lacedaemonian territory with such success that the Lacedaemonians, though reluctant to break their treaty with Athens and officially resume hostilities, announced that any of their citizens who wished could raid Athenian holdings. In a similar spirit, the Corinthians began their own hostile actions against the Athenians, motivated by private disputes. However, the other Peloponnesian states chose to remain neutral, avoiding any direct engagement in these rising conflicts.

During this period, the Melians seized an opportunity to strike against their besiegers. In a daring night raid, they attacked a section of the Athenian fortifications near the marketplace, managing to kill some of the Athenian soldiers stationed there. They then brought in as much corn and other provisions as they could gather, retreating before dawn to maintain their position. This attack prompted the Athenians to increase their vigilance and strengthen their defenses around the city to prevent any further attempts.

As summer drew to a close, winter approached with renewed tensions. The Lacedaemonians planned to invade Argive territory, but upon reaching the border, they found the sacrificial omens unfavorable for crossing. Reluctantly, they turned back, abandoning the campaign for the time being. This unexpected retreat heightened suspicion within Argos, where certain citizens were already viewed with distrust. Fearing conspiracy, the Argives detained some individuals they deemed suspicious, though others managed to escape arrest.

Meanwhile, the Melians launched a second nighttime raid on another section of the Athenian fortifications, which was only lightly guarded. This success was short-lived, however, as Athens soon sent reinforcements under the command of Philocrates, son of Demeas. With this strengthened force, the Athenians intensified their siege efforts, applying increased pressure on the Melians. Eventually, with their resources dwindling and no hope of relief, the Melians were betrayed from within, leading to their unconditional surrender to Athens.

The consequences were severe. The Athenians executed all Melian men of fighting age and sold the women and children into slavery. Afterward, they claimed Melos for themselves, sending out five hundred Athenian colonists to settle the island and establish control over its lands.

Book VI

Chapter XVIII

Seventeenth Year of the War—The Sicilian Campaign—Affair of the Hermae—Departure of the Expedition

During that winter, the Athenians decided to prepare for another expedition to Sicily, one far larger than the one previously led by Laches and Eurymedon, with the intent of conquering the entire island if possible. Most Athenians, however, knew little of Sicily's vastness, nor of its many diverse inhabitants, both Greek and non-Greek. They underestimated the scale of the campaign, not realizing that they were about to embark on a war almost as challenging as the one they waged against the Peloponnesians. Sicily was immense—the journey around the island in a merchant ship took close to eight days.

Despite its size, it lay only two miles from the Italian mainland, barely separated by the sea.

The island's history and its settlers were varied. According to the earliest accounts, Sicily was first inhabited by the Cyclopes and the Laestrygones. However, I cannot specify what race they belonged to, where they came from, or where they eventually went. For that, I leave readers to rely on poetic tradition and popular legends. The Sicanians seem to have been the next group to settle on the island, though they claim they were the original inhabitants, the true natives of the land. However, evidence suggests they were Iberians, driven out by the Ligurians from the area around the river Sicanus in Iberia. Sicily was even named "Sicania" after them, replacing its earlier name of Trinacria, and they continue to inhabit the island's western regions to this day.

Later, following the fall of Troy, some Trojans who had escaped from the Achaeans arrived in Sicily by ship and settled near the Sicanians. They became known collectively as the Elymi, establishing towns called Eryx and Egesta. Alongside them were some Phocians who, after being driven off course by a storm, were carried first to Libya and then eventually to Sicily, where they joined the Elymi.

Another group, the Sicels, crossed over from Italy, fleeing from the Opicans, according to tradition. It's said they made the journey on rafts, timing their passage to match favorable winds blowing down the strait, though they may have used other methods of travel. Today, there are still Sicels in Italy, and the region got its name, "Italy," from Italus, a king of the Sicels. After crossing over in great numbers, the Sicels defeated the Sicanians in battle, forcing them to relocate to the southern and western parts of the island. With their arrival, the island's name changed from Sicania to Sicily. The Sicels claimed the richest lands, holding central and northern Sicily for almost three hundred years before any Greeks arrived. They continue to occupy those regions today.

Phoenician settlers also established themselves around the island, setting up trading posts on the promontories and small islands near the shore to conduct trade with the Sicels. However, as Greek settlers began to arrive in greater numbers, the Phoenicians abandoned most of these trading posts, consolidating their settlements at Motye, Soloeis, and Panormus near the Elymi. Their choice of location was partly due to the security offered by their alliance with the Elymi and partly because these areas were the closest points to Carthage, allowing easier travel between Carthage and Sicily.

These were the barbarian groups established in Sicily, as described. Among the Greeks, the first to arrive were the Chalcidians from Euboea, led by their founder Thucles. They founded the city of Naxos and built the altar dedicated to Apollo Archegetes, which stands outside the town even now. This altar is used by deputies for the games, who offer sacrifices on it before departing from Sicily. The following year, Archias, one of the Heraclids from Corinth, founded Syracuse. He began by driving the Sicels from the island where the inner city of Syracuse now stands—though this area is no longer surrounded by water. Over time, the outer town expanded within the city walls and became densely populated.

Meanwhile, Thucles and the Chalcidians left Naxos five years after Syracuse was founded, driving the Sicels out by force to establish the cities of Leontini and later Catana. The Catanians selected Evarchus as their founder. Around the same time, Lamis arrived in Sicily from Megara with a new colony. He initially founded a settlement called Trotilus, beyond the Pantacyas River. After leaving Trotilus, he joined the Chalcidians at Leontini for a short period, but they eventually expelled him. Following this, Lamis and his group founded Thapsus. Upon Lamis's death, his followers were driven out of Thapsus and founded the city known as the Hyblaean Megara. Hyblon, a Sicel king, invited them there and granted them land. The settlers lived in Hyblaean Megara for 245 years, until the Syracusan tyrant Gelo expelled them from both the city and the surrounding countryside. A century after they first settled there, however, they had sent out

Pamillus to establish Selinus, with assistance from Megara, their mother city.

Gela was founded by two leaders, Antiphemus from Rhodes and Entimus from Crete, who together led a colony to Sicily forty-five years after Syracuse was established. The town took its name from the Gelas River, and the location of its original fortified citadel was named Lindii. The institutions they adopted were Dorian in nature. About 108 years after Gela's foundation, the Geloans established the city of Acragas (later known as Agrigentum), named after the nearby river. They chose Aristonous and Pystilus as their founders and introduced their own political institutions to the new colony.

Zancle was originally founded by pirates from Cuma, a Chalcidian city in the land of the Opicans. Later, settlers from Chalcis and other parts of Euboea arrived and helped populate the area. The founders were Perieres from Cuma and Crataemenes from Chalcis. The city's original name, Zancle, was given by the Sicels, inspired by its sickle-like shape (the Sicilian word for sickle being "zanclon"). However, the original settlers were eventually expelled by a group of Samians and other Ionians who had come to Sicily, fleeing from the Persian invasion. Before long, the Samians were themselves expelled by Anaxilas, the tyrant of Rhegium. Anaxilas repopulated the city with a mixed community and renamed it Messina, after his own native region.

Each of these settlements contributed to the rich and complex patchwork of cultures and communities that came to define Sicily.

Himera was established by colonists from Zancle, led by Euclides, Simus, and Sacon. The majority of these settlers were Chalcidians, though they were joined by some exiled Syracusans called the Myletidae, who had been forced out of Syracuse after losing in a civil conflict. The spoken language in Himera became a blend of Chalcidian and Doric, but the city's institutions and customs followed the Chalcidian model. The Syracusans went on to found Acrae and Casmenae, establishing Acrae seventy years after Syracuse and founding Casmenae almost twenty years after Acrae. Later, they founded Camarina approximately 135 years after Syracuse's establishment, with Daxon and Menecolus as its leaders. However, after Camarina's revolt, the Syracusans forcefully expelled its inhabitants. Some years later, Hippocrates, the tyrant of Gela, received the territory of Camarina as ransom for a group of Syracusan prisoners and resettled the city, claiming himself as its founder. Eventually, Camarina was again depopulated by Gelo, only to be settled a third time by the Geloans.

These were the peoples—both Greek and non-Greek—inhabiting Sicily, an island of considerable size that the Athenians now aimed to invade. Their true ambition was to conquer the entire island, though they justified their actions by claiming they sought to assist their allies and kin. They were particularly spurred on by envoys from Egesta, who appealed to Athens with renewed urgency. Egesta had entered into conflict with its neighbors, the Selinuntines, over disputes involving marriage alliances and territorial boundaries. The Selinuntines, in turn, had formed an alliance with the powerful Syracusans, who began pressing Egesta aggressively by both land and sea.

The Egestaeans reminded the Athenians of the alliance formed during the previous Leontine war, when Laches had led Athenian forces. They urged Athens to intervene by sending a fleet to their aid. Among the arguments they presented, they stressed that if Syracuse went unpunished for depopulating Leontini and undermining Athens's remaining allies in Sicily, the Syracusans could eventually consolidate control over the entire island. Such a development, they argued, would pose a significant threat to Athens. If Syracuse grew strong enough, it could join forces with the Peloponnesians and other Dorian allies, thereby endangering Athenian dominance. Given that the Syracusans were also Dorians, they might one day come to aid their Dorian kin in the Peloponnese, as well as the very people who had originally founded their colony, with the ultimate aim of challenging Athenian power.

The Egestaeans thus urged the Athenians to support their allies in Sicily and take a stand against Syracuse. They further promised to fund the war effort, assuring Athens that they had sufficient financial resources for the campaign. These arguments were repeated regularly by the Egestaeans and their supporters at Athenian assemblies, until the Athenians finally voted to send envoys to Egesta. The mission was to confirm whether the Egestaeans truly possessed the wealth they claimed, stored in their treasury and temples, and to assess the current state of the conflict with Selinus.

The Athenian envoys were duly sent to Sicily, while in the same winter, the Lacedaemonians and their allies (excluding the Corinthians) launched a minor incursion into Argive territory. They caused limited destruction, seizing a few yokes of oxen and taking some corn. They also resettled the Argive exiles at Orneae, leaving behind a small garrison to protect them. Before departing, the Lacedaemonians arranged a truce that prohibited both the Orneatae and the Argives from harming each other's lands. Having made these arrangements, the Lacedaemonian forces returned home.

Shortly thereafter, the Athenians arrived with a fleet of thirty ships and a force of six hundred heavy infantry. Joined by the Argives, who mobilized all their forces, they marched to Orneae and laid siege to the garrison stationed there. The siege lasted one day, but the defenders managed to slip away during the night while the besiegers were camped at a distance. The next morning, realizing that the enemy had escaped, the Argives demolished Orneae and withdrew. The Athenians, having completed their mission, returned home by sea.

Meanwhile, the Athenians launched a separate operation, transporting some of their cavalry along with Macedonian exiles to Methone, near the Macedonian border, where they ravaged the territory of King Perdiccas. In response, the Lacedaemonians sent envoys to the Thracian Chalcidians, encouraging them to join Perdiccas in opposing Athens. The Chalcidians, however, declined, maintaining their truce with Athens, which renewed every ten days.

Thus ended the winter, along with the sixteenth year of the war chronicled by Thucydides.

With the arrival of spring, the Athenian envoys returned from Sicily, accompanied by representatives from Egesta, who brought with them sixty talents of uncoined silver to fund a month's pay for sixty Athenian ships they hoped would be dispatched to aid them. At the Athenian assembly, the Egestaeans and returning envoys gave a glowing—though inaccurate—report on the situation in Sicily, particularly regarding the wealth supposedly available in Egesta's temples and treasury. Persuaded by these accounts, the Athenians voted to send a fleet of sixty ships to Sicily. Command was entrusted to Alcibiades, son of Clinias; Nicias, son of Niceratus; and Lamachus, son of Xenophanes, who were granted full authority. Their orders were to assist Egesta against Selinus, restore Leontini if possible, and handle all other affairs in Sicily as they saw fit to benefit Athens.

Five days later, a second assembly was held to discuss the swift preparation of the fleet and to grant any additional resources requested by the generals. Nicias, however, who had been assigned command reluctantly and believed that the expedition was unwise, took the opportunity to address the assembly. He was concerned that Athens, spurred by superficial arguments, was embarking on an overly ambitious campaign to conquer all of Sicily—a daunting task.

Nicias began by urging the assembly to reconsider the entire expedition. Although the purpose of the meeting was to discuss preparations for sailing, he argued that they should first question whether it was wise to send the ships at all. He warned against hastily committing to a war that had no direct relevance to Athenian interests and allowing themselves to be swayed by the appeals of foreigners. While acknowledging that this expedition might bring him personal honor, he maintained that he was not speaking out of personal fear or self-interest. In his view, a man who looked after his own wellbeing was no less patriotic, since such a person would desire the success of his country for his own security as much as anyone.

Nicias insisted that he would not compromise his principles by speaking in favor of an enterprise he did not believe in, and he urged the assembly to value their existing possessions over the uncertain promise of new conquests. While he knew his words might seem ineffective against the strong current of Athenian ambition, he urged them to consider that their eagerness was ill-timed and that their aspirations might be more difficult to realize than they anticipated. He ended by urging caution and a sober assessment of their goals and resources.

"I maintain that by setting out for Sicily, you risk leaving behind many enemies here, only to gather more enemies abroad and bring them back with you. Perhaps you believe that our treaty can be relied upon, but that is a dangerous assumption. This so-called treaty remains in effect only so long as we stay quiet. It has become more symbolic than real, given the schemes of certain men both here and in Sparta. If we were to suffer a serious setback anywhere, our enemies would not hesitate for a moment to strike. Remember that this treaty was imposed on them after their own disaster, and it is less honorable for them than it is for us. Moreover, there are several unresolved issues within the treaty itself, and some of the most influential states have yet to formally accept it. Some of these cities remain openly hostile, while others are restrained only by truces renewed every ten days. Given these conditions, if our power is divided—as we are preparing to do by sending forces to Sicily—these states may join forces with the Sicilian cities and attack us with newfound vigor, seizing the opportunity presented by our divided focus.

"A wise leader should take these considerations seriously and not risk entangling a state already in a precarious position. It's reckless to reach for new territories before we've fully secured the ones we already hold. Recall that the Chalcidians in Thrace have been in rebellion for years, and we have yet to subdue them. Meanwhile, some of our allies on the mainland offer only uncertain loyalty. And here we are, rushing to help the Egestaeans, while the rebels who have wronged us for so long remain unpunished.

"Conquering Sicily, even if successful, would be a hollow victory. The Sicilians, due to their sheer numbers and distance from us, would be difficult, if not impossible, to keep under control. It is foolish to fight a people whom we could not effectively govern even if we defeated them, especially since a failure would leave us worse off than before. As for the Sicilian Greeks, if Syracuse were to dominate the island—despite the fears Egesta raises about that prospect—I believe they would actually be less of a threat to us than they are now. Currently, they could be tempted to join the Lacedaemonians as independent states. But as one consolidated power, they would be less likely to challenge us, knowing that the very allies they seek in the Peloponnesians could one day turn on them. By aiding in the destruction of our empire, they would simply invite their own downfall at the hands of those same allies. The Greeks in Sicily would likely fear us most if we stayed away entirely; their respect would diminish the moment we showed any sign of weakness by going there and then leaving in haste.

"We know that distant powers often inspire admiration precisely because they remain untested. But any setback we experience in Sicily would quickly erode that respect, and the Sicilians would then align with our enemies here to turn against us. You've already seen how this works: the Lacedaemonians and their allies, whom you once feared, became targets of your disdain after your unexpected victories. Emboldened by these successes, you now aim to conquer Sicily. Instead of letting the misfortunes of our rivals go to our heads, we should first work to break their resolve completely before allowing ourselves to feel secure. Consider that the disgrace the Lacedaemonians have endured only fuels their determination to regroup and redeem themselves. Military honor has always been their guiding principle, and their disgrace drives them to seek any chance to undermine us and restore their standing.

"So, if we're wise, our true priority should not be aiding the barbarian Egestaeans in Sicily. Our focus should be on defending ourselves as effectively as possible against the oligarchical ambitions of Lacedaemon."

"We should remember that we are only now enjoying a much-needed respite from a devastating plague and years of war—a relief that has greatly benefited both our lives and our properties. This peace should be used to strengthen our own interests here at home, rather than risking them on behalf of exiles who paint the best possible picture to suit their needs, who merely speak grandly but leave others to face the danger. If they succeed, they'll show no genuine gratitude, and if they fail, they'll bring ruin not only upon themselves but upon those who aided them.

"And if any man here—especially someone young, newly appointed to command, and eager for the glory of it—urges you toward this expedition for his personal gain, take heed. Perhaps such a person wishes to bolster his public image or gain admiration for his expensive horses and lifestyle, hoping this campaign might ease his financial burdens. Do not allow someone like this to pursue his private ambitions at the expense of the state. Such people harm the public fortune even as they exhaust their own. This matter is far too serious for a young man to decide or to rush into without forethought.

"I see men like these, sitting here beside the one who called this assembly, and I cannot help but feel alarmed. In response, I call upon any older men here, seated beside one of these ambitious figures, not to let themselves be intimidated or silenced out of fear of being seen as cowards if they vote against the war. Remember that success rarely comes from wishful thinking, but rather from careful planning. Let us not chase after this reckless dream of conquest. Instead, as true patriots who care for our state now facing unprecedented danger, let us stand firm against this motion. Let us agree to leave the Sicilian cities within the limits that now separate us—the Ionian Sea for the coastal voyage, and the Sicilian Sea across the open waters—allowing them to hold their territories and resolve their own disputes. Let the Egestaeans, who entered into conflict with the Selinuntines without

Athens's consultation, be advised to conclude their affairs independently. In the future, we should avoid alliances with those who can demand our help in their need, yet cannot offer us the same support when we need it.

"And you, Prytanis, if you truly care for the well-being of our city and wish to demonstrate good citizenship, I urge you to put this matter to a second vote and ask the people once more for their decision. If you are hesitant, fearing a breach of protocol, consider that with so many willing to second your action, no real penalty is likely to follow. Instead, you will serve as a physician to our misled city. Remember that the virtue of those in office is, in short, to bring as much benefit to the state as they can—or, at the very least, to do no harm."

Such were the words of Nicias. While a few Athenians argued in support of his view, the majority who spoke favored proceeding with the expedition and standing by their original decision. The most enthusiastic supporter of the campaign, however, was Alcibiades, son of Clinias, who not only sought to counter Nicias as his political rival but also resented the criticisms leveled against him in Nicias's speech. Moreover, Alcibiades harbored grand ambitions: he aspired to command an expedition that would bring Sicily and perhaps even Carthage under Athenian control, thereby increasing his own wealth and prestige through these achievements.

Alcibiades's standing among the citizens allowed him to live extravagantly, especially in maintaining his horses and indulging in other expenses beyond his means. This lifestyle eventually contributed to the downfall of Athens itself. Over time, the people, troubled by his excessive behavior, began to view him as a threat—a potential tyrant—and their mistrust grew. Though he managed public affairs effectively, his private conduct alienated many, prompting them to entrust the city's welfare to others, a decision that soon led to disastrous consequences.

At present, however, Alcibiades rose to address the assembly, offering the following counsel to the Athenians.

"Athenians, I have every right to command—let me begin there, as Nicias has singled me out—and I believe I am worthy of that command. The very things for which I am criticized bring honor to my family, to myself, and profit to our city. When the Greeks expected to see Athens ruined by the war, they instead found her even more magnificent than imagined, largely because of how I represented her at the Olympic Games. I entered seven chariots into the races, a feat no private citizen had attempted, and I won the first prize, while also securing second and fourth place. I ensured that every aspect of my presentation was grand and befitting of such a victory. These displays are considered honorable, and they leave a lasting impression of strength and prosperity.

"Even my displays of splendor here in Athens—providing choruses or other public contributions—may inspire envy among my fellow citizens, but to outsiders, they convey strength, just as my displays at Olympia did. This isn't idle vanity; it's a way to enhance Athens's reputation at my own expense, not just for my personal benefit but for the benefit of the city. It isn't unreasonable for someone in my position to distinguish himself from others. Misfortune is borne alone, as we know, and no one courts a man in adversity. By that same token, a person in prosperity should be able to accept the envy it brings. If anyone would demand equality with me, let them first ensure that everyone lives equally, then I might agree. But history shows that prominent figures, although sometimes disliked in their time, are later revered. Posterity eagerly claims connection with them, and their cities honor them not as strangers or troublemakers, but as national heroes and patriots.

"These are the ideals I aspire to, and even if some speak against me in private, I ask whether anyone here handles public matters more effectively than I do. I brought together the strongest cities in the Peloponnese without putting Athens at great risk or cost. I forced the

Lacedaemonians to stake their fate on a single day at the Battle of Mantinea; although they won that battle, their confidence has never fully recovered.

So, in my younger days, my so-called wild ideas found strong reasons to face the might of the Peloponnesians, and through my energy, I gained their trust and succeeded. Don't worry about my age now—while I'm still young and in my prime, and Nicias is doing well, make full use of both of us. Don't back down from your plan to sail to Sicily just because you're worried about facing a powerful force there. The cities in Sicily are made up of all kinds of people who quickly change their rules and adopt new ways of doing things. Since they lack a strong sense of loyalty to their land, they aren't well-armed and haven't settled down properly. Each person there thinks they can get something from the government either by clever words or by stirring up conflicts, and, if disaster strikes, they're prepared to just leave and settle somewhere else. With a population like this, you won't find unity or organized action. Most likely, they'll join us one by one if they're given a fair offer, especially if they're already divided by internal fights, as we've heard.

Besides, the Sicilian Greeks don't have as many heavily armed soldiers as they claim, just like the Greeks in general didn't turn out to be as numerous as each state thought, and Hellas greatly overestimated their numbers. From all I hear, the states in Sicily will be as I describe, and I haven't even mentioned all our advantages. Many non-Greek groups will likely join us, driven by their dislike of the Syracusans. Nor will the powers at home stop us, if we judge correctly. Our ancestors, with these very same opponents—and with the Persians against them too—were able to build an empire relying solely on their naval strength. The Peloponnesians have never had less hope of defeating us than now. Even if they are optimistic, though they're strong enough to invade our land if we stay here, they can't harm us at sea. We'll leave a navy behind that can match theirs.

Given all this, what reason could we have to hold back, or what excuse could we give to our allies in Sicily for not helping them? They're our allies, and we're obligated to help, without demanding that they help us first. We didn't bring them into our alliance so they could support us in Greece, but so they could trouble our enemies in Sicily and prevent them from coming over to attack us. That's how empires are built, both by us and by everyone else who has held one, through a willingness to support all—whether foreigners or Greeks—who ask for our help. If everyone just waited or carefully chose whom to help, we would make few new conquests and would risk losing the ones we already have. People don't just defend against a stronger enemy; they often make the first move to prevent the attack. And we can't decide the exact point where our empire should stop; we're in a position where we can't just hold onto what we have—we must work to expand it. If we stop ruling others, we risk being ruled ourselves. And we can't think of inactivity in the same way as others do unless we're willing to change our ways and become like them.

Be certain, then, that by going on this journey abroad, we'll actually strengthen our power back home. Let's carry out this expedition and show the Peloponnesians how little we care about the peace we're currently enjoying by setting sail for Sicily. This will either make us rulers, as we likely can be, of all of Greece by gaining the support of the Sicilian Greeks, or, at the very least, it will ruin the Syracusans, which will benefit both us and our allies. Our navy will allow us the choice to stay if we succeed or to return whenever we want since we'll have control over the sea against all the Sicilian cities combined. Don't let Nicias's strategy of doing nothing, or his efforts to pit the young against the old, sway you from your goal. Instead, in the way our ancestors did, let young and old come together in unity to push our success forward. Remember that neither youth nor age can achieve much alone, but together, youthful energy, mature caution, and careful planning are strongest. And if we fall into idleness, like anything that sits still too long, our city will wear down, and we'll lose our skill in everything we do. Each new challenge brings new knowledge and helps us learn to defend ourselves not just in words but in action. In short, I believe that a city as naturally active as ours would find no quicker way to ruin than to suddenly adopt a policy of inaction. The safest way to live is to stick as closely as possible to the character and values that define us.

These were the words of Alcibiades. After hearing him, as well as the Egestaeans and some exiles from Leontini, who came forward to remind them of their oaths and ask for help, the Athenians became even more eager to go on the expedition than before. Nicias, realizing it was pointless to try to discourage them with his earlier arguments, thought he might still change their minds by showing just how costly the plan would be. He came forward once more and spoke as follows:

"I see, Athenians, that you're fully committed to this expedition, so I hope everything turns out as we wish. I'll now share my opinion about the situation. From what I've heard, we're preparing to face cities that are large, independent, and not looking to change. They wouldn't easily give up their freedom to accept our rule, nor are they in desperate circumstances that would make them welcome a change in leadership. To consider only the Greek cities, there are many on just this one island. Besides Naxos and Catana, who may join us because of their ties with Leontini, there are seven other cities that are armed and prepared much like we are, especially Selinus and Syracuse, the main targets of our mission. These cities are full of heavy infantry, archers, and light-armed soldiers. They have plenty of warships with large crews to man them, and they also have wealth, partly in private hands and partly in the temples of Selinus, as well as offerings from some of the non-Greek people at Syracuse. But their greatest strength over us lies in their large numbers of horses and in the fact that they grow their own grain at home, instead of relying on imports like we do.

To face a force like this, we can't rely on just a weak navy; we'll also need a large land army to go with us if we hope to achieve something worthy of our goals. Without enough ground troops, we risk being kept away by their many cavalry, especially if the cities unite against us. We can't depend only on the Egestaeans for horses to defend ourselves. It would be shameful to be forced to retreat or have to send back for reinforcements because we didn't plan properly from the start. Therefore, we need to set out with a strong enough force, as we're heading far from home on a mission unlike any in the past. In previous missions, we could rely on allies nearby in Greece, who could quickly send supplies if needed. But this time, we're cutting ourselves off and going to an entirely foreign land, where, for four winter months, it won't even be easy to send a messenger back to Athens.

So, I believe we should take a large number of heavy infantry, both from Athens and from our allies, not only from our subjects but also from anyone in the Peloponnese who will join us, whether for loyalty or pay. We also need many archers and slingers to counter the Sicilian cavalry. At the same time, we must have overwhelming naval strength to ensure we can bring in supplies easily. We should carry our own grain, like wheat and barley, in merchant ships, along with bakers paid to work for us, so that if we're delayed by weather, our troops won't go without food. Not every city will be able to provide for a force as large as ours. We should also bring every other supply we can, so we don't have to rely on others. Most importantly, we must take as much money as possible from Athens, as the wealth reportedly waiting for us in Egesta is probably more of a rumor than a reality.

Even if we leave Athens with forces nearly matching those of the enemy and surpassing them in some areas, it will still be challenging to conquer Sicily or even ensure our own safety. We shouldn't ignore the fact that we're going to a place full of strangers and potential enemies, and anyone taking on such a mission should expect to either take control of the territory as soon as he lands or face hostility from all sides. Because of this risk, and knowing that we'll need both wise decisions and a lot of luck—a difficult thing for any person to depend on—I want to be as prepared as possible before we sail. I aim to make our force as secure as it can be, which I believe is the best choice for Athens as a whole and for those of us going on this expedition. If anyone thinks otherwise, I am willing to hand over my command to them.

With this, Nicias finished speaking, hoping that the enormity of the preparations required would dampen the Athenians' enthusiasm, leading them to rethink the voyage. He thought that by highlighting the huge demands of the mission, he would either deter them altogether or, if they still insisted on proceeding, ensure that they went in the safest and best-prepared way possible. However, the Athenians reacted quite differently than he had anticipated. Instead of being put off by the grand scale of the undertaking, they felt even more excited and determined to go forward with it. Rather than taking his warnings as discouragement, they interpreted his advice as sound, believing that if the preparations were as thorough as he suggested, the journey would be exceptionally secure and successful.

Everyone seemed captivated by the allure of the expedition. The older men believed that with such a large and well-equipped force, they would either easily conquer the territories they planned to attack or, at the very least, avoid any kind of disaster. Those in the prime of life were eager for the adventure, yearning to see new lands and confident they would return home safely. For the common people and the soldiers, the excitement came from the prospect of immediate pay, coupled with the chance to expand their empire, which they imagined would provide them with a steady stream of wages and wealth in the future. The overwhelming enthusiasm of the majority silenced the few who harbored doubts or misgivings. These individuals, fearing that any opposition would make them seem unpatriotic, refrained from speaking out against the mission and instead kept their opinions to themselves.

At last, one of the Athenians stepped forward and directly addressed Nicias, urging him not to delay or offer any further excuses but to tell them openly what forces and resources he thought would be necessary for the expedition. Nicias, reluctant but recognizing the futility of further resistance, responded that he would need some time to discuss the details with his colleagues. Nevertheless, based on his initial judgment, he advised that they would need to set sail with at least one hundred warships. The Athenians should provide as many transport ships as they deemed necessary, with additional vessels to be requested from their allies. He estimated that they would need no fewer than five thousand heavily armed soldiers, both Athenian and allied, and ideally even more. The rest of the forces would need to be proportionate to this, including archers from both Athens and Crete, as well as slingers and any other specialized forces that might prove useful, all of which would be prepared under the generals' guidance.

Upon hearing Nicias's outline, the Athenians immediately agreed to grant full authority to the generals over all aspects of the expedition. They entrusted them with complete freedom to determine the size of the army and to manage the preparations as they saw fit, confident that this would best serve the interests of Athens. With this decision made, the preparations began in earnest. Messages were dispatched to allies, and rosters were drawn up at home. Having recently recovered from the ravages of the plague and the prolonged war, Athens now had a new generation of young men ready for service and a reserve of wealth accumulated during the truce, making it easier to gather the necessary resources for the expedition.

In the midst of these feverish preparations, a shocking event occurred that unsettled the city. One night, nearly all the stone Herms in Athens—customary squared statues with carved faces, placed at the doorways of houses and temples—were found with their faces defaced and mutilated. This act of desecration was both surprising and deeply troubling, as no one knew who had done it or why. In response, the city offered large public rewards to anyone who could identify the perpetrators. Additionally, it was decreed that anyone aware of any other sacrilegious acts should come forward with information without fear of retribution, whether they were a citizen, foreigner, or even a slave. The incident was taken very seriously, as it was considered an ill omen for the expedition. Many feared that it was not merely an isolated act of vandalism but part of a larger conspiracy aimed at overthrowing the democracy and sparking a revolution.

Accordingly, several resident aliens and household servants came forward with information, though not directly about the Hermae. Instead, they spoke of earlier acts of vandalism against other statues, which were reportedly damaged by a group of young men during drunken celebrations. They also mentioned instances of mock rituals supposedly imitating sacred ceremonies, held secretly in private homes. Among those accused of these acts was Alcibiades, and his involvement became a convenient opportunity for his enemies—those who could not bear his influence over the people and saw him as an obstacle to their ambitions. These adversaries seized on the accusations, exaggerating them and loudly insisting that the sacrilege against the Hermae and the mockery of the mysteries were deliberate steps in a plot to overthrow the democracy, all allegedly orchestrated by Alcibiades. They pointed to his bold and undisciplined lifestyle as supposed proof of his anti-democratic intentions.

Alcibiades immediately denied these charges, and even before departing on the expedition, he offered to stand trial to clear his name. He insisted that if he were found guilty, he should be punished; however, if proven innocent, he should retain his command without further impediment. He strongly objected to the idea of facing accusations in his absence, pleading with them to either execute him immediately if they truly believed he was guilty or else allow him to leave for the expedition with a clean slate. He also argued that it was unwise to send him to lead such a large force with serious charges unresolved, as such doubts could affect both him and the army's morale. But his opponents, aware that he would likely gain the support of the troops if tried right away, feared that the public would sympathize with him, especially since many already credited him with securing the support of the Argives and some of the Mantineans for the campaign. They worked to prevent his proposal from moving forward, presenting other speakers who argued that Alcibiades should not delay the army's departure and could instead face trial upon his return within a set timeframe. Their strategy was to have him recalled later for a trial on even graver charges, which they could more easily fabricate while he was away. As a result, it was decided that Alcibiades would indeed set sail as planned.

Shortly after, the fleet prepared to depart for Sicily, with the expedition set to launch in midsummer. Most of the allies, along with the grain transports, smaller vessels, and other support ships, had already been ordered to assemble at Corcyra, from where they would cross the Ionian Sea as a united force to reach the Iapygian promontory. On the appointed day, as dawn broke, the Athenians, along with any allies present, gathered at the port of Piraeus and began manning the ships in preparation for departure. Almost the entire population of the city came down to the harbor—citizens and foreigners alike. Each family from the countryside accompanied their own: friends, relatives, or sons. They walked alongside them, sharing both hopeful words and quiet fears, dreaming of the victories they wished their loved ones to achieve or worrying they might never see them return, given the long journey ahead. At this final moment, as they were about to part ways, the risks of the expedition became painfully real to many, more so than when they had initially voted in favor of it. Yet the impressive strength of the fleet and the lavish preparation of every aspect of the mission provided some comfort.

As for the foreigners and the larger crowd, they were drawn by the sheer spectacle. The fleet's assembly and the sight of such a formidable armament made for an awe-inspiring event, a scene that surpassed anything they had ever witnessed, almost seeming too grand to believe.

This fleet that set sail was by far the most elaborate and costly force that any single Greek city had ever sent out. In terms of sheer numbers of ships and heavy infantry, it wasn't greater than the fleet Pericles led against Epidaurus or the one Hagnon took against Potidaea, both of which had consisted of four thousand Athenian infantry, three hundred cavalry, and one hundred warships, with additional support from fifty Lesbian and Chian ships and many other allies. However, those previous expeditions had been prepared for shorter missions and were outfitted with far fewer supplies. This current force was designed for an extended campaign, both on land and at sea, and it was equipped to remain operational for as long as necessary.

The fleet's preparation involved great expense from both the state and individual captains. The state treasury paid each sailor a daily wage of one drachma, supplied empty ships, including sixty warships and forty transport vessels, and secured the most skilled crews available. Captains added their own incentives, offering bonuses beyond the state's pay to the rowers and crew, while also spending generously on decorative elements and specialized equipment for their ships. Each captain strove to make his vessel the most visually impressive and the fastest, creating a sense of friendly rivalry and driving everyone to ensure their ship was a model of elegance and speed.

Meanwhile, the land troops were chosen from the best rosters, each striving to ensure that their weapons and personal armor were well-maintained and of high quality. This generated a sense of pride and competition among the troops, both on land and at sea. As a result, the spectacle of this Athenian armament gave other Greeks the impression that this was not just a military expedition, but a grand display of Athenian power and wealth.

If someone were to calculate the full cost of the campaign, including both public funds and private investments, they would be astonished at the sheer amount of resources devoted to it. The state had already spent significant sums on initial preparations, and was now sending additional funds with the generals. Individual soldiers, traders, and ship captains had also invested heavily in their equipment, supplies, and additional funds to support themselves for a lengthy journey, far beyond the state-provided wages. Merchants and other travelers brought goods to trade, adding to the overall wealth being carried out of Athens. In total, many talents of silver and gold were leaving the city, making this venture famous not only for its boldness and visual splendor but also for the strength and ambition behind it. This was the farthest-reaching mission Athens had ever attempted, with the highest aims given the resources they had committed.

When the ships were fully manned and loaded with everything necessary for the expedition, a trumpet sounded, calling for silence. Instead of each ship performing prayers individually, the entire fleet joined together in a unified ceremony, led by the voice of a herald. Bowls of wine were prepared across the fleet, and the soldiers and officers poured libations from gold and silver cups. The crowds onshore—citizens, foreigners, and well-wishers alike—joined in the prayers, hoping for the expedition's success. After the hymn was sung and the ritual libations were completed, the fleet set out to sea. First, they organized in a line, then, in a show of excitement and competitive spirit, they raced one another as far as Aegina, each striving to outpace the other, before continuing on to Corcyra, where the rest of their allied forces were gathering in anticipation of the mission.

Chapter XIX

Seventeenth Year of the War—Parties at Syracuse—Story of Harmodius and Aristogiton—Disgrace of Alcibiades

Meanwhile, in Syracuse, news of the Athenian expedition began arriving from various sources, though few took it seriously at first. An assembly was held where different speakers took turns either supporting or dismissing the reports about the Athenians' plans. Among them, Hermocrates, son of Hermon, who believed he knew the truth, addressed the assembly with the following words:

"Although you may not believe me any more than those who have spoken before, and although I understand that people who share warnings often receive only skepticism and sometimes scorn, I cannot remain silent when I see our city at risk. I'm confident that I have more insight into the situation than most. Surprising as it may seem, the Athenians are indeed coming against us with a significant military and naval force. They claim to be supporting the Egestaeans and restoring Leontini, but their real objective is to conquer all of Sicily, starting with Syracuse. They believe that, if they capture our city, the rest of the island will soon fall under their control as well.

"Prepare yourselves, then, to see the Athenians arriving shortly, and focus on how best to defend against them with the resources we have. Don't be caught off guard by dismissing this news as exaggeration or allow doubt to lead you into neglecting the safety of the city. But those who do believe me shouldn't be frightened by the strength or audacity of the Athenians. They won't be able to do us more harm than we can do to them, and in fact, their large force could actually work to our advantage. The greater their numbers, the more alarmed the other Sicilian cities will be, and this fear may lead them to join us more readily.

"If we manage to defeat the Athenians or drive them away, thwarting their grand ambitions (for I am not at all concerned that they will succeed), it will be an extraordinary achievement for us. And in my opinion, this outcome is not at all unrealistic. History has shown that large forces, whether Greek or foreign, rarely succeed when they venture far from their homeland. Even if their numbers are vast, they cannot outmatch the combined strength of the people here in Sicily, along with neighboring regions, especially if we unite against them. If they end up struggling for resources in this foreign land, they may weaken themselves, and the credit for defending against them will go to us, even if their own overreach is the true cause of their difficulties.

"Consider, too, that it was precisely under similar circumstances that these Athenians rose to power after the Persian king's defeat. Athens became a celebrated city simply because it was the target of the Persian invasion, and chance played a significant role in that victory. There's no reason we cannot turn a similar fate to our advantage in this instance as well."

"Let us, therefore, begin our preparations here with firm resolve. We must reach out to some of the Sicels, confirming their loyalty and securing alliances, while persuading others to join us. We should also send envoys across Sicily to make clear that this threat affects us all and send messages to Italy, urging them to join us or at the very least refuse any cooperation with the Athenians. It may also be wise to reach out to Carthage; they are certainly aware of the risk the Athenians could pose to them someday and might see the danger to Sicily as a warning of their own possible future. The Carthaginians may not act openly, but they may help us quietly, in one form or another, since they have abundant resources, especially in gold and silver, which power wars as it powers all other things. With their wealth, they are better positioned than most to lend support if they choose.

"We must also reach out to Lacedaemon and Corinth, asking them to come to our aid as quickly as possible and to continue pressing the war in Greece. However, in my opinion, the best course of action, though it may not be readily accepted by our peace-minded nature, is something I must bring up regardless. If we Sicilian Greeks, united or at least with as many allies as we can muster, launch our entire navy, bring enough provisions for two months, and meet the Athenians at Tarentum and the Iapygian promontory, we could force them to fight just for the right to cross the Ionian Sea before they even reach Sicily. Such a move would unsettle their forces, making them realize that we have a strong defensive position at Tarentum, ready to receive us, while they face the risk of crossing a wide sea with their massive fleet, struggling to keep formation over such a long journey. This would make them vulnerable to our attacks if they drift into smaller, isolated groups.

"Furthermore, if they decide to lighten their ships and gather their fastest vessels to confront us, we could either strike them when they are worn from rowing or, if it suits us better, retreat to Tarentum. They, meanwhile, would be stranded with limited provisions brought solely for a quick battle, which would leave them in a difficult position in barren lands. They would either face a siege or be forced to hug the coast, abandoning part of their fleet and growing further disheartened by the uncertainty of whether any cities will even accept them. I believe that such an approach alone might deter them from even departing from Corcyra. Faced with the need to scout our numbers and locations, they would waste time until winter arrived or, overwhelmed by the unexpected, would abandon the expedition altogether—especially since their most capable general is reportedly reluctant to lead this campaign and would likely seize any credible reason to turn back if faced with a serious show of force from us.

"Our presence would also be amplified by rumor, I am sure, as they would hear exaggerated accounts of our numbers, and fear would naturally grow from these reports. There is a powerful psychological effect in being the first to show resistance; those prepared to stand and defend themselves inspire greater fear because their readiness signals determination. This would be exactly the case with the Athenians now. They come against us assuming that we will not fight back, likely judging us harshly for not aiding the Lacedaemonians against them before. But if they encounter a surprising level of resolve from us, they will be shaken, not by our actual strength, but by the unexpected show of courage.

"I strongly urge you to embrace this spirit, but if that's not possible, then do not delay any further in preparing comprehensively for war. Remember that the best way to show contempt for an enemy is through bravery in action. For now, the most sensible approach is to let our preparations reflect the seriousness of the threat, as this offers the best assurance of safety. We must act as though the danger is imminent. I am fully convinced that the Athenians are coming to attack us; indeed, they are already on their way and nearly upon us."

These were the words of Hermocrates. Meanwhile, the people of Syracuse found themselves deeply divided. Some argued that the Athenians would never come and that Hermocrates's warnings were baseless. Others asked what real harm the Athenians could do that the Syracusans wouldn't repay them tenfold if they dared to attack. Some took the entire affair as little more than a joke, mocking the idea of an

Athenian invasion. In short, only a few among them took Hermocrates's warning seriously or felt any real concern about the future. Amidst this debate, Athenagoras, who was the popular leader and held considerable influence among the people, stood up to speak and offered the following response:

"For my part, when it comes to the Athenians, anyone who doesn't hope they'll be as misguided as these rumors suggest, or that they might come here only to be subdued by us, is either a coward or a traitor. As for those spreading these alarming stories, I'm more struck by their foolishness than their boldness, if they truly think we can't see through their intentions. The truth is, they have their own private fears and hope to unsettle the entire city, thinking that if everyone is scared, their own anxieties will go unnoticed. In short, these reports have no credibility; they don't emerge naturally but are invented by people who constantly stir up unrest in Sicily. If you're wise, you won't base your decisions on the claims of these people, but instead, you'll consider what rational men, with a real understanding of matters—like I believe the Athenians to be—would logically do.

"Now, it's highly improbable that the Athenians would leave the Peloponnesians behind them, with the war in Greece not even concluded, only to start a new conflict of equal difficulty here in Sicily. In my view, they're likely just relieved that we haven't gone to attack them ourselves, given that we are a collection of large and powerful cities. But let's say, for argument's sake, that they do come, as some say they will. I believe Sicily is much better equipped to endure a war than the Peloponnesians ever were, and our city alone is more than a match for this so-called invading army, even if it were twice as large.

"I know that they won't have any cavalry with them—only perhaps a handful of horses from the Egestaeans, if that. Nor could they bring enough heavy infantry to match ours, especially since their ships will already be hard-pressed to make it all the way here, even if they're traveling light. And that's without mentioning all the other supplies they would need to maintain a campaign against a city as formidable as ours, which would require no small quantity of resources. In fact, my confidence is so strong that I don't see how they could hope to avoid complete defeat even if they somehow brought along an entire city as large as Syracuse and tried to establish a base on our borders. And yet they imagine they can succeed with all of Sicily set against them, bringing only a makeshift camp of tents and bare essentials, from which they wouldn't dare venture far due to the threat posed by our cavalry.

"But the Athenians, as I have every reason to believe, are focused on safeguarding their interests back home, while people here are fabricating stories that have no basis in truth and never will. This isn't the first time I've seen these individuals, unable to act through real deeds, resort to spreading false reports and even worse rumors to intimidate you and seize control of the government. This pattern repeats itself time and again. I fear that, if they keep trying, they may eventually succeed, especially if we fail to take action while these schemes are still in their infancy. If we wait until the offenders are known and only then attempt to counter them, it may be too late. Consequently, our city rarely finds peace, facing as many internal disputes as external threats, with occasional fits of tyranny and disgraceful conspiracies in the mix.

"However, with your support, I will do all in my power to prevent this from happening in our time. My goal is to win the trust of you— the majority—and to bring those who plot such mischief to justice, not only when caught red-handed, which can be difficult, but even for harboring such ambitions. For if we wish to be safe, we must punish an enemy not only for what he does but also for what he plans to do. The first to let down their guard are always the first to suffer the consequences. I will keep a close eye on these few and hold them accountable, not merely for their actions but also for their intentions, warning them as needed. This approach, in my view, is the most effective way to turn them from their harmful paths.

"And tell me, as I have asked before, what is it that you seek, young men? Do you wish to hold office immediately? The law forbids it—and not to demean you, but because it recognizes that experience is necessary before leadership. Do you feel insulted by not being considered equal under the law to the broader population? Yet, how can it be right for every citizen, despite differences in readiness or experience, to have the same privileges? The laws were made for good reason, to ensure that those governing are equipped to do so effectively.

"Some might say that democracy is neither wise nor fair and that only those with wealth are suited to rule. But I argue the opposite: the very essence of democracy is that it includes everyone in the state, whereas oligarchy represents only a small faction. True, the rich may best guard property, and the wise may offer the soundest advice, but only the broader populace can fully hear and judge matters fairly. In a democracy, each of these talents—of wealth, wisdom, and fair judgment—finds its rightful place, individually and together. An oligarchy, on the other hand, shares the risks with the majority but keeps all the benefits for itself. This is precisely what some of you, particularly the powerful and ambitious among the young, aspire to achieve, though it's impossible to realize such ambitions in a great city like ours."

"Even now, you foolish men—the most senseless among the Greeks I know—if you truly do not grasp the wickedness of your plans, or worse, if you do understand it and still pursue it, you are either reckless or outright criminal. But even now, if you cannot bring yourselves to regret your actions, at least learn from reason and turn your energy toward benefiting the country. Remember that the prosperity of the country benefits everyone, including those among you with ambition and ability, who stand to gain more from its success than the average citizen. But if you continue with these other plans, you risk losing everything. Abandon these rumors and falsehoods; the people see your intentions clearly and won't tolerate them. If the Athenians arrive, this city will meet them with the strength and pride it is known for. We have generals who will manage this situation well. If, as I believe, these reports turn out to be baseless, then the city won't be panicked into a needless submission to those who seek to rule over it. Instead, the city will investigate these claims carefully and judge your words as if they were actions. Rather than surrendering its freedom by listening to you, the city will safeguard it, ensuring it always has the means to command respect."

These were the words of Athenagoras. At this point, one of the generals stood up and put a stop to further debate, offering these words regarding the issue at hand: "It does not benefit us to engage in personal attacks or to encourage our people to listen to accusations against one another. Instead, we should focus on the reports we've received and consider how each of us, individually and collectively, can best prepare the city to defend itself. Even if there is no threat, there is no harm in ensuring that the city is well-stocked with horses, arms, and all the necessities of war. We will manage this, organizing and inspecting these provisions, while also reaching out to other cities to gather intelligence and address any further preparations that seem necessary. Some of these actions are already underway, and we will keep you informed of any developments."

After these words, the Syracusans dispersed from the assembly.

Meanwhile, the Athenians, along with all their allied forces, had reached Corcyra. Here, the Athenian generals conducted another review of the fleet and organized the order of anchoring and encampment. To ensure smoother logistics, they divided the entire fleet into three sections, assigning one to each general. This division was intended to avoid the logistical strain of moving all the ships at once, which could lead to shortages of water, food, or space at the ports they would stop at. By having each division under a separate commander, the fleet would remain better organized and easier to manage.

They then dispatched three ships to Italy and Sicily to determine which cities might be open to receiving them, instructing these scouts to meet the main fleet along the route and provide updates before any landings.

Following these preparations, the Athenians set out from Corcyra and began the journey to Sicily. The fleet now consisted of 134 galleys in total, along with two additional Rhodian vessels with fifty oars each. Of these, 100 ships were Athenian, including 60 warships and 40 troop carriers, while the rest came from Chios and other allied states. The army comprised 5,100 heavy infantry, including 1,500 Athenian citizens from the military rolls and 700 Athenian Thetes serving as marines, with the remainder made up of allied forces, some of whom were Athenian subjects. Among them were 500 Argives and 250 Mantineans, both groups serving as paid troops. Additionally, the force included 480 archers, 80 of whom were Cretans; 700 slingers from Rhodes; 120 light-armed exiles from Megara; and a single horse transport carrying 30 horses.

With this formidable force, the Athenians embarked on their campaign, ready to cross to Sicily and face whatever awaited them.

Such was the impressive force of the first armament that sailed to Sicily for the war. Thirty cargo ships, loaded with grain and carrying the necessary personnel—bakers, stonemasons, carpenters, along with the tools to build fortifications—accompanied the fleet, along with one hundred smaller boats requisitioned for service. In addition, numerous other boats and trade ships joined voluntarily, seizing the opportunity to conduct business along the way. This entire convoy departed Corcyra, making a coordinated crossing of the Ionian Sea.

The fleet landed at the Iapygian promontory and Tarentum, then proceeded along the Italian coast. The Italian cities generally closed their markets and gates against them, offering only the most basic hospitality—water and permission to anchor briefly. Tarentum and Locri were even more resistant, providing no assistance at all. Eventually, the fleet arrived at Rhegium, the farthest point of Italy. Here, though they weren't permitted within the city walls, they set up camp just outside in the sacred precinct of Artemis, where a market was established for their provisions. They pulled their ships ashore and rested, maintaining a cautious peace as they opened negotiations with the Rhegians. They appealed to them as fellow Chalcidians, urging them to support their Leontine allies. The Rhegians, however, declined to take sides, stating that they would wait to see the stance of the other Italian cities and align with the general consensus.

With this response, the Athenians began considering their next moves for the Sicilian campaign, but they first awaited the return of the ships sent ahead to Egesta to confirm whether the promised funds were indeed available, as reported by the Athenian messengers.

In the meantime, solid reports reached the Syracusans from various sources, including scouts they had sent to gather intelligence. The news confirmed that the Athenian fleet was stationed at Rhegium. Faced with this undeniable proof, the Syracusans abandoned their skepticism and threw themselves wholeheartedly into preparations. They organized guard patrols and sent envoys to the Sicels to secure their support. They stationed garrisons at strategic posts across the countryside, reviewed the city's horses and weaponry, and ensured that every essential was in order for a war that could break out at any moment.

Soon, the three ships returned from Egesta to Rhegium with disheartening news: rather than the large sums of money promised, only thirty talents could actually be produced. The generals felt a significant blow at this early setback, compounded by Rhegium's refusal to join the expedition, despite being the first city they had approached and the one they expected to support them the most, given its kinship with the Leontines and longstanding friendship with Athens. While Nicias had anticipated this disappointing news, his two colleagues were completely taken aback.

The Egestaeans had used a clever deception to mislead the initial Athenian envoys sent to verify their resources. When these envoys visited, the Egestaeans brought them to the temple of Aphrodite at Eryx, where they displayed a collection of silver treasures—bowls, wine-ladles, censers, and many other items—that created an impression of far greater wealth than their true worth. They also went further by privately hosting the crews of the Athenian ships, gathering all the gold and silver cups available in Egesta and borrowing others from neighboring Phoenician and Greek towns. Each host presented these items as though they were his own, and, with everyone displaying similar valuables at these gatherings, the effect was dazzling. The Athenian sailors returned to Athens full of stories about the riches they had witnessed.

However, when word spread that Egesta could not provide the promised funds, the soldiers turned their ire on those among them who had been fooled by this spectacle and had, in turn, convinced others.

Meanwhile, the generals gathered to discuss their next steps. Nicias argued that their best course was to head directly to Selinus, the primary target of the campaign. Upon arrival, they could assess whether the Egestaeans were able to fund the entire force as initially promised. If the Egestaeans could not, they should at least be expected to provide provisions for the 60 ships they specifically requested. With this support, they could attempt to resolve the conflict between the Egestaeans and the Selinuntines, either by force or negotiation. Following this, Nicias proposed that they sail along the coast, stopping at other cities to showcase Athenian power, reinforcing their commitment to allies, and, if feasible, finding ways to aid the Leontines or sway other cities to their side. Then, they would return to Athens without risking undue losses or exhausting Athenian resources in a prolonged campaign.

Alcibiades countered, insisting that a mission of this scale should not end in retreat without significant achievements. He proposed that they send envoys to every city except Selinus and Syracuse, working to incite the Sicels to rebel against Syracuse and secure alliances with others to gain access to supplies and reinforcements. According to Alcibiades, their first priority should be securing Messina, strategically positioned at Sicily's entry point. Messina would offer an ideal harbor and base for their operations. Once they had a clear sense of which cities would stand by them, they could move to attack Syracuse and Selinus. In Alcibiades' view, only if Selinus reached a peaceful resolution with Egesta and Syracuse ceased its opposition to the Leontines should they consider refraining from conflict.

Lamachus offered a third perspective, arguing for an immediate and direct strike on Syracuse. He reasoned that they should engage Syracuse under the city's very walls while its people were still unprepared and the initial panic was intense. Armies at their first arrival tend to inspire the greatest fear; if too much time passed without action, the enemy's courage would recover, and the initial threat would lose its edge. By striking while Syracuse was still shaken by their presence, the Athenians would have the highest chance of achieving victory and instilling deep terror in the Syracusans through the sheer display of their numbers. No other moment would appear as intimidating to the enemy, and the immediate danger of battle would heighten the psychological impact. They might also catch many Syracusans in the surrounding fields, still unconvinced of their imminent arrival. At such a time, as the enemy scrambled to bring their belongings into the city, the Athenians would find ample plunder if they deployed with full force before the city.

By taking swift action, Lamachus argued, they would make the other Sicilian states less likely to side with Syracuse, persuading them instead to join the Athenians without waiting to see who emerged stronger. He proposed making Megara, an uninhabited location not far from Syracuse by land or sea, their naval base—a strategic position both for retreat and for launching attacks on Syracuse.

After speaking in this manner, Lamachus ultimately supported Alcibiades' plan. Alcibiades then set out on his own ship to Messina to propose an alliance but met with refusal; the Messinians replied that they could not allow him inside their city walls, though they would set up a market for him outside. With this, Alcibiades returned to

Rhegium. Upon his return, the generals organized a fleet of sixty ships from the larger force, provisioning them with supplies, and set sail along the coast toward Naxos, leaving the remainder of the fleet and one general stationed at Rhegium. Welcomed by the Naxians, they continued on to Catana. However, the Catanian inhabitants denied them entry, as a pro-Syracusan faction held influence within the city, so the fleet proceeded to the Terias River. There, they made camp overnight and the next day sailed in single file toward Syracuse with all their ships, except for ten which they sent ahead to enter the Great Harbor. These advance ships were instructed to scout for any enemy fleet and to announce, by a herald on board, that the Athenians had arrived to restore the Leontines to their homeland, as allies and kin of Athens. The proclamation encouraged any Leontines residing in Syracuse to leave without fear and join the Athenians, their friends and supporters. After delivering this message and surveying the city, its harbors, and the surrounding areas that could serve as operational bases in the war, they returned to Catana.

An assembly was then held in Catana, where the inhabitants again declined to admit the main Athenian force but invited the generals to enter and present their case. While Alcibiades was addressing the assembly, and the citizens were fully engaged in the proceedings, Athenian soldiers took advantage of the distraction, breaking through an inadequately barricaded side gate and slipping unnoticed into the town, where they quickly gathered in the marketplace. The pro-Syracusan faction, small in number, was alarmed at the sight of the Athenian soldiers within the city and withdrew. With this group gone, the remaining Catanian citizens voted in favor of an alliance with the Athenians, inviting them to bring the rest of their forces from Rhegium. The Athenians then sailed back to Rhegium, collected their full armament, and returned to Catana, where they immediately set to work establishing their camp.

Meanwhile, they received word from Camarina, suggesting that the town might join them if they arrived there. They also learned that Syracuse was preparing a fleet. In response, the Athenians sailed along the coast toward Syracuse with their entire armament to investigate. Upon reaching Syracuse, however, they found no fleet being prepared, so they continued along the coastline to Camarina, anchoring along the shore. They sent a herald to the Camarinaeans, but the city refused them entry, explaining that their oaths allowed them to admit only a single Athenian vessel unless they requested more. Frustrated, the Athenians sailed back along the coast. Along the way, they landed to raid Syracusan territory but suffered some losses among their light infantry when Syracusan cavalry arrived to defend the area. After this encounter, they returned to their camp at Catana.

Upon returning to Catana, the Athenians found that the Salaminia, a state ship from Athens, had arrived with orders for Alcibiades. He was commanded to sail back to Athens to face charges, along with several other soldiers accused of sacrilege in connection with the mysteries and the mutilation of the Hermae. After the departure of the expedition, the Athenians had been relentless in their investigation into these sacrilegious acts. Their heightened suspicion led them to accept any accusation without thorough scrutiny, arresting and imprisoning some of the city's most esteemed citizens on the testimony of questionable informers. The popular mood favored a thorough inquiry, with many preferring to risk questioning reputable individuals rather than allowing anyone potentially guilty to go unpunished, simply due to the unreliability of the accusers.

The people's wariness stemmed from their collective memory of the oppressive tyranny under Pisistratus and his sons, and they remembered how this rule had only ended thanks to the intervention of the Lacedaemonians—not through their own efforts or the actions of Harmodius and Aristogiton, as popular legend suggested. This constant awareness kept them in a state of vigilance, prompting them to treat anything suspicious with the utmost seriousness.

In fact, the well-known act of Aristogiton and Harmodius had its origins in a personal dispute rather than purely political motives, as I will explain here to show that the Athenians, like others, often misinterpret their own history and rulers. Pisistratus ruled Athens as tyrant until his death, after which his eldest son, Hippias, succeeded him, contrary to the common belief that Hipparchus held power. At the time, Harmodius was celebrated for his youthful beauty, and Aristogiton, a middle-class citizen, was his devoted lover. When Hipparchus, son of Pisistratus, approached Harmodius with romantic intentions, Harmodius rejected him. Harmodius shared this with Aristogiton, who grew furious and, fearing that Hipparchus might attempt to seize Harmodius by force, began plotting to overthrow the tyranny within the limits of his means.

Unsuccessful in winning over Harmodius after a second attempt, Hipparchus refrained from using force but decided to humiliate Harmodius in a subtle manner. In truth, the Pisistratid rule was not harsh or oppressive toward the general populace; rather, they promoted wisdom and virtue and were moderate in their demands, collecting only a twentieth of citizens' income. They adorned the city with splendid monuments, waged wars, and offered sacrifices in the temples. Most civic institutions continued as before, with the only major alteration being that key offices were held by members of Pisistratus's family.

During one of the family's terms in the annual archonship, Pisistratus, son of Hippias and grandson of the original tyrant, dedicated two altars: one in the marketplace to the Twelve Gods and another to Apollo in the Pythian precinct. Although the altar in the marketplace was later expanded by the Athenians, obscuring its original inscription, the inscription in the Pythian precinct remains partially visible and reads:

Pisistratus, the son of Hippias,

Sent up this record of his archonship

In precinct of Apollo Pythias.

I assert confidently, based on careful accounts, that Hippias was the eldest son of Pisistratus and thus the primary heir to power. This is evident from the records; Hippias appears to be the only legitimate son who had children. Inscriptions on the Athenian Acropolis recall the crimes of the tyrants, mentioning five children of Hippias by his wife Myrrhine, daughter of Callias, son of Hyperechides, but none for Thessalus or Hipparchus, supporting the idea that Hippias, as the eldest, would have been the first to marry.

Furthermore, Hippias's name consistently appears first on the commemorative pillar, directly after his father's, naturally positioning him as the eldest and reigning tyrant. It is unlikely that Hippias could have assumed power so smoothly had Hipparchus been in command at the time of his assassination, as he would have had to establish authority from scratch on that very day. However, he had long held control over the citizens and had experience commanding mercenaries, which allowed him to solidify his rule with ease, unlike a younger sibling without experience in authority. Ironically, it was Hipparchus's tragic fate that led future generations to mistakenly credit him with the title of tyrant.

To continue with the story of Harmodius: after Hipparchus's advances were rejected, he decided to insult Harmodius as planned. First, he invited Harmodius's sister, a young girl, to carry a basket in an important procession—a high honor in Athenian society. Then, at the last minute, he denied her participation, publicly claiming she had never been invited and was unworthy. This slight outraged Harmodius, and Aristogiton, who was already deeply invested for Harmodius's sake, became even more enraged. Together, they began laying plans with a small circle of conspirators, choosing to strike during the great Panathenaea festival, the only day when citizens could legally carry arms in the procession without arousing suspicion. The plan was for Harmodius and Aristogiton to make the first move against the tyrant's bodyguard, with their accomplices following immediately. Though their group was small for security reasons, they believed their example would inspire others present to rise up and reclaim their freedom.

When the day of the festival finally arrived, Hippias and his bodyguard were outside the city in the Ceramicus, arranging the procession. Harmodius and Aristogiton, with daggers hidden and ready, were prepared to act. But suddenly, they saw one of their fellow conspirators conversing casually with Hippias, who was known for his accessibility. They immediately feared their plan was exposed and that their arrest was imminent. Driven by a desire for vengeance, especially against Hipparchus, who had humiliated them and provoked this entire scheme, they decided to act recklessly and entered the gates, heading toward him. They found Hipparchus near the Leocorium and, in a fit of fury—Aristogiton fueled by love and Harmodius by the insult inflicted on his family—they struck him down, killing him on the spot. In the commotion that followed, Aristogiton initially escaped but was eventually captured and executed with little mercy, while Harmodius was killed immediately.

Upon receiving word of the assassination, Hippias, who was still in the Ceramicus, did not rush to the scene. Instead, he headed straight for the armed citizens in the procession, who were at a distance and unaware of what had just happened. Composing himself so as not to betray any alarm, he instructed them to move to a specific location without their weapons, giving the impression he had something important to announce. Once they had gathered, he ordered the mercenaries to confiscate their arms, then selectively arrested those he suspected of being part of the plot or anyone found carrying daggers, as the traditional weapons for the procession were the shield and spear.

Thus, it was a combination of wounded pride and sudden fear that led Harmodius and Aristogiton to act rashly, igniting a conspiracy that would change Athenian history. In the aftermath, Hippias tightened his control over the city, now more suspicious and fearful of his people. He executed many citizens and began preparing for an eventual escape should a revolution arise. Though he was Athenian by birth, Hippias arranged for his daughter, Archedice, to marry Aeantides, son of the tyrant of Lampsacus, as they held significant influence with King Darius of Persia. Archedice's tomb remains in Lampsacus, bearing this inscription:

"Archedice lies buried in this earth,

Hippias her sire, and Athens gave her birth;

Unto her bosom pride was never known,

Though daughter, wife, and sister to the throne."

Hippias continued to rule Athens for three more years but was deposed in the fourth by the Lacedaemonians, aided by the exiled Alcmaeonidae. He fled to Sigeum and later to Lampsacus, with the protection of Aeantides, and ultimately sought refuge at the court of King Darius. Twenty years later, in his old age, he returned with the Persian army, accompanying them to Marathon, a final chapter in his long and tumultuous life.

With these events weighing heavily on their minds, and recalling rumors and stories they'd heard, the Athenians became increasingly distrustful and suspicious of those implicated in the mysteries scandal. Convinced that these incidents were part of a larger conspiracy aimed at establishing an oligarchy or monarchy, public sentiment grew increasingly hostile. Many prominent citizens had already been imprisoned, and instead of calming, the public's fury continued to rise, resulting in more arrests each day. Eventually, one of the prisoners— believed to be the most deeply involved—was persuaded by a fellow detainee to confess. Whether his admission was true remains uncertain, as even to this day no one has definitively determined who committed the acts. Nevertheless, this fellow prisoner argued that, guilty or not, it would be wiser for him to confess and seek clemency, thereby freeing the state from its cloud of suspicions. He suggested that a confession, under promise of immunity, would be far safer than facing a trial under such conditions.

Following this counsel, the prisoner confessed, implicating himself and several others in the desecration of the Hermae. The Athenians, relieved to have finally uncovered what they believed to be the truth, released him and all those he hadn't named, while bringing the accused to trial. Those captured were executed, and those who had fled were condemned to death in absentia, with rewards offered for their capture. Although it remained unclear if these individuals had truly been guilty, the city as a whole felt a palpable sense of relief.

Meanwhile, public sentiment toward Alcibiades grew even more hostile, driven by the same enemies who had opposed him before he left. Now, with the Athenians believing they had uncovered the truth about the Hermae, they were more convinced than ever that Alcibiades was also behind the affair of the mysteries, seeing both as linked in a plot against the democracy. At this tense moment, a small force of Lacedaemonians advanced as far as the Isthmus, supposedly coordinating with the Boeotians. This movement was interpreted by the Athenians as further evidence of Alcibiades's guilt; many believed the Lacedaemonians had come on his invitation to support a planned coup. Fearing betrayal, the Athenians became so alarmed that some citizens even spent a night armed in the Temple of Theseus within the city walls.

Suspicion spread even to Alcibiades's friends in Argos, who were accused of plotting against the democratic government there. In response, the Athenians handed over the Argive hostages held on the islands to the Argive authorities, who promptly executed them. All around, new suspicions seemed to arise against Alcibiades, convincing the Athenians that he must be tried and, if found guilty, executed. They sent the state ship Salaminia to Sicily to summon Alcibiades and others implicated to return and face trial. Importantly, the instructions were not to arrest him but to command his return, avoiding any disruption among the troops or giving the enemy cause to capitalize on the instability. The Athenians also hoped to retain the support of the Mantineans and Argives, who were believed to have joined due to Alcibiades's influence.

Alcibiades, along with his accused companions, embarked on his own ship and sailed with the Salaminia from Sicily, appearing to comply with the summons. However, once they reached Thurii, he and his companions slipped away, fearing the harsh prejudice awaiting them in Athens. The Salaminia's crew searched for them in Thurii for some time, but finding no trace of them, they finally set sail back to Athens. Now a fugitive, Alcibiades crossed from Thurii to the Peloponnese in a small boat. The Athenians, upon hearing of his escape, passed a sentence of death in absentia on Alcibiades and his associates.

Chapter XX

Seventeenth and Eighteenth Years of the War—Inaction of the Athenian Army—Alcibiades at Sparta—Investment of Syracuse

The Athenian generals remaining in Sicily now divided their forces into two groups, each commander taking one part by lot, and together they set out for Selinus and Egesta. Their aims were to assess whether the Egestaeans would fulfill their promises of financial support and to investigate the nature of the conflict between Selinus and Egesta. Sailing along the Sicilian coast, with the shoreline to their left toward the Tyrrhene Gulf, they stopped at Himera, the only Greek city on that part of the island. When the Himerans denied them entry, they continued their journey. Along the way, they seized Hyccara, a small Sicanian coastal town that was at war with Egesta, enslaving the inhabitants and handing over the town to the Egestaeans, some of whose cavalry had joined the Athenians. The Athenian army then traveled overland through Sicel territory toward Catana, while their fleet sailed along the coast with the enslaved captives on board.

Meanwhile, Nicias proceeded directly from Hyccara to Egesta, where he completed his assigned tasks and received a sum of thirty talents before reuniting with the rest of the forces. They sold the captives, earning an additional one hundred and twenty talents, and then sailed to their Sicel allies to encourage them to send reinforcements. Meanwhile, half of the Athenian force advanced on the hostile town of Hybla in Gela's territory, though they were unsuccessful in capturing it.

As summer ended, the Athenians began preparing for an offensive against Syracuse, while the Syracusans readied themselves to march out against the invaders. When the Athenians failed to launch an immediate assault, as the Syracusans had initially feared, the Syracusan confidence grew with each passing day. Observing the Athenians journeying far away to other parts of Sicily and even failing to take Hybla, the Syracusans grew bolder and began mocking the Athenians. They urged their own generals to lead them to Catana, since the Athenians seemed reluctant to face them at Syracuse. Syracusan cavalry regularly rode close to the Athenian camp, taunting them and asking if they had really come to settle in foreign lands instead of restoring the Leontines to their homeland.

Noting these developments, the Athenian generals devised a plan to lure the Syracusan forces out of their city. Their goal was to draw the Syracusans as far from the city as possible, then sail along the coast by night to seize a favorable position unopposed. They knew that attempting a direct landing under the Syracusan forces' watch or advancing by land openly would leave them vulnerable to the Syracusan cavalry, a force they themselves lacked. In a face-to-face battle, the Syracusan horse could easily harass their light troops and supporting personnel. However, if they could establish a position near the Olympieum, as some Syracusan exiles in the Athenian army had suggested, they could neutralize the impact of the Syracusan cavalry.

To enact their strategy, the generals devised a clever ruse. They sent a loyal agent to Syracuse, a man whom the Syracusan generals believed to be aligned with their cause. This agent, a native of Catana, claimed to come on behalf of certain known Syracusan sympathizers within Catana who were familiar to the Syracusan leadership. He reported that the Athenians were spending their nights within Catana, separated from their weapons. If the Syracusans would set a day to march at dawn with their full force and attack, he assured them that their supporters within Catana would close the gates, set fire to the Athenian ships, and allow the Syracusan forces to storm the Athenian camp and breach its defenses. This, he said, would be supported by many Catanians already preparing to act, and it was from these allies he claimed to have come.

The Syracusan generals, who had already planned to march on Catana even without this new information, readily believed the report without further investigation. They immediately set a day for their arrival and dismissed the messenger. With the Selinuntines and other allies having joined their ranks, they ordered all available Syracusan forces to prepare for a full-scale march. Once their preparations were complete and the appointed day neared, the Syracusans set out for Catana, spending the night along the Symaethus River in the territory of Leontini.

Meanwhile, the Athenians, learning of the Syracusan advance, quickly embarked all their forces, along with any Sicel allies and other supporters, on their ships and sailed under the cover of night toward Syracuse. As dawn broke, the Athenians were disembarking near the Olympieum, ready to secure their position. The Syracusan cavalry, which had ridden ahead to Catana, found that the Athenian forces had already departed by sea. Turning back, they relayed the news to the infantry, and the entire Syracusan army redirected their march toward Syracuse to defend the city.

With the Syracusans still at a distance, the Athenians established themselves in a tactically advantageous position, selecting a site that would enable them to initiate combat at their discretion and limit the effectiveness of the Syracusan cavalry. On one side, their position was shielded by walls, houses, trees, and a marsh; on the other, it was bordered by cliffs. The Athenians also cut down nearby trees and used them to build a palisade along the shore to protect their ships. Additionally, they gathered stones and wood to hastily construct a small fortification at Daskon, the most exposed part of their camp, and dismantled the bridge over the Anapus River. All these fortifications were completed without interference, as no Syracusan forces appeared until the Syracusan cavalry arrived, followed later by their full infantry. The Syracusans advanced close to the Athenian position but, observing that the Athenians did not engage, crossed the Helorine Road and made camp for the night.

The next day, the Athenians and their allies prepared for battle, forming up as follows: their right wing consisted of Argive and Mantinean soldiers, the Athenians held the center, and the remaining allies occupied the left. Half of their forces were drawn up eight ranks deep in the front, while the other half formed a hollow square of equal depth near the tents, ready to reinforce any units under heavy pressure. Inside this square, they placed the camp followers for additional protection.

The Syracusans organized their heavy infantry sixteen ranks deep, consisting of their mass levy and allied forces, with the Selinuntines providing the strongest contingent. Next to them were the Geloan cavalry, numbering two hundred, along with twenty horse and fifty archers from Camarina. The Syracusan cavalry, numbering twelve hundred, was stationed on the right flank with the darters positioned beside them.

Just as the Athenians were about to launch their attack, Nicias moved along the lines, delivering words of encouragement to the assembled forces and their allies:

"Soldiers, there is little need for a lengthy exhortation among warriors such as yourselves, who stand here ready to face battle together. The strength of this army alone speaks more convincingly than any speech, for when we have Argives, Mantineans, Athenians, and the finest of the islanders side by side, we have every reason to feel assured of victory. Our foes are a mass levy facing seasoned troops like ours, and though they may scorn us, they lack the skills to match their boldness.

"Remember, we are far from home, with no friendly land nearby save what you can secure with your swords. While our enemies fight for their own country, we fight in foreign lands, where we must win or face the harsh reality of having no retreat, surrounded as we are by their numerous cavalry. Keep in mind your reputation and march confidently into battle, knowing that the urgency and necessity of our situation are far more daunting than any threat they pose."

After this speech, Nicias immediately led the Athenian army forward. The Syracusans, not expecting an immediate attack, were caught off guard; some had even returned to the nearby town. They rushed back, joining the main body as quickly as they could. The Syracusans could not be faulted for lack of spirit or courage, either in this or other battles; however, while their bravery matched that of the Athenians, they lacked the same level of military expertise. In the face of a seasoned enemy, their resolve wavered when their knowledge and experience fell short. Despite their unpreparedness, the Syracusans took up arms promptly and moved to confront the Athenians.

The battle began with the light troops—stone-throwers, slingers, and archers from both sides—who skirmished back and forth, alternately driving each other back. Then the soothsayers stepped forward with the usual sacrificial offerings, and the trumpeters sounded the call to arms for the heavy infantry. The Syracusans fought to defend their homeland and their individual lives and freedom, while the Athenians fought to conquer a foreign land and safeguard their own from harm through victory. The Argives and independent allies fought for the chance to return home, and the subject allies, driven by a desire for self-preservation, fought for victory to ensure their survival and for the hope of lighter terms under Athenian rule.

The armies closed in and engaged in fierce, close-quarters combat, neither side yielding ground. Suddenly, thunderclaps, lightning, and heavy rain struck the battlefield. For the inexperienced Syracusans, many of whom were fighting their first battle, these natural events added to their fear. For the Athenians and their allies, more seasoned in warfare, these phenomena were seen as merely the effects of the season. The real concern for them was the fierce resistance from the Syracusan forces. Eventually, the Argives broke through the Syracusan left flank, followed by the Athenians routing their opponents, splitting the Syracusan forces and driving them to flight.

The Athenians pursued cautiously, held back by the numerous and still-intact Syracusan cavalry, which pushed back any Athenian heavy infantry straying too far from the main body. The Athenians advanced only as far as was safe, then regrouped and set up a victory trophy. Meanwhile, the Syracusans reassembled as best they could along the Helorine road, placing a garrison of their own citizens at the Olympieum to prevent the Athenians from seizing the treasures housed there, while the rest retreated to the city.

The Athenians, however, refrained from approaching the temple, instead gathering their dead, whom they laid upon a pyre, and passing the night on the battlefield. The following day, they returned the bodies of the Syracusan dead—about two hundred and sixty men, including allies—under a truce, and collected their own fallen, around fifty Athenians and allies. After gathering the spoils, they returned to Catana. Winter had now set in, and it seemed impractical to lay siege to Syracuse until reinforcements of cavalry could be brought from Athens and levies raised from allies in Sicily to offset their current inferiority in mounted troops. Additionally, they required funds, either raised locally or sent from Athens, and hoped to bring more Sicilian cities to their side, anticipating that some might be swayed after the recent victory. Supplies, including grain, and other provisions would also be needed for a spring campaign.

With these objectives in mind, they sailed to Naxos and Catana to winter there. Meanwhile, the Syracusans burned their dead and convened an assembly. Hermocrates, son of Hermon, a distinguished leader known for both his intelligence and courage in warfare, addressed the citizens. He urged them not to lose heart over the recent defeat, explaining that it was their lack of training, not their spirit, that had caused the setback. Given their inexperience, the Syracusans had, in fact, fared better than might have been expected, as most of them were artisans, unskilled in the art of war, facing some of the most seasoned soldiers in Greece.

Hermocrates argued that the defeat was partly due to having too many generals—fifteen in total—who issued conflicting orders, compounded by the disorganization and lack of discipline among the troops. He proposed that they should elect a few skilled commanders with full powers and use the winter to prepare thoroughly, equipping as many soldiers as possible with armor and focusing on rigorous training. With courage already in their hearts, proper discipline would give them a strong chance of defeating the Athenians. He pointed out that both discipline and courage would improve with experience and that skill would lend greater confidence to their bravery.

Hermocrates recommended that they take an oath to allow these chosen generals complete control of the campaign, which would ensure better organization, secrecy, and accountability.

The Syracusans listened to Hermocrates and approved all his suggestions, and they elected three generals: Hermocrates himself, Heraclides, son of Lysimachus, and Sicanus, son of Execestes. They also sent envoys to Corinth and Lacedaemon to request a force of allies to join them, and to persuade the Lacedaemonians to commit earnestly to waging war against the Athenians for their sake, so that the Athenians would either be forced to withdraw from Sicily or would be less able to send reinforcements to their forces already there.

Meanwhile, the Athenian forces stationed at Catana immediately sailed to Messina, expecting the city to be betrayed to them. However, the intrigue ultimately came to nothing. Alcibiades, who knew of the plot, foresaw that he would be exiled after being recalled by Athens, and thus disclosed the plot to the Syracusan supporters in Messina, who promptly executed those behind it. They then rose up with others of their faction and succeeded in preventing the Athenians from being admitted to the city. The Athenians waited for thirteen days but, lacking provisions and exposed to adverse weather conditions, they returned without achieving their objective and sailed back to Naxos, where they prepared winter quarters by establishing mooring places for their ships and building a palisade around their camp. During this time, they also dispatched a galley to Athens to request funds and cavalry reinforcements for a renewed campaign in the spring.

During the winter, the Syracusans took steps to fortify their defenses. They constructed an extension to their city walls to enclose the statue of Apollo Temenites along the side facing Epipolae, intending to make any future siege longer and more difficult in the event of a defeat. Additionally, they built forts at Megara and the Olympieum and lined sections of the coast with palisades to deter enemy landings. Knowing that the Athenians were wintering at Naxos, the Syracusans gathered their forces and marched to Catana, where they devastated the surrounding land, set fire to the Athenian encampment and tents, and then returned home.

They soon learned that the Athenians had sent an embassy to Camarina, relying on an alliance that had been established previously under Laches, hoping to persuade the Camarinaeans to join their side. The Syracusans, suspecting that the Camarinaeans had only reluctantly contributed to the previous battle, feared that the recent Athenian success would sway them into joining Athens on the basis of their old friendship. In response, they quickly dispatched envoys of their own to counter this move. Hermocrates and other representatives from Syracuse arrived at Camarina just as Euphemus and his fellow Athenian envoys arrived, and the Camarinaeans called an assembly to hear both sides. Hoping to influence the Camarinaeans against the Athenians, Hermocrates addressed them as follows:

"Camarinaeans, we have not come here out of fear that you may be intimidated by the Athenian forces but rather out of concern that you may be persuaded by what they intend to say to you before you have heard anything from us. They have come to Sicily under the pretense you already know, but with intentions we all suspect; in my opinion, they are here not to restore the Leontines to their homes but to seize ours. It is beyond reason to believe that they would aim to restore in Sicily the cities they are laying waste in Hellas, or that they would genuinely support the Leontine Chalcidians on the grounds of shared Ionian heritage while keeping the Euboean Chalcidians, of whom the Leontines are a colony, in servitude.

"No, their intentions here are simply an extension of the policy that has been so effective for them in Hellas. After being chosen as leaders of the Ionians and other Athenian-allied states to wage war against the Mede, they began finding pretexts to accuse their allies—some for failing in military service, some for conflicts with each other, and others whenever any excuse could be found—until, one by one, they subdued them all. In the end, the Athenians fought not for the liberty of the Hellenes, nor did the Hellenes fight for their own freedom, but rather so that the Athenians could replace the Mede's control with their own, forcing the Greeks to serve them. In reality, the Greeks simply exchanged one master for another, one who may indeed be wiser, but who used that wisdom for even greater oppression."

"But we have not come here merely to expose to you the misconduct of a state as obviously guilty as Athens. Rather, we are here to reproach ourselves, because, despite having witnessed how other Greeks in Hellas have fallen under Athenian domination by failing to support each other, and now seeing the same tactics being applied to us—under the guise of restoring our Leontine kin and supporting our allies in Egesta—we still fail to stand united and resolutely show the Athenians that they face neither Ionians, Hellespontines, nor islanders, who, accustomed to servitude, have alternated between submission to the Mede and other rulers, but rather free Dorians from the independent Peloponnese, residing here in Sicily. Or do we wait to be conquered piece by piece, each city one at a time? We know that we cannot be overcome except in this way, and yet we witness the Athenians using precisely this strategy: dividing us with words, luring some into alliances that lead to open conflict, and enticing others with flattering promises suited to their particular circumstances. And do we imagine that when misfortune strikes a distant fellow Greek, the danger will never reach us? Or that whoever suffers first will suffer alone?

"To the Camarinaean who believes that it is Syracuse, not he, who is the true enemy of Athens, and who feels reluctant to risk himself for our sake, I would remind him that he fights on Syracusan soil not merely for Syracuse's sake, but equally for his own. Moreover, he will fight more securely if he joins the struggle now alongside us rather than facing it alone later, once we have been subdued. Understand that the Athenians seek not so much to punish Syracuse's hostility as to use us as a cover to win Camarina's friendship. And to those who envy or even fear us (for powerful states are always both envied and feared), and who therefore wish Syracuse to be weakened but not destroyed, for their own security, let me point out that such a wish is impossible. One can control one's desires, but not the circumstances that follow. Should their calculations fail, they may find themselves lamenting their own predicament, longing for the days when they merely envied our strength. This regret will be futile if they now abandon us and refuse to share in these dangers, which, though they appear different in name, are in fact identical for both our cities; what seems to be merely the preservation of Syracusan power is in reality Camarina's own salvation. Camarinaeans, as our closest neighbors and those next in line for Athenian aggression, it was expected that you, of all people, would have foreseen this. Rather than offering Syracuse the limited support you now do, you should have joined us proactively, providing the assistance in Syracuse that you would have requested in Camarina had the Athenians arrived there first. You ought to be rallying us against the invader. But thus far, neither you nor any others have made any real effort in this direction.

"Perhaps fear compels you to try to satisfy both us and the invaders, using your alliance with Athens as an excuse. Yet you formed that alliance not against friends, but against enemies who might threaten you, and to support Athens when wronged by others—not when, as now, they themselves are the aggressors against their neighbors. The Rhegians, Chalcidians as they are, refuse to assist in restoring the Chalcidian Leontines; would it not be strange if, while they see through this flimsy pretense and act cautiously, you—with every reason to do the same—were to ally with your natural enemies and join forces with their bitterest foes to destroy those whom nature has made your kin? This is far from acting justly. Instead, you should support us without fearing the Athenian force, which holds no true danger if we stand united, but becomes menacing only if we allow them to succeed in dividing us. After all, even when they defeated us in a single battle, they left without achieving their ultimate aim.

"Together, then, we have no reason to lose heart but, instead, newfound motivation to form an alliance, especially as we can expect reinforcements from the Peloponnesians, whose military expertise surpasses that of the Athenians. Let me emphasize that your policy of neutrality—being allies with both sides—is neither safe for you nor fair to us. It is not as balanced as it seems. Should the vanquished fall, and the victors triumph, your so-called neutrality will mean little more than abandoning the defeated to their fate and allowing the conquerors to continue unopposed. It would be far more honorable to ally with those who have been wronged and who are also your kin, thereby protecting Sicily's collective interests and helping the Athenians avoid falling into wrongdoing against their allies."

"In conclusion, we Syracusans declare that it serves no purpose for us to rehearse to you or anyone else the dangers and motives we all recognize as well as you do. Rather, we implore you, and, should our plea fail, we firmly state that we are under threat from our relentless foes, the Ionians, while being abandoned by you, our fellow Dorians. If the Athenians conquer us, they will owe their success to your choice but will claim the glory themselves, leaving you as little more than a stepping stone to their triumph and the very prize that enabled them to achieve it. On the other hand, if we succeed and are victorious, you will bear responsibility for having brought us to such peril. Consider carefully, then, and now choose between the temporary security of submission and the chance to win alongside us, thus avoiding the disgrace of an Athenian yoke and the enduring enmity of Syracuse."

These were the words of Hermocrates. Next, Euphemus, the Athenian envoy, responded as follows:

"Although our original purpose in coming here was simply to renew our prior alliance, the remarks of the Syracusan envoy compel us to address the matter of our empire and the legitimacy of our claim to it. The speaker has unwittingly offered the strongest evidence in our favor by calling the Ionians the 'eternal enemies of the Dorians.' This is indeed the case. As Ionians, we sought the means to escape domination by our more numerous and neighboring Dorian rivals from the Peloponnese. After the Persian Wars, with a fleet at our disposal, we liberated ourselves from Lacedaemonian control, who had no more right to command us than we to command them, beyond the fact of momentary strength. Having been appointed to lead the former subjects of the Persian King, we retained that role, believing it the surest defense against Peloponnesian encroachment. Thus, in truth, we have not acted unjustly in subduing the Ionians and islanders, whom the Syracusans claim we have enslaved. These 'kinsfolk' of ours joined the Persian in an attempt to conquer their own motherland— us—while we, by contrast, sacrificed our wealth and abandoned our city for freedom.

"Therefore, we deserve our leadership because we offered the greatest fleet and unwavering commitment to the Hellenes, while our 'kinsfolk' aided the Persians. Beyond the fault of treachery, we strive to fortify ourselves against the Peloponnesians. We make no empty claims of a right to rule based on having defeated the barbarian alone, nor do we claim to have risked all solely for the freedom of our allies, but equally for our own. It is only natural for each to prioritize his security. Our current presence in Sicily likewise arises from a concern for our own safety, which we see as intertwined with yours. This is the very rationale the Syracusans challenge us on, and you regard with undue caution, knowing that when fears arise, momentary eloquence may sway a crowd, but actions must ultimately align with interests.

"Thus, just as fear preserves our rule in Hellas, so does it bring us here with our allies, to establish order in Sicily and prevent subjugation, not to enslave. Let no one imagine that we act out of interest in you alone, unconnected to our own needs, since by strengthening your defenses against Syracuse, we lessen the threat of Syracusan interference in the Peloponnesian struggle. In this way, you are directly relevant to us. Therefore, it is entirely reasonable that we restore the Leontines, strengthening them not as subjects, like their Chalcidian relatives in Euboea, but as capable allies who can oppose the Syracusans from their own borders. In Hellas, we stand alone against our enemies. As for the claim that it is inconsistent for us to liberate Sicily while controlling Chalcis, consider that the Chalcidians serve us best by being unarmed and contributing financially, while here, the Leontines and our other allies can only aid us effectively if they remain independent."

"Moreover, for tyrants and imperial states, no action is deemed unreasonable if it serves their advantage, and no one is considered kin unless reliable; friendship and enmity are merely matters of timing and circumstances. Here in Sicily, our goal is not to weaken our allies, but to use their strength to hinder our enemies. Why should you doubt this? In Hellas, we treat our allies based on their usefulness to us: the Chians and Methymnians govern themselves and provide ships, while most others have tougher terms and pay tribute in money; some, though islanders and easy to subdue, are completely free because of their strategic locations near the Peloponnese. In managing the affairs of Sicily, we are therefore guided by our interest and, as we say, by fear of the Syracusans. The Syracusans aim to rule over you, using our presence to create suspicion and unity among you, intending that once we depart, having accomplished nothing, they can dominate Sicily either by force or through your isolation. If you ally with them, they will inevitably become the masters here, for such a consolidated power would be far beyond our capacity to counter once unified, and they would easily overpower you once we are gone.

"Any other interpretation contradicts the facts. When you first asked us to intervene, your argument was that Athens itself would be at risk if you fell under Syracusan domination. It is inconsistent to now distrust the very reasoning with which you persuaded us, or to let fear undermine your resolve simply because we have arrived with a stronger force against that same city. Those you should truly mistrust are the Syracusans. We cannot remain here without your cooperation, and if we were to act treacherously and subject you, we could not maintain control over you due to the vast distance and the difficulty of overseeing large, populous towns resembling mainland territories. But the Syracusans, residing close to you, not in a temporary camp but in a city larger than our current force, consistently plot against you, never missing an opportunity to act on their ambitions, as they have demonstrated with the Leontines and others. They have the audacity, as though addressing fools, to ask you to assist them against the very power that prevents this domination and has maintained the freedom of Sicily thus far. We, on the other hand, offer you a far more genuine security by asking you to preserve our shared safety. Consider that even without allies, the Syracusans will always have access to you because of their proximity, while you may not again have such an opportunity to defend yourselves with an alliance as large as ours. Should you let us depart without success or, worse, defeated due to your suspicions, you will find yourselves yearning to have even a small contingent of us back when the moment has passed, and our presence can no longer aid you.

"But we trust, Camarinaeans, that the accusations of the Syracusans will not sway you or others. We have laid out the full truth concerning the suspicions held against us and will briefly summarize to clarify our position. We maintain that we rule in Hellas not to be ruled ourselves, and that we come to Sicily as liberators to avoid future threats from Sicilians. We are compelled to intervene widely because we face numerous threats. Now, as before, we have arrived as allies to those among you who face injustice, not uninvited, but at your request. Therefore, rather than attempting to judge or censor our actions, which would now be difficult to change, take advantage of what aligns with your interests in our policy and character. Understand that, far from being harmful to all, our policy actually benefits the majority of Hellenes. Thanks to it, all peoples, even in places where we are absent, who either fear or consider aggression are held in check—some by the expectation of our aid, others by the danger posed by our potential arrival. This forces moderation upon aggressors and provides safety for others without them having to exert themselves.

"Do not reject the security that is available to all who seek it, and which we now offer you. Follow the example of others and, instead of remaining perpetually defensive against the Syracusans, join with us, and for once let them feel the threat."

These were the words of Euphemus. The Camarinaeans' reaction was shaped by a mixture of sympathies and apprehensions. While they felt inclined to support the Athenians, wary only of the possibility that Athens might eventually aim to dominate Sicily, they had traditionally been hostile toward their neighboring city, Syracuse. However, precisely because Syracuse was so close, they feared them more than the Athenians and were anxious about the Syracusans achieving victory even without their help. Thus, they initially sent the small contingent of cavalry mentioned, intending to assist Syracuse just enough to avoid fully committing, and decided to provide only minimal support in the future. For the present, though, they wished to avoid appearing dismissive toward the Athenians, especially given Athens' recent success in battle, and therefore responded diplomatically to both sides.

Accordingly, the Camarinaeans answered that, as both parties were officially their allies, it seemed most consistent with their sworn obligations to remain neutral at that time. Satisfied with this answer, both the Athenian and Syracusan ambassadors departed.

Meanwhile, as Syracuse continued its war preparations, the Athenians remained camped at Naxos, working to negotiate alliances with as many Sicels as possible. Those living in the lowlands and under

Syracusan influence generally stayed distant, but the tribes in the interior, who had always maintained independence, mostly joined the Athenians, bringing corn and, in some cases, even money for the army. The Athenians marched against the Sicels who refused to ally with them, forcing some into alliance; with others, they were thwarted when the Syracusans sent garrisons and reinforcements to support them. Later, the Athenians moved their winter quarters from Naxos to Catana, rebuilding the camp that the Syracusans had burned and remaining there for the rest of the winter. They also dispatched a ship to Carthage, proposing an alliance in hopes of securing support, and another to Tyrrhenia, as some cities there had offered assistance voluntarily. Additionally, the Athenians sent requests to the Sicels and Egesta for as many horses as possible and prepared essential materials like bricks, iron, and other supplies needed for constructing a siege wall, with plans to begin offensive actions by spring.

Meanwhile, the Syracusan envoys, on their way to Corinth and Lacedaemon, attempted to rally support from the Italian states along the coast, warning them that the Athenians' actions posed a threat to Italy as much as to Syracuse. Upon reaching Corinth, the envoys appealed to their shared ancestry to win Corinthian support. The Corinthians immediately pledged full support and sent their own representatives with the Syracusans to Lacedaemon to persuade the Spartans to engage more openly in the war with Athens and to send reinforcements to Sicily.

The Corinthian and Syracusan envoys arrived in Lacedaemon, where they found Alcibiades and his fellow exiles. Alcibiades had traveled from Thurii across the sea, first to Cyllene in Elis, and then to Lacedaemon. He had come at the Spartans' invitation and had first obtained a safe conduct, as he feared hostility due to his involvement in the events at Mantinea. Alcibiades, along with the Corinthian and Syracusan envoys, presented their requests before the Lacedaemonian assembly. They succeeded in persuading the Lacedaemonians to take action; however, while the ephors and other officials resolved to send representatives to Syracuse to prevent the city from falling to the

Athenians, they showed no inclination to dispatch military support. At this point, Alcibiades took the floor to stoke the Lacedaemonians' resolve further, delivering the following address.

"I must first address the prejudice that exists against me to prevent it from clouding your judgment on the public matters at hand. The relationship between our family and yours as proxeni, which our ancestors renounced due to certain grievances, was one I personally tried to renew through acts of goodwill, particularly following your disaster at Pylos. Despite this, although I remained well-disposed toward you, you chose to negotiate peace with Athens through my political opponents, strengthening their position and undermining mine. Thus, you had no right to reproach me when I turned to the Mantineans and Argives and sought other opportunities to counteract and harm your interests. Now, the time has come for those among you who once harbored resentment against me to consider the matter with clearer perspective.

"Likewise, those who misjudged me because of my support for the people should not believe their dislike was justified. We have always been opposed to tyranny, and in opposing arbitrary power, we naturally aligned with the popular party. Since Athens is a democracy, it was essential to respect this structure in most matters. Nevertheless, we strived to be more restrained than the excesses of the era allowed, while others—who, like now, sought to mislead the masses—pushed for my exile. Our party aimed to serve the interests of the entire people, guided by the conviction to preserve the democratic system under which Athens had reached its peak of prosperity and freedom. Intelligent men among us understood the flaws of democracy, as did I, perhaps more so, since I have reason to complain about it. But one cannot change what is obviously flawed in a system without introducing greater risks, especially in the face of your hostility.

"With that said, I now direct your attention to the vital issues at hand, on which I can speak with some authority. The goal of our campaign in Sicily was initially to subjugate the Siceliots, then to move on to the Italiots, and finally to target the empire and city of Carthage. If we succeeded in these, or even most of them, our plan was to attack the Peloponnese, bolstered by a new force of Hellenes from those regions, with additional troops from among the barbarians, particularly the Iberians and others, known to be the fiercest warriors. We planned to build more ships, as timber was abundant in Italy, and, with our naval power, to blockade the Peloponnese by sea and attack its cities by land. Some we intended to storm, others to surround with siege works, until we could subdue the entire region. This would allow us to establish dominion over all Hellenic territories. The resources— money and food—for this ambitious plan would be provided by our new territories, independent of our revenues in Athens.

"You now understand our objectives, laid out by someone who knows them best. And rest assured, the remaining Athenian generals in Sicily will continue to pursue these aims if they are able. But Sicily will undoubtedly fall unless you intervene, as I will now explain. While the Siceliots could still be saved if united, the Syracusans alone, having lost a battle with their entire force and blockaded by sea, cannot withstand the Athenian armament now on their shores. If Syracuse falls, all of Sicily will follow, and Italy soon after. The same threat I mentioned will inevitably reach you. Let no one therefore think that only Sicily is at stake; Peloponnese is also in jeopardy unless you act quickly by following my counsel. You must send reinforcements by ship to Syracuse, soldiers capable of rowing and fighting as heavy infantry when they land. More importantly, a Spartan commander should accompany them to impose discipline and ensure all are committed to the cause. With this support, your current allies will grow more confident, and those wavering will be encouraged to join you. Meanwhile, you should openly wage war here, so that the Syracusans know you are mindful of them, boosting their resolve, while the Athenians become less capable of reinforcing their forces.

"Additionally, you should fortify Decelea in Attica, a blow that the Athenians fear above all others, and one they have yet to experience in this war. The surest way to harm an enemy is to attack their most vulnerable point. Knowing their own weaknesses, they will fear this the most. Fortifying Decelea will benefit you while creating considerable hardship for your opponents. There are many aspects to this, but I will focus on the main ones. Most of the property in the area would either fall into your hands through conquest or surrender, while the Athenians would lose their revenue from the Laurium silver mines, the income from their lands and law courts, and, crucially, the tribute from their allies, who would pay less regularly as their fear of Athens wanes and they witness your vigorous engagement in the war.

"Lacedaemonians, the swiftness and determination with which these actions are carried out rests on you; as for their feasibility, I am confident of their success, and I see little chance of error in my judgment."

"I hope none of you will think less of me for standing now with those who are enemies to Athens, despite having once been known as a patriot. Nor should you dismiss my words as the eager ramblings of an exile. I was exiled not for wrongdoing but by the injustice of those who forced me out. My greatest enemies are not you, who only harm your foes, but those in Athens who drove a friend to become an adversary. Patriotism is not a sentiment I feel in the face of injustice, but one I cherished when I was respected as a citizen. I do not see myself as attacking a country that is still mine; instead, I aim to reclaim one that is no longer truly my own. The true patriot is not one who passively surrenders his homeland when wronged but one who desires it so deeply that he will go to any lengths to recover it.

"So, Lacedaemonians, I ask you to use me without reserve in whatever dangers or challenges may arise. Remember the common argument that if I could harm you greatly as an enemy, I could benefit you just as much as a friend, given that I know Athenian plans inside out, while yours were previously only guessed at. Consider this as your most critical decision: dispatch expeditions to both Sicily and Attica without delay. A fraction of your forces will secure key cities in Sicily and strike a fatal blow against the present and future power of Athens.

Afterward, you will rest in safety, possessing supremacy over all Hellas, based not on coercion but on consent and goodwill."

These were Alcibiades' words. The Lacedaemonians, already contemplating an advance on Athens but hesitating, now became resolute upon hearing these details directly from someone who knew Athens best. They decided to focus on fortifying Decelea and sending reinforcements to Sicily immediately. Gylippus, son of Cleandridas, was appointed as commander to support the Syracusans. He was instructed to coordinate closely with them and the Corinthians to ensure swift and effective aid to the island. At Gylippus' request, the Corinthians prepared two ships to be dispatched immediately to Asine and began readying additional vessels to be deployed as needed. With these plans in place, the envoys left Lacedaemon.

In the meantime, an Athenian galley arrived from Sicily, sent by the generals requesting additional funds and cavalry. After reviewing the request, the Athenians agreed to provide the necessary support and approved the dispatch of resources and troops for the campaign. Thus ended winter, marking the close of the seventeenth year of the war chronicled by Thucydides.

At the onset of the following summer, the Athenians in Sicily departed from Catana, sailing along the coast to Megara, a territory whose original inhabitants had been expelled by the Syracusans under their tyrant Gelo. Here, the Athenians landed, ravaging the land. Following an unsuccessful attempt to seize a Syracusan fort, they moved on with their fleet and forces to the river Terias. Pushing inland, they devastated the plains and set the fields ablaze. After clashing with a small Syracusan force, defeating them, and erecting a trophy, they returned to their ships.

Afterward, the Athenians returned to Catana for provisions, then marched with their full force on Centoripa, a Sicel town, which they captured by agreement before burning the grain stores of the Inessaeans and Hybleans. Upon returning to Catana, they found their reinforcements from Athens had arrived: two hundred and fifty cavalrymen with their gear (though without horses, which were to be obtained locally), thirty mounted archers, and three hundred talents of silver.

In that same spring, the Lacedaemonians advanced against Argos, marching as far as Cleonae, but an earthquake struck, causing them to retreat. Following this, the Argives invaded the region of Thyreatis on their border and took a substantial amount of loot from the Lacedaemonians, which they later sold for no less than twenty-five talents. Later in the summer, a significant event unfolded in Thespiae when the commons attempted to overthrow the ruling faction. Their effort failed, and reinforcements arrived from Thebes, capturing some rebels while others sought refuge in Athens.

During that summer, the Syracusans received word that the Athenians had been reinforced with cavalry and were preparing to march against them. Realizing that without control of Epipolae—a high, steep area overlooking the city—the Athenians could not easily besiege them even if victorious in battle, they decided to secure its access points. Epipolae, or "Overtown" as it was called, was visible from within Syracuse, and the only feasible path for an ascent lay on one side, as the rest of the terrain dropped steeply down to the city. Early one morning, the Syracusans gathered in full force along the meadows by the river Anapus. With new generals, including Hermocrates, recently in command, they held a review of their infantry. From this assembly, they selected a group of six hundred elite soldiers under Diomilus, an exile from Andros, to guard Epipolae and be ready to assist wherever needed.

Meanwhile, that same morning, the Athenians disembarked at a location called Leon, just under a kilometer from Epipolae, having landed from Catana undetected. They anchored their fleet at Thapsus, a nearby peninsula with a narrow isthmus, within striking distance of Syracuse by both land and water. The Athenian fleet quickly fortified the isthmus and held position at Thapsus, while the land forces hurried to Epipolae. They ascended via Euryelus before the

Syracusans, still occupied with their review in the meadow, could respond. Diomilus and his six hundred troops rushed to meet them, but they had a distance of nearly five kilometers to cover. Advancing in disorder, the Syracusans engaged the Athenians at Epipolae but were defeated, with approximately three hundred men, including Diomilus, killed. The Syracusans withdrew to the city, and the Athenians erected a trophy, returning the fallen Syracusans under a truce. The following day, the Athenians descended toward Syracuse, but seeing no opposition, they retreated to construct a fort at Labdalum on the edge of the Epipolae cliffs, facing Megara, which would serve as a storage site for their supplies and money whenever they advanced.

Not long afterward, additional cavalry joined the Athenians from Egesta (three hundred men), the Sicels, Naxians, and other allies (about a hundred), raising their total cavalry to six hundred and fifty, including two hundred and fifty riders from Athens who had received horses from the Egestaeans and Catanians or purchased their own. Leaving a garrison at Labdalum, the Athenians advanced to Syca and rapidly began constructing the central part of their siege wall, called the Circle. The Syracusans, alarmed by their swift progress, decided to attack, hoping to interrupt the work. However, their generals noticed that their forces struggled to form up and were in disarray, so they withdrew to the city, leaving only a portion of their cavalry outside to hinder the Athenians from gathering stones or straying too far from their main position. The Athenians eventually countered, sending a force of heavy infantry supported by all their cavalry, which routed the Syracusan horse, prompting them to set up a trophy to commemorate this victory.

The following day, the Athenians continued their siege works, extending the wall northward from the Circle, gathering stone and timber as they proceeded towards Trogilus along the shortest line from the great harbor to the sea. Seeing the Athenians' progress, the Syracusans, led by Hermocrates, opted against direct engagements and instead began building a counter-wall below the Athenian Circle. This cross-wall was designed to block the Athenians' wall construction and buy the Syracusans time. They started their defensive line from the city, cutting down olive trees and erecting wooden towers. Since the Athenian fleet had not yet sailed into the great harbor, the Syracusans still controlled the coastline, forcing the Athenians to transport supplies overland from Thapsus.

The Syracusans, confident that their counter-wall of stockades and stone was now sufficiently developed, felt it could effectively block the Athenians' progress. Observing that the Athenians were highly focused on completing their own siege wall and preferred not to split their forces to engage the Syracusans at the counter-wall, they withdrew most of their troops back to the city, leaving only a single tribe to guard the new construction.

Meanwhile, the Athenians saw an opportunity to disrupt their adversaries. They began by destroying the underground pipes that supplied Syracuse with drinking water, hoping to weaken the city's defenses and morale. Then, biding their time, they waited until midday, when the heat and the apparent inactivity of the Athenians had led most of the Syracusans to relax, retreating into their tents or even back into the city. With only a light guard at the stockade, the Athenians seized the moment. They assembled a force of three hundred select soldiers along with some light-armed troops outfitted especially for speed and maneuverability, instructing them to charge swiftly toward the counter-wall. Simultaneously, the rest of the Athenian army advanced in two separate divisions: one led by a general toward the city, prepared to repel any potential sortie, and the other, commanded by the second general, made its way toward the stockade by the postern gate.

The elite force of three hundred Athenians reached the stockade at top speed, catching the Syracusan defenders off guard. The guards abandoned their posts and retreated to the safety of the outer defenses surrounding the statue of Apollo Temenites. The Athenian pursuers followed them into this fortified area. However, upon breaking into the sanctuary, the Athenians were met with a fierce counterattack. The Syracusans rallied and managed to repel them, forcing the attackers back out of the defenses. A few Argive and Athenian soldiers were killed in the ensuing clash, leading the Athenians to withdraw. Nonetheless, they succeeded in tearing down the Syracusan counter-wall, dismantling the stockade, and removing the stakes, which they brought back to their own fortifications. They capped their efforts by erecting a trophy, symbolizing their success in the skirmish.

The following day, the Athenians set out from the Circle to fortify a cliff on Epipolae overlooking the marshy area adjacent to the great harbor. They recognized this as the shortest route for extending their siege wall down across the marsh and into the plain, where it could reach the harbor. Meanwhile, the Syracusans countered by mobilizing a second line of defense, constructing another stockade that stretched from the city and across the marsh. Alongside this, they dug a trench to obstruct the Athenians' attempts to extend their wall to the sea.

As soon as the Athenians completed fortifying the cliff, they prepared to assault this new stockade and trench. They instructed their fleet to sail from Thapsus into the great harbor of Syracuse to offer naval support. Early at dawn, the Athenian army descended from Epipolae into the plain. To cross the marshy ground, they laid wooden planks and doors over the firmest sections and advanced steadily. By sunrise, they had captured most of the ditch and stockade, save for a small section that they later seized.

A fierce battle ensued. The Athenians triumphed over the Syracusan forces, which split in retreat: the right wing fell back to the city, while the left wing made for the river. Seizing this moment to intercept, three hundred elite Athenians sprinted toward the bridge, hoping to cut off the Syracusans' escape route. But the Syracusans, rallying around their remaining cavalry, turned and counterattacked, successfully pushing back the Athenian force. This sudden reversal caused a shock among the Athenian ranks, particularly within the first tribe on their right wing, leading them to falter.

Lamachus, seeing the turmoil, moved swiftly to reinforce his troops. Bringing a handful of archers and some Argive allies, he crossed a ditch to join the fray, but in his haste, he found himself isolated with only a small contingent. In this vulnerable position, he and a few of his men were killed. The Syracusans, sensing an advantage, quickly recovered the bodies of Lamachus and his men, transporting them safely across the river. They then retreated as the rest of the Athenian forces approached, ending the encounter with their fallen leader secured from enemy hands.

When the Syracusans who had initially fled back to the city saw the situation shifting, they rallied, forming a line against the Athenians, and also sent a contingent to the Circle on Epipolae, hoping to take it while it was lightly defended. These forces successfully captured and destroyed the Athenian outwork, which extended about a thousand feet. However, the main fortification, the Circle itself, was preserved by Nicias, who had been left there due to illness. Nicias, realizing that they lacked enough defenders to hold back the Syracusans in a traditional fight, instructed his attendants to set fire to the siege engines and timber piled in front of the wall. This tactic proved effective, as the flames deterred the Syracusans from advancing any further, forcing them to retreat.

Meanwhile, reinforcements arrived from the main Athenian forces below, who had just repelled the Syracusan troops confronting them. At the same time, the Athenian fleet, as ordered, sailed from Thapsus into the great harbor. Seeing these movements, the Syracusan forces on the heights quickly withdrew, and the entire Syracusan army returned to the city, recognizing that their current strength was insufficient to prevent the Athenians from extending their wall to the sea.

Following this victory, the Athenians erected a trophy on the battlefield and returned the Syracusan dead under a truce, receiving in exchange the body of Lamachus and those who had perished alongside him. With their naval and land forces now fully assembled, they resumed construction on their double wall from Epipolae down to the coast, encircling the Syracusans more effectively. Supplies began pouring in from across Italy to support the Athenian forces, and many Sicel tribes that had been waiting to see how events would unfold now joined the Athenians as allies. Additionally, three Tyrrhenian ships, each equipped with fifty oars, arrived to reinforce them, boosting the Athenians' morale and fortifying their position.

The Syracusans, increasingly demoralized by their situation and dismayed by the lack of expected reinforcements from Peloponnese, began to lose hope in their ability to resist. Some even considered negotiating terms of surrender with Nicias, who had assumed full command after the death of Lamachus. Although no formal decision was reached, discussions of capitulation circulated widely, both within the city and with Nicias directly, as it was natural for men under siege and facing deteriorating conditions to consider such options. Internal suspicion grew, with accusations of poor leadership or even treachery aimed at the Syracusan generals responsible for their recent losses. Consequently, these generals were removed from command, and Heraclides, Eucles, and Tellias were appointed in their place.

Meanwhile, Gylippus, the Lacedaemonian general, along with a fleet of Corinthian ships, had arrived off the coast of Leucas, with intentions of hastening to Sicily's aid. Alarmed by exaggerated reports that Syracuse was already fully encircled, Gylippus doubted the feasibility of a rescue mission in Sicily and shifted his focus to preserving Italy. He quickly crossed the Ionian Sea to Tarentum with a small force—only Pythen's Corinthian ship, two Lacedaemonian vessels, and two additional Corinthian ships—leaving instructions for the Corinthian fleet to follow with reinforcements from Leucas and Ambracia. At Tarentum, Gylippus approached the Thurians, invoking his father's former ties as a citizen, but failing to sway them, he resumed his journey along the Italian coast. However, he was caught in a severe northerly wind near the Terinaean Gulf and, after enduring harsh conditions, was forced back to Tarentum, where he repaired the ships most damaged by the storm.

Although Nicias received word of Gylippus's arrival, he, like the Thurians, dismissed the small fleet as insignificant, assuming it was likely engaged in piracy rather than part of a larger operation and thus made no immediate preparations to counter it.

Around the same time, the Lacedaemonians, along with their allies, launched an invasion of Argos, ravaging much of the land. In response, the Athenians sent thirty ships to assist the Argives, marking a clear and open violation of their truce with Lacedaemon. Prior to this, Athens had limited its involvement in the Argive-Mantinean alliance to raids from Pylos and small incursions elsewhere in Peloponnese, carefully avoiding attacks directly on Laconian territory. Despite repeated requests from the Argives to join them in briefly invading Laconia, Athens had consistently refrained from doing so. Now, however, with Phytodorus, Laespodius, and Demaratus commanding, the Athenian fleet landed forces at various Laconian locations—Epidaurus Limera, Prasiae, and other coastal areas—plundering the countryside, thereby giving the Lacedaemonians a much stronger justification to renew hostilities with Athens. After both the Athenian fleet and the Lacedaemonian forces withdrew, the Argives took advantage of the opportunity to invade the Phlisaid, devastating the area and killing several inhabitants before returning home.

Book VII

Chapter XXI

Eighteenth and Nineteenth Years of the War—Arrival of Gylippus at Syracuse—Fortification of Decelea—Successes of the Syracusans

After refitting their ships, Gylippus and Pythen resumed their journey, sailing from Tarentum to Epizephyrian Locris. Here, they received more accurate intelligence that Syracuse was not yet completely encircled, and that an arriving army could still break through at Epipolae. After weighing their options, they debated whether to risk entering by sea or, alternatively, to sail towards Himera, gather reinforcements from the Himeraeans and any others willing to support them, and proceed overland to Syracuse. Ultimately, they chose the latter, mainly because the Athenian ships Nicias had dispatched to intercept them had not yet arrived at Rhegium. Thus, before the Athenian squadron could reach its post, the Peloponnesians crossed the strait, stopping briefly at Rhegium and Messina, before reaching Himera.

Once there, Gylippus successfully persuaded the Himeraeans to join the war effort, not only by providing troops but also by arming the sailors from his ships, which had been beached at Himera. They coordinated with the Selinuntines, agreeing upon a rendezvous point for their forces. The Geloans promised a small contingent, while some Sicel tribes also agreed to join, partly due to the recent death of Archonidas, a pro-Athenian Sicel king, and partly impressed by Gylippus's resolve in traveling from Lacedaemon. Gylippus's assembled force now included about seven hundred sailors and marines armed for combat, one thousand heavy infantry and light troops from Himera, a contingent of one hundred horse, additional forces from Selinus, and Sicel allies numbering roughly one thousand. Thus, prepared, he set out for Syracuse.

Meanwhile, the Corinthian fleet from Leucas hurried to reinforce them, with Gongylus, one of their commanders, setting out last with a single ship but arriving first in Syracuse, just before Gylippus. Gongylus found the Syracusans about to convene to deliberate on ending the war, but he intervened, instilling renewed hope by informing them that more ships were en route, and that Gylippus, son of Cleandridas, had been appointed by the Lacedaemonians as commander of the reinforcement. Encouraged by this, the Syracusans immediately marched out with their entire force to meet Gylippus, who was now close by.

Gylippus, after seizing the Sicel fort of Ietae on his way, organized his forces and reached Epipolae, ascending by the Euryelus pass as the

Athenians had previously done, and advanced on the Athenian defenses with the support of the Syracusan army. His arrival proved timely, as the Athenians were in the final stages of constructing a double wall stretching six or seven furlongs down to the great harbor, with only a small section remaining unfinished near the shore. The wall toward Trogilus, facing the opposite sea, had stones prepared for most of the distance, with some parts half-built and others already completed, putting Syracuse in a precarious situation.

Despite their initial shock at the sudden arrival of Gylippus and the Syracusans, the Athenians quickly reorganized into battle formation. Gylippus, stopping at a distance, sent a herald to propose that the Athenians withdraw from Sicily with their possessions within five days. The Athenians dismissed this offer with disdain, sending the herald away without a reply. Both sides now readied for combat, though Gylippus noticed that the Syracusan ranks were in disarray and struggled to form up. Consequently, he led his troops to more open ground, where they could regroup, while Nicias kept the Athenians close to their own fortifications rather than advancing.

Seeing that the Athenians remained stationary, Gylippus moved his army to the stronghold near the Temple of Apollo Temenites and camped there for the night. The following morning, he arranged his forces in front of the Athenian walls, aiming to prevent any intervention, and dispatched a separate force to assault Fort Labdalum, a key Athenian outpost. Fort Labdalum was swiftly captured, with the Syracusans killing all those found within, as the location was out of sight from the main Athenian position. On that same day, the Syracusans also captured an Athenian galley anchored in the harbor.

These setbacks placed the Athenians on the defensive, underscoring the urgency of their situation and marking the beginning of an intensified Syracusan resistance under the strategic guidance of Gylippus.

Following this, the Syracusans and their allies embarked on building a single wall from the city, extending diagonally across

Epipolae, intending to obstruct the Athenians from completely encircling the city. By this time, the Athenians had extended their own wall down to the sea and were now advancing their fortifications up onto the heights. Recognizing that a portion of the Athenian wall was weak, Gylippus launched a nighttime assault. However, the Athenians who were bivouacked outside the walls were quickly alerted and emerged to counter the threat, forcing Gylippus to withdraw his forces without engaging further.

In response, the Athenians raised their wall to fortify it further and positioned their own troops to guard this vulnerable section. They distributed their allies along the remaining sections of their defenses. Nicias, seeking to improve their strategic advantage, decided to fortify Plemmyrium, a promontory directly opposite the city, narrowing the mouth of the Great Harbour. By doing so, he aimed to facilitate the blockade by reducing the distance needed to monitor the Syracusan fleet, sparing them from having to respond from the far end of the harbor with each enemy movement. With Gylippus's arrival, Nicias had also begun to focus on the naval aspect of the war, as the Athenians now saw their prospects on land diminished. Nicias, therefore, transported some ships and troops across to Plemmyrium, establishing three forts there where he stationed most of their supplies and moored their larger vessels and warships.

However, this move introduced new hardships for the Athenian crews. Water had to be collected from distant sources, and the sailors could not forage for firewood without the risk of being cut off by Syracusan cavalry, who held the countryside and stationed a portion of their forces at the town of Olympieum to prevent Athenian incursions from Plemmyrium. Meanwhile, Nicias learned of the imminent arrival of the remaining Corinthian fleet and dispatched twenty ships to intercept them near Locris, Rhegium, and the entrance to Sicily.

Gylippus, in the meantime, continued the construction of the counter-wall across Epipolae, even using the stones the Athenians had stockpiled for their own fortifications. He also frequently assembled his forces in front of the Athenian lines, presenting a battle formation, prompting the Athenians to do the same. Finally, Gylippus judged the time right for an attack, and a fierce hand-to-hand battle erupted. The Syracusan cavalry, unable to operate effectively in the tight confines of the battlefield, was sidelined, resulting in a Syracusan defeat. After the battle, the Syracusans requested permission to retrieve their dead, while the Athenians erected a trophy in victory.

Following the loss, Gylippus addressed his soldiers, acknowledging that the fault lay with his strategy rather than their efforts. He had led them too close to the fortifications, which limited the use of their cavalry and light troops. He vowed to correct this in their next engagement, encouraging them with the belief that they matched the Athenians in physical strength and held the moral advantage as Peloponnesians and Dorians facing Ionians, islanders, and a mixed foreign force.

Seizing the first chance to re-engage, Gylippus led his forces out once more. Nicias and the Athenians recognized that it was crucial to prevent the completion of the Syracusan cross-wall, as it was nearing the point where it would intersect with their own. Should it extend any further, it would negate the strategic purpose of their investment, rendering victories in battle futile. Thus, the Athenians moved out to confront the Syracusans. This time, Gylippus positioned his heavy infantry farther from their fortifications than in the previous encounter, also deploying his cavalry and light troops on the Athenians' flank where the two walls converged in open ground.

In the ensuing battle, the Syracusan cavalry routed the Athenian left wing, which was stationed opposite them, leading to a full retreat of the Athenian army back within their defenses. The Syracusans took advantage of their victory and used the following night to extend their wall past the Athenian defenses, effectively neutralizing the Athenian siege efforts. With this cross-wall in place, the Syracusans could no longer be encircled, denying the Athenians the possibility of a complete investment, even if they managed to win future battles.

Following these events, the twelve remaining ships from Corinth, along with vessels from Ambracia and Leucas, managed to enter the harbour under the command of Erasinides, a Corinthian. These ships had skillfully evaded the Athenian naval blockade and reinforced the Syracusans in completing the final section of the cross-wall, a critical structure that further hindered the Athenian siege efforts. Meanwhile, Gylippus embarked on a campaign across Sicily to gather additional land and naval forces, persuading cities that had previously been neutral or lukewarm to join the cause. Syracusan and Corinthian envoys were also dispatched to Lacedaemon and Corinth, urgently requesting more troops. They suggested using any available means— whether merchant ships, transport vessels, or other methods—to deliver reinforcements to Sicily, particularly as they knew the Athenians were also seeking reinforcements. In the meantime, the Syracusans began preparing a fleet and conducting naval exercises, intending to challenge the Athenians by sea and showing a newfound confidence in their military situation.

Nicias, witnessing the enemy's increasing strength and his own forces' growing difficulties, decided to send a comprehensive message to Athens. He had already sent frequent reports of each development, but he now deemed it essential to communicate more urgently. Realizing they were in a critical position, he felt that without a timely recall or substantial reinforcements, they had little hope of survival. Concerned that oral messengers might fail to convey the gravity of the situation—whether due to forgetting details, misunderstandings, or wanting to downplay the severity—Nicias chose to write a detailed letter. This would ensure that his perspective reached Athens accurately, allowing the Athenians to make an informed decision based on the true state of affairs.

After dispatching his emissaries with the letter and supplementary verbal instructions, Nicias resumed managing the army, now focusing on defensive strategies and avoiding unnecessary risks. As the summer drew to a close, Athenian general Euetion, in coordination with Perdiccas, launched an offensive against Amphipolis, bringing a large force of Thracians. Though unsuccessful in taking the city, he managed to blockade it from the river by establishing a base at Himeraeum with a fleet of galleys.

The winter arrived, and Nicias's envoys reached Athens. There, they conveyed his verbal messages, answered any questions, and presented his letter. The city clerk read Nicias's letter aloud to the Athenians, who listened intently to the following message:

"Our previous operations, Athenians, have been reported to you in several dispatches. Now, it is essential that you understand our current predicament, so that you may respond accordingly. Initially, we defeated the Syracusans, our primary adversaries, in most encounters and successfully constructed the defensive positions we currently occupy. However, the arrival of Gylippus from Lacedaemon with a combined army from the Peloponnese and allied cities in Sicily altered the situation. We won the first battle against him, yet on the following day, his army, augmented with numerous cavalry and light-armed troops, overpowered us, forcing us to retreat within our fortifications.

"As a result of the substantial forces opposing us, we have been compelled to halt our circumvallation efforts and adopt a defensive stance. Even within our lines, we cannot fully deploy our forces, as a considerable number of our heavy infantry are preoccupied with the defense of these fortifications. Meanwhile, the enemy has managed to construct a cross-wall that extends past our lines, making a complete investment of Syracuse impossible without a major offensive to break through this barrier. Ironically, while we are called the besiegers, we are effectively besieged from the land side, as the enemy's cavalry prevents us from moving freely in the countryside."

In the letter, Nicias conveyed the dire reality of the Athenians' circumstances in Sicily, highlighting the escalating challenge of their position and the urgent need for Athenian reinforcements or a strategic recall.

In addition to these difficulties, an embassy has already been sent to Peloponnese to procure reinforcements, while Gylippus has been rallying support within Sicily itself. His mission includes persuading cities currently neutral to join the war effort, as well as securing reinforcements from allies in troops and naval supplies. It seems they are planning a joint assault on both our lines and our fleet by sea. You may be surprised at the mention of a naval attack, but they have come to realize the effect that time has had on us—our ships, long at sea, are worn and decaying, and our crews are depleted. The original strength and quality of our navy have diminished, as it has become impossible to pull our ships ashore to properly careen them. The enemy's fleet, equal to or even surpassing ours in numbers, is always poised to attack, forcing us into a constant state of readiness. They can be seen drilling, and since they are not bound to maintain a blockade, they are able to rest and dry their ships, keeping them in better condition than ours.

Even if we had additional ships, we would find it hard to spare any from the demands of the blockade. The flow of supplies is already challenging to maintain, as we struggle to secure provisions without being intercepted by Syracuse; any slight lapse would make it even harder. Moreover, our crews continue to suffer losses from several sources: many of our men are lost to ambushes by the Syracusan cavalry while out foraging for fuel or water, which they must now collect from distant locations. Our slaves, who once feared us, are now emboldened by the decline in our dominance and desert in increasing numbers. Our foreign sailors, witnessing the unexpected appearance of a formidable navy against us, have been demoralized. Those who initially joined under compulsion now seek every opportunity to return to their home cities, while those enticed by promises of high pay with little danger find an easy escape, deserting to the enemy or making use of Sicily's vast expanses to evade service. Some sailors even engage in commerce themselves, bribing captains to take

Hyccaric slaves aboard in their place, thus further diminishing our fleet's efficiency.

As you know, the period during which a naval crew maintains peak performance is short, and it is difficult to replace those experienced in timing and coordination. However, the greatest challenge for me, in my position, is the natural resistance of Athenian sailors to authority, which prevents me from taking necessary disciplinary measures to address these problems. We also have no reliable means of replenishing our crew, unlike the enemy who can draw recruits from numerous sources. We are forced to rely on the men we brought from Athens, as our allies here—Naxos and Catana—are unable to supply us. Only one further misfortune could worsen our situation: the defection of our Italian suppliers. If they perceive that you are not committed to reinforcing us, they may well side with the enemy. This would cut off our supplies, forcing us to abandon our position due to starvation, and would allow Syracuse to conclude the war without the need for further conflict.

"I could, of course, have written to you in a way that might have sounded more reassuring, yet nothing could have been more beneficial than this candid account if your aim is to understand the real conditions here before making any decisions. I am aware that it is in your nature to prefer hearing a favorable report; however, experience has shown that if such reports fail to align with outcomes, blame quickly falls on the one who presented them. For this reason, I deemed it best to lay out the truth plainly.

"You should not think that either your generals or your soldiers have lost the ability to contend with the forces originally set against them. Instead, consider that we are now facing the threat of a broad alliance throughout Sicily, coupled with the arrival of additional troops from Peloponnese, while the forces we currently command struggle even to meet the challenges posed by our existing enemies. Therefore, a prompt and decisive choice is required: either recall us or dispatch another fleet and army, doubling our strength and providing substantial financial resources. I also ask you to send a successor to take over my duties, as a severe affliction in my kidneys renders me unfit to hold command. I believe I have earned some indulgence from you, as I provided valuable service in previous commands when I was in better health. Nevertheless, whatever course you decide, execute it with utmost speed as soon as spring begins. The enemy will soon receive reinforcements from Sicily, and, if unchecked, those from Peloponnese will arrive after some delay. Without timely intervention, the former will reach us before your reinforcements, and the latter, as they did previously, may evade your forces entirely."

These were the contents of Nicias's letter. After hearing it, the Athenians rejected his request to resign. Instead, they appointed two additional colleagues, Menander and Euthydemus, who were already serving in the field, to assist Nicias so that he would not bear the full weight of command alone in his illness. The assembly then voted to dispatch additional forces by both land and sea, drawing recruits from the Athenians on the muster roll and from allied contingents. To support Nicias, they selected Demosthenes, son of Alcisthenes, and Eurymedon, son of Thucles, as his new colleagues.

Eurymedon was sent off promptly around the winter solstice with ten ships and one hundred and twenty talents of silver, bearing instructions to inform the army that reinforcements were forthcoming and that support for their needs was in hand. Demosthenes, meanwhile, remained in Athens to organize the new expedition. He awaited the onset of spring before departing, summoning troops from allied territories, and gathering money, ships, and heavy infantry at home.

Additionally, the Athenians dispatched twenty ships around Peloponnese to hinder any reinforcements from reaching Sicily from Corinth or Peloponnese. Encouraged by favorable reports from their envoys on the changing situation in Sicily, the Corinthians now felt emboldened, convinced that their previously dispatched fleet had contributed to this improvement. They began preparing to send heavy infantry by merchant vessels to Sicily. The Lacedaemonians took similar steps for the other cities in Peloponnese. The Corinthians also manned a fleet of twenty-five ships, intending to challenge the Athenian squadron stationed at Naupactus. Their aim was twofold: to probe the possibility of an engagement with the Athenians there, and to divert Athenian attention, making it more challenging for them to monitor and obstruct the departure of their merchant vessels destined for Sicily.

While the Lacedaemonians finalized preparations for their invasion of Attica, driven both by their own resolve and the urging of their Syracusan and Corinthian allies, they were determined to block the reinforcements Athens was preparing to send to Sicily. Alcibiades strongly advocated for the fortification of Decelea and a renewed, vigorous campaign, which added further impetus. But above all, the Lacedaemonians felt confident because they believed that Athens, now facing two simultaneous wars—one with them and another with the Sicilians—would be easier to defeat. They were also emboldened by their conviction that Athens had been the first to violate the truce.

During the prior conflict, the Lacedaemonians had felt that they themselves were primarily at fault, recalling the Theban incursion into Plataea during peacetime, as well as their rejection of Athens' offer for arbitration, which, according to their treaty, should have precluded warfare. Reflecting on these past errors, they saw their setbacks, such as the disaster at Pylos, as a form of retribution and took them to heart. However, as the years passed, hostilities from Pylos became incessant, and the Athenian fleet from Argos raided and ravaged several regions, including Epidaurus and Prasiae. The Athenians repeatedly dismissed Lacedaemon's calls for arbitration on disputed points in the treaty, leading the Lacedaemonians to conclude that Athens was now guilty of the same offenses they had previously committed. Their resentment grew, and they renewed their enthusiasm for war.

During the winter, the Lacedaemonians began amassing iron from their allies and preparing equipment for the fortification at Decelea.

At the same time, they raised additional forces domestically and requisitioned others across Peloponnese to be transported by merchant vessels to support their allies in Sicily. Winter came to a close, marking the end of the eighteenth year of this ongoing conflict chronicled by Thucydides.

With the onset of early spring, sooner than usual, the Lacedaemonians and their allies launched an invasion of Attica under the command of Agis, son of Archidamus, king of the Lacedaemonians. They commenced by ravaging the outskirts of the Athenian plain and soon set about fortifying Decelea, dividing the work among the various allied cities. The strategic location of Decelea, approximately thirteen to fourteen miles from Athens and a similar distance from Boeotia, allowed the fort to threaten the Athenian plains and the wealthiest lands, remaining visible from Athens itself. As the Peloponnesians and their allies fortified Decelea in Attica, forces back home also dispatched heavy infantry to Sicily.

The Lacedaemonians contributed six hundred chosen troops, comprising Helots and Neodamodes (freedmen), led by Eccritus, a Spartan. Meanwhile, the Boeotians sent three hundred heavy infantry under the command of two Theban generals, Xenon and Nicon, as well as Hegesander, a Thespian. This contingent was among the first to venture into open sea, departing from Taenarus in Laconia. Shortly after, the Corinthians dispatched five hundred heavy infantry, a mix of Corinthian citizens and Arcadian mercenaries, under the leadership of Alexarchus, a Corinthian commander. The Sicyonians simultaneously sent two hundred heavy infantry under Sargeus, a Sicyonian commander. Meanwhile, the twenty-five Corinthian ships, prepared during the winter, remained stationed opposite the twenty Athenian ships at Naupactus. Their purpose was to distract the Athenians, keeping them occupied with the Corinthian galleys while the merchant vessels, carrying the reinforcements, successfully embarked from Peloponnese.

While the Athenians actively fortified Decelea, they simultaneously launched new naval operations in the early spring. They sent out a fleet of thirty ships under Charicles, son of Apollodorus, around the Peloponnese with instructions to stop at Argos to request Argive heavy infantry as stipulated by their alliance. Concurrently, they dispatched Demosthenes to Sicily, as previously planned, with a fleet comprising sixty Athenian ships, five Chian vessels, twelve hundred Athenian heavy infantry, and additional forces from allied islands, including whatever resources could be obtained from other subject allies useful for the campaign. Demosthenes was ordered to rendezvous with Charicles, conduct joint operations on the Laconian coast, and await reinforcements at Aegina while Charicles collected the Argive troops.

Around this same period in spring, Gylippus arrived in Syracuse, accompanied by as many reinforcements as he could muster from allied Sicilian cities. Convening the Syracusan populace, he urged them to prepare for a naval confrontation, believing that a victory at sea could be pivotal. Hermocrates also encouraged his fellow Syracusans, asserting that the Athenians' naval dominance was not an inherent trait but rather born out of necessity when faced with the Persian threat. The Athenians, he argued, were more accustomed to land combat than maritime warfare, much like the Syracusans themselves, and their naval prowess had only developed as circumstances demanded. By confronting the Athenians at sea, the Syracusans could undermine Athenian confidence, turning their usual strategy of intimidation back upon them. The unexpected sight of Syracusan ships challenging the Athenian fleet, Hermocrates suggested, would shock and unsettle the enemy, giving the Syracusans an edge despite their relative inexperience.

Spurred by these words, the Syracusans resolved to engage in a naval battle and began preparing their fleet. When all was ready, Gylippus led the Syracusan army out under the cover of night, planning to attack the Athenian forts at Plemmyrium from the land side. Meanwhile, thirty-five Syracusan ships sailed from the great harbor to engage the Athenians, while another forty-five vessels maneuvered from the smaller harbor, aiming to converge with the first group and launch a combined assault on Plemmyrium, creating a two-front distraction for the Athenian forces.

Responding swiftly, the Athenians manned sixty of their ships, deploying twenty-five against the Syracusan thirty-five in the great harbor and dispatching the remaining vessels to intercept those approaching from the arsenal. The battle unfolded at the mouth of the harbor, with both sides fighting fiercely: the Syracusans trying to break through, while the Athenians sought to block their entry.

While the Athenian defenders stationed at Plemmyrium were drawn to the sea to monitor the naval skirmish, Gylippus launched a sudden dawn attack on the forts. He captured the largest fort first, followed by the two smaller ones, whose defenders retreated upon seeing the rapid fall of the primary fortification. Some of the defenders from the first fort managed to escape by boat, but their passage back to camp was fraught with difficulty, as the Syracusans were then prevailing in the great harbor and even sent a swift galley to pursue them. However, as the battle turned in the Athenians' favor, the remaining defenders retreated along the coast with greater ease.

In the harbor, the Syracusan ships initially managed to force their way through the Athenian line but, entering in disarray, collided with one another. This misstep handed the advantage to the Athenians, who not only defeated the disorganized Syracusan fleet but also overcame the squadron that had initially held the upper hand in the great harbor. The Athenians sank eleven Syracusan ships, capturing the crews of three while the others were mostly killed. They themselves lost only three vessels. After towing the wrecked Syracusan ships to shore, they erected a trophy on the small islet opposite Plemmyrium and then returned to their camp in victory.

Despite their naval defeat, the Syracusans benefited considerably from capturing the forts at Plemmyrium, erecting three trophies to mark the victory. They dismantled one of the two forts captured last, but strengthened and stationed garrisons in the remaining two. The fall of Plemmyrium had resulted in significant losses for the Athenians: numerous soldiers were either killed or captured, and a substantial amount of valuable resources was seized. Since the Athenians had used Plemmyrium as a storage depot, the Syracusans captured large quantities of merchant goods and grain, as well as extensive supplies belonging to the Athenian captains. They also took masts, ship fittings, and equipment for forty Athenian galleys, along with three ships that had been docked on the shore. This loss of Plemmyrium proved disastrous for the Athenian forces, as it severely compromised their control over the harbor entrance. With Syracusan ships now patrolling the area, bringing in supplies became increasingly perilous, requiring naval skirmishes to secure even the most basic provisions. The overall effect on the Athenian army was demoralizing, spreading a sense of disheartenment and anxiety.

Following this, the Syracusans sent out a fleet of twelve ships led by Agatharchus, a Syracusan commander. One ship carried ambassadors to the Peloponnese to deliver reports of the favorable state of Syracusan affairs and to urge an intensification of hostilities against Athens. Meanwhile, the remaining eleven vessels set course for Italy, having heard of supply ships en route to the Athenians. These Syracusan ships managed to intercept and destroy most of these incoming supply vessels, burning a substantial stockpile of timber in Caulonia intended for Athenian ship construction. Afterward, the Syracusan fleet proceeded to Locri, where they encountered a Peloponnesian merchant ship carrying Thespian heavy infantry. Taking these troops on board, they sailed back along the coast toward Syracuse. The Athenians, who had stationed twenty ships at Megara in anticipation of such movements, attempted to intercept them but managed to capture only one vessel with its crew, while the others successfully reached Syracuse.

A series of skirmishes also occurred in the harbor as the Athenians attempted to remove a stockade that the Syracusans had driven into the sea near the old docks. This stockade enabled Syracusan ships to anchor safely within, protected from Athenian attacks. To dismantle this barrier, the Athenians brought forth a large, heavily fortified vessel equipped with wooden turrets and screens. They used boats to secure ropes around the piles, then pulled and broke them, while some divers sawed the piles from below. Throughout this operation, the Syracusans bombarded the Athenians from the docks, while the Athenians returned fire from their large vessel. After sustained effort, the Athenians managed to remove most of the piles, though some of the submerged ones, invisible from the surface, continued to pose a hazard for ships passing through. Despite the danger, divers were eventually able to cut even these submerged piles, although the Syracusans continued to replace them.

This phase of the siege saw constant innovation and countermeasures on both sides, with each army devising new tactics and defenses, given their close proximity. Frequent skirmishes, raids, and other engagements became daily occurrences as both sides sought every possible advantage. During this period, the Syracusans dispatched embassies to allied cities, including Corinth, Ambracia, and Lacedaemon, with representatives urging their allies to assist in the war effort. They reported the capture of Plemmyrium and emphasized that their recent naval setback was due not to enemy strength but to a lack of organization on their part. The Syracusans expressed renewed optimism, imploring allies to send reinforcements of ships and troops. With the Athenians rumored to be sending fresh forces, the Syracusans hoped to eliminate the current Athenian contingent before these reinforcements arrived, a victory they believed would effectively end the war.

While the conflict raged on in Sicily, Demosthenes had finally gathered the reinforcements he would lead to the island. Setting out from Aegina, he sailed toward Peloponnese, where he joined forces with Charicles and the thirty Athenian ships already stationed there. They embarked a contingent of heavy infantry from Argos and headed to Laconia. Their first move was to raid part of Epidaurus Limera, after which they landed on the Laconian coast, opposite Cythera, near the temple of Apollo. Here, they laid waste to the surrounding lands and fortified a narrow isthmus, hoping to create a base similar to Pylos where Helots, the oppressed underclass of the Lacedaemonians, could desert and seek refuge. This base was intended to facilitate raiding expeditions into Laconian territory. Demosthenes helped secure this new position before quickly sailing on to Corcyra to rally additional allies there, intending to head without delay to Sicily. Charicles, meanwhile, remained to complete the fortifications, station a garrison, and then return home with his thirty ships and the Argive forces.

During this same summer, Athens received a contingent of thirteen hundred Thracian targeteers, fierce swordsmen from the tribe of the Dii, who were meant to reinforce Demosthenes in Sicily. However, arriving too late for this purpose, the Athenians decided to send them back to Thrace, as retaining them for the war at Decelea proved prohibitively expensive, with each man receiving a drachma per day. Since the fortification of Decelea by the entire Peloponnesian army that summer, its garrisons, which rotated between the allied cities at fixed intervals, had inflicted significant damage upon the Athenians. Unlike the previous short-lived invasions, this occupation rendered Attica a permanent battleground, with frequent raids that devastated property and resulted in the loss of countless lives. Agis, the Lacedaemonian king, was stationed at Decelea and vigorously pursued the war, ensuring continuous harassment. This permanent enemy presence cost the Athenians their entire territory: over twenty thousand slaves—many skilled artisans—had fled, and they lost most of their livestock. Even the daily patrols of Athenian cavalry, tasked with defending the countryside, took a toll, as the rocky terrain led to injuries and exhaustion among the horses.

Additionally, the Athenians faced severe logistical challenges. Previously, provisions from Euboea could be transported swiftly overland from Oropus via Decelea; now, however, they were forced to bear the expense of shipping supplies around Sunium by sea. This costly maritime route slowed down essential imports, transforming Athens from a vibrant city into something resembling a fortress under siege. Year-round, the Athenian populace suffered under the weight of their defenses, with every citizen except the cavalry serving regular guard shifts during the day and full-scale watch duties at night, covering both the fortifications and the walls. Yet what weighed most heavily upon them was the unprecedented dual-front war, straining them to limits previously unimaginable. It seemed incomprehensible that, while under siege by the Peloponnesians entrenched in their own land, they would continue the siege of Syracuse—a city comparable in size and strength to Athens—rather than recalling their forces from Sicily. This spectacle of Athenian resilience defied all assumptions about the city's resources and tenacity. At the war's onset, most Greeks thought Athens could withstand a year or two, perhaps three, if the Peloponnesians launched an invasion. Now, seventeen years since that initial invasion and despite suffering all the ravages of war, they had ventured across the sea to undertake a new conflict as challenging as the one they already faced at home against the Peloponnesians.

This dire combination—the substantial losses from Decelea and the costly demands of sustaining their expanding campaigns—led to Athens' financial strain. Consequently, the Athenians replaced their traditional tribute from subject states with a new tax, levying a twentieth on all imports and exports by sea. This tax was expected to yield higher returns, as their expenditures had risen significantly with the prolonged war, while their revenues dwindled.

The Athenians, not wishing to incur further expense amid their financial strain, quickly arranged for the Thracians who had arrived too late to accompany Demosthenes to Sicily to return to Thrace. They placed them under the command of Diitrephes, with orders to cause as much damage to enemy territories as possible while passing along the coast, particularly through the Euripus Strait. Diitrephes first landed them at Tanagra, where they swiftly carried off some spoils. That evening, he sailed across the Euripus from Chalcis in Euboea, and early the next morning disembarked his forces near Mycalessus in Boeotia. He led the Thracians in an attack on the town at daybreak, moving under cover of darkness to within two miles of the city by the temple of Hermes. At dawn, they launched their assault, catching the townspeople unprepared, as Mycalessus was small, unwalled in places, and poorly defended. Trusting in its distance from the coast, the townspeople had not considered the possibility of a raid, leaving parts of their wall in disrepair and the gates open.

The Thracians, upon entering Mycalessus, immediately began a brutal massacre. They sacked homes and temples alike, showing no mercy to the inhabitants—men, women, children, and even the animals in their path fell to their blades, with every sign of the unrestrained bloodlust characteristic of Thracian warfare. In their ferocity, they stormed into a local schoolhouse, slaughtering a large number of children who had just gathered. The suddenness and intensity of the assault left the city in utter devastation, a tragedy unmatched in scale and horror.

As word of the massacre reached Thebes, the Thebans dispatched troops to intervene. They intercepted the Thracians before they could retreat far, reclaiming the plunder and forcing the invaders back to the Euripus, where their ships were waiting. The worst of the slaughter occurred as the Thracians attempted to re-embark; unable to swim, many perished in the water, and those on the boats, seeing the carnage onshore, moved further out to avoid the reach of enemy arrows. Despite this, the Thracians defended themselves with notable resilience, skillfully forming ranks and fending off attacks from the Theban cavalry as they attempted their retreat. Some who remained in Mycalessus were captured or killed by the Thebans. Out of the thirteen hundred Thracians, two hundred and fifty fell, while the Thebans lost about twenty men, including some cavalry and the Boeotarch Scirphondas. The losses suffered by the Mycalessians, however, were particularly heavy and grievous.

Meanwhile, Demosthenes, who had set sail for Corcyra after fortifying the position in Laconia, encountered a Corinthian merchant vessel at Phea in Elis, intended to transport Corinthian heavy infantry to Sicily. Although he managed to destroy the ship, the soldiers on board escaped and eventually continued their journey in another vessel. From there, Demosthenes made his way to Zacynthus and Cephallenia, where he took on a detachment of heavy infantry. He then summoned Messenian allies from Naupactus and crossed over to Acarnania, stopping at Alyzia and the Athenian-held town of Anactorium. While there, he met Eurymedon, who had just returned from Sicily after delivering funds to the Athenian forces. Eurymedon informed him of the latest developments, including the troubling news that the Syracusans had captured Plemmyrium.

Conon, the Athenian commander stationed at Naupactus, also joined them, bringing an urgent message. He reported that the Corinthian fleet of twenty-five ships stationed across from him seemed ready to resume hostilities and requested additional support, as his own eighteen ships were insufficient to counter the Corinthian threat. Responding to this plea, Demosthenes and Eurymedon dispatched ten of their best ships to bolster Conon's squadron at Naupactus. Eurymedon, who had now officially become Demosthenes' colleague, sailed to Corcyra to instruct the Corcyraeans to prepare fifteen ships and enlist additional heavy infantry. Meanwhile, Demosthenes gathered a contingent of slingers and javelin-throwers from Acarnanian territories, in preparation for the campaign to Sicily.

Meanwhile, the envoys who had previously departed from Syracuse to rally support after the capture of Plemmyrium succeeded in their efforts and were preparing to bring the collected forces to Syracuse. Nicias, however, became aware of their movements and immediately contacted the Centoripae, Alicyaeans, and other Sicel allies controlling the mountain passes, urging them to prevent the advancing army from passing through. This route was the only possible path for the enemy forces, as the Agrigentines had refused them passage through their territory. Heeding Nicias' request, the Sicels laid three separate ambushes along the route. Surprising the approaching Siceliot army, they attacked without warning, killing around eight hundred men, including all of the envoys except one Corinthian. This Corinthian survivor managed to lead the fifteen hundred remaining troops to safety in Syracuse.

Around the same period, reinforcements arrived in Syracuse from other parts of Sicily. The Camarinaeans sent five hundred heavy infantry, three hundred darters, and an equal number of archers, while the Geloans contributed crews for five ships, four hundred darters, and two hundred cavalry. With these reinforcements, almost the entirety of Sicily, aside from the neutral Agrigentines, ceased their previous passive stance and joined actively in Syracuse's fight against the Athenians.

Following the Sicel ambush, the Syracusans decided to delay any immediate attacks on the Athenians. Meanwhile, Demosthenes and Eurymedon, who had now organized their forces from Corcyra and the mainland, set out across the Ionian Gulf with their assembled armament. They made their first stop at the Iapygian promontory and then moved on to the Choerades Isles, located off Iapygia, where they enlisted an additional hundred and fifty Iapygian darters from the Messapian tribe, provided by their ally Artas, the Messapian leader, with whom they renewed a longstanding friendship.

From the Choerades Isles, they continued to Metapontium in Italy, where they persuaded the Metapontines to contribute three hundred darters and two galleys. With this reinforcement, they sailed further along the coast, eventually arriving at Thurii. Here they found that a recent internal conflict had driven out the faction hostile to Athens, so they took advantage of the situation to remain and regroup, mustering and reviewing their entire force to ensure that no soldiers had been left behind. In addition, they successfully encouraged the Thurians to fully commit to their campaign, forging a defensive and offensive alliance with Athens in light of the current circumstances.

At around this same period, the Peloponnesians stationed with their twenty-five ships opposite the Athenian squadron at Naupactus—tasked with protecting the passage for transports to

Sicily—had completed their preparations for battle. They increased their fleet with additional vessels until they were nearly equal to the Athenians in numbers and then anchored off Erineus in Achaia, in the region of Rhypes. Positioned in a crescent-shaped formation, they set their land forces, provided by the Corinthians and allied troops, on the projecting headlands on either side, while the fleet, led by Polyanthes of Corinth, filled the space between, effectively blocking the entrance.

The Athenian fleet under Diphilus, with thirty-three ships from Naupactus, sailed out to engage them. At first, the Corinthians did not advance; however, they eventually judged the moment favorable, raised the signal, and moved forward to engage the Athenians. The ensuing clash was fiercely contested. Though the Corinthians lost three ships, they succeeded in damaging seven of the Athenian vessels by ramming them prow to prow. The Corinthians had strengthened the forepart of their vessels specifically for this purpose, allowing them to shatter the Athenians' bows in direct collisions.

Following this closely contested battle, both sides refrained from declaring a definitive victory. Although the Athenians gained control of the wrecks—thanks to a favorable wind that drove the remnants of the battle out to sea—the Corinthians did not pursue them further. No side made prisoners, and the Corinthians and Peloponnesians, being close to shore, easily escaped without any of their vessels being sunk, while the Athenians also suffered no total loss of ships.

The Athenians eventually returned to Naupactus, and the Corinthians immediately set up a trophy on the shore, claiming victory due to the greater number of enemy ships they had damaged. They felt justified in their claim, reasoning that avoiding outright defeat was, in itself, a triumph. Meanwhile, the Athenians also saw their position as favorable and erected a trophy as victors in Achaia, about three and a half kilometers from Erineus, the Corinthian base. This marked the conclusion of the action at Naupactus.

Turning back to Demosthenes and Eurymedon, the two Athenian generals, after seeing the Thurians ready with their force of seven hundred heavy infantry and three hundred darters, ordered the fleet to proceed along the coast towards Croton's territory. They held a review of all their land forces along the river Sybaris, then led them through Thurian lands. Upon reaching the river Hylias, they were met by a message from the Crotonians, who stated they would not permit the army to pass through their land. In response, the Athenians turned toward the coast, setting up camp near the mouth of the Hylias River, where they rejoined their fleet. The next day, they embarked again and sailed along the coast, making stops at each city except Locri, eventually reaching Petra in Rhegian territory.

Meanwhile, hearing of the Athenians' approach, the Syracusans resolved to make a renewed assault, employing both their fleet and the ground forces they had been gathering for this purpose, aiming to strike decisively before the Athenians arrived. Having analyzed lessons from the previous sea engagement, they made significant modifications to their navy. They reduced the breadth of their ships' prows to make them more compact and solid, and strengthened the cheek structures, reinforcing the hulls with six-cubit stays that extended inward and outward. This design was modeled on the alterations the Corinthians had made to their prows before their engagement with the Athenian squadron at Naupactus. The Syracusans believed these sturdier prows would give them a tactical advantage over the Athenian ships, which were lightly built at the bows, as they had been designed more for maneuvers like circling and flanking than for direct prow-to-prow collisions.

With the battle set to take place in the large but restricted harbour, the Syracusans saw these modifications as essential. By charging head-on, their reinforced prows would smash the weaker Athenian bows, making use of the narrow space in the harbour that would limit the Athenians' favored tactics, such as breaking through the line or circling around. The Syracusans aimed to prevent the Athenians from attempting these maneuvers by controlling the harbour space, pushing the Athenians toward the shore where they would have limited room to retreat. Meanwhile, the Syracusans would hold the central area of the harbour, preventing the Athenians from spreading out and forcing them into confined waters where confusion and collisions would be inevitable. This compact formation, allowing the Syracusans to control the entry and exit, especially with Plemmyrium as a hostile position, would make any Athenian retreat through the harbour's narrow mouth nearly impossible.

Confident in their new modifications and tactics, and emboldened by the previous naval encounter, the Syracusans launched a coordinated assault by land and sea. Gylippus led a contingent of troops to approach the Athenian wall near the city, while the forces stationed at the Olympieum, consisting of heavy infantry, cavalry, and light-armed troops, advanced on the Athenians from the opposite side. The Syracusan fleet then launched from the harbour.

Initially, the Athenians believed they were facing only a land assault, and were alarmed when they saw the Syracusan ships advancing as well. The Athenians hurriedly divided their forces: some men positioned themselves along the walls to face the advancing infantry, others prepared to counter the Syracusan cavalry and light-armed troops approaching from the Olympieum, while another group rushed to man their ships or gathered on the shore to defend the fleet. Once their ships were ready, the Athenians set out with seventy-five ships to face the roughly eighty Syracusan vessels.

The battle extended through much of the day with both sides making advances and withdrawals without a decisive outcome, though the Syracusans managed to sink one or two Athenian vessels. After hours of skirmishing with neither side gaining a substantial advantage, both forces eventually withdrew, with the land forces also pulling back from the walls.

The following day, the Syracusans remained inactive, revealing no immediate plans for another assault. However, Nicias, recognizing that the previous day's battle had been indecisive and suspecting the Syracusans might attack again, ordered the Athenian captains to repair any damaged ships. To strengthen their defenses, he instructed them to anchor merchant ships in front of the stockade that extended into the sea, positioning them about sixty meters apart to form a protected area. This arrangement would allow any Athenian vessel under pressure to retreat safely, then reenter the fray when ready. These defensive adjustments occupied the Athenians throughout the day, continuing until nightfall.

The following day, the Syracusans began their operations earlier, repeating their combined attack by land and sea. The two sides spent much of the day as before, facing each other and skirmishing without a clear breakthrough. Eventually, Ariston, son of Pyrrhicus, a Corinthian known for his skill as a helmsman in the Syracusan fleet, suggested a strategic adjustment to their naval commanders. He advised them to send word to the city officials, requesting that the market be set up near the shore as quickly as possible and instructing vendors to bring all available food to sell directly by the sea. This arrangement would allow the crews to land, eat immediately near the ships, and launch a second attack the same day, catching the Athenians off guard.

Following Ariston's suggestion, a messenger was dispatched, and the city swiftly organized the market at the shore. The Syracusans then suddenly withdrew their fleet back to the town, where they landed and quickly took their meal nearby. Observing their retreat, the Athenians assumed the Syracusans had conceded defeat and returned to the city. With this false confidence, they disembarked leisurely, thinking the fighting was done for the day, and set about eating and other activities. But unexpectedly, the Syracusans soon re-boarded their ships and launched a renewed assault. The Athenians, taken by surprise and many of them still fasting, scrambled in disarray to reassemble their crews and put to sea, managing with difficulty to prepare for the attack.

For a while, both sides held a defensive stance, neither willing to initiate the engagement. Finally, the Athenians, unwilling to be worn out by continued waiting, decided to take the offensive. They let out a cheer and advanced into combat. The Syracusans met them head-on, implementing the new tactic they had devised, charging directly into the Athenian prows. Their solidly reinforced beaks struck with such force that they shattered a large portion of the Athenian ships' bows. Meanwhile, Syracusan fighters stationed on the decks inflicted heavy damage with their missiles, while a significant portion of their force used small boats to maneuver close to the Athenian ships. From these boats, they rowed up alongside the Athenian vessels, aiming darts at the rowers and obstructing the oars, further weakening the Athenian position.

In the end, the Syracusans emerged victorious, forcing the Athenians to retreat through the passage between their merchant ships and back to their own base. The Syracusan ships pursued them up to the merchant vessels, but were stopped by beams equipped with weighted dolphins—large metal counterweights designed to crush any ship that ventured too close. Two Syracusan ships, caught up in the fervor of their victory, ventured too near and were destroyed, with one of them even captured along with its crew. Nonetheless, the Syracusan forces had achieved a decisive win, sinking seven Athenian ships, disabling many others, and either killing or capturing a large portion of their crews. Confident in their newfound superiority at sea, the Syracusans set up trophies commemorating both engagements, now hopeful for continued success by land as well.

Chapter XXII

Nineteenth Year of the War—Arrival of Demosthenes—Defeat of the Athenians at Epipolae—Folly and Obstinancy of Nicias

Demosthenes and Eurymedon arrived from Athens to help with about seventy-three ships, including some from foreign lands, nearly five thousand soldiers, both Athenians and their allies, and a large group of soldiers skilled in using darts, as well as slingers, archers, and everything else that might be needed. When the Syracusans and their allies saw them coming, they were deeply troubled, realizing that there was no end to the dangers they faced. Even though Athens was already struggling with the fortification at Decelea, another strong army arrived, nearly as large as the first one, proving once again the vast power of Athens. At the same time, the Athenians, who had been there earlier and were now suffering from setbacks, began to feel some hope return to them.

Demosthenes observed the situation and was determined not to repeat Nicias's approach. Nicias had wasted time in Catana, instead of attacking Syracuse directly when he first arrived. This delay let the Syracusans shake off their initial fear, and they had time to call for Gylippus to come with reinforcements from Peloponnese—a call they might not have made if Nicias had attacked immediately. The Syracusans had initially believed they could handle the Athenians alone and would only have realized their need for help once they were already surrounded. At that point, even if they had called for help, they would not have been able to use it as effectively. Remembering this, Demosthenes knew that his best chance was to strike while his army still held an advantage in scaring the enemy. Noticing that the Syracusan counterwall, which blocked the Athenians from surrounding the city, was only a single wall, Demosthenes decided to capture the path up to Epipolae. With control of that path, he believed he could seize the enemy camp with little resistance, as no one would be prepared to defend against him. Moving quickly, he aimed to end the war swiftly. He would either succeed in capturing Syracuse or bring the army back, avoiding the continued loss of Athenian lives and resources in the process.

To start, the Athenians went out and devastated the lands around the Anapus River. Both on land and sea, they were victorious, with the Syracusans offering only minor resistance from their cavalry and dart-throwers based at the Olympieum. After this, Demosthenes decided to first attack the counterwall with siege engines. However, as the Syracusans set fire to the machines and repelled the Athenians from various points along the wall, Demosthenes decided not to delay any longer. He secured agreement from Nicias and the other commanders and prepared to execute his plan to attack Epipolae. Since approaching during the day would make it difficult to go unnoticed, he ordered five days' worth of supplies and gathered all necessary tools, including carpenters and masons, as well as arrows and other supplies for building fortifications if the attack succeeded. After the first night watch, he set out with Eurymedon, Menander, and the entire army, leaving Nicias to defend the camp.

They climbed up the hill of Euryelus, where the previous army had ascended, without being seen by the enemy guards. Reaching the fort the Syracusans had stationed there, they took control and killed part of the garrison, though many managed to escape, raising the alarm across the three enemy camps on Epipolae. One camp held the Syracusans, another was occupied by other Sicilians, and the third by the allies. Additionally, six hundred Syracusans who formed the original garrison for Epipolae moved forward to confront the attackers. They met Demosthenes and the Athenians and fought hard but were eventually defeated. The Athenians pushed on, eager to finish the assault while their determination was still high. Some among them immediately attacked the counterwall, abandoned by its defenders, and began tearing down the battlements.

The Syracusans, their allies, and Gylippus, along with his troops, moved to reinforce their comrades from their fortifications. At first, they were taken aback by the unexpected night attack, which threw them into confusion, and they began to retreat. However, as the Athenians advanced with increasing confidence and less caution, trying to force their way through the unengaged portion of the enemy forces without allowing time for the opposition to regroup, the Boeotians rallied and struck back. They attacked the Athenians, broke through their ranks, and forced them into a chaotic retreat.

The Athenians found themselves in complete confusion and uncertainty, so that it was almost impossible to get any clear report from either side about what was happening. In daylight, at least, soldiers have a better idea of what's going on, though even then they hardly know much beyond what is happening right around them. But in a nighttime battle—especially this one, which was the only major clash fought in darkness during the entire war—how could anyone know what was really going on? Although there was a bright moon, they could see each other only as people do by moonlight; they could make out the shapes of bodies, but they couldn't be sure if they were looking at a friend or an enemy. There were large numbers of heavily armed soldiers packed into a small space. Some of the Athenians had already been beaten, while others who had not yet fought were coming forward for their first attack. Many others were just arriving or still climbing up, not knowing which way to go. Because of the disorder ahead, everything was now a tangle of noise and chaos, making it hard for anyone to understand what was happening.

The victorious Syracusans and their allies were shouting loudly to encourage each other since this was the only way to communicate in the dark, and they attacked anyone who came near them. Meanwhile, the Athenians were desperately searching for each other, mistaking everyone in front of them for an enemy, even if it was some of their own fleeing comrades. They kept asking each other for the password, which was their only way of identifying allies. But this constant asking only added to their confusion, with many asking at once, and the password was quickly known to the enemy, while the Athenians couldn't easily discover the Syracusan one. This was because the Syracusans, having won, were not scattered and were less likely to be mistaken for the enemy. As a result, if the Athenians came across an enemy group that was weaker, it managed to slip away because it knew the Athenian password. But if the Athenians didn't know the right answer to the Syracusan password, they were killed. What made things even worse for them was the singing of the paean, which caused confusion because it sounded nearly the same on both sides. The Argives, Corcyraeans, and other Dorians in the Athenian army struck fear into the hearts of the Athenians whenever they sang their paean, almost as much as the enemy did.

Once they were thrown into this chaos, they ended up clashing with each other all over the battlefield, with friends fighting friends and citizens attacking fellow citizens, frightening each other and even coming to blows until they could barely be separated. In the frantic retreat, many soldiers fell to their deaths by throwing themselves over the cliffs, as the way down from Epipolae was narrow. Those who made it down safely into the plain had better chances of escaping. Many from the first Athenian force managed to get away since they knew the area well, but some of the newcomers got lost, wandered around the countryside, and were captured and killed in the morning by Syracusan cavalry.

The following day, the Syracusans proudly set up two trophies to mark their victory. One was placed on Epipolae, where the Athenians had initially ascended, and the other on the spot where the Boeotians had first checked the Athenians' advance. In accordance with a truce, the Athenians were allowed to retrieve their dead. Many Athenian and allied soldiers had been killed, yet there were even more arms collected than could be attributed to the number of those fallen. This was because some Athenians, forced to jump down from the cliffs without their shields, had managed to escape and survive, while others hadn't been so fortunate.

Buoyed by this unexpected victory, the Syracusans regained their confidence. They quickly sent Sicanus with fifteen ships to Agrigentum, where a revolution was underway, hoping to persuade the city to join their cause. Meanwhile, Gylippus took a land route across Sicily to gather reinforcements, now encouraged by the success at Epipolae and hoping that with enough support, he could capture the Athenian lines by force.

Meanwhile, the Athenian generals held a council to discuss the recent defeat and the overall weakened state of their army. They recognized that their attempts had largely failed, and the soldiers had grown weary of the prolonged stay. Sickness was widespread in the camp due to the marshy and unhealthy conditions and the sickly season, making the entire situation feel bleak. Demosthenes argued that they should no longer remain in such a dire position; his initial aim in attacking Epipolae had been to swiftly seize control, and with that attempt now failed, he recommended they leave immediately while they still had the upper hand at sea. He suggested that instead of wasting resources here, they could return and redirect their efforts toward fighting the forces building fortifications in Attica. Continuing the siege in Syracuse, he argued, was simply a waste of money and lives.

This was the opinion of Demosthenes. Nicias, however, though he acknowledged the challenges they faced, was hesitant to openly admit their weakness or to have news of their plan to retreat spread to the enemy, fearing it would make their withdrawal even more difficult. Nicias believed that if they continued the siege, the Syracusans' situation might soon deteriorate more than theirs. Their extensive control of the sea, thanks to their navy, gave the Athenians a strong advantage. Additionally, Nicias had received confidential messages from a faction within Syracuse that wished to betray the city to the Athenians and urged him not to abandon the siege.

Because of this secret encouragement and a general desire for clarity on the best course of action, Nicias publicly argued against a retreat. He explained that he was certain the Athenians back home would not want them to return without formal approval. He knew that those who would judge their actions back in Athens, not having seen the conditions firsthand but relying on hearsay, would be swayed by the persuasive speech of the first critic to denounce them. Many of the same soldiers who were currently decrying their difficult situation, Nicias warned, would, upon returning to Athens, claim just as loudly that the generals had betrayed them or taken bribes. He knew the Athenian mood all too well and declared that rather than face a dishonorable and unjust trial at home, he would prefer to die a soldier's death on the battlefield if it came to that. Besides, he argued, the Syracusans were in an even more desperate position than the Athenians. Their resources were drained from having to pay mercenaries, maintain defensive posts, and sustain a large navy for over a year. Syracusans had already spent two thousand talents and taken on heavy debts, and even a slight loss of their force would put them in jeopardy. Unlike the Athenians, who were financially secure, the Syracusans depended heavily on paid mercenaries rather than troops compelled to serve by loyalty.

Nicias therefore urged that they remain and continue the siege rather than withdraw in defeat, arguing that the Athenians held a considerable advantage in financial resources and should not abandon their position without giving the enemy's endurance a final test.

Nicias spoke with confidence because he had accurate information about the financial troubles faced by Syracuse, along with knowledge of the strong Athenian faction there that was continuously sending him messages urging him not to abandon the siege. He also felt more assured than before regarding the effectiveness of his fleet and believed it was capable of achieving success in their endeavors.

On the other hand, Demosthenes firmly opposed the idea of continuing the siege. He argued that if they could not withdraw the army without formal approval from Athens and were required to remain, they should relocate to Thapsus or Catana. These locations would provide their land forces with a broader area to raid, allowing them to sustain themselves by plundering the enemy's resources. Additionally, he pointed out that their fleet would benefit from the open sea rather than the confined waters that favored the enemy; in wider spaces, the Athenians could utilize their naval skills effectively and have the freedom to maneuver without being trapped when advancing or retreating.

In any case, Demosthenes was strongly against remaining where they were and insisted on making the move immediately, without any delay. Eurymedon agreed with this assessment. However, Nicias continued to voice his objections, which created a sense of uncertainty and hesitation among the group. They began to wonder if Nicias had received additional information that could explain his strong stance.

Chapter XXIII

Nineteenth Year of the War—Battles in the Great Harbour—Retreat and Annihilation of the Athenian Army

While the Athenians stayed in place without taking action, Gylippus and Sicanus arrived in Syracuse. Sicanus had failed to take over Agrigentum, as the party supporting the Syracusans was forced out before he could reach them, while he was still at Gela. But Gylippus arrived with a large group of soldiers gathered in Sicily, along with the heavy infantry that had been sent from Peloponnese in merchant ships earlier that spring, who made their way to Selinus from Libya. They had been blown off course by a storm to Libya, and after getting two ships and guides from the Cyrenians, they sided with the Euesperitae, who were under siege by the Libyans, and defeated the Libyan forces. Then they moved along the coast to Neapolis, a Carthaginian trading hub, which is the closest point to Sicily, just a two-day and one-night journey away. From there, they crossed over to Selinus. Upon their arrival, the Syracusans prepared to attack the Athenians by both land and sea.

The Athenian generals, seeing that more enemy troops had arrived and that their own situation was worsening, especially with many soldiers falling sick, began to regret not leaving earlier. With Nicias no longer opposing the idea as strongly—only asking for no open voting—the generals secretly ordered everyone to be ready to leave the camp at a set signal. Once everything was ready, they were about to set sail when a full moon eclipse occurred. Most of the Athenians, alarmed by this, insisted that they should wait; and Nicias, who was deeply superstitious, refused even to consider leaving until they had waited the full period of thrice nine days required by the soothsayers.

Because of this, the besieging forces had to stay in place, and the Syracusans, learning what had happened, were now even more determined to press their advantage. The Athenians themselves had shown they no longer felt superior on either sea or land; otherwise, they would not have planned to leave. Additionally, the Syracusans did not want the Athenians to settle elsewhere in Sicily, where they could become a more difficult threat. Instead, the Syracusans wanted to force them into a sea battle, where they had a stronger position. They prepared their ships and practiced for as many days as they felt necessary. When the time came, they launched an attack on the Athenian lines. When a small group of Athenian heavy infantry and cavalry came out to defend, the Syracusans cut off some of the infantry and chased the rest back to their lines, where the Athenians lost seventy horses and a few infantry soldiers.

The Syracusans withdrew their forces for the day, but on the following day, they returned with a fleet of seventy-six ships and their land forces, advancing on the Athenian lines. The Athenians went out to meet them with eighty-six ships, and the two sides engaged in close combat. The Syracusans and their allies first broke through the center of the Athenian fleet, then surrounded Eurymedon, the commander of the right wing, who had sailed closer to shore in an attempt to encircle the enemy. They killed him and destroyed the ships with him. After this, they chased the entire Athenian fleet back to shore.

Gylippus seeing the enemy's fleet defeated and Carried ashore beyond their defenses and camp, he hurried to the breakwater with some of his troops to cut off the men as they landed, making it easier for the Syracusans to haul away the ships on their own ground. The Tyrrhenians, who were guarding this area for the Athenians, saw the enemy approaching in a scattered formation, and rushed out to confront them. They attacked and drove them back, pushing them into the marsh of Lysimeleia. Soon after, a larger force of Syracusans and their allies arrived, and fearing for their ships, the Athenians came out to defend them. They engaged the Syracusans, defeated them, chased them back, and killed a few of their heavy infantry. Most of the Athenian ships were saved and brought close to their camp, but eighteen were captured by the Syracusans and their allies, with all their crews killed.

The enemy then attempted to set fire to the rest of the Athenian ships using an old merchant vessel filled with bundles of sticks and pine wood. They set it ablaze and let it drift towards the Athenians, with the wind blowing directly in their direction. Alarmed for their ships, the Athenians quickly found ways to stop the fire, putting it out and preventing the burning ship from coming closer, thus escaping the danger.

Afterwards, the Syracusans set up a trophy to celebrate their naval victory and the heavy infantry they had defeated at the Athenians' lines, where they had captured their horses. The Athenians also raised a trophy for routing the Syracusan foot soldiers who had been driven into the marsh by the Tyrrhenians, as well as for their victory with the rest of the army.

The Syracusans had now achieved a clear victory at sea, a victory they had feared they wouldn't gain after Demosthenes had arrived with reinforcements. The Athenians, now deeply discouraged, were filled with disappointment and regret for having joined the campaign. These cities they were fighting were similar to their own in character, democratic like themselves, equipped with ships and cavalry, and considerably large. The Athenians had not managed to sway them by suggesting changes in their governments, nor had they succeeded in overpowering them with their larger forces. Now, failing in most of their efforts and suffering a defeat at sea—a place where they hadn't expected to lose—they found themselves in greater difficulty than ever before.

Meanwhile, the Syracusans began to sail freely around the harbor, deciding to block its entrance so that the Athenians couldn't escape, even if they tried. The Syracusans no longer thought only about defending themselves; now they aimed to prevent the enemy from escaping, realizing that they had become stronger and that a victory over the Athenians and their allies on both land and sea would bring them great honor in Greece. This would mean that the rest of Greece would either gain freedom or be relieved from fear, as Athens's remaining forces would no longer be able to continue the war. The Syracusans would be seen as the ones who brought this freedom, gaining respect not only from the people of their time but also from future generations.

This struggle held great significance for many reasons. Not only would they be defeating the Athenians but also their numerous allies. And they would not win alone—they would share this victory with their fellow fighters, standing alongside the Corinthians and Lacedaemonians. They had put their city at the forefront of danger and had taken a lead role in achieving naval success.

Indeed, there had never been so many different peoples gathered together before a single city, except for the large forces assembled by Athens and Sparta in this war. Here are the states that came to Syracuse, either to help conquer Sicily or to defend it. Their alliances weren't based on shared heritage as much as on interests or, in some cases, necessity. The Athenians, being Ionians, willingly fought against the Dorians of Syracuse; joining them were the Lemnians, Imbrians, and Aeginetans—settlers from Aegina who followed Athenian laws and customs, as well as the Hestiaeans from Hestiaea in Euboea.

Some joined because they were subjects of Athens, some as independent allies, and others as mercenaries. Among the subjects were the Eretrians, Chalcidians, Styrians, and Carystians from Euboea, along with the Ceans, Andrians, and Tenians from the islands. The Milesians, Samians, and Chians came from Ionia. The Chians, however, were independent allies who didn't pay tribute but contributed ships. Most were Ionians, originally descended from the Athenians, except the Carystians, who were Dryopes, and though obligated to fight, were still Ionians facing Dorians.

There were also Aeolians: the Methymnians, who provided ships instead of tribute, and the Tenedians and Aenians, who paid tribute. These Aeolians were fighting against their Boeotian founders, who were on the Syracusan side, out of obligation, while the Plataeans, the only Boeotians fighting against other Boeotians, did so for a valid reason. Among the Rhodians and Cytherians—both Dorians—the latter, colonists of Sparta, fought with the Athenians against their fellow Spartans under Gylippus. The Rhodians, being Argives by ancestry, found themselves fighting against the Dorian Syracusans and their own relatives, the Geloans, who sided with the Syracusans.

From the islands near the Peloponnese, the Cephallenians and Zacynthians joined the Athenians as independent allies, though their island positions left them with little choice because of Athens's control over the sea. Meanwhile, the Corcyraeans, Dorians of Corinthian descent, openly fought against the Corinthians and Syracusans, who were their colonists and shared their lineage. Although they claimed to be forced, they actually joined willingly, motivated by their deep hostility towards Corinth. The Messenians, who were then based in Naupactus and Pylos—both controlled by the Athenians—also joined the war, along with a few Megarian exiles now fighting against the Megarian Selinuntines.

Many others joined voluntarily. For the Dorian Argives, it was less about alliances and more about their dislike of the Spartans and the immediate personal gains each could achieve by siding with the Ionian Athenians against other Dorians. The Mantineans and other Arcadian mercenaries, accustomed to fighting whoever they were directed against, saw the Arcadians with the Corinthians as equally their enemies. The Cretans and Aetolians also fought for pay, with the Cretans even willing to fight against the Rhodians who had once joined them in founding Gela. Some Acarnanians were also paid to fight, though many came mainly out of loyalty to Demosthenes and friendship with the Athenians, who were their allies.

These groups all came from the Hellenic side of the Ionian Gulf. From Italy, there were the Thurians and Metapontines, drawn into the conflict by the harsh demands of a time of upheaval; from Sicily, the Naxians and Catanians joined in, along with the Egestaeans who had called on the Athenians for aid. Most of the Sicels, and outside Sicily, some Tyrrhenian enemies of Syracuse and Iapygian mercenaries, also took part.

Such were the diverse peoples who had joined the Athenians. Facing them, the Syracusans had their own allies: first, their neighbors the Camarinaeans and then the Geloans, who lived nearby. Moving past the neutral Agrigentines, they had the Selinuntines, who were situated on the other side of the island. These Selinuntines lived on the side of Sicily that faced Libya. Coming from the direction of the Tyrrhenian Sea, the Himeraeans also joined them, being the only Greek inhabitants in that area and the only people from that side of the island to assist the Syracusans. These Sicilian allies who joined the war were all Greeks and Dorians, and each maintained their independence. Among the local non-Greek allies, only the Sicels stood with the Syracusans, although some Sicels had switched their allegiance to the Athenians.

From outside Sicily, the Syracusans had support from various Greek states. The Lacedaemonians sent a Spartan commander, along with a force of Neodamodes, or freedmen, and Helots. The Corinthians, who were the only outside allies to contribute both land and naval forces, also brought troops from their allies in Leucas and Ambracia. They even provided Arcadian mercenaries hired specifically for this battle, while some Sicyonians were forced to participate. Additionally, from beyond the Peloponnese, the Boeotians also joined the fight. Yet, when compared to these foreign reinforcements, the Sicilian cities contributed far more in every aspect—supplies of heavy infantry, ships, and cavalry were abundant, and an enormous crowd of supporters rallied to defend their lands. Even in comparison with all these gathered forces combined, the Syracusans themselves contributed the most to the defense of the island, both because of their large and powerful city and because they were in the gravest danger, which drove them to fully mobilize their people.

These were the reinforcements assembled on each side, with no further allies expected. The Syracusans and their allies, energized by their recent victory in the naval battle, were now set on achieving the ultimate triumph by capturing the entire Athenian fleet and preventing their escape by either land or sea. With this in mind, they began blocking off the entrance to the Great Harbour, using boats, merchant vessels, and galleys arranged side by side across the nearly mile-wide mouth of the harbor. They took every possible measure to prepare in case the Athenians tried to fight at sea again, with plans that were bold and ambitious.

The Athenians, noticing the Syracusans closing off the harbor and becoming aware of their further preparations, held an urgent council of war. Their generals and officers gathered to assess the dire situation, the most pressing concern being that they no longer had provisions on hand. They had sent word to Catana not to send any more supplies, under the mistaken belief that they would be leaving soon, and without control of the sea, they had no means of restocking. After discussing their limited options, they decided to abandon their upper defenses and build a cross-wall to secure a smaller area close to the ships, just enough to store provisions and shelter the sick. The plan was to put every available man into their fleet, regardless of the ship's condition, and engage the Syracusans at sea. If they won, they would sail to Catana; if they lost, they would burn their ships, form a close order on land, and retreat to the nearest friendly place, whether Greek or non-Greek.

Once this decision was made, the Athenians moved quickly to put it into action. They gradually withdrew from the upper defenses and started manning every vessel, requiring all able-bodied men to board. This effort allowed them to prepare around one hundred and ten ships, onto which they loaded archers and javelin throwers from the Acarnanians and other foreign allies. Every other necessary preparation was made, limited only by the resources at hand and the demands of their plan. As they completed these final steps, Nicias, observing the soldiers' lowered morale from their recent, resounding defeat at sea and their anxious desire to settle the matter quickly due to the lack of provisions, called them all together to boost their spirits. He began to address them, speaking with a tone of encouragement and resolve.

"Soldiers of Athens and our allies, the coming battle holds the same importance for each of us, for our lives and our homelands are at stake as much as for the enemy. If we win, each of us has the chance to see his native city again, wherever it may be. Do not lose heart, nor act like those who, after failing once, expect nothing but disaster. Instead, let the Athenians among you, who have faced many battles, and the allies who have joined us in numerous campaigns, recall the unpredictability of war and believe that fortune may yet turn in our favor. Prepare to fight as bravely as the numbers you see here call for.

"We have prepared everything we could against the cramped fighting conditions in the narrow harbor and the attacks we suffered from the soldiers on the enemy's decks. With the guidance of our helmsmen, we have devised plans and made adjustments within our means. A greater number of archers and javelin throwers will join the fight onboard, and we have filled the ships with more soldiers than we would in open-sea battles, where heavier vessels can be a disadvantage. But here, where we are forced into a ship-based land battle, all this additional force will be an asset. We've also made structural modifications to counter theirs. Against their thick ramming prows, which have caused us the greatest trouble, we now have grappling-irons that will stop them from pulling back after striking, as long as our soldiers on deck stand firm. We are forced into this kind of fight, and it's in our best interest not to retreat and not to allow the enemy to either, especially as the shore, apart from the sections our troops hold, is enemy ground.

"With this in mind, fight on with all your strength, and do not let yourselves be pushed ashore. Once you are alongside an enemy ship, resolve to stay engaged until you've cleared their deck of heavy infantry. This command is especially for the soldiers on deck, as this close fighting is their duty, and we know our land forces are generally stronger. As for our sailors, I urge and implore you not to be overly discouraged by past setbacks. Now that we have stronger decks and more vessels, keep in mind how valuable it is to hold onto the respect you have earned. Many of you, though not Athenians by birth, have been embraced as Athenians due to your understanding of our language and ways, gaining honor throughout Hellas. You've shared in the benefits of our empire and earned more respect than any other allies under our protection. Now, in this critical hour, we ask you not to abandon that empire, to prove your superiority over the Corinthians, whom you have defeated often, and over the Sicilian Greeks, none of whom dared face us when our navy was at its strongest. Show them that even in these difficult times, your skill can outmatch the energy and luck of any other opponent.

"To the Athenians among you, I remind you of one last thing: no more ships like these are left at home in our docks, nor are there any more able-bodied soldiers waiting in reserve. If you do not win today, our enemies here will sail straight to Athens, and our people at home, weakened and without these reinforcements, will be unable to fend off attackers bolstered by new allies. Here, you will fall into the hands of the Syracusans, and I needn't remind you of their intentions. Meanwhile, your families at home will fall under the power of the Lacedaemonians. With the fate of both here and at home resting on this one battle, now is the time, more than ever, to stand firm. Remember that as you board these ships, you are the entire army and navy of Athens. You are all that remains of the state and the great name of Athens. If any of you has an edge in skill or bravery, now is the moment to show it—for your own sake and to save all of us."

Following his speech, Nicias immediately ordered the ships to be manned. Meanwhile, Gylippus and the Syracusans, observing the Athenians' preparations, realized they were planning to engage at sea. They also learned about the Athenians' grappling-irons, designed to latch onto their ships. To counter this, they covered the prows and upper portions of their vessels with hides, hoping the slippery surface would cause the grappling-irons to slide off rather than catch hold. Once ready, the generals, along with Gylippus, addressed their forces with the following words:

"Syracusans and allies, the greatness of our past accomplishments and the vital stakes in the upcoming battle are well known to many of you—otherwise, you wouldn't have thrown yourselves into this struggle with such enthusiasm. Yet, for any among you who may not fully appreciate the importance of our position, let us make it clear. The Athenians came here intending not only to conquer Sicily but, after that, to extend their dominance over the Peloponnese and the rest of Hellas. They already control the largest empire ever known to the Greek world, surpassing anything in recent or ancient times. Here, however, they met an unexpected resistance—you, the first people to face them on the water and to challenge their fleet, which has made them masters everywhere else. You've already beaten them in previous sea battles, and there is every reason to believe you will defeat them again now.

"When men suffer a setback in the area they consider their greatest strength, it wounds their confidence more deeply than if they had never held themselves superior in the first place. This shock to their pride makes them more likely to yield, diminishing their morale beyond their actual loss of strength. This is likely the case now with the Athenians, who are feeling the sting of having been humbled at sea by a force they had thought inferior.

"Our situation is entirely different. The confidence that first gave us courage, even when we were inexperienced, has only grown stronger. Added to this is the firm conviction that we are indeed the best sailors of our time, having conquered the very people who once held that title. This double assurance fills each of us with renewed hope, and where hope is greatest, so too is the eagerness to act. They may have tried to imitate our equipment and tactics, but these are familiar elements of our own warfare, and we have prepared ways to counter them effectively. Their attempt to crowd heavy infantry and javelin throwers—men accustomed to land battles—onto their decks will only work to our advantage. These soldiers, many of them Acarnanians and others, are not used to standing still at sea and will find it challenging to aim and use their weapons in such conditions. This unfamiliarity will only create confusion and disorder among their ranks, throwing them off balance.

"And for those of you who might feel intimidated by the sheer number of Athenian ships, know this: in a narrow space, such an abundance of vessels is more of a disadvantage than an advantage. They will be slower in maneuvering and more vulnerable to our attacks. Indeed, the truth of the matter, as we have credible reason to believe, is that their heavy losses and worsening situation have left them desperate. They have little faith in their remaining forces and have resolved to try their luck in this one last gamble. Their aim is to either break through and escape by sea or, failing that, to retreat by land, knowing that their current condition cannot get much worse.

"The fortunes of our greatest enemies have clearly faltered, and their forces are in disarray as I've described. Let us, then, go into battle with fierce determination, believing that when it comes to defending oneself against adversaries, nothing is more fitting than fully satisfying our anger by punishing the aggressor. Indeed, as the saying goes, nothing is as sweet as revenge upon an enemy, and that satisfaction is now within our reach. These Athenians are our foes, and you all know well how truly hostile they are; they have come here to enslave our land. Had they succeeded, they would have brought the most dreadful fates upon our men, the greatest disgrace to our children and wives, and the heaviest shame upon our entire city. None of us, then, should feel any pity or think we are better off if they manage to leave without further harm to us. If they win, they will carry on as they had planned; but if we succeed in defeating them and ensuring the lasting freedom of Sicily, our victory will be unparalleled. And this battle is a rare opportunity—one in which failure brings only minimal loss, while victory will bring the highest reward."

Following this stirring address, the Syracusan generals and Gylippus, noticing that the Athenians were preparing their ships, immediately moved to man their own fleet in response. Meanwhile, Nicias, deeply troubled by the gravity of the situation, felt the weight of the impending danger as they approached the crucial moment of setting out from the shore. Like many in moments of crisis, he was seized by the sense that, despite all he had done, there was still something left to accomplish, and though he had spoken to his men, he felt he had not said enough. Driven by this urgency, he went to each captain individually, addressing them by their family names, their own names, and the names of their tribes. He implored them not to tarnish their own hard-earned reputations, nor to let down the honor that their ancestors had established.

He reminded them of their homeland, a place of unparalleled freedom where each person had the right to live as they chose. He urged them to remember what they were fighting for and used every possible appeal that could strengthen their resolve, speaking of their wives, their children, and the gods of their nation. In such a dire moment, Nicias did not worry whether his words might sound ordinary or predictable. He raised his voice and invoked these ideas, fully believing they would inspire courage in the midst of their fear. With this final encouragement, he felt he had not spoken as he wished but as well as he could under the circumstances.

After this, Nicias withdrew, leading his men to the shore and arranging them in as long a line as possible to offer visible support and bolster the morale of those aboard the ships. Meanwhile, Demosthenes, Menander, and Euthydemus, who were now in command on the water, set off from their camp. They sailed directly toward the barrier across the harbor's mouth, making their way to the narrow passage that remained open, determined to break through and secure their escape.

The Syracusans and their allies had already launched nearly the same number of ships as before. A portion of their fleet guarded the narrow harbor outlet, while the rest positioned themselves around the harbor's perimeter, aiming to surround and attack the Athenians from all directions. On land, their infantry stood ready at any point where Athenian ships might try to come ashore. The Syracusan fleet was under the command of Sicanus and Agatharchus, each leading one wing, with Pythen and the Corinthians stationed in the center.

As the Athenians approached the barrier, they struck fiercely with the first wave of their attack, overpowering the defending ships and attempting to break apart the barriers' fastenings. But soon the Syracusans and their allies closed in from every side, and the fight spread beyond the barrier to fill the entire harbor. This battle was fiercer and more tenacious than any that had come before. Every rower was deeply committed, responding to the boatswains' calls with urgency, while the helmsmen showcased exceptional skill in maneuvering, each pushing themselves to outdo the others. Once the ships came alongside one another, the soldiers on board fought with equal determination, striving not to be outperformed. In every role, each man tried to be the best, competing to demonstrate his worth.

With so many ships fighting in such a confined space—nearly two hundred vessels in the harbor—the usual tactics of ramming with the prows were rare, as there wasn't room to back away or break through the enemy lines. Instead, ships frequently collided with each other by chance, whether fleeing or pressing an attack on a third vessel. As a ship approached, the men on deck would hurl a hail of darts, arrows, and stones, but once they came side by side, the soldiers turned to close combat, attempting to board the enemy's vessel and engage hand-to-hand. In the cramped harbor, many ships found themselves charging one opponent on one side while being rammed by another on the opposite side, sometimes with two or more ships becoming entangled around a single vessel. This forced the helmsmen to split their attention between offense and defense, managing threats from multiple directions at once. The loud crash of ships colliding filled the air, creating a chaotic noise that not only struck fear but drowned out the orders of the boatswains.

The boatswains on each side, caught in the fervor of the battle, shouted constant commands and encouragement to their crews. They urged the Athenians to break through, reminding them that now, if ever, was the time to summon all their courage and fight for a safe return home. To the Syracusans and their allies, they cried that it would be a glorious feat to trap the enemy within the harbor and, through victory, elevate the honor of their own lands. Meanwhile, the generals on both sides, watching over the battle, called out the names of captains if they saw any ship pulling back toward shore without a clear reason. The Athenian generals called out, asking if their men thought the enemy-controlled shore was safer than the sea they had worked so hard to conquer. The Syracusan generals questioned their men, wondering if they were retreating from Athenians desperate to escape, knowing full well that their enemies were looking for any way to flee.

Meanwhile, the two armies on shore, watching the intense and undecided struggle, were caught in a torment of emotions, each side consumed by hopes and fears. The Syracusan natives, eager to secure a complete and lasting victory, were driven by the thirst for glory, while the Athenian invaders, already wounded by past losses, dreaded finding themselves in an even worse predicament. For the Athenians, whose entire fate now rested on their fleet, the fear they felt was beyond anything they had previously endured. As they watched the battle unfold, their hopes rose and fell in rhythm with the shifting tides of combat. Close to the action but unable to see the full scope of the fight, they focused on isolated scenes—some watching their comrades gain ground and cheering, calling on the gods for deliverance, while others saw their forces falter and cried out in despair, their anguish as bystanders even more intense than the soldiers fighting on the ships.

Others still fixed their gaze on parts of the battle where victory was undecided, where neither side could gain the upper hand. These spectators swayed with the strain of their anxieties, their bodies reflecting the inner turmoil of minds caught between faint hope and near-certain ruin. Of all, these suffered the worst, tormented by the constant swing between safety and destruction that seemed within arm's reach, yet always eluded them. In short, the Athenians on shore felt every possible emotion as they watched the uncertain outcome of the sea-battle. The air was filled with a blend of sounds—shouts of encouragement, desperate cries, triumphant cheers of "We're winning!" and despairing cries of "We're losing!"—a chorus of voices that rose from thousands caught in the throes of great peril. The soldiers in the fleet experienced a similar turmoil, as uncertainty, hope, and dread surged through them until the outcome became clear.

Finally, after a long and fiercely contested battle, the Syracusans and their allies broke through and sent the Athenian ships fleeing. With great cheers and shouts of victory, they chased the Athenians back to shore in full retreat. The remnants of the Athenian navy scattered in every direction, each ship seeking refuge on land. Those who were not captured or killed at sea rushed from their ships to the safety of their camp. The Athenian army, no longer divided by individual fears but united by a shared panic, let out a collective wail of anguish and ran toward the shore. Some rushed to aid the battered fleet, while others moved to protect the last defenses of their camp. But the largest number, overcome by terror, began to prepare for a desperate escape, their thoughts turning toward any possible means of survival.

This moment of panic surpassed anything the Athenians had ever experienced. They were now enduring a fate almost identical to what they had once inflicted upon the Lacedaemonians at Pylos: just as the Spartans had been trapped on the island when their fleet was lost, so the Athenians now faced the same hopelessness, with no chance of escaping by land unless by some miracle.

The sea battle had been fiercely fought, with heavy losses on both sides in ships and men. But now, victorious, the Syracusans and their allies gathered the remains of the wreckage and retrieved their dead from the water before sailing back to their city in triumph, where they set up a trophy to mark their victory. The Athenians, utterly crushed by their defeat, did not even think to request a truce to recover their own dead or wreckage. Their minds were solely focused on escape, hoping to depart that very night. Demosthenes, however, approached Nicias and urged him to make one more attempt. He suggested they gather their remaining ships and try to break through at dawn, reasoning that they still had more seaworthy ships than the enemy—about sixty vessels to the Syracusans' fewer than fifty.

Nicias agreed, but when they tried to assemble the sailors, they refused to board. Their spirits were so broken by the crushing defeat that they could no longer bring themselves to believe in any possibility of success.

Seeing no other choice, the Athenians now resolved to retreat by land. Meanwhile, Hermocrates, a Syracusan leader, suspected their intention and realized the potential danger in allowing such a large force to escape. If the Athenians were able to reach another part of Sicily and regroup, they might continue the war from there. Hermocrates took his concerns to the Syracusan authorities, urging them not to allow the Athenians to leave under cover of night. He proposed that all Syracusan forces, along with their allies, should march out immediately to block the roads, guard the passes, and trap the Athenians on their route.

The authorities agreed completely, recognizing the strategic importance of stopping the Athenians' escape. However, they also doubted that they could rally the people to act on such short notice. The Syracusan citizens were celebrating their victory at sea with festivities, as it was a festival day dedicated to Heracles. Most were indulging in revelry and drink, basking in the thrill of triumph, and would hardly be willing to take up arms and march out at that moment. With these obstacles in mind, the magistrates deemed it impossible to execute Hermocrates' suggestion.

Determined not to let the Athenians slip away, Hermocrates devised a ruse to delay their departure. He feared that if the Athenians managed to pass through the difficult terrain during the night, they might get too far ahead to be caught. As night fell, Hermocrates sent a few trusted friends to the Athenian camp, along with some horsemen. These men approached within earshot of the camp and, pretending to be Athenian sympathizers, called out to some of the soldiers. They instructed them to inform Nicias that the Syracusans were guarding the roads and advised him to delay the retreat until daybreak, when he could proceed with less risk. This message sounded credible to the Athenians, especially since Nicias already had contacts within the city who sent him information. Relieved by the warning, the Athenian generals postponed their departure, trusting the message and assuming it was genuine.

Having delayed their departure for the night, the Athenians then decided to spend the following day preparing for the journey. They gave their soldiers time to gather only the most essential items, leaving behind everything that was not strictly necessary for their survival. This delay allowed the Syracusans and Gylippus to move swiftly. They marched out and began blocking the likely routes the Athenians would take through the countryside, setting up defenses at strategic points like river crossings and other natural barriers. They positioned their forces to intercept the Athenian army wherever they thought it would be most effective.

Meanwhile, the Syracusan fleet approached the shore where the Athenian ships were beached. The Athenians had already burned a few of their own ships to prevent them from being captured, but the rest lay stranded on the sand. The Syracusans, unopposed, secured these remaining ships, towing them back to their own city without interference, thus adding the Athenian vessels to their own fleet.

After all the preparations were deemed complete, Nicias and Demosthenes led the Athenian army out of their camp on the second day following the sea battle. The departure was a scene of profound sorrow, not only because they were abandoning the field in defeat—having lost their ships, seen their hopes shattered, and placed both themselves and Athens in grave peril—but also because of the painful sights they were forced to leave behind. Unburied bodies lay scattered around the camp, and as each soldier recognized a fallen friend, he was struck with fresh waves of grief and horror. But the sight of the wounded and sick left behind was even more disturbing; to the living, these suffering comrades seemed far more pitiable than the dead.

The wounded pleaded with those departing, crying out and begging to be taken along, calling to each friend, comrade, or family member they could see. Some clung desperately to their tent-mates, trying to follow as long as their strength allowed, and when they could go no further, they collapsed, crying out to heaven in despair as they were left behind. The whole army was overcome with grief, and many were torn by conflicting emotions—drawn by the need to leave yet struggling with sorrow, unable to turn their backs even in an enemy's land where they had already suffered so terribly. As they marched, their minds were weighed down by self-reproach and the bitter awareness of their situation. The entire army, numbering nearly forty thousand, resembled a starving town escaping after a prolonged siege.

Every man carried whatever he could that might be useful, and even the heavily armed soldiers and horsemen, contrary to their usual custom, carried their own provisions. Some did so because they had no servants left, while others, having witnessed many desertions, no longer trusted the few servants who remained. Despite these precautions, most carried insufficient food, as the camp's supplies had been nearly exhausted. The disgrace of their defeat and the severity of their suffering weighed heavily on them all, even though the fact that they endured it together offered some small solace. In that moment, however, the burden of their misery was overwhelming, especially when they remembered the grandeur of their departure, filled with hope and pride, and compared it to the utter humiliation of their return. This was, by far, the greatest defeat ever to befall a Greek army. They had come with the intention of subjugating others but were now retreating in fear of enslavement themselves. They had sailed forth with songs of praise and solemn prayers, but now they marched back under ominous signs, relying on their heavy infantry rather than their once-mighty fleet. Instead of trusting in the sea, they now feared it, forced to travel by land. Yet even with these heavy losses and shattered hopes, the looming dangers made their current suffering seem almost bearable.

Nicias, observing the army's low morale and the profound change in their spirit, walked through their ranks, offering encouragement wherever he could. As he moved from one group to another, he raised his voice louder and louder, driven by a deep earnestness and the desire to lift the spirits of as many men as possible. He spoke words of comfort and urged them not to lose hope, striving to rally their courage despite the bleakness of their situation.

"Athenians and allies, even now, in this difficult situation, we must continue to hold on to hope. There are those who have survived worse troubles than these, and we should not be too harsh on ourselves, either for the misfortunes that have struck us or the undeserved suffering we now endure. I, who stand among you not any stronger—indeed, you can see my own state of illness—and in my circumstances am perhaps equal to any of you, face the same danger as the least of you. My life has been one of sincere devotion to the gods and of fairness and justice toward others, without having wronged anyone. For this reason, I still hold onto a strong hope for the future; our misfortunes do not terrify me as much as they could. In fact, I believe we might yet see relief: our enemies have had their share of good fortune, and if any god was displeased with our expedition, surely we have suffered more than enough punishment by now.

"Remember that many others before us have attacked their neighbors and done as people do, without facing suffering beyond what they could bear. We may rightfully expect a kinder fate from the gods, for we are now more deserving of their pity than of their anger. Look around you and take heart in the strength and numbers of the heavy infantry marching at your side. Do not surrender to despair; remember that wherever you go, you bring a city with you. No place in Sicily could easily withstand or drive out a force like ours once we settle. Each one of you is responsible for the order and safety of this march, and let every man's focus be that any ground he may need to defend must be fought for and held as if it were his homeland and fortress.

"We will press on both day and night, as our provisions are low. If we can reach one of the friendly Sicel towns, whose loyalty to us has been maintained by fear of the Syracusans, then you can consider yourselves safe. We have sent word ahead to them with instructions to meet us with supplies. In short, soldiers, know that you must summon your courage, as there is no nearby refuge for cowardice. If you push through and escape the enemy here, you will have the chance to see once more the things you hold dear. Those among you who are Athenians will have the chance to restore the greatness of our state, fallen as it may be. For it is men who make a city—not walls or ships that stand empty of the people within."

As Nicias gave this address, he moved through the ranks, bringing back to their place any soldiers he saw straying from the line. Demosthenes did the same for his own division, urging his troops with similar words of encouragement. The army formed a hollow square, with Nicias's division leading and Demosthenes's division bringing up the rear. The heavy infantry protected the outer perimeter, while the baggage carriers and the main body of the army moved within the formation for greater security.

When they reached the ford of the river Anapus, they encountered a force of Syracusan soldiers and their allies, stationed to block their passage. However, the Athenians managed to drive off this opposing force, securing a way across the river. They continued their march, though constantly harassed by Syracusan cavalry and hit by missiles from the light troops. That day, the Athenians made about four and a half miles' progress, stopping for the night on a hill to rest.

The next morning, they set out early and advanced about two more miles, descending into a plain where they set up camp. This location was chosen to allow them to gather food from the surrounding houses and to collect water, as there was a long stretch ahead where water would be scarce. Meanwhile, the Syracusans moved ahead and began fortifying the path the Athenians would need to take. They chose a steep hill known as the Acraean cliff, which had rocky ravines on either side, making it a strategic chokepoint.

The following day, as the Athenians moved forward, they found themselves hindered by a constant barrage of missiles and attacks from the Syracusan cavalry and light-armed troops, who had reinforced their numbers. After a prolonged struggle, the Athenians were forced to fall back to their previous camp, unable to advance further. Supplies were now dwindling, and they couldn't leave their camp freely due to the Syracusan cavalry.

At dawn the next day, the Athenians set out once again, attempting to force their way up the fortified hill. There, they encountered the Syracusan infantry, standing several shields deep and blocking the narrow pass. As the Athenians launched an assault, they were met with a rain of missiles from the steep hillside, which took a heavy toll. Unable to breach the fortifications, they eventually withdrew to rest.

During this pause, a storm swept in, with thunder and rain—a common occurrence in early autumn—that further discouraged the Athenians. They saw this as an ominous sign, a warning of impending disaster. Meanwhile, Gylippus and the Syracusans sent a portion of their forces to fortify the rear of the Athenian position, aiming to trap them. But the Athenians quickly dispatched men to counter this maneuver, stopping the Syracusans from completing their works. After this, they moved further toward the plain and settled there for the night.

The next day, as the Athenians advanced, they found themselves surrounded by Syracusan forces on all sides. The Syracusans pressed their attack relentlessly, wounding many Athenians as they fell back, attacking when the Athenians tried to move forward and closing in if they attempted to retreat. They focused particularly on harassing the rear guard, hoping to break the Athenians gradually and spread panic throughout the army.

For a long time, the Athenians held their ground under this pressure, managing to push forward by four or five furlongs before finally stopping to rest in the open plain. The Syracusans, having inflicted considerable damage, then withdrew to their own camp for the night.

During the night, Nicias and Demosthenes, observing the dire condition of their army—short on every necessity and with many soldiers wounded from the relentless attacks—decided to change their plan. They determined to light as many fires as possible to disguise their movement, then lead the army away by a different route. Instead of continuing along the path they had initially intended, they directed their forces toward the sea, moving in the opposite direction from the one being watched by the Syracusans. This route would take them not toward Catana but across Sicily to the other side, toward the towns of Camarina, Gela, and other Greek and non-Greek settlements in that region.

Following their plan, they lit numerous fires in the camp and set out under cover of darkness. Armies—especially large ones—are often prone to fear and confusion during night marches through enemy territory, with the enemy nearby, and the Athenians soon fell into one of these panics. Nicias's leading division managed to stay together and moved steadily ahead, while Demosthenes's division, comprising more than half the army, fell into disorder and became separated. By dawn, Nicias and his troops had reached the sea and proceeded along the Helorine road, pushing forward with the aim of reaching the river Cacyparis. Here, they intended to move inland along the river, hoping to rendezvous with the Sicels they had called upon for support.

Upon arriving at the Cacyparis, however, they encountered a Syracusan force that was in the process of blocking the river crossing with a wall and a palisade. The Athenians managed to break through this guard and cross the river, then continued on to another river called the Erineus, following the guidance of their local allies.

Meanwhile, at daybreak, the Syracusan and allied forces discovered that the Athenians had slipped away. Many blamed Gylippus, accusing him of deliberately letting the Athenians escape. Without delay, they set out in pursuit, easily tracking the Athenians' route. By midday, they caught up to them, first reaching Demosthenes's division, which had fallen behind due to the confusion of the night march. Demosthenes's troops, marching more slowly and in disarray, were immediately engaged by the Syracusans. The Syracusan cavalry surrounded Demosthenes's division with little difficulty, taking advantage of its separation from the rest of the army, trapping them in one location.

Nicias's division, meanwhile, had managed to advance about five or six miles ahead, as he was pressing his troops onward as quickly as possible, believing that their best chance of survival lay not in stopping to fight unless absolutely necessary, but in retreating swiftly. His strategy was to avoid engagement as much as possible, only turning to fight if forced. Demosthenes, however, faced more constant harassment from the Syracusan forces, as his position at the rear made him the first to be exposed to their attacks. When he realized the Syracusans were closing in, he stopped advancing to organize his troops for battle. But this delay allowed the enemy to fully encircle him, trapping him and his soldiers in a narrow area enclosed by walls, with roads on either side and dense olive groves surrounding them. The Syracusans unleashed a relentless hail of missiles from all sides.

The Syracusans chose this tactic of attacking from a distance instead of engaging directly, recognizing that close combat would favor the Athenians, who would fight desperately when cornered. Confident in their imminent victory, the Syracusans sought to conserve their own forces, avoiding unnecessary risks and keeping themselves fresh for the final push. Their success seemed so certain that they saw no need to take chances, relying on this method to wear down and capture the Athenians in a decisive and orderly manner.

After bombarding the Athenians and their allies with missiles all day, Gylippus and the Syracusans saw that their enemy was exhausted from wounds and hardships. Recognizing this, they made a proclamation, offering freedom to any of the islanders in the Athenian ranks who wished to defect. A few soldiers from nearby towns took the offer. Following this, Demosthenes negotiated a surrender for the rest of his forces, agreeing to lay down their arms on the condition that no one would be executed, imprisoned, or deprived of basic necessities. In total, about six thousand men surrendered, laying down the money they carried, which filled four shields. They were promptly taken into custody by the Syracusans and escorted back to the city.

Meanwhile, Nicias and his division reached the river Erineus that same day. Crossing over, they positioned themselves on high ground on the opposite bank. The next morning, the Syracusans caught up with them and announced that Demosthenes and his forces had surrendered, urging Nicias to follow suit. Nicias, doubtful of the news, requested a truce to verify the report, sending a horseman to confirm. When the messenger returned with the confirmation, Nicias sent a proposal to Gylippus and the Syracusans, offering to repay all the expenses they had incurred during the war if they allowed his army to depart. He even offered Athenian hostages—one for each talent owed—until the sum was repaid. However, the Syracusans and Gylippus rejected the offer and attacked Nicias's division as they had done Demosthenes's, surrounding them and raining missiles down on them until nightfall.

Like their comrades before them, Nicias's men were in desperate need of food and other supplies. Still, they held out, hoping to resume their retreat under cover of darkness. As they began to take up their arms, however, the Syracusans noticed the movement and raised their battle hymn, alerting the Athenians that they had been detected. Forced to abandon the plan, most of them set down their arms again, though about three hundred men managed to break through the guards and flee during the night.

At dawn, Nicias rallied his army and began moving again, with the Syracusans and their allies pressing in from every side, hurling missiles and striking them down with javelins. The Athenians continued forward toward the Assinarus River, desperate to escape the relentless attacks of the Syracusan cavalry and other forces. Exhausted and tormented by thirst, they believed that crossing the river would bring them relief. But as they reached the riverbank, discipline collapsed; driven by sheer desperation for water, they surged forward in a chaotic mass, each man trying to be the first to cross, making it difficult to cross at all. As they crowded together, they trampled each other, some falling immediately to the javelins, others stumbling over baggage and being unable to rise.

On the opposite bank, which was steep, Syracusan forces waited, pelting the Athenians with missiles as they crowded in the river below. The Peloponnesians descended upon them, especially targeting those in the water, turning the river into a scene of carnage. Despite the water being fouled with mud and blood, the Athenians, driven by thirst, continued to drink, even fighting one another to reach it.

At last, when bodies lay piled in the riverbed, and much of the army was either killed at the river or intercepted by the cavalry, Nicias surrendered to Gylippus, whom he trusted more than the Syracusans. He offered himself to Gylippus and the Spartans, begging them to end the slaughter of his soldiers. Gylippus responded by ordering his men to take prisoners rather than kill. The remaining soldiers were captured alive, except for a significant number hidden by the Syracusan troops for themselves. A detachment was sent to capture the three hundred who had escaped during the night; these were also brought in with the rest.

While the number of captives officially declared as public property was modest, a large number were secretly taken as personal spoils, and Sicily was soon filled with these prisoners, who were not part of the terms granted to Demosthenes's division. In addition, a vast number of Athenians were killed outright in the final carnage, marking one of the bloodiest episodes of the Sicilian campaign. Many others had perished in skirmishes during the retreat, and those who managed to escape either served as slaves or eventually made their way to freedom, finding refuge in places like Catana.

The Syracusans and their allies gathered the spoils of war and as many captives as they could capture, then returned triumphantly to the city. Most of the Athenian and allied prisoners were placed in the quarries, as this seemed the most secure way to keep them under guard. However, Nicias and Demosthenes were killed, despite the objections of Gylippus, who had hoped that taking the Athenian generals back to Sparta would be the ultimate mark of his victory. Demosthenes was particularly despised by the Spartans due to his role in the events at the island and Pylos, while Nicias was respected for his efforts to secure peace and release Spartan prisoners, which had earned him goodwill from Sparta. This reputation had given Nicias confidence in surrendering to Gylippus, believing that he would be spared. However, some Syracusans who had secretly corresponded with Nicias feared that he might reveal compromising information under interrogation. Others, particularly the Corinthians, worried that Nicias's wealth might allow him to bribe his way to freedom and live to oppose them again. These groups influenced the decision to have both Nicias and Demosthenes executed. Thus, Nicias, a man who least deserved such a fate due to his lifelong commitment to virtue, met an unjust end.

The prisoners in the quarries endured extreme hardship at the hands of the Syracusans. Packed tightly into the confined space without shelter, they suffered under the scorching sun and the suffocating air during the day, only to face cold, damp nights as autumn set in. This sudden shift in temperatures led many to fall ill. With limited space, they were forced to carry out all activities in the same crowded area. The bodies of those who succumbed to their wounds, illness, or the harsh conditions lay piled up, creating unbearable stench and squalor. Hunger and thirst were constant afflictions; for eight months, each prisoner received only half a pint of water and a pint of grain per day. No form of suffering was spared to these captives. They remained in this state for about seventy days, after which the Syracusans sold all prisoners, except the Athenians and any Sicilian or Italian Greeks who had joined the Athenian expedition.

The total number of prisoners taken is difficult to estimate precisely, though it was certainly no less than seven thousand. This victory in Sicily was the greatest Greek accomplishment of the war and, indeed, one of the most notable in Greek history—a triumph that brought the greatest glory to the victors and the greatest calamity to the defeated. The Athenians were beaten on every front, suffering total destruction. Their fleet, their army, all their hopes—everything was annihilated, and only a few of the vast expedition managed to return home. Such were the devastating events in Sicily.

Book VIII

Chapter XXIV

Nineteenth and Twentieth Years of the War—Revolt of Ionia— Intervention of Persia—The War in Ionia

When news of the disaster reached Athens, the people refused to believe it at first. Even the most credible soldiers who had escaped the battle and provided clear accounts were met with skepticism, as such a total destruction seemed beyond belief. When the truth could no longer be denied, the Athenians' reaction was one of anger toward the orators who had promoted the expedition, as though they had not voted for it themselves. They also turned their fury on the soothsayers, oracle-readers, and all those who had assured them that Sicily could be conquered. Already beset with troubles from every direction, Athens was now gripped by an unprecedented fear and despair.

The losses were felt painfully both by the state as a whole and by each citizen personally: so many soldiers, both infantry and cavalry, had perished, with no reserves left to replace them. They saw, too, that their naval resources were severely depleted, with insufficient ships, money, and crews to defend themselves. They feared that their victorious enemies in Sicily would soon sail directly to Piraeus, spurred by their recent success, while their adversaries closer to home would intensify preparations to attack Athens by sea and land, supported by Athenian allies who had revolted.

Nevertheless, Athens resolved to resist with what resources remained. They decided to gather timber and funds to rebuild their fleet, to strengthen bonds with their allies—especially securing Euboea—and to reorganize the city's affairs more economically. They also elected a council of elders to advise on matters as they arose. In typical democratic fashion, the Athenians, seized by fear, resolved to act with newfound prudence.

These decisions were put into action immediately. Summer had ended, and with the onset of winter, all of Greece was abuzz with news of Athens' catastrophe in Sicily. Previously neutral states felt compelled to join the fight against Athens, reasoning that if the Sicilian expedition had succeeded, Athens might have turned its sights on them. They saw an opportunity to join the war at a moment when it seemed likely to end quickly and when involvement would add to their honor. The Lacedaemonians' allies were more eager than ever to bring the long struggle to a close. Above all, the subjects of Athens were ready to rebel, judging the situation with strong emotion and refusing to believe that Athens could survive the coming summer.

Encouraged by the prospect of a powerful alliance in the spring with the Sicilian states—who had recently expanded their navy—Sparta gained confidence from all sides. The Lacedaemonians resolved to throw themselves fully into the conflict, believing that victory would not only save them from the threat Athens would have posed had it conquered Sicily, but would also allow them to enjoy undisputed supremacy over Greece.

Their king, Agis, moved swiftly that winter, taking some forces from Decelea to gather contributions from the allies to support the fleet. As he marched toward the Malian Gulf, he exacted money from the Oetaeans, seizing their cattle in retaliation for their past hostilities.

Despite protests and resistance from the Thessalians, Agis coerced the Achaeans of Phthiotis and other Thessalian subjects in that region to provide money and hostages, which he then sent to Corinth. His objective was not only to secure resources but also to persuade these populations to join the confederacy against Athens.

Meanwhile, the Lacedaemonians issued an order to their allied cities, calling for the construction of a fleet of one hundred ships. They assigned quotas: twenty-five ships each from themselves and the Boeotians, fifteen from the Phocians and Locrians combined, fifteen from the Corinthians, and ten each from the Arcadians, Pellenians, and Sicyonians as a group, as well as the Megarians, Troezenians, Epidaurians, and Hermionians collectively. Alongside this, they made extensive preparations to begin active hostilities in the spring.

In Athens, the response was no less determined. As winter set in, the Athenians gathered timber, accelerated their ship-building efforts, and fortified Sunium to ensure safe passage for their grain ships. To concentrate resources, they dismantled the fort they had constructed in Laconia on their way to Sicily and implemented strict austerity measures, reducing all expenses deemed non-essential. Above all, they took extra precautions to prevent any further revolts among their allies.

While both sides worked tirelessly to prepare for the renewed conflict, the Euboeans, seeing the Athenians' weakened position, sent envoys to Agis during the winter to propose a revolt from Athens. Agis welcomed their approach and called for Alcamenes, son of Sthenelaidas, and Melanthus to come from Sparta and take command in Euboea. They arrived with about three hundred Neodamodes, and Agis began arranging their crossing. However, before they could proceed, representatives from Lesbos arrived, also seeking to revolt from Athens. Supported by the Boeotians, the Lesbians persuaded Agis to shift his attention to their cause. Agis redirected Alcamenes, initially designated for Euboea, to govern in Lesbos, promising them ten ships, with the Boeotians committing to provide the same number. Agis, stationed at Decelea and commanding a powerful army, had the autonomy to dispatch troops and raise men and funds as he saw fit. During this time, his authority was such that the allies deferred to him even more than to the Spartan government, as his military strength instilled immediate fear and respect wherever he moved.

While Agis was occupied with arrangements in Lesbos, the Chians and Erythraeans, also ready to rebel against Athens, took their appeal directly to Sparta. They were accompanied by an envoy from Tissaphernes, the commander of King Darius's forces in the maritime regions, who invited the Peloponnesians to cross over, promising to support their army financially. King Darius had recently demanded that Tissaphernes pay his overdue tribute, which he had struggled to collect from the Greek cities due to Athenian interference. Tissaphernes calculated that by weakening Athens, he could ensure better tribute payments and secure an alliance with Sparta. Moreover, he aimed to fulfill the King's command to capture Amorges, the rebel son of Pissuthnes, who was defying Persian rule on the Carian coast.

While the Chians and Tissaphernes thus Around the same time, Calligeitus, son of Laophon from Megara, and Timagoras, son of Athenagoras from Cyzicus—both exiles from their cities and residing at the court of Pharnabazus, son of Pharnaces—arrived in Lacedaemon. They were on a mission from Pharnabazus to secure a fleet for the Hellespont, hoping to achieve the same goal as Tissaphernes: to incite the cities under their governance to revolt against Athens. This would allow Pharnabazus to collect tribute and establish an alliance with the Lacedaemonians on behalf of the Persian King.

With both Tissaphernes and Pharnabazus seeking Spartan support, intense competition broke out in Lacedaemon over whether the fleet and army should first be sent to Ionia and Chios, or to the Hellespont. However, the Lacedaemonians ultimately favored the Chians and Tissaphernes, supported by Alcibiades, a family friend of Endius, one of that year's ephors. In fact, the family of Endius derived its Laconic name from Alcibiades, who was a close associate. Nevertheless, before taking any action, the Lacedaemonians sent Phrynis, one of the Perioeci, to Chios to verify if they truly possessed the ships and resources they claimed. Phrynis returned confirming the reports, and the Lacedaemonians promptly entered an alliance with the Chians and Erythraeans, voting to send them forty ships. The Chians, they claimed, already had sixty vessels on the island.

Initially, the Lacedaemonians planned to send ten of the forty ships directly, under the command of Melanchridas. However, after an earthquake, they appointed Chalcideus in his place and reduced the fleet to five ships from Laconia. Thus, the winter ended, closing the nineteenth year of this war as Thucydides recounts it.

As the next summer began, the Chians, eager to avoid discovery by the Athenians, pressed for the fleet to be dispatched without delay. The Lacedaemonians responded by sending three Spartans to Corinth to hasten the transfer of the ships across the Isthmus to the sea on the Athenian side. Their orders included that all vessels, even those Agis was preparing for Lesbos, should sail to Chios. Altogether, thirty-nine ships from allied states were mobilized.

Meanwhile, Calligeitus and Timagoras, representing Pharnabazus, refrained from participating in the mission to Chios or contributing the twenty-five talents they had brought to support the expedition, instead planning to sail separately with a distinct force later. Agis, observing that the Lacedaemonians were resolved on supporting Chios first, decided to align himself with their plan. The allies gathered in Corinth held a council and agreed on a sequence for the campaign: they would sail first to Chios under Chalcideus, who was preparing five ships in Laconia; next to Lesbos, under Alcamenes, whom Agis had designated; and finally to the Hellespont under the command of Clearchus, son of Ramphias.

To divert Athenian attention, they planned to transfer only half the ships across the Isthmus initially, sending those out immediately so that the Athenians would focus less on the first squadron and more on those crossing afterward. This was done with little secrecy, as they held the Athenians in contempt for their lack of a capable fleet. Following this strategy, twenty-one ships were promptly moved across the Isthmus.

Eager to set sail, the Peloponnesians faced a delay as the Corinthians insisted on waiting to celebrate the Isthmian festival, which was taking place at that time. Agis suggested they bypass the festival's truce by letting him lead the expedition alone, but the Corinthians refused, causing further postponement. Meanwhile, suspicions grew in Athens regarding the Chians' intentions. To investigate, they sent Aristocrates, one of their generals, to confront the Chians, who denied any wrongdoing. To affirm their loyalty, the Athenians ordered the Chians to send a contingent of ships as proof of their alliance. Complying, the Chians sent seven ships, as the majority of their citizens were unaware of the secret negotiations with the Peloponnesians, and those in the know were reluctant to commit until they saw a firm Peloponnesian presence, fearing that the delay might mean the fleet wouldn't come at all.

During this period, the Isthmian games proceeded, and the Athenians, invited to attend, used the opportunity to scrutinize the situation in Chios more closely. When they returned to Athens, their suspicions were confirmed, and they quickly took steps to monitor and prevent any Peloponnesian fleet from leaving Cenchreae without their knowledge. After the festival concluded, the Peloponnesians finally set sail with twenty-one ships to Chios, commanded by Alcamenes. The Athenians intercepted them with an equal force, drawing them into open waters. However, the Peloponnesians soon turned back before a full engagement unfolded, and the Athenians returned as well, cautious about the seven Chian ships in their fleet. Shortly after, the Athenians assembled a force of thirty-seven ships and pursued the Peloponnesians along the coast, driving them into Spiraeum, a deserted Corinthian port near the Epidaurian border. One Peloponnesian ship was lost at sea, but the remaining ships anchored in the port.

Seizing this opportunity, the Athenians launched an attack, assaulting both from the sea and from the shore. A fierce and chaotic battle followed, resulting in the Athenians disabling most of the Peloponnesian vessels and killing Alcamenes, though they suffered minor losses of their own. Following the fight, the Athenians divided their forces: a detachment remained to blockade the enemy fleet, while the rest anchored on a nearby islet, setting up camp and requesting reinforcements from Athens. The Peloponnesians were soon joined by the Corinthians, who had come to support the ships, and later by other nearby allies. Recognizing the challenge of holding a blockade in such a deserted place, the allies debated whether to burn their own ships. Ultimately, they opted to pull the ships ashore and station their land forces around them until a better chance to escape could arise.

When Agis heard of the defeat, he sent a Spartan named Thermon to assist. The Lacedaemonians first learned of the fleet's departure from the Isthmus after Alcamenes was instructed by the ephors to send a horseman to report this milestone. Fired up by the news, they planned to send five additional ships under Chalcideus, with Alcibiades joining him. But before they could act, word arrived that the fleet had taken refuge in Spiraeum. Disheartened by this early setback in their Ionian campaign, they abandoned the idea of dispatching more ships and even considered recalling those that had already departed.

Seeing the hesitation among the ephors, Alcibiades once again persuaded Endius and the others to continue with the expedition. He argued that they could complete the voyage before the Chians learned of the fleet's setback. Once he arrived in Ionia, he assured them, he could easily convince the cities to revolt by highlighting Athens' weakened state and Lacedaemon's commitment to their cause. He emphasized to Endius privately that it would bring great honor to have been the one to incite Ionia's revolt and secure an alliance with the Persian King, rather than leaving this distinction to Agis (who was a rival of Alcibiades). Persuaded by Alcibiades, Endius and the other ephors gave their consent, and Alcibiades set sail immediately with five ships, accompanied by the Lacedaemonian Chalcideus, making the voyage with all possible speed.

Around this same time, sixteen Peloponnesian ships returning from service in Sicily under Gylippus encountered twenty-seven Athenian vessels near Leucadia. These Athenians, commanded by Hippocles, son of Menippus, were on the lookout for the Sicilian fleet. After a brief clash in which one Peloponnesian ship was lost, the remaining ships managed to evade capture and sailed safely to Corinth.

Meanwhile, Chalcideus and Alcibiades captured every vessel they encountered on their journey to prevent any word of their arrival from reaching Ionia. They released the detained ships at Corycus, their first stop on the mainland. There, they were joined by some Chian allies who advised them to sail directly to the city of Chios without advance notice. Following this advice, they arrived unexpectedly at Chios, catching the larger population by surprise. However, a select few who were part of the conspiracy had arranged for the city council to be in session at their arrival. Chalcideus and Alcibiades then addressed the council, assuring them that more ships were en route (though they omitted mention of the fleet blockaded at Spiraeum). Believing them, Chios immediately revolted from Athens, followed shortly afterward by the city of Erythrae.

After securing Chios and Erythrae, three ships sailed to Clazomenae, where they succeeded in inciting another revolt. The Clazomenians, anticipating the possibility of conflict, began fortifying a mainland site called Polichna to provide a refuge from their island home if necessary.

While the revolted cities busily fortified and prepared for war, news of Chios's defection reached Athens swiftly. The Athenians saw this as a grave and undeniable threat, realizing that their other allies might soon follow suit, especially given that Chios was the largest and most influential of their allies. In their alarm, they immediately lifted the restriction on using the thousand talents they had held in reserve throughout the war. They decided to employ these funds to rapidly outfit a large number of ships. Under the command of Strombichides, son of Diotimus, they dispatched eight ships from the fleet blockading Spiraeum, which had temporarily left their post after failing to catch Chalcideus's vessels. Shortly after, they sent twelve more ships under Thrasycles from the same blockade. Additionally, they recalled the seven Chian ships that had been part of the blockade at Spiraeum, freeing the slaves on board and confining the freemen. To maintain the blockade, they quickly manned ten new ships and sent them to replace the departing vessels, while also deciding to prepare thirty more. Their determination was unflagging, sparing no effort to bring assistance to Chios.

Meanwhile, Strombichides arrived at Samos with his eight ships, joined by a Samian vessel, and sailed to Teos, demanding that the city remain neutral. Around this time, Chalcideus left Chios with twenty-three ships and headed for Teos, accompanied by land forces from Clazomenae and Erythrae, who marched along the shore in support. Learning of this, Strombichides promptly departed Teos before Chalcideus arrived, and upon sighting the approaching fleet, fled toward Samos, pursued by Chalcideus. Initially, the Teians refused entry to the land forces, but after the Athenians withdrew, they allowed them in. The forces waited for Chalcideus to return from his chase; when he did not appear, they began dismantling the wall that the Athenians had built on Teos's landward side, aided by a few barbarians led by Stages, an officer under Tissaphernes.

After chasing Strombichides into Samos, Chalcideus and Alcibiades returned to Chios, where they armed the crews of the Peloponnesian ships and left them there, then manned twenty additional ships with replacements from Chios. With this force, they set sail to incite Miletus to revolt. Alcibiades, who had allies among Miletus's leaders, aimed to secure the city's defection before reinforcements arrived from Peloponnese, hoping to spread rebellion through Ionia with the backing of Chios and Chalcideus. His goal was to achieve this for the glory of Chios, Chalcideus, himself, and his ally Endius, who had supported the mission. Undetected until they neared their destination, Chalcideus and Alcibiades reached Miletus just before Strombichides and Thrasycles, who had arrived with twelve additional ships from Athens and joined forces in pursuit. Their arrival triggered Miletus's revolt.

The Athenians, arriving in pursuit with nineteen ships, found Miletus closed off and instead stationed themselves on the nearby island of Lade. At this point, following the revolt of Miletus, Tissaphernes and Chalcideus formalized the first alliance between the Persian King and the Lacedaemonians, marking a new chapter in the war.

The Lacedaemonians and their allies agreed to a treaty with the Persian King and Tissaphernes, under the following terms:

1. All lands and cities currently held by the King, or once held by the King's ancestors, shall remain the King's. The Athenians shall be prevented by both the King, the Lacedaemonians, and their allies from receiving any revenue or benefits from these territories.

2. The King, along with the Lacedaemonians and their allies, shall jointly conduct the war against the Athenians. No peace agreement with Athens shall be made unless it is mutually agreed upon by both the King and the Lacedaemonians and their allies.

3. Any cities or territories that rebel against the King shall be considered enemies of the Lacedaemonians and their allies. Likewise, any territories that revolt from the Lacedaemonians and their allies shall be treated as enemies by the King.

This was the formal alliance between the Lacedaemonians and their allies with the Persian King and Tissaphernes. Following this agreement, the Chians quickly mobilized ten additional ships and set sail for Anaia. Their aim was twofold: to gather intelligence about the situation in Miletus and to encourage more cities to join the revolt. However, they soon received an urgent message from Chalcideus, warning them to return immediately, as Amorges was approaching by land with his army. Obeying the summons, they turned back and headed toward the temple of Zeus. Along the way, they spotted another Athenian fleet—ten ships under the command of Diomedon, who had been dispatched from Athens after Thrasycles. The sight of the Athenian ships forced the Chians to flee; one of their ships made it safely to Ephesus, while the rest took refuge in Teos.

The Athenians managed to capture four of the Chian ships, which had been abandoned on the shore, as the crews managed to escape into the countryside. The remaining Chian ships found safety within the walls of Teos. After this encounter, the Athenian squadron sailed back to Samos, while the remaining Chian fleet, now accompanied by their land forces, launched a campaign along the coast, successfully bringing Lebedos and Erae into revolt against Athens. Having accomplished these objectives, both the Chian fleet and the army returned home.

Around this same period, the twenty Peloponnesian ships blockaded at Spiraeum by an equal number of Athenian vessels suddenly broke free. In a surprise sally, they managed to defeat the Athenian blockading force, capturing four Athenian ships. They then sailed back to Cenchreae, where they prepared once more for a journey to Chios and Ionia. At Cenchreae, they were joined by Astyochus, who had been sent from Lacedaemon to take over as high admiral. Astyochus now held the supreme command over the Peloponnesian fleet, solidifying their naval leadership.

Meanwhile, with the land forces departing from Teos, Tissaphernes himself arrived with his own troops to ensure that all remaining sections of the Athenian-built wall around Teos were demolished. Once this was accomplished, he withdrew his forces. Shortly after Tissaphernes left, Diomedon arrived with ten Athenian ships. He arranged a truce allowing the Teians to admit his forces just as they had allowed the enemy, giving him access to the city. Diomedon then sailed along the coast to Erae but, failing to capture the town, returned to his base.

Around this time, a significant uprising took place in Samos. The common people, with the support of some Athenians stationed there in three vessels, rose up against the ruling upper class. In the ensuing conflict, the Samian commons executed about two hundred members of the aristocracy and exiled another four hundred. They then took control of the land and properties of the exiled elite. Recognizing their loyalty, the Athenians granted the Samian commons full independence. The new government in Samos was composed solely of commoners, excluding the landholding aristocrats from any role in public affairs. Additionally, strict marriage restrictions were imposed, forbidding members of the commons from marrying into the aristocracy, thereby consolidating the commons' control over the city's future.

Later that same summer, the Chians, still zealous and undeterred, continued their efforts to incite revolts among Athenian-held cities. Confident in their own strength and wishing to draw as many others into the conflict as possible, they set out with thirteen of their own ships for Lesbos. This move was in line with instructions from Lacedaemon, directing them to rally Lesbos and then proceed toward the Hellespont. Simultaneously, the Peloponnesian land forces stationed with the Chians, along with allied forces in the area, advanced along the coast toward Clazomenae and Cuma, led by Eualas, a Spartan commander. The Chian fleet, under Diniadas—a member of the Perioeci—first arrived at Methymna, successfully inducing it to revolt, and left behind four ships to secure their hold. With the remaining vessels, they continued to Mitylene, which also joined the rebellion.

Meanwhile, Astyochus, the Lacedaemonian admiral, departed from Cenchreae with four ships as planned and made his way to Chios. Three days after his arrival, an Athenian fleet of twenty-five ships reached Lesbos, led by Diomedon and Leon, the latter having recently arrived from Athens with ten reinforcements. Astyochus, upon hearing of their presence, immediately took a Chian vessel and set sail for Lesbos to offer assistance. Arriving at Pyrrha and then at Eresus the following day, he learned that Mitylene had fallen to the Athenians in a swift and unexpected assault. The Athenians had entered the harbor suddenly, overpowered the Chian ships stationed there, landed troops, and routed the forces opposing them, swiftly taking control of the city.

Astyochus received this information from Eresian locals and from the crew of the Chian ships that had previously been left at Methymna under Eubulus. These ships had fled upon the capture of Mitylene, and he encountered three of them, with one vessel having already been seized by the Athenians. Realizing that Mitylene was already lost, Astyochus chose not to proceed there. Instead, he strengthened the defenses of Eresus, arming its population. He also sent his heavy infantry, led by Eteonicus, to march overland toward Antissa and Methymna, while he sailed with his ships along the coast, accompanied by the three Chian vessels, hoping to rally support among the Methymnians to continue their resistance.

However, events in Lesbos continued to turn against him. Recognizing the unfavorable situation, Astyochus withdrew, returning with his forces to Chios. The troops who were originally bound for the Hellespont also returned to their respective cities. Shortly afterward, six additional Peloponnesian allied ships, which had been stationed at Cenchreae, joined the forces gathered at Chios.

In the meantime, the Athenians, having restored control over Lesbos and reestablished the status quo, turned their attention to Polichna, a fortified site on the mainland where the Clazomenians had been preparing a defensive position. The Athenians attacked and captured Polichna, then forced the Clazomenians to return to their island settlement, sparing all except for those leaders responsible for the revolt, who took refuge in Daphnus. Through this action, Clazomenae was brought back under Athenian control, ending the short-lived rebellion.

That summer, the Athenians stationed at Lade with their twenty ships, blockading Miletus, launched an assault on Panormus in Milesian territory. During this skirmish, they killed Chalcideus, the

Lacedaemonian commander, who had attempted to repel them with only a small force. Three days later, the Athenians sailed back to erect a victory trophy, though the Milesians quickly dismantled it, as the Athenians did not control the surrounding land.

Meanwhile, Leon and Diomedon, commanding the Athenian fleet from Lesbos and other nearby posts—namely the Oenussae islands off Chios, and the forts of Sidussa and Pteleum in the Erythraean territory—kept up an aggressive campaign against Chios. Their ships carried heavy infantry pressed into service as marines. Landing at Cardamyle and Bolissus, they defeated the Chians who confronted them in open battle, causing heavy casualties. The Athenians then raided the area, and shortly afterward, they triumphed over the Chians in two more battles, one at Phanae and another at Leuconium. After these defeats, the Chians ceased attempting to meet the Athenians in open combat, leaving the Athenians free to devastate the countryside, which had long been flourishing since the days of the Persian Wars.

The Chians, one of the wealthiest and most prosperous peoples after the Lacedaemonians, had a reputation for wisely managing their success and ordering their city securely as it grew. Even in this revolt, they had acted with caution, entering into the conflict only after securing strong allies and judging that Athens, weakened after the Sicilian disaster, was facing a critical moment. Yet, like many others, they underestimated Athenian resilience. Believing in Athens' impending collapse, they were caught off guard by the unexpected turn of events.

As they suffered from Athenian blockades at sea and pillaging on land, some Chian citizens began conspiring to bring the city back under Athenian control. Learning of the plot, the Chian authorities refrained from immediate action but instead called in Astyochus, the Spartan admiral stationed at Erythrae, who brought with him four ships. They then quietly devised a strategy to suppress the conspiracy, considering measures such as taking hostages to ensure the city's loyalty.

During these events in Chios, a large Athenian force departed from Athens. This force included a thousand Athenian heavy infantry, fifteen hundred Argives (with five hundred light troops outfitted with armor by the Athenians), and an additional thousand allied soldiers. They embarked on forty-eight ships, some of which were transports, under the command of Phrynichus, Onomacles, and Scironides. Reaching Samos, they crossed over and set up camp near Miletus.

In response, the Milesians marched out to face them, fielding eight hundred heavy infantry, supported by Peloponnesian troops who had arrived with Chalcideus, along with Tissaphernes' mercenaries and cavalry, led personally by Tissaphernes. The Argives, confident and disdainful, charged forward against the Milesians, assuming that these Ionians would quickly break. However, the Milesians held their ground and inflicted significant losses on the Argives, killing nearly three hundred of them. On the other wing, the Athenians prevailed over the Peloponnesians and drove back the barbarians and the rest of the force. Seeing their allies routed, the Milesians withdrew into the city without further engagement.

This battle was marked by a striking reversal, with Ionians on both sides triumphing over Dorians: the Athenians defeated the Peloponnesians, while the Milesians bested the Argives. After setting up a victory trophy, the Athenians prepared to lay siege to Miletus by constructing a wall around the city, which lay on an isthmus. They hoped that, by capturing Miletus, they could easily persuade other cities to join them in defection from the Lacedaemonians.

Around dusk, news reached the Athenians that a fleet of fifty-five ships from Peloponnese and Sicily was expected to arrive imminently. This fleet included twenty-two ships contributed by the Sicilian allies, urged by the Syracusan leader Hermocrates, who pushed for a decisive blow against Athenian power. Of these ships, twenty came from Syracuse and two from Selinus. Meanwhile, the ships that had been outfitted in Peloponnese were now ready, and both contingents were placed under the command of Therimenes, a Spartan, to deliver to Astyochus, the overall admiral.

The fleet initially made port at Leros, an island near Miletus. There, learning that the Athenian forces were actively stationed outside Miletus, they redirected into the Iasic Gulf to better understand the situation. That night, Alcibiades arrived on horseback at Teichiussa, a coastal spot in the Milesian territory along the gulf where the fleet had anchored. He brought firsthand accounts of the recent battle, in which he had fought alongside the Milesians and Tissaphernes. Alcibiades advised the Peloponnesian commanders that, if they intended to secure Ionia and sustain their campaign, they needed to hasten to Miletus and prevent the Athenians from fortifying the city. His urgent counsel underscored the strategic importance of Miletus to the survival of the entire Ionian alliance against Athens.

The Peloponnesian fleet decided to relieve Miletus the following morning. However, Phrynichus, the Athenian commander, had already received accurate intelligence from Leros about the approaching fleet. When his fellow commanders expressed their willingness to engage in battle, Phrynichus strongly opposed the idea. He refused to allow them—or anyone else, if he could prevent it—to take such a risk without proper preparation and clear knowledge of the enemy's exact numbers and strength. In his view, recklessly confronting a larger fleet was not only unnecessary but could jeopardize Athens itself. For Phrynichus, there was no shame in retreating strategically; it was far worse to be defeated and expose Athens to both humiliation and serious danger. After their recent setbacks, Phrynichus argued, Athens should only take the offensive when absolutely necessary and with overwhelming strength, not as a matter of pride or bravado.

Phrynichus ordered his troops to swiftly gather the wounded, supplies, and soldiers they had brought, leaving behind any goods taken from enemy territory to lighten their load. He directed them to sail to Samos, where they could consolidate their forces and choose the best opportunities for engagement. As he had spoken, so he acted, demonstrating his prudence not only in this situation but in every command he held. Thus, that evening, the Athenians withdrew from Miletus, leaving their victory unfinished. Meanwhile, the Argives, still resentful over their recent defeat, departed directly for home from Samos.

The following morning, the Peloponnesians set sail from Teichiussa and entered Miletus, finding the Athenians already gone. They stayed a day, then took with them the Chian ships, which had been previously chased into port with Chalcideus, and returned to Teichiussa to retrieve equipment they had left ashore. Tissaphernes soon joined them with his land forces and encouraged them to launch an attack on Iasus, a city held by his enemy, Amorges. Taking his advice, they launched a surprise assault on Iasus, catching the residents off guard, as they had assumed the fleet belonged to the Athenians. In the ensuing battle, the Syracusan forces distinguished themselves. Amorges, an illegitimate son of Pissuthnes and a rebel against the Persian King, was captured alive and handed over to Tissaphernes, who planned to deliver him to the King, as per his orders.

Iasus, a wealthy city of long standing, was thoroughly plundered by the Peloponnesian forces, who amassed substantial loot. The mercenaries in Amorges's service, many of whom hailed from the Peloponnese, were spared and incorporated into the Peloponnesian army. Tissaphernes received control of the city, including all its inhabitants—free and enslaved—at an agreed price of one Doric stater per person. After securing Iasus, the Peloponnesians returned to Miletus. Pedaritus, son of Leon, had been dispatched by the Lacedaemonians to command at Chios, and he was sent overland to Erythrae with the mercenaries formerly under Amorges. Philip was appointed governor of Miletus.

As summer ended and winter set in, Tissaphernes took steps to fortify Iasus, then moved on to Miletus, where he fulfilled his promise to pay the fleet a month's wages at the rate of an Attic drachma per man per day. However, he soon declared his intention to reduce the pay to three obols until he could consult the King about continuing the full drachma rate. Hermocrates, the Syracusan general, protested this reduction. Therimenes, who was only overseeing the fleet's delivery to Astyochus and not acting as its full admiral, was less concerned about the pay issue. Eventually, it was agreed that five ships' wages would be paid at the higher rate, while the rest of the fleet would receive three obols per man, with Tissaphernes committing thirty talents per month for the fifty-five ships. For any additional ships, he would pay at the same rate, ensuring support for the Peloponnesian fleet.

During the same winter, the Athenian forces at Samos received a reinforcement of thirty-five ships from Athens, commanded by Charminus, Strombichides, and Euctemon. Gathering their fleet, including the squadron stationed at Chios, they planned a twofold operation: a naval blockade against Miletus and a simultaneous expedition to attack Chios with both sea and land forces. To assign duties, they drew lots, and Strombichides, Onamacles, and Euctemon were chosen to lead the mission against Chios. They set sail with thirty ships and a portion of the thousand Athenian heavy infantry who had previously been stationed at Miletus. Meanwhile, the main Athenian force, consisting of seventy-four ships, remained at Samos, continuing to dominate the sea as they advanced toward Miletus.

Astyochus, stationed in Chios and overseeing the collection of hostages after the recent conspiracy there, adjusted his plans when he learned that Therimenes had arrived with a new fleet and that the Peloponnesian alliance was gaining strength. Setting sail with ten Peloponnesian ships and ten Chian ships, Astyochus attempted an attack on Pteleum, which ultimately failed. From there, he moved along the coast to Clazomenae, where he ordered the city's Athenian supporters to relocate inland to Daphnus and join the Peloponnesians. This command was echoed by Tamos, the Persian King's deputy in Ionia. However, when the Clazomenians ignored the directive, Astyochus launched an assault on their unfortified town. His efforts to capture it were thwarted, and a strong gale carried him to Phocaea and Cuma. Meanwhile, the remaining ships took shelter on nearby islands—Marathussa, Pele, and Drymussa—where they spent eight days due to persistent winds. During this time, they looted the stored goods of the Clazomenians and eventually rejoined Astyochus at Phocaea and Cuma.

While stationed there, Astyochus received emissaries from Lesbos, who sought to renew their revolt. Although Astyochus was inclined to support them, he encountered resistance from the Corinthians and other allies, who were wary due to past failures in Lesbos. After some deliberation, Astyochus departed with his fleet for Chios, though they were scattered by a storm and arrived separately.

Meanwhile, Pedaritus, who had been journeying along the coast from Miletus, arrived at Erythrae and then crossed with his forces to Chios. There, he found approximately five hundred soldiers who had previously been left behind by Chalcideus with the five ships and their equipment. Shortly afterward, Lesbians once again expressed interest in joining the revolt. Astyochus seized this opportunity, urging Pedaritus and the Chians to mobilize their fleet and lead the Lesbians in revolt, thereby expanding the Peloponnesian alliance and inflicting harm on the Athenians even if they failed to secure Lesbos. However, the Chians were unresponsive, and Pedaritus flatly refused Astyochus's request to use the Chian vessels, thereby stalling the plan for an uprising in Lesbos.

Astyochus, after issuing stern warnings to the Chians that he would refuse to assist them if they encountered trouble, took five Corinthian ships, one from Megara, another from Hermione, and those he had brought from Laconia, and set sail for Miletus to assume his role as admiral. That night, he anchored at Corycus in the Erythraean region. Unbeknownst to him, the Athenian fleet from Samos was also anchored on the other side of a hill, only a short distance away, though neither fleet was aware of the other's presence.

During the night, Astyochus received an urgent message from Pedaritus warning that some recently freed Erythraean prisoners had come from Samos, allegedly intending to betray Erythrae. Astyochus immediately reversed course and returned to Erythrae, narrowly avoiding an encounter with the Athenian fleet. Pedaritus joined him there, and upon investigating the supposed plot, they realized the story was fabricated to allow the prisoners' escape from Samos. They dropped the matter, and Astyochus continued to Miletus, while Pedaritus returned to Chios.

Meanwhile, the Athenian fleet, rounding Corycus, encountered three Chian ships near Arginus and promptly pursued them. A storm struck, and although the Chians managed to reach a safe harbor with difficulty, the three Athenian ships leading the chase were wrecked near Chios. The crews were either killed or captured. The remaining Athenian ships took shelter in Phoenicus harbor, at the base of Mount Mimas, before later proceeding to Lesbos, where they began preparations for a fortification project.

Around the same winter period, the Spartan Hippocrates set sail from Peloponnese with a fleet of ten Thurian ships commanded by Dorieus, son of Diagoras, accompanied by one Lacedaemonian and one Syracusan vessel. They arrived at Cnidus, which had already rebelled under Tissaphernes's influence. Upon learning of their arrival, orders from Miletus directed them to station half their fleet at Cnidus and to patrol the waters around Triopium, a promontory of Cnidus sacred to Apollo, capturing merchant vessels from Egypt. When the Athenians discovered this, they launched a raid from Samos and seized the six guard ships stationed at Triopium, though the crews escaped. The Athenians then attacked Cnidus itself, which was unfortified, almost capturing the town. The following day they renewed their assault but with less success, as the defenders had bolstered the fortifications overnight and had received reinforcements from the escaped crew members. After plundering the countryside, the Athenians returned to Samos.

Around this time, Astyochus arrived at Miletus to take command of the Peloponnesian fleet. The camp there remained well-provisioned, with the troops still holding the significant spoils obtained from their raid on Iasus and receiving consistent pay. The Milesians displayed strong enthusiasm for the war effort. However, the Peloponnesian commanders found their initial agreement with Tissaphernes, made by Chalcideus, lacking and overly favorable to Tissaphernes. While Therimenes was still present, they negotiated a new agreement with Tissaphernes, Darius, and the sons of the King. The new terms of the treaty were as follows:

1. The Lacedaemonians and their allies shall neither wage war against nor harm any regions or cities belonging to King Darius, or that previously belonged to his father or ancestors. Similarly, they shall not demand tribute from such cities. In return, King Darius and his subjects shall not wage war against or harm the Lacedaemonians or their allies.

2. Should the Lacedaemonians or their allies need assistance from the King, or if the King requires aid from the Lacedaemonians or their allies, they are entitled to act together on any mutually agreed terms.

3. Both the Lacedaemonians and the King shall jointly prosecute the war against the Athenians and their allies. Should they agree to peace, both shall make peace together.

4. The King shall bear the expense of any troops stationed in his territory that he has requested for his support.

5. If any state that is a party to this agreement with the King attacks his territory, the other states shall work to stop the aggressors and aid the King to the best of their ability. Likewise, if any region under the King's rule or within his domain attacks the Lacedaemonians or their allies, the King shall intervene to prevent it and assist them to the fullest extent of his power.

Following the new treaty, Therimenes handed control of the fleet over to Astyochus and set out in a small boat, where he ultimately disappeared and was lost. Meanwhile, the Athenian forces moved from Lesbos to Chios, where, having established control both by sea and on land, they began fortifying Delphinium. This location, naturally defensible on the land side and equipped with multiple harbors, was also close to the city of Chios, making it an ideal strategic position.

In Chios, the population remained inactive and divided. After suffering multiple defeats, the Chians were weakened and embroiled in internal discord. Pedaritus had executed members of Tydeus's faction, accusing them of sympathizing with Athens, and forced an oligarchy on the city. This led to a pervasive atmosphere of mistrust, with the citizens doubting both their own strength and that of Pedaritus's mercenaries to effectively resist the Athenians. Despite these divisions, they sent a plea for assistance to Astyochus at Miletus, but he refused to aid them. Pedaritus, in turn, accused Astyochus of betrayal and reported him to the authorities in Lacedaemon. While this conflict persisted, the Athenian fleet at Samos continued to challenge the enemy fleet at Miletus, though they eventually returned to Samos when it became clear that Astyochus would not engage.

During the same winter, twenty-seven Lacedaemonian ships, outfitted through the efforts of the Megarian Calligeitus and the Cyzicene Timagoras to support Pharnabazus, set sail for Ionia around the winter solstice. The fleet was commanded by the Spartan Antisthenes, and the Lacedaemonians also sent eleven Spartans as advisors to Astyochus, including Lichas, son of Arcesilaus. Upon their arrival at Miletus, their orders were to oversee the campaign's progress and decide whether to dispatch the ships, or more if necessary, to Pharnabazus at the Hellespont, appointing Clearchus, son of Ramphias, to lead this force. They were also authorized to make Antisthenes the new admiral if they deemed it appropriate, as Pedaritus's letters had cast suspicion on Astyochus.

The fleet departed from Malea, crossing the open sea and stopping at Melos, where they encountered ten Athenian ships. They managed to capture and burn three empty vessels, but concerned that the remaining Athenian ships would report their position to the Athenians at Samos—as indeed happened—they altered their course, heading toward Crete. Lengthening their route as a precaution, they eventually reached Caunus in Asia. Feeling more secure there, they sent word to the fleet at Miletus, requesting an escort for safe passage along the coast.

The Chians, led by Pedaritus, persisted in urging Astyochus to bring the fleet to relieve them, despite his reluctance. They reminded him of his duty not to abandon the most significant ally in Ionia while it was besieged by land and sea, its territory ravaged, and its large slave population defecting to the Athenians. Many slaves, harshly punished under normal circumstances, took advantage of the Athenian presence, defecting to their side and using their knowledge of the land to wreak havoc. The Chians argued that Astyochus should intervene immediately, as the Athenian fortifications at Delphinium were still incomplete, giving them a brief window of opportunity to disrupt the enemy's position before they strengthened their defenses further.

Astyochus, seeing the general consensus among his allies, prepared to respond to their call for help. However, just then, news arrived from Caunus that twenty-seven ships had come from Peloponnese with Lacedaemonian commissioners. Realizing the importance of escorting this reinforcement, which would bolster their sea power, and mindful that these commissioners were also sent to observe his conduct, Astyochus decided to prioritize meeting them. He abandoned the plan to assist Chios and set course for Caunus. Along the way, he made a stop at Meropid Cos, a city weakened by a recent earthquake—the strongest in recent memory. Astyochus sacked the city, taking its goods while sparing the free citizens who had fled to the mountains, before continuing on to Cnidus.

Arriving at Cnidus, Astyochus received pleas from the Cnidians, urging him not to let his fleet disband but to press on immediately toward twenty Athenian ships under Charminus. These ships were stationed near Syme, Chalce, Rhodes, and Lycia, specifically to intercept the very reinforcements Astyochus was escorting from Caunus. The Athenians, alerted to the fleet's approach by their allies at Melos, had dispatched Charminus to lie in wait.

Astyochus, seizing the chance to ambush the Athenian force before they were fully prepared, pressed forward through the night to Syme, hoping to catch them by surprise at sea. However, rain and fog caused his fleet to scatter and become disorganized. By dawn, only his left wing was in sight of Charminus, who mistook it for the expected ships from Caunus. With part of his twenty ships, Charminus quickly advanced, attacking and sinking three ships while damaging others. The Athenians initially gained the upper hand, but when the remainder of Astyochus's fleet appeared on the horizon, they found themselves surrounded. In the ensuing confusion, the Athenians lost six ships before retreating to Teutlussa, also known as Beet Island, and finally regrouped at Halicarnassus.

Following the battle, the Peloponnesians regrouped at Cnidus with the newly arrived twenty-seven ships from Caunus. Together, they erected a trophy at Syme to commemorate their victory and returned to anchor at Cnidus.

Upon hearing of the battle, the Athenians at Samos sailed to Syme with their entire fleet. Finding no opportunity for direct confrontation with the Peloponnesians, who remained at Cnidus, the Athenians instead collected any remaining ship equipment left at Syme. After a brief stop at Lorymi on the mainland, they returned to Samos.

Meanwhile, the Peloponnesian fleet gathered at Cnidus for necessary repairs. The eleven Lacedaemonian commissioners met with Tissaphernes, who had come to discuss grievances with the previous agreements. The most vocal critic was Lichas, who argued that neither the treaty made by Chalcideus nor that by Therimenes could be upheld. He condemned the King's claim to all territories once ruled by his ancestors, a demand that effectively subjected regions such as the islands, Thessaly, Locris, and everything up to Boeotia to Persian control, thus replacing Greek liberty with Persian domination. Lichas urged Tissaphernes to negotiate a more favorable treaty, rejecting any Persian funds tied to such terms.

Tissaphernes, angered by Lichas's rejection of the existing agreements, departed in a rage, leaving the negotiations unresolved.

Chapter XXV

In the twentieth and twenty-first years of the war, the Peloponnesians, prompted by influential leaders on the island of Rhodes, decided to sail there. They hoped to gain a strategic foothold on the powerful island, known for its large number of seamen and substantial land forces, and believed that this move would allow them to sustain their fleet without needing to rely on subsidies from Tissaphernes. Setting out from Cnidus, they arrived with ninety-four ships at Camirus in Rhodes, causing great alarm among the general population, who were unaware of the plan and fled in panic, especially since their town lacked fortifications. The Lacedaemonians then gathered the people of Camirus, Lindus, and Ialysus, persuading the Rhodians to break ties with Athens and ally themselves with the Peloponnesians. In response, the Athenians swiftly set out from Samos with their fleet to preempt the Peloponnesians, arriving close to the island but just missing their opportunity. They withdrew to Chalce, then returned to Samos, from which they conducted raids against Rhodes, launching attacks from Chalce, Cos, and Samos.

After securing Rhodes, the Peloponnesians levied a contribution of thirty-two talents from the Rhodians. Then, pulling their ships ashore, they remained inactive for eighty days. Meanwhile, behind the scenes, political tensions were escalating. Ever since the death of Chalcideus and the battle at Miletus, Alcibiades had come under suspicion by the Peloponnesians, and Lacedaemon had even sent orders to Astyochus to kill him. Alcibiades, a personal enemy of Agis and increasingly distrusted, was alarmed by these developments and fled to Tissaphernes, where he quickly turned against the Peloponnesian cause and became an influential adviser to the Persian satrap.

Under Alcibiades's influence, Tissaphernes cut the Peloponnesian soldiers' pay from an Attic drachma to three obols per day and even delayed payments. Alcibiades convinced him to justify this by claiming that even Athens, with its long experience in naval warfare, paid only three obols to prevent the seamen from spending excessively on luxuries that would weaken their resolve. He added that delayed payments were an effective means of ensuring loyalty, as it would discourage desertion. Alcibiades also advised Tissaphernes to secretly bribe the captains and commanders of allied cities, securing their quiet support, a strategy that succeeded with most leaders except the Syracusans, with Hermocrates standing firm for the alliance's interests.

As more cities began to request funds, Alcibiades harshly dismissed them on behalf of Tissaphernes. He criticized the Chians, the wealthiest people in Hellas, accusing them of expecting foreign forces to not only risk their lives but also finance their defense, despite Chios's own wealth. He argued that other cities had paid substantial sums to Athens before their revolt and should therefore willingly contribute the same, if not more, now that they were seeking their own independence. He also reminded them that Tissaphernes was funding the war from his own pocket and thus had every reason to be cautious with expenses. However, he assured them that once funds arrived from the Persian king, they would receive full pay and the cities would be adequately supported.

Alcibiades further counseled Tissaphernes to avoid hastily concluding the war or bringing in the full strength of the Phoenician fleet he was preparing. He advised against paying more Greek troops and thus placing both naval and land power in a single party's hands. Instead, he suggested that Tissaphernes let each side keep one realm of power, allowing the King to shift support as needed to balance the other if one became troublesome. If both sea and land forces were controlled by one faction, the King would have no reliable counterbalance unless he entered the war directly, which would be costly and risky. Instead, the King could let the Greeks exhaust each other at minimal expense and risk.

Alcibiades argued that Athens was, in fact, a more manageable ally than the Peloponnesians. The Athenians focused primarily on sea power and had no interest in territorial conquests, which suited the King's aims; they were willing to support Persian control over the Greek cities in Asia, while the Peloponnesians had come with the declared purpose of "liberating" those same cities. The Lacedaemonians, if unchecked, might try to liberate Greek communities under Persian rule, and it was improbable they would stop at liberating Greeks from Athenians alone. Therefore, Alcibiades recommended weakening both Athens and Sparta and, after reducing Athenian power as much as possible, promptly driving out the Peloponnesians altogether.

Tissaphernes largely accepted Alcibiades's strategy, judging from his subsequent actions. He kept the Peloponnesians short on funds, discouraged them from fighting at sea, and undermined their morale by pretending the Phoenician fleet's arrival was imminent, which would supposedly tilt the odds in their favor. This tactic led the Peloponnesian fleet, once powerful, to lose its edge, while Tissaphernes's aloofness toward the war became increasingly obvious.

Alcibiades gave this advice not only because he considered it sound but because he hoped it would pave the way for his eventual return to Athens. He knew that by not directly harming Athens, he might one day persuade the Athenians to recall him. He saw his best opportunity for this if he could show that he had Tissaphernes's favor. His strategy proved effective: as news spread that Alcibiades held significant influence with Tissaphernes, the Athenians at Samos, largely on their initiative (though also encouraged by Alcibiades), began to entertain the idea of restoring him. Alcibiades even sent word to some of the leading figures in the Athenian forces, suggesting they inform those most capable that he would be willing to return and secure Tissaphernes's alliance if they replaced the flawed democracy with a more stable oligarchy. The captains and other influential leaders in the Athenian armament quickly took to the idea of dismantling the democracy.

The idea of shifting power away from the democracy first began to circulate within the Athenian military camp at Samos, eventually reaching Athens itself. Some representatives crossed over from Samos to speak directly with Alcibiades, who promised that, if they abandoned the democracy, he could secure the friendship of both Tissaphernes and, ultimately, the Persian King. This plan sparked hope among the higher classes, who had suffered greatly from the ongoing war and now saw a path to both gaining control of the government and defeating their enemies. Upon returning to Samos, these emissaries organized their supporters into a faction, informing the troops openly that, with Alcibiades back and the democracy removed, the King would become their ally and provide funds to support them. Although some of the soldiers were initially uneasy with these maneuvers, they remained calm, enticed by the prospect of Persian financial backing.

The oligarchic faction, having disclosed Alcibiades's plan to the wider assembly, reconvened to discuss it more deeply among themselves and with other allies. While many viewed Alcibiades's proposal as beneficial and reliable, Phrynichus, still serving as a general, stood apart. He mistrusted Alcibiades's motives, believing that his return was driven by personal ambition rather than any genuine preference for oligarchy over democracy. Phrynichus argued that Alcibiades only sought to modify Athens's government to facilitate his own return and questioned whether such a change was wise. He felt the Athenians should avoid internal strife above all.

Phrynichus also believed the King had little incentive to ally with Athens, as the Peloponnesians were now strong at sea and already controlled key cities within the Persian Empire. The King, he argued, would likely side with the Peloponnesians, whom he could trust more. Furthermore, Phrynichus doubted that oligarchy would inspire Athens's allies to rejoin them or strengthen the loyalty of those still aligned with Athens. These allies, in his view, preferred the freedom they currently had under their own systems—whether democratic or oligarchic—over submitting to a new government imposed from

Athens. Many of these allied cities, he pointed out, harbored deep mistrust toward the "better classes," seeing them as the originators of policies that often harmed the alliance. If the oligarchic elites took charge, Phrynichus argued, they would only increase the oppression of the allies, who saw the general populace as their protector against such abuses.

Despite Phrynichus's warnings, the faction moved forward with Alcibiades's plan, deciding to send Pisander and others to Athens to propose both Alcibiades's return and the end of the democracy. Their goal was to establish an alliance with Tissaphernes by transforming Athens's political structure.

Phrynichus, seeing that a proposal to restore Alcibiades was likely to gain approval among the Athenians, feared retribution from Alcibiades for his opposition. To preempt this, he devised a risky plan: he secretly sent a letter to the Lacedaemonian admiral, Astyochus, still stationed near Miletus. In it, Phrynichus revealed Alcibiades's efforts to win Tissaphernes over to the Athenian side and disclosed the entire scheme, asking Astyochus to consider this an acceptable act of self-defense against his enemy, even if it harmed his own city.

However, rather than acting against Alcibiades, Astyochus took the letter to Alcibiades and Tissaphernes in Magnesia, effectively becoming an informant and, as rumors suggested, receiving pay from Tissaphernes to provide updates on such matters. This was also likely why he didn't press Tissaphernes more forcefully about unpaid wages for the Peloponnesians. Upon hearing of Phrynichus's betrayal, Alcibiades immediately sent a letter to the Athenian authorities at Samos, condemning Phrynichus's actions and urging them to execute him.

Panicked by Alcibiades's denunciation, Phrynichus sent another letter to Astyochus, reproaching him for leaking his earlier message. He proposed a new plan to redeem himself: he would set up an attack on the Athenian camp at Samos, which was unfortified, thus offering the Lacedaemonians an easy victory. Justifying this proposal by his dire need to save his own life, he laid out the specific methods he would use to expose the Athenian camp's vulnerability.

Astyochus, however, again revealed Phrynichus's plans to Alcibiades, who immediately sent another letter warning of Phrynichus's betrayal. Phrynichus, anticipating this letter, quickly acted on his own: he warned the Athenian army that the enemy intended to attack their camp, citing its lack of fortifications and the scattered positioning of their fleet. As general, he had the authority to order immediate defenses, and thus the Athenians fortified Samos more quickly than they otherwise might have. When Alcibiades's letter finally arrived, accusing Phrynichus of betrayal and warning of the same attack, it only seemed to confirm Phrynichus's foresight, leading many to believe Alcibiades was merely trying to frame Phrynichus due to their mutual animosity.

Meanwhile, Alcibiades worked to sway Tissaphernes toward an Athenian alliance. Although Tissaphernes feared the Peloponnesians, who currently had more ships in Asia, he found Alcibiades's arguments increasingly compelling, especially after a falling-out with the Peloponnesians at Cnidus over Therimenes's treaty. The rift had intensified, with the Peloponnesians stationed at Rhodes, and Lichas of Sparta explicitly rejecting any agreement that would grant the King control over all territories historically claimed by him or his ancestors, a stance that validated Alcibiades's original arguments about the risks of the Lacedaemonians' promise to "liberate" all Greek cities.

While Alcibiades worked to win over Tissaphernes with all the energy the situation demanded, the Athenian envoys sent from Samos with Pisander reached Athens. They presented their case before the people, summarizing their points and particularly emphasizing that if Alcibiades were recalled and the government reformed, they could secure the King's support and overpower the Peloponnesians. Opponents of the proposal, including Alcibiades's detractors, objected strongly, calling it a scandal to restore him by changing the constitution. The Eumolpidae and Ceryces also protested, invoking the gods and recalling the reason for Alcibiades's exile—the sacrilegious mistreatment of the sacred mysteries.

Amid these objections, Pisander stepped forward and addressed his opponents one by one, posing a crucial question: given that the Peloponnesians had as many ships at sea as the Athenians, more allies, and both the King and Tissaphernes providing financial support, did they hold any hope of saving the state unless they could persuade the King to side with Athens? Each admitted they saw no alternative. Pisander then asserted plainly, "This alliance is impossible without changing our government to a more moderate form, concentrating power in fewer hands, and thus gaining the King's trust. And for this, we must recall Alcibiades, who is the only one capable of securing such an arrangement. The priority now is to secure the state; we can alter the government again once we are safe."

Initially, the people were deeply troubled by the idea of establishing an oligarchy. But as Pisander made it clear that this was their last remaining option, they set aside their fears for the immediate crisis and decided to proceed. They approved a motion for Pisander and ten others to travel and negotiate the best terms they could with Tissaphernes and Alcibiades. In a related action, the people—following Pisander's accusations—removed Phrynichus from command along with his colleague Scironides, replacing them with Diomedon and Leon. Pisander's charges held that Phrynichus had betrayed Iasus and Amorges, but the true intent was likely Pisander's distrust of Phrynichus's ability to handle the delicate situation with Alcibiades. Pisander also reached out to all political clubs within the city—groups that usually coordinated in legal and electoral matters—and urged them to unite in an effort to overthrow the democracy. With preparations in place to act swiftly, Pisander departed with his team to meet Tissaphernes.

That same winter, Leon and Diomedon, now with the fleet, launched an assault on Rhodes. They found the Peloponnesian ships beached and, after landing and defeating the Rhodian forces who attempted to resist, withdrew to Chalce, establishing it as their base instead of Cos for better surveillance of the Peloponnesian fleet. Soon, Xenophantes, a Lacedaemonian from Pedaritus at Chios, arrived with urgent news that the Athenians had completed their fortifications, and that without immediate support from the full Peloponnesian fleet, Chios would be lost. The Peloponnesians, thus alerted, prepared to go to their aid.

Meanwhile, Pedaritus led an offensive against the Athenian defenses at Chios with his mercenaries and the Chian forces. They managed to capture a section of the defensive works and seize some of the ships beached along the shore. However, the Athenians soon launched a counterattack, first driving back the Chians, then decisively defeating Pedaritus's remaining forces. Pedaritus himself was killed in the battle, along with many of his troops, and a large quantity of their weapons was also captured.

Following these developments, the Chians found themselves under even tighter siege by land and sea, as the Athenians intensified their blockade. Conditions worsened inside the city, with severe shortages of food leading to great suffering among the inhabitants. Meanwhile, Pisander and the Athenian envoys finally arrived at the court of Tissaphernes to negotiate the much-anticipated treaty. Their discussions with Tissaphernes were, however, covertly sabotaged by Alcibiades, who was increasingly skeptical of Tissaphernes's sincerity. Although Tissaphernes seemed to consider the Athenian alliance, he was wary of antagonizing the Peloponnesians outright and wished to prolong the war as Alcibiades had advised, thus draining both sides.

Alcibiades, sensing Tissaphernes's hesitation, employed a deliberate strategy to make the negotiations fail without appearing to be at fault himself. He presented Tissaphernes's terms to the Athenians in a way designed to make them seem excessively burdensome. In my view, this approach aligned well with Tissaphernes's own interests, as he feared openly committing to either side. Meanwhile, Alcibiades wanted the Athenians to see the failure of the treaty as the result of their unwillingness to yield rather than his inability to persuade Tissaphernes.

In the initial discussions, the Athenians conceded to the demands, agreeing to cede all of Ionia and several nearby islands to the King. But as negotiations progressed, Alcibiades pushed further, making demands he knew would be too much for the Athenians to accept. At the third meeting, he introduced the demand that the King be allowed to construct ships and sail freely along his own coasts with as large a fleet as he desired. This was too much for the Athenians, who had already bent as far as they could. Realizing that further concessions would compromise their security, they angrily abandoned the negotiations, feeling duped by Alcibiades, and returned to Samos.

After this failed negotiation, Tissaphernes, seeking to maintain some influence over the Peloponnesians, traveled along the coast to Caunus to bring their fleet back to Miletus and provide them with pay. He aimed to strike a new arrangement with them that would preserve a balance without committing fully to their cause. Tissaphernes worried that a lack of pay would force the Peloponnesians into an engagement that could lead to a decisive defeat or a depletion of their crews, leaving Athens victorious without his assistance. He also feared they might pillage the nearby territories in desperation for provisions. Accordingly, Tissaphernes resumed his strategy of keeping the warring factions in equilibrium by restoring payments to the Peloponnesians and arranging a third treaty, with the following stipulations:

In the thirteenth year of Darius's reign, while Alexippidas was serving as ephor at Lacedaemon, the Lacedaemonians and their allies reached an agreement in the Maeander plain with Tissaphernes, Hieramenes, and the sons of Pharnaces, to define the terms between the King, the Lacedaemonians, and their allies.

1. The territories of the King in Asia shall remain fully under his authority, with the King free to govern his lands as he deems appropriate.

2. The Lacedaemonians and their allies shall neither invade nor inflict harm upon the King's domains, and likewise, the King shall neither invade nor inflict harm upon the lands of the Lacedaemonians and their allies. Should any members of the Lacedaemonian alliance invade or harm the King's territories, the rest of the Lacedaemonians and their allies shall act to prevent it. Similarly, if forces from the King's domains should invade or harm the lands of the Lacedaemonians or their allies, the King shall act to stop it.

3. Tissaphernes shall provide financial support for the ships currently stationed here, in line with the terms of the agreement, until the King's own fleet arrives. Once the King's ships arrive, the Lacedaemonians and their allies will have the choice to either fund their own fleet or continue receiving support from Tissaphernes. If they choose to continue accepting financial support from Tissaphernes, they shall repay him the funds received at the conclusion of the war.

4. Following the arrival of the King's ships, the naval forces of both the Lacedaemonians and their allies, as well as those of the King, shall jointly conduct the war in accordance with the decisions of Tissaphernes and the Lacedaemonians and their allies. If they choose to pursue peace with the Athenians, such peace shall also be pursued collectively.

The treaty thus established a coordinated alliance between the Lacedaemonians and the Persian King, balancing each party's interests in the war.

As winter neared its end, the Boeotians seized Oropus through betrayal. This town, strategically positioned opposite Eretria and held by an Athenian garrison, had been a continual source of frustration for Eretria and the Euboeans. With Oropus under Boeotian control, the Eretrians then traveled to Rhodes, urging the Peloponnesians to bring their fleet to Euboea. However, the Peloponnesians prioritized aiding the beleaguered Chians. They set sail from Rhodes with their entire fleet but, upon spotting the Athenian fleet near Triopium, each side avoided direct confrontation, allowing the Athenians to return to Samos and the Peloponnesians to proceed to Miletus. Realizing that Chios could not be relieved without a naval engagement, they refrained from any further action. Thus ended the winter and, with it, the twentieth year of the war chronicled by Thucydides.

As spring arrived, Spartan commander Dercyllidas was dispatched with a small force over land to the Hellespont to incite Abydos, a Milesian colony, to revolt. Meanwhile, the Chians, under increasing pressure from the Athenian siege and lacking leadership since the death of Pedaritus, were forced to mount a sea offensive. While Astyochus was still stationed at Rhodes, a new commander, the Spartan Leon, arrived at Miletus with a reinforcement of twelve ships, including a mix from Thurii, Syracuse, Anaia, Miletus, and Leon's own vessel. The Chians, gathering their forces, occupied a strong position on land while their fleet of thirty-six ships engaged thirty-two Athenian vessels in a fierce battle. Though the Chians and their allies appeared to have a slight advantage, they ultimately withdrew to the city as darkness fell.

Soon after, Dercyllidas reached Abydos, successfully securing its revolt along with Lampsacus just two days later, with support from the Persian satrap Pharnabazus. Responding to the alarming news, Strombichides set sail from Chios with twenty-four Athenian ships, including transports with heavy infantry, and captured unfortified Lampsacus at the first assault. Taking prisoners, he restored the free inhabitants to their homes and then advanced on Abydos. Although Abydos resisted and his attacks were unsuccessful, Strombichides positioned his forces at Sestos on the Chersonese, which had once been controlled by the Medes, designating it as the defensive center for the entire Hellespont.

During this period, the Chians strengthened their naval dominance, emboldening the Peloponnesians in Miletus and Astyochus, especially after news of the recent sea battle and the Athenian squadron's departure with Strombichides reached them.

Taking two ships, Astyochus sailed along the coast to Chios, assembled the fleet stationed there, and advanced with the entire force toward Samos. However, upon finding that the Athenians refrained from confronting him—due to internal discord and suspicion within their ranks—he turned back to Miletus. Around this time, Athens underwent a political upheaval, replacing its democracy with an oligarchy.

When Pisander and his envoys returned from Tissaphernes to Samos, they worked to consolidate support for their cause, even persuading the influential class in Samos, who had once resisted oligarchic rule, to support a similar government. Concurrently, the Athenians at Samos, after discussing their situation, chose to abandon Alcibiades as he declined to join their efforts and was seen as unsuited for the oligarchy. Committed to protecting their interests, they resolved to carry on the war independently, raising money from their personal fortunes and using all available resources to sustain their fight.

Following these resolutions, they sent Pisander and half of the envoys back to Athens, instructing them to establish oligarchies in the cities they encountered en route. The remaining envoys were sent to other dependent cities to propagate the new governance. Diitrephes, who was stationed near Chios, was dispatched to Thrace to oversee the cities there and abolished democracy in Thasos. However, within two months of his departure, the Thasians began fortifying their city, weary of Athens' aristocratic influence and eager for Lacedaemon's support. Many Thasians, previously exiled by the Athenians and aligned with the Peloponnesians, conspired within the city to bring in a Lacedaemonian squadron and secure Thasos' revolt.

These developments ran counter to what the oligarchs in Athens had anticipated. Many of the Athenian-controlled cities, upon gaining a moderate level of autonomy, quickly pursued complete independence, unmoved by Athens' promise of political reforms. In fact, the attempt to impose oligarchic rule often spurred these cities to seek full freedom rather than aligning themselves with Athenian governance.

As Pisander and his companions traveled along the coast, they dismantled democracies in the cities they encountered, as planned, enlisting some local heavy infantry as allies. Upon reaching Athens, they found that much of their revolutionary work was already underway. A group of younger men had formed a clandestine faction, targeting and assassinating Androcles, a prominent leader of the common people and a key figure in the banishment of Alcibiades. They believed that eliminating Androcles, a strong advocate for the democratic cause, would help pave the way for Alcibiades' return and forge an alliance with Tissaphernes. Other individuals deemed troublesome were similarly eliminated in secrecy.

Publicly, the conspirators declared that only those actively serving in the war should receive pay and that only five thousand citizens, capable of personally and financially contributing to the state, should participate in governance. However, this was merely a slogan to pacify the masses, as the real control was intended for the revolutionaries themselves. The Assembly and Council continued to convene, but only discussed matters pre-approved by the conspirators, who directed the speakers and scripted their statements in advance. The climate of fear and the conspirators' large numbers silenced opposition. Anyone daring to voice dissent soon faced death, without investigation or justice for the suspects, leaving the people in a state of intense fear. The sheer size of Athens, the lack of mutual trust, and exaggerated perceptions of the conspirators' numbers further crippled resistance. The popular faction was paralyzed, suspicious of one another, with conspirators embedded in ranks that no one would have suspected of supporting an oligarchy. This division among the commoners only served to protect the oligarchs and allowed them to act with impunity.

Pisander and his associates wasted no time in completing their task. They convened the Assembly and proposed appointing ten commissioners with full authority to draft a new constitution, with the plan to present their governance model on a set date. When the day arrived, the conspirators gathered the assembly at Colonus, in Poseidon's temple just outside the city, under strict control. The commissioners then introduced a single proposal allowing any Athenian to suggest measures without fear of reprisal, backed by penalties for those who might try to prosecute or intimidate them for doing so.

With the way thus prepared, the conspirators announced an overhaul: all current offices and paid positions under the existing democratic system were terminated. Five men were to be selected as leaders, who would then choose a group of one hundred, with each of these members selecting three more, ultimately forming a council of four hundred members. This body would assume complete authority, governing as they deemed fit, and summoning the proposed assembly of five thousand citizens only when they saw fit.

The resolution to bring down the democracy was formally introduced by Pisander, who played the leading public role in executing the plan. Yet the true architect of this political transformation was Antiphon, a man highly esteemed in Athens for his intellect and strategic skill. Known for his sharp mind and persuasive rhetoric, Antiphon avoided taking a visible role in the Assembly, as his intelligence made him mistrusted by the common people. However, he was frequently sought by those who needed assistance in legal matters, both in the courts and in the Assembly, where he guided them with unmatched counsel. When the oligarchy later fell and Antiphon was tried for his involvement in its establishment, he delivered what was considered one of the most powerful defenses known up to that time.

Phrynichus was another fervent advocate for the oligarchic cause. His distrust of Alcibiades, and his awareness of Alcibiades' secret dealings with Astyochus in Samos, led him to commit fully to the cause, believing that no oligarchic government would ever reinstate

Alcibiades. Once committed, Phrynichus proved to be the most resolute supporter in times of risk. Theramenes, son of Hagnon, was also a prominent figure in dismantling the democracy, known for his skill in both planning and debate. Guided by leaders of such insight and capability, the plan, though ambitious, advanced steadily, despite the immense challenge of curtailing Athenian liberty nearly a century after the fall of the tyrants—a liberty the people had grown accustomed to, and a period in which Athens had governed over its own subjects.

The Assembly formally approved the new constitution without dissent, and was then dismissed. The installation of the Four Hundred into power proceeded methodically. With the enemy positioned at Decelea, Athenians were routinely stationed on the city walls or at various defensive posts. On this day, however, those not part of the conspiracy were allowed to return home, while conspirators were instructed to stay close to their posts without drawing attention and to be prepared to seize arms in the event of any resistance. Additionally, there were contingents from Andros, Tenos, three hundred Carystians, and some settlers from Aegina who had come armed specifically for this purpose and were instructed to assist if needed.

With these arrangements secured, the Four Hundred entered the council chamber, each carrying a concealed dagger, and escorted by one hundred and twenty young men, ready to act if violence proved necessary. They approached the Councillors of the Bean, the existing governing body, and ordered them to take their remaining pay and vacate their offices. The Four Hundred even brought funds for the rest of the councillors' term, which they distributed as the Councillors exited.

With the withdrawal of the Council, which did not attempt any resistance, and the wider citizenry remaining silent, the Four Hundred took control of the council chamber without opposition. Initially, they established their leadership formally by selecting their Prytanes (executive officers) through a lottery, and, observing tradition, they offered prayers and sacrifices to the gods upon assuming their offices. However, as they settled into power, they rapidly deviated from the democratic system. Operating with force rather than consent, they undertook actions starkly opposed to prior democratic norms, acting with a harshness that had been rare. Though mindful not to provoke matters concerning Alcibiades—particularly avoiding any recall of exiles that might disrupt their plans—the Four Hundred used their power to silence dissent. They selectively executed a few individuals they deemed problematic, imprisoned others, and exiled some more, ensuring a strict control over the city.

To strengthen their hold, they also sought to establish peace with Lacedaemon, thinking that Agis, the Spartan king stationed in Decelea, might view their government as more stable and predictable than the shifting public will of the Athenian commons. Thus, they sent emissaries to Agis, expressing a desire for peace and hoping he would favor negotiating with them over dealing with the volatile democracy. However, Agis suspected that the city's calm was only a façade, doubting that the Athenian people would so quickly abandon their long-cherished freedom. Convinced that a strong Spartan show of force would unsettle the city, Agis refused their overtures and instead requested reinforcements from the Peloponnese. Soon after, he led these additional troops, along with his forces stationed at Decelea, straight to the very walls of Athens. His intent was clear: by pressuring the city, he hoped to spark an uprising that would ease his conquest or, in the best case, prompt Athens to surrender without battle. He was especially hopeful that he could seize the city's Long Walls, as he believed they would lack sufficient defenders in the current disarray.

However, Agis's assumptions about unrest in the city proved incorrect. The citizens observed his approach without reacting, and the Athenian forces quickly organized a counterattack. Cavalry, supported by heavy infantry, light-armed troops, and archers, advanced and skirmished with Agis's men. They succeeded in killing a number of his soldiers who ventured too close and managed to capture weapons and fallen bodies. Realizing that Athens was neither divided nor vulnerable as he had expected, Agis finally withdrew, leading his army back to its former position at Decelea. He then dismissed the reinforcements and returned them to the Peloponnese.

After this display, the Four Hundred, undeterred, decided to pursue peace more earnestly. They sent another embassy to Agis, who this time was more receptive. He advised them to extend their overtures to Lacedaemon itself, suggesting that a direct approach to the Spartan leadership might yield the negotiations they sought. Eager to secure a resolution, the Four Hundred quickly sent delegates to Lacedaemon to formally negotiate a peace treaty.

In response to the establishment of the oligarchy at Athens, ten envoys were sent to Samos to address the army. Their mission was to reassure the soldiers that the new government was not intended to harm the city or its citizens but was a necessary step to save Athens in the midst of crisis. They explained that the government supposedly included not just the Four Hundred, but a larger body of five thousand citizens, though Athens had never managed to assemble such a large number to discuss important matters due to its many campaigns and foreign engagements. The envoys were instructed to emphasize this point and address any other concerns of the army, as the new government feared, rightly, that the seamen might resist the oligarchy and potentially spark its downfall.

At Samos, events concerning the oligarchy were already taking an unexpected turn, with significant developments unfolding around the same time as the Four Hundred's plotting in Athens. The segment of the Samian population that had previously risen against the upper class, identifying as the democratic faction, had now shifted alliances. Persuaded by Pisander during his visit and encouraged by Athenians conspiring in Samos, they took oaths in support of an oligarchical order, with a faction of three hundred preparing to strike against their fellow citizens, now seen as supporters of democracy. They took the extreme step of killing Hyperbolus, a notorious Athenian ostracized not for his influence but for his notoriety as a disruptive presence. Charminus, an Athenian general, along with some others, aided in this act and joined the conspiracy, planning a full assault on the democratic supporters in Samos.

However, news of the impending attack reached the democratic faction. They urgently appealed to two generals, Leon and Diomedon, both respected among the commons and only reluctantly associated with the oligarchy, as well as to Thrasybulus, a galley captain, Thrasyllus, a soldier among the heavy infantry, and other known adversaries of the conspirators. They implored them not to stand by and watch the destruction of their allies and the loss of Samos, the last remaining bastion of Athenian power. These democratic sympathizers took up the cause, rallying the soldiers individually to prepare for resistance, especially focusing on the crew of the Paralus. The Paralus, composed entirely of Athenians and free citizens, had long harbored anti-oligarchical sentiments, even when no oligarchy existed. Leon and Diomedon, meanwhile, made strategic arrangements, leaving ships for the democrats in case they needed protection.

When the Three Hundred launched their assault, these forces were ready. The soldiers, especially the Paralus crew, came swiftly to the aid of the people, leading to a decisive victory for the Samian democrats. In the aftermath, they executed about thirty members of the Three Hundred and exiled three principal instigators of the plot, but granted amnesty to the rest. With this victory, Samos was firmly established as a democratic state moving forward, a stronghold of Athenian democracy in defiance of the oligarchical takeover in Athens.

The ship Paralus, with Chaereas, son of Archestratus, an Athenian involved in recent events at Samos, was quickly sent to Athens by the Samians and the Athenian army to deliver news of the developments there. The crew was unaware that Athens was now under the control of the Four Hundred oligarchs. Upon the Paralus' arrival, the Four Hundred swiftly detained a few members of the crew, seized the ship, and reassigned the remaining men to a troopship for guard duty around Euboea. Chaereas, perceiving the situation, managed to escape before being detained and returned to Samos, where he delivered a grim account of events in Athens to the soldiers, painting an exaggerated picture of harsh repression. He claimed that the oligarchs punished any dissenters with brutality, insulted soldiers' families, and intended to arrest and possibly execute the relatives of those in the army who opposed their rule. His report included numerous other embellishments designed to inflame the troops.

This alarming news initially drove the army into a fury, with many proposing to strike at the oligarchic leaders and anyone associated with them. However, the soldiers eventually refrained from this course, influenced by those urging moderation and warning them not to risk everything by internal conflict with the enemy so close. Thrasybulus, son of Lycus, and Thrasyllus, leaders of the democratic movement, now took decisive steps to formalize democratic governance at Samos. They bound the soldiers under solemn oaths—especially targeting those with oligarchic leanings—to support a democratic government, to remain unified, to aggressively continue the war against the Peloponnesians, and to stand opposed to the Four Hundred in Athens, cutting off all ties with them. This oath was extended to include all adult Samian citizens, integrating them fully into the democratic cause and sharing equally in both the risks and benefits of their united struggle. The soldiers saw no other path to survival but through resolute solidarity, fully understanding that either the Four Hundred or the enemy's success would spell their doom.

Thus, a fierce struggle emerged, with the army at Samos striving to uphold democracy against the Four Hundred, who sought to impose oligarchy on the military forces. Immediately, the soldiers convened an assembly to dismiss former generals and captains they distrusted, replacing them with leaders they could rely on, including Thrasybulus and Thrasyllus. Rallying together, they encouraged one another not to despair over the city's revolt from them, arguing that the dissenters back home were far fewer and less resourceful than themselves. They pointed out that, with the fleet at their disposal, they retained the means to enforce tribute from the subject cities of their empire, as effectively as if they were operating from Athens itself. Samos, their new base, was a powerful stronghold, one which had nearly deprived the Athenians of naval supremacy before. As for the Peloponnesians, their situation remained unchanged, with the fleet still dominating the sea.

They also noted that having the fleet at Samos actually put them in a stronger position than the oligarchic government back home, which depended on their forward base at Samos to control access to Piraeus. Should the Four Hundred refuse to restore democratic rule, the army at Samos could more easily deny the city access to the sea than vice versa. In fact, the city was proving less critical to the war effort than expected, as it provided neither supplies nor valuable counsel, with the soldiers having to secure resources on their own. The home government, in abolishing their ancestors' democratic traditions, had failed them; meanwhile, the army upheld those very traditions and was prepared to pressure Athens to do the same. They saw themselves as possessing counsel equal to that of the city, if not superior.

Additionally, they considered that if they could guarantee Alcibiades' safety and facilitate his return, he would eagerly work to secure the King's support for their cause. And should they face absolute defeat, they held a trump card: with their fleet, they had the option to withdraw to new territories where they could establish themselves in cities and lands of their own choosing.

The Athenians, encouraging one another with these discussions and bolstering their resolve, continued preparing for war with as much energy as ever. Meanwhile, the ten envoys that the Four Hundred had sent to Samos halted upon learning the situation, remaining quietly at Delos.

Around this time, unrest began to grow within the Peloponnesian fleet stationed at Miletus, with voices accusing Astyochus and Tissaphernes of sabotaging their efforts. Many criticized Astyochus for his reluctance to engage in a naval battle, either in the past when they were at full strength and the Athenian fleet was small, or now, when they had heard that the Athenians were divided and their forces not yet consolidated. Instead, Astyochus had delayed, waiting for the Phoenician fleet promised by Tissaphernes—a fleet that had yet to materialize and seemed increasingly unlikely to do so. Adding to the discontent, Tissaphernes failed to deliver consistent and full payments to their navy, causing significant hardship and frustration among the forces. The Peloponnesians, especially the Syracusans, insisted that they could wait no longer and urged for a decisive battle.

Taking note of these growing complaints, Astyochus and the allied commanders had already decided in council to prepare for an engagement. When word arrived about the recent turmoil at Samos, they resolved to act swiftly. Mobilizing their entire fleet of one hundred and ten ships, they commanded the Milesians to join the attack by marching along the coast toward Mycale. Setting sail in that direction, the Peloponnesian fleet aimed to confront the Athenians decisively.

The Athenian fleet, consisting of eighty-two ships stationed at Glauce, a point in Mycale close to Samos, noticed the Peloponnesian approach and withdrew to Samos. They felt their fleet was too outnumbered to risk a decisive battle. Moreover, they had received intelligence from Miletus that the Peloponnesians were eager for battle and were expecting reinforcements from the Hellespont under Strombichides, who had been summoned with ships from Abydos. The Athenians thus chose caution, retreating to Samos, while the Peloponnesians reached Mycale, where they set up camp alongside the land forces from Miletus and nearby regions.

The following day, the Peloponnesians were preparing to advance on Samos when they learned that Strombichides had indeed arrived with additional ships from the Hellespont. This news prompted the Peloponnesians to retreat immediately to Miletus, wary of confronting a now-reinforced Athenian force. Buoyed by their reinforcements, the

Athenians, totaling a fleet of one hundred and eight ships, soon launched an offensive against Miletus, hoping for a conclusive engagement. Yet, finding no one willing to meet them in battle, they ultimately returned to Samos.

Chapter XXVI

In the same summer, right after these events, the Peloponnesians, feeling unprepared to engage the enemy with a combined fleet and uncertain about securing enough funds to maintain such a large number of ships, especially with Tissaphernes proving unreliable with payments, decided on a different course. They dispatched Clearchus, son of Ramphias, with a contingent of forty ships to join Pharnabazus, according to initial directives from Peloponnese. Pharnabazus had extended an invitation and was ready to provide financial support, and Byzantium had also signaled its willingness to revolt. To avoid detection by the Athenian forces, the Peloponnesian ships took an open-sea route; however, they encountered a storm. Most ships, under Clearchus, made it to Delos and then backtracked to Miletus. Clearchus subsequently set out overland to the Hellespont to assume command. Meanwhile, ten ships led by Helixus, a Megarian, successfully reached the Hellespont and managed to incite Byzantium to revolt.

When the Athenian commanders at Samos received word of these developments, they quickly deployed a squadron to defend the Hellespont, leading to a clash with eight ships on each side off the coast of Byzantium.

During this time, the leaders at Samos, with Thrasybulus as a primary advocate, focused on restoring Alcibiades. Thrasybulus had held this view firmly since the change in government and finally managed to convince the soldiers to support Alcibiades' recall and grant him amnesty. With this decision made, they dispatched Thrasybulus himself to bring Alcibiades back from Tissaphernes' court to Samos, firmly believing that their best hope for survival lay in persuading Tissaphernes to abandon the Peloponnesians. In an assembly at Samos, Alcibiades spoke to the troops, lamenting his personal misfortunes due to his exile, then pivoted to public matters. Through a compelling speech, he ignited their hopes, claiming immense influence over Tissaphernes. Alcibiades sought to make the oligarchic government in Athens wary of him, to expedite the breakup of the political clubs, and to secure greater loyalty from the Samos forces. At the same time, he aimed to damage the Peloponnesians' trust in Tissaphernes, thereby undermining their hopes.

To this end, Alcibiades promised the soldiers lavishly, claiming that Tissaphernes had given him his word that if he could trust the Athenians, they would have a steady supply of resources as long as he had any means left—even offering to melt down his silver couch if necessary. He assured them that Tissaphernes would also direct the Phoenician fleet currently stationed at Aspendus to aid the Athenians, not the Peloponnesians, provided Alcibiades could return to guarantee their loyalty.

Hearing Alcibiades' stirring words, the Athenians promptly elected him as a general alongside the existing commanders and handed over the management of all their affairs to him. This decision breathed new life into the hopes of every soldier in the camp, who saw in Alcibiades the key to both their survival and the chance to exact vengeance on the Four Hundred back in Athens. The spirit of the troops was electrified, with a fresh confidence that led many to believe they were now more than capable of overpowering their immediate enemies. Inflamed by these sentiments and the promises made by Alcibiades, some soldiers began clamoring to set sail directly for Piraeus, eager to confront the Four Hundred without delay.

However, Alcibiades firmly opposed this idea, despite the push from many within the ranks. Now appointed as general, he asserted his authority, stating that he would first go to Tissaphernes to devise a strategic plan for conducting the war rather than make an impulsive move against Athens. After the assembly, Alcibiades promptly left for Tissaphernes, deliberately acting in a way that suggested a strong and trustworthy alliance between himself and the Persian satrap. He sought to further impress upon Tissaphernes that his newly restored position endowed him with significant influence, allowing him either to be a beneficial ally or a formidable adversary. Through this maneuver, Alcibiades skillfully aimed to make both the Athenians fearful of Tissaphernes' potential role and to leverage his new status to intimidate Tissaphernes with his own Athenian backing.

Meanwhile, the Peloponnesians at Miletus soon received news of Alcibiades' reinstatement as general of the Athenian forces, which only heightened their dissatisfaction and distrust of Tissaphernes, who was already unpopular for failing to uphold his financial commitments. Having previously declined to fight when the Athenians appeared before Miletus, Tissaphernes had also become even less diligent in providing regular pay. Now, with Alcibiades returned to favor, suspicions of Tissaphernes' motives grew among the Peloponnesians, with soldiers and leaders alike discussing how they had never received their pay in full and how the money they did receive was given sporadically. They feared that without either engaging in a conclusive battle or relocating to a base with a more reliable supply line, desertions would increase among the ship crews. Blaming Astyochus for pandering to Tissaphernes' interests for his own gain, many saw him as responsible for their poor conditions.

Tensions reached a boiling point when Astyochus found himself confronted by a group of angry Syracusan and Thurian sailors, many of whom were free men and notably vocal in demanding overdue pay. When Astyochus responded with threats rather than placation, even raising his baton toward Dorieus, who had spoken up for his own men, the sailors grew furious. In their frustration, a mob of sailors rushed at Astyochus, forcing him to seek safety at an altar before the situation escalated into outright violence.

While this confrontation took place, the Milesians seized a fort that Tissaphernes had recently constructed within Miletus, expelling the Persian garrison stationed there. This act of defiance against

Tissaphernes won the support of the allied forces, especially the Syracusans, who saw it as a step toward autonomy. However, Lichas, a Lacedaemonian, openly disapproved of the Milesians' actions, arguing that the Greek states within the King's territory should continue to accommodate Tissaphernes, or at the very least avoid hostilities, until the war concluded in their favor. This statement further fueled Milesian resentment toward Lichas, whose actions and other similar views had already caused discontent. When Lichas fell ill and died not long after, the Milesians even refused to allow his body to be buried in the location chosen by the Lacedaemonians and their allies, revealing their lingering animosity toward him and the ongoing strain within the alliance.

The tensions within the Peloponnesian forces had reached their peak as a result of Astyochus's unpopularity and Tissaphernes's failure to provide timely support. At this critical juncture, Mindarus arrived from Lacedaemon to replace Astyochus as admiral, assuming full command of the fleet. Seizing this moment, Astyochus prepared to sail back to Sparta. Meanwhile, Tissaphernes, the Persian satrap whose actions had increasingly stirred discontent, sent with him a trusted associate named Gaulites—a Carian who spoke both Greek and Persian—to convey grievances and attempt to discredit the accusations anticipated from the Milesians, who were also en route to Sparta to denounce him. Notably, they were accompanied by Hermocrates, who had long held animosity toward Tissaphernes over unpaid wages to the troops. Hermocrates was determined to expose Tissaphernes as an ally of Alcibiades and as an enemy of the Peloponnesian cause.

Astyochus and the Milesians set sail with Hermocrates, while Alcibiades, after conferring with Tissaphernes, returned to Samos. It was here that envoys from the Four Hundred in Athens arrived to explain the recent shift in governance and to reassure the forces stationed there of their loyalty to the Athenian state. However, when the envoys attempted to speak to the soldiers in assembly, they were met with fierce resistance; the troops, already incensed by rumors of abuses and betrayals, initially called for the envoys' execution as traitors to the democracy. Only after much effort were the envoys able to proceed, at which point they began their defense.

The envoys argued that the changes made by the Four Hundred were not meant to undermine Athens but rather to preserve it in its time of peril. They pointed out that during the recent invasion, they had had every opportunity to surrender the city to the enemy, yet they had not done so. Furthermore, they clarified that the recent changes were temporary and that the full assembly of the Five Thousand would soon assume its role in governance. They also refuted Chaereas's claims that the families of the soldiers had been abused or mistreated, assuring the troops that their relatives and property remained safe. Despite these assurances, the soldiers remained unconvinced, especially as conflicting rumors and views circulated. The prevailing sentiment leaned toward launching an immediate expedition against Piraeus.

It was at this moment that Alcibiades, for the first time, performed a critical service to Athens, quelling the rage of the soldiers. He spoke forcefully against the plan to attack Athens itself, pointing out that such a move would lead to a disastrous weakening of Athenian control in Ionia and the Hellespont, making it easy prey for the Peloponnesians. Recognizing the soldiers' anger toward the Four Hundred, Alcibiades nevertheless persuaded them to direct their efforts against the external enemy, urging them not to turn their wrath inward in a way that would benefit Sparta. He argued that instead of the Four Hundred, the Council of Five Hundred should be restored, and the assembly of the Five Thousand should retain its authority, so that Athens might continue to find resources to support the army.

Alcibiades reminded the soldiers of the delicate situation, stressing that they should present a united front to the enemy and keep up the fight, knowing that the survival of Athens depended on their efforts. He also held out hope for a future reconciliation between the opposing factions in Athens, pointing out that as long as both sides remained intact, there was still a chance for the city to heal itself. This message from Alcibiades shifted the focus of the soldiers, and they began to look past their personal grievances, recognizing that a larger purpose was at stake.

Shortly after, an envoy arrived from Argos, pledging the support of the Argive democrats to the Athenian forces at Samos. Alcibiades thanked the Argives and requested that they remain ready to provide assistance when called. The Argives were accompanied by the crew of the Paralus, who had been dispatched by the Four Hundred to patrol Euboea but had instead taken a daring course of action. As they passed through Argos, they captured Athenian envoys—Laespodias, Aristophon, and Melesias—who had been sent by the Four Hundred to negotiate with Sparta. Turning the envoys over to the Argives as traitors, the Paralus crew chose not to return to Athens, fearing retribution. Instead, they brought the Argive envoys to Samos on their own ship, effectively siding with the forces stationed there.

This surprising development from the crew of the Paralus strengthened the resolve of the forces at Samos, as the commitment from Argos underscored the support for democracy both in Samos and among certain factions back in Athens. The loyalty of the Paralus crew served as a morale booster, affirming to the soldiers at Samos that they were not alone in their commitment to the democratic cause. Meanwhile, with Alcibiades as their leader, the Athenians stationed at Samos turned their focus entirely toward the external threats, determined to secure the safety of Athens from both internal and external dangers.

During this same summer, the return of Alcibiades and Tissaphernes's conduct had fueled the Peloponnesians' suspicions to new heights, making them firmly believe that the satrap had aligned himself with the Athenians. In response to these accusations, Tissaphernes appeared to be trying to clear his name by embarking on a journey to Aspendus, where he claimed he would personally fetch the Phoenician fleet, asking Lichas, a prominent Spartan, to accompany him. In his absence, he appointed Tamos to oversee payments for the Peloponnesian forces. However, the exact purpose of Tissaphernes's trip to Aspendus and his failure to bring the fleet to aid the Peloponnesians sparked considerable speculation.

Some believed Tissaphernes was acting on a calculated plan to exhaust Peloponnesian resources by delaying their pay, as Tamos proved to be even more inconsistent than his superior. Others thought he merely brought the Phoenician fleet to Aspendus to extort money from the Phoenicians and then release them, having never intended to use their fleet at all. Yet another theory was that he aimed to deflect the Peloponnesians' suspicions by creating a show of summoning the fleet and then leaving it at Aspendus under the pretense of logistical issues.

From my perspective, it's evident that Tissaphernes's primary motive was to prolong the conflict without actually aiding either side decisively. If his intent had been genuine, he could have brought the Phoenician fleet to support the Lacedaemonians and, given the fleet's strength, potentially tipped the balance in their favor. Instead, he delayed, claiming that the assembled ships were fewer than the King had initially ordered. This excuse alone made it clear that Tissaphernes preferred a strategy of delay, neither fully supporting the Lacedaemonians nor allowing them to suffer a defeat that would have ended the war prematurely.

Meanwhile, Alcibiades, having learned of Tissaphernes's journey to Aspendus, sailed there himself with thirteen ships. He claimed that he could achieve a great benefit for the Athenians at Samos by either bringing the Phoenician fleet to their side or at least ensuring it didn't fall into Peloponnesian hands. Given his familiarity with Tissaphernes's intentions, Alcibiades likely knew the fleet would never be deployed. By appearing to challenge Tissaphernes's loyalty, he effectively pressured the satrap into maintaining his apparent alliance with the Athenians.

While Alcibiades sailed east, the envoys from the Four Hundred at Athens arrived in Samos, where they relayed Alcibiades's encouragement to the troops, urging them to stay strong against the enemy and promising hopes of reconciliation. This news significantly strengthened the resolve of those within the Four Hundred who were already disillusioned with the oligarchy and seeking a safe way to distance themselves from its leadership. Among these critics were prominent figures such as Theramenes and Aristocrates, who had initially supported the oligarchy but now expressed concerns about the concentration of power in the hands of only a few, arguing for a government in which the Five Thousand were given real authority, not just nominal inclusion.

Their stated objective of expanding the government to involve the Five Thousand in governance was, however, largely a pretense; the true motivation for many of these men was personal ambition. Within an oligarchy that had arisen from democracy, the struggle for dominance became even more cutthroat, as each member aspired to be superior to his peers, while under a democracy, the disappointment of losing was less personal since one was not necessarily bested by an equal. For some, the increasing power of Alcibiades at Samos and their own belief in the weakness of the oligarchy inspired them to act, and so began a race among them to win favor with the common people and position themselves as the leaders who would restore their rights.

Meanwhile, the leaders within the Four Hundred who were most opposed to any democratic reforms—Phrynichus, who had clashed with Alcibiades while commanding at Samos; Aristarchus, a staunch opponent of the commons; and figures like Pisander and Antiphon—intensified their efforts to consolidate their control. These individuals, who had immediately pushed for peace with Lacedaemon upon assuming power, had sent representatives to negotiate with the Spartans, and when news reached them of the democratic resurgence at Samos, they felt their position slipping. Realizing that even their closest allies were starting to turn against them, they hastily dispatched

Antiphon, Phrynichus, and others with strict orders to secure peace with Lacedaemon on any reasonable terms.

Concurrently, they accelerated construction on the wall at Eetionia. This structure, as Theramenes and his supporters argued, seemed less intended to protect Piraeus from the returning Athenian forces from Samos and more designed to permit entry for an invading enemy fleet. Eetionia, being a narrow mole by the mouth of the Piraeus harbor, connected with an existing land wall. Together, these fortifications could control the harbor entrance, allowing a small force to secure it with ease. They fortified an adjacent warehouse area where incoming grain had to be unloaded and distributed, creating a centralized hold over food supplies. All this granted the oligarchs tight control over the port, potentially making it easier to allow an enemy fleet in if the need arose.

Theramenes had long criticized these moves, suspecting that the wall's true purpose was not for the city's protection but as a means for the Four Hundred to maintain control by inviting in the Spartans if they felt it necessary. When the envoys returned from Lacedaemon without securing a peace agreement, Theramenes became more vocal, asserting that the wall would lead to the city's destruction. Tensions were further heightened by the presence of forty-two Peloponnesian ships anchored off the coast of Laconia near Las, poised to sail for Euboea. This fleet, commanded by Agesandridas, included ships from Italian and Sicilian cities like Locri and Tarentum, which had come at the invitation of the Euboeans.

Theramenes publicly claimed that this squadron was not primarily intended to support Euboea but rather to aid those fortifying Eetionia, suggesting that an invasion by the Peloponnesians was imminent. He warned that unless immediate measures were taken, the city would be caught off guard and fall. Theramenes's accusations were not without basis; it was true that some within the Four Hundred harbored a secret plan. Their primary goal was to maintain the oligarchy while preserving the empire. If this wasn't possible, they aimed to keep their fleet and city walls intact to remain self-sufficient. Should both of these options fail, they were willing to strike a deal with the Spartans, surrendering their fleet and defenses, and securing the government—even if this meant accepting Spartan control—as long as their lives and positions of power remained intact.

Driven by urgency, the oligarchs hurried to finish the wall at Eetionia, adding posterns, gates, and other structures designed to admit the enemy fleet should it arrive. They knew that time was limited and were desperate to have these defenses completed to secure their own grip on power. Initially, dissent against these plans was limited to a few people who murmured in secret. But when Phrynichus returned from his embassy to Lacedaemon, he was ambushed in the marketplace and fatally stabbed by a member of the Peripoli. He collapsed before he had made it far from the council chamber. The assassin managed to escape, but one of his accomplices, an Argive, was captured and tortured by the Four Hundred. Despite their efforts, they could not extract the name of the mastermind, learning only that he knew of gatherings at the house of the Peripoli's commander and other locations. With no further evidence, they dropped the matter.

This incident emboldened Theramenes, Aristocrates, and their allies, both within the Four Hundred and outside it. With the conspiracy now exposed, they prepared to take action. Meanwhile, the Peloponnesian fleet that had set sail from Las reached Epidaurus, raiding Aegina along the way. Theramenes argued that, if they were truly bound for Euboea, they would not have stopped to raid Aegina or lingered at Epidaurus without some deeper motive. He suggested that these maneuvers were meant to support the oligarchic agenda in Athens, proving his suspicions correct.

No longer able to remain passive, Theramenes and his supporters began to make their move openly. A group of heavy infantry stationed in Piraeus and working on the wall at Eetionia, led by Aristocrates and his tribe, seized Alexicles, a general loyal to the Four Hundred. They took him to a nearby house and held him captive. Their effort was supported by Hermon, the Peripoli commander at Munychia, and others in Piraeus, with the majority of the heavy infantry backing them.

When word of Alexicles's capture reached the Four Hundred, who were in session, those loyal to the oligarchy were outraged and wanted to rush to the arms depots. They turned their anger towards Theramenes and his faction, accusing them of betrayal. Theramenes defended himself, offering to help secure Alexicles's release, and left for Piraeus, accompanied by one of the generals from his side, along with Aristarchus and some young cavalry officers. Panic ensued on both sides. In the city, rumors spread that Piraeus had fallen and that Alexicles had been killed; in Piraeus, there were fears of an imminent attack from the city.

Older men and city leaders tried to keep people from rushing to arms, calming the situation to prevent an open clash. Thucydides the Pharsalian, an official representative of the city, stepped forward to mediate. He reminded everyone of the real enemy, just outside the city walls, waiting for any opportunity to exploit internal chaos. His appeal had the desired effect, helping to diffuse the situation and prevent bloodshed.

Meanwhile, Theramenes arrived in Piraeus, visibly angered at the heavy infantry's actions, though some suspected his fury was more for show. Aristarchus and those supporting the Four Hundred reacted with genuine outrage. However, the heavy infantry continued their work, undeterred, and openly questioned Theramenes about the purpose of the wall at Eetionia, asking if he truly believed it was built for the city's benefit. When they suggested that it would be better to demolish it, Theramenes cautiously agreed, saying that he supported whatever they believed was in the city's best interest.

With Theramenes's tacit approval, the heavy infantry, joined by the people of Piraeus, immediately climbed onto the fortification and began tearing it down. As they worked, they called upon others to join them, proclaiming that everyone who wished to see governance by the Five Thousand, rather than by the Four Hundred, should help. To avoid direct confrontation, they avoided phrases that might explicitly call for the return of democracy, fearing that the Five Thousand might indeed be real and might include powerful individuals among their ranks.

This ambiguity served both the Four Hundred and the conspirators in Piraeus well. The Four Hundred preferred not to make it known whether the Five Thousand were real or fictitious, as their absence kept power concentrated in their hands, while the illusion of their existence instilled fear and caution among the populace. For their part, the heavy infantry exploited this ambiguity, appealing to a shadowy "Five Thousand" that represented a more inclusive government than the oligarchic Four Hundred, without openly rallying for a return to full democracy.

The following day, despite their alarm, the Four Hundred met in the council chamber as usual, attempting to maintain control over the city. Meanwhile, the heavy infantry in Piraeus, after freeing Alexicles and demolishing the fortification, gathered with their weapons at the theater of Dionysus near Munychia. There, they held an assembly and decided to march into the city, ultimately halting at the Anaceum. Here, they were met by delegates from the Four Hundred who approached them individually, seeking to quell the uprising. These delegates spoke to the more moderate members of the heavy infantry, urging restraint and promising that the government would soon reveal the Five Thousand, who would rotate members into the Four Hundred, allowing broader participation. They pleaded with them to avoid tearing the city apart and risking Athens falling to its enemies.

After much discussion, the heavy infantry began to calm, realizing that the larger danger lay in the potential ruin of the city. Moved by these appeals, they agreed to convene a new assembly at the theater of Dionysus on an agreed-upon day, hoping to restore harmony among themselves and within the government.

When the day arrived and preparations for the assembly were underway, sudden news spread through the city: forty-two ships under

Agesandridas had been sighted sailing from Megara along the coast of Salamis. This news ignited the fears that Theramenes and his faction had previously warned about, reinforcing suspicions that these ships were indeed targeting the controversial fortifications at Eetionia. The people believed they had acted wisely in tearing down the wall, as Agesandridas's presence seemed to confirm the threat.

It is possible that Agesandridas had coordinated with sympathizers within the city, as he had previously hovered around Epidaurus and nearby areas, likely waiting for internal turmoil in Athens to present an opportunity. Whether this timing was intentional or merely opportunistic, the Athenians now faced a dire crisis. Realizing that they were no longer just facing an internal threat but were now at risk of an enemy invasion directly at the harbor of Piraeus, the Athenians took immediate action.

In a flurry of activity, the populace surged toward Piraeus to prepare for defense. Those already at the harbor scrambled to board the ships stationed there, while others launched additional vessels or hastened to defend the harbor walls and the entrance. Men poured down from all parts of the city, every citizen aware that the threat of enemy ships at their very doorstep demanded their full attention. In this way, Athens—united in the face of an immediate external threat—mobilized to protect itself, setting aside the internal divisions that had so recently consumed it.

Meanwhile, the Peloponnesian fleet continued its movement, rounding Sunium and eventually anchoring between Thoricus and Prasiae before reaching Oropus. In Athens, amidst the turmoil of internal strife, the urgency to defend Euboea was overwhelming, as the island had become essential to their survival, particularly after they were cut off from Attica. Forced to act swiftly, they hastily assembled a fleet with poorly trained crews, dispatching Thymochares to Eretria with a number of ships. Upon reaching Euboea, these reinforcements joined the existing Athenian fleet, bringing the total to thirty-six ships.

However, Agesandridas had timed his approach well. After his crews had dined, he set sail from Oropus, a mere seven miles from Eretria by sea. The Athenians, upon spotting the approaching fleet, scrambled to man their ships, but found themselves caught off-guard. The Eretrians, who had plotted with Agesandridas, had ensured that provisions were scarce in the marketplace, forcing the Athenian sailors to venture to the outskirts to purchase food. This tactic delayed the Athenians just long enough for the Peloponnesian fleet to arrive, catching them unprepared and forcing them to hurriedly launch their ships.

As the battle commenced near the Eretrian harbor, the Athenians held their ground for a short while. But soon, the Peloponnesians gained the upper hand, and the Athenians were routed, forced to flee towards the shore. Tragically, many who sought refuge in Eretria found themselves betrayed by the city they assumed was friendly; the Eretrians slaughtered those who entered. Some managed to escape to an Athenian fort in Eretrian territory or fled to Chalcis, but the losses were devastating. Agesandridas and his forces captured twenty-two Athenian ships, killing or capturing the crew members, erecting a trophy to mark their victory. With this triumph, they quickly incited the revolt of the entire island of Euboea—save for Oreus, which remained under Athenian control—and reorganized the island's affairs.

When news of the disaster reached Athens, the reaction was one of unprecedented panic. No prior calamity, not even the devastating defeat in Sicily, had instilled such fear. The Athenian empire seemed to be unraveling: Samos was in revolt, they lacked both ships and men to defend their territory, and the city itself was rife with internal divisions that could erupt into conflict at any moment. The loss of Euboea was particularly crushing, as it was more valuable to Athens than even Attica, providing essential resources. The prospect of the Peloponnesians capitalizing on their victory by sailing directly for Piraeus—the city's most vulnerable point due to the absence of a defensive fleet—loomed ominously.

The Athenians feared that the Peloponnesians, emboldened by their success, might indeed press forward to Piraeus. Should they do so, they could have further destabilized the city's already fragile unity. Alternatively, if they had laid siege to the city, they might have forced the fleet in Ionia, despite its opposition to the oligarchy, to return home in defense of Athens and their families. In the meantime, the Peloponnesians would have easily seized control over the Hellespont, Ionia, the islands, and everything stretching as far as Euboea— essentially, the entire Athenian empire.

Yet, once again, the Peloponnesian reluctance proved fortunate for Athens. True to their cautious nature, the Lacedaemonians did not seize the moment. Their measured, often sluggish approach contrasted sharply with the bold and agile spirit of the Athenians, a characteristic that consistently served Athens well, especially in maintaining a maritime empire. It was this disparity, exemplified by the Athenians' quick adaptability and willingness to take risks, that kept Athens afloat. Ironically, the Syracusans, who resembled the Athenians in their audacity and vigor, had shown similar strengths in their conflict with them. Thus, in this moment of crisis, it was the cautious character of their enemies that allowed the Athenians a brief respite, enabling them to regroup and contemplate their next moves in defense of what remained of their empire.

Upon receiving the news of their recent losses, the Athenians promptly manned twenty ships and called for an immediate assembly at the Pnyx, their traditional meeting place. In this first assembly, they deposed the Four Hundred and transferred the government to a newly established body of Five Thousand. Membership in this group was limited to those who could provide a suit of armor, a criterion aimed at creating a more balanced representation of those able to defend the state. They also decreed that no one in public office should receive pay, and if anyone did, they would be considered cursed. In the following assemblies, they took steps to solidify their new government, including the election of lawmakers and the drafting of measures to shape a stable constitution.

This new constitution marked a period in which Athens experienced what many regarded as one of the best forms of government in its history. For the first time in recent memory, the interests of the wealthy and the common people were harmoniously blended, enabling the city to recover from its many hardships and begin to rebuild its strength. The citizens also passed measures for the recall of Alcibiades and other exiles, urging them to rejoin the Athenian cause and contribute vigorously to the war effort. Representatives were sent to both Alcibiades and the army stationed at Samos, emphasizing the urgency of their return and commitment to the conflict.

In the wake of this political shift, the prominent leaders of the former oligarchy, including Pisander, Alexicles, and their allies, fled to the fortified stronghold of Decelea, which was under Spartan control. Only Aristarchus, one of the generals, did not immediately retreat. Instead, he took a group of foreign archers and quickly made his way to Oenoe, a fort on the Boeotian border then under siege by the Corinthians. The Corinthians were angered over the loss of a party recently defeated by the fort's defenders and had called upon the Boeotians to assist in their siege.

Upon arriving at Oenoe, Aristarchus used his position to deceive the garrison. He claimed that Athens had negotiated a settlement with the Lacedaemonians and that, as part of this agreement, Oenoe was to be surrendered to the Boeotians. Trusting him as an Athenian general and having no knowledge of recent developments in the city due to the ongoing siege, the garrison accepted his word and agreed to evacuate under a truce. Thus, the Boeotians gained control of Oenoe without further resistance.

With this, the oligarchic regime effectively came to an end, and the civil unrest that had plagued Athens began to subside. The state's leadership stabilized, and Athens was able to focus its resources once more on the external threats it faced, marking the close of a turbulent chapter in its history.

To return to the Peloponnesians stationed in Miletus, the situation was becoming increasingly challenging. No funds were forthcoming from any of the representatives left by Tissaphernes after he departed for Aspendus, where he had ostensibly gone to secure the Phoenician fleet. Yet, there was no sign of either Tissaphernes or the promised ships. Philip, sent along with Tissaphernes, and another Spartan officer, Hippocrates, stationed at Phaselis, wrote urgently to Mindarus, the Peloponnesian admiral, reporting that the Phoenician fleet was not coming and that Tissaphernes had essentially deceived and neglected them. During this period of inaction and frustration, Pharnabazus was consistently pressing them to come to his aid, showing great zeal in offering the fleet supplies and encouraging revolts in the cities under his jurisdiction still loyal to Athens. Pharnabazus was optimistic that with the Peloponnesian support, he could compel these cities to shift allegiance.

Mindarus, finally yielding to Pharnabazus's persistent invitations and recognizing the opportunity to create a stronger foothold, decided to act swiftly. Around mid-summer, he mobilized his fleet of seventy-three ships, preparing to avoid detection by the Athenians at Samos and sail for the Hellespont, where sixteen of their ships had already gone earlier in the season and had made initial moves in the Chersonese. However, his fleet was soon caught in a sudden storm, which forced them to take shelter at Icarus for several days. After five or six days of rough weather, they resumed their course and eventually reached Chios.

At the same time, Thrasyllus, stationed with the Athenian fleet at Samos, had already received intelligence of Mindarus's departure from Miletus. He set out at once with fifty-five ships, hoping to reach the Hellespont before the Peloponnesians could. When he learned that Mindarus had temporarily stopped at Chios, he believed they might remain there, at least for a time. To monitor the Peloponnesian movements closely, Thrasyllus posted scouts in strategic locations on Lesbos and the nearby mainland. He then coasted along to Methymna, preparing the necessary supplies, including provisions like meal, to launch an attack from Lesbos if the Peloponnesians stayed at Chios.

Meanwhile, Thrasyllus decided to address a growing threat from Eresus, a town on Lesbos that had recently revolted. The revolt had been orchestrated by influential Methymnian exiles who had brought around fifty heavy infantry from Cuma, along with additional mercenaries from the mainland, totaling about three hundred soldiers. They chose Anaxander, a Theban, as their leader, appealing to the historic connection between Thebans and Lesbians. These forces first attempted to capture Methymna but were repelled by Athenian guards sent from Mytilene. Undeterred, they crossed the mountains and succeeded in winning Eresus over to their cause. In response, Thrasyllus resolved to gather his entire fleet and attack Eresus to reclaim it.

Meanwhile, Thrasybulus had arrived at Eresus ahead of Thrasyllus, bringing five ships from Samos as soon as he heard that the Methymnian exiles had crossed over. Unfortunately, he arrived too late to prevent the capture of Eresus. He anchored his ships in front of the town, soon to be joined by two additional vessels returning from the Hellespont and the Methymnian fleet, bringing their total force to sixty-seven ships. With this substantial fleet assembled, they immediately began preparations, gathering engines and all available siege equipment to make a determined assault on Eresus, aiming to regain control of the town and secure their hold over Lesbos.

Meanwhile, Mindarus and the Peloponnesian fleet, having stocked provisions for two days and receiving additional funds from the Chians—a sum of three Chian pieces of money per man—departed from Chios on the third day, moving quickly to avoid encountering the Athenian fleet at Eresus. Choosing a cautious route, they sailed close to the shore of Lesbos, keeping the island on their left instead of venturing into open waters. First, they stopped at Carteria in the Phocaeid, where they rested and dined, and then proceeded along the coastline of Cumaea. They took their evening meal at Arginusae, situated on the mainland opposite Mytilene, and despite the late hour, continued their journey under the cover of night.

Their voyage took them past a series of coastal landmarks—Harmatus, across from Methymna, where they paused to dine again, and then swiftly onwards, passing through Lectum, Larisa, Hamaxitus, and nearby settlements. By the time they reached Rhoeteum just before midnight, they had successfully entered the Hellespont. A few of their ships took anchorage at Sigeum and other nearby spots, marking their strategic spread across the area.

Meanwhile, the Athenian forces stationed at Sestos were alerted to the fleet's approach by the sudden intensification of fire signals on the opposite shore. With the enemy's arrival imminent, the eighteen Athenian ships at Sestos set out immediately, navigating close along the coast of the Chersonese to reach Elaeus. Their intent was to evade the Peloponnesian fleet by keeping a safe distance at sea.

As dawn approached, they sighted Mindarus's fleet advancing. Though they attempted to escape, only a portion managed to flee toward Imbros and Lemnos. Four of the slower Athenian ships were caught near Elaeus: one ran aground near the temple of Protesilaus and was captured along with its crew, while two more were seized, their crews having abandoned them; the fourth was run ashore on Imbros and set ablaze by the enemy.

The Peloponnesians, now strengthened by the addition of sixteen ships from Abydos, brought their fleet's total to eighty-six vessels. With this force, they attempted an assault on Elaeus, though their efforts were in vain. Failing to take the city, they returned to Abydos.

During this time, the Athenians at Eresus were unaware of the Peloponnesians' covert movement past them, and continued their siege on the town. Upon receiving the urgent news of the enemy's approach to the Hellespont, they immediately abandoned the siege and redirected all efforts toward intercepting the Peloponnesian fleet. En route, they intercepted two of the Peloponnesian ships that had ventured too far out in their eagerness and now found themselves within the Athenian fleet's path. The Athenians then anchored at Elaeus, regrouped with the ships that had taken refuge at Imbros, and spent the next five days preparing meticulously for the anticipated battle that was now imminent.

The battle unfolded as follows: the Athenians sailed in a tight formation close to the shore, moving toward Sestos. Noticing this maneuver, the Peloponnesians launched from Abydos to confront them directly. Both fleets extended their flanks in anticipation of an imminent clash. The Athenians, with seventy-six ships, stretched along the Chersonese coastline from Idacus to Arrhiani, while the Peloponnesians, with eighty-six ships, deployed from Abydos to Dardanus. On the Peloponnesian side, the Syracusan vessels held the right wing, while Mindarus himself commanded the left wing with the best sailors. The Athenian left was led by Thrasyllus, and their right by Thrasybulus, with other commanders stationed strategically across the fleet.

Eager to secure the advantage, the Peloponnesians initiated the battle, attempting to outflank the Athenians by pushing their left wing to cut off the Athenian right wing from escaping the straits. Their objective was to press the Athenian center against the shore, where it could be more easily captured or destroyed. The Athenians, seeing this tactic, expanded their own line and sailed faster to prevent being outflanked, extending their ships until the leftmost vessels passed beyond the point of Cynossema. However, this maneuver stretched and weakened their center, as they had fewer ships than their opponents, and the angle of the coastline at Cynossema prevented them from observing the full scope of the battle on the opposite side.

Seizing the moment, the Peloponnesians struck the Athenian center hard, forcing several Athenian ships ashore, where the Peloponnesian sailors disembarked to pursue the beached vessels. Thrasybulus on the right and Thrasyllus on the left were unable to assist the beleaguered center. Thrasybulus was occupied with a considerable number of Peloponnesian ships opposing him, and

Thrasyllus's line of sight was obstructed by the point of Cynossema. Additionally, Thrasyllus was engaged with Syracusan and other enemy ships that matched his force.

As the Peloponnesians grew more confident in their apparent victory, they began to scatter, losing their disciplined formation as they chased down the Athenian ships. Observing this disorder, Thrasybulus ceased his lateral movement, turned his ships around, and launched a fierce counterattack on the now-disorganized enemy ships facing him. He swiftly routed these scattered Peloponnesian vessels and forced most into a chaotic retreat. Meanwhile, Thrasyllus's squadron on the left had managed to push back the Syracusans, who, upon seeing their allies flee, turned and joined the general retreat.

In the end, the Athenian strategy of exploiting the Peloponnesians' overconfidence and disarray paid off. They turned a seemingly lost battle into a decisive counterattack, scattering the Peloponnesian forces and sending them into full retreat.

The rout was now decisively in favor of the Athenians. Most of the Peloponnesians sought safety by fleeing first to the river Midius, and then retreating to Abydos. The Athenians managed to capture only a few enemy ships since the narrowness of the Hellespont allowed the Peloponnesians a short escape route to safety. Nevertheless, this victory came at an ideal time for Athens, lifting the morale of a fleet that had been plagued by minor defeats and the crushing loss in Sicily. With this battle won, the Athenians regained confidence in their navy and ceased to view the Peloponnesians as formidable sea opponents.

In total, they seized eight Chian vessels, five from Corinth, two from Ambracia, two Boeotian ships, and one each from Leucas, Lacedaemon, Syracuse, and Pellene, while sustaining the loss of fifteen of their own. The Athenians erected a victory trophy at Point Cynossema, gathered the wreckage, and returned the dead to the enemy under a truce. They quickly sent a galley back to Athens with the news of their victory. The arrival of this galley, bearing unexpected good tidings amid the recent disasters of Euboea and the turmoil in Athens, rejuvenated the spirits of the Athenians. They began to believe that with a renewed effort, they might still have hope of triumph.

Four days after the sea battle, the Athenians stationed in Sestos, having hastily refitted their ships, sailed against Cyzicus, which had recently revolted. Near Harpagium and Priapus, they spotted and swiftly engaged eight vessels from Byzantium anchored near the shore, overpowering the enemy forces stationed there. After securing the ships, they proceeded to recapture the unfortified town of Cyzicus, extracting monetary contributions from the inhabitants.

Meanwhile, the Peloponnesians departed from Abydos to Elaeus to recover their damaged ships. They retrieved those that were salvageable, though several had been burned by the inhabitants of Elaeus. Hippocrates and Epicles were dispatched to Euboea to gather the Peloponnesian squadron stationed there for further support.

Around this same period, Alcibiades returned to Samos from Caunus and Phaselis with his thirteen ships, reporting that he had successfully blocked the Phoenician fleet from assisting the Peloponnesians. Moreover, he claimed to have strengthened the Athenians' standing with Tissaphernes. Alcibiades then recruited nine additional ships and collected significant funds from the Halicarnassians, fortifying Cos and establishing a garrison and a local governor before returning to Samos as autumn approached.

Upon learning that the Peloponnesian fleet had moved from Miletus to the Hellespont, Tissaphernes hurriedly left Aspendus and made his way back to Ionia. Meanwhile, the people of Antandros, an Aeolian community, transported heavy infantry from Abydos across Mount Ida into their town, motivated by their grievances against Arsaces, the Persian lieutenant of Tissaphernes. This same Arsaces, under the guise of a friendly gathering, had deceitfully invited the prominent Delians—who had been exiled from Delos by the Athenians—to join his forces. Once they were assembled, he ambushed and killed them with his soldiers, a ruthless act that raised the suspicions of the Antandrians, who feared a similar betrayal. Weighed down by the burdens he imposed, they expelled Arsaces's garrison from their citadel.

Tissaphernes, now aware of the Peloponnesians' actions in Antandros and his ejected garrisons in Miletus and Cnidus, recognized the severity of the discord between them. He grew increasingly concerned about further conflicts and also resented Pharnabazus's growing rapport with the Peloponnesians, suspecting that the latter might achieve more against Athens in less time and at lower cost. Determined to address these grievances, Tissaphernes decided to meet with the Peloponnesians in the Hellespont. His aim was to defend his actions concerning the Phoenician fleet and other accusations and to mend the rift as best as he could. Stopping first at Ephesus, he offered sacrifices to Artemis before continuing his journey.

THE END

Of The Nature of Things

Titus Lucretius Carus

Book I

Proem

Mother of Rome, delight of gods and men,
Dear Venus, who beneath the stars that glide
Fills the vast oceans and fertile lands with life.
Through you alone, all living things are conceived,
Through you they rise and see the great sun above.
Before you, Goddess, as you draw near,
Stormy winds retreat, and heavy clouds disperse.
For you, the Earth blooms with fragrant flowers,
For you, the calm waters of the seas smile,
And the serene sky glows with soft light for you.
When springtime dawns and gentle west winds blow,
The birds of the air, moved by your power,
Announce your coming, O divine one,
And wild herds leap joyfully through the fields,
Or swim freely in rushing streams.
Every creature feels your spell,
Following wherever you choose to lead them.
Through seas, mountains, rivers, and green forests,
You inspire love in every heart.
Through your power, life is born again,
Each kind producing its own.
And since you alone guide the universe,
And without you, nothing reaches the light of day,
Nothing beautiful or joyful can exist,
I ask you to share in this work I now write.
It is for Memmius, whom you have graced
With every virtue and charm.
Grant my words an immortal beauty,
And bring peace to the lands and seas.
You alone can calm the rage of war
And bring harmony to humanity.

Even mighty Mars, the god of war,
Cannot resist your eternal power.
Often, he throws himself into your arms,
Overcome by love's unending pull.
There, gazing at you with longing,
His strength and ferocity fade.
With your words and embrace,
You can soothe his fiery heart,
And guide him toward peace.
O glorious Goddess, grant peace to the Romans,
A peace that this troubled time so desperately needs.
For without peace, I cannot focus on this work,
Nor can the noble Memmius attend to the needs of the state.
While humankind lay crushed across the lands,
Burdened beneath Religion's heavy hand,
She loomed above, her terrifying face
Glowering down from the boundless skies.
But it was a Greek who dared to stand,
Who first raised mortal eyes against her power.
Neither the fame of gods nor lightning's flash,
Nor the thunder's roar from ominous skies,
Could shake his will. Instead, these spurred him on,
Filling his fearless heart with fiery resolve
To tear apart the barriers of Nature's gates.
Through his courage and wisdom, he prevailed.
He journeyed far beyond the flaming walls
That marked the boundaries of our known world,
Exploring the vast, unmeasured universe.
From there, he returned as a conqueror,
Revealing truths of what can come to be,
What cannot, and by what unchanging laws
Each thing is bound, held firm through endless time.
And thus, Religion now lies trampled down,
And his triumph lifts us toward the heavens.
I know how hard it is to shape in Latin verse

The profound discoveries of the Greeks,
Especially since our language lacks the words
For concepts so strange and new.
Yet your worth, and the joy I expect from your friendship,
Urge me onward, despite the toil it brings.
Through sleepless nights, I search for fitting words
And verses to reveal, in shining clarity,
The hidden truths that lie at Nature's core.
So I ask you to come with an open mind,
Free from distractions, focused, and untroubled,
Lest you dismiss my offering too soon,
Before understanding its meaning and worth.
For this is for you: the ultimate law of gods and skies,
The origin of all things, the seeds of creation.
From these, Nature brings forth all that exists,
Nurtures it, multiplies it, and finally,
Returns each thing to its primal state when it ends.
These fundamental elements we call
The atoms of creation, seeds of matter,
Or primal bodies—the building blocks of the world.
I fear you may think we walk an impious path,
Wandering into thoughts that defy the sacred.
But often, it is religion itself
That leads to the foulest acts of humankind.
Recall the tale of Aulis, where the greatest chiefs,
The leaders of the Danaans,
Defiled the altar of the virgin goddess Diana.
They stained it with the blood of Agamemnon's daughter,
Slain in cruelty.
She felt the garland upon her maiden hair,
The ribbons falling gently to her cheeks,
And saw her grieving father by the altar.
The priests, hiding the knife, stood by in silence,
While the crowd wept at the sight of her.
Terror-stricken, her legs gave way,

And she fell to the ground. Even her role
As the first to call him "father" could not save her.
They lifted her trembling body
And carried her to the altar—not with hymns
Or joyful songs for a wedding day,
But as an innocent girl, condemned by sin.
On that day, her father struck her down,
Turning his daughter into a sacrificial offering,
All to gain favorable winds for the fleet to Troy.
Such are the horrors that blind faith can bring.
And there may come a time when you, too,
Driven by the fear of omens and prophecies,
Will seek to break away from us.
Even now, these seers weave false dreams,
Threatening your plans and filling your life with fear.
They wield such power because men do not know
That all suffering could have an end.
If they did, they would find strength,
A way to stand firm against such terrors.
But as it is, no tools, no knowledge exist,
Because people fear eternal torment after death.
They do not understand what the soul truly is—
Whether it is born with the body,
Or comes into us at birth,
And whether it dies with us,
Or journeys to shadowy caves in the underworld.
Perhaps, as some say, it passes into animals,
A belief even our great poet Ennius held,
Who first brought the laurel crown of Helicon
To the Italian people, earning eternal renown.
Yet even Ennius, in his immortal verse,
Speaks of the dark halls of Acheron,
Claiming no souls or bodies return from there,
Only pale, ghostly figures.
He tells how Homer's spirit rose to him,

Weeping bitterly,
And revealed the secrets of Nature's origin.
Let us, then, with steady minds,
Seek to grasp the truth of the skies above—
The laws that guide the sun and moon.
Let us study the forces that drive life below.
But most of all, let us strive to understand
What the mind and soul are made of,
And what it is that terrifies us so deeply,
Whether in the grip of sleep or illness,
That we see and hear, as if close by,
The long-dead, whose bones rest beneath the earth.

Substance is Eternal

This fear, this darkness in the human mind,
Cannot be dispelled by the rising sun,
Or the bright rays of morning's light,
But only by understanding Nature and her laws.
And Nature begins with this truth:
Nothing is ever created from nothing.
People fear the unknown because they look at the sky and earth,
Unable to explain their workings,
And believe divine powers must be at play.
But once we understand that nothing comes from nothing,
We can begin to see the truth of how all things arise—
Not through the tools of gods, but through natural laws.
Imagine if anything could come from anything:
Fish might spring from the land,
Humans might rise from the sea,
Birds might burst fully formed from the air,
And wild creatures might roam,
Producing offspring of entirely different kinds.
Fruits would grow on random trees,
And life would exist without order or reason.

But this does not happen,
Because all things are born from fixed seeds,
Each following its own nature and origin.
Why else would roses bloom only in spring,
Grain ripen in summer,
And grapes mature in autumn?
It is because the seeds of life combine at the right times,
And the earth, ready and fertile,
Brings forth her creations when conditions are just.
If things came from nothing,
They could appear at random,
Without cause or season,
And grow without nourishment or time.
Imagine if life sprang up without any process:
A baby could immediately grow into an adult,
Or a tree could suddenly emerge from the ground,
Fully grown.
But Nature does not work this way.
Everything grows gradually,
Preserving its kind through steady development,
Feeding and flourishing only from its own matter.
This shows us that nothing can grow without a source,
Just as crops need rain to thrive,
And living things need food to survive.
Without these, life would cease to sustain itself.
Thus, it is more reasonable to believe
That all things share fundamental elements—
Like the letters that form many words—
Than to think anything can exist without origins.
Why doesn't Nature create humans tall enough
To walk across the seas,
Or strong enough to tear down mountains,
Or capable of living forever?
Because all things are made from fixed, unchanging matter,
Bound by the rules of their creation.

The fields we till yield more crops than those left untouched,
Not because of miracles,
But because our labor awakens the seeds within the earth.
If nothing required seeds or care,
The earth would spontaneously produce
More beautiful and abundant forms on its own.
So, admit this truth: nothing comes from nothing.
All things have their origins,
And all return to their basic forms when they end.
Nothing truly perishes into nothingness.
If something were completely mortal,
It could vanish instantly without force.
But we see that everything endures
Until an external force breaks it apart
Or internal decay dissolves it.
If time could destroy all matter completely,
Life would never return.
The earth could not sustain us with food,
Nor could rivers and oceans remain full,
And the stars would lack fuel to shine.
But because matter is eternal,
The world continues to renew itself.
Even rain, which seems to vanish,
Returns as crops, trees, and fruit,
Feeding animals and humans alike.
Cities thrive, children grow,
Forests echo with birdsong,
And cattle rest content in the fields.
From these cycles of life,
Nature creates one thing from another,
Never allowing anything to exist
Without the death of something else.
And now, since I have taught that things cannot
Be born from nothing, nor, once born,
Return to nothing, doubt not my words,

Though your eyes cannot see the smallest seeds of matter.
Consider instead those forces we know exist,
Yet remain invisible to sight.
The winds, unseen, lash against our faces,
Driving great ships to ruin and tearing the clouds apart.
They whirl wildly across the land, scattering trees,
Or roaring through the mountains with deafening blasts.
Their howls shriek ominously as they wreak destruction,
Though we cannot see them, their power is clear.
Like rivers swollen by heavy rains,
The winds sweep all before them.
The torrents rush down from the hills,
Carrying fragments of trees and rocks,
Crashing against piers and bridges with unrelenting force,
Until even the strongest structures give way.
The waters surge, hurling debris far and wide,
Destroying all that stands in their path.
Just so, the winds scatter and break,
Driving everything before them,
Or spiraling into whirlwinds,
Lifting all they catch in their twisting grasp.
The winds are unseen, but they are no less real,
Their works and ways as mighty as the rivers.
We know, too, the scents of things that reach our noses,
Yet never see their particles come.
We feel the warmth of fire, the chill of frost,
And hear the voices of men,
Though their forms are not visible to our eyes.
These, too, must be made of matter,
For only physical things can touch the senses.
Consider how clothing hung by the shore grows damp,
The moisture seeping in unseen.
And when laid out beneath the sun,
The fabric dries, yet we see not the water depart.
It scatters into particles too small for sight.

Or take the ring worn on the finger,
Thinning slowly beneath with passing years.
Drops falling from a roof wear grooves into stone,
And the iron plowshare, dragged through fields,
Wastes away little by little, unseen.
Even the stone-paved roads grow smooth
From the countless steps of passing feet.
Bronze statues at the city gates
Have hands worn thin by the touch of many travelers.
We see the marks of time upon these things,
But we cannot see the tiny bits that break away.
In the same way, Nature builds all things,
Adding little by little, unseen by any gaze.
No eye can trace the growth of trees,
Or the steady maturing of life,
Nor can we see the gradual decay
As time and age wear all things down.
Salt waves gnaw at towering cliffs,
But the smallest changes escape our sight.
Thus, Nature works through forces unseen,
Her processes hidden, yet ever present.

The Void

But know this: creation is not crammed or blocked,
For in all things, there exists a void—
An empty space, intangible and unseen.
This truth, once known, will guide you often,
Saving you from endless doubt and wandering,
And from losing faith in what I have explained.
If there were no void, nothing could move,
For matter's nature is to block and halt.
Without an open space to flow into,
No thing could shift or find a starting place.
But look at the world—the oceans, the land,

The vast expanse of the heavens above—
So much moves in so many ways before our eyes,
And if there were no void, all would be still,
Matter trapped, compressed, unable to stir.
Even the most solid things are not without void.
In rocks and caves, water trickles through,
And beads of moisture collect like tears.
Trees grow, bearing fruit in their season,
As nutrients pass upward from the roots
Through trunks and branches to nourish every part.
Voices penetrate walls, reaching our ears,
Frost seeps into our very bones.
Such things are only possible because of void—
For bodies must have space to pass through.
Why else do some objects weigh more than others,
Though their sizes appear the same?
If a ball of wool and a lump of lead
Contained the same amount of matter,
They would weigh the same. But they do not.
Lead is heavier because it holds less void,
While the wool, full of emptiness, weighs less.
The difference in weight reveals the truth:
Matter and void are always intermingled.
Some argue that water gives way before fish,
Allowing them to swim by creating space.
They claim the water rushes back to fill the gap,
And so, they say, motion is possible
Even if everything is completely full.
But this belief is false.
Where could the fish move if no space existed?
And how could water shift aside
If the fish had nowhere to go?
Without void, nothing could begin to move at all.
When two solid bodies strike and separate,
A gap forms between them, filled by air.

But even air, rushing in with gusty speed,
Cannot fill the gap instantly.
It moves to one place first, then spreads to the rest.
Some might say this happens because air condenses,
But they are mistaken. If air were compressed,
It would create voids elsewhere as it shrank,
And no true filling would occur.
Without void, air could not collapse on itself,
For matter cannot contract infinitely.
Thus, despite objections, the truth stands firm:
There is a void in all things.
I could present many arguments to prove this,
But these few examples should suffice.
They are the footprints that will guide you,
Like a hound tracking a hidden trail.
Once you sense the path, you can follow it,
Thought by thought, uncovering hidden truths.
But if you stray or hesitate,
Even by a little, I warn you, Memmius,
You may find yourself lost.
Still, fear not: I will pour forth proofs in abundance,
Drawing from the wellspring of my mind.
Yet time moves swiftly, and I worry
That life itself may leave us
Before I can reveal to you
Every answer your questions deserve.

Nothing Exists Per Se Except Atoms and The Void

But now, to continue weaving the tale begun,
All of nature, self-sustained, consists
Of two main things: of bodies and the void
In which they rest and move about.
For common sense among all humankind
Declares that body must exist.

If this deep-rooted belief should fail,
We'd have no foundation to prove anything else,
No place to begin our reasoning.
And without the void—empty space,
Where bodies move and find their place—
Nothing could exist or change position.
As I have shown, without such space,
Motion would be impossible.
Beyond these two—bodies and void—
Nothing exists that is separate from both.
There is no third kind of thing in nature.
Anything that exists must be something—
If it can be touched, no matter how slight,
It adds to the sum of bodies, large or small.
If it cannot be touched and allows all things
To pass through it unhindered,
Then it must be what we call the void.
Moreover, whatever exists must either act,
Be acted upon, or provide the space
In which things move and exist.
Bodies act and are acted upon;
Void provides the space to move.
Thus, there is no third nature, no other kind,
Besides bodies and void,
That can be sensed or understood
By the reasoning of the mind.
Name whatever you like throughout creation;
You will find it is either a property of these two,
Or an accident caused by them.
A property is something inseparable from a thing,
Without which it cannot exist:
Weight belongs to rocks, heat to fire,
Flowing to water, tangibility to bodies,
And intangibility to the void.
But poverty, wealth, slavery, freedom,

War, peace, and other such conditions,
Which come and go while the nature of things remains,
These we rightly call accidents.
Even time does not exist by itself;
We perceive its passage through changes in things:
What has happened, what is happening now,
And what will come next.
No one feels time apart from motion
Or the stillness of objects.
When we speak of Helen's abduction,
The siege and fall of Troy,
We do not claim these acts exist by themselves,
But rather as events tied to people and places.
Those who lived them have long since passed,
Carried away by the relentless flow of time.
Thus, all past actions are accidents—
Some of humankind, others of the world.
Without matter and the space of the void,
Even the fire of love that burned
In the heart of Alexander of Troy,
Ignited by Helen's beauty,
Could not have sparked that great conflict.
The wooden horse would never have been built,
And the fires that consumed Troy
Would never have risen from its ruins.
From this, you see that every act and event
Does not exist on its own.
It is neither a body nor the void,
But an accident of both—
Dependent on the matter and space
Where all things happen and exist.

Character of The Atoms

Bodies, once more,

Are of two kinds: some are primal seeds,
The indivisible germs of all creation,
And others are unions formed by these primal seeds.
Those primal seeds, the first building blocks,
Cannot be destroyed; they endure by their own solidity.
It may seem strange to think that anything
Could possess a truly solid frame,
When lightnings pierce through walls of houses,
Voices and shouts travel through barriers,
Iron glows white-hot in fire,
And even rocks burn and shatter under fierce heat.
Rigid gold softens and melts in the flames,
Bronze yields and flows under intense heat,
And warmth or cold seeps through silver cups.
Hold such a cup in your hand, and you'll feel
The warmth or chill of the water within,
Passing through the metal's shining surface.
So it seems nothing is truly solid.
Yet reason and the nature of things compel us
To see that there must exist
Bodies of solid, everlasting structure—
The seeds of things, the primal particles
From which the entire universe is built.
First, we know there are two kinds of things:
Bodies, and the space where bodies exist.
Each is distinct and cannot mix with the other.
Where there is empty space, no body can be,
And where a body resides, there is no void.
Thus, the primal particles must be solid,
Free of any void within.
But since void exists in all created things,
Those things made of solid matter
Must have spaces between their parts.
No matter can contain void within itself
Unless it is formed of tightly bound particles.

Only matter with a solid structure
Can hold and shape the void.
Therefore, matter, with its enduring solidity,
Must be eternal, even if all else—
Every creation in the universe—dissolves away.
If there were no void at all,
The world would be a single, solid mass.
Without matter to fill empty spaces,
The world would be nothing but a void.
Thus, nature is a balance of body and void,
With neither being entirely full nor empty.
There must be particles capable of alternating
Between the empty and the full.
These particles cannot be broken from the outside
By blows or cuts, nor torn apart from within.
They cannot be destroyed by fire, cold, or dampness—
The forces that erode weaker things—
For without void, nothing can be crushed,
Split apart, or broken down.
The more void within a thing,
The more vulnerable it becomes to destruction.
But the primal particles, being entirely solid,
Stand unshaken.
If matter had not been eternal,
Long ago, all things would have perished,
Returning to nothingness.
And from nothing, nothing could ever be created.
But since I have shown that nothing comes from nothing,
And nothing returns to nothing,
The primal seeds must possess an immortal frame.
When anything meets its end,
It is dissolved back into these seeds,
Which remain, ready to build anew,
Supplying the universe with the materials
For endless creation.

Bodies, once more,
Are of two kinds: some are primal seeds,
The indivisible germs of all creation,
And others are unions formed by these primal seeds.
Those primal seeds, the first building blocks,
Cannot be destroyed; they endure by their own solidity.
It may seem strange to think that anything
Could possess a truly solid frame,
When lightnings pierce through walls of houses,
Voices and shouts travel through barriers,
Iron glows white-hot in fire,
And even rocks burn and shatter under fierce heat.
Rigid gold softens and melts in the flames,
Bronze yields and flows under intense heat,
And warmth or cold seeps through silver cups.
Hold such a cup in your hand, and you'll feel
The warmth or chill of the water within,
Passing through the metal's shining surface.
So it seems nothing is truly solid.
Yet reason and the nature of things compel us
To see that there must exist
Bodies of solid, everlasting structure—
The seeds of things, the primal particles
From which the entire universe is built.
First, we know there are two kinds of things:
Bodies, and the space where bodies exist.
Each is distinct and cannot mix with the other.
Where there is empty space, no body can be,
And where a body resides, there is no void.
Thus, the primal particles must be solid,
Free of any void within.
But since void exists in all created things,
Those things made of solid matter
Must have spaces between their parts.
No matter can contain void within itself

Unless it is formed of tightly bound particles.
Only matter with a solid structure
Can hold and shape the void.
Therefore, matter, with its enduring solidity,
Must be eternal, even if all else—
Every creation in the universe—dissolves away.
If there were no void at all,
The world would be a single, solid mass.
Without matter to fill empty spaces,
The world would be nothing but a void.
Thus, nature is a balance of body and void,
With neither being entirely full nor empty.
There must be particles capable of alternating
Between the empty and the full.
These particles cannot be broken from the outside
By blows or cuts, nor torn apart from within.
They cannot be destroyed by fire, cold, or dampness—
The forces that erode weaker things—
For without void, nothing can be crushed,
Split apart, or broken down.
The more void within a thing,
The more vulnerable it becomes to destruction.
But the primal particles, being entirely solid,
Stand unshaken.
If matter had not been eternal,
Long ago, all things would have perished,
Returning to nothingness.
And from nothing, nothing could ever be created.
But since I have shown that nothing comes from nothing,
And nothing returns to nothing,
The primal seeds must possess an immortal frame.
When anything meets its end,
It is dissolved back into these seeds,
Which remain, ready to build anew,
Supplying the universe with the materials

For endless creation.
So primal seeds possess a solid unity,
Without which they could not endure
Through endless ages and infinity of time,
Ensuring the replenishment of worn-out worlds.
If nature allowed things to break apart forever,
The bodies of matter would by now
Have been reduced so completely by ancient decay
That nothing new could ever be formed,
No living thing could grow, or reach its prime.
For everything is destroyed more quickly than it is made,
And so, if infinite time has passed already,
It would have shattered and dissolved all things long ago.
There would be nothing left to rebuild or renew
The world we see around us today.
But notice this: a fixed limit must exist
To prevent the breaking down of matter.
We see it in the way everything is continually renewed,
Each in its season, each reaching its peak,
Its flower of life, before it fades.
Again, if there were no boundary
To the decay of the material world,
Then all bodies, of every kind,
Would have endured from the beginning of time
Until now, untouched by destruction.
But if, as you believe, they are fragile by nature,
It makes no sense that they could have lasted so long,
Enduring through endless ages,
Subject to the countless blows of chance and change.
So, observe in this account of creation
How, even though the particles of all matter
Are solid and unbreakable,
They combine to form things that are soft:
Air, water, earth, and fiery vapors.
This is made possible by the void within things,

Which allows them to flow and function.
If, however, the primal seeds themselves were soft,
It would be impossible to explain
How such solid things as basalt and iron
Could ever be formed.
Without a firm foundation of solidity,
They would lack the strength to exist at all.
The primal seeds, powerful in their simplicity,
Remain solid and unyielding.
When tightly bound together,
They create objects of unbreakable strength,
Able to endure against all forces.
Moreover, every kind of thing in nature
Has fixed limits for its growth and lifespan.
Nature has decreed what each can do,
What each can never do.
No fundamental change occurs; everything abides
Within its limits, passing on its traits,
Spring after spring. The birds reveal their stripes,
Their spots, their forms, unchanging in their kind.
This proves that all things must be made
Of matter that cannot be altered or destroyed.
If the primal seeds could be conquered or changed,
Then nothing would be certain—
No living thing could be reliably born,
Nor would there be laws to govern
What each thing can and cannot do,
What boundaries they cannot cross.
The generations, kind after kind,
Could not so faithfully reproduce
The habits, motions, and ways of life
Of their ancestors.
Thus, primal seeds remain unchanging,
Bound by eternal laws,
Ensuring that all things retain their nature,

And life continues without disruption.
Of that first matter, which our senses cannot see,
There exists a smallest point, a limit beyond division.
This indivisible minimum of nature is not
A thing apart, standing on its own,
Nor can it ever be so, for it is always part of another—
A first and single element, from which others align,
Joined in close-packed order, forming
The essence of all matter.
These smallest particles are not separate,
But tightly bound to one another,
Unable to break away from the whole.
Thus, the primal seeds possess a solid unity,
Their indivisible parts tightly joined,
Not by mere combination, but by their eternal singleness.
Nature preserves these seeds as the foundation of all things,
Allowing no rupture, no decrease, no decay.
Moreover, if there were no minimum size,
Even the smallest bodies would be infinite,
For a half of a half could still be halved endlessly.
What, then, would be the difference
Between the whole and the smallest part?
None—for both would consist of infinite pieces.
Reason denies this, for the mind cannot grasp
A boundless division without end.
Thus, we must accept that there are smallest, indivisible units,
The minimums of nature.
And if these exist, we must also accept
That primal particles are solid and eternal.
For if Nature, the creator of all things,
Broke everything into parts so small
That they lacked any structure or substance,
She could not build anything anew.
What lacks parts cannot form connections,
Cannot possess the weight, motion, or collisions

Necessary to create and sustain the world.
Thus, these indivisible seeds—solid, eternal,
And irreducible—serve as the building blocks
Of all creation, enabling things to exist
And continue through infinite time.

Confutation of Other Philosophers

Those who claim that fire alone is the substance of all things,
That the entire universe arises only from fire,
Have strayed far from the truth of reason.
Foremost among them is Heraclitus,
Famed for his cryptic words that dazzle the foolish,
Though serious seekers of truth find little wisdom there.
For the ignorant are often drawn to that which is obscured,
Marveling at distorted language,
Believing as truth whatever flatters their ears
Or comes wrapped in fine and polished phrases.
But how, I ask, can the infinite variety of things exist
If all comes from fire, simple and pure?
It matters not if fire is condensed or rarefied;
Its nature would still remain the same—
Burning heat in every form.
When compressed, the fire might burn hotter;
When dispersed, it might burn more gently.
But beyond such changes, nothing else could arise.
Certainly not the vast variety of earth's forms
Or the diversity of all we see.
If they admit a void exists,
Fire could indeed be condensed or rarefied.
But fearing the contradictions this would create,
They reject the idea of void,
Straying far from the path of truth.
Yet if void were entirely absent,
All matter would be compact and immobile,

A solid mass without motion or change.
Fire could not cast its light or heat outward,
Proving that its particles are not tightly packed.
And if they claim fire transforms into other things
Through some combination or alteration,
Then fire itself would cease to exist,
And with it, all heat would perish.
From nothing, the world could not arise again,
For if anything changes beyond its bounds,
It dies to what it was before.
Thus, something must remain unchanged,
A foundation enduring beneath the world's transformations,
Ensuring all things do not collapse into nothingness.
Primal particles exist, eternal and unchanging,
Which rearrange themselves to create new forms.
Through their motion, order, and connection,
Matter transforms, taking on new natures.
But these seeds themselves are not fire,
For if they were, no transformation could occur.
Even if particles shifted, left, or joined anew,
If they all retained fire's nature,
Only fire would ever be created.
Instead, primal bodies collide and combine,
Their motions and arrangements giving rise
To fire, or to other forms entirely,
Changing what they produce without themselves
Becoming like the things they create.
To say that all is fire, and nothing else exists,
Is a thought bordering on madness.
For the senses, which perceive fire,
Also perceive all other things just as clearly.
If fire alone is real, the senses would be deceived,
Yet it is through the senses that we know fire itself.
How then can we trust fire while rejecting all else?
This reasoning is flawed and self-contradictory.

Why dismiss everything else but allow fire?
Or, equally absurd, deny fire and accept all else?
Both paths are equally misguided.
Those who claim the universe is made of fire,
Or air, or water, or earth alone,
Have wandered far from the truth.
Even those who mix air with fire, or water with earth,
Or claim all four elements combine to create all things,
Miss the mark.
Empedocles of Acragas first introduced this idea,
A thinker from the three-cornered isle of Sicily,
Surrounded by the mighty Ionic seas,
Where the waves crash against the rugged coasts,
And swift ocean currents divide the land from Italy.
Here, Charybdis swirls in its deadly grasp,
And Aetna rumbles with fiery wrath,
Threatening to spew its flames anew,
Hurling lightnings skyward in a fiery storm.
Though Sicily is rich and bountiful,
Renowned for its strength and heroes,
It has produced nothing more revered or divine
Than this one man.
His lofty voice, inspired and pure,
Sings of truths so great and profound,
That he seems more god than man.
Yet he, and those others mentioned before,
Though lesser in insight, skill, and wisdom than he,
Even as they unveiled much noble truth,
And spoke from the heart's shrine,
Pronouncing holier and sounder responses
Than ever issued from the Delphic oracle,
Still stumbled over the question of first elements,
And great was their fall—great minds brought low.
First, they denied the existence of void,
Yet still allowed for motion in things,

And admitted the existence of soft, fluid forms—
Air, dew, fire, earth, animals, and grains—
All composed without the presence of void.
Next, they claimed no end exists to the division of bodies,
No boundary to the cutting down of matter.
They refused to see that all things must have limits,
Even the smallest particles invisible to sight.
If the boundaries of the unseen are real,
Then surely there must be minimums,
Beyond which division cannot go.
Moreover, they held that the primal germs were soft,
Subject to birth and decay, mortal in their being.
If that were true, then all things
Would eventually dissolve into nothingness,
And from nothingness arise again,
A cycle contrary to reason and truth.
Their doctrines, thus, stand far from reality.
Further, the primal bodies they propose
Are hostile to one another,
As poisons mixed and opposing forces clash—
Rains, winds, and lightning scatter in storms,
Driving each other apart in chaos.
If all things are made of four elements,
And dissolve back into the same four,
How can these elements be called primal?
By the same reasoning, all things themselves
Could be considered the seeds of the four.
For fire, earth, air, and water
Constantly transform into one another,
Interchanging their forms and natures
Throughout eternity.
Yet, if fire, earth, air, and water meet
Without losing their distinct natures,
They cannot form the world we see:
No breath, no trees, no living things.

Instead, this wild heap of elements
Would display their separate forms—
Air visibly mixed with earth,
Unquenched heat clashing with water.
To create the world, the primal germs
Must have hidden, unseen qualities,
Free from alien elements that might distort
Or weaken the new forms they create.
But these thinkers start from the heavens.
They claim fire becomes the winds of air,
Air gives birth to rain,
Rain forms the earth,
And the earth returns, reversing the process:
Moisture becomes air, air becomes heat,
And the cycle continues endlessly,
From the heavens to earth and back again.
Yet the primal germs cannot act in this way.
There must be something immutable,
Unchanging, to prevent the world
From dissolving into nothing.
For any change beyond natural bounds
Brings instant death to the thing that was.
Thus, the things they describe—
Fire, air, water, and earth—
Must themselves derive from other,
Unchanging and indestructible elements,
To avoid the collapse of all things into naught.
Why not, then, suppose that there are bodies
With a nature so fixed and enduring
That they can create fire,
And with a slight change in arrangement,
By adding or removing a few,
Or altering their motion and order,
They can give rise to air, water, earth, and all,
Interchanging forms forever?

"But look," you say, "the facts are clear to see—
All things grow into the winds of air,
And everything is nourished by the earth.
Unless the seasons bring their timely rains,
Filling the soil beneath dark thunderclouds,
And unless the sun provides its warmth and light,
No grains, no trees, no breathing creatures grow."
True—and unless man takes in food and drink,
His body would waste, his strength would fail,
And life would dissolve from bones and flesh alike.
It is beyond doubt that we are nourished
By certain things, just as other things are fed
By sources unique to their own natures.
This happens because the many primal seeds,
Shared among countless things, are mixed in different ways.
It's no surprise, then, that diverse things
Are sustained by diverse sources.
Moreover, it matters greatly how the primal seeds
Are combined with one another—what positions they take,
What motions they give and receive among themselves.
These same seeds form the sky, the sea, the land,
Rivers, the sun, trees, and living beings,
But their combinations and movements differ,
Producing endless variety in what is made.
Consider even these verses here,
Made from letters common to many words.
Yet each verse and word differs in meaning and sound,
Simply because of the order in which the letters are arranged.
If such variety can arise from mere letters,
How much more can the primal seeds of matter achieve
Through their infinite combinations?
Now let us examine the "homeomeria"
Of Anaxagoras, a concept with no name
In our Italian tongue, though the idea itself
Is not difficult to explain.

Anaxagoras claims that all things are formed
From minute versions of themselves:
Bones are made of tiny bones, flesh from tiny bits of flesh,
Blood from drops of blood, and gold from grains of gold.
He imagines earth as bits of earth,
Fire as tiny fires, water as tiny waters,
And so on with all substances.
Yet he denies the existence of void in things,
And allows no limit to the division of matter.
On these points, he seems no less mistaken
Than those we discussed before.
Moreover, the particles he describes are too fragile—
If these primordial particles are the same in nature
As the things they form,
And if they are subject to the same decay,
What could prevent their annihilation?
What would endure against the grip of death?
The fire? The water? The air?
The blood, the bones? None of these,
For all would share the mortality
Of the objects we see perish before our eyes.
Yet the proofs above already show
That nothing can return to nothing,
And nothing can arise from nothing.
Since food nourishes and builds the body,
You must understand that our veins, blood, and bones
Are formed from particles unlike themselves.
If someone claims that food contains tiny particles
Of veins, bones, and flesh,
Then all food—solid or liquid—must itself
Be made of these same varied substances.
Thus, bread or water would need to contain
Small bits of bone, flesh, and blood.
If everything that grows from the earth
Were already contained within it,

The earth itself must be composed
Of all these different materials,
Holding within it the diversity of life it sustains.
Apply the same reasoning to other things:
If flame, smoke, and ash lie hidden in wood,
Then wood, too, must be a compound
Of many alien substances,
Containing these forms unseen.
Here lies a subtle way to evade the truth,
One that Anaxagoras claims for himself.
He argues that all things are mixed within all,
And only that which dominates in number
Or lies nearest to hand comes into view.
But this idea is far removed from reason.
If it were true, then grains, crushed by millstones,
Should sometimes yield a trace of blood,
Or fragments of other substances that nourish our bodies.
Rocks grinding against each other
Should ooze with gore. Similarly, herbs
Ought to drip with sweet milk,
Flavored like that from a ewe's udder.
Breaking clods of earth would reveal
Scattered bits of grains, leaves, and roots.
Splitting logs of wood should uncover
Ash, smoke, and hidden fire.
But since experience shows none of this occurs,
It proves that things are not mixed with things in this way.
Rather, seeds, shared by many things,
Are combined in countless ways within all matter.
"But," you say, "on windy hills,
The treetops sometimes rub together,
Driven by fierce southern gales,
Until they blaze with bursts of flame."
True indeed—but fire is not stored inside the wood.
Instead, the seeds of heat lie dormant,

And when friction draws them out and unites them,
The fire is kindled, igniting the forests.
If fire were already formed and hidden within the trees,
The flames could never remain concealed.
They would constantly burn the woods,
Reducing all the forest to ash.
This shows, as I explained earlier,
How much depends on the arrangement of seeds—
How they are combined with others,
What positions they hold,
And what motions they give and receive.
For these same seeds, rearranged,
Can create both fiery and wooden things,
Just as a small shift in the letters of a word
Produces entirely different meanings.
Consider again: if everything you see
Could only exist by containing particles
With exactly the same properties as the whole,
Then your argument destroys the very seeds of things.
You would have to claim that the primal germs themselves
Could laugh, shed tears, or express emotions,
Like living beings breaking into fits of laughter,
Or weeping with salty tears down their cheeks.

THE INFINITY OF THE UNIVERSE

Now listen further! Attend with sharper mind!
I know how dark the path may seem,
But the hope of praise has struck my heart,
Piercing like a thyrsus deep into my soul.
At that moment, sweet love for the Muses stirred,
And now, inspired, I wander boldly,
Exploring paths untrodden by others,
Discovering pure, untouched fountains of thought.
I drink deeply, I pluck fresh flowers,
And weave for my brow a crown of truth,
Taken from lands the Muses have never adorned.

First, I teach of great and mighty things,
Stripping away the strangling coils of fear,
Freeing the mind from dread religion's grasp.
Next, I sing of the darkest themes in words
Made clear, imbued with the charm of the Muses,
For good reason:
As doctors, when treating children with bitter wormwood,
Coat the rim of the cup with sweet honey,
So the unthinking child may drink,
Unaware of the bitterness within,
Yet emerge strengthened and healed,
So too have I, knowing these truths may seem harsh,
Dressed them in sweet verse, the honey of the Muse,
Hoping to hold your mind long enough
To guide it toward understanding
The nature and order of all things.
Now that I have explained how solid matter,
Eternal and unyielding, flies forever
Through infinite time,
Let us examine whether these seeds,
And the space they inhabit,
Are finite or infinite in nature.
We must explore the vast expanse of void,
The boundless abyss where all things occur.
The sum of all existence has no limits,
For if it did, it would need a "beyond."
And a "beyond" cannot exist without something
To border and contain it.
If there were a boundary, we must ask:
What lies beyond it?
If you say "nothing," then the boundary itself is void,
And void is infinite.
Imagine you stand at the edge of this supposed limit,
And hurl a spear beyond.
Does it fly onward, piercing the beyond,

Or is it stopped by some unseen wall?
Either answer proves there is no boundary,
For if the spear flies, space continues;
If it stops, something beyond resists it.
Thus, the universe stretches endlessly,
Without an edge or limit to contain it.
If space were finite,
The infinite weight of matter
Would collapse into a single point,
And the universe, unable to spread,
Would not exist. There would be no sky,
No sun, no earth, no seas.
Instead, matter is in constant motion,
Flowing from all directions, endlessly supplied.
Even the mighty thunderbolts
Cannot traverse this infinite void
Nor find an end to their course.
Things bound things, but nothing bounds the All.
Air surrounds mountains, sea ends at land,
Land meets the sea again—but the totality
Has no outer limit.
The nature of all existence is infinite,
Balanced by body and void.
If it were otherwise,
The universe would collapse,
Matter scattered without union,
Unable to form the world we see.
Primal particles, eternal and in motion,
Have tried every possible arrangement
Since time immemorial,
And through their collisions and unions,
The world as we know it emerged,
Sustained by the ceaseless supply of seeds.
The rivers replenish the seas,
The sun warms the earth to bring forth life,

And breathing creatures grow and thrive.
But these cycles depend on infinite space
And an endless reserve of matter.
If the supply were finite,
All things would dissolve,
As creatures die without food.
The blows that unite the universe,
Though constant, cannot preserve it all;
Some particles escape,
And new ones must take their place.
Thus, an infinite supply of matter,
Moving through infinite void,
Is the only way the universe persists,
Boundless, eternal, and ever in motion.
In these matters, my dear Memmius,
Do not yield to the common and mistaken claims:
That all things press inward to a single center,
And thus the nature of the world stands firm,
Unshaken by any outward blows,
Incapable of being divided or dispersed.
They argue that all heights and depths
Constantly press toward this central point—
As if anything could rest upon itself,
Or support itself in this way.
They also contend that the heavy bodies
Beneath the earth are somehow pressed upward,
Resting upside down upon the underside of the earth,
Much like the reflections we see in water.
They claim that living creatures beneath us
Walk head downward, yet do not fall
Into the sky below, just as we do not
Spontaneously fly upward into the heavens.
According to them, when those creatures
Look toward their sun, we see our stars of night.
And they believe their seasons of the sky

Mirror our own, with days and nights divided equally.
But these are vain dreams, embraced by fools,
Born of perverse reasoning and false beliefs.
For in a boundless world,
There can be no fixed center.
Even if such a center existed,
Nothing could settle there permanently,
For no force would hold it in place
More than any other could dislodge it.
The void itself, infinite and yielding,
Allows no fixed position, no resting point.
It must give way equally to weights,
Wherever their motions lead.
In the void, bodies cannot remain still,
Deprived as they are of any force to anchor them.
Nor can void offer support,
For its nature is to yield and give way.
Thus, no craving for a center
Could bind things together in such a manner.
Moreover, those who claim that not all bodies
Press toward the center,
But only earth and water—
The seas, rivers, and all things
Encased in earthly form—
Contradict themselves.
They argue that thin air and hot fire
Are driven outward from the center,
And that this outward motion feeds the ether,
Filling it with bright stars
And fueling the sun's flame in the sky.
They suggest that heat, fleeing from the center,
Gathers above and creates these celestial fires.
Yet this same logic would demand
That tree branches could not sprout leaves,
Unless their nourishment rose slowly upward

From the earth below.
These claims, built on faulty reasoning,
Crack under scrutiny,
For the world, boundless and infinite,
Knows no center, no fixed order of weight or motion,
And no single point to which all things gravitate.
Lest, like the winged flames of fire,
The walls of the world dissolve and flee,
Scattered into the boundless void,
And all that exists should follow after—
Lest the heavens, with their thundering vaults,
Burst apart and splinter skyward,
And the earth, slipping from beneath our feet,
Collapse into ruin. Its solid mass,
Torn apart along with heaven's wreckage,
Would scatter its primal seeds,
Drifting forever through the immeasurable void,
Leaving behind no trace, no remnants—
Only desolate space and invisible atoms.
For wherever you imagine the primal seeds lacking,
That very place becomes the doorway of death,
Through which all matter will rush and scatter
Outward, into nothingness.
If you reflect on these truths,
Guided by reason with but little effort,
One thing after another will reveal itself,
And the path will grow clear before your gaze.
No blind night will obscure your understanding,
Nor hinder your vision of nature's farthest reaches.
Thus, one truth will light another,
And knowledge will kindle torches of its own.

Book II

Proem

It is sweet, when on the vast and stormy sea
The winds churn up the waves, to watch from land
Another's struggle, distant from your own,
Not because we take delight in others' pain,
But for the joy of seeing troubles spared from us.
It is sweet, too, to witness mighty armies
Clashing in battle across the open plains,
While we ourselves are safe from risk and harm.
Yet nothing is more sweet, more goodly,
Than to stand on the high, serene plateaus,
Fortified by wisdom's walls, and look below
At other men, wandering far and wide,
Searching in vain for life's elusive path.
Some strive for genius, others chase after rank,
Laboring through days and nights in endless toil,
Seeking power, mastery over the world.
O wretched minds of men! O blinded hearts!
In what great dangers, in what shadows of life,
Do you waste your fleeting years!
How can you not see that Nature seeks for nothing
Except to keep pain from the body
And fill the mind with peace, free from fear and care?
We see, then, that the body needs but little:
Only enough to drive away pain
And provide a modest share of simple joys.
For Nature craves no lavish luxury.
It is no less sweet, if golden statues
Do not line the halls, holding lamps aloft,
If the house glitters not with gold and silver,
And no gilded ceilings resound to the lyre.
It is enough to recline with friends on soft grass,

By a flowing stream, beneath the shade of a great tree,
Refreshing our bodies with simple pleasures—
Most sweet of all when springtime graces the earth,
Sprinkling flowers across the green.
Nor will a fever leave your body sooner
If you toss upon a couch of purple silk
Than if you lie on a poor man's humble bed.
Since treasures, rank, and glory bring no ease
To the body's sufferings,
They bring no more comfort to the mind.
Unless, perhaps, you find joy in the sight
Of your legions gathering on the Field of Mars,
Or your fleets deploying across the seas,
The spectacle momentarily silencing
The fears of death and dispelling dread.
But if we reflect, we see this pomp is hollow—
A mockery, a fleeting show.
The dread of death does not fear swords or armies,
Nor does it shrink from golden thrones or purple robes.
Even amidst kings and rulers of the world,
Dread walks undaunted, mingling among them.
Can there be any doubt that such fears arise
Not from wealth or power, but from the mind itself?
For all of life labors in the dark.
Just as children tremble in the shadows of night,
Fearing what they cannot see,
So do we, in the full light of day,
Dread things no more real or terrible
Than the phantoms children invent in the dark.
This terror, this darkness in the mind,
Cannot be dispelled by the rising sun,
Nor by the bright arrows of morning light.
Only nature's laws, understood,
Can bring such fears to an end.

Atomic Motions

Now come, and let me guide your steps
To untangle how the primal seeds
Give birth to all the varied world,
And how, when formed, it dissolves again—
What force compels these acts, and what speed
Drives the seeds through the vast, infinite void.
Attend closely and yield to my words.
For matter does not cling together tightly,
Nor is it packed so dense as to remain unchanged.
We see how everything ages and decays,
How time erodes all things,
How objects wither and pass from sight.
Yet the total sum of matter endures,
Unharmed, because the seeds departing from one
Diminish it, while joining another,
Replenishing what they reach.
This endless exchange ensures the world's renewal:
What dies in one place gives life to another.
Thus, nations rise and fall, generations pass,
Each one like a runner handing on
The torch of life to the next.
But if you believe the primal seeds can stop
And, from rest, give birth to motion anew,
You stray far from truth's path.
For all seeds move through the infinite void,
Driven by their own weight or struck by others.
When these seeds meet and clash,
They often rebound, leaping apart,
Solid and unyielding in their nature,
Nothing behind them halting their motion.
Consider further: nowhere in the vastness
Of all existence is there a bottom,
No final resting place for primal seeds.

The infinite void extends without measure,
Boundless in all directions.
Thus, primal seeds can never find rest;
They are forever driven by ceaseless motion.
Some collide and rebound, leaving gaps;
Others cluster more tightly,
Their shapes interlocking in firm bonds.
Those bound closely form the roots of rocks,
The brute strength of iron, and other dense matter.
The seeds that leap far apart, leaving large gaps,
Create thin air and the radiant light of the sun.
And many others, cast off from unions,
Wander the void, unlinked and unaccepted,
Without a place in the structure of things.
This ceaseless dance of seeds mirrors
What we see with our own eyes:
When sunlight streams into a darkened room,
Tiny motes are revealed, tumbling in the light,
Battling, colliding, parting,
Chased up and down in endless motion.
From this, imagine the ceaseless tossing
Of primal seeds in the mightier void—
A small reflection of their vast, unseen dance.
These tumbling motes in sunlight
Hint at the hidden movements of primal matter.
For even in the smallest specks,
You can see how unseen blows
Drive them to change course,
To rebound, to scatter in all directions.
This restless motion begins with the primal seeds,
Moving of their own accord.
From their blows, they stir the smallest unions,
Closest in size to themselves,
And these in turn move the next larger bodies,
Until motion climbs stage by stage

To reach the objects visible to us.
Thus, from the unseen atoms,
Motion spreads outward, step by step,
Until it reaches the world we observe,
Though the original forces driving it
Remain hidden from view.
Do not wonder, Memmius,
Why, while the seeds of things are in constant motion,
The world as a whole seems to stand still,
Except when its entire frame visibly moves.
The nature of these primal atoms lies
Far beyond the reach of human senses;
Since we cannot see them,
Their movements remain hidden from our eyes.
Consider even the things we can observe—
How often their motions are concealed by distance.
On a far hillside, flocks of sheep may graze,
Wandering as the dew-drenched grass calls to them,
While lambs, full-bellied, frolic and lock horns in play.
Yet from afar, all appears as a still white blur,
A motionless gleam against the green hill.
Or imagine mighty legions spread across the plains,
Engaged in mock warfare, their polished brass
Gleaming in the sun, the ground trembling
Under their rhythmic march. Their shouts echo
From mountain walls to the stars above,
While cavalry charges send tremors through the earth.
But from some high vantage point,
The great army appears at rest,
A shining stillness upon the fields below.
Now consider the speed of matter's atoms,
And from this example, learn how swift they move:
When dawn first sprinkles light across the land,
And birds flit through the forest,
Filling the air with their liquid notes,

The sun rises, and suddenly its light
Spreads to clothe the world in radiance.
Yet, the sun's light and warmth do not travel
Through a void; they push through the dense air,
Slowed as they cleave the waves of atmosphere.
These rays move as a mass, tangled together,
Each particle restraining the others,
Checked by resistance as they advance.
But the primal atoms, solid and indivisible,
Travel through the void unhindered.
Unbound by external forces,
They race straight toward their goal,
Swift and unimpeded.
Their simple, compact nature allows them
To move far faster than the sun's light,
Covering vast expanses of space
In the time it takes sunlight
To fill the sky with its glow.
There is no need to trace each atom's path
To understand the laws of their motion.
Yet some, ignorant of matter's workings,
Claim that the seasons and the fruits of the earth
Exist only by divine will,
That gods adjust the world's workings to suit mankind,
Providing grains, life's pleasures, and the allure of love
To ensure the propagation of the human race.
They argue that the gods created all things for man,
But in doing so, they stray far from reason.
Even without knowledge of primal seeds,
I dare assert—by observing the heavens,
And by countless other proofs—
That the world was not crafted by divine hands
For humanity's sake.
For great are the flaws with which the world is burdened.
These faults, Memmius, I will later explain in detail.

For now, let us continue unraveling
The nature of motion and the truths it reveals.
Now, let me show you this truth, Memmius:
Nothing corporeal can rise upward by its own force
Or move against gravity's pull.
Let not the upward leap of flames deceive you,
For they ascend not by their own will,
But are driven by external forces.
Flames grow upward as they consume fuel,
Just as trees and plants reach skyward,
Though their weight always presses downward.
When fire climbs through a house,
Leaping from beams and timbers,
It is not moving freely—
It is pushed upward by the heat beneath.
Have you not seen how blood spurts upward
From a wound in the body,
Or how water hurls back timber and beams,
No matter how forcefully they are pushed beneath its surface?
The deeper they are submerged,
The more violently they rebound,
Emerging far above the surface,
Yet their weight always pulls them downward.
So too with flames:
Though they seem to rise,
Their motion results from external forces,
Not from an intrinsic upward pull.
Look to the meteors sweeping the skies,
Trailing long lines of fire.
Do not their flames follow paths provided by nature?
Do not stars fall toward the earth,
And does not the sun,
Though high in heaven,
Send its heat downward to warm the ground?
Lightning, too, cuts through the rain,

Zigzagging from cloud to earth,
Its fiery energy descending.
In all this, we must also grasp this truth:
As the atoms fall through the infinite void,
They do not always follow perfect straight lines.
At indeterminate times and places,
They swerve ever so slightly from their paths.
Without this subtle deviation,
All atoms would fall endlessly downward,
Parallel like raindrops in a bottomless void,
Never colliding, never creating anything.
Some argue that heavier atoms fall faster,
Striking lighter ones to create the collisions
That bring the world into being.
But this view falters,
For in the void, where no resistance exists,
All atoms, regardless of weight,
Fall at the same speed.
In water or air, heavier objects fall faster
Because the medium resists lighter bodies less.
But in the void, where nothing resists,
All move equally, without obstruction.
Thus, no collisions can occur simply from weight,
And without collisions, nature could create nothing.
Therefore, atoms must swerve slightly—
A minute deviation, almost imperceptible.
This swerve, slight as it is,
Allows them to meet, collide, and create motion.
Without this swerve,
All movement would be predetermined,
Each motion linked to another in an unbroken chain,
And free will would not exist.
But we see it does.
When we move as we desire,
It is not because of external force

Or predetermined cause.
Consider the horses at the starting gate:
They rear with eagerness to race,
But their bodies do not leap forward at once.
Their matter must first be roused,
From the mind's command to the limbs,
Until their motion matches their will.
Contrast this with motion forced upon us,
When external blows drive us against our will.
In such cases, our inner force resists,
Pulling back on the reins,
Redirecting the body's course
To align with our desires.
This power to resist,
To act freely despite external forces,
Must originate in the atoms themselves.
If the primal seeds lacked this capacity,
All motion would be fixed,
A mere consequence of weight and impact.
Thus, we see that freedom—
The ability to act without compulsion—
Is born of the atoms' subtle swerve.
In no fixed place or time,
This slight deviation breaks the chain of necessity,
Allowing for choice, will, and the creation of all things.
The stock of matter has never been more tightly packed,
Nor has it ever been divided by wider gaps.
For nothing can be added to it, and nothing can be taken away.
Thus, as the elemental particles move today,
So they moved in ages past,
And so they shall move forevermore.
What was born long ago shall be born again,
Under the same conditions and laws,
To grow and flourish according to Nature's
Unchanging and eternal decrees.

The sum of all things cannot be altered,
For nothing exists outside the universe—
No place for matter to escape,
No external source to supply fresh atoms,
To intrude upon the established order,
Change the essence of things,
Or reverse their motions.

Atomic Forms and Their Combinations

Now come, and grasp what follows:
Understand the countless forms and shapes
Of the ancient seeds of the universe.
They differ vastly, not just in a few cases,
But in endless variety.
These primal particles do not share
A single uniform appearance.
It is no wonder, since their number is infinite,
As I have shown—without limit or sum.
It must follow that they cannot all
Be marked by the same outline or shape.
Consider humanity, the flocks of fish
Swimming silently in streams,
The joyful herds grazing the fields,
The wild beasts, and the myriad birds—
Some flitting through water-bound haunts
By rivers, springs, and pools,
Others darting from tree to tree
In untamed forests.
Take any creature you choose,
From any kind or group,
And you will see each one differs in form,
Distinct from all others of its kind.
Without this diversity,
Mothers could not recognize their young,

Nor offspring their mothers—
Yet we see this happen every day,
As clearly among animals as among humans.
Behold, at the altars of the gods,
Where incense burns,
A yearling calf falls to the ground,
Its breast streaming warm blood.
Meanwhile, the orphaned mother roams
The green woodlands,
Searching the earth for her lost young.
She tracks its cloven hoofprints,
Scanning every place for signs,
Until, finding none, she halts.
Filling the leafy paths with her cries,
She returns to the stall,
Driven by relentless longing.
Not the tender willows,
Nor the fresh, dew-kissed grass,
Nor the gentle streams
Gliding along the banks
Can soothe her or ease her pain.
No other calves grazing nearby
Can distract her heart—
Her mind clings fiercely
To what is known and hers alone.
So too, the young of goats,
With their bleating throats,
Seek out their horned dams,
And the lambs their ewes.
Unfailingly, each finds its place,
Pressing to its proper teat,
As nature wills.
Even among grains of wheat,
No single kernel is identical to another—
Some subtle difference

Marks each one apart.
Likewise, on the seashores,
Where soft waves kiss the thirsty sands,
You will find no shell or conch
Perfectly alike in shape.
Thus, the seeds of all things,
Born of nature, not crafted by hand,
Do not conform to a single pattern.
They drift, diverse in form,
Each shaped uniquely,
Without a fixed mold or design.
It is easy to understand, dear Memmius,
Why the fires of lightning penetrate more deeply
Than the flames we kindle from earthly pine.
The celestial fire is composed of finer particles,
More subtle and delicate,
Allowing it to pass through spaces
That our denser fire cannot breach.
Consider how light passes through the horn
Of a lantern, while rain is kept at bay.
This is because the particles of light
Are finer than those of water.
Observe also how wine flows swiftly
Through the holes of a colander,
While olive oil moves sluggishly.
This happens because the oil's particles
Are larger or more entangled,
Slowing their separation and movement.
The same principle applies to all matter—
Finer particles move freely,
While larger, hooked elements are slower to pass.
Notice how honey or milk pleases the tongue
With its smooth and rounded nature,
While wormwood or centaury repels with bitterness.
The agreeable substances are formed of smooth atoms,

While the harsh and sharp are made of jagged shapes,
Tearing at the senses as they enter the body.
All sensations arise from these differences:
Smooth forms bring pleasure,
While rough forms cause irritation and pain.
Consider the difference between the sound
Of a sweet melody played on strings
And the harsh screech of a saw—
Surely, their atoms differ in shape and structure.
Likewise, the odors that pierce the nostrils
From burning flesh are not the same
As the fragrant scent of saffron or incense.
The pleasant and the foul, the beautiful and the vile,
Are all made of different forms,
With smoothness producing charm,
And roughness creating distress.
Some sensations lie between these extremes—
Such as the tartness of wine or the bitterness of herbs.
These arise from elements that are neither entirely smooth
Nor fully hooked, but slightly angled,
Tickling the senses without tearing them.
Fire and ice also differ in the shapes of their atoms,
As their effects on the body clearly show.
For touch, above all, is the ultimate sense—
Whether pain or pleasure arises
From something external or internal,
From collisions of atoms or their orderly flow.
Touch alone reveals the true nature of matter,
Showing how diverse forms cause diverse sensations.
The hardest substances—diamond, flint, iron—
Are built from hooked atoms,
Interlocked like branches,
Resisting blows and force.
Meanwhile, liquids, with their smooth and rounded atoms,
Flow freely, their particles unable to cohere.

Popcorn kernels in the hand flow like water,
Their roundness enabling easy movement.
Yet even in fluids like ocean brine,
Rough particles are mixed with smooth ones,
Giving the bitter taste.
The rough particles do not cling together,
But their globular nature allows them to roll
And still rasp the senses.
Proof of this mixture lies in the separation
Of sweet water from salt.
As water filters through the earth,
The rough, briny particles cling to the soil,
While the smooth, sweet ones flow freely,
Emerging as fresh springs.
Smoke, clouds, and flames also disperse easily,
Made of atoms that are not tightly linked.
Their pointed forms pierce through air,
Stone, and body alike,
Yet remain unbound to one another.
Having explained these truths,
Let us turn to another:
Though atoms vary in shape,
Their variations are finite.
If their forms were infinite,
Some seeds would grow infinitely large,
For endless variation would require endless parts.
Imagine atoms composed of three parts—
Rearranging their top, bottom, left, and right
Will yield only a finite number of shapes.
To create new forms, additional parts would be needed,
And with each new form, more additions required.
This would lead to infinite size,
Which we know cannot exist.
Thus, atoms are finite in form,
Bound by nature's laws,

And their differences, though vast,
Do not extend to infinity.
Now consider this, Memmius:
The dazzling robes of barbaric lands,
Their hues steeped in the Meliboean purple,
Dyed with the shellfish of Thessaly,
Would pale beside brighter, newer colours,
If such could be conceived.
The radiant feathers of peacocks,
Their golden generations streaked with brilliance,
Would be overshadowed by a fresher splendor.
The scents of myrrh, the sweetness of honey,
Would lose their allure.
Even the swan's song,
Or Apollo's hymns upon the lyre's strings,
Would be silenced by a sound more divine.
If ever something finer than the finest,
Or loathlier than the worst,
Could emerge to the senses,
The balance of things would be undone.
But such is not the case.
All things are bounded, limited—
Their forms, colours, scents, and sounds
Confined by nature's eternal laws.
The extremes of heat and cold
Stand fixed upon the path of seasons,
And between them lie every shade,
Every degree of warmth and chill.
Creation itself is governed by this law,
Differing only by finite changes,
Bound always by the limits of frost and flame.
From this truth, let us draw another:
The primal seeds of things,
Though varied in shape and form,
Are infinite in number.

Since their shapes are finite in kind,
Those sharing the same form must be infinite,
Else the supply of matter would fail.
From everlasting to today,
These eternal atoms endure,
Unbroken by time's ceaseless blows,
Sustaining the world without end.
Though some creatures are rare,
Like the elephants of India,
Whose ivory walls shield the land within,
They thrive elsewhere in abundance,
Balancing the scales of life.
Even if we imagined a being unique,
One of its kind across all lands,
Its existence would still require
An infinite reserve of matter
To form, to grow, and to sustain itself.
Without infinite seeds of its kind,
How could it survive in the vast chaos of the void,
Amidst the countless tides of matter?
Just as after a mighty shipwreck,
The ocean scatters beams, oars, and splinters of wood
Across distant shores,
So too would finite seeds,
Flung through endless ages,
Fail to unite or persist.
Yet we see things born,
We see them grow and thrive.
This proves the infinite nature
Of the primal seeds in every kind,
Providing the matter for all existence.
Neither creation's forces
Nor destruction's power reigns eternal.
Birth and death wage an unending war,
A balance of forces in ceaseless struggle.

Sometimes life's vitality prevails;
Sometimes it is overcome.
At the edge of life's beginning,
The cries of infants pierce the dawn,
While the laments of death
Echo in the shadows of every night.
Day and night, birth and death,
Have ever been entwined.
Hold this truth firmly in mind:
Nothing visible or known to us
Is made of a single kind of seed.
Everything is composed of mixed elements,
And those with more powers and properties
Contain the greatest diversity of seeds.
The earth, above all,
Holds within her the seeds
Of water, fire, and life itself.
From her springs the cool rivers,
The blazing fires of Aetna,
The grains and trees that nourish mankind,
And the grasses and pastures
That sustain the beasts of the wild.
For this, she is called
The great mother of gods,
The parent of beasts and men.
The ancient poets sang her praises,
Hailing her as the source of all creation.
Seated in her chariot above the airy realms,
She drives her team of lions, teaching all
That the vast earth hangs poised in empty space,
Needing no other earth to hold its weight.
To her chariot are yoked the wild beasts,
Symbolizing that even the most savage offspring
Must be tamed and guided by a parent's care.
A turret-crown encircles her head,

Signifying her fortressed cities,

For she sustains their strength and safety.

And today, adorned with the same emblem,

Her sacred image is borne solemnly

Through many lands, worshipped as divine.

Nations far and wide revere her as

The Idaean Mother, following the ancient rites.

They escort her with Phrygian bands,

Honoring the legend that grain first spread

From those regions to the world.

To her they dedicate the Galli,

The emasculate priests, to show

That men ungrateful to their mothers,

Or violators of her sacred majesty,

Are unfit to bring life into the world.

The Galli come, with wild frenzy,

Beating hollow cymbals and tambourines.

The blaring horns cry out with raucous bray,

And the pipes stir their minds to madness

With piercing Phrygian melodies.

They bear sharp knives, wild symbols of their zeal,

Meant to terrify the impious

With the fearsome power of the goddess.

When the Mother is carried through the cities,

She blesses all with silent grace.

People line the streets, scattering coins of brass and silver,

Showering her and her attendants

With a snowfall of roses.

Armed troops accompany her,

Known to the Greeks as the Phrygian Curetes.

Dancing with bloody mirth,

They clash brass on brass,

Their crested helmets nodding fiercely.

This armed procession recalls the story of Crete,

Where, as the tale goes, the Curetes drowned

The infant cries of Zeus with their rhythmic dance,
Beating their weapons to shield the child
From Saturn's devouring jaws.
Others say the armed retinue honors
The Mother's lesson: that men must defend
Their homelands with valor,
Guarding their parents with courage and pride.
Yet such tales, however beautifully told,
Stray far from reason.
The gods must dwell in eternal peace,
Untouched by mortal woes,
Needing neither our gifts nor our service.
The earth, insensate and eternal,
Is no goddess, but rather the source
Of life's materials. She holds within her
The seeds of countless forms,
Birthing all that lives and grows.
Those who name the ocean Neptune,
Or call the grain-crops Ceres,
May speak in metaphor,
So long as they keep their souls
Free from the stains of blind religion.
Look to the flocks, the herds, and the horses,
Grazing together on a single plain,
Beneath one sky, drinking from one stream.
Each lives in its own form and nature,
Faithfully repeating the traits of its kind,
Generation after generation.
In every plant and every river,
In all creatures great and small,
Diverse materials and seeds reside,
Shaped uniquely to form their distinct natures.
Every living being, without exception,
Is composed of bones, blood, veins,
Moisture, flesh, and muscle—

All built from elements
Diverse in shape and form.
Even fire, when it blazes,
Reveals its secret power:
Atoms within its frame
Release heat and light,
Scattering sparks and embers wide.
If you examine the world with reason,
You will see how everything hides within itself
The seeds of many forms,
Diverse and interwoven.
Observe how certain things are given
Colour, flavour, and scent combined—
Chiefly in burnt offerings,
Where fire reveals the hidden essence
Of their nature.
Thus, all things must be composed of diverse shapes.
The smell of scorching enters our senses,
While the bright color from dye remains apart;
And flavor, distinct from both,
Affects us differently still.
From this, it is clear that color, flavor, and scent
Are made of differing elemental shapes.
These varied forms combine into one,
And things exist through the mingling of seeds.
Yet not all things can combine in every way,
For if they could, monstrous forms would arise—
Half-human creatures with beastly parts,
Or trees growing from the bodies of men,
Sea creatures fused with land animals,
And the earth giving birth to Chimeras,
Breathing fire from hideous jaws.
But such beings are never born,
Because all things come from fixed seeds
And follow a fixed ancestry.

Nature ensures that each creature,
From the food it consumes,
Absorbs only the atoms suited to its kind.
These atoms, once within,
Join and produce the proper motions
That sustain the creature's life.
Meanwhile, nature expels foreign particles,
Those unsuitable for the body,
Which cannot integrate or support its functions.
Invisible bodies are cast out,
Impulsed by the force of blows,
Unfit to bond or sustain vital motion.
These laws do not bind living forms alone;
They govern all things, everywhere,
Distinguishing and defining the world.
Just as all things in creation are,
In their very nature, each unlike the other,
So too must their atoms differ in shape.
Not because only a few share the same form,
But because, as a general rule,
No one thing is exactly like all others.
In these verses, you see many elements
Common to many words—letters repeated,
Yet the words and lines remain distinct,
Built from different combinations.
Not every word is made of identical elements,
But rather, each has its unique pattern.
So it is with all things in nature:
While many seeds are shared across forms,
Their specific combinations
Create entirely different wholes.
Thus, humankind, grains, and joyful trees
Are each composed of distinct atoms.
Moreover, since the seeds differ,
So too must their intervening spaces,

The pathways they form, their connections,
Weights, impacts, collisions, and motions.
These distinctions do not merely define
The living forms of the world;
They also separate the ocean from the land,
Hold the heavens apart from the earth,
And maintain the harmony of all things.

Absence of Secondary Qualities

Thus must you understand that primal seeds,
The basic forms of things, lack hue and dye.
Do not suppose that white things shine because
Their atoms too are white, nor black things dark
Because their seeds are black. This thought is false.
For matter holds no colour of its own—
Neither like the objects formed nor unlike.
And should you think that mind or sense imparts
A hue to these first bodies, you are lost,
Far from the truth. For even those born blind,
Who've never seen the sun or light of day,
Can feel and recognize through touch alone
The forms of things, though colours mean no more.
What we perceive in dark is yet untinged;
No colour comes to us when light is gone.
If every colour shifts and changes shape,
And nothing keeps its hue unaltered still,
Then primal seeds cannot be stained with hues,
For they must hold their form eternally,
Or all would crumble back to nothingness.
A change in essence spells the end of things.
Thus, seeds must be devoid of tint or shade,
Or all we see would vanish into void.
Yet though they lack all hue, these primal forms,
By their arrangements, make all colours bloom.

A blackened thing may turn to gleaming white
As atoms shift, combine, and rearrange—
Much like the ocean changes, dark to light,
When winds upheave and churn its tranquil waves.
But if the sea were made of only blue,
No storm or motion could transform its hue.
If primal seeds could bear the stain of red,
Or green, or white, or blue, then just as shapes
Of cubes retain diversity within,
Each ocean wave would show a patchwork hue,
A thousand shades at odds with one another.
But objects we behold are pure in tone—
No patchwork waters shimmer in the sea.
Furthermore, colours do not birth themselves.
White does not come from white, nor black from black,
But rather, all derive from varied seeds,
Combined and altered in their size and shape.
And since no colour lives without the light,
These primal seeds, which dwell in shadowed void,
Must ever lack the vivid glow of hues.
See how the hues of doves and peacock tails
Shift subtly with the angle of the sun.
The green of emerald mingles with the red,
The golden bronze gives way to glowing white,
Depending on the play of beams and rays.
So colours are but fleeting forms of light,
A product of the sun's swift-moving touch.
Moreover, objects worn and torn to bits
Lose colour as they crumble into dust.
A linen cloth, unraveled thread by thread,
Reveals how dyes dissolve and fade away
Long before matter falls to primal seeds.
Thus, colours vanish as their forms degrade,
Proving they do not dwell within the core.
As not all things emit a sound or scent,

Nor all can touch or taste, so not all bear
The property of colour. Mind alone
Can sense and know these things without such traits.
And primal seeds, the building blocks of all,
Must lack both sound and scent, both warmth and cold,
For they emit no essence from themselves.
Just as a fragrant balm must first be mixed
With oil devoid of scent, lest it corrupt
The pure and subtle perfume it should hold,
So too must primal seeds be free of hues,
And scents, and flavours, lest they alter forms.
The seeds are bare, their power unadorned,
Yet from them rise all things in varied hue.
The rest; and yet, since all these things are mortal—
The pliant, being soft of body and yielding;
The brittle, with frames that crumble into dust;
The hollow, full of pores and easily broken—
They must be separate from primal elements,
If we are to establish an immortal foundation
Beneath the world, where the sum of all safety
And stability may rest, lest all things
Return to nothingness and perish utterly.
Now also, whatever we observe possessing sense
Must undeniably be formed of elements
Devoid of sense themselves. And the evidence,
So clear and immediate to all who see,
Does not refute this notion nor oppose it;
Rather, it leads us to this truth by hand,
Compelling belief that all living beings
Are born from lifeless elements, as I assert.
Indeed, we see live worms arise from foul dung
When the soaked earth rots after heavy rains;
And everything changes form in the same way.
Behold: rivers and grass, and lush pastures,
Are transformed into cattle; the cattle, in turn,

Into our own bodies; and from our bodies,
Wild beasts and winged birds grow mighty.
Thus nature converts all food into living forms,
Creating senses in these frames,
Just as she transforms dry logs into flame.
Do you not see, therefore, how greatly it matters
In what order the primal seeds are arranged,
With what other seeds they mix and combine,
And what motions they give and receive?
But now, what doubt strikes your sceptical mind,
Forcing you to argue against belief
That sense can arise from senseless atoms?
Surely, it is this: you see liquids, earth, and wood,
Even when combined, fail to create feeling life.
Thus, it will be helpful to remind yourself:
I never claimed that sense is born
Under all conditions or from every substance
That composes things capable of feeling.
What matters here is first the size of the seeds
That make up the thing endowed with sense;
Then, the shapes they carry; and finally,
Their positions, motions, and arrangements.
In wood and clods, these conditions are absent.
Yet even these, when softened by the rain,
Can give rise to writhing grubs, because the atoms
Within them, disarranged by the new factor,
Recombine in such a way as to create life.
Next, those who claim that sensing beings can
Only be formed from other beings that feel,
When soft they fashion them, for all sensation
Is linked with flesh, with sinews, and with veins—
And these, as we observe, are formed soft,
Endowed with frames destined to perish.
Yet even if they could endure forever,
Their sense would still be partial, tied to parts,

Or they'd be judged to share a sense akin
To that which animates the living whole.
But parts alone cannot themselves perceive,
For every sense within each member points
Back to the unity of something greater.
A severed hand, or any limb removed,
Cannot sustain sensation of its own.
Thus, these parts must resemble living beings
To hold the power of sense within themselves,
Each part in harmony with vital feeling,
Sensing all things precisely as we do.
If so, how could they serve as primal seeds,
The indestructible roots of all creation?
For living beings are subject to decay,
And mortal things cannot eternal be.
And even were they, by their unions all,
They'd yield but swarms of living things alone—
A chaos thronged with men, beasts, herds, and flocks.
For simply by conglomeration none
Can birth a thing new-made and separate.
And if, within a living frame, they lose
Their own sensation, taking on another,
Why grant them such a quality at all,
Only to strip it from them afterward?
Recall the proof: we see that fowls' eggs change,
Becoming chicks; and teeming worms arise
When sodden earth is drenched with soaking rain.
It's plain that sense can spring from insensate things.
And if some argue sense can thus emerge
By change, or through a certain kind of birth,
Know first: no birth occurs unless there comes
A union of the elements before,
No change unless they intertwine and meet.
For sense cannot inhabit any frame
Before its living nature is composed—

Since all its matter, scattered and dispersed
In rivers, air, and earth, cannot unite
To form the vital motions needed to
Ignite the spark of sensing life within.
And further, if some violent external blow
Strikes hard enough, it shatters every frame,
Confounding mind and body, as the seeds
Are loosened from their order and their motion halts.
Until these structures shake and scatter wide,
Undoing the vital threads of life itself,
The soul is driven out through every pore.
What else, when struck, could matter possibly do
But break apart, loosening from itself?
And yet, when gentler blows disturb the frame,
The vital motions often can prevail—
Restoring order, calming chaos, calling
Each part back to its proper place again,
Quelling the near dominion of death's sway,
And kindling once more sensations almost lost.
Else how could life reclaim its footing near
The very brink of death, turning away
From that abyss, rather than fully passing?
Furthermore, pain arises when matter,
Jostled within the body's joints and vitals,
Quivers and shakes against its natural state.
Delight, by contrast, blooms when all returns
To proper place, and smoothness soothes the form.
Thus primal seeds can feel neither pain nor joy,
For they lack the composition required
To suffer or to savor sweet delight.
If sense were necessary in all things
That lend sensation to the living whole,
What then of those fixed elements from which
Humanity is formed? Shall we believe
They laugh aloud, or weep, or question what

They themselves are made of? By such logic,
Each primal germ would need to come from others,
Endlessly regressing into nonsense.
Follow this reasoning: if a laughing man
Need not arise from laughing elements,
Nor thinking minds from sapient seeds, why, then,
Cannot sensation spring from senseless things,
Joined and arranged in proper form and motion?

Infinite Worlds

Once more, we all are born from seeds of heaven,
That same great Father, who bestows on earth,
Our nurturing mother, drops of liquid life,
Impregnating her womb to bear her broods—
The golden grains, the joyous shrubs and trees,
The human race, and all the wild beasts' kin.
She yields the food that feeds all living frames,
Sustains their lives, and helps them propagate;
Thus earning well the name of mother true.
What springs from earth sinks back to earth again;
What's sent from ether, homeward speeds once more
To heaven's embrace. Yet death annihilates
Nothing entirely: bodies never perish.
She only breaks their bonds, and then re-forms
The primal seeds in fresh configurations.
Thus, forms and colours shift, sensations come
And go, and life itself takes fleeting shape.
So thou may'st learn how much it matters, friend,
With what companions, in what structure held,
The primal seeds unite, and how they move.
For nothing that we see adrift today,
Born or destroyed, remains in its essence
Fixed within the eternal atoms' core.
Why, even in these verses that I craft,

The meaning rests on where and how I place
Each letter: sky and sea, the lands and streams,
The sun, the grains, the trees, and living forms—
All take their being from these same base shapes.
And what distinctions simple order makes!
So too in nature: change the intervals,
The ways of motion, paths, and weights, or bonds
Between the seeds, and all must change in turn—
The things themselves must differ utterly.
Now to sound reason turn thy open mind.
Strange truths demand a readiness to hear,
For they present the world in novel guise.
Yet nothing is so simple, at the start,
That it seems easy; nor so great, at first,
That it astounds forever. Mortal men
Soon grow accustomed, little by little,
To marvels vast and wondrous as they are.
Consider how the heavens stretch above,
The bright, clear skies, the constellations' dance,
The moon's soft glow, the blazing sun's fierce light:
Were these revealed to mortals suddenly,
If unforeseen, what wonder would there be!
What awe-struck whispers would the nations share!
Yet now, though grand, they scarcely draw our gaze.
So, cast not reason from thy mind in scorn,
Nor spurn this truth because it seems so new.
Instead, with sharpened judgment weigh its worth.
If it prove true, then yield thy heart to it;
If false, prepare thy arguments with care.
For now my human mind seeks far beyond,
To fathom the vast reaches lying past
The ramparts of this world, the boundless void,
Where thought itself leaps forward, swift, unbound.
First, understand that the universe has no bounds—
No end above, below, nor to the sides,

As reason shows and Nature's truths proclaim.
The infinite abyss of space extends,
And countless seeds, unnumbered, ceaselessly
In endless motion drift throughout the void.
It's folly, then, to think this earth and sky,
This single world of ours, were formed alone,
While all those seeds beyond remain inert,
Their power unused, their purpose left undone.
For just as seeds collided here by chance,
Combining randomly, without design,
To form this world, so countless other worlds
Must rise in other realms of boundless space.
For matter flows abundant, free, and vast,
And space lies open, offering no restraint.
Thus, many earths, suns, skies, and seas exist,
And races born of myriad kinds abound,
Scattered across the cosmos, endlessly.
No single kind of thing exists alone,
For all are members of a greater race—
Beasts roaming mountains, men upon the plains,
The fish in streams, the birds that skim the air—
Each springs from countless like itself. And so,
The earth and stars, the sun and moon, are joined
By countless others of their kind, unseen,
Scattered in regions vast beyond our ken.
Perceiving this, thou'lt see that Nature moves
Free from the tyranny of haughty gods.
No hand divine directs her course, nor voice
Commands the sum of her immeasurable frame.
For who could guide such boundless realms, or wield
The reins of endless matter, sky, and fire?
Who could at once light myriad suns, or shake
The heavens with thunder, while still tending all?
Indeed, how often has the lightning struck
The temples of the gods, or storms laid low

Their shrines, while blameless mortals bore the blows
Of such chaotic, aimless acts of force?
These sights, more reasoned than all fabled tales,
Reveal the truth: Nature herself, unbound,
Creates and ends, assembles and dissolves,
Without divine direction or decree.
From time's first dawn, new matter has flowed in,
To build the earth, expand the heavens' vault,
And fill the sea. Each element combines,
Joining its kind—earth thickening with earth,
Moisture merging with moisture, fire with fire.
This ceaseless process, guided by no will,
Extends the universe and shapes its bounds.
Yet limits hold: each thing can grow no more
When Nature reaches her appointed end.
For when the inward flow of nourishment
Equals the outward loss of vital seeds,
The body halts its climb, and life begins
Its slow descent toward decay and death.
As growth recedes, the tides of age prevail,
And what expands with ease now wastes away,
Unable to sustain its former strength.
So all things perish: either worn by time,
Eroded by external blows, or drained
By dwindling stores of life. Their fleeting forms
Are carried off by Nature's endless flow,
While she, unbroken, works to forge anew.
Thus, too, the mighty walls of this vast world
Shall crumble down, their ramparts stormed and breached,
Their fragments scattered through the boundless void.
For food sustains all things, renewing life;
Yet now no food suffices to uphold,
No veins contain the measure that is needed,
No Nature yields as much as time demands.
Even now, the earth—so weary, worn with age,

That once bore forth all life in teeming floods—
Now scarcely brings to birth her smallest forms.
She who of old gave life to mighty beasts,
And nourished every race upon her plains,
Now falters in her power to renew.
For never from the heavens' vaulted heights
Did golden chains let mortal beings down,
Nor did the sea, nor rocks lashed by the waves,
Bring forth these lives; the earth, the mother, bore them—
She still sustains, as once she gave them birth.
It was her hand that first bestowed the grain,
The joyful vineyards, and the pastures green,
Which now, though aided by our tireless toil,
Reluctant grow, their bounty slow and scant.
We yoke the oxen, wear our bodies down,
And spend the strength of sturdy farmer's hands;
The iron tools grow dull, and yet the soil
Grants little yield, begrudging every ear.
The aged ploughman shakes his head in grief,
And sighs to see his labours yield no gain.
He dreams of days long past, when life was full,
When less was asked, and yet the earth gave more.
He praises now the fortunes of his sires,
And, prattling on, recalls how simpler men
Once lived in plenty on their smaller fields.
The vine-planter, too, with weary heart, laments,
And rails against the seasons and the skies,
Not seeing that all things, by slow degrees,
Are fading, wasting, slipping to their end.
For all that's born must journey to the tomb,
Each worn and spent by time's unyielding march.

Book III

Proem

O thou who first did lift so bright a torch,
Illuminating dark paths of human thought,
Thy wisdom shines a beacon, guiding men
To seek the true and shun the shades of fear.
I follow thee, great glory of the Greeks,
Not as a rival, but a devotee,
Eager to tread the noble paths thou laid,
As one who loves the master's work would do.
For how can sparrows vie with mighty swans,
Or lambs unsteady match the coursing steed?
Thou art the father, fountain of our truths,
Bestowing precepts from thy treasured scrolls.
As bees do sip the blossoms of the fields,
We drink thy golden wisdom, ever fresh,
A feast for thought, eternal in its worth.
When thy profound, godlike reason first unveiled
The workings of the universe entire,
The terrors of the mind were swept away;
The walls of this vast world fell open wide,
Revealing all the wonders of the void.
The gods emerged in their celestial calm,
Free from our woes, their peace untouched by strife,
Dwelling in realms beyond the winds and storms,
Where neither frost nor tempest breaks their rest.
No longer does my gaze behold the shades
Of Acheron, nor does the earth's expanse
Obstruct my view of all that lies below.
Through thee, I find a new and holy awe,
A trembling joy at nature's perfect law,
So plainly laid before the eyes of men.
And now, my verse must turn to delve the soul,

To teach the nature of the mind and life,
And banish fear of Acheron's dark gates,
Which clouds with dread the brightness of our days,
And poisons life's delights with shadowed grief.
For though some claim they dread not death itself,
Declaring shame and poverty their fears,
Their actions and their prayers betray the lie.
Exiles, fugitives, and outcasts alike,
Despised and stained with every wretchedness,
Still seek the gods with sacrifices grim,
Offering prayers and rites in bitter straits.
Their words, their masks, fall shattered in despair,
Revealing minds enslaved to fear of death.
The lust for wealth, the hunger after power,
The endless toil that leads to fleeting gain,
These too are rooted in the dread of death.
Men, fleeing want and disgrace, heap corpse on corpse,
Amassing riches at the cost of kin,
Hardened by fear to acts of cruel despair.
From envy, hatred grows; from greed, deceit;
From dread of death, the bonds of trust are torn,
And every virtue trampled underfoot.
For children fear the shadows in the dark,
And grown men tremble at the light of truth.
This terror of the mind, this ancient night,
No dawn can chase away, no gleam of gold,
But only wisdom, grasped through nature's laws.

Nature And Composition of The Mind

First, let us probe this question: the mind,
That intellect which governs human life,
Is part of man, no less than eyes or hands,
No less than feet or any vital limb.
But some declare its seat is nowhere fixed,

And name it "harmony"—a state derived,
Not of a part, but from the whole entire.
Thus do they claim that health within the flesh,
Although no single part can claim its seat,
Is yet the body's state. So mind, they say,
Resides as harmony, diffused throughout.
Yet, mightily, I hold their error plain.
For oft the body, seen and palpable,
Is sick, yet in the mind a joy remains;
Or else the mind in sorrow lies entrapped,
While limbs and frame enjoy a sweet repose.
Just as the foot may throb while head is whole,
So too the mind or body feels alone.
And when in slumber deep, the weary limbs
Lie lax and void of sense, the mind within
Still stirs itself, in dreams it wanders far,
Embraces phantoms, joys, and suffers cares.
Consider this: when body is undone,
With flesh consumed, the limbs still sometimes hold
A semblance of their life; yet, when a breath
Or heat's small remnants from the frame are gone,
All life departs, the structure falls to dust.
Thus life depends not on all parts alike,
But on those seeds of warmth and vital wind,
Which, fleeing, leave the body dead and cold.
So too the soul, a corporeal thing, must be,
A part within the body, not mere "harmony."
And now, since nature of the mind and soul
Dwells in the body as a vital part,
We must dismiss this notion borrowed hence
From Heliconian minstrels—let it serve
For music's art, not for the seat of life.
Mind and the soul, though joined as one, yet show
A double nature: one the sovereign power,
Which we call "mind," residing in the breast,

Where joy and terror spring and reason rules;
While through the limbs the soul obeys the mind,
A scattered presence moved by its command.
The mind alone perceives, and when it stirs,
It stirs itself, and neither body nor soul
Necessitates its mirth or pain; and yet,
When struck by fiercer shocks, the whole must feel:
A trembling spreads, the pallor pales the skin,
The voice is lost, the tongue falls silent, ears
Ring loudly, darkness veils the failing eyes,
And limbs collapse, as terror wracks the frame.
At times, such fear may even bring to death.
Thus, clear it is: the soul, conjoined with mind,
Forthwith transmits the mind's disturbance through
The limbs and body, proving them entwined.
From this, too, follows that the soul and mind
Are of a corporeal substance, since they move
And move the body, which no act can touch
Except by physical force. The spear that strikes
Our frame may miss the life itself, yet still
May stagger thought and set the mind adrift,
Till strength returns. Such anguish of the mind
Proclaims its nature too must be corporeal.
Thus have I shown the mind and soul, as parts
Of man corporeal, hold sway within,
And not as fleeting "harmony" dissolved
When man himself dissolves into the void.
The nature of the mind and soul, I tell,
Is wrought of finest particles, so small
And light, their motion outruns all we see.
For nothing moves as swiftly as the mind:
What it proposes, it begins at once,
Far faster than what hands or eyes can do.
Thus, such agility must spring from seeds
Exceedingly fine, smooth, and round, to move

At even the slightest touch or impulse weak.
Observe the flowing water: with a breath,
Its waves respond, for all its stock consists
Of rolling, rounded forms. Yet honey moves
Much slower; its structure, rougher, clings together,
Its atoms larger, rougher than the stream.
The lightest breeze will scatter poppy seeds,
Yet cannot shift the weight of stones or grain.
So by this rule, the smoother and more fine
The body's seeds, the swifter its response;
The rougher and more heavy, the more still.
Since mind is swift beyond all else we know,
Its seeds must be the smallest, roundest kind.
This truth, once grasped, illuminates the rest.
When life departs, when mind and soul withdraw,
The body's shape and weight remain unchanged.
All goes with death but sense and vital heat.
Thus, the soul's form must be compact and fine,
Its atoms woven subtly through the veins,
The nerves, the very marrow of the limbs.
For just as fragrance fades without a trace,
Or savour leaves the food yet alters not
Its weight or form, so soul, composed of seeds
So delicate, departs unseen, unfelt,
Leaving the body's outward semblance whole.
Yet soul and mind are not one simple form.
An aura subtle mingles there with heat,
And heat with air—a triple nature bound.
Heat, being rare, permits the airy seeds
To intermingle, forming one fine weave.
But these alone could never yield the sense,
The thought, the consciousness that life requires.
To this must join a fourth, unnamed, unknown,
More mobile, smooth, and subtle still than all.
This fourth conveys the motions that awake

Sensation; it is stirred the first, and then
Transfers its impulse to the heat and air,
Which rouse the blood and nerves, and finally
Reach to the marrow, spreading joy or pain.
Thus, sensation courses through the flesh,
Yet rarely penetrates beyond the skin;
For when it does, the soul, perturbed too much,
Begins to scatter through the body's pores.
So fragile is the balance that sustains
Our life, and yet, by nature's wise design,
Most shocks are stopped before the vital core,
Preserving life and granting us repose.
The soul and body, intertwined as one,
Hold shared dominion till their joint life's done.
Their union, like the fragrance in the myrrh,
Cannot be parted lest the whole deter.
From birth, the seeds of life are closely bound,
With mutual motions all their sense is found.
The soul, though fine and made of smallest parts,
Instructs the body, guides its vital arts.
Through every vein and nerve, it weaves its thread,
And, with the body, learns the path it's led.
For when the mind is struck by joy or pain,
The body echoes, stirred in every vein.
No single part can sense apart sustain,
Nor can the soul alone perception gain.
Each motion, thought, and sense is mutual born,
Each to the other bound till death is sworn.
To rend the soul away would break the frame,
And leave the body ruined, robbed of flame.
Like fragrant frankincense destroyed by force,
The sundered life cannot retain its course.
If any claim the body feels no pain,
And sense is soul's domain alone to reign,
They clash with fact: for eyes perceive the light,

And bodies flinch at wounds or burning blight.
Should soul alone be keeper of the sense,
The body's part would claim no consequence.
Yet, when the soul departs, the frame decays,
For it no longer serves the vital ways.
To say the soul peers outward, through the eyes
As through mere doors, with truth cannot align;
For when the light's too bright, we squint and fail,
And doors, unhampered, would not thus prevail.
If eyes were only portals to the mind,
Then with them closed, we'd clearer vision find.
From birth, the soul and body learn to share
Their powers, as each depends upon the pair.
No sense arises from a single source,
But through their blending comes the vital force.
Thus, see the truth: their lives are intertwined,
And neither lives without the other's kind.
The soul and mind, as partners deeply twined,
Compose the essence of our mortal kind.
Though mind stands sovereign, holding life's command,
The soul, its ward, obeys its guiding hand.
Without the mind, the soul cannot remain;
Together they depart, as life does wane.
Democritus, though wise, yet missed the trace,
Proposing soul and body's shared embrace.
For soul, more subtle, scattered, light, and few,
Cannot by bulk the body's form imbue.
Its primal seeds, dispersed with gaps between,
Are finer still than dust, or gossamer seen.
Thus, sensations come with measures vast,
For countless atoms must their signals cast
To stir the soul and make its presence felt,
By pounding motions where their clashes melt.
The body's coarser elements require
More frequent hits to kindle soul's desire.

The mind, however, reigns above the soul,
Its intellect retains the body's whole.
If mind remains, though limbs are torn apart,
Life lingers still, sustaining vital heart.
Yet when the mind is lost, the soul takes flight,
Abandoning the frame to death's cold night.
As vision rests upon the eye's clear core,
Its pupil bright, though injured parts implore,
So too the soul and mind in union dwell,
Each vital to the other, bound as well.
Destroy the mind, the soul will cease its claim,
And life's bright flame will vanish all the same.
This sacred bond, this deep entwined duet,
Sustains the frame, where life and soul are met.

The Soul is Mortal

The soul and mind, united, frail, and bound,
Are mortal both, as proofs in nature found.
Now hear, as sweet toil yields these truths to thee,
How they arise, dissolve, and cease to be.
The soul, composed of atoms small and fleet,
Exceeds in fineness smoke or vapor's sheet.
Like incense curling high from altars' glow,
Its substance, subtle, swiftly tends to go.
When vessels break, their liquids spill or seep;
When fog disperses, winds their fragments keep.
So too the soul, if loosed from mortal clay,
Fades quicker still and scatters far away.
The body forms the soul's supporting vase;
When shattered, both dissolve to void and space.
If blood's escape leaves veins and flesh undone,
How shall mere air, more tenuous, hold as one
The fragile soul? It parts as body fades,
Like mist dissolved by morning's warming rays.

Observe, as age unfolds, the mind and frame
Together grow, and together bear the same
Inevitable decay. In tender youth,
The mind is weak; in age, it seeks no truth.
When limbs grow frail, and strength begins to wane,
The mind too falters, tethered to the strain.
Disease, which plagues the flesh, afflicts the mind;
Their fates are linked, as nature's laws designed.
Grief, fear, and madness seize the mind with might,
And such afflictions end in death's dark night.
For as the body's pangs the soul confound,
So mortal pains the fleeting mind unbound.
See how the fiery wine within can weave
Its chaos through the veins, make strength deceive:
Limbs stumble, tongues stammer, eyes grow dim,
And thoughts are drowned as senses fade and swim.
If such a transient cause the mind can shake,
A greater blow its fragile bonds would break.
Witness the man who, seized by sudden throes,
Writhes, sputters, foams, and in convulsion goes.
The soul, disturbed by body's dire distress,
Reveals its nature: mortal, powerless.
Thus mind and soul, as body, find their end,
To winds dispersed, where primal atoms blend.
The soul, when ravaged, foams as if to spew
Its essence forth, like waves in tempest's brew
Where winds compel the seas to rage and toss.
It groans, torn by the poison's cruel cross,
Which drives the seeds of voice in hurried flight
Through well-worn paths, escaping to the light.
Reason falters; mind and soul are rent,
Their harmony undone, their strength near spent.
Yet when disease retreats, its venom fades,
The man, though reeling, slowly sense regains.
Thus, mind and soul, when trapped in fleshly frame,

Are fragile, wracked by sickness and by shame.
How then could these, exposed to open air,
Immortal battle with the winds out there?
The healing arts restore the mind's distress,
Confirming mortal roots in its recess.
For what can alter nature's primal plan
Save rearrangement of its form and span?
Yet what is deathless cannot lose or gain;
Its essence fixed, unchanging will remain.
But mind, when changed by sickness or by cure,
Shows mortal bounds no shift can long endure.
Mind and body, bound in common fate,
Are vessels joined, their essence integrate.
As severed limb or eye cannot persist
Detached from life, they rot and cease to exist.
So, too, the soul apart can never be,
For bound it is in body's frailty.
The union prospers both in life's design;
No sense endures if one must disentwine.
As eyes removed no longer see the day,
So soul and mind, alone, would lose their sway.
For deep within the body they're confined,
Their motion trapped in flesh, their fate entwined.
Once freed, the soul dissolves to mist or air,
Unable life's sensations to repair.
The frame disbands, its essence seeps away,
And mind and soul to scattered winds decay.
Thus death, the sunderer of life's tight bond,
Dissolves the soul to fragments far beyond.
When life departs, the body's ruin tells
How mind and soul had intertwined so well.
No single moment marks their swift retreat;
They fail in parts, their dissolution discrete.
Were they immortal, they'd not shrink nor flee,
But shed the frame, intact, like snakes shed skin to free.

Yet even in life, the soul can seem to fade,
A shadow tottering in the frame decayed.
When faintness grips, the body bends and falls,
The mind withdraws, and silence fills the halls.
How then, when loosed from fleshly bounds, can soul
Retain its essence, stripped of life's control?
Such truths unravel error's feeble guise:
The mortal soul cannot immortal rise.
Its fragments lost, its tethered power dissolved,
Its fleeting life, in body's ruin, resolved.
If soul immortal entered with the birth,
Why hold we not the memories of earth
Before we lived this life? Why no recall
Of deeds once done, if soul retains it all?
Should mind so alter, every trace effaced,
Is this not death by other name replaced?
Thus, what was once, hath perished, gone to naught,
And what now lives, by nature's hand is wrought.
Why, too, does soul, if death it cannot know,
Shrink not entire, as body comes to woe?
When limbs grow cold and sense retreats from skin,
Why gathers it not close, held safe within?
Yet no such seat of concentrated soul
Appears to rally when the dying toll
Creeps slow through flesh; instead, as parts decay,
The soul, like breath, dissolves and drifts away.
Observe the field where soldiers clash in fight,
And chariot scythes bring ruin in their might:
A severed arm still twitches on the ground,
A foot, cut free, its curling toes astound.
The head, once hewn, maintains its gaze, until
The final spark departs and all is still.
Shall we then claim each fragment keeps its soul?
Would many souls inhabit but one whole?
Absurd! The soul, as body, splits and dies,

Its mortal nature shown before our eyes.
And mark the serpent, sliced in writhing parts,
Its severed lengths still animated, starts
Each toward the other, jaws in futile quest
To join again and soothe the wound's unrest.
Are these now hosts of souls in pieces spread?
Or was the single soul, like body, shed?
What of the man who fades as death encroaches,
Each limb in turn the chill of death approaches?
The nails turn blue, the feet lose sense and life,
The creeping cold ascends in gradual strife.
The soul does not withdraw to one last place;
It fragments, like the body, and efface
Itself entirely as breath slips to the winds—
No trace remaining where its presence thins.
And if, as some may falsely hold, the soul
Gathers its essence inward, makes it whole,
Then should the seat of such collected power
Burn bright with life, a final blazing hour.
But no such spark, no focus of the mind,
Emerges; only dissolution blind.
Thus mortal must the soul be, since it dies
In step with flesh, its parting seen through eyes.
Lastly, if immortal were the soul,
And births it entered whole, its sacred role,
Why not retain some trace of lives before,
Some memory of what came ere this shore?
Yet blank our minds, and naught remains to show
The footprints of the paths we used to know.
If memory's power has wholly changed or failed,
What is that but death by other veil?
Thus must we see, from reason's steadfast guide,
The soul that was is gone; what lives, new-tied.
Moreover, if the soul should enter frame
Just at the moment body springs to life,

Why does it grow as if by nature's aim,
Entwined with flesh, with blood, with nerves so rife?
If it were foreign, placed as in a cave,
And not a partner fused with living form,
How could it share the pain the body gave—
The aching tooth, the ice-cold water's harm?
The body's flesh, its bones, its very teeth
Share with the soul the joys and pangs of sense.
From this, 'tis clear, they're twined, not placed beneath—
Not transient, but born of joint essence.
And when the soul departs, dissolving ties,
It cannot leave the body whole, unscathed.
The weaving threads of life it thereby flies,
And with the severance, both are unmade.
If soul, as some might fancy, trickles in,
Seeping through pores, absorbed through all the frame,
Then it, like water mingling, must begin
To scatter, perish—merge and lose its claim.
For what dissolves within another's form
Cannot survive, nor hold its own estate.
Thus, too, the soul, from dissolution born,
Finds in the body's death its destined fate.
And what of life within the corpse's clay?
Does soul remain, or leave its seeds behind?
If fragments linger when the soul's away,
Then soul is mortal, as its parts unwind.
But if it flees intact, with none to stay,
Whence crawl the worms, the teeming forms of life?
Does soul from outward bring these beasts to clay,
Or bubble they from death's dissolving strife?
Should souls descend to animate decay,
How could one soul give rise to such a host?
Are treaties made in realms where spirits play,
Where first to come claims entry, others lost?
Or must they toil to forge new forms from seeds,

Dismissing peace to war for mortal needs?
The fox's cunning, lion's raging heart,
The deer's innate and ancestral fleeing—
Each shows the mind with body grows, takes part,
In traits inborn, not later entering being.
Were souls immortal, swapping forms at will,
The hawk might quake before the gentle dove,
The stag might hunt the hound through forest still,
And men might shun their hate, and beasts learn love.
If souls retain their wisdom, why do men
Not bear the knowledge of their prior state?
The child begins as blank, and only then
Through growth and frame learns reason, small or great.
Were soul unchanged, a steed's newborn would know
The mastery of gallops through the plain.
But minds are shaped by bodies, as they grow,
And when they falter, minds too feel the strain.
And if the soul with body wax and wane,
Must they not share a common mortal thread?
For what immortal would such growth sustain,
Or flee from age, as though by frailty led?
And why should countless souls await in strife
To fill the forms of creatures yet unborn,
Contending madly for a fleeting life,
While others linger in immortal scorn?
No treaties bind the souls in such a race;
No orderly descent could guide their ways.
Instead, as body wanes, so wanes its grace;
And soul, entwined with flesh, fades with its days.
For bound together, born as one, they die,
The mortal shell and mind, beneath the sky.
Again, a tree can't flourish in the air,
Nor clouds reside beneath the ocean's swell,
Nor fish take root upon the fields of earth,
Nor blood course through the rigid veins of stone,

Nor sap in boulders thrive: all things are fixed,
Bound to their proper natures and their place.
So too the mind cannot exist alone,
Apart from body, nor sustain itself
Without the thews and pulsing streams of life.
Were it conceivable to stand apart,
It might as well take root within the head,
The chest, the feet—no matter where it dwelled—
So long as it remained a part of man.
But even here, within this mortal frame,
The soul and mind are stationed and confined,
Each in its own domain, to grow and act.
How then imagine them to dwell apart,
Unbound by blood and body, yet endure?
To think the mortal bound to the divine,
Entwined, enduring both decay and time,
Is folly's height. What could be more opposed—
The fleeting joined with the eternal flame?
If soul were deathless, it would surely stand
Immune to blows, impervious to decay,
Its essence formed of indivisible parts,
Like primal seeds we've spoken of before.
Or else, like void, it might escape all harm,
Unyielding to the touch of any force.
Or, lastly, it would be eternal still,
For lack of space to scatter and dissolve—
As is the sum of all, boundless and whole.
But should one claim the soul eternal proves
Through some defense against dissolving blows—
That naught can harm its essence, or that harm
Is felt and then expelled before it breaks—
Such claims dissolve when viewed in mortal life.
For when the body sickens, so does soul;
And when the frame endures its biting pains,
The soul, in tandem, bears the torment too.

The past, as well, torments the soul with guilt;
Old crimes resurface, gnawing bitterly.
Add to these woes the frenzy of the mind,
Its sinking into torpor, or its loss
Of memories once cherished and retained.
Even sleep—a brief oblivion each night—
Suggests how soul can waver, fade, and sink.
What then of death, which ends all mortal ties?
How could the soul survive, when even here
It quakes beneath the weight of fear and pain?

Folly of The Fear of Death

Therefore, death to us is nothing, nor a thing to fear,
For the nature of the mind is mortal and no more.
Just as in the ages long before our birth,
When Carthage's hosts clashed in mighty war,
And the trembling world hung in uncertain fate,
We felt no pangs, nor knew the strife of nations.
So, when the union of body and soul dissolves,
And we are no more, nothing can harm or touch us,
Even if earth and sea should merge in chaos
And heaven tumble down upon the ruins.
For once dissolved, the senses cannot suffer,
Nor the self lament its own extinguished light.
If perchance one fears the soul may linger still,
Detached from body but imbued with feeling,
Let them reflect: it is only in this union,
This bond of soul and body, that life and pain exist.
When this bond breaks, the self is gone forever,
Its motions stilled, its thoughts dispersed to naught.
Even were time to gather our scattered atoms,
Rebuilding our frame and reigniting life,
That second self would not concern the first—
For the thread of memory, once severed, cannot join.

The selves we were in yesterdays long past
Are nothing to us now; we grieve them not.
Reflect on this: the atoms that form us now
Have wandered many times before, forming
Countless shapes and lives, only to dissolve again.
If we recall no pain from those lost selves,
Why should we dread the loss of this one now?
For only the living can feel harm or woe;
Death, which ends life, bars such feelings too.
He who grieves his future corpse is plagued by folly,
Imagining his self in lifeless flesh,
Picturing his body torn by beasts or fire.
Yet no one exists within the corpse to suffer;
No self remains to mourn its disarray.
The dead feel nothing. What harm is there, then,
To lie in flames, or earth, or brutes' wild jaws?
Why should the honeyed tomb, the icy slab,
Or crushing soil torment what cannot sense?
Consider this, then, to free the mind from grief:
"Thee now no more the warm embrace shall welcome,
Nor children's laughter fill thy heart with joy.
Thou shalt no longer strive nor hold dominion."
But add: "And thou no longer carest for these things."
For he who sees that death is endless sleep,
A rest eternal without pang or longing,
Will lay aside his fears of what may come,
Knowing the mind's release is but repose.
Death is sleep eternal, a scattering of self,
The atoms dispersed, their motions ceased forever.
And just as sleep demands no self or being,
So too does death demand even less—
For none awaken once life's icy pause has struck.
This too, men often say, reclining at their ease,
Amid the wine cups, garlanded with blooms awry:
"Brief is this joy we mortals glean; it flies

Too soon, and once it's gone, it comes no more."
As if, in death, the worst of all our ills
Were parched tongues thirsting, or some lack endured.
But if, perchance, great Nature raised her voice,
And thus reproached us with a stern rebuke:
"O mortal, what afflicts thee so that thou
Dost yield to plaints and tears in face of death?
If all the days behind thee brought delight,
And all thy life was not a wasteful flow,
Why not, content as one who leaves a feast,
Depart from life with calm, untroubled heart?
But if thy joys were squandered, unfulfilled,
And life offends thee, why prolong the chain,
Only to lose again what once seemed sweet?
Why not make end, and free thyself from toil?
For naught remains that I can give thee now,
No new delights, nor days unlike the past,
Though thou shouldst conquer all the bounds of time,
And endless years should stretch before thy feet."
What could we answer to this just appeal?
Would not her words stand firm, her counsel true?
Yet should some elder soul, grown ripe with years,
Lament his fate with louder cries than fit,
Would not her voice rise sharper still to chide:
"Cease your weeping, fool! Restrain your moans!
The sum of life's delights is now fulfilled;
Yet ever you disdain the goods at hand,
While craving more that cannot come to you.
Thus, life has slipped away, incomplete, in vain,
While death now waits beside you, close at hand.
Why linger here, unsated of the feast,
When time has come for you to make your way?
Yield with grace, and give your place to those
Who follow, as once others made room for you."
Justly, I think, would Nature reason thus,

And rightfully reproach; for ever new
Must rise from old, and one thing give to others
Room to grow and thrive. None are consigned
To black Tartarus—no endless void devours—
But substance ever serves the generations,
A ceaseless chain of life that rises, falls,
And rises yet again.
Look back: before our birth, the eternal past
Was nothing to us—silent, unperceived.
So, too, shall time to come, when we are gone,
Mirror that past, unbroken and serene.
What horror lies in that? What grief can stir
At such a fate? Is it not calmer far
Than any dreamless sleep, untroubled and secure?
And truly, those torments they tell of in Acheron,
The depths of the underworld, are here in life.
No Tantalus, struck by empty fear,
Cowers beneath a rock suspended in the air;
But rather, a baseless dread of the gods
Plagues humanity, and each fears the fall
Of misfortune that fate might send their way.
No vultures feed forever on Tityus,
Sprawled out in Acheron, nor can they find
Eternal banquet in his mighty breast.
Even if his limbs spanned the whole wide earth,
He could not endure perpetual pain,
Nor nourish such devourers endlessly.
Instead, our own Tityus is the lover
Torn by relentless anguish, gnawed within
By unfulfilled desires, his soul laid bare.
And we see Sisyphus, not in some distant hell,
But here among us—he who strives for power,
Who courts the people's favor, seeks the rods,
The axes of high office, only to fall,
Beaten, dejected, time and time again.

This is to push the stone with wearying toil
Up the steep hill, only for it to roll
Back down again into the plain below.
Likewise, to sate an ungrateful mind,
To fill it with pleasures yet find it never full—
As the seasons bring forth their varied fruits,
And still we hunger endlessly for more—
Is like the Danaids in their endless task,
Pouring water into a sieve that never fills.
Cerberus, the Furies, Tartarus' dark pit,
And its fiery waves—they exist not there,
Nor ever could. But here on earth we see
The fear of justice, the dread of retribution.
The dungeon, the scourge, the infamous leap
From the rock of shame, the rack, the flames, the lash—
All these are real, and yet, even in their absence,
A guilty conscience wields its own cruel whip,
Tormenting the mind with fear of what may come,
Of heavier punishments after death's veil falls.
Indeed, the fools' own lives are Acheron on earth.
Say to yourself at times: "Even good Ancus
Left the sunlight behind, though greater than I.
And kings, lords of vast dominions, have fallen,
Yielding their power to the grasp of death.
He, too, who bridged the sea with his armies,
Who marched his cavalry over the waves,
Mocking the roar of the ocean's tides,
Poured out his soul, no less than the lowliest slave.
Scipio's son, terror of Carthage, lies
In the dust, his bones mingling with the earth,
No different from the humblest in his house.
Add to this roll the discoverers of arts,
The companions of the Muses, such as Homer,
Who now sleeps, sceptered no longer, among the dead.
Democritus, seeing his mind grow dim with age,

Gave himself willingly to death. And even
Epicurus, who surpassed all men in wisdom,
Extinguished like a star beneath the sun's bright light.
Wilt thou, then, hesitate and shrink from death,
When life itself is but a living death for thee?
Thou who in slumber dost waste the greater part
Of thy brief years, and even awake dost dream,
Haunted by phantoms, burdened by empty fears,
Unknowing what ails thee as cares toss thee about,
Like a drunkard staggering, mind clouded, astray."
If men could feel, as deeply as they bear
The weight that presses heavy on their minds,
The causes of their anguish and their grief,
And why their hearts are burdened so with woe,
They would not live as now, so lost, so blind,
Uncertain what they seek, yet seeking still,
Endlessly shifting place, as though escape
Could lighten what they cannot leave behind.
The man who tires of home flees from his halls,
Only to find no solace far away;
He hastens back, his weary steps retraced,
And finds no joy at home. He speeds along,
Driving his chariot down to country fields,
As though to douse some blazing fire—and yet,
Upon arrival, yawns or falls asleep,
Seeking escape in dreams, or rushes back
To town again, in restless, aimless flight.
Thus every man flees from himself—his self
That none may flee, for it clings ever close,
Loved and loathed, and always misunderstood.
Sickened and weary, man knows not the cause;
But should he see it clearly, then, at last,
All else forgotten, he would seek to know
The nature of the world, for here the stakes
Are more than fleeting moments—they are all

Of time, eternity, and mortal fate,
What lies beyond the shadow cast by death.
And yet, when all is said, what madness drives
This fevered lust for life that grips us so,
Binding us fast in terrors and in toils?
Death is unyielding; none may turn its course;
Its hour is fixed, and we must face its gate.
Yet still we labor at the selfsame tasks,
Repeating, circling back, forever bound,
Finding no new delight to forge from life.
The things we long for, when they are denied,
Seem best of all; yet when at last they're ours,
Some other want consumes us, and we thirst
For yet another fleeting dream. We chase,
Unceasing, life's illusions, yet remain
Ever unsure what future days may bring,
What chance may hold, or what the end shall be.
Nor can we, by prolonging life, reduce
The span of death awaiting us; no hour
Can we subtract from what eternity
Has claimed, nor steal one moment from its grasp.
Thus, mortal man, live out thy numbered days,
As many as thy lot allows; yet still,
Eternal death awaits thee, just the same.
He who has died but yesterday shall lie
No shorter time in death's eternal shade
Than he who passed a thousand years before.

Book IV

Proem

I wander far afield, sustained by thought,
Through untrod paths of the Pierian Muse,
Where none before has ventured. Here I thrive,

Delighting in untainted springs, to drink
Their waters deep; I joy to pluck new blooms,
To weave a crown of fresh, ungarlanded flowers
For this my brow, from regions yet untouched
By hands of men or homage of the Muse.
First, for I speak of mighty themes, and strive
To free the mind from coils of dread belief
That fetters it with fear. Then, too, I frame
Clear song on darksome topics, touching all
With the Muse's charm—a purpose fair and true.
For just as healers, seeking to bestow
A bitter draught of wormwood on young boys,
First sweeten all the rim with honeyed gold,
That childish folly, coaxed by pleasant taste,
Might take the healing bitter to the heart,
And be restored to health through gentle guile:
So I, perceiving that my doctrine seems
To many harsh and heavy, filled with dread,
And seeing how the common throng recoils
In horror from it, have adorned my words
With melodies of Muse and honeyed song,
To charm and hold thy mind upon these truths,
Till thou hast learned the nature of all things
And understood their purpose and their worth.

Existence and Character of The Images

But since I've taught already of what kind
The seeds of things must be, and how distinct
In varied forms they flit, with motion stirred
Eternal, shaping all, and since I've shown
The nature of the mind, its bond with flesh,
Its growth, its life, its final dissolution,
I turn now to a theme of utmost weight:
That there exist those forms, those airy shapes,

The images of things—these subtle films
That skim the outer surface, scale-like, thin,
And through the air flit lightly, here and there,
To stir our minds, awake or lost in sleep.
These, when we dream, or in the shadows peer,
Take on strange shapes of wonder, forms of dread,
And move us deeply, making some believe
That souls escape from Acheron's dark bounds,
That shades walk forth among the living still,
And part of us persists beyond the grave.
But no—when mind and body are undone,
Their elements return to primal seeds,
And naught of us remains to roam or wail.
I say that from all things there stream abroad
Fine effigies, faint images, like skins,
Shed from their outermost. These waft and glide
Through space, unseen, until they strike our sense
And conjure shapes that stir our intellect.
This truth, though subtle, reason makes it plain.
Behold the visible: the smoky wreaths
That curl from burning logs, the heat that waves
Above a fire, the sheen a serpent sheds—
All these are proofs that surfaces give off
Thin layers, parts, or vestments of their form.
And finer still, these effigies may pass,
Unseen, unbroken, as a perfect whole,
Bearing the shape and semblance of their source.
Consider too the hues of stretched-out awnings,
Which, in the sunlight of a theatre,
Diffuse their colors on the crowd below.
These dyes, sent forth from surfaces, attest
That objects cast their essence out in streams,
And finer still than color's subtle glow
Are those thin shapes that form the mirrored world.
The images reflected in a glass,

In water, or a polished plate of bronze,
Prove that such forms exist. They come to us,
Invisible in single frame, but dense
When many flow in constant, quick succession,
To recreate the likeness of the source.
Thus, effigies of objects stream and move,
Too slight to see alone, yet strong enough
To fill the senses with their fleeting touch.
Consider now the size of smallest things:
Some creatures are so minute that even less
Than their third part evades the naked eye.
What then of organs nestled deep within?
How fine their fibers, smaller still the seeds
That form their essence, life, and thought itself!
And scents confirm this truth: a bitter herb,
The southernwood, or wormwood's pungent leaf,
Exhales its tang from surface to the air.
A touch, though faint, releases subtle streams,
Proclaiming that the smallest parts exist
And act upon us, though they stay unseen.
Then why not rather grasp that countless images
Flit everywhere, in endless modes, unseen,
Bodiless, through the vast expanse of air?
But lest thou think these images arise
From objects only, know that others form,
Self-born, within the airy skies of earth,
Shaped and reshaped in countless fleeting forms,
Shifting appearances at every turn.
Behold the clouds that gather thick on high,
Darkening the serene expanse of heaven.
We see their shapes—giants, beasts, or mountain peaks—
Rolling across the sun and trailing shade.
Such forms, though momentary, show how swift
And manifold are images that arise,
Flow forth, and vanish into nothingness.

Forever from all things an outer stream
Flows forth—thin films, textures of form and hue.
When these strike objects, as with polished glass,
They pass, unbroken, forming mirrored shapes.
But roughened surfaces, like wood or stone,
Rend these effigies and scatter them.
Yet when they meet smooth mirrors, nothing breaks;
Instead, they bounce back, reflecting forms.
So swiftly does this process play, that ere
Thy eye perceives, the mirrored shape appears,
Proof that such images from objects flow,
Fine, fleeting, and incessantly renewed.
Think, too, how light from sun to earth arrives
In but a moment, filling all the world.
So must the images of things be borne,
In manifold directions, swift and sure,
Answering each surface turned to meet their path.
For sudden storms obscure the tranquil sky,
And blackened clouds, as if from Acheron,
Surround the heavens in a murky night.
Such vast assemblies of forms and fleeting shades—
How small a part is any single image!
Now mark the swiftness of their flight through air.
Objects of lightest mass, of smallest form,
Move swiftest—like the beams of sun and heat.
These particles, propelled by endless blows,
Pass freely through the spaces of the air,
Pushed by the force of those that follow close.
Thus too must images in swiftness move,
Their rareness and their lightness bearing them
Through boundless space, with nothing to impede.
Consider this: if rays of sun can pass
From heavenly heights to earth in but an instant,
What of those images that merely skim
The surface, hurled away without delay?

How much more swiftly must they travel forth,
Unbarred by obstacles, propelled by force!
Thus do we see, as stars reflect in pools
Beneath the open sky, the images
Of heaven's constellations flash below.
So swift the journey of these phantom forms,
From ether's height to earth's awaiting gaze.

The Senses and Mental Pictures

Bodies send streams perpetually to sense—
Be it scent, heat, or spray from ocean waves
That gnaw at walls along the briny coast.
Voices, too, disperse their sound through air,
While taste's sharp tingle meets us by the sea
Or bitter wormwood stirs the tongue's recoil.
From all things, streams of nature radiate,
Each borne incessantly, filling space around.
So ceaselessly our senses are engaged,
Alert to see, to smell, to touch, to hear.
And since we grasp a square by touch in dark
As surely as in daylight's clearer view,
It follows both are caused by images,
By forms that strike the senses in their kind.
Thus sight and touch confirm: these outer films,
These tenuous effigies, must dart from things,
Fitting the shape of objects that they leave.
These images, invisible yet real,
Traverse the air in countless forms and hues,
Yet only through the eyes their truth is caught.
Wherever sight is turned, they strike the gaze,
Revealing form, position, and their range.
For when they speed, they displace the air between,
Driving it through the channels of the eye,
Until the force informs us: "This is near,"

Or: "This lies farther off," gauged by the length
Of air displaced before their brushing flight.
Marvel not that we see a single thing,
Though countless particles in streams converge;
For as the wind upon us strikes as one,
Though countless breaths compose its moving force,
Or as a rock touched shows its solid form,
Not hue or dust, so does the image tell
The unified impression of the whole.
And why, within a mirror, deep and clear,
The world reflects as though removed in space?
Understand the mechanism at play:
The image strikes the glass and, bouncing back,
Displaces air between our gaze and it.
This air conveys the vision, making seem
The shape we see recedes behind the plane.
Thus twofold airs—the nearer and the far—
Grant depth to vision in the glass's truth.
And when the right becomes the left in view,
The cause is simple: images rebound,
Reversed as masks when cast upon a frame,
Returning to present the opposite.
From glass to glass, reflections ripple on,
Till twisted angles multiply the forms
And further turn the left to right again.
Or curved mirrors keep the right aligned,
Bending the image back with faithful cast.
These images seem joined to us in step,
Walking our gait, mimicking our stance,
Because from regions whence we turn away
No more are they reflected back to sight.
Bright light repels the gaze; the sun confounds,
Its mighty beams descending swift through air,
Assaulting eyes and breaking their fine threads.
Seeds of fire within such piercing rays

Strike pain upon the sight, much as disease
Can taint the vision of the jaundiced eye,
Painting the world with hues of sickly yellow.
From shade, we glimpse the luminous beyond,
As light flows swiftly in to cleanse the dark,
Opening pathways for the images
That stream from objects in the sun's embrace.
But from the light, no gaze can pierce the dark,
For heavy shadows flood the eye instead,
Blocking the subtle channels vision needs,
Thus rendering the obscured world unseen.
When from afar we gaze upon the towers
Of cities squarely built, they seem as round.
This happens since the distant angles lose
Their sharp distinction, softened by the air
That blunts and scatters their advancing forms.
When edges fade, the stones appear as shaped
By some turner's wheel, though faintly so,
Not truly rounded, but with shadowy semblance.
Likewise, our shadow seems to follow us,
Matching our steps and mimicking our form,
Though it is naught but air deprived of light.
When we obstruct the sun's rays on the ground,
The earth, reft of illumination there,
Gains shadow while our movement clears a path
For sunlight to return. Thus shadows shift,
Illusions born of constant interplay
Between the light and our obstructing forms.
But senses do not err in such events.
Their task is only to perceive the place
Where light exists or shadows fall; they serve
Our reason, which must judge what truth lies there.
Blame not the eyes for faults of mind or thought,
Nor deem all senses prone to errancy.
A ship at anchor seems to move when we

In motion pass; the hills and fields appear
To flee astern as sails drive forward flight.
The stars seem fixed in heaven's arching dome,
Though ever in their paths they circle wide.
The sun and moon, steadfast to our view,
Yet sweep across the sky in ceaseless course.
Between two mountains' peaks, a gap reveals
A fleet's escape, though distance blurs their truth,
Making them seem a single island joined.
Children, dizzy from their games, perceive
The spinning world as whirling round their heads,
And roofs and walls as threatening to fall.
At dawn, the sun appears near mountain crests,
Its fiery orb tinging their rugged tips,
Yet oceans stretch vast leagues between the two,
And countless lands divide their seeming nearness.
A shallow pool, mere inches deep, reflects
The heavens' breadth, as if beneath the earth
A mirrored sky lies sunk in endless space.
In rivers swift, the standing horse appears
To drift upstream, its motion all reversed,
As if the flowing waters bore it back.
A portico, though level in its length,
Contracts into a cone when seen afar,
Its columns narrowing to a vanishing point.
The distant sun, rising or setting, seems
To leap from waves or plunge into their depths,
A trick of sight for those who lack the scope
To see the wider world of land and sea.
Ships anchored in the port seem strangely bent,
Their hulls submerged appearing curved or torn,
While masts above the waterline stand straight.
Winds shifting clouds at night give constellations
The false appearance of another course,
Though stars remain upon their fixed orbits.

With pressure underneath one single eye,
The world appears to double—twain the lamps,
Twain the forms of all about the room.
In sleep, we wander far in dreams, convinced
We wake and move, though still our bodies lie
Enclosed in night's unbroken, silent dark.
These errors spring from mind, not sense itself,
Which perceives what is but adds no falsehood.
The mind, by inference, confuses truth,
Conflating what it sees with what it thinks,
And thus belief, untethered, twists the facts.
Yet senses faithfully convey the world—
The rest is in our reasoning alone.
If one should claim that nothing can be known,
He cannot know if even this is true,
Since he admits to knowing naught at all.
With such a one, no dialogue remains;
He stands inverted, feet where head should be.
Yet grant he knows this single point—I'll ask:
From whence comes knowledge of the true and false?
What test has proven doubtful things distinct
From certain truths, if all the world he sees
Has shown no sign of what is truly real?
The senses first must form our grasp of truth,
For no criterion, higher, more secure,
Exists to judge the senses false or true.
What greater arbiter than these can stand?
Shall reason—born of senses, rooted there—
Contradict its own foundation, sense,
And prove itself as false as what it doubts?
Or shall the ears reproach the eyes, or touch
Deny the ear, or taste refute the skin,
Or scent dispute the tongue? Not so, indeed.
Each sense its sphere commands: the eye for sight,
The ear for sound, the tongue for taste, the touch

For warmth or cold, for soft or hard, and nose
For smells. Distinct their powers and tasks remain,
And none can convict another of deceit.
No sense can disprove itself, for trust
Is due to each in equal measure still.
What sense reports is true—its own domain
Is sovereign, judged by none but what it shows.
If reason falters, failing to explain
Why distant towers seem round though near they're square,
It harms us less to theorize amiss
Than to renounce the senses' primal faith.
For life itself would crumble, if we dared
Distrust what senses plainly show. Without
Their guidance, how would we avoid the brink
Of cliffs or other dangers? How discern
The safe from perilous paths?
As buildings fail,
If plumb-lines deviate or squares mislead,
So too must life collapse if senses err.
Reason, like bricks mislaid, would topple all,
And life, unmoored, would falter in the void.
Thus, those who war against the senses' truth
Are vain, their arguments as false as flawed.
Now let us show how senses recognize
Their objects, each perceiving its own realm.
A sound, a voice, is heard when, striking ears,
It moves the sense through matter of its own.
For sound, as much as voice, must have a form,
A body, since it strikes and scrapes the ear.
Who shouts or screams will feel their throat grow rough,
The windpipe rasped, the passage tightly strained
As thicker streams of sound push through their bounds.
This friction, proof of sound's corporeal force,
Shows sense and body joined, their union sure.
Thus, senses stand as sentinels of truth,

Their trust the bedrock of our lives and thought.
No greater judge than these can guide our way;
No stronger proof exists to light the path.
Voice and words, indeed, are made of matter,
For they can tire the body, cause its loss.
Prolonged discourse, from morning's early glow
To evening's shade, drains strength and wastes the frame,
Especially when loud with ringing shouts.
Thus voice must be corporeal, a force
Whose particles escape and wane with use.
The nature of a voice—its smooth or rough—
Depends upon the shapes of primal seeds.
A trumpet's hollow roar is rough and harsh,
While flutes of Berecynthian pipes emit
A buzzing boom, and swans' lament at dusk
Pours forth a liquid wail. From deep within,
We force these sounds; the mobile tongue crafts words,
And lips, through shaping motions, give them form.
So, when the voice has little space to cross,
It reaches ears distinct and clear, intact.
But over distance, air confounds its form,
And winds distort its flight, dissolving words—
A scattered sound is heard, but sense is lost.
One voice may rouse a multitude of ears,
Its single burst divided into parts,
With each fragment carrying the tone and form
To waiting listeners. What misses ears
Is lost to winds; what strikes on solid walls
Returns as echoes, mocking our own calls.
In lonely places, cliffs reflect our cries,
Returning words in mimicry, as though
Companions called from distant, unseen paths.
At times, the rocks repeat a single cry
Sixfold or more, their echoes bounding back,
Conjuring myths of fauns or woodland gods,

Their revels breaking silence with their song.
Thus, myths arise in lonely, shadowed woods,
Born of men's fears or need to fill the void.
Yet, no marvel lies in sound that passes
Through walls unseen, for voice can thread through gaps
And winding passages where sight may fail.
Doors closed may dull the words but let them through,
For voice, unlike an image, does not break
When turned aside; it travels, bending paths.
Its many parts divide and scatter wide,
Like sparks from fire bursting into flames,
Filling hidden spaces with their din.
But images, sent forth in straight lines,
Cannot pierce walls; hence why the eye sees naught
Though ears may catch the sound from beyond.
Now turn to taste and tongue, the seat of flavor.
When chewing food, we squeeze out subtle streams,
As one might press a sponge soaked full with water.
These streams disperse within the porous tongue,
Whose intricate paths discern the smooth or rough.
Smooth bodies please, caressing as they pass;
Rough ones sting and irritate the sense.
Yet flavor's pleasure halts at tongue and palate;
Once food descends the throat, the joy is gone,
Its role reduced to fueling flesh and frame.
What matters is digestion, nourishment—
Not how the taste was savored at the start.
Thus, voice and taste, though tied to body's bounds,
Reveal the nature of corporeal forms:
A union of material and the senses,
Where matter flows to touch, to speak, to feed.
Indeed, where one from overwhelming anger
Is struck by fever, or otherwise
Feels the intense force of some illness,
There, the whole body is thrown into disarray,

And the arrangement of its parts shifts—
So the things that once brought certain tastes
No longer do so, while others take their place,
More suited now to enter the pores
And create sourness. Both types, in truth,
Are found together in honey—
Something we've already proven before.
Now come, and I'll explain how smells
Reach and affect the nose.
First, it's important to know
That countless tiny particles
Stream from objects and spread freely,
Touching everything around them.
But each living thing is affected differently;
Some are drawn to one scent, others to another—
All because their senses are built differently.
Bees are led by the scent of honey;
Vultures by the smell of corpses.
Dogs follow scents to track wild animals,
While the white goose,
Which saved the Roman citadel,
Can smell the presence of humans from far away.
In this way, each creature is guided
By the smells suited to it—
To find food or avoid poison,
And thus continue to survive.
But this variety isn't limited to smell
Or even to taste. The way we see things
And the colors we perceive
Aren't the same for all creatures.
For example, lions—fierce as they are—
Can't bear to look at a rooster.
The rooster, with its flapping wings,
Chasing away the night,
And calling out to announce the morning,

Drives the lions to flee.
This is because the rooster's body contains particles
That, when they enter the lions' eyes,
Pierce them with unbearable pain.
Yet, these same particles don't harm human eyes,
Either because they don't penetrate
Or because they pass through so quickly
That they can't linger and cause damage.
To speak again of smells:
Some travel farther than others,
But none go as far as sound or voice—
Not to mention light, which travels faster still.
Smells move slowly,
And disappear as they mix into the winds.
First, because they are released with effort
From deep inside objects (we know this because
Grinding, breaking, or burning something
Releases stronger smells,
Showing that odors come from deep within).
Second, smell is made of larger particles than sound,
Since it cannot pass through stone walls,
While sound easily can.
This is why it's harder to locate the source of a smell—
It cools and scatters in the air,
So that by the time it reaches us,
It's weakened and harder to trace.
Even dogs, skilled at tracking scents,
Can sometimes lose their way.
Now, let me explain how images move the mind.
Countless thin images of objects
Float in every direction, so fine
That they merge in midair,
Like strands of spiderweb or thin sheets of gold.
These images are far thinner
Than those that strike the eyes,

For they pass through the body's pores
And directly affect the mind,
Triggering sensations.
This is why we see things like centaurs,
The monstrous Scylla, or Cerberus—
Or even the faces of people long dead.
These images form partly from the air,
Partly from objects around us,
And partly from combinations of shapes.
For example, no real centaur exists,
But when the image of a man and a horse
Come together, they combine to create one.
In the same way, other strange shapes are formed,
And when these light, subtle images strike the mind,
They stir it, creating vivid impressions.
This happens just as it does with sight:
As the eyes see objects through films,
So too does the mind perceive them
Through even finer, subtler films.
This explains why we can "see" things like lions
Not just with our eyes,
But also with our minds.
When we sleep, the body rests,
But the mind stays active,
Still affected by these films,
Which is why we dream of people or things,
Even of those who are no longer alive.
The senses, asleep, cannot tell truth from illusion,
And memory, also dormant,
Doesn't remind us that these visions aren't real.
So, we believe what we see in dreams.
And further, it's no surprise that images appear
To move their arms and other parts in rhythm.
Often in dreams, we see them doing this.
When one image disappears,

And another takes its place in a new pose,
It seems as if the first image changed its gestures.
This change must happen quickly—
So fast, and with so many images available,
That in the briefest moment the mind can perceive,
Countless pieces of images arrive to replace the old.
Sometimes, an entirely different image appears.
What seemed to be a woman might suddenly
Turn into a man.
A new face or even a different age may appear,
But sleep and forgetfulness
Make sure we don't question this strange shift.
There's much to explore and explain here,
If we truly want to understand.
First, why does the mind,
When it decides to think of something,
See that thing immediately?
Do the images wait for our command?
Does an image appear
Exactly when we wish it to—
Whether we think of the sea, the land, or the sky?
Do scenes of gatherings, parades, feasts, or battles
All form instantly at our word?—
Even when, at the same time and place,
Another mind might be thinking of something
Completely different?
And what of this:
When we dream of images moving,
Stepping forward in rhythm,
Swinging their arms with smooth, quick motions,
And turning their heads as they keep time—
Are these images truly skilled in art,
Wandering around with perfect training,
Just so they can perform for us at night?
Or is this the truth instead:

In even the smallest moment of time we can imagine—
The time it takes to say a single word—
There are many smaller moments hidden within,
Which reason can uncover.
So it is that in the briefest instant,
Countless images are nearby, ready to appear,
Each one in its own form.
When one image vanishes,
And another takes its place in a different pose,
It seems as though the first image changed its movements.
And because these images are so delicate,
The mind focuses only on the ones it chooses to see,
While the rest disappear entirely,
Except for the ones the mind prepares itself to notice.
The mind does prepare itself,
Hoping to see what comes next—
And that's why this happens.
Haven't you noticed how the eyes,
When trying to see something very small,
Will strain to focus,
Unable to see clearly otherwise?
Even with ordinary objects,
If you don't pay attention,
It's as if they are far away and out of reach.
So, it's no wonder that the mind ignores the rest,
Except for what it has chosen to focus on.
In this way, we draw big conclusions
From small details,
And often trap ourselves in our own misunderstandings.

Some Vital Functions

In these matters,
We ask you to avoid one great mistake:
Do not assume that the eyes were created

So we could see, or that thighs and knees,
Designed to bend and rest upon the feet,
Were made so we could walk smoothly ahead.
Do not think that forearms joined to upper arms,
Or the hands on either side,
Were given to us so we could handle tasks.
This way of thinking is backwards,
For nothing in the body is made for a purpose;
Rather, things are born, and their uses follow.
No one could see before eyes were created,
And no one could speak before the tongue existed.
The tongue came into being before speech,
And ears existed long before they heard sound.
All our body parts, it seems, were there
Before they were put to any use,
So they could not have been made for their uses.
Instead, fighting hand-to-hand,
Twisting and breaking joints,
And wounding limbs with blood and gore,
All existed long before
Shining spears were invented.
Nature taught humans to avoid injuries
Long before the left arm was trained
To lift a shield for protection.
And resting the tired body
Came far earlier than soft beds.
Quenching thirst existed long before cups.
The things made to help us live—
Like beds, shields, and cups—
Were created later, for their usefulness.
But senses and body parts were different.
They existed first and only later
Revealed their uses.
This is why it's impossible
To argue that our senses and limbs

Were created with specific purposes in mind.
Likewise, it's not surprising
That all living creatures seek food
As part of their nature.
I've already explained how tiny particles
Stream out constantly from objects,
In countless forms and patterns.
This is especially true for living beings,
Whose constant motion sends particles out—
Through breath when they pant,
And through sweat when they toil.
The body loses material this way,
Growing weaker, and pain follows.
So, food is consumed to restore the body,
To fill in the gaps in the joints,
And to renew its strength.
Food enters the body and satisfies
The open hunger running through limbs and veins.
At the same time, liquid spreads
To every part of the body that needs moisture.
It calms the burning heat inside,
Quenching the fire that scorches us.
This is how thirst is washed away
And hunger is eased.
Now, let me explain
How we can step forward when we wish,
How we move our limbs,
And how our bodies carry their weight.
Listen closely.
First, an image of walking
Appears in the mind, as I said before.
This image inspires the will to act,
Since no one acts without first imagining
What they want to do.
When the mind decides to walk,

It sends a signal to the soul,
Which is spread throughout the body.
This happens easily,
Because the soul is closely connected to the mind.
Next, the soul sends a signal to the body,
And step by step,
The whole body begins to move.
At the same time, the body adjusts,
Allowing air—so light and nimble—
To flow through open pores
And spread everywhere inside.
These two forces, working together,
Move the body forward, like a ship
Driven by both oars and the wind.
There's no mystery here.
Even the smallest, finest particles
Can move something as large as the human body.
The wind, though invisible and delicate,
Drives massive ships.
One hand can steer such a ship,
And a small rudder can turn it wherever you please.
Likewise, heavy loads, large and numerous,
Can be lifted and moved
By pulleys and wheels with minimal effort.
Now, how sleep spreads its calm
Through our limbs and gives the mind a break from its troubles,
I'll explain in verses sweeter than many others—
Like the soft song of a swan,
Much better than the loud clamor of cranes
Among the airy clouds of the south wind.
So, give me your sharp attention and an open mind,
So you won't deny the truth of what I say
Or turn away in disbelief,
Unable to grasp these spoken truths.
Sleep comes mainly when the energy of the soul

Has scattered throughout the body,
Some of it leaving outward,
And some retreating deep inside.
This makes our limbs loosen and droop.
There's no doubt that the soul gives us our senses,
And when sleep blocks those senses,
It's because the soul is disturbed and partly expelled.
But not entirely—
Otherwise, the body would collapse into
The cold stillness of death.
If no part of the soul were left within,
Even in hiding, like fire buried under ashes,
How could the senses reawaken?
Just as flames rise again from hidden embers,
So too does sense return when the soul stirs anew.
Now I'll explain how this strange state happens,
How the soul becomes confused
And the body grows weak.
Listen carefully so my words don't vanish into the wind.
First, the outer parts of the body,
Exposed to the touch of moving air,
Are constantly struck by tiny gusts.
For this reason, most creatures
Are protected by skin, shells, tough calluses, or bark.
But this same air also affects the inner parts
When creatures breathe in and out.
Thus, the body is buffeted both inside and out,
As the air's blows enter through tiny pores
And reach the body's core elements.
Over time, this leads to a kind of collapse.
The fundamental particles of body and soul
Are thrown into confusion.
When this happens, some of the soul is expelled,
Some retreats into hidden recesses,
And some scatters throughout the body,

Unable to unite or move together.
Nature blocks the pathways and connections,
And so the sense withdraws deep inside.
With nothing left to support it,
The body weakens, the limbs grow heavy,
The arms and eyelids droop,
And even as you lie in bed,
Your knees buckle and lose their strength.
Sleep often follows eating,
Because food has a similar effect to air,
Spreading through the veins as it's digested.
The deepest sleep comes when you're full or exhausted,
Because the body's particles are most disrupted then,
Bruised by the effort of work or digestion.
Thus, three things happen:
The soul sinks deeper,
It is partially expelled,
And its movements become scattered and divided.
Whatever tasks a person focuses on most during the day—
Whatever they've spent time on or strained their mind over—
Often appears in their dreams.
Lawyers dream of pleading cases and citing laws.
Commanders dream of battles and leading troops.
Sailors dream of struggling against the wind.
Even I dream of writing this book,
Studying the nature of the world
And recording what I discover here on these pages.
So every pursuit and art tends to appear in dreams,
Mocking and taking over the minds of men.
Even animals are affected.
Horses, though stretched out and asleep,
Will sweat and strain as if racing for a prize.
Hunting dogs, in their soft slumber,
Will suddenly move their legs, growl, bark,
And sniff the air as if catching the scent of prey.

Sometimes, even when awake,
They chase after imagined stags,
Believing they see them fleeing ahead,
Until the illusion fades and they come to their senses.
Young puppies, bred for the home,
Sometimes jerk awake,
As if startled by unfamiliar faces.
The fiercer the breed,
The more intense their dreams and actions in sleep.
Birds, too, will flee in the night,
Flapping their wings in fear,
Dreaming of hawks swooping down to attack.
Even humans,
Whose minds tackle great challenges,
Will continue their mighty tasks in sleep.
Kings dream of storming cities or falling into captivity,
Fighting on the battlefield,
Or crying out as if their throats were cut.
Some wrestle and groan,
Filling the air with wild cries,
As if attacked by lions or panthers.
Some speak aloud in their sleep,
Revealing their plans or even confessing their crimes.
Others dream of dying,
Or of falling headlong from a mountain,
And wake up frantic and confused,
Their minds still shaken from the dream.
A thirsty man might dream
Of sitting beside a spring or river,
Drinking deeply, trying to gulp the entire stream.
Children, overtaken by sleep,
Might dream they're lifting their clothes
Beside a chamber pot,
Only to wet the bed and soak
Their fine Babylonian sheets.

Young men, just entering adulthood,
With their bodies newly producing seed,
Are often visited in sleep
By images of beauty—
Visions of fair faces and radiant forms
That stir their bodies and release the seed,
Leaving stains behind as if the act itself
Had truly been carried out.
And as said before,
That seed is awakened in us when mature age
Has strengthened our bodies…
Just as different causes bring motion to different things,
So too does one force stir the human seed,
Driving it to flow out from the man.
As soon as it leaves its starting place,
It moves through the whole body, passing
Through the limbs and frame,
Gathering in specific parts of the muscles.
It energizes and excites the man's genitals.
The aroused regions swell with seed,
And with this comes the desire to release it
Toward the object of longing,
That which the body so eagerly seeks—
The object that love has made the mind obsessed with.
Almost every man is drawn toward his own wound,
And the blood flows toward the place from which
The blow of love was struck.
If the source of desire is near,
That fiery passion reaches directly for it.
In the same way, someone struck by Cupid's arrows—
Whether by a boy with soft, delicate limbs
Or by a woman radiating love
Through every part of her body—
Strives to reach the one who caused his longing.
He burns to unite with them,

To release into their body
The fluid that was stirred within his own.
For this silent craving promises a sense of joy.

The Passion of Love

This craving is what we call Venus in us.
From this arises all the charms of love.
From this, the first drop of joy seeps into human hearts—
A joy soon followed by cold, creeping worry.
Even if the one you love is far away,
Images of them linger near,
And their sweet name echoes in your ears.
But you must push these images away,
Chase off whatever feeds your love,
Turn your mind elsewhere,
And release the seed gathered within you into other bodies.
Do not cling to thoughts of a single love
Or hoard your desire for one pleasure—
This only brings pain and unavoidable sorrow.
For just as a wound, if nourished,
Grows deeper and harder to heal,
So too does love burn more fiercely each day.
The suffering worsens with time,
Unless you counter the wounds of love with new blows—
Soothing them while they are fresh
By pursuing other loves freely
Or redirecting your restless mind elsewhere.
The man who avoids love entirely
Still enjoys the gifts of Venus.
He takes the pleasures free of penalties.
Indeed, the joys of Venus are purer
For those with a calm, steady soul
Than for those sick with love's torment.
Even in the moment of passion,

Lovers are restless and uncertain.
They cannot decide where to first indulge their hands or eyes.
The parts they long for, they grip too tightly,
Harming the body they desire.
They press their teeth against her lips
And crush mouth into mouth with eager kisses.
This is because their pleasure is not pure—
It hides stings beneath it,
Urging them to hurt the very thing
That sparked their love-madness.
Yet Venus soothes the pain with tender caresses,
And the mix of affection tempers the fury of passion.
Lovers hope that the same body that kindled their fire
Can also extinguish it.
But nature insists otherwise.
For love is the one craving that grows fiercer
The more it is fed.
Food and drink enter the body
And can fill the parts that hunger for them,
Satisfying thirst and hunger with ease.
But beauty and charm send nothing real into the body—
Only fleeting images, empty and insubstantial,
A vain hope that often vanishes like smoke in the wind.
It is like a thirsty man dreaming of water:
He reaches for it, yet finds nothing to quench
The burning thirst in his body.
He chases illusions of liquid,
Straining in vain, thirsting even as he gulps down
The image of a stream.
In the same way, love deceives lovers
With empty images.
They cannot satisfy their lust
Just by gazing at the body they desire.
Nor can their hands, wandering across tender skin,
Draw out the pleasure they seek.

Even when they finally embrace,
Their bodies entwined,
Sharing the bloom of youth
And feeling the height of physical joy,
When Venus is about to sow her seed in the fields of woman,
They lock themselves tightly together,
Mixing saliva, breathing into each other,
Pressing teeth to lips.
Yet all this is in vain.
They cannot dissolve into each other's bodies,
Cannot fully merge or become one.
Often, they seem to struggle and strain for this,
Clinging desperately in Venus' grip,
Until their bodies seem to melt away,
Overcome by the force of their delight.
But when the lust stored in their muscles
Has been spent,
There comes a brief pause,
A momentary calm in the raging heat.
Yet soon the same madness returns.
The old craving burns anew,
Driving them to seek again what they cannot grasp—
An elusive remedy for their torment.
In this uncertain state, they waste away,
Wounded by a pain they cannot see.
To this, we must add
That they waste their strength and grow weak from the effort;
They spend their futile years
Living under someone else's control,
Neglecting their duties,
Letting their good reputation falter,
While their wealth is lost on luxurious things—
Babylonian tapestries,
Exquisite perfumes,
And dainty Sicyonian shoes

That adorn her feet.
Emeralds of green light are set in gold;
Rich purple dresses, worn often,
Grow shabby and soaked with Venus' sweat.
The hard-earned property of their ancestors
Is turned into headbands, fine headdresses,
And garments from Alidens or Cean isles.
Lavish banquets are laid out,
With rare cloth, fine food, games of chance,
Goblets, perfumes, crowns, and garlands.
All of this is in vain,
Because from the fountain of these pleasures
Always bubbles a drop of bitterness.
This bitterness torments them among their delights,
When their mind, stricken with remorse,
Gnaws at itself for wasted years and ruinous indulgence—
Or because she leaves them doubting her loyalty,
Dropping sly hints that burn like fire
And cling to their eager hearts.
Perhaps they think she looks at others too much,
Or notice a trace of a laugh on her face.
These troubles come even in successful love,
But in unrequited or failed love,
The miseries are too many to count.
This is why it's better to take precautions beforehand,
As I've already shown,
And guard against love's enticements.
It's easier to avoid falling into love's traps
Than to escape once entangled,
When you're caught in the strong nets of Aphrodite.
Even when you're caught with tangled feet,
You can still escape—
Unless you stand in your own way,
Ignoring the flaws of the one you adore.
People, blinded by passion,

Invent virtues that don't exist.

So, we see many crooked or unattractive people

Held in high regard by their infatuated lovers.

These lovers advise each other to honor Venus,

Thinking their friends are smitten with true beauty—

While blind to their own delusions.

A dark-skinned woman is called "golden like honey";

A dirty, smelly one is said to be "carelessly elegant."

The one with catlike eyes is "a little Pallas";

The skinny, wiry one is "a gazelle."

The short and pudgy woman is "charming, like one of the Graces";

The big, bulky one is "impressive, commanding admiration."

The stuttering one "has a sweet lisp";

The mute woman is "modest";

And the loud, sharp-tongued woman is "witty and spirited."

The scrawny, sickly one becomes "delicate";

The coughing, dying one is "fragile and refined."

A woman with a thick chest and heavy breasts is said to be "like
    Ceres nursing Bacchus."

The pug-nosed lady is "a feminine Silenus."

The one with swollen lips is praised as "a luscious kiss."

It would take forever to list all such delusions.

Even if her face is beautiful

And Venus' charm lights her whole body,

You must remember—there are others like her.

You lived without her before,

And she does nothing that others don't.

Even this woman, so praised,

Hides herself behind perfumes,

Which even her maids laugh at behind her back.

Yet the lover, shut out from her,

Lays flowers at her doorstep,

Anoints her doorposts with perfume,

And kisses the threshold in despair.

If at last he's admitted,

One whiff of her scent might drive him away,
Searching for excuses to leave.
His long-planned complaints dissolve,
And he curses himself
For ever believing she deserved so much devotion.
Women are aware of this,
Which is why they try harder to hide
Their less glamorous realities
From the men they wish to ensnare.
But no matter how they try,
You can uncover these truths with careful thought.
If she is kind and graceful,
Overlook her flaws in return—
This is only fair for mortal love.
Not every woman pretends to love.
Many genuinely desire shared pleasure,
Embracing their lovers with true passion
And urging them to enjoy love's race together.
Animals, too, feel this same instinct.
Cattle, birds, wild beasts,
Sheep, and mares all yield to males
Because their nature burns with desire.
They gladly accept the joy of Venus' embrace.
And don't you see how creatures,
Bound by mutual pleasure,
Struggle even against their bonds?
Dogs at crossroads, panting to separate,
Strain to pull apart
Even as Venus' chains hold them fast.
This wouldn't happen if not for the shared joy
That drags them back and holds them.
Thus, mutual pleasure ties them together
And binds them to one another.
When the male's seed mingles with the female's,
If the female seizes control,

The offspring resembles her more.
If the male's seed dominates,
The offspring resembles him.
Sometimes, the child is an equal blend,
Taking features from both parents.
This happens when the seeds mix harmoniously,
Aroused and driven by Venus' passion.
In some cases, offspring resemble grandparents,
Or even great-grandparents.
This happens because parents carry
Hidden traits passed down from their ancestors.
These hidden particles combine in different ways,
Producing features, voices, and hair
That reflect the family line.
A female child can come from a father's seed,
And a male from the mother's.
Gender, like faces and bodies,
Does not arise from a single source.
Each birth comes from two seeds,
And the child takes more from the parent
It resembles most—
Whether male or female.
Nor do the divine powers deny any man
The joy of fathering children,
So that he is never called "father"
By his sweet offspring,
Or spends his life in barren love forever.
This is what many believe,
And so they gloomily sprinkle altars with blood,
Making them fragrant with burnt offerings,
Praying that their wives may be made fertile
Through abundant seed—
But they trouble the gods and sacred rituals in vain.
For some men are sterile because their seed is too thick,
While others have seed that is too watery and thin.

The thin seed cannot cling to the right places;
Instead, it trickles away and is wasted.
Meanwhile, overly thick seed is unfit,
Either failing to shoot forth properly,
Not reaching the right place,
Or, even if it does, mixing weakly with the woman's seed.
The harmony of Venus' union matters greatly here.
Some men impregnate certain women more easily,
And some women conceive more readily with specific men.
Indeed, many women who were sterile
In previous marriages have later found mates
With whom they could bear children,
Blessing their homes with sweet offspring.
Likewise, husbands whose fertile wives
Could not bear them children
Have found other partners whose nature aligns with theirs,
Granting them sons to brighten their old age.
It is crucial that the seeds
Mingle harmoniously for procreation.
Thicker seeds must mix with thinner ones,
And thinner with thicker,
For successful conception.
Diet also plays an important role in this process.
Certain foods can thicken the seed within the body,
While others make it thinner and weaker.
Additionally, the way love is made
Matters greatly as well.
It is commonly thought that women
Conceive more easily in positions
Like those of four-legged animals,
With the breasts downward and the hips raised.
This posture helps the seed
Reach the proper places.
Women should avoid excessive motion or playfulness during
   intimacy,

As this can hinder conception.
If a woman moves too joyfully,
Arching her body and tossing herself wildly,
She disrupts the natural course of the seed,
Deflecting it from where it needs to go.
Courtesans often move this way intentionally,
Preventing pregnancy while increasing pleasure for their clients.
But such practices are unnecessary for wives,
Whose goal is often to conceive.
Sometimes, it happens—through no divine intervention
Or arrows of Venus—that a plain and unremarkable woman
Wins a man's love.
Her actions, accommodating nature,
And tidy habits can endear her to him,
Making her a companion for life.
Long familiarity can also foster love.
Even as a stone, struck repeatedly by gentle blows,
Eventually weakens and cracks,
So too does a heart yield to love
When exposed to kindness and habit over time.
Do you not see how drops of water,
Falling consistently on stones,
Eventually wear through them?

Book V

Proem

O who can craft with mighty heart a song
Worthy of the greatness of these discoveries?
Or who can find words strong enough
To give proper praise to the one
Who left us heirs to such vast treasures,
Discovered and revealed by his own effort?
Surely no mortal man could do this.

For if he must be named according to the majesty
Of these great findings, then he was a god—
Listen to me, illustrious Memmius—a god,
Who first discovered the way of life
Now called philosophy.
By his skill, he lifted life
Out of the wild waves of chaos and darkness
And anchored it in calm harbors,
In the light of reason and peace.
Compare this to the discoveries of others:
According to the tales,
Ceres gave us the gift of grain,
And Bacchus the juice of grapes for wine.
But even without these gifts, life could continue,
As some peoples live without them still.
But happiness and well-being were impossible
Without freeing the mind.
That is why this man rightly seems to us a god—
He who spread the sweet comforts of life
Across all lands, soothing the minds of men.
And if you think the labors of Hercules
Were greater than these,
Then you stray far from reason.
What harm could the mighty jaws
Of the Nemean Lion cause us now?
Or the Boar of Arcadia with its bristling hide?
Or the Cretan Bull, or the Hydra,
That venomous monster of Lerna,
Surrounded by its deadly snakes?
What threat could the three-bodied Geryon pose,
Or the Stymphalian birds of the marshes?
What danger is there from the fire-breathing steeds
Of Thracian Diomedes,
Roaming the lands of Bistonia and Ismara?
Even the great serpent,

Guarding the golden apples of the Hesperides,
Coiled around its tree with immense bulk—
What harm could it inflict on us now,
On the distant shores of the Atlantic?
None of these monsters,
Even if they lived and were undefeated,
Could bring us harm today.
For the earth still swarms with savage beasts,
And the forests and mountains
Are filled with dangers even now.
Yet we avoid those places with ease.
But if the mind is not freed,
What conflicts and fears rage within us!
How great the struggles and dangers of the soul!
The agonies of desire tear men apart.
How overwhelming the fears!
Pride, greed, and reckless indulgence
Bring endless slaughter in their wake,
Along with debauchery and laziness.
Therefore, the man who overcame these evils,
Who freed the mind with words alone—
Not with weapons—
Shouldn't he rightly be ranked among the gods?
All the more because he spoke
Of the immortal gods themselves
With divine wisdom,
Revealing the truths of the world
And explaining its nature.

Argument of The Book and New Proem
Against A Teleological Concept

And now, following in his footsteps,
I continue his reasoning,
Explaining through my words the laws

That govern how all things are formed,
How they must follow those laws
And cannot escape the eternal decrees of time.
We've seen that among mortal things,
The mind is born from the body,
Fragile and unable to endure
Through the infinite ages.
We've also discussed how dreams bring images
That confuse the mind,
Making us think we see people
Who are no longer alive.
So far, we have come to this point:
The order of my plan now requires me
To explain how the universe itself
Is made of mortal matter, born in time,
And how its parts—earth, sky, oceans, stars,
Sun, and moon—came together.
I will also explain what living creatures
Sprang from the earth,
Which never came to life at all,
And how humans began to name things
And develop language to communicate.
I'll tell how the fear of gods arose in their hearts,
Leading to the creation of temples, altars,
Sacred groves, lakes, and idols of the gods.
I will also describe how nature guides
The courses of the sun and moon,
So that we don't mistakenly believe
That they move of their own free will,
Or that their paths are planned by gods
To sustain crops and life on earth.
Even those who know the gods live carefree lives
Sometimes wonder how things work,
Especially the movements of the heavens.
This doubt often drives them back to fear

And makes them believe again
In harsh, all-powerful gods.
Such men fail to understand
What can and cannot be,
And by what laws all things are bound,
Each with its proper limits set in time.
But now, lest I delay you with empty promises,
Look first at the sea, land, and sky:
O Memmius, see their threefold nature—
Three vast bodies, so different,
Yet all will one day be destroyed.
One single day will bring annihilation,
And the great structure of the world,
Which has endured for countless ages,
Will collapse.
I know this idea may seem strange and incredible,
That the sky and earth could someday end.
It is a difficult truth to explain,
As with any new idea,
One that cannot be seen or touched.
For the senses are the easiest way
To open belief in the human mind.
But still, I will speak.
Perhaps the fact itself will compel belief,
And you may soon witness a time
When the earth shakes with violent upheaval.
May nature, the great guide,
Keep these disasters far from us,
And may reason, not the events themselves,
Convince us that all things can be destroyed
And crash down in ruin.
Before I begin explaining this further,
I will share truths more solid and clear
Than anything the Oracle of Delphi ever proclaimed.
These truths will console you,

So you won't be trapped by religion,
Thinking that the earth, sun, sky, sea,
Stars, and moon must last forever,
Or that they are divine and eternal.
For some believe that those who explore
The truths of the universe
And challenge the heavens' walls,
Wishing to darken the brilliant sun,
Deserve punishment for their arrogance—
A belief as old as the myths of the Giants.
But this is far from true.
The sun, moon, and stars are not divine;
They are unworthy of being counted among the gods.
Instead, they serve as examples of things
That lack life, motion, and thought.
It is absurd to think
That judgment and reason could exist
In things like fire, water, or air—
Just as a tree cannot grow in the sky,
Clouds cannot form in the sea,
And fish cannot live on land.
Every part of the world has its place and purpose.
So too, the mind cannot exist alone,
Separated from the body.
If it could, why not imagine
A mind in the head, shoulders, or even the feet?
But since the soul and mind exist only in this body,
Arranged within its proper parts,
We must reject the idea
That they can survive outside the body.
They cannot dwell in rotting earth,
In the sun's fire,
In water,
Or in the distant reaches of the sky.
These elements have no divine sense,

For they cannot be quickened with life.
Likewise, you must never believe
That the sacred homes of the gods exist
Anywhere in this earthly world.
The nature of the gods is far too subtle,
Too removed from our senses,
And barely understood even by the mind.
Since they are beyond the touch of human hands,
They cannot grasp anything tangible to us.
For anything that cannot be touched itself
Can never touch something else.
This means their dwelling places
Must also be unlike ours—
Subtle and fitting for such a delicate essence.
I will prove this to you later in greater detail.
Further, to claim that the gods created
This magnificent world for the sake of humanity,
And that we should therefore praise their work,
Calling it worthy of admiration,
Or that it is sacrilege to question or overturn
What has been established by ancient divine will—
Such ideas, Memmius, are pure folly.
What gratitude could we offer
That would benefit the immortal, blessed gods,
Enough to make them act on our behalf?
Or what new reason, after so long a time,
Could persuade them—
Who have lived in eternal peace—
To alter their way of life?
It is those who are dissatisfied with the old
Who seek change,
But beings who have known only endless contentment—
What could spark in them a desire for something new?
And what harm would it have caused us
If we had never been born?

It's not as if we were trapped in misery,
Waiting in darkness for the dawn of creation!
Whoever has been born naturally wishes to live
As long as life is sweet,
But for those who never lived,
What difference does it make to them
That they were never born?
How could the gods have had a model
For creating the world in the first place?
How could they have conceived
What humans should be like,
Or imagined what they wanted to create?
How would they have known
The properties of the primal elements,
Or how those elements could combine
To form the world,
If nature herself had not first provided examples?
For countless ages,
The primordial particles of the universe
Have been in motion,
Colliding in every possible way.
By combining and separating,
They have continually tested
What could be created.
It is no surprise that they eventually settled
Into the arrangements we see today,
Sustaining the world through endless renewal.
Even if I did not know the nature
Of these primal particles,
I would still confidently assert—
Based on the patterns of the skies
And many other observations—
That the universe was not created
By any divine power.
The many flaws of nature make this clear.

First, consider all the regions under the vast sky.
Much of it is taken up by mountains,
Forests filled with wild beasts,
Cliffs, barren swamps, and oceans
That separate the lands with vast stretches of water.
Of the remaining space, nearly two-thirds
Are rendered uninhabitable
By unbearable heat or eternal frost.
Even the land left for farming
Would be overrun with brambles and weeds
If human effort did not resist it.
For survival, people have long toiled,
Sweating under the burden of their tools,
Splitting the soil with plows and mattocks,
Struggling to make the earth yield its bounty.
Unless we turn the fertile soil with the plough
And knead the earth, bringing it to life,
Crops would not grow on their own,
Rising into the free, bright air.
Even then, after our hardest labor
Has brought them to leaf and blossom,
The blazing sun may scorch them with deadly heat,
Or sudden rains, chilling frost,
Or violent winds may destroy and twist them.
Beyond this, why does nature foster
On both land and sea
The dreadful breeds of savage beasts,
Enemies of the human race?
Why do the seasons bring sickness and disease?
Why does untimely death strike so often?
Look at the newborn child:
Like a castaway washed ashore by raging waves,
He lies naked on the ground,
Speechless and in desperate need of help,
When nature first brings him

Into the light of day.
Torn from his mother's womb with birth-pangs,
He fills the air with plaintive cries—
A fitting beginning for one
Who must journey through so many hardships in life.
But all the flocks, herds, and wild beasts
Come into the world fully equipped.
They need no rattles,
No soothing words from a nurse's playful chatter.
They do not require different clothes
To adapt to changing weather.
They need no weapons or high walls
To protect what they have.
For the earth itself,
And nature, the creator of the world,
Provides abundantly for them all.

The World is Not Eternal

And first,
Since the bodies of earth, water, air,
And fiery exhalations (these four elements
That make up everything we see)
Are all born and have a perishable nature,
The entire world must also be understood
As perishable.
For truly, anything whose parts and pieces
Are born in time and have a limited lifespan
Must itself have been created in time
And must eventually perish.
So, when I see the largest parts of the world—
Its mightiest features—being consumed and renewed,
I know that the sky above
And the earth beneath had a beginning in time
And will, in time, come to an end.

And in case you think
I am making this claim lightly or to suit myself—
Because I argue that earth and fire are mortal,
That water and air also perish,
And that these are born again and grow anew—
Consider the evidence.
First, certain parts of the earth,
Parched by relentless sun
And trampled under countless feet,
Release clouds of fine dust,
Which the strong winds carry into the air.
Other parts of the soil are washed away
By heavy rains and swelling rivers
That erode their banks.
Moreover, whatever the earth gives
To nourish and grow life,
It takes back in return.
And since the earth, the mother of all,
Is also the common grave of all things,
You can see her resources diminish
Only to be replenished with new growth.
As for the sea, streams, and springs,
They overflow with fresh water
Again and again.
This endless renewal of water
Requires no explanation—
The constant movement of countless waters
Proves it clearly.
Whatever water rises up
Is immediately carried away,
So there is never an overflow.
This happens partly because
The strong winds and the sun's heat
Reduce the seas by evaporation,
And partly because water seeps underground

Through the earth.
Saltwater is filtered out,
And the fresh water gathers again
At the sources of rivers.
From there, it flows onward,
Pouring over the land through channels
Carved by ancient floods.
Now, about the air:
It constantly changes, hour by hour,
In countless ways.
Whatever rises as dust or vapor from things
Is carried into the vast ocean of the air.
If air did not, in turn, return to replenish things
By giving back matter as it absorbs it,
Everything by now would have dissolved
And turned entirely into air.
But the air is continuously created
From the things around us
And flows back into them,
Since all things are in a constant state of flux.
Likewise,
The endless source of liquid light,
The ethereal sun, floods the heavens
With a constant flow of new radiance,
Replacing the light as soon as it shines.
Whatever beams stream from the sun
Are lost the moment they fall elsewhere.
You can understand this from simple examples:
When clouds begin to pass beneath the sun
And seem to split its rays in two,
The lower beams disappear entirely,
Casting shadows wherever the clouds roll.
This shows that light constantly needs renewal,
With each beam perishing as soon as it flashes forth.
Without this replenishment,

Nothing could remain visible under the sun.
Even earthly sources of light, like lamps and torches,
Behave the same way. Their gleams dart forth,
Flickering alive with their flames,
While new light continually replaces the old.
The destruction of one flame
Is masked by the swift birth of another,
So the light never truly leaves the area it illuminates.
Thus, we must believe that the sun, moon, and stars
Emit their light from constantly renewing sources.
The flames that first rise always perish one by one,
Preventing us from imagining them as eternal.
Do you not see, as well,
How even stones are defeated by time?
How tall towers collapse into ruin,
And massive boulders crumble?
How the shrines of gods and their idols crack and decay?
Even divine power cannot hold back
The inevitable march of fate,
Nor can it defy the fixed decrees of nature.
Look at the monuments of heroes, now in ruins,
And hear them ask if you still doubt
That they too grow old.
See the shattered rocks falling
From high mountains,
Unable to withstand the forces of time.
If these had endured since eternity past,
Resisting every assault of the ages,
They would not suddenly collapse now.
Now, consider this whole world—
The vast structure surrounding the earth.
If it produces all things within itself,
As some claim, and reclaims them upon their destruction,
Then it must itself be born of mortal matter.
For whatever gives part of itself to sustain other things

Must eventually diminish and be replenished
When it takes things back.
Moreover, if the earth and sky had no beginning—
If they had always existed—
Why, before the Theban war or the fall of Troy,
Did no poets sing of other great events?
Why have so many heroic deeds been forgotten,
Lost to time, without eternal monuments to preserve them?
Surely, this is because the universe is new,
Having only recently begun.
Even now, some arts are still evolving.
New devices are continually being added to ships,
Musical instruments were only recently invented,
And the understanding of nature and the universe
Was discovered not long ago.
I, too, have only just begun
To express these truths in the Roman tongue,
Bringing this knowledge to my people.
But if you believe that all these things
Existed in the same way before,
Only to be destroyed by fiery eruptions,
Massive earthquakes, or floods
That overwhelmed the earth and its cities,
Then you must admit,
Defeated by the argument,
That the earth and sky will someday
Be destroyed as well.
For if such great catastrophes
Have afflicted the world before,
It stands to reason that some even greater disaster
Could cause its ultimate collapse.
This is no different from how we know
That humans are mortal—
Because we all suffer the same illnesses
That claimed the lives of those who came before us,

Removed from life by nature.
Whatever lasts forever must either
Resist all forces, being made of solid matter
That allows nothing to break it apart—
Like those seeds of matter
We've discussed before—
Or exist free from harm,
Like the void, which cannot be touched or struck.
The void endures because it cannot be broken,
And it provides no resistance to blows.
Alternatively, something could last forever
If there were no space around it
For its parts to break apart and scatter—
Like the universe as a whole,
Which has no external place
Where its pieces could flee or dissolve.
Nor are there bodies outside the universe
To strike it and destroy it.
But the world is not made of solid matter,
As it contains void mixed throughout.
Nor is it entirely void,
And there are still forces from the infinite beyond—
Mighty whirlwinds of matter
That could batter the world into ruin,
Or other catastrophic forces
That might shatter its walls.
There exists infinite space,
A vast and boundless abyss,
Into which the universe's foundations
Could be hurled and destroyed.
Some external force could still strike them
And bring everything to ruin.
Thus, the door to destruction is not closed
For the heavens, the sun, the earth,
And the deep seas.

It stands wide open,
Glaring at them with a monstrous grin.
This is why we must admit
That these things were born in time.
For objects made of mortal matter
Could not have survived
The countless assaults
Of infinite past ages without breaking apart.

Again, the four great elements of the world—
Earth, water, air, and fire—
Clash constantly in a fierce and endless war.
Don't you see that their struggle could one day end?
What if the sun and its heat
Finally gained control
And evaporated all the water?
They are constantly trying to do this,
Though they haven't succeeded yet.
The rivers, fed by endless seas,
Continue to replenish the water,
Threatening the world with floods
From the ocean's deep reservoirs.
But the winds and the sun's heat
Work to dry up the seas,
Hoping to stop the waters
Before they succeed in their goal.
This vast struggle continues,
Each force balancing the other,
Locked in battle over the fate of the world.
At times, fire has been victorious.
Once, as the tale goes,
Water ruled over the earth.
Fire triumphed in the story of Phaethon,
Who lost control of the sun's fiery chariot
And set the skies and lands ablaze.

Then Jupiter, in his wrath,
Struck Phaethon down with a thunderbolt,
And his father, the sun,
Seized the flaming reins,
Tamed the horses,
And restored order to the universe—
As the ancient poets of Greece tell us.
But this tale seems far from the truth.
Fire prevails only when
A greater number of fiery particles rise
From the infinite beyond.
At other times, fire is subdued,
Or it consumes the world
In burning heat.
Likewise, water has had its victories.
As the story goes,
Floods overwhelmed humanity,
Drowning men beneath their waves.
But when the force of water receded—
Its fury turned aside—
The rains stopped,
And rivers calmed their rage.

Formation of The World And Astronomical Questions

But now, I will explain how the gathering of first particles
Created the vast universe—
The earth, the sky, the endless seas,
The sun's path, and the moon's orbit.
It was not through some plan or deliberate thought
That these primal elements placed themselves
In their proper order.
Nor did they agree upon how they would move.
Instead, the particles of matter—

Countless and varied—
Have been moving and colliding
For infinite ages, driven by their own weight
And the constant blows they endured.
Through these endless movements and combinations,
The particles eventually formed unions and motions
That gave rise to the great structures of the world:
The earth, the sea, the sky,
And all living creatures.
In that ancient time,
The sun's blazing wheel had not yet risen
To light the heavens.
No constellations, no oceans,
No sky, no earth, no air,
And nothing that resembled the world we know.
There was only a chaotic mass—
A storm of disordered particles,
Colliding and conflicting with one another.
Their random motions and varied shapes
Prevented them from joining together
In stable and harmonious ways.
Over time, similar particles began to gather,
Separating into distinct groups
And forming the world's major elements.
The heavens lifted high above the land,
The sea spread out its waters,
And pure fires of the upper sky
Clustered together in their own realm.
First, the heaviest and most entangled particles—
The earthy ones—
Settled in the middle,
Forming the solid ground.
The more they interlocked,
The more they pushed out
The lighter particles,

Which became the sea, the stars, the sun,
The moon, and the boundaries of the world.
These lighter elements were made of smaller, smoother particles.
The fiery ether, escaping through countless pores in the earth,
Rose upward,
Carrying the stars with it.
This process is similar to how lakes and streams
Release mists into the air,
Or how the earth smokes
When the sun's golden rays at dawn
Begin to warm the dew-covered grass.
As these vapors gather overhead,
They form clouds,
Which weave a cover across the sky.
In the same way, the light, diffuse ether
Spread out on all sides,
Bending and curving into a dome
That encased everything below.
Next came the sun and moon,
Their globes suspended in the air,
Midway between the earth and the ether.
They were too heavy to remain aloft
In the highest ether,
But too light to sink to the ground.
Thus, they revolve in their paths,
Becoming part of the greater whole,
Like some parts of the human body move
While others remain still.
As these elements separated,
The earth collapsed inward,
Forming the vast basins
Where the oceans now stretch.
Day by day, the sun's rays and ether's tides
Pressed and shaped the earth,
Condensing it further toward its center.

This process squeezed out salty moisture,
Which flowed into the oceans,
And released particles of heat and air,
Which rose to form the bright, glowing heavens.
The plains sank lower,
While the mountains grew taller,
Their rocky foundations resisting the forces of compression.
Thus, the earth became stable,
Its heavy and coarse matter settling at the bottom,
Like dregs sinking in a liquid.
The oceans, air, and ether above
Were left pure and separate,
Each lighter than the one beneath it.
Ether, the lightest and most fluid of all,
Floats above the winds,
Unaffected by their chaos.
While the winds below clash and whirl,
The ether glides steadily,
Carrying its fires in a smooth and constant motion.
The steady flow of ether
Is like the Pontus sea,
Which moves with fixed tides,
Maintaining its endless rhythm as it glides forward.
And so,
For the earth to remain at rest
In the middle of the universe,
It must lose weight gradually and shrink,
Being connected from its very beginning
To another substance below it—
Bound tightly to the vast realms of air,
On which it depends and where it resides.
For this reason, the earth does not weigh down
On the air beneath it.
Just as a man's body does not feel
The weight of his own head pressing on his neck,

Or the body's full weight pulling on the feet,
We do not notice the earth pressing on the air.
Instead, we feel only external weights—
Those placed upon us—causing discomfort,
Even if they are lighter than our own body.
This shows that the inherent nature of a thing
Always determines its effect.
Thus, the earth is no foreign object
Dropped from another universe
Onto alien air.
It was formed alongside the air
As part of the world's creation,
Just as our limbs are part of our bodies.

***

Furthermore, when the earth is shaken violently
By a great thunder,
It also shakes everything above it.
This could not happen unless the earth
Was firmly connected
To the air and sky.
They are bound together with common roots,
United since their origin.
Don't you see how the subtle energy of the soul
Supports the heavy weight of the body?
It does this because it is joined to the body,
Bound to it as one.
In the same way,
What power could lift our body into a leap
Without the energy of the mind guiding the limbs?
So, you see how a subtle force,
When connected to something heavy,
Can be incredibly strong—
Just as the air is bound to the earth,
And the mind to the body.

***

Now let us consider what makes the stars move.
If the heavens spin as a massive sphere,
Then it must be that air presses on the poles—
Both above and below—
Holding and enclosing them in place.
Additionally, air might flow across the top of the sphere,
Pushing it in the same direction as the stars,
Or it might stream beneath it,
Turning the sphere upward,
Much like rivers turn waterwheels.
It's also possible that the heavens remain still
While the stars themselves move,
Perhaps driven by swift currents of ether
Encased within the sky.
These ether tides might flow
In search of escape,
Carrying the stars along their paths.
Or, it could be that an external stream of air
Flows from a distant source,
Driving the stars onward,
Or that the stars themselves
Move under their own power,
Traveling wherever their "fuel" invites them,
Sustaining their fiery bodies as they go.
It's hard to say with certainty
Which of these causes moves the stars in our world.
But I can show that in the universe at large,
Different worlds may follow different plans.
One of these causes must apply here,
Moving the constellations we see.
Yet to determine which one is true
Is not an easy task—
It requires careful, step-by-step reasoning.

***

The sun's disk is likely neither much larger
Nor its blaze much smaller than it appears.
From the distances at which light and heat reach us,
Neither the flame's size nor its brightness
Seems diminished.
Thus, the sun's heat and radiance
Touch our bodies just as they appear.
Its form and size, as seen from earth,
Are likely very close to their actual dimensions.
As for the moon,
Whether it shines by reflecting the sun's light
Or glows with its own radiance,
Its shape and size remain as they appear to us.
All distant objects seem blurred
When viewed through layers of air,
Yet the moon's bright and well-defined form
Indicates it is visible to us on earth
Exactly as it is.
Lastly,
The fires of ether—those stars we see from earth—
May be slightly larger or smaller than they seem,
But only by the tiniest margin.
Fires we see here on earth
Change size only slightly when viewed from afar,
So long as they remain bright and distinct.
Similarly, the stars above likely maintain
Almost exactly the size we perceive.
Nor should it surprise us
That the small sun can emit such vast light,
Flooding the oceans, lands, and sky,
Bathing the entire world in fiery warmth.
It's possible that the light comes from a vast wellspring,
A single source that spreads its radiance outward.

In this way, the fiery particles
From the entire world gather and flow together
To form a single, powerful stream of heat and light.
Do you not see how even a small spring of water
Can flood meadows and fields?
Similarly, the heat of the sun,
Though its fire may be small,
Can fill the air with fierce warmth,
Especially if the air is ready to be kindled—
Just as we see an entire field of grain
Or stubble catch fire from a single spark.
The sun, gleaming on high,
May also have an invisible fire surrounding it,
Unseen by the eye,
But adding greatly to the power of its rays.
There is no single, definite explanation
For how the sun moves from summer
To its winter position in Capricorn
And back again to Cancer at the solstice.
Nor do we fully know why the moon
Crosses the same distance each month
That the sun takes a year to traverse.
The most likely explanation comes
From the teachings of Democritus,
Who argued that objects closer to the earth
Move more slowly because
The rotational force of the sky weakens
As it nears the ground.
The sun, lying below the blazing stars,
Is left behind as the heavens whirl above it.
The moon, being closer to the earth than the sun,
Lags even farther behind.
The slower the motion of the heavens below,
The more the moon falls behind the stars.
This is why the moon seems to return

To the same position in the Zodiac
More quickly than the sun,
Since the stars overtake her more often.
It could also be that streams of air,
Blowing alternately at fixed times,
Push the sun from summer to winter
And back again.
One stream might drive the sun
Toward the cold of winter,
While another sends it back
To the heat of summer.
The same reasoning could explain the movement
Of the moon and stars,
Which may be carried along
By alternating air currents,
Much like clouds are blown
In different directions at different heights.
Why shouldn't the stars in the ether
Be moved by opposing streams of air,
Just as clouds are moved below?
Night envelops the world in darkness
When the sun, after its daily journey,
Reaches the farthest edges of the sky,
Its fires spent and weakened
By their long passage through the air.
Or it may be that the same force
That drives the sun above the earth
Then compels it to travel below.
Morning, at its appointed hour,
Spreads rosy light across the heavens,
Either because the sun, returning beneath the earth,
Prepares to rise and light the sky,
Or because fiery particles gather together,
Forming a new sun at the start of each day.
Some say the fires seen on mountaintops at dawn

Combine into a single orb,
Creating the sun anew each morning.
It's not surprising that fiery particles
Could stream together at a fixed time,
Reforming the sun's brilliance.
Many things happen at regular intervals:
Plants sprout and shed their flowers,
Children lose their baby teeth,
And young men grow soft beards at a certain age.
Even thunder, snow, rain, and winds
Follow fixed patterns,
Arriving in their seasons.
From the very beginning of the world,
These causes have operated in regular cycles.
And now, just as they did then,
These events continue to follow
Their fixed order and sequence.
Likewise,
Days may grow longer as nights grow shorter,
And nights may extend as daylight fades.
This might happen because the sun,
Traveling under the earth and across the sky,
Follows two arcs—one longer, one shorter—
Dividing the ether unequally.
As it moves, it adds light to one part of its path
While taking it away from another,
Until it reaches the point in the heavens
Where day and night become equal again.
When the sun is halfway between
The northern and southern winds,
The sky keeps its two goals balanced evenly,
Thanks to the steady position of the Zodiac,
Through which the sun travels in a year,
Illuminating the heavens and the earth
With its slanted rays.

This, at least, is what astronomers tell us,
Using their diagrams to chart the stars
And map the Zodiac's constellations.
Or perhaps the air beneath the earth
Is denser in some places,
Slowing the sun's fiery beams
So they cannot easily rise.
This would explain why winter nights linger so long
Before the many-rayed badge of the day appears.
It might also be that, as seasons change,
The fires that fuel the sun
Sometimes stream together more quickly,
Sometimes more slowly.
Thus, some claim that each day
A new sun is born at dawn.
The moon may shine because
It reflects the rays of the sun.
As it moves farther from the sun's position,
It reveals more of its light to us,
Until, opposite the sun across the sky,
It gleams fully.
When the moon rises,
It watches the sun set.
Then, as it moves closer to the sun again,
Its light fades gradually,
Its glowing face turning away from us.
This is how those who think the moon is a sphere,
Traveling between the sun and the earth,
Explain its phases.
Alternatively, the moon might have its own light,
Revealing its changing shapes
Through other mechanisms.
Perhaps another dark, invisible body
Travels with the moon,
Blocking its light in three different ways.

Or the moon could rotate on its own axis,
Half of it glowing with light,
While its spinning reveals and hides
Different parts of its surface over time.
This idea, supported by Babylonian astronomers,
Contradicts the theories of Greek astrologers.
Yet, both views could hold some truth,
And there's no clear reason to favor one
Over the other.
It's also possible that each day
A new moon is created and then destroyed,
Its shapes following a fixed sequence.
This would align with the regular cycles
We see in nature:
Springtime arrives with Venus,
And her winged companion leads the way.
Mother Flora follows,
Scattering colors and sweet fragrances.
Summer brings heat and the dry touch of Ceres,
Along with northern breezes.
Then comes autumn with Bacchus,
And finally winter,
Chilling the earth with its icy breath.
If so many things happen in fixed cycles,
It is not surprising that a moon
Could also be born and destroyed at regular intervals.
Similarly, the eclipses of the sun and moon
May have various causes.
Why should the moon be the only body
Capable of blocking the sun's light
By placing itself between the earth and the sun?
Couldn't another dark object,
Always invisible to us,
Be responsible for such phenomena?
And why couldn't the sun itself

Lose its fire temporarily
As it passes through regions
Hostile to its flames,
Only to regain its light afterward?
Likewise, when the earth casts its shadow,
Blocking the sun from the moon,
This might not be the only explanation for lunar eclipses.
Why couldn't another body
Pass below the moon
Or above the sun,
Interrupting their light?
Even if the moon glows with its own light,
Why couldn't it grow dim in certain parts of the sky,
Traveling through regions that weaken its radiance?

Origins of Vegetable and Animal Life

And now, to what remains!
Since I've explained how the motions of the sun and moon
Come about, and how they may falter,
Veiling the land in shadow
When they seem to blink,
Only to shine again with bright radiance,
I will return to the early days of the world.
I'll tell how the young earth, in her first moments,
Brought forth life, raising it to the light
And entrusting it to the winds.
At first, the earth gave rise to grass,
Covering the hills and plains
With green shoots.
The meadows sparkled with vibrant colors.
Then came the trees,
Spurred by a great impulse
To grow tall into the air.
Just as feathers, hair, and bristles

Are first to grow on animals,
So the earth first sprouted grasses and shrubs,
And later gave birth to countless living creatures
In countless forms.
These creatures could not have fallen from the sky,
Nor emerged from the salty pools of the sea.
Earth has rightly earned the name "Mother,"
Since all life comes from her.
Even now, life forms in the soil,
Shaped by rain and the heat of the sun.
It's no wonder that, in those early days,
More and larger creatures arose,
Born in the fresh, young years of earth and sky.
First came birds,
Hatching in springtime and leaving their eggs behind,
Just as crickets today shed their shells
And go on living.
Then the earth brought forth
Other living beings in abundance.
The land was rich with heat and moisture,
And in suitable places, womb-like cavities formed,
Attached to the earth by roots.
When the young creatures inside
Reached the age to seek the air,
They broke free, escaping the dampness of the ground.
At that time, the earth supplied them with food.
Like a mother's milk,
The earth's pores released nourishing juices,
Just as a woman's body produces milk
After childbirth.
These early creatures found warmth in the soil
And softness in the grass,
Without suffering from harsh cold,
Scorching heat, or violent winds.
In those days, the young earth

Protected life from such extremes.
How fitting is the name "Mother Earth,"
For she gave birth to humankind,
As well as the beasts of the mountains
And the birds of the skies.
But, like any mother,
Her ability to give life diminished with age.
Time changes the nature of all things,
And nothing remains the same forever.
All things come and go.
Nature transforms everything:
Some things decay and wither,
While others rise and flourish.
Thus, as time passes,
The earth takes on new roles.
What she once created,
She can no longer produce,
And what she never bore before,
She may bring forth today.
In those ancient times,
The earth also gave rise to strange creatures—
Monsters with bizarre forms and limbs.
There were beings that were neither male nor female,
Lacking characteristics of either sex.
Some had no feet, others no hands.
Some were dumb horrors without mouths,
Or blind creatures with no eyes.
Some were so malformed
That their limbs were fused to their bodies,
Preventing them from moving,
Escaping harm, or seeking what they needed.
Earth produced such monsters in vain.
Nature refused to let them thrive.
They could not mature, find food,
Or reproduce.

For life requires certain conditions:
There must be food,
A way for reproductive seeds
To move through the body,
And the physical means for male and female
To unite and propagate life.
And after monsters passed away,
Many creatures could not stay, unable
To survive or grow a lasting line.
For every creature that you see,
Living, breathing, as they be,
Has, from earliest days, survived,
By clever tricks, or strength, or flight.
Many kinds are still alive today
Because they serve in some helpful way,
Entrusted now to human care.
Strength has kept fierce lions alive
And other beasts that inspire fear;
Foxes live by clever schemes,
While stags are saved by speed and grace.
Faithful dogs, with hearts alert,
And animals bred for strength and work,
The woolly sheep and horned cattle too,
All are guarded under human watch.
For they fled from savage beasts,
Seeking peace and food in rest,
A life where they need not labor hard,
A reward for their service true.
But beasts without these gifts to give—
Those that could not thrive alone
Or serve in ways that made them safe—
Were left exposed to harsher fates,
Chained by nature to doom's hold,
As prey and prize for others' needs,
Until their kind met utter end.

No Centaurs were, nor could there be,
Creatures made of double form,
Mixed with limbs not built alike,
Yet somehow strong in every way—
For even if your mind is slow,
You'll see that horses, by year three,
Stand in the peak of strength and speed;
A child, by then, is still so small,
Sometimes seeking his mother's care,
An infant yet. And later on,
When strong and sturdy horse limbs fail,
Youth is only then taking root
In boys, with down upon their cheeks.
So never think that human kind
And horse could join to make Centaurs,
Or Scyllas, half-dog and half-fish—
Or others mixed in strange design,
For their parts could never blend;
Their ages, needs, and growth don't match.
They wouldn't share one lust or taste,
For just as goats can eat the plant
That poisons men, each kind is set.
Flame burns lions just the same
As it scorches any flesh or blood.
So how could Chimaera's form—
With lion front, dragon tail, and goat between—
Breathe fire from its body so?
And those who claim such beings were born
When earth was young and sky was fresh
Base their words on tales alone.
They say that rivers of gold once flowed
Through lands and trees bore gems as fruit,
Or that humans walked as giants tall,
Able to wade through oceans deep
Or spin the heavens in their hands.

But even though, in ancient times,
Earth held seeds of every life,
This is not proof that creatures mixed,
With parts of all kinds bound as one.
Even now, each plant and tree
Sprouts from the earth in its own way;
They cannot join into one kind—
Each follows its own nature true,
Bound by nature's fixed decree.

ORIGINS AND SAVAGE PERIOD OF MANKIND

But mortal man
Was hardier then, in the old plains,
As well he should be, born from earth
That was stronger too; he was built
With bigger, sturdier bones within,
And flesh bound tight with solid sinews,
Unaffected by heat or cold,
Or strange foods, or aches and pains.
And as many suns rolled by,
They lived a roaming life like beasts.
No one then guided curved plows,
Or tilled the soil with iron tools,
Or planted shoots in the turned-up earth,
Or trimmed the old branches from trees.
What the sun and rains brought forth,
What earth itself created freely,
Was enough to please their simple hearts.
Among the oak trees full of acorns
They refreshed themselves for a time;
The wild berries of the arbutus,
Now ripening red in winter's chill,
The old earth yielded then more full.
And many coarse foods, back then,
The fresh, young world provided,
Enough for those poor, early folk.

Rivers and springs summoned them
To quench their thirst, as now the hills
Call down to the creatures of the wild
With water rushing far and wide.
They also sought the Nymphs' grottos—
Woodland shelters they found while roaming—
From which they knew that streams slid out,
Splashing, soaking rocks with moss,
And bursting forth across the plains.
They didn't yet know how to make fire
To guard against the cold, nor use
The furry skins of beasts as clothes;
They huddled in groves, in caves, in woods,
Or hid in thickets to shield their backs,
Driven to flee the sting of wind
And pounding rains. Nor could they yet
Understand the common good,
Or share any customs, any laws:
Whatever fortune brought to each
They kept alone, trained by instinct
Only to survive and thrive.
And in the woods, Venus joined
The lovers' bodies; the woman gave
Either from a shared desire,
Or from the man's wild, insistent urge,
Or from a gift—perhaps acorns, ripe pears,
Or berries from the arbutus tree.
And trusting strength in hands and legs,
They'd chase the beasts that roamed the forests;
They caught many, but a few escaped,
Fleeing into their hiding places...
With thrown stones and heavy branches
Twisted and gnarled. When night arrived,
They'd lie down, like bristly boars,
Their wild bodies on the bare earth,

Rolling themselves in leaves and boughs.
They did not call out to the sun
Or the fields in loud lament,
Quaking in the night's shadows;
But, silent and buried in sleep,
They waited until dawn brought light
And the sun's rosy flames. From youth,
Seeing the dark and light come back
In turns, they had no fear at all
That night would last forever, that light
Of the sun would vanish for good.
Their worries instead were more of beasts,
The savage animals that often
Turned their sleep to frightful scenes,
Forcing them to leave their caves
As boars with foaming mouths or strong lions
Pushed them from beds of scattered leaves.
Yet even then, much as today,
They left the fading light of life.
In those times, a person might be seized
By beasts, devoured alive,
Echoing in the forests as he watched
His living flesh become a grave;
While those who escaped would scream,
Pressing hands to their wounded flesh,
Begging for eternal rest,
Till, lacking any help at hand
To ease their pain, they died from it.
But not in those early days would war
Destroy great armies in a day,
Nor did raging seas then crash
Entire ships upon the rocks.
The ocean raged in vain,
Its fury ending empty, and with ease
It let go of its threats;

Nor did the calm sea's gentle waves
Tempt men toward disaster:
The bold skill of ship-sailing
Was unknown in those early days.
Again, back then a lack of food
Would drain men's strength to death; today
It's excess that overwhelms.
Unknowing, they once poured poison
For themselves; now, with more skill,
They pass the drink to others.

Beginnings of Civilization

Afterwards,
When they had gained huts, pelts, and fire,
And when the woman joined the man,
Withdrew with him to share one home,
And children born from them were known,
Then humankind began to soften.
For now fire warmed their shivering frames,
And made them less strong to bear the cold
Under the open sky; and Love
Softened their rough and shaggy ways.
Children's chatter and gentle kisses
Soon broke their proud, wild nature down.
Then neighbors began to join as friends,
No longer wanting to harm or suffer,
And urged for women and children, too,
Mercy from fathers, while they showed
With cries and gestures how it was fit
To show compassion for the weak. And still,
Though full harmony was not yet found,
A good part of men kept their faith—
For otherwise, mankind would long ago
Have perished utterly, and none

Would have survived the passing years.
Lest perhaps,
You ponder this in silent thought,
Let me say that lightning first brought fire
To earth for mortals, spreading flames
Across the lands. For even now we see
So many things flash into flame,
Struck by lightning's celestial power.
And also, when a tree with many branches,
Swaying from winds, rubs to and fro
Against the branches of a nearby tree,
There, by the power of rub and rub,
Fire is created; at times outbursts
The scorching heat of flames, when boughs
Chafe against tree trunks. Either cause
Could well have given fire to mortal men.
Next, food to cook and soften in flame,
The sun taught them, as they often saw
How warmth could mellow things it touched
With its bright and fiery rays
Across the fields.
And day by day
The stronger, wiser men would teach
Them to change their old way of life
With fire and new devices. Kings began
To found cities and to build strongholds
For protection, places safe for themselves,
Dividing flocks and fields for each
According to beauty, strength, and mind—
For beauty was prized then, and strength
Held supreme rights. After that, wealth
Was discovered, and gold revealed,
Which soon stripped honour from the strong and fair;
For men, however fair in form
Or brave, would mostly choose the rich.

But if men lived by better reason,
They'd find great wealth in a simple life,
Content with what they have; for I believe
There's never a lack of little in the world.
But men desired power and fame
So they could lay firm foundations
And live quietly in wealth—
In vain, in vain; for, in the race to climb
To the heights of honour, they make
Their path so terrible; and once they reach
The top, envy, like a thunderbolt,
Will strike, hurling them headlong down
Into darkest Tartarus with scorn; for all
Summits and highest regions
Smoke as if scorched by envy's flames;
So it is far better to obey in peace
Than to seek mastery of affairs
And possession of empires. Let it be;
And let the weary exhaust themselves,
All to no end, fighting on
The narrow path of human ambition;
Since all they know is from others' words,
All they seek is from what they hear,
And not from what they think. And this folly
Is no greater today, nor will it grow,
Than it was long ago
And thus, kings were slain,
And the ancient majesty of golden thrones
And haughty scepters lay cast down in dust;
Crowns, once splendid on royal heads,
Became bloody beneath common feet,
Groaning for their lost glories—for once feared,
They were now trampled under with greedy zeal
By the crowd. So, down to the dregs,
All things fell to the brawling mobs,

As each man sought to rule alone. Then some
Wiser minds taught men to form
The magistrates' office and to frame
Laws that all might choose to follow.
For humankind, weary of a life
Ruled by brute force, was tired of feuds;
And so it soon, of its own free will,
Gave way to laws and strictest codes. Since then,
Each man, in anger, no longer took
A vengeance harsher than what fair laws
Would now allow, they loathed the life
Led by force alone. From this arose
The fear of punishments that taints each gain
Of wickedness, for force and deceit
Circle back on the one who used them.
Not easy is it for a person
Who breaks the peace to live a calm,
Composed life. For though he may escape
The wrath of gods and men, he must still fear
That it will not stay hidden—for indeed,
Many, often babbling in dreams,
Or raving in sickness, have let slip
Their secrets and confessed their sins.
But nature itself
Urged men to speak in different sounds,
And need and use shaped the names of things,
Just as speechless years compel young children
To make gestures with their hands,
Pointing here and there at what's before them.
For each creature knows, by instinct,
How best to use its powers. Before
The bull-calf's horns have barely budded,
He starts to butt and fiercely thrust.
Panther cubs and lion whelps,
With claws and teeth not fully formed,

Already begin to fight and claw.
We see all young birds use their wings
And seek to fly with early flutters.
Thus, to think that, in those days, one man
Gave things their names, teaching others
First words, is foolishness. For why would he
Name each thing by words while others, too,
Could have made such sounds? And if others
Had not already used such words,
How did he know their use himself,
Or alone have this power to name things?
One man could scarcely make
A whole crowd remember his names.
It is not easy to persuade
The deaf on what they need to do.
They would not accept nor endure
Endless strange sounds in their ears. And why,
In the end, would it seem so strange
That humans (who had voice and tongue)
Should use various words for things,
Led by their differing senses?—
For even speechless herds, and even
The beasts of the wild, send forth different sounds
When in fear, in pain, or in joy.
You can know this from simple facts:
When great-jowled hounds, maddened, begin
To bare their teeth and snarl, they make
A sound far different from their barks
That echo through the fields.
And when they lick their young with love,
Or play with gentle, snapping bites,
They whimper softly, far different from
The sounds they make when, alone in the house,
They howl or cringe from blows.
Or take the neighing of the horse—

Is it not different when the stallion
In his prime, driven by Love,
Raves among the mares, or snorts
A call to battle, or whinnies
In fright with trembling limbs?
Finally, the dappled birds,
The hawks, ospreys, and sea-gulls,
Searching for food along the waves,
Cry differently at different times—
When they fight for food, or struggle
With prey in their grasp. There are birds
That change their calls with the weather—
The ancient crows or flocks of rooks
Are said to cry out for rain,
Or to call for winds and storms. Thus, if moods
Move the speechless beasts to make
Different sounds, then surely much more
Would mortal men, even then,
Use many sounds to name each thing..
And now what cause
Has spread belief in gods abroad
Through mighty nations, and filled cities full
Of high altars, leading to the practice
Of solemn rites in due season—rites which still
Flourish amid the great affairs of state
And at the heart of civic life,
Rites that plant a trembling awe in humankind,
Raising new temples to the gods from land to land
And drawing crowds to them on holy days—
It's not so hard to explain. For even then
People saw, with minds awake,
Visions of gods in mighty forms; and more,
In their sleep, they saw bodies of wondrous size.
Thus, they attributed to these beings
Awareness and life, as they seemed to move,

To speak grand words befitting their power.
Men believed they had eternal life,
For their images appeared constantly
And did not change; and mainly because men thought
That beings of such mighty power
Could not be overcome by any force.
They thought them full of happiness,
For the fear of death troubled them not,
And in dreams men saw them do great things
Without suffering or weariness. Besides,
They saw how the heavens followed a set course,
How seasons changed in steady cycles,
But did not understand the causes. So,
They took refuge in the idea that all
Was guided by the gods' will, and believed
The heavens were the gods' dwelling place, for there
The night, the moon, and all the stars
Are seen to move—moon, day, and night, and night's
Ancient constellations and bright fires,
The shooting stars, clouds, sun, rain,
Snow, winds, lightning, hail,
The rumblings and the hollow roar
Of thunder's mighty threats forevermore.
O humankind unhappy!—when it assigned
Such deeds to the gods, adding fierce wrath!
What pain did men on that sad day bring
To themselves, and what wounds for us,
What tears for generations yet to come!
O humankind, this is not true piety:
To approach altars with veiled head,
To bow before a stone,
To fall to earth, arms outstretched,
Before shrines of the gods, nor to stain
Altars with blood from four-footed beasts,
Nor to link one vow to another. But rather this:

To look on all things with a calm mind
And clear understanding. For when we look up
At the sky's vault, and the vast world beyond,
And ether high over the twinkling stars,
And think of the sun's and moon's paths,
Then into our already burdened hearts
Rises a new fear: whether, perhaps,
The gods' mighty powers turn round and round
The far-off constellations. For lack
Of knowledge troubles the puzzled mind:
Did the world have a beginning,
And will there be an end? How long can
The world's walls withstand this constant strain
Of movement, or will they, blessed forever,
Glide through endless ages untouched
By the vast powers of immeasurable time?
What man, fearing the gods,
Does not shrink, whose limbs do not tremble,
When the dry earth quakes under the force
Of thunderbolts, and rumbling shakes the sky?
Do not all people tremble, and kings,
Even the proudest, hold themselves tight,
Afraid that something done or said in folly
Is now to be repaid? When fierce winds
Sweep a fleet across the sea,
Dashing it along with soldiers and beasts,
Does not the leader seek the gods' peace,
And beg for calm winds and friendly seas?—in vain,
For often, swept up in raging storms,
He is borne helpless to a fatal shore.
Yes, it seems that some hidden power
Always tramples on the affairs of men,
Grinding down the highest honors,
Mocking their rods and axes with scorn.
And when the earth shakes from end to end,

And cities collapse, or are on the brink,
What wonder then that mortals bow low
And give the gods, in earthly matters,
Almighty powers to govern all?
Now for the rest: copper, gold, and iron
Were discovered, with silver's weight
And lead's power, when the burning heat
Of great fires devoured the forest trees
Upon the mighty mountains, struck
By lightning from the sky, or perhaps because
Men, fighting in the woods, threw flames
To frighten and confuse their foes,
Or because they sought to clear rich fields
For pasture, or to hunt for game
And thrive on the spoils they gained.
(For hunting by pitfall or by fire came first,
Before the art of encircling the coverts
With nets or chasing with trained dogs.)
Whatever the cause, when fire's crackling heat
Had devoured the forest roots below,
And baked the earth with blazing flames,
Then from deep veins began to flow
Rivulets of silver and of gold,
Of lead and copper, pooling soon
In hollow places on the ground.
And when men saw the cooled lumps shining
With a splendid gleam upon the earth,
Moved by that smooth, bright delight,
They dug them out and saw how each
Held the shape of its earthen mold.
Then came the thought that these same lumps,
If melted by heat, could take any form,
Or be drawn into points or sharpened edges,
Yielding tools that could chop down forests,
Carve beams and planks, bore holes,

And drill through wood. They began to work
With tools of silver and gold at first,
Alongside copper's impetuous strength;
But in vain—for silver and gold,
Too soft, could not endure the strain
Like copper in that hard labor. Back then,
Copper was prized, while gold lay dull,
Blunt-edged and useless. Now copper lies low,
And gold is raised to loftiest honors.
Thus do the ages roll, changing the worth
Of things: what once was prized
Becomes of little value, while something
Rises from contempt to glory,
Treasured more each day, and praised
As a wondrous honor.
Now, Memmius,
How iron was discovered, you may
Easily imagine. Man's earliest arms
Were hands, nails, teeth, stones and branches—
Broken from forest trees—and flame and fire
As soon as they were known. Then came
The discovery of iron and copper;
Copper was used before iron, since
It was more abundant and easier to shape.
With copper they began to till the soil,
To rouse the waves of war,
To inflict great wounds, and seize
Another's flocks and fields. Thus armed,
They conquered all that lay defenseless.
Then, slowly, the iron sword replaced
The bronze one, and the copper sickle
Fell to scorn. With iron they cleaved
The earth, and warfare became equal.
And soon men learned
To ride horses armed, guiding them with reins,

With free right hands, long before they tried
The chariot's dangers; yokes of two horses came
Before the yokes of four, or chariots
With scythes where men-at-arms would stand.
Then the Punic folk trained elephants—
Those monstrous Lucanian beasts, terrifying,
With serpent-like trunks and towers on their backs—
To withstand the wounds of war, to strike fear
Into the mighty ranks of Mars. Thus sad Discord
Brought forth one terror after another,
Spreading horror among the nations,
And day by day adding to the grim art of war.
They even tried
Bulls in battle, and sent wild boars
Against their foes. Some sent forth
Mighty lions, with armed trainers
To guide and hold them, but in vain—
For once in a frenzy of slaughter,
They would fly wildly through the ranks,
Their dreadful crests shaking on their heads,
Leaping here and there. No rider could calm
His panicked horse or rein it back to face the foe.
The infuriated lionesses would leap,
Rending those who met them face to face,
Or from behind would drag down others,
Wrapping their powerful claws around them,
Until, defeated by wounds, they fell to earth.
Bulls would toss their allies,
Goring horses with their horns,
And pressing threatening heads to the ground;
Boars would strike with sharp tusks,
Splashing blood on spears shattered in their flesh,
Felling infantry and horse in chaos.
There you might see beasts rearing up,
Hooves pawing the air in vain—

Until, with tendons cut, they'd fall heavily,
Strewn across the ground. Even those well-trained
Foamed with fury amidst wounds, cries,
Flight, and panic; men could not
Rally their numbers. All types of beasts
Fled apart, just as in today's battles
The wounded Lucanian oxen do,
Having caused so many deaths among their friends.
(If, indeed, they did this at all—
I can hardly believe men didn't foresee
The foul disaster this would bring.
But this we may hold as true, happening
In diverse worlds created in different ways,
More likely somewhere far from here.)
But men did this less in hopes of winning
Than to give their foes cause for woe,
Even if it led to their own ruin,
For they were few in number and lacked arms.
Now, rough clothes made of twisted strands
Came long before woven coverings;
And weaving came later than iron itself,
Since iron is needed for weaving's craft,
And without it, none could make the polished tools—
The treadles, spindles, shuttles,
And yarn beams sounding as they work.
And nature first compelled men
To work the wool before women's hands:
For the male of the species excels in skill,
Far cleverer in such things—until at last
The rugged farmers scorned these tasks
And soon were eager to hand them down
To women's hands, while they grew strong
In the hard labor of the fields.
But nature herself,
Mother of all, was the first sower,

The first to graft; for berries and acorns,
Falling from trees, would sprout below
With swarms of tiny shoots in season.
Thus men grew fond of grafting slips
Onto branches, and planting shrubs
In the fields. Then they would try
New ways of tilling the soil they loved,
And notice how the earth improved
The taste of wild fruits under care.
Day by day they cleared the woods,
Moving higher up the mountain slopes
And leaving the plains below for crops—
There, on flatlands and hills, they grew
Meadows, cisterns, crops of grain,
And joyful vineyards, and laid out belts
Of silvery-green olive trees,
Marking the landscape far and wide,
As you see today with lovely rows
Of fruit trees that men plant and ring
With thriving hedges.
And by the mouth,
Imitating birds' liquid notes,
Men learned to make sounds long before
The measured songs and verses
That delight the ears. The whistling wind
Through hollow reeds first taught
The peasants how to blow through stalks
Of hollow hemlock. Then, bit by bit,
They learned sweet melodies, like those
Played on pipes by singing fingers,
Echoing through deep, untrodden groves,
In forest meadows and the stillness
Of shepherd's fields. Thus, time brings forth
Each thing little by little among men,
And reason raises it to light.

These tunes soothed and gladdened mortals
When they were full from meals—for songs
Are sweetest then. And often, lying
With friends on soft grass beside a river,
Underneath a tree's wide branches,
They refreshed themselves with ease,
Especially when the weather smiled,
And flowers painted the green grass around.
Then came laughter, jokes, and talk,
For the rustic muse was in her prime;
Then lively Mirth would prompt them all
To crown their heads and shoulders with
Chaplets of flowers and leafy vines,
To dance along with swaying limbs,
Clownishly stamping the earth,
Which brought forth laughter and joy—
Such merry acts in their glory then,
Being new and strange. And wakeful men
Found comfort for sleepless hours
In drawing forth varied notes,
Modulating melodies, running lips
Along the tuned reeds, which even now
The watchmen guard in faithful measure,
Honoring old traditions. Yet they find
No greater joy than the woodland folk
In ancient times. For whatever we have
Seems best, if sweeter things are unknown—
Until some later, better find
Changes our desires anew,
And dims the worth of yesterday.
And thus
Began the loathing of the acorn; thus
Were beds of grass abandoned, and leaves
Scattered for rest were left behind.
Thus, too, the pelts of beasts fell from grace—

Once a robe of honor, which, I suppose,
Stirred up such fierce envy then
That the first wearer met his end,
Ambushed by foes; and that prize, torn
To shreds by greedy hands, stained with blood,
Was ruined beyond all use or gain.
In olden days it was pelts, and today
It's purple and gold that burden men's lives,
With cares and weary struggles for wealth.
Wherefore, I think, the greater blame
Rests on us today: the earth's bare sons,
Without pelts, would shiver from the cold;
But we could well live without
Our purple robes embroidered with gold,
And still manage with simple clothes.
Thus, man toils on in vanities,
Wasting his years in idle cares—
For truly, he has not learned
The true end of gathering wealth, nor knows
How far pleasure may grow.
Desire for better and for more
Has carried men to the depths,
And stirred the mighty waves of war.
The sun and moon, those watchmen of the world,
With their bright lamps circling round
The vast, revolving sky, have taught
Mankind that seasons come again,
And that all follows a fixed order.
Already men lived surrounded
By strong towers; they tilled the land
Marked by boundaries; already
The sea bloomed with sail-winged ships;
Already men, through treaties and pacts,
Had allies and confederates, when poets
First began to record heroic deeds in verse.

And not long before this, letters were devised—
Thus, our age is unable to look back
Except by reason's trace of what came before.
Sailing the seas, tilling fields,
Building walls, making laws, forging arms, roads,
Clothing and such, all prizes and delights
Of finer life, poems, paintings, sculptures
Of polished beauty—all these arts were learned
Through practice and the mind's experience,
As men advanced step by step.
Thus time brings forth each thing
Little by little into the world of men,
And reason lifts it to the shores of light.
For one thing after another, men saw
Grow clear by intellect, till now,
Through their arts, they've reached the peak.

Book VI

Proem

'Twas Athens first, renowned in name,
That once gave humankind the harvest's sheaves,
Reordered life, decreed the laws,
And first brought comforts to the world,
When she gave birth to a man so wise,
Who poured out wisdom from his truthful lips.
His glory, though he's dead, lives on,
For those divine discoveries of old
Raised his fame high up to the sky.
For when he saw that almost everything
Which mortals most urgently require
Was close at hand, that life was safe
And men had wealth, honor, and praise,
And noble fame for worthy sons,

Yet still, within their homes, they bore
Anxious hearts that vexed their lives,
And raved with cries of endless pain,
Then he, the master, understood
That it was the vessel, cracked and flawed,
Which spoiled all good it took within—
Partly because it was leaky,
And could not ever be filled to the brim,
And partly because it stained with bitter taste
Whatever entered it. So he, the master,
Through his words of truth, did cleanse
The hearts of men and set clear bounds
To lust and fear, and showed the way
To the highest good we seek,
Guiding us by a straight-cut path,
And showing from which gates each ill
Might enter human life, whether by chance or fate,
Since nature destined it so. And he proved
That most of human suffering rolls in vain
Within the breast, grim waves of care.
For just as children tremble in the dark
And fear all things unseen, so we,
In the light, dread many things no more
Fearsome than the fantasies children fear
In darkness. This terror, this shadow of the mind,
Is not dispelled by sunlight's fiery beams
Or arrows of the morning, but only by
Nature's aspect and her laws.
Therefore, I will continue now to weave
In verse this task I've undertaken.
And since I've taught you that the world's great vault
Is mortal, and that the sky was formed
In time, and that all within it moves
By need and must go on,
The most I have unraveled; what remains,

Take now as well; for once we rise
To mount the winds' chariot,
The storms calm, and all things once raging
Are changed now, with fury stilled;
Other movements through earth and sky
Which mortals see (often with anxious,
Quaking thoughts) abase their minds
With dread of gods, pressing them down,
For in ignorance they yield all things
To gods' rule, believing them to reign.
For even those who know that gods live free
From care, still wonder by what means
Things can proceed (especially those things
In the sky above). And thus they fall back
To the old fears and again submit
To harsh masters, thinking them almighty—
Wretched, not knowing what can be and what cannot,
Nor by what law each thing has limits set,
Its bounds so deeply rooted in Time.
And so they wander, led astray
By blind reasoning. And, Memmius, unless
You cast out of your mind these thoughts,
Unworthy of gods, alien to their peace,
Then often will the majesty of gods
Seem harmful to you, as your thoughts degrade them—
Not because gods would be outraged
Or thirst for vengeance, but because
You torment yourself, thinking the gods,
Serene and calm, roll waves of wrath;
And you will never approach their shrines
With a tranquil mind, nor will you receive
Those images that from their holy forms
Are carried into human minds,
Reflecting their divine nature.
What kind of life would follow, you can see;

But that pure reason may drive away
Such a life far from us, much remains
To polish in my verse, though much has poured
Already from me. Behold, the law and form
Of the sky are to be grasped by reason;
There are the tempests and bright lightnings—
Why they happen and from what cause
They move—that you may no longer tremble,
Dividing the sky in anxious thoughts
For auguries, and wondering whence comes
The flying flame or to which side of heaven
It turns, or how it finds its way
Through walls, or how, after its force is shown,
It speeds forth again—
Men do not know these causes,
And think divinities are at work.
Do thou, Calliope, ingenious Muse,
Delight of mortals, joy of gods,
Show me the path as I press on
To the white line of my goal,
That I may win the crown,
With you, my guide!

Great Meteorological Phenomena, Etc.

And first of all,
Thunder shakes the blue depths of heaven,
When the ethereal clouds, racing high,
Clash together as winds battle fiercely.
For no sound ever comes from the serene
Regions of the sky; but wherever dense clouds
Gather in force, there more often comes
A crash with mighty rumbling. And again,
Clouds cannot be as dense as stones and wood,
Nor as fine as mist or drifting smoke,

For if they were, they'd either fall, pulled down
By sheer weight, like stones, or be too weak,
Like smoke, to hold their mass together,
To retain within them snow and hailstorms.
And they send forth, across the open sky,
A sound above, like a linen awning stretched
Over mighty theaters, which gives a crack
When struck by gusts between poles and beams.
Sometimes, too, when torn by playful winds,
It raves, making sounds like tearing sheets
Of paper; even this noise you can hear
In thunder, or the sound as when winds
Whip and buffet in the air a cloth
Or sheets of paper flying loose.
For sometimes the clouds do not crash head-on,
But move side-by-side, brushing each other's sides
With motions slow and contrary,
Creating that dry sound that grates
On our ears, drawn out until the clouds
Have passed from their close embrace.
And again,
It often seems as though all things shake
At the shock of heavy thunder, and the high walls
Of the wide heavens suddenly split apart,
Riven asunder, when a fierce blast
Of hurricane wind has all at once
Twisted into a cloud mass, and enclosed,
Spins tighter and tighter, forcing the cloud
To grow hollow with a thickening crust.
For when the power and force of wind
Weakens that crust, then the cloud, split in two,
Bursts with a hideous crash and boom.
No wonder, for a small bladder filled with air,
When it suddenly bursts, can make a sound as loud.
There's reason, too,

Why clouds make sounds as winds blow through them:
We often see clouds with rough, jagged edges,
Or branching into many forked shapes,
Much like when sudden gusts of wind
Sweep through dense forests, making leaves rustle
And branches crash. It happens too at times
That the fierce force of a hurricane
Tears through a cloud, breaking it apart with a blow.
For what a blast of wind can do above
Is clear from what we see on earth,
When a lesser wind twists tall trees
And tears them madly from their roots.
Besides, within the clouds are waves that crash,
Giving off a rumbling roar,
Like the loud surf breaking along deep streams
Or upon the great sea. It happens, too, when
A thunderbolt's fiery energy
Falls from one cloud into another;
If the cloud is full of moisture, it quenches
The fire with a mighty noise,
Just as hot iron plunged into cold water
Sizzles and cools. But if a drier cloud
Receives the fire, it will suddenly ignite,
Burning with monstrous sound,
As if flames driven by whirling winds
Raced across laurel-crowned mountains,
Setting the trees ablaze with a fierce assault.
There is nothing that crackles in flame
With sound more fearsome to man
Than Apollo's sacred laurel.
Often, too, the crashing of ice
And the swift downpour of hail send out a sound
Among the mighty clouds above; for when
The wind has packed them tight, each towering
Rain-cloud, frozen and mingled with hail,

Breaks and booms…
Likewise, it lightens when clouds collide,
Striking forth seeds of fire with their clash,
As if stone struck stone or steel;
Then, too, light leaps out, and sparks
Of fire scatter in shining bursts.
But we hear the thunder after we see the flash,
For sound forever reaches our ears
More slowly than sight meets our eyes—
As you can see from this example:
When you see someone far away
Chopping a tree with a two-edged ax,
You'll see the swing of the blow before
The sound reaches your ears; so too,
We see the lightning flash before
We hear the thunder, even though both
Are born together from the same clash
And by the same cause.
Thus,
The clouds light up the lands with their flashes,
And the storm trembles with bursts of flame.
When the wind has swept into a cloud
And, whirling within, has twisted it hollow
With a thick crust, it heats up quickly
From its swift motion—just as you see
How movement itself can overheat
And ignite objects: even a leaden ball,
Hurtling through space, can melt.
Therefore, when the fiery wind splits
The black cloud, it scatters seeds of fire,
Pressed out by force, bursting forth in flames;
Then follows the detonation, reaching our ears
After the sight meets our eyes.
This happens when clouds are piled high,
Layered upon one another with great force—

And do not be deceived by the view below,
Where we see only their broad base,
Not how high they tower. Watch when
The winds drive clouds across the horizon,
Like mountain ranges moving along,
Or see them massed around tall peaks,
Anchored in calm, winds stilled around:
Then you may know their mighty masses,
And view their caverns, as if built of cliffs;
When the storms have filled them utterly,
Prisoned in clouds, they roar around,
Blustering like savage beasts, sending
Growls through the clouds from side to side,
Whirling within to find an outlet,
Gathering seeds of fire until they burst
In forked flashes from the broken clouds.
Again, from this cause it comes to pass
That swift, golden streams of fire
Plunge downward to the earth: for clouds
Hold abundant seeds of fire;
When clouds are dry, they appear mostly
Flame-colored, resplendent in hue.
And indeed, they must take to themselves
Many seeds from sunlight, glowing bright.
So, when the wind has thrust these clouds together,
It presses forth the seeds of fire,
Making flames flash with colors bright.
Likewise, it lightens when clouds grow thin;
When the wind gently unravels them,
The seeds of light must naturally fall,
Lighting the sky without the dreadful roar
And crashing terror of storms.
To continue,
What nature thunderbolts possess
Is made clear by the marks they leave,

The scorched brands of their fiery heat,
And the fumes of sulfur rising around.
All these are marks not of wind or rain, but fire.
They often ignite the roofs of houses
And, inside rooms, hold fierce dominion
With swift flames. Know that nature fashioned
This fire subtler than all other fires,
With minute and darting bodies—a fire
That nothing can withstand:
The thunderbolt, so mighty, passes through
Walls and barriers as easily as voices pass through air,
Piercing stones and bronze, melting them
Instantly, melting bronze and gold,
And causing wine to vanish suddenly
From jars left intact. Its heat makes porous
The sides of the earthen wine jars,
Seeping within and scattering the elements
Of the wine in a quick dissolution—
A feat which even the sun's fiery rays,
For all their strength, could not accomplish.
So much more agile and overpowering is this force.
Now, in what way are these forces formed,
With such fierce strength as to split towers apart,
To topple houses, wrench beams and timbers,
And cast down monuments of heroes' past,
To take breath forever from men,
And to lay cattle low across the fields—
Yes, by what power lightnings do all this,
All this and more, I'll now reveal,
And keep you no longer with mere promises.
Thunderbolts must be conceived as born
In those thicker clouds piled high above;
For from the clear sky and lighter clouds
They never strike. This fact is clear:
When dense clouds gather across the sky,

So thick we might think the darkness of Acheron
Had risen and filled the vault of heaven—
So heavy do those storm clouds loom,
When tempests begin to forge their thunderbolts.
And often, far out at sea,
A black thunderhead, like a pitch-dark cataract
Falling from heaven, bulges thick
And drops with a mighty roar on the waves,
Bringing tempests heavy with thunder
And hurricanes; crammed so full with fire
And wind, that even those on land shudder
And seek cover. Therefore, as I said,
These storms must be thought to rise far above us,
For clouds would not cast such heavy dark
Unless built high, towering heap on heap,
To block out the sun. Nor could they bring
So much rain to flood rivers and fields,
If ether weren't crowded with clouds stacked high.
Then, here we find winds and fires combined—
Thus come the long lightning bolts and loud thunder.
For, as I've shown before, cavernous clouds
Hold countless fiery seeds, and they must
Draw many more from sunlight's heat.
So, when wind gathers clouds in one region
And presses out fiery seeds, mingling with fire,
That wind becomes a whirlwind in the cloud's
Deep belly, spinning tightly within
And sharpening the thunderbolt in fiery furnaces.
For the wind ignites in two ways:
Its own swift motion heats it, and the fire's
Repeated touch makes it burn. Then,
When wind's energy is fully heated,
And fierce fire moves deep within, the bolt,
Now ripened, bursts the cloud apart,
And flashes forth, illuminating with forking light

All around. Then follows a clap so heavy,
The vaults of the sky seem to burst apart,
Engulfing the earth. A quake spreads fearfully
Across the land, and far through the skies
Run the long rumbles. For in that moment
The whole tempest quakes, shaken through,
And roaring echoes fill the air. From this shock
Falls such resounding rain that all dark ether
Seems to turn to water, flooding fields
Back to their primal state, as rain pours down
From bursting clouds and hurricanes,
When the thunder, from a burning bolt,
Cracks through the sky. At times,
A force of wind from outside strikes
Into a cloud already hot with fire,
And when it bursts that cloud, down comes
That coil of flame we still call,
With our forebears' word, a thunderbolt.
The same thing happens on any side
Where that force sweeps forth. Sometimes, too,
A wind, though hurled forth without flame,
Ignites in flight, gathering heat as it goes,
Losing larger particles that can't pass
Through the air's bulk as swiftly as others—
And gathering smaller ones from the air,
Which, mingling, create fire as they fly:
Just as a leaden ball can grow hot in flight,
Losing cold particles and gaining warmth
From the air. Sometimes the force of a blow
Creates fire, when a cold wind strikes forth
Without flame. No wonder, for with a fierce blow
It releases fiery elements, streaming out
From the wind itself and from whatever
Receives the strike, as when fire springs forth
From steel striking stone. Though the steel is cold,

Its seeds of heat speed out swiftly.
And so, an object struck by a thunderbolt
Can catch flame, if it is suited to burn.
Yet we shouldn't think the force of wind
Entirely cold—this power sent from high
With such strength; and if not kindled by fire
On its course, it still arrives mixed with heat.
And now, the speed and stroke of thunderbolt
Is so tremendous, and with glide so swift
These thunderbolts descend, because their force
First gathers itself within the clouds,
Building up for their powerful release.
Then, when the cloud can no longer hold
The intense force pressing within, it bursts,
And so the bolt flies forth with such fierce power,
Much like a shot from Roman catapults.
Know too, this force is made of elements
Both small and smooth, so nothing resists it easily;
It darts between and penetrates the pores of things,
Without delay from countless collisions,
Flying onward with a swift, unstoppable surge.
Next, since every weight by nature falls downward,
The bolt's speed doubles, and the rush grows wild,
As the weight joins with the blow, shaking to pieces
All that blocks its path as it travels on.
And, because it moves along in one continuous surge,
It gains new speed as it goes,
And this constant momentum adds power,
Driving all the fiery seeds of thunder
Into a single, straight course,
Casting them onward, one by one.
And sometimes, it pulls from the air around
Certain bodies, which by their own blows
Further spark its velocity. And, behold,
It passes through objects unharmed,

Moving through many things without breaking them,
For the liquid fire flies through their pores.
Yet it pierces what it strikes when the bolt's atoms
Meet just where the atoms of other things
Are tightly joined. Further, it easily melts brass
And quickly fuses gold, because its force
Is made of such minute, smooth parts
That it winds its way within with ease,
And, once inside, quickly loosens all bonds
And unties every knot holding them together.
And most often in autumn, the heavens shake,
The star-studded vaults, and all the earth below—
And again in spring, when flowers unfold:
For in the cold season, there is little fire,
And winds are sparse in summer, while clouds
Have less bulk. But in those seasons in between,
The diverse causes of thunderbolts unite;
For then, cold and heat cross paths,
Raising discord in the air, which billows
In furious tumult with fire and wind—
Both of which the clouds need to form thunderbolts.
For spring brings the first touch of warmth and the last of cold,
So elements that oppose must clash,
And, when mixed, rage with chaotic fury.
And when the year brings summer's last warmth
Mixed with the earliest chill, in autumn's time,
Then, too, fierce cold and heat wrestle hard.
These seasons are called "cross-seas"—and no wonder
That thunderbolts prevail and storms rise then,
Since both sides rage in dubious war,
One with flame, the other with winds and rain mixed in.
This, O Memmius, is to see through
The true nature of fire-filled thunderbolts;
O this is to know by what blind force
Each effect is made, and not to unwind

Etrurian scrolls for tokens of gods' will,
Asking whence the flaming bolt has come,
Or to which part of heaven it turns,
Or how it winds through walls,
Or, after proving its force there,
How it speeds forth again, or what ill
It brings from high heaven. For if Jupiter
And the gods shake the shining vaults
With dread, and hurl fire where they will,
Why strike not the wicked in punishment,
So they may breathe forth flames in pain,
A warning for all? Why instead is he,
Guiltless, yet caught in the fiery storm,
Lifted by a whirlwind, though innocent?
Why then do bolts strike barren places,
Wasting their force? Do they practice their aim,
Strengthening their arms? Why let the Father's spear
Strike earth in vain? Why, too, does he allow it,
Nor keep it for his enemies? Why often
Aim at high places? Why do we find
Marks of lightning on mountain tops?
Why then does he strike the sea—
What guilt have waves or the vast deep
Of foam and spray? And if he wishes
To make us cautious of the bolt, why not
Give us the sight to see it come?
Or, if he seeks to catch us unawares,
Why thunder first in a distant sky,
So we may flee? Why rouse the dark air
With rumblings from afar? And how
Can one believe he strikes in many ways?
Do you think it never happens that
Thunderbolts strike in more than one place?
Yet it often has, and will again, as rain
Falls over many regions, so too do bolts

Fall at the same time across different lands.
Why does Jupiter never cast a bolt
When skies are clear? Does he descend
With the clouds to decide the shot himself?
And why, with his destructive bolt,
Does he break apart the holy shrines of gods,
Destroy his splendid thrones, and shatter
The images of his own divinities,
Robbing them of glory with violent wounds?
But to return apace,
It's easy now to see how those "bellows" fall,
As the Greeks have called them, discharged from above
Onto the seas. For at times from the sky,
A column descends upon the waters, pushed down,
Around which waves seethe in furious turmoil,
Stirred by powerful gusts; and any ship caught
Within that churning is placed in grave danger,
Thrown by the tempest. This happens when the force
Of the wind cannot burst through the cloud it strikes,
And instead pushes the cloud down in a column
Upon the sea, like a fist pressing down,
Stretching toward the waves. When the wind finally
Rips through the cloud, it pours down upon the sea,
Stirring up wondrous waves with swirling whirl,
Dragging the cloud's soft body downward.
And when it reaches the surface of the deep,
The whirl plunges itself into the water
With monstrous roar, forcing it to seethe.
At times, too, that vortex of wind enfolds
Itself in clouds, gathering particles from the air,
Forming a "bellows" descending from the sky.
When it bursts on land, it releases an immense
Force of whirlwind and blast. But since it forms
Rarely on land, where hills break its path,
It's seen more often out on the open sea,

Across the free horizons.
The clouds take shape
When in the upper regions of the sky,
Particles gather suddenly as they fly—
Rougher ones that, though loosely linked,
Hold each other firm. These form small clouds
That join and swell, drawn by the winds,
Until a storm's fury forms. It happens, too,
That mountains close to the sky smoke more often
With dark clouds, for as the mists begin to form,
The winds drive them upward before the eyes
Can see them, until they reach the peaks;
Then they gather in thicker mass,
Rising from the mountain's peak up to the sky.
Indeed, as we climb high mountains, we see
How windy those upper regions are.
Clothes hung out along the shore, when wet,
Show that nature lifts from the sea below
Unnumbered particles. Thus it is clear
That many particles rise from the salt waves
To build the bulk of clouds, for sea moisture
Is akin to that of clouds. From rivers, too,
And from the land itself, mists and steam
Rise like breath, covering the sky in a murk
That slowly gathers to form clouds.
Additionally, the heat from the starry ether
Weighs down upon them, condensing them
Under the blue sky into clouds. Sometimes,
Particles even come from far Beyond
To form the clouds and flying thunderheads.
For I have shown that particles are infinite
And fly with tremendous speed, passing through
Space beyond our grasp. It's no wonder, then,
That darkness and storms swiftly cover
The oceans and lands, bulking thunderheads

Hanging above, for everywhere through
The ether's narrow channels, or the "breathing-holes"
Of the upper world, the elemental particles
Have exits and entrances.
Now come,
And I'll tell how rain condenses in clouds
And pours upon the land in heavy showers.
First, I'll persuade you that water's seeds
Rise together with the clouds, growing alike—
Both clouds and water increase proportionately,
As our bodies grow with blood and sweat
And moisture within us. Clouds also draw
Moisture from the broad sea as winds
Carry them, like floating fleeces of wool.
Thus, rivers also lift moisture into the clouds.
When water's seeds gather in abundance,
The crowded clouds struggle to release rain
For two reasons: wind presses them together,
And the great mass of storm clouds urges rain
To pour. And when the winds winnow the clouds,
Or the sun strikes them, they release
Their rainy moisture, distilling drops
Like wax that melts under a fire's heat.
Heavy rains fall when clouds are weighed down
By their mass and the force of wind. Rains
Continue when water's seeds are stirred,
And clouds pile layer on layer,
While the earth exhales its moisture.
When the sun shines amid dark storms,
Its rays strike the blackened rains, and there,
In the dark clouds, the bright bow appears.
And now, as to things
Not yet mentioned here, which grow by themselves
Or form within the clouds—
Snow and wind, hail and hoarfrost, chill with ice,

And the freezing power that hardens lakes and pools,
Binding rivers in winter's icy grip—
It's easy still to see and understand
How these all happen and how they are born,
Once you understand the functions given
To the procreating atoms of the world.
Now come, and hear the law of earthquakes;
First, know that under the earth, as above,
Are caverns full of wind, dark pools,
Deep abysses, cliffs, and jagged rocks,
And rivers rolling rapidly below,
With waves and crashing stones. For it's clear
That earth must be of like form in every part.
Thus, with these things set underneath,
The earth above trembles with big tumblings,
When time erodes the huge, underground caves.
Whole mountains fall, and from the spot
Of that massive jolt, tremors quiver out wide.
For houses shake when jarred by a cart
Of little weight, and furniture leaps
When wheels hit a block in the street.
Sometimes, too, when heavy soil rolls down
From mountain slopes into dark pools,
The land rocks from the water's swell,
Just as a basin rocks until the liquid
Within settles still, with no undulation.
And besides,
When winds gather in the hollow depths,
Pressing mightily from one spot,
They push against high caverns until
The earth bulges in that direction;
Then buildings above lean ominously,
And beams hang forward, ready to fall.
Yet people still doubt that a time may come
For the world's end, though they see

Such bulging and breaking of the ground!
If not for the winds blowing back again,
Nothing could halt the collapse. But because
Winds alternate, charge, and retreat,
Earth more often threatens than brings about
A complete collapse. She leans to one side,
Then sways back; after teetering forward,
She returns to her seat of balance.
This is why buildings rock, with roofs
Shaking more than middle floors,
Middle more than the lowest,
And lowest least of all.
This same great quaking
Arises when wind and fierce air,
Either from outside or deep below,
Force themselves into the earth's caves,
Churning wildly until their stirred-up power
Breaks out, ripping deep chasms in the ground—
As happened once in Syrian Sidon,
And once in Aegium of the Peloponnese,
When the wild force of air burst forth,
Overthrowing those cities with earth's convulsion.
Many a walled town has fallen this way,
And many cities have sunk below the sea,
Engulfed with all their people. If the air
Does not break forth, then its wild rush
Disperses through the earth's countless pores,
Shaking her whole form—just as a chill,
Seeping to our bones, makes us shake.
Therefore, people run through cities in fear,
Dreading the roofs above, fearing the caverns below,
Lest the earth split open suddenly,
Gaping wide with a tremendous maw,
Swallowing everything in ruin.
Let people go on believing that earth and sky

Will remain secure forever; yet at times,
Danger forces a goad of fear—
One fear among many—that the earth might slip,
Suddenly vanishing beneath their feet,
Hurried down into the abyss,
Dragging all of existence in a world's wreckage.

EXTRAORDINARY AND PARADOXICAL TELLURIC
PHENOMENA

Firstly, men marvel why the ocean's bulk
Grows not bigger and bigger, though vast waters
Pour down into it, and every river flows
From every realm to the sea;
Add the random rains and gusty storms
That sprinkle every sea and land,
And add the springs themselves:
Yet all these added to the ocean's sum
Are but the increase of a single drop.
So it's less a wonder that the sea,
The mighty ocean, does not rise.
Besides, the sun draws off a mighty part—
We see its burning rays dry clothes wet with rain;
And we behold the sun over seas far outspread,
Drying the waters bit by bit.
So even though the sun takes a small part from any spot,
Across the vast waves it removes much.
Then, too, winds sweeping over the waters
Bear away much moisture—
We often see highways dry overnight,
And soft mud crusted over by dawn.
I've told you that clouds carry off moisture too,
Lifted from the vast ocean, sprinkling it about
Over all lands when rain falls,
Driven by winds that carry misty vapors.
Lastly, since the earth is porous, and lies
Near the seas, touching their shores,

Water must seep from briny ocean into the lands
Just as it flows from land to sea.
For brine is filtered out, and fresh water
Seeps back again, reappearing at river sources,
Returning to the land in flowing streams
Through channels cut long ago.
Now, the cause
For why vast fires blow forth from Aetna's mouth,
I will unfold; for with no small force
The fiery storms rose there, reigning over
Sicilian fields, drawing the upturned faces
Of nearby peoples, who saw the sky afar
A-smoke and sparking, filling their hearts with dread
Of what new thing nature was creating.
In such matters,
It's wise to look far and wide, to see how vast
The universe is, and to recognize
How small a part of it is this sky of ours—
No larger, truly, than one man compared
To the entire earth. If you understand
This cosmic truth, you will cease to wonder
At many things. Who among us marvels
When a fever gathers heat in a man's joints,
Or other painful ailments attack his limbs?
For soon the foot swells blue and sore,
Or sharp pain seizes teeth and eyes;
The sacred fire breaks out, burning all it touches
And creeping over the body. No wonder here,
Since earth and sky bring forth enough seeds of harm
To fuel countless diseases.
Thus, we must suppose that earth and sky, too,
Receive from the infinite enough of all things—
Enough for earthquakes, typhoons over land and sea,
Aetna's fires overflowing, or a blaze in heaven.
For that happens too; the vaults of the sky

Glow with fire, and heavier rains pour,
When seeds of water gather from infinity.
"But such fires are massive!" you may say.
True, but many a river seems huge to one
Who has never seen a larger.
Thus, trees and men seem large,
And whatever we see as biggest in each kind
We think is "huge"; yet all these, along with land,
Sea, and sky, are nothing to the all-encompassing
Universe.
Now, I will explain at last
How that fierce flame bursts forth from Aetna.
First, the mountain's nature is hollow,
Propped by basaltic caverns, and in these
Caverns are air and wind.
Wind forms when air is stirred
By violent agitation; when this air
Heats up and rages, it makes the earth
And rocks hot, striking off
Swift flames that lift themselves,
Hurtling upwards through the mountain's throat
Into the sky, scattering burning blasts,
Ashes, and pitch-black smoke,
While heaving up boulders of wondrous weight—
Leaving no doubt it's the air's
Tumultuous force. Besides, the sea
At the mountain's roots breaks its waves,
Sucking back its surf.
Grottoes run from the sea below
Into the mountain's base,
And from here you must believe they travel...
Conditions force both water and air
To penetrate deeply from the open sea,
Then blow outward, lifting flames on high,
Casting boulders up from the depths,

And raising clouds of sand. At the top
Are "bowls," as people there call them,
What we in Rome would name the throats or mouths.
There are some things for which one cause alone
Is not enough—there may be several,
And one among them must be true.
For if you saw someone lying dead from afar,
You'd have to consider all causes of death
To name his true end; for he may not have died
By steel or poison, nor from cold or disease,
Yet something of this sort must have happened—
And we must reason the same in many cases.
Toward summer, the Nile swells up,
Overflowing the plains—a singular river,
Watering Egypt alone. In the mid-summer heat,
It often floods the land, either because
The Etesian winds blow northward that season,
Forcing back its waves, swelling its waters,
And halting its flow. These winds from the icy north
Drive straight up the river. That river flows
From sultry lands to the far south,
Where sun-darkened people live with sun-baked skin.
Or perhaps sandbanks pile against its mouths,
Blocked by winds driving sand inland,
So the river's outlet becomes less free,
And its floods less swift. Or it may be that rains
Fall more abundantly at its source,
Since the Etesian blasts drive clouds inland.
When clouds gather in the central heat of day,
They're pressed against high mountains, forced to mass.
Or, perhaps, its waters grow far away
In the Ethiopian mountains, when the sun's
Warming rays melt the white snows down into the valleys.
Now come, and I'll explain the Birdless spots
And Birdless lakes, and what nature they hold.

First, they're called "birdless" because they're harmful
To all birds. When birds fly above these places,
They lose their strength and fold their wings,
Drooping their necks as they fall,
Plummeting to the earth if such is the nature
Of the spot, or into water if Birdless lake lies below.
At Cumae, there is such a place, where mountains smoke,
Filled with the scent of sulfur, steaming springs rising.
And there is one within Athens' walls,
On the Acropolis' summit, beside
The temple of Tritonian Pallas, where crows
Will not fly, even when smoke rises from offerings—
They flee not from the goddess's wrath,
As Greek poets once told the tale,
But from the nature of the place itself.
In Syria, too, they say there's a spot
Where four-footed animals collapse
Once they step within, as if struck down
For the gods below. All these wonders work
By natural law, their causes clear to see.
Let no one think these places are gateways to Orcus,
Or imagine gods of the underworld
Drawing souls to Acheron's dark shores—
As stags, it's said, use their scent
To draw hidden snakes from shadowed lairs.
How far from reason such ideas stray!
Now I'll try to explain the truth.
Firstly, as I've often said,
The earth holds atoms of every kind;
All things rise from it—
Many life-giving, fit for food,
And many which bring disease and hasten death;
Many seeds of many kinds, in many forms,
Since earth mingles and releases them all.
We've shown that some things suit certain creatures,

Based on nature, texture, and shape.
You see how many things are oppressive, foul,
And harmful to us in many ways:
Some irritate the ears,
Some fill the nostrils with harsh scents,
Or poison the breath we draw.
Some are loathsome to touch or see,
Others disgusting to taste.
Some weaken the limbs
Or drain the soul within.
Some trees cast a shade so noxious
That they bring headaches to those resting below.
On Helicon's hills, a tree grows that kills
By the stench of its flowers.
The sharp smell of a freshly snuffed lamp
Can put to sleep a person
Afflicted with convulsions.
The scent of castor makes a woman drowsy,
Her handiwork slipping from her fingers,
If she inhales it at certain times.
If you linger too long in hot baths,
Over-full, you might faint suddenly;
And the heavy fumes of charcoal
Can cloud the brain without a drink of water.
When fever seizes the limbs,
Even the smell of wine is unbearable.
Have you not seen how earth itself produces sulfur
And thickens bitumen with its stench?
What noxious odors rise from Scaptensula below,
Where men dig for silver and gold,
Or from the deadly air in gold mines?
What pale, ghastly look it gives them!
Many die quickly, the life drained from them,
Forced by grim necessity to work there.
Thus, this earth releases many toxic fumes,

Breathing them into the visible world.
Thus, Birdless places release
A fatal essence to flying creatures,
Rising from the earth to poison the air.
When birds fly into this unseen danger,
They're struck down, losing control,
And fall to where the fumes arose.
Once down, this poison drains life from every limb,
First striking them with dizzying weakness,
Then, once they've fallen to the source,
They release their souls, the toxic fumes too thick.
At times, the power of Birdless places
Displaces the air between birds and the ground,
Leaving nearly a void. When birds enter,
Their wings lose lift, falling useless.
Unable to hold themselves up,
They're forced by nature's weight to fall,
Prostrate upon the near-empty space,
Their life seeping out from every pore.
Further, well water is colder in summer
Because the earth, heated, releases into the air
Whatever fiery seeds it may hold within.
The more the ground loses heat,
The colder the water stays deep below.
Yet in winter, when the earth contracts
Under cold's grip and grows dense and solid,
It presses its own heat down into the wells.
They say at the shrine of Hammon there's a spring
That's cold in daylight but warms by night.
Men wonder at this and claim it heats
From a hidden sun beneath the ground,
Covered by night's dark shroud—
A notion far from reason. For when the sun,
Beaming on open waters, has no power
To warm their surface with his scorching light,

How, then, can he, hidden beneath the earth,
Boil water to make it burn with heat?
Especially since he can't even send his warmth
Through the walls of houses with ease.
What's the true cause? Here's the likely answer:
The earth around that spring is porous, more so
Than usual ground, and many seeds of fire
Lie close by. When night's dewy shades
Chill the earth, it contracts and squeezes out
These fiery seeds into the spring,
Which heat the water's steam and touch.
Then, when the sun rises and his rays warm the soil,
The seeds of fire return to their hidden places,
And the warmth retreats, leaving the spring cold.
Moreover, the sun's rays strike the water,
Making it thinner as dawn arrives;
Thus, it releases any fiery seeds it holds,
Just as it sheds frost and melts its ice.
There is also a cold spring that lights
Tow from a distance, making it flame.
Even a pitch torch flares when held near its waves,
As it floats before the breeze. This marvel is
No wonder, for within this water, many seeds
Of heat must rise from the earth's depths,
Flowing up through the spring and into the air—
Yet not in numbers enough to warm the water.
These seeds gather, though scattered through the liquid,
And ignite into flame above.
Much like a spring near Aradus, amid the sea,
Where sweet water bubbles out,
Surrounded by salt waves. Elsewhere, the vast ocean
Gives sailors fresh water in their time of need,
Issuing sweet streams among the salt waves.
In this way, seeds of fire may rise
Through this spring and kindle on the tow;

As they gather and cling to the torch,
They ignite readily, since tow and torches themselves
Hold many hidden seeds of fire.
Have you not seen, when you hold
A wick close to a lamp, it catches flame
Before it touches the fire? The same with a torch.
Many things, touched only by heat,
Flare from a distance before reaching true flame.
This we must suppose also happens in this spring.
Now to other matters!
I'll explain why iron is drawn by the stone
The Greeks call "magnet" from the land of Magnesia,
Where its origin lies. This stone is wondrous—
It can hold a chain of rings hanging down,
Swaying in the wind, one linked to another,
Each feeling the stone's power to bind,
Its strength flowing down.
In such things, much must be known
Before we can explain this power;
We must examine it from every side.
So I urge you to listen closely.
First, from everything we see,
Particles flow out constantly,
Touching the eyes to bring sight,
Odors to the nose, warmth from the sun,
Spray from waves that eat away
The coastlines. And echoes flow
Through the air. At the sea,
A salty taste comes to the mouth,
And when we watch wormwood mixed,
Its bitterness stings us.
So from everything flows something,
Spreading all around us without rest,
For we constantly see, smell,
And hear all things at hand.

Now let me remind you how porous
All things are. In my first verse,
I proved this truth—it's essential
To understand that all is body and void.
In caves, rocks above drip moisture;
Our bodies sweat, hair grows, and veins
Carry food down to the nails.
Cold and heat move through bronze,
Silver, and gold goblets we hold.
Sounds pass through walls of stone;
Odors, cold, and fire's heat penetrate iron.
And so, at times, harmful influences
Enter our world from afar. Tempests gather
From both earth and sky, only to return there—
For all things must be porous, designed to absorb.
Furthermore, not all particles from things around
Have the same qualities we can perceive,
Nor do they suit every substance alike.
For instance: the sun scorches the earth,
Melts ice, and softens snow on mountain tops.
Wax under heat turns to liquid; fire will melt
Copper and fuse gold, but shrivels hides and flesh.
Water hardens iron fresh from fire, yet softens
The same hides and flesh, which heat had hardened.
Wild olive trees seem like ambrosia to goats,
Though their leaves are bitter food for humans.
Pigs recoil from marjoram and scented oils,
Which seem like poison to them but refresh us.
While mud disgusts us, it delights pigs,
Who roll from belly to back, contented.
Now, one more thing to clarify before
Explaining what's at hand. Different things
Contain different kinds of pores in unique shapes,
Sized and shaped specifically for their purpose.
In creatures, we see this through the senses,

Each capturing its own unique quality:
Sounds travel to one place, flavors to another,
Scents to a third. Some things seep through rock,
Others through wood or gold or glass. Some
Bring heat, others color or form, moving through
Various paths according to their nature.
With these ideas established,
It's easier to explain why a magnet attracts iron.
First, the magnet emits a stream of particles
That displaces the air between the stone and iron.
As that space empties, the iron's own particles
Rush to fill the void, pulling the iron ring with them,
Since iron holds its parts so tightly bound.
This force draws the ring until it connects,
Bound by an invisible link to the magnet.
The air behind helps to push it along,
Moving through iron's tiny pores like wind through sails.
When the iron reaches the void, it continues,
Driven by the surrounding air's constant motion.
Sometimes, iron even resists the magnet,
Repelled as if it alternates between fleeing and following.
I've seen Samothracian rings leap and iron filings
Bubble and froth in brass bowls above the magnet.
This happens because the brass obstructs the flow,
And the magnetic current, finding no path,
Pushes iron away, stirring it as it struggles
Against the obstruction. While other metals,
Like gold, remain unmoved, iron is uniquely suited
To the magnet's force, as its structure complements
The magnet's particles.
Now, turning to diseases, their spread, and origin:
We know life-giving particles exist alongside
Particles that bring decay. When these gather,
They corrupt the air, spreading a pestilence
That falls upon humans and animals alike.

It can descend from above, like clouds or fog,
Or rise from the earth, which, after heavy rains
Or intense heat, can emit decay.
Notice how travelers often fall ill in foreign lands,
Affected by the unfamiliar air and water.
Each region has a unique climate:
The Britons differ from Egypt's people,
Or the Pontic coast from sunny Gades,
As each area shapes its inhabitants.
Each disease, too, is bound to a place:
Elephantiasis near the Nile,
Affects the feet in Attica, and the eyes in Achaea.
These afflictions arise from the nature of the air,
Which, when it shifts or grows tainted, moves like a cloud,
Creeping across the land, altering what it touches.
When such a foreign atmosphere mingles with ours,
It infects and corrupts it. The blight settles
On crops and livestock or hangs in the air,
Waiting for us to inhale. So, like us,
Cattle and sheep suffer pestilence too,
Whether we journey to strange lands or they bring
A poisoned air to us, disrupting our health.

THE PLAGUE ATHENS

It was this kind of disease, this deadly plague,
That once swept through Cecropian lands,
Turning plains into fields of bones, emptying roads,
Draining Athens of its people. It came from afar,
Rising out of Egypt, crossing air and sea,
Until it descended on all of Pandion's folk.
Soon, many were struck by the sickness and death.
At first, they felt their heads burning with fever,
Their eyes blazing red, throats blackened inside,
Oozing blood, and their voices choked
By ulcers. The tongue, weakened and sore,
Dripped blood, rough and slow to speak.

When that sickness spread through their throats,
Down into their chests and to their hearts,
Every part of life began to collapse.
Their breath grew foul, like rotting corpses,
And soon, every ounce of strength faded,
And every power of the mind, too.
Pain and despair, with endless groans,
Were constant companions to their suffering.
Day and night, they vomited in waves,
Their exhausted bodies breaking down.
Their skin wasn't fever-hot to the touch;
Instead, it felt warm, covered in red sores,
Branded with blisters like "sacred fires"
Burned into their skin. Inside, their bodies
Burned down to the bone, as if a furnace
Raged in their stomachs. No relief was enough—
They craved cool air and breezes, always.
Some even threw themselves into icy rivers,
Diving in with mouths open wide, desperate,
But a shower of water seemed like mere drops.
Their thirst was unquenchable. They lay, drained,
Silent, while doctors, helpless, muttered low,
Seeing their patients stare with open, sleepless eyes,
Already marked for death.
In those days, death brought many signs:
The mind twisted by dread and despair,
The face fierce and delirious, tormented ears
Ringing, breaths short or labored,
Sweat soaking the neck, the spit turning thick
And bitter, the throat rattling with a cough.
The fingers curled, the body shook,
The cold crept from feet upward.
Near the end, their faces hollowed,
The eyes sunken, temples drawn,
Skin cold and stiff, twisted into a grimace,

Muscles swollen around the brows—
And soon after, they would lie rigid in death.
By about the eighth or ninth day,
They'd give up the struggle for life.
If anyone survived that bout of death,
Still they'd be plagued by sores and sickness,
Their bellies releasing black, foul fluids,
Or blood seeping from their noses,
While pain throbbed in their heads, draining
All strength and flesh from their bodies.
If they managed to outlast this bleeding sickness,
It still attacked their muscles, their joints,
Even their private parts.
Some, so terrified of death, lived on
But only after surgeons removed their limbs.
Others, though lopped of hands and feet,
Held on to life, and some lost their eyes—
Such was their fierce fear of dying.
And some, besides, lost all memory,
Forgetting even themselves.
Bodies lay unburied, piling up,
And birds and animals would shy away,
Fleeing the deadly stench; or, if they fed,
They'd soon fall sick and die. Through those days,
Hardly a bird appeared, and the wild beasts
Were seldom seen, overcome by disease.
Most often, the loyal dogs lay dying in the streets,
Breath leaving their bodies painfully—
Such was the plague's grip. No single cure
Could work for all: what saved one
Might doom another, and what let one
Breathe freely might bring death to the next.
But worst of all, the most pitiful part,
Was this: once someone felt themselves
Trapped by the disease, they lost all hope,

Their hearts heavy with dread, as if they already
Saw their own funeral. They'd give up the fight.
People infected each other constantly,
Like flocks of sheep or herds of cattle,
And this made the dead pile up faster.
Some, fearing death, avoided their sick friends,
Choosing to flee rather than risk their lives.
But this only brought its own punishment,
For soon after, they too fell to the same neglect,
Abandoned and alone, and they died.
Yet those who stayed to care for their sick,
Compelled by duty, fell ill too, worn out
By the infection and by the unending cries
Of the dying. This kind of death
Was the price of nobility.
Funerals were hurried, neglected,
Rushed along as families competed
To bury their dead as quickly as they could.
And people, struggling to bury their dead,
Piled body upon body in heaps.
Weary from sorrow and tears, they would return home,
Only to fall ill themselves from grief.
There was no one left untouched—no one
Escaped those dreadful times without
Facing sickness, death, or heartbreak.
Even the shepherds, cattle herders,
And strong plowmen grew weak,
Their bodies huddled in dark corners of huts,
Succumbing to squalor and disease.
Often, you could have seen lifeless children
Clinging to their parents' bodies,
Or children lying beside the corpses
Of mothers and fathers, giving up life.
And from the countryside, floods of sick,
Sick farmers streamed into the city,

Carrying their misery with them, crowding
Every space. More and more, death
Filled the packed city, claiming lives in droves.
Bodies lay strewn along the streets,
Dragged and rolled by thirst to die beside
Fountains, their last breaths choked
By a desperate need for water.
Everywhere, in the city squares,
On roads, you could see half-dead bodies,
Covered in grime, barely more than bones,
Dying from sheer neglect, clothed in rags,
Skin stretched over bones, already like
Corpses rotting in filth and vile sores.
The temples, too, were full of bodies,
Crowded with corpses, once holy places
Now filled with death, each shrine packed
With the dead—sacred spaces that had once
Welcomed worshipers now overwhelmed by plague.
People no longer honored the gods;
The suffering was too great to think of worship.
In the city, the usual burial rites were gone,
And those devout customs of the past
Were abandoned in a frenzy of fear.
Each person buried their dead in haste,
Doing whatever they could manage.
The chaos and poverty drove people
To desperate acts. In a panic, they'd place
Their loved ones on strangers' funeral pyres,
Setting the torch beneath, fighting each other
With cries and bloody brawls,
Desperate to lay to rest those they'd loved in life.

Thank You for Reading

Dear Reader,

We hope this timeless classic has sparked your imagination and enriched your literary journey. Now that you've turned the final page, we want to share a vision for the future of reading—one where every classic you've ever wanted to explore is at your fingertips, in a format that best suits your life.

We'd like to invite you to gain immediate, unlimited digital & audiobook access to hundreds of the most treasured literary classics ever written—along with the option to secure deluxe paperback, hardcover & box set editions at printing cost. Together, we can spark a new global literary renaissance alongside our small, independent publishing house called "The Library of Alexandria."

Thousands of years ago, the Library of Alexandria stood as a beacon of knowledge—until it was lost to history. We aim to reignite that spirit of preservation and discovery right now, in the modern age—only this time, it's accessible to all, in every language and every format.

Picture a world where every timeless classic, novel, poem, or philosophical treatise is not only available to read but also updated for today's readers—modernized, translated into any language or dialect, and ready to enjoy in any format you choose, whether that is in an eBook, audiobook, paperback, or deluxe hardcover & box set version a printing cost.

By joining our movement to rebuild the modern Library of Alexandria, you become part of an unprecedented mission to offer:

- **Unlimited Audiobook & eBook Access to the Greatest Classics of All Time**

  Instantly explore thousands of legendary works, from Plato and Shakespeare to Jane Austen and Leo Tolstoy. All are instantly ready to read or listen to, giving you a complete literary universe at your fingertips.

- **Paperback & Deluxe Editions at Printing Costs:**

Purchase any title in a paperback, deluxe hardbound, or deluxe boxset edition at printing costs, shipped right to your doorstep. Curate your personal library of Alexandria with editions worthy of display—crafted to last, designed to captivate, and delivered straight to your door.

- **Modern translations for Contemporary Readers in all languages and dialects**

Discover a vast selection of classics reimagined in clear, current language—no more struggling with outdated phrases or obscure references. Next to the original versions, we aim to offer translations in as many languages and dialects as possible.

As we continue our translation efforts and add new languages, readers everywhere can connect with these works as if they were written today. By bridging linguistic divides, you're contributing to ensuring that these timeless stories become more meaningful, accessible, and inspiring for people across the globe.

- **Your Personal Library of Alexandria:**

Over the months and years, you'll curate a unique physical archive of classics—each volume a testament to your taste, curiosity, and love of knowledge. It's not just about owning books—it's about curating a cultural legacy you'll cherish and pass down for generations to come.

- **Join a Global Literary Renaissance:**

Your support fuels an ongoing mission: allowing us to reinvest in offering deluxe print editions (including special boxsets) at their true cost, broaden the range of available formats and translations, and extend the reach of these works to new audiences worldwide. By joining today, you're not just preserving a legacy of masterpieces; you set in motion a powerful wave of literary accessibility.

We are more than a publisher—we're a movement, and we can't do it alone. Your support lets us scale our mission, preserving and reimagining history's greatest works for tomorrow's readers.

Become a Torchbearer of knowledge.

Thank you for picking up this book and allowing us into your literary journey. As you turn the pages, know that you're part of something larger: a global effort to keep these stories alive, share their wisdom across borders and generations, and spark a true cultural revival for the modern era.

If this resonates with you—please consider taking the next step by visiting:

www.libraryofalexandria.com

With gratitude and a shared love of knowledge,

The Modern Library of Alexandria Team

Visit:

www.libraryofalexandria.com

Or scan the code below:

www.ingramcontent.com/pod-product-compliance
Lightning Source LLC
Chambersburg PA
CBHW011803010726
47498CB00009B/2854